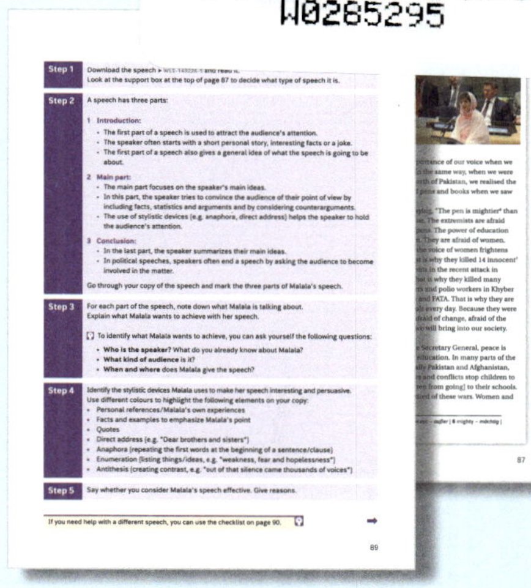

Step by step trainiert kleinschrittig ausgewählte Kompetenzen und Skills, die auch für die kommenden Jahrgänge relevant sind.

Reading tour mit spannenden Lesetexten!

Photo tour mit starken Bildern und interessanten Texten!

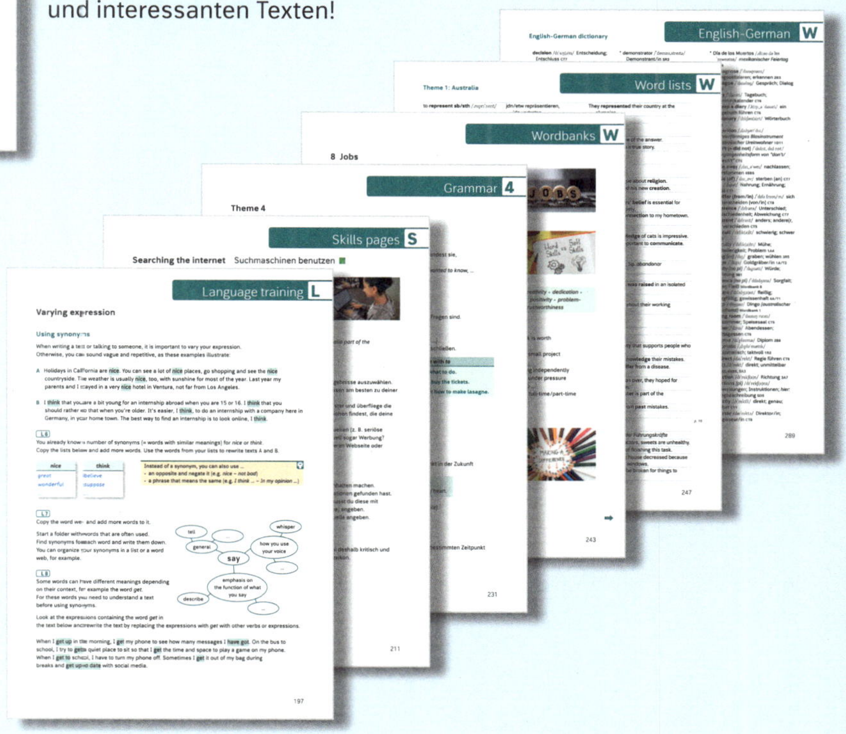

Language training Tipps und Übungen zur Vertiefung der Sprachkompetenz

Skills pages konkrete Hilfen zu allen Kompetenzen

Grammar Erläuterungen zu sprachlichen Strukturen

Wordbanks nützliche Wörter und Redewendungen zu einzelnen Themen

Word lists Wortlisten zu den Kapiteln

Dictionary Wörterbuch (Englisch-Deutsch)

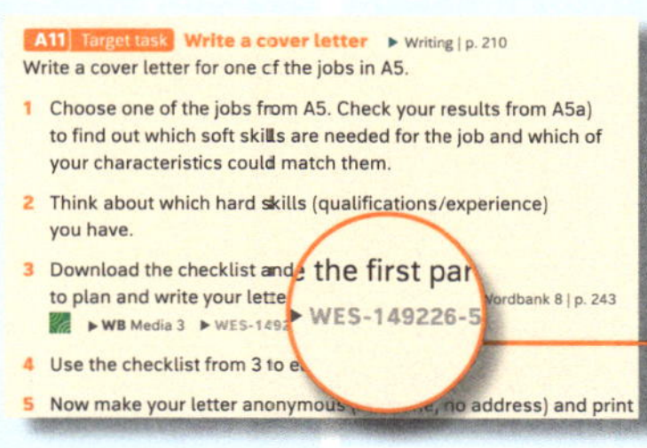

Für zusätzliche Materialien gibst du einen der folgenden **Webcodes** auf www.westermann.de/webcode ins Suchfeld ein:

WES-149226-1 Audio-Tracks für Schülerinnen und Schüler

WES-149226-2 Materialien zur Medienbildung

WES-149226-3 Lösungen zu den *Target task tools* und zu *Diff and train*

WES-149226-4 Videos zu Grammatikthemen und die *Grammar*-Anhänge aus Camden Town 5-8

WES-149226-5 Materialien zu einzelnen Aufgaben

Alternativ kannst du auch diesen QR-Code scannen:

westermann

CAMDEN TOWN

9 (G8)

CAMDEN TOWN

9 (G8)

Autorinnen und Autoren: Stephanie Claussen, Pamela Hanus, Christoph Reuter, Sylvia Wauer
Unter Mitwirkung der Fachredaktion Englisch Gymnasium.
Berater der Fachredaktion Gymnasium: Florian Nuxoll
Fachliche Beratung: Roswitha Henseler, Thomas Rahn, Dana Reimer, Ulrike Selz, Prof. Dr. Karin Vogt

Zusatzmaterialien zu Camden Town 9 (G8)

Für Lehrerinnen und Lehrer:

Textbook 9 (G8) für Lehrkräfte	978-3-14-149258-3
Workbook 9 (G8) mit Lösungen	978-3-14-149265-1
Teacher's Manual 9 (G8)	978-3-14-149251-4
Differenzierungsmaterial 9 (G8)	978-3-14-149329-0
Vorschläge für Lernerfolgskontrollen 9 (G8)	978-3-14-149272-9
Audio-CD 9 (G8) mit DVD für Lehrkräfte	978-3-14-149279-8
Online-Diagnose zu Camden Town 9	www.onlinediagnose.de

Für Schülerinnen und Schüler:

Workbook 9 (G8)	978-3-14-149233-0
Workbook 9 (G8) mit interaktiven Übungen	978-3-14-149414-3
Vocab Practice 9 (G8)	978-3-14-149244-6
Interaktive Übungen	978-3-14-149411-2

Das digitale Schulbuch und digitale Unterrichtsmaterialien für Schülerinnen und Schüler und für Lehrkräfte finden Sie in der BiBox – dem digitalen Unterrichtssystem passend zum Lehrwerk. Mehr Informationen über aktuelle Lizenzen finden Sie auf www.bibox.schule.

Druck A[1] / Jahr 2024
Alle Drucke der Serie A sind im Unterricht parallel verwendbar.

Redaktion: Ella Collier, Bettina Hammersen-Schiffner, Daniel Harnett, Kerstin Klemm, Linda Knief, Lucas Mees, Dr. Heike Michaelis
Redaktion Reading tours Theme 1, 3 und 5: Tanja Mees
Redaktion Grammar-Anhang: Caroline Byrt
Layout: LIO Design GmbH, Braunschweig
Illustrationen: Ulf Marckwort, Kassel
Umschlaggestaltung: LIO Design GmbH, Braunschweig
Druck und Bindung: Westermann Druck GmbH, Georg-Westermann-Allee 66, 38104 Braunschweig

ISBN 978-3-14-**149226**-2

Dear students,

Welcome to *Camden Town* 9!

This year's book has a modular structure, in other words, you and your teacher are free to decide the order in which you complete the five Themes.

The focus will be on developing the skills you need for the "Oberstufe".

- You will practise your language skills in both the Themes and the Diff and train section (p. 145ff.), with additional tasks available in the Language training section (p. 194ff.). The Wordbanks (p. 237ff.) can help you to expand your vocabulary.
- You will work on many different types of texts. The Step by step pages focus on the types of text that are relevant for the "Oberstufe" (e.g. characterization and summary).
- The Skills pages (p. 202ff.) offer tips on how to deal with the different kinds of tasks, e.g. speaking or writing tasks.
- Target tasks, two per Theme, will help you see how much progress you have made.
- Five Reading tours offer exciting extracts from young adult literature – a graphic novel, a short story, a play and two novels.

Enjoy *Camden Town* 9!

Inhalt

		Zielaufgaben (Target tasks)	Kompetenzen
	Theme 1	**Australia**	
12	Intro: G'day Australia!		**Listening:** die Bedeutung von Wörtern mit Hilfe eines Hörtextes erschließen
14	Part A: In the past?	**Target task:** einen Zeitungsartikel zusammenfassen	**Listening:** einem Sachtext Informationen entnehmen **Speaking:** Arbeitsergebnisse austauschen **Reading:** einem Sachtext Informationen entnehmen | Steckbriefe vergleichen | einem Zeitungsartikel Informationen entnehmen
19	Target task tools	*Unterstützendes Übungsangebot zur Erarbeitung der Target task*	
20	Part B: School exchange down under	**Target task:** eine Präsentation vorbereiten und halten	**Listening:** einem Podcast Informationen entnehmen **Speaking:** sich über einen Aufenthalt in Australien austauschen | Schulen in Deutschland und Australien vergleichen | eine Präsentation halten **Reading:** einem Blogeintrag Informationen entnehmen | einem Sachtext Informationen entnehmen
25	Target task tools	*Unterstützendes Übungsangebot zur Erarbeitung der Target task*	
26	Photo tour	*New Zealand (Fotomaterial und Informationen)*	
28	Reading tour	*Night Feet (Auszug aus einer Kurzgeschichte)*	
32	I can ...	*Selbsteinschätzung nach Abschluss des Kapitels*	
33	Step by step	*Schrittweises Training weiterführender Kompetenzen*	**Speaking:** ein Bild beschreiben, interpretieren und präsentieren
	Theme 2	**Teenage life**	
38	Intro: Teens then and now		**Listening:** einem Interview Informationen entnehmen **Speaking:** Infografiken beschreiben | Arbeitsergebnisse austauschen | eine Aussage zu Teenagern diskutieren
40	Part A: Growing up in a digital world	**Target task:** einen Erfahrungsbericht schreiben	**Speaking:** Umfrage durchführen | *zigzag debate* führen | eine Aussage zur Handynutzung diskutieren **Reading:** Cartoon analysieren | einem Zeitungsartikel Informationen entnehmen | einem Blogeintrag Informationen entnehmen
45	Target task tools	*Unterstützendes Übungsangebot zur Erarbeitung der Target task*	
46	Part B: Finding your way	**Target task:** eine Filmkritik verfassen	**Listening:** einer Buchbesprechung Informationen entnehmen | einem Hörbuch Informationen entnehmen **Speaking:** über den Inhalt eines Buches spekulieren | Standbilder aus einem Film analysieren **Reading:** einem Romanauszug Informationen entnehmen | einer Filmkritik Informationen entnehmen
51	Target task tools	*Unterstützendes Übungsangebot zur Erarbeitung der Target task*	
52	Reading tour	*Check, please! (Auszug aus einer Graphic Novel)*	
58	I can ...	*Selbsteinschätzung nach Abschluss des Kapitels*	
59	Step by step	*Schrittweises Training weiterführender Kompetenzen*	**Writing:** einen Romanauszug zusammenfassen

	Sprachliche Mittel
Writing: eine *class wall chart* erstellen | einen kurzen Kommentar zu einem geposteten Foto schreiben | ein Quiz erstellen **Viewing:** einem Videoclip Informationen entnehmen	**WORTSCHATZ:** Australian English-British English **STRUKTUREN:** R: *tenses* **DIFF**
Writing: einen Zeitungsartikel zusammenfassen **Viewing:** einem Videoclip Informationen entnehmen **Mediation:** Informationen auf Deutsch wiedergeben **DIFF** **Media:** eine Internetrecherche durchführen	**WORTSCHATZ:** Australische Geschichte • biografische Informationen **STRUKTUREN:** R: Passiv
Writing: einen Blogeintrag kommentieren **Mediation:** Informationen auf Deutsch wiedergeben | Fragen zu einem deutschsprachigen Artikel auf Englisch beantworten **DIFF** **Media:** eine Internetrecherche durchführen | eine Präsentation aufnehmen **CULTURE BOX** School of the Air	**WORTSCHATZ:** Vergleiche • Natur und Umweltschutz • Schulen in Australien **STRUKTUREN:** adverbiale Nebensätze • R: indirekte Rede mit Zeitverschiebung **DIFF** • *connectives* **DIFF**
Reading: Infografiken Informationen entnehmen **Viewing:** einem Videoclip Informationen entnehmen	**WORTSCHATZ:** Infografiken • Teenager • Diskussion **STRUKTUREN:** R: Bedingungssätze, Typ 2 **DIFF**
Writing: einen Erfahrungsbericht schreiben **Viewing:** einem Videoclip Informationen entnehmen **Mediation:** Informationen auf Deutsch wiedergeben **DIFF** **Media:** sich mit Social Media und der eigenen *screen time* auseinandersetzen	**WORTSCHATZ:** Social Media • Cartoons **STRUKTUREN:** R: Modalverben und Ersatzformen • R: *tenses* **DIFF**
Writing: ein Interview verfassen/ein Skript für einen Fernsehbericht verfassen | eine Filmkritik verfassen **Viewing:** Filmtrailer recherchieren und Szene daraus interpretieren **Mediation:** einer deutschsprachigen Filmkritik Informationen entnehmen und sie auf Englisch wiedergeben **DIFF** **Media:** Skript erstellen | eine Internetrecherche durchführen **CULTURE BOX** Mental health education	**WORTSCHATZ:** Vorlieben/Abneigungen • Film • Filmkritik **STRUKTUREN:** Partizipialkonstruktionen

Inhalt

		Zielaufgaben (Target tasks)	Kompetenzen
	Theme 3	**Human rights for all?**	
66	Intro: Young people's rights		**Speaking:** sich über Rechte austauschen | ein Interview durchführen/eine kurze Präsentation halten **Reading:** Fotos Texten zuordnen
68	Part A: "The right to be protected from harm"	**Target task:** eine Stellungnahme verfassen	**Listening:** einem Podcast Informationen entnehmen **Speaking:** Fotos beschreiben | Grafiken beschreiben | über eine Aussage diskutieren **Reading:** Schlagzeilen Informationen entnehmen | Stilmittel erkennen | einem Sachtext Informationen entnehmen | ein Gedicht lesen und interpretieren
73	Target task tools	*Unterstützendes Übungsangebot zur Erarbeitung der Target task*	
74	Part B: "The right to have an adequate standard of living"	**Target task:** eine Geschichte fortschreiben	**Speaking:** über den Inhalt eines Buches spekulieren | einer Zusammenfassung Informationen entnehmen | Spekulationen zu einer Romanfigur anstellen | ein Rollenspiel durchführen
79	Target task tools	*Unterstützendes Übungsangebot zur Erarbeitung der Target task*	
80	Reading tour	*Trell: Nothing But the Truth (Romanauszug)*	
86	I can ...	*Selbsteinschätzung nach Abschluss des Kapitels*	
87	Step by step	*Schrittweises Training weiterführender Kompetenzen*	**Reading:** eine Rede analysieren
	Theme 4	**Chances and opportunities**	
92	Intro: Teen jobs		**Listening:** einer Radiosendung Informationen entnehmen **Speaking:** ein Rollenspiel durchführen | eigene Vorlieben oder Abneigungen nennen
94	Part A: Finding a job	**Target task:** ein Anschreiben verfassen	**Listening:** einem Podcast Informationen entnehmen **Speaking:** über zukünftige berufliche Vorstellungen sprechen | eine Entscheidung begründen **Reading:** Stellenanzeigen Informationen entnehmen | einem Lebenslauf Informationen entnehmen **Writing:** einen Lebenslauf schreiben | ein Anschreiben überarbeiten | ein Anschreiben verfassen
99	Target task tools	*Unterstützendes Übungsangebot zur Erarbeitung der Target task*	
100	Part B: A good impression	**Target task:** ein Bewerbungsgespräch führen	**Speaking:** über eine Entscheidung diskutieren | ein Bewerbungsgespräch führen **Reading:** einem Sachtext Informationen entnehmen
103	Target task tools	*Unterstützendes Übungsangebot zur Erarbeitung der Target task*	
104	Photo tour	*English as a global language (Fotomaterial und Informationen)*	
106	Reading tour	*Forty-Five Minutes (Auszug aus einem Drama)*	
112	I can ...	*Selbsteinschätzung nach Abschluss des Kapitels*	
113	Step by step	*Schrittweises Training weiterführender Kompetenzen*	**Writing:** eine Charakterisierung schreiben

	Sprachliche Mittel
Viewing: einem Videoclip Informationen entnehmen **Media:** eine Internetrecherche durchführen	**WORTSCHATZ:** Menschenrechte
Writing: eine Zeitungsüberschrift erstellen | einen Kommentar verfassen **Viewing:** einem Videoclip Informationen entnehmen **Media:** eine Internetrecherche durchführen CULTURE BOX The Second Amendment and "Stand-your-ground" laws	**WORTSCHATZ:** *gun culture* • Grafiken • Stilmittel • Meinungsäußerung **STRUKTUREN:** *personal passive* **DIFF** • R: notwendige und nicht-notwendige Relativsätze **DIFF** • R: *contact clauses* **DIFF** • R: *relative clauses referring to a sentence* **DIFF**
Reading: einem Romanauszug Informationen entnehmen | die Erzählperspektive in einem Romanauszug erkennen **Writing:** einen Bericht schreiben | eine Geschichte fortschreiben	**WORTSCHATZ:** Soziale Gerechtigkeit • Schule **STRUKTUREN:** R: indirekte Rede **DIFF**
Reading: persönlichen Berichten Informationen entnehmen **Writing:** einen Dialog schreiben **Media:** eine Radiosendung aufnehmen	**WORTSCHATZ:** Vorlieben/Abneigungen • Jobs **STRUKTUREN:** R: indirekte Rede (Fragen) **DIFF**
Viewing: einem Videoclip Informationen entnehmen **Mediation:** Informationen aus einer deutschsprachigen Ferienjob-anzeige/einem deutschsprachigen Artikel auf Englisch wiedergeben **DIFF** **Media:** einen Lebenslauf als Video erstellen CULTURE BOX International job applications	**WORTSCHATZ:** Jobs • Vorlieben/Abneigungen • Zukunftspläne • Soft Skills/Hard Skills • Bewerbung **STRUKTUREN:** *let/make sb do sth, have sth done* • *future progressive* **DIFF** • *future perfect* **DIFF**
Viewing: einem Videoclip Informationen entnehmen **Media:** ein Video mit Bewerbungstipps erstellen	**WORTSCHATZ:** Bewerbung • Gespräch **STRUKTUREN:** R: Bedingungssätze, Typ 3

Inhalt

		Zielaufgaben (Target tasks)	Kompetenzen
	Theme 5	**The North of England**	
120	Intro: Art and culture in the North		**Listening:** einem Hörtext Informationen entnehmen **Speaking:** Vorlieben nennen | eine Reiseroute planen und präsentieren **Reading:** Sachtexten Informationen entnehmen |
122	Part A: Manchester	**Target task:** eine Debatte führen	**Speaking:** Vorlieben nennen | eine Debatte führen **Reading:** Sachtexten Informationen entnehmen | einem Zeitungsartikel Informationen entnehmen | Merkmale unterschiedlicher Zeitungstypen erkennen
127	Target task tools	*Unterstützendes Übungsangebot zur Erarbeitung der Target task*	
128	Part B: Take a stand	**Target task:** einen Zeitungsartikel schreiben	**Listening:** einem Telefongespräch Informationen entnehmen **Speaking:** über die Pläne einer Person spekulieren | eine Sprachnachricht aufnehmen | eine Szene mit verteilten Rollen vorlesen
133	Target task tools	*Unterstützendes Übungsangebot zur Erarbeitung der Target task*	
134	Photo tour	*Stories from the North (Fotomaterial und Informationen)*	
136	Reading tour	*The Summer We Turned Green (Romanauszug)*	
140	I can ...	*Selbsteinschätzung nach Abschluss des Kapitels*	
141	Step by step	*Schrittweises Training weiterführender Kompetenzen*	**Writing:** einen Leserbrief schreiben

Anhang

145	Diff and train	*Differenzierungs- und Trainingsanhang* Theme 1 **145** Theme 2 **151** Theme 3 **164** Theme 4 **173** Theme 5 **182**
194	Language training	Assuming and speculating **194** Varying sentence structure **195** Varying expression **197** False friends **201**
202	Skills pages	Listening **202** Reading **203** Speaking with others **205** Giving a presentation **206** Writing **208** Searching the internet **211** Viewing **212** Mediation **213** Working with others **214**
216	Grammar	*Erläuterung der grammatikalischen Strukturen*
235	Grammatical terms	*Grammatikalische Begriffe*

	Sprachliche Mittel
Mediation: Informationen aus englischsprachigen Sachtexten/einem Artikel auf Deutsch wiedergeben **Media:** Empfehlungen für kulturelle Veranstaltungen aufzeichnen | eine Internetrecherche durchführen CULTURE BOX Brexit **DIFF**	**WORTSCHATZ:** kulturelle Angebote
Writing: eine Zeitleiste erstellen **Viewing:** einem Videoclip Informationen entnehmen	**WORTSCHATZ:** Geschichte • Vorlieben/Abneigungen **STRUKTUREN:** R: Infinitiv mit oder ohne *to* **DIFF** • adverbiale Bestimmungen im Satz **DIFF**
Reading: einem szenischen Text Informationen entnehmen **Writing:** eine Szene fortschreiben | einen Zeitungsartikel schreiben	**WORTSCHATZ:** Umwelt- und Klimaschutz • Aktivismus **STRUKTUREN:** Gerundium oder Infinitiv mit *to* • *emphatic 'do'* **DIFF** • Gerundium nach Präpositionen **DIFF**

237	Wordbanks	1 Nature and environment **237** 2 History **238** 3 Cartoons **239** 4 Social media **239**	5 Film **240** 6 Expressing your opinion **241** 7 Statistics **242** 8 Jobs **243**
245	Word lists	*Wortlisten zu den Kapiteln*	
277	English-German dictionary	*Wörterbuch Englisch-Deutsch*	
330	Names	*Eigennamen*	
333	English sounds The English alphabet	*Lautschrift und Alphabet*	
334	Ähnliche Wörter	*Ähnliche Wörter im Englischen und Deutschen*	
336	Class instructions	*Arbeitsanweisungen*	
337	Irregular verbs	*Unregelmäßige Verben*	
340	Quellenverzeichnis		

Inhalt

Verweise

▶ **DIFF** Training D1 | p. 145	Verweis auf differenzierendes Zusatzangebot
▶ Wordbank 2 | p. 238	Verweis auf eine *Wordbank*
▶ Listening | p. 202	Verweis auf eine *Skills page*
▶ G9 | p. 231	Verweis auf den Grammatikanhang
L 1/1 | **S** 1	Verweis auf einen Audio-Track: Track 1 der Audio-CD 1 für Lehrkräfte/Audio-Track 1 für Schülerinnen und Schüler ▶ WES-149226-1
▶ **WB** 3 | p. 4	Verweis auf eine Übung im *Workbook*
▶ WES-149226-1	Verweis auf Online-Materialien unter www.westermann.de/webcode

Symbole

	Diese Aufgabe vermittelt Medienkompetenz.
	Diese Aufgabe trainiert Sprachmittlung.
	Videoclip
	Partnerarbeit
	Gruppenarbeit
A2	Aufgabe A2 ist obligatorisch.
A6	Aufgabe A6 ist obligatorisch und dient der Vorbereitung der *Target task* in Part A.
A12	Aufgabe A12 ist fakultativ.
b)	Teilaufgabe b) ist fakultativ.

Die Inhalte von Camden Town stellen ein Angebot dar. Die Auswahl der Aufgaben und Übungsteile richtet sich nach dem Lehrplan des jeweiligen Bundeslandes bzw. den Schwerpunkten des schulinternen Curriculums.

1

Australia

In this Theme you will ...

- get to know different aspects of Australia's past and present
- summarize a newspaper article
- read a blog about a school exchange
- learn about school in Australia
- find out about the effects of climate change in Australia
- give a short presentation

1 G'day Australia!

1 Great Barrier Reef

2 Uluru

3 Cricket

4 Sydney: Opera House and Harbour Bridge

1 Australia ▶ WB 1, 2 | p. 4

a) What comes to your mind when you think of Australia?
Collect ideas in class. The photos can help you. Note down your ideas.

b) Start a class wall chart on Australia. Write each of these categories on a separate poster.

cities • geography • culture/history • nature/environment • sport

Note down your ideas from a) and put up the posters in your classroom. Add more information as you learn more about Australia in this Theme. You can add more categories, too. ▶ Class wall chart | p. 214

2 Welcome to Australia ▶ Viewing | p. 212 ▶ DIFF Training D1, D2 | p. 145 ▶ WB 3 | p. 4

a) Watch the video clip and explain what is special about Australia's capital city.

b) Form two groups. Each group concentrates on different aspects.
Group A: general facts about Australia, nature/environment, sport
Group B: cities, geography
Watch the video again. Note down your results, then share them with the other group.
Add your results to your class wall chart from Intro 1b).

c) Choose two photos from these pages. Imagine you are travelling in Australia and are posting the photos on social media. Write a short comment for each photo and add at least three hashtags.
▶ Wordbank 1 | p. 237

d) Find the places from photos 1, 2, 4 and 6 on the map at the back of the book.

5 Bushfires

6 Melbourne

7 Quokka

8 The Outback

3 Australian English

L 1/1 ▶ WB 4 | p. 5

a) Look at the following Australian words and phrases. Listen to some dialogues in which they are used.

sanger • brekky • g'day • footy • put a sock in it • to be stoked • barbie • arvo • roo • no worries

b) Write the Australian words and phrases in a grid. Then listen to the dialogues again and write down the British English equivalents. You can use a dictionary if you need help.

Australian English	British English
sanger	*sandwich*
brekky	...

c) Go online and find five more Australian English words and phrases. Share your results in class and add them to your grid from b).

4 A quiz about Australia

▶ DIFF Training D3 | p. 145 ▶ WB 5 | p. 5

Prepare a quiz about Australia for a partner. Think of at least five multiple-choice questions.

- Go online to search for information and note it down.
- For each question, note down three answers. Of course, only one of them is correct!
- Swap your quiz with a partner's and answer the questions.
- Check your answers with your partner.

Media
You can use digital tools to create a quiz.

▶ WB Media 5 ▶ WES-149226-2

A1 British prisoners in Australia

▶ Wordbank 2 | p. 238 ▶ WB 6, 7 | p. 6

a) Before you watch the video, match these words and definitions. ▶ DIFF Training D4 | p. 146

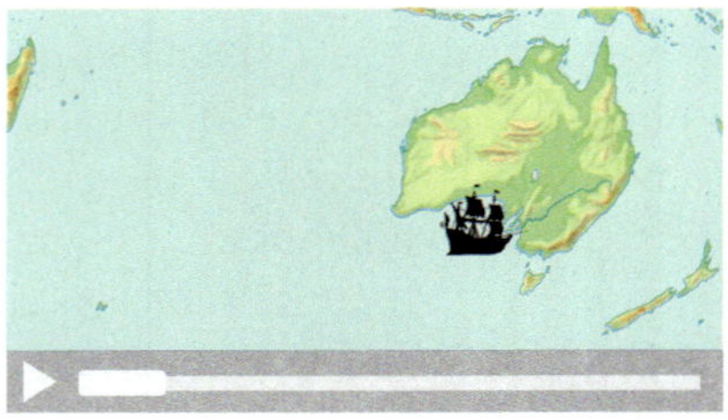

1	to benefit from	**A**	to come to an end
2	convicts	**B**	too full
3	colony	**C**	connected to/with
4	to cooperate	**D**	to work together
5	to expire	**E**	to profit from
6	former	**F**	belonging to an earlier time
7	to found	**G**	having always lived in a place
8	indigenous	**H**	to take the first steps in building sth
9	overcrowded	**I**	a country under control of another country
10	related to	**J**	people who were found guilty of a crime

b) Group work (3): Choose two dates/periods of time each. Watch the video and note down information on "your" dates. Exchange the information in your group and make a timeline.
▶ DIFF Easy alternative D5 | p. 146

1700s/1800s 1770 1787 1788-1868 1810 1830s

c) What impact did the British colonization of Australia have on the country and on its indigenous people?

A2 Australian flags

L 1/2 ▶ Listening | p. 202 ▶ DIFF Training D6, D7 | p. 146

Since 1995, Australia has had three official flags: the Australian national flag, the Australian Aboriginal flag and the Torres Strait Islander flag.

a) Listen and explain what ...

1. is special about the stars in the Southern Cross on the Australian national flag.
2. the yellow circle on the Australian Aboriginal flag represents.
3. the green and blue stripes on the Torres Strait Islander flag stand for.

b) The star under the Union Jack is called the "Commonwealth Star".

- Research and explain what it means for a country to be part of the Commonwealth.
- Find three other examples of countries which are currently members of Commonwealth.
- Australia has been discussing leaving the Commonwealth. Research the current status.

A3 Aboriginal Australians

▶ DIFF Training D8 | p. 147 ▶ WB 8, 9 | p. 7

Information relay: Divide the class into two groups. ▶ Information relay | p. 214

1 Each group reads the information on page 15, focusing on one aspect:

- Group 1 notes down information about Aboriginal Australians' culture and their way of life
- Group 2 notes down information about how British settlers impacted Aboriginal Australians' lives

2 When you have taken your notes, go to your relay point and wait for someone from your own group to join you. Check anything you are unsure of and compare your notes.
If necessary, add information to your notes.

3 Then go to a third relay point and wait for someone from the other group to join you.
Explain to each other what you found out in 2.

Aboriginal Australians

Together with the Torres Strait Islander peoples, Aboriginal peoples were the first to live in Australia and are one of the oldest living civilizations in the world. They came to Australia more than 50,000 years ago. At that time, sea levels were much lower than today and Australia and Asia were connected by land bridges.

However, Aboriginal Australians have their own stories about how it all began. These stories are based on *The Dreaming*: the foundation of Aboriginal religion and culture which also explains how the world and life was created by the ancestor spirits. After the creation of the universe, the ancestor spirits became part of nature and live on mountains, in trees, rivers and lakes. Some of these places, like Uluru, are sacred places. These beliefs also explain the close connection that Aboriginal Australians feel to their land and to all living things. Through storytelling, Aboriginal Australians pass down knowledge from generation to generation. This includes information about where to find water and how the seasons affect animals and plants.

When the first British settlers arrived in Australia in 1788, there were about 600 different Aboriginal groups. Each group spoke their own dialect of one of the over 200 Aboriginal languages. Many Aboriginal Australians spoke two or more languages and could communicate with other groups.

The British settlers forced the Aboriginal Australians off their land. Many died from starvation or diseases that the Europeans had brought to the continent.

In the 20th century the Australian government forced Aboriginal Australians to abandon their traditional way of life. Against their will, more than 100,000 indigenous children were taken from their parents and raised by foster families or in government institutions. These children were later referred to as the "Stolen Generations".

Aboriginal Australians protested against this mistreatment for many years. It wasn't until the 1960s that Aboriginal Australians were given the right to vote and were finally recognized as Australian citizens. However, this did not mean that they were widely accepted by society and had the same standard of living or the same opportunities as others. It took another 30 years until Australian society began to acknowledge the horrible treatment Aboriginal Australians had suffered. In 1996 Australia held the first *National Reconciliation Week*. Two years later, the first *National Sorry Day* was held. The two events are celebrated every year from 26 May to 3 June. In 2008 the Australian prime minister apologized formally for the past mistreatment of Aboriginal Australians.

Although there are many success stories, like Olympic gold medal winner Cathy Freeman, a lot of Aboriginal Australians still experience discrimination and racism today. They face higher rates of poor health, poverty and social problems compared to non-indigenous Australians.

A4 Three profiles ▶ DIFF Training D9 | p. 147 ▶ WB 10 | p. 8

a) Read the profiles. Explain what the three people have in common.

A Isaiah Dawe

Isaiah grew up in 17 different foster homes in New South Wales and experienced abuse during that time. As a young adult, he founded a non-profit mentoring organization "ID. Know Yourself" to support Aboriginal children who, like him, do not live with their families. According to Isaiah, knowing yourself means knowing what you are capable of, knowing your worth and what you can achieve in this world. He regularly posts information under #BreakTheCycle.

B Shadeene Evans

Shadeene was born and raised in Borroloola, a tiny, very isolated community in the Northern Territory. She grew up in the Mara tribe, hunting and fishing with her dad and has a brother and two sisters. At age 12, she was given the chance to join the John Moriarty Football programme. Although it was a great opportunity that would change her life, it also meant moving 3,000 km away from her family and adjusting to life in Sydney. Shadeene currently plays soccer for Adelaide United and for the Australia Women's National Under-20 Team.

C Adam Briggs

Adam Briggs, known as "Briggs", is a successful Australian rap musician. Rap is a way for him to express both the importance of having pride in one's identity and his anger at racism in Australia, which he and his family experienced on a daily basis in the small, isolated town he grew up in. Music helped him through difficult times at school, where he experienced discrimination and did not receive any support. The tattoo on his forearms, which reads "Yorta Yorta", represents his Indigenous heritage. He has released several albums and has won many Australian music awards. He is also the director of an organization that supports the development of Indigenous young people in the creative industries.

b) Analyse how overcoming difficulties has influenced the lives of the three people.

c) Choose one of the profiles and write down three questions that you would like to ask Isaiah, Shadeene or Adam. Search the internet to find answers to your questions. If you cannot find an answer, imagine what they might say.

d) Research other publicly known Aboriginal Australians and write a brief profile. Compare your profiles in class and discuss what they have in common and what is different.

A5 In the news ▶ DIFF Training D10 | p. 147 ▶ WB 11 | p. 8

Read the newspaper article and explain ...

- why Australia Day is celebrated on 26th January,
- why some people protest against the anniversary,
- what protesters demand.

Australia Day polarizes nation

by Rosalind Cresswell for *The Canberra Bugle*
27th January, 2022

Yesterday, tens of thousands of people across the country protested the anniversary of the British colonization of Australia. 26th January is officially known as Australia Day, but is often referred to as Invasion Day by many Aboriginal activists and their supporters.

Despite poor weather in Brisbane, protesters of all ages gathered at Queens Gardens to join the protest march through the city's central business district. Part of the march was a large Indigenous flag, carried by more than 20 people. When the crowds arrived in Musgrave Park, chants of "Always was, always will be Aboriginal land" could be heard. Historically, Musgrave Park was a sacred place to the Native Murri people. Speeches, music and dance performances continued late into the evening.

Meanwhile, early on Wednesday morning, in the city of Melbourne at Catani Gardens in St Kilda, a statue of British naval officer James Cook was sprayed with red paint. Police who came to assess the damage found posters with slogans such as "Abolish Australia Day." So far, no suspects have been found.

For a long time now, there have been heated debates over how the arrival date of the first British ships at Port Jackson in present-day Sydney in 1788 should be remembered. Protesters point out that the British built their colony on land which was forcefully taken from Indigenous Australians. "Governments should abolish Australia Day celebrations or possibly change the date to another day," commented Deborah Sandy, Indigenous elder and co-organiser of the Brisbane protest.

"Reflect, respect and celebrate" was the motto for Australia Day in the national capital of Canberra. The day was marked by a mix of protests, celebrations, and the welcoming ceremony for new citizens. Across the country, more than 16,000 immigrants from 150 nations received their Australian citizenship.

"Australia is the most successful multicultural and multi-faith nation on Earth," Prime Minister Scott Morrison proclaimed in a speech at one ceremony.

"Today, on this Australia Day, I feel a deep sense of gratitude. Gratitude for a history that spans 65,000 years; a continent of unmatched beauty and wonder; a democratic tradition that is the foundation of our freedom; and the multicultural and multi-faith communities that add so much to our national life," he added.

Changing the date of Australia Day might be a helpful first step in addressing the wrongs of the past committed by British colonialists.
Better still would be real change in society – an acknowledgement of the hardships Indigenous communites have faced and continue to face, as well as striving for a more just and equal society for all Australians, no matter their background.

A6 Revision: The passive
▶ G2R | p. 220 ▶ DIFF Training D11 | p. 148 ▶ WB 12 | p. 9

a) Passive sentences are often used in newspaper articles to report what happened. Find examples in A5. If you cannot remember how to form the passive, check G2R on page 220.

b) Read these pieces of news and rewrite them using the passive.

1 On Australia Day, many buildings will hang flags and colourful decorations.
2 Sydney will light up its opera house with a spectacular First Nations artwork.
3 Aboriginal activists are leading protest marches in Sydney, Melbourne and Canberra.
4 Two young men had sprayed the Cook statue with red paint.
5 In recent years, many people have criticized politicians for not changing the date of Australia Day.

A7 Preparing a summary
▶ WB 13 | p. 9

When you want to write a summary, you can start by dividing the text into meaningful parts. Then you take notes on the main points in each part. Look at the first part of the article from A5 and the notes:

> Yesterday, tens of thousands of people across the country protested the anniversary of the British colonization of Australia. 26th January is officially known as Australia Day, but is often referred to as Invasion Day by many Aboriginal activists and their supporters.

- *big protest against Australia Day*
- *Australia Day is the anniversary of British colonization*
- *Australia Day is often called Invasion Day by Aboriginal activists*

Now divide the rest of the article from page 17 into meaningful parts and take notes. You can download the article with this webcode:
▶ WES-149226-5

Before you take notes, ...
1 read each part and make sure you understand it.
2 highlight the main information.

A8 Target task Write a summary (newspaper article)
▶ Writing | p. 209

Write a summary of the newspaper article from page 17.
The checklist ▶ WES-149226-5 can help you.

1 Write an introduction. Make sure you include:
- the author,
- title,
- type of text,
- the place and date of publication, and
- the main idea.

You can start like this:
In her article "Australia Day polarizes nation", which was published in ... on ..., Rosalind Cresswell ...

2 Write the main part. You can use your notes from A7 to help you.
- Focus on the basic facts, not details.
- Use your own words.
- Use the present tense.
- Don't use direct speech. ▶ WB 14 | p. 10
- Don't give your opinion.

Connect your ideas with different conjunctions. Vary your sentence structure (e.g. use passive sentences).

Need help? Look at page 19. T1 T2

Target task tools for A8: Write a summary (newspaper article)

T1 Words and phrases for your summary

Read the phrases below. Decide whether they are part of the introduction (1) or the main part of a summary (2).

Ben Miller's article "See you in Sydney", published in May 2023 in the Morning Sun, deals with ... • The author describes/points out/argues ... • In her article "Moon River", which was published in ..., the author Julie Smith ... • He moves on to explain ... • She opens the article by describing ... • At the end, the author expresses hope that ... • According to the author, the main problem is ...

T2 Summarizing

Read this extract of a newspaper article and the different summaries of it. Use the checklist ▶ WES-149226-5 to decide which summary is the best. Explain why.

In 1849 Edward Hargraves, a sailor, farmer and shop owner, sailed from Sydney to California for the gold rush, but did not manage to find any gold. When he returned to Australia two years later, he headed straight inland to the colony of New South Wales to find gold. With the help of a few other men, Hargraves found a small amount of gold a few weeks later at a place he named Ophir. News of the gold find was soon published in the Sydney Morning Herald, and within just a few months about 40,000 diggers arrived in Ophir. The gold rush had begun!

The government of the colony of Victoria offered a £200 reward to anyone who could find gold within 200 miles of Melbourne. Soon gold was discovered in Clunes, and then at Ballarat, Castlemaine and Bendigo. Gold was also discovered in Tasmania (1852), Queensland (from 1857) and the Northern Territory (from 1871). In the 1890s, a new series of gold rushes began when huge gold fields were found at Kalgoorlie and Coolgardie in Western Australia.

Before 1851, Australia was a relatively unknown British colony where about 400,000 people lived. The discovery of gold changed all that. In 1871, Australia's population had grown to over three million. 40 percent of the world's gold production came from Australia at the time and the profits were an enormous boost to the Australian economy.

A *The author describes how the discovery of gold helped Australia to become an economically successful country. The gold rush took place in New South Wales (Ophir), in Victoria (Clunes, Ballarat, Castlemaine), in Tasmania, Queensland, the Northern Territory and in Western Australia (Kalgoorlie and Coolgardie).*

B *In the extract, the author explains the effect of discovering gold in Australia in the 1850s. It brought gold-seekers from around the world to the colonies. The first big discoveries of gold were made at Ophir in New South Wales, and then at Ballarat and Bendigo Creek in Victoria. The gold rushes led to growth in Australia's population and economy.*

C *Without Edward Hargraves, Australia would not have become a rich country with such a big population. Hargraves was an adventurous and courageous man. He was fed up with his life as a farmer and wanted to get rich. Although he did not succeed in finding gold in California, he had more luck in Australia. I think he was an interesting person.*

1 School exchange down under

B1 Going abroad

▶ Milling around | p. 214

Milling around: Would you like to spend some time in Australia as an exchange student?
Talk to at least three people and tell each other …

- why you would like/wouldn't like to go to Australia,
- where you would like to go and why,
- what you might gain from living in a different country.

If you don't want to spend any time in Australia, say if you would prefer another country and explain why.

B2 Theo's blog

▶ Reading | p. 203 ▶ WB 15-17 | p. 10

a) Read Theo's blog and name at least three topics he writes about.

b) Look at the map at the back of the book to find the Australian place where Theo lives.
Work with a partner. Go online and find five interesting facts about the city.
Note them down, then share your results in class.

c) Match the following definitions and synonyms with words from the blog.

▶ DIFF Easy alternative D12 | p. 148 ▶ DIFF Training D13, D14 | p. 148

a person that lives in a place • a school for children between the ages five and twelve • designing and building machines or structures • flying planes • one half of the earth

www.theosaustralianadventure/blog/posts/my_s

Theo's Australian Adventure!

Subscribe to my blog
Listen to my podcast

Latest posts

- **My school**
- Sights and places
- Cairns
- My new home
- My host family
- Arriving in Australia

20th February

5 min | ♥ 321 | 12 comments

G'day and welcome to my blog!

My name is Theo and I'm from Tübingen, Germany. I've been an exchange student in Australia for a few weeks now and I've been using my blog to share my experiences and adventures down under! Today's entry is about my school, Greenway State College in Cairns.

Cairns is a city in the north of Queensland with about 150,000 inhabitants. The best thing about Cairns is its location – there are loads of great places and sights nearby, for example the Great Barrier Reef. Personally, I love the Skyrail, an almost 8-km-long tourist cableway running above a tropical rainforest.

Greenway State College has students in years 7 to 12 and, like lots of other schools in Australia, it's a private school. Up to Year 6, all public and private school kids go to primary school, and then secondary school starts in Year 7. But there are exceptions! As many of you will know, most Australians live on the coast, but some children who live in the Outback don't have a school anywhere nearby. The only way they can get an education is by signing up for School of the Air.

My school day begins at around seven o'clock. At the start, it felt strange having to put on my school →

www.theosaustralianadventure/blog/posts/my_s

uniform every morning, but now that I've got used to it, I find it quite practical. It means I don't have to decide what to wear! Most Australian schools have their own school uniforms, and many even have a small shop where you can buy them.

After breakfast, I take the bus to school. Classes start at nine o'clock – much later than in Germany, yay! Many school subjects are just like the subjects at German schools: maths, English, geography, history and foreign languages. There's no German at my school, but you can learn French and Japanese.

There are several short breaks and a long lunch break. The weather is usually good, so we often sit on the grass outside.

In the afternoon, you can choose from a wide range of electives. Every school has different electives, but most schools offer a range of interesting subjects. I was amazed at some of them, for example engineering and aviation. I don't know any German schools where you can take flying lessons! At my school, you can choose between psychology, drama, film and TV, design and many more.

But my personal favourites are aquatic practices and marine science. In aquatic practices we learn snorkelling, fishing and aquatic safety. You can even get your boat licence – I really want to do that!

Marine science is about marine organisms, their environment and how to protect them. We also learn about oceans, for example how oceans were formed, their movement and how this affects the weather. Navigation is also part of the course. It's quite difficult! The best thing about marine science is that we're going on a trip to a coral reef next week – I'll tell you all about it, of course!

One more thing about Australian schools: sport is very important here. There are loads of options to choose from, for example tennis, surfing, golf, triathlon, rowing and dance. Some schools even have their own swimming pools, tennis courts or boats!

By the way, in Australia the summer holidays start in December and go until the end of January. That may sound strange, but it's because we're in the southern hemisphere. Traditionally, on the last day before the summer holidays, students go to the beach and jump into the ocean wearing their school uniforms!

One last thing about the summer here in Australia. When I arrived just before Christmas last year, the first thing I saw were Christmas decorations on the beach. Crazy, right?

That's it for today, guys!
What else would you like to know about Australia? Let me know in the comments!

PS I have just recorded a new podcast:
Tips for your trip to Australia. *Check it out!*

B3 Australian schools

In comparison with ...
In contrast to ...
While ...
Unlike students in Germany, ...

a) Use the information from Theo's blog to compare German and Australian schools.

b) Add information about Australian schools to your class wall chart.

c) Round robin: Explain whether you would like to spend a year at Theo's school in Australia.
▶ Round robin | p. 215

d) In what way can Theo benefit from his stay? Compare your ideas with your answers from B1.

e) Write a comment for Theo's blog. ▶ WB Media 2 ▶ WES-149226-2

B4 School of the Air

a) The *School of the Air* is sometimes called "one of the greatest Australian inventions". Read the culture box and explain the statement.

b) Describe the challenges students of the *School of the Air* face.

c) There is another organization caring for remote areas, the *Royal Flying Doctor Service*. To find out more, go online and add relevant information to your class wall chart. ▶ DIFF Easy alternative D15 | p. 149

School of the Air

Culture box

The *School of the Air* was invented for children who live in remote areas of Australia, for example in the Outback, where there are no nearby schools. The first lessons were broadcast from Alice Springs in 1951. Today, the *School of Air* operates from 16 towns and cities to make sure that almost every part of the country can be reached. The school at Katherine, for example, covers an area of just over 800,000 km². In comparison, Germany covers an area of 357,000 km².

A typical school day begins with instructions from the teacher via internet or radio. When the lesson is over, students continue working on their own. Many students use the internet if they have a good internet connection.

The *School of the Air* is very successful. On the one hand, studies show that the students are very well educated. On the other hand, the *School of the Air* also has a very important impact on its students' social lives. For many students in the Outback, the *School of the Air* is the only opportunity to interact with children and teenagers of the same age. Once or twice a year, students travel to meet their classmates and teachers – a highlight for many students!

B5 Adverbial clauses ▶ G4R | p. 223 ▶ WB 18 | p. 12

Adverbial clauses can be used to give a text a logical structure and make it more interesting to read. Use the conjunctions to complete the sentences.

just as • since • so that • because • although • as if • before • while

1. Theo has started a blog **XXX** he wants to tell other students about his time in Australia.
2. Theo's host family is very friendly, **XXX** he imagined them to be.
3. Theo looked at the Christmas decorations on the beach **XXX** he couldn't believe his eyes.
4. Students at Theo's school choose aquatic practices as an elective **XXX** they can get a boat licence.
5. **XXX** he goes to school, Theo showers, puts on his school uniform and has breakfast.
6. Theo thinks the uniform is practical **XXX** he had to get used to it.
7. **XXX** Cairns has about 150,000 inhabitants, Tübingen has about 90,000.
8. Every Australian school offers different sports courses **XXX** sport is very important in Australia.

B6 Theo's tips L 1/3 ▶ Listening | p. 202 ▶ DIFF Extra D16 | p. 150 ▶ WB 19 | p. 12

a) Theo has recorded a podcast for people who want to travel to Australia. Listen to the podcast and note down which tip he claims is the most important.

b) Listen again and take notes on each tip. Explain which of the tips you consider the most important.

c) Your cousin wants to travel to Australia. Summarize Theo's tips in German and send your cousin a voice message. ▶ WB Media 7 ▶ WES-149226-2

B7 A trip to Fitzroy Island

▶ DIFF Training D17, D18 | p. 150 ▶ Reading | p. 203 ▶ WB 20, 21 | p. 13

a) Read Theo's blog entry. Explain why he had a lot to think about when he got back from his trip.

b) Scan the blog entry and describe …

- the importance of the turtle rehabilitation centre,
- why the Great Barrier Reef is in danger.

Add relevant information to your class wall chart.

c) Scan the blog entry again and list phrases Theo uses to talk to the reader directly (e.g. *Today, I want to tell you about …, You may already know that …; Why is that? Well, …, …*).

www.theosaustralianadventure/blog/posts/Fitzro

Theo's Australian Adventure!

✉ Subscribe to my blog
🎧 Listen to my podcast

Latest posts

- **Fitzroy Island**
- ✈ Cairns
- ✈ My school
- ✈ My new home
- ✈ Sights and places
- ✈ My host family

1st March

5 min | ♥ 108 | 7 comments

Hey guys,

In my last blog entry, I told you that one of my electives is marine science. Today, I want to tell you about our trip to Fitzroy Island, which is a tropical island with a rainforest about 45 minutes from Cairns. You may already know that it's listed as a national park. It has a turtle rehabilitation centre, a great beach and a coral reef that is part of the Great Barrier Reef. No wonder it's a popular tourist destination!

Our school always organizes a trip to Fitzroy Island in September or October. Why is that? Well, the dry season runs from May to October, and at that time of year the sky is clearer and the sea is calmer than during the wet season. Also, from November to May is stinger season! There aren't too many stingers around Fitzroy Island, but you really might not want to take the risk!

When we arrived, Dr Li Symmonds, a marine biologist, picked us up and took us to the turtle rehabilitation centre – a great experience! You should definitely go if you ever have the chance to visit Fitzroy Island! The centre helps injured turtles, nursing them back to health and releasing them back into the ocean.

Unfortunately, humans are the reason why so many turtles get injured. Turtles are hit by boats, get caught in fishing nets or plastic, or eat microplastics that make them sick.

After lunch, we got to try out our aquatic skills and go snorkelling. It was just awesome – so many fish and corals!!!

In the afternoon, we learned more about corals and the Great Barrier Reef. Did you know that baby corals look like tiny jellyfish? They float around in the water until they find a place to attach to, usually a coral reef. When they land, they begin to build themselves a shell, which is made of calcium carbonate, also known as limestone. →

www.theosaustralianadventure/blog/posts/Fitzro

Dr Symmonds also told us why zooxanthellae – very tiny animals – are important for corals. They live on and inside the coral. Corals eat them and zooxanthellae give them their colour. Different corals like different zooxanthellae – and that's why they have different colours. Isn't that cool?

As you probably know already, the Great Barrier Reef contains the world's largest collection of coral reefs. There are more than 350 types of coral as well as all kinds of fish and birds. But did you know that the Great Barrier Reef is so big that you can see it from space? Check out this photo. Awesome, right?

Unfortunately, the Great Barrier Reef is in great danger. Tourism, ships and farming have caused a lot of harm to the reef, but the biggest threat is climate change and the higher water temperatures it brings. The corals become stressed and stop eating the zooxanthellae, and as a result, the corals lose their colour and die. This is called coral bleaching. Dr Symmonds told us that the Great Barrier Reef could be dead within the next 30 years – a terrible tragedy.

To prevent this, people on Fitzroy Island have come up with ideas for how to save their precious environment. For example, the Reef Restoration Foundation specializes in growing new heat-resistant corals that aren't affected by warmer temperatures. Volunteers watch out for pollution, animal pests and coral bleaching in the ocean around the island. Plastic cups, plates and straws are banned, and there are regular beach-cleaning events.

When we got back to Cairns in the evening, all of us had a lot to think about. Fitzroy Island is amazing, but you just can't ignore what we humans are doing to the natural environment.

B8 Target task Prepare and give a three-minute talk

▶ Presentation | p. 206 ▶ Wordbank 1, 2 | p. 237

Prepare and give a three-minute talk that provides information on one of these Australian topics:

- sights
- nature
- people
- culture
- sports
- …

You can also use your class wall chart for other ideas.

1 Search for information online, then paraphrase the results. ▶ **WB** Media 5 ▶ WES-149226-2
2 Use the checklist ▶ WES-149226-5 to plan the structure of your talk (introduction, main part, conclusion). The list will provide you with useful phrases as well.
3 Use the phrases from B7c) to make your talk more interesting for your audience.
4 Prepare cue cards with keywords that you can refer to while giving your talk.
5 Use the checklist to make sure that you have considered everything you need for your talk.
6 Practise giving your talk.
7 In groups present your topics. Remember to make eye contact with your classmates and to stay within the time limit.
8 Use the checklist to give feedback.
▶ **WB** 22 | p. 14

Media
Alternatively, you can record your talk and send it to a partner/your teacher for feedback.
▶ **WB** Media 7 ▶ WES-149226-2

Need help? Look at page 25. T1

Target task tools for B8: Prepare and give a three-minute talk

T1 Searching the internet: Paraphrasing search results

When researching a topic on the internet, you often find too much information.
This is why you should paraphrase your search results.

- ✓ If possible, highlight the information you are looking for.
- ✓ Use your own words to paraphrase the information.
- ✓ Instead of copying the original text, you can ...
  - use synonyms,
  - shorten sentences, for example by using participle constructions,
  - combine sentences, for example by using connectives (*because, after, when, ...*).
- ✓ Don't note down unnecessary information.

a) Read the first part of a text about South Australia and compare it with the paraphrased text.

Adelaide is the capital city of the Australian state South Australia and one of the biggest cities in Australia.

Early history

The Indigenous Kaurna people, one of many Aboriginal nations in South Australia, originally inhabited the area where Adelaide is located today. The Kaurna are also known as Coorna, Kaura, Gaurna and other variations.
More than 20 Kaurna clans lived in the place where Adelaide is located today. They called it Tartanya and lived in huts and mound settlements.

Adelaide was originally inhabited by the Indigenous Kaurna people. They called the area Tartanya.

b) Download the second part of the text and read it. Highlight the main information about the 19th century. ▶ WES-149226-5.

19th century

In 1834 the British Parliament passed the South Australia Act. This law stated that South Australia could be used as a British province and that new settlers would be financially supported.
On 28 December 1836, Captain John Hindmarsh issued the proclamation that South Australia was now a British province.
Hindmarsh's private secretary George Stevenson had written the text aboard the *HMS Buffalo*. The document was printed by Robert Thomas (1782-1860), who came from England with his family on the *Africaine* and arrived at Holdfast Bay on 8 November 1836. Thomas owned a printing press, which he brought with him. It was the first printing press ever to reach South Australia. The press was a Stanhope Invenit No. 200, which was on display at the State Library until 2001.
The event on 28 December 1836 is commemorated in South Australia as Proclamation Day.

c) Paraphrase the information you highlighted in b).

1 New Zealand

Photo tour

1

2

3

4

5

6

7

8

9

10

A New Zealand is approximately 1,500 km south-east of Australia. The two countries have a similar colonial history, with the result that both are English-speaking and have similar flags. The Australian flag has six white stars, whereas the New Zealand flag has four red stars, but both flags have a Union Jack in the top left-hand corner.

B New Zealand, also known as *Aotearoa* in Māori, is made up of two main islands, the North Island and the South Island, as well as approximately 600 smaller islands. Aside from snowy mountain ranges, volcanoes and hot springs, farms, historic villages and cities, New Zealand also has a coastline of over 15,000 km, one of the longest in the world, with many beautiful beaches.

C New Zealand is also known for its national parks. One of the most famous destinations in New Zealand is Milford Sound fiord, located in Fiordland National Park. It combines breathtaking mountain scenery, waterfalls, deep water full of marine life and the lush green vegetation typical of the subtropical climate of the South Island. You can explore Milford Sound by boat.

D New Zealand has much more to offer than just natural beauty, with lots of exciting towns and cities to explore. The largest city, Auckland, boasts an impressive skyline right on the seafront, with its instantly recognizable Sky Tower. Around 1.5 million people live in Auckland, and it is a very multicultural city with one of the highest proportions of foreign-born citizens in the world.

E The capital city of New Zealand is Wellington, in the south-west of the North Island. Wellington attracts many visitors with its museums, waterfront cafés and beautiful scenery, as well as the famous Wellington Cable Car. It has the least pollution of any capital city and is also the world's windiest city.

F Wellington is home to New Zealand's parliament buildings, including The Beehive, which is famous for its distinctive shape. Today, New Zealand is a parliamentary democracy with the British monarch as the Head of State. Britain's presence in New Zealand began in 1840, when New Zealand became a British Crown colony after the signing of the Treaty of Waitangi. However, a growing number of European settlers in New Zealand wished to be in control of their own decisions, and sixteen years later they had gained self-government with their own prime minister. But it was only after World War II that they became citizens of New Zealand rather than of Britain.

G After the British had started colonizing New Zealand, the rights of the Indigenous Māori peoples were often ignored. The British made laws that allowed them to take land from the Māori and forced the Māori to sell their land to the settlers. In 1939, only 1% of the South Island and 3% of the North Island belonged to the Māori. Today, the New Zealand government protects and promotes Māori language and culture. There are certain parts of New Zealand where Māori culture is particularly present, for example in Rotorua. Rotorua is a city situated near many hot springs with geysers and brightly coloured natural pools that are sacred to the Māori.

H One Māori ritual you might have heard of is the *haka*. It's a ritual dance and includes chanting, stamping, clapping and strong facial expressions. It is believed that the *haka* was originally a war dance used to scare the enemy. Today, it is performed at different special events and before each game of New Zealand's national rugby team.

I The kiwi is a bird that can't fly and can only be found in New Zealand. Since precolonial times, the kiwi has been considered special by the Māori, who used kiwi feathers in their ceremonial dances. The bird has since become a national symbol. New Zealanders are also often referred to as 'Kiwis'.

J With its diverse landscapes and natural beauty, New Zealand is a popular filming location. The popular fantasy films *The Lord of the Rings* and *The Hobbit* were all filmed in New Zealand. After the success of the films, a decision was made to keep the *Hobbiton* film set as a tourist attraction. You can visit the set and see the colourful hobbit houses set into the hill.

P1 ▶ Reading | p. 203

a) Read the texts and match them to the photos.
b) Start a grid. Collect information on the topics in the box.

history • Māori culture • nature • society • tourist attractions

P2 L 1/6 | S 3 ▶ Listening | p. 202

Think about what the numbers might refer to and match them to the descriptions below. Then listen to the podcast to see if you were right. Correct your answers if necessary.

approx. 5,000,000 • 1642 • approx. 1300 • 176 • 16.5 • approx. 1,600 • 1769

year the first Europeans arrived • types of Māori language • inhabitants • percentage of total population who are Māori • first human settlement • distance north to south (km) • year the first British people arrived

P3

a) Listen to the podcast again and add information to your grid from P1.
b) Imagine you had the opportunity to travel to New Zealand. Use the information from your grid to say what you would like to see and do. Give reasons.

1 Night Feet

Meet Me at the Intersection *is a collection of short stories, memoirs and poems for young adults, written by authors from diverse backgrounds. The authors' backgrounds include Indigenous peoples, People of Colour, members of the LGBTIQA+ community or people living with a disability.*

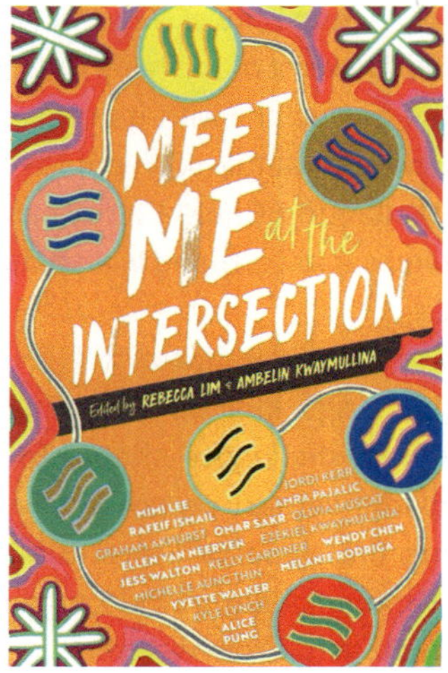

R1

a) Speculate why the book editors have chosen authors from these groups.

b) One of the short stories in the collection is *Night Feet*, written by Ellen van Neerven. Look up the author on the internet. State which of the above groups the author belongs to and speculate on how van Neerven's own biography might be reflected in the story.

R2 ▶ Reading | p. 203

Read extract A from the short story *Night Feet*.

a) Note down what the protagonist, Bella, reveals about herself and her family situation.

b) Choose three adjectives to describe Bella.

ambitious • confident • determined • diplomatic • focused • insecure • laid-back • outgoing • resourceful • selfish • sensible • sociable

c) Work with a partner. Explain your choice of adjectives with reference to Bella's actions and thoughts. Discuss the circumstances that have influenced Bella's life and shaped her character.

A The scholarship was due today and Dad wasn't home. If I didn't get the scholarship money I wouldn't be going to the Nationals[1]. I tried turning my back to the window and began finishing my application. Every scrape[2] outside could be him.

Dad didn't have a phone. One day he propped his old Nokia up on a ledge[3] above the creek and got my brother and me to take turns throwing rocks at it. We both missed twice and he grew impatient. Knocked it off the cliff[4] himself.

Hours went by too quickly as I lost time cleaning up the kitchen, heating soup on the stove, thinking he'd return for lunch. It was afternoon, and I was still missing a few lines when I remembered we didn't have a printer and I had a game at 8.30 pm.

I filled my backpack, putting in my unwashed strip[5], shin pads[6] that had been lying outside on the barbecue, and two bottles of water. Importantly, I had a hair tie and a thin band to push back my fringe. I went back and wrote a hurried last sentence on my application. I finished with the words *I love it*, but did I? This had felt like the most important thing in the world once, but last night, today, it had all slipped away. What would happen if I didn't get the money to go to Canberra? I had relied on Dad to be home to work out how we'd get the application in; he would have planned how we'd print it. I would have to work it out for myself.

I'd catch the bus to the library in town, because the post office near it closed later than the local one did. I knew, because Mum used to work there.

There were more people outside the library than in, sitting at the café, standing against the walls talking and hooked into the wi-fi. I hurried through the doors, printed my application and went straight out, with minutes left to post it. [...]

1 Nationals – *landesweiter Wettkampf* | **2** scrape – *Kratzer* | **3** ledge – *Felsvorsprung* | **4** cliff – *Klippe* | **5** strip – *Trikot* | **6** shin pad – *Schienbeinschoner*

I had half an hour until the train to the soccer field and I walked back to the café at the library. I ordered myself a coffee. I'd never had coffee before, but after a sleepless night and with the need for a load of energy tonight, I thought it was a good time to start. I did worry about dehydration, but I had two water bottles, and they could be refilled. With Dad's voice, I said, gruffly, 'Cappuccino, thanks'. I ordered it to go, as they looked like they were packing up. I'd be the machine's last kiss. When they handed it to me, I went and sat in the garden, and watched the people. There was a young black man, African, walking around. I admired his red, new-looking sneakers, a pair like the ones I wanted but Dad would never give me. I could hear the beat of his music, see the yellow buds in his ears. He was wearing a white T-shirt and grey jeans. He looked at me. I sculled the coffee, hot and sudden in my throat. My father's habit. Mum always said to him, *You burn yourself. You'll have no taste buds left for my casserole.*

The coffee tasted nice, and I already felt less tired. There was a breeze filtering through the garden, caressing[7] my thighs[8]. I chucked the cup in the bin and decided it was time to get changed into my football shorts in the toilets. I stopped for a moment, reopened my bag and took a sip from my water bottle. 'Keep sipping before the game,' Brisbane Roar captain Jade North had said when he came to visit the club. 'Don't gulp.'

I loved North. I rarely had affection for a defender but I loved him because he was a blackfella[9] and a real workhorse. I rested my bag on the slab of concrete on the side of the café. A sitting spot tucked away. This was the corner where I'd had my first kiss, last year, and the feeling of it always returned. I put my bottle down, and the wind picked it up and took it, and it rolled in the direction of the African boy. He caught it easily and handed it back.

'Thanks,' I smiled. 'Crazy wind, hey?'

He nodded. He still had his earphones in but I couldn't hear the music anymore. As I packed my bag up, he took a step closer and said, 'Hey, how you going[10]?'

'Good,' I said. 'And you?'

'Good. Just waiting for friends and that. Where are you from?' he asked.

I half-smiled at the predictability[11] of the question. The easy answer, and what felt true, was to say, 'From here'.

But they always wanted to know more. He didn't buy it, licking his lips.

'My mother's Italian, my father's Aboriginal.'

'Ah,' he said, and repeated it for clarity.

'And where are you from?' I asked. It was only fair.

'I'm from West Africa,' he said, guarded, and of course it was a line from him. What was West Africa?

'What's your name?' he said, looking at me with some sort of understanding.

'Bella. Yours?'

'Akachi,' he mumbled self-consciously.

It took three times to pronounce it properly, but I wanted to. I looked in his eyes.

'I asked because you look different,' he said.

Again, I could have rolled my eyes at the predictability. We looked at each other. I was used to these sorts of moments of connection. Lines of dialogue came in to my head. *Welcome, brother. Thank you, sister.*

'You study, work?'

'I'm still at school,' I said. How old did this fella think I was?

'Oh. Yeah. I study and work.'

'You doing anything interesting tonight?' I asked.

'Waiting for friends. We're going out to the city. I go here to check my emails. You here often?'

'Not really.' I reckoned I should come here more often. 'I've got to get changed,' I said, pointing away.

'Okay,' he said. 'Nice to meet you.' And he made the effort to give me one of the handshakes I'd always wanted, made me feel like one of the boys.

7 to caress – *streicheln* | **8** thigh – *(Ober)schenkel* | **9** blackfella – *indigener Australier* | **10** How you going? *(AusE)* – *Wie geht es dir?* | **11** predictability – *Vorhersagbarkeit*

R 3

a) Dramatic reading: Work with a partner. Act out the dialogue between Bella and Akachi. Emphasize the way in which they react to each other.

b) Present your version of the dialogue to another pair and give each other feedback.

c) Explain how Bella feels about Akachi. Why do you think this?

R 4

Read extract B of the story.

a) List the reasons why Bella is disappointed with the game.

b) Explain how she deals with this disappointment. What does that reveal about her character?

R 5

Study the relationship between Bella and her father. Say what you find unusual or surprising about it.

B

I was playing on the left wing[1]. My second position. Covering[2] for missing girls. I didn't mind that much. I knew I'd still get my chances. Although I did feel a little self-conscious. I had been chosen to represent State. I was my team's biggest weapon. But I wasn't put where I was most effective. I looked at the two girls playing there, Casey was one of them.

She was a defender by birth and always would be. I was angry at the decision. There were no scouts, I didn't have to prove anything, but, at the same time, I did.

[...]

It was 1—1 at half-time. We weren't happy. Our keeper was trying to pick us up. Casey and I weren't even making jokes like we normally did.

I was better than the girl I was playing. Loads better. But she had her dad egging her on from the sideline. 'Round her!'

I thought my dad would do that if he was there. Except his favourite cheer was 'C'mon!' At one point of the match, she did round me. Conned[3] me, took off, went running into miles of space. I felt foolish and couldn't catch up. I chased her down to the corner flag, but I was nowhere close to making any sort of contact. It didn't cause a goal or anything, but I was annoyed.

I got a message from the coach to swap positions with Casey and jump up front. *Here we go.* I started to get some good touches. Control the match. Put my girls in for some good chances. But on the other end, we copped it. Mistake after mistake, and we were down 3—1. Terrible. I still tried. Whenever Bronte had it in her paws, I took off to make myself an option, got all the high balls.

Lack of sleep was catching up on me. And I was cramping[4]. My calves[5] were stiff.

Towards the end of the game, when both coaches were subbing, and the players were no longer running to get the ball when it went past the sideline, I got the ball in a good position.

Casey was behind me, and I gave it to her quickly, hoping to get it back. Yes! She put it through the hole. I was right in on goals. At the keeper again! But the ball bounced off, to Donna, who hit it well. It pushed off the post but I was running so hard at it I didn't see it and there were hands on my shirt and I was on the ground and the ball was in the net. Where did it come off? My knee? Chest? My girls were around me.

I had got my goal, sort of, but it didn't feel any kind of sweet. Before anything else could happen, the ref blew the whistle for the end of the game.

'Where's your dad?' Casey said as we walked barefoot across the field. I realised how drenched in sweat[6] my jersey[7] was.

'I don't know,' I replied.

'We'll take you home,' Casey's mum said.

1 left wing – *linker Flügel* | **2** to cover – *übernehmen* | **3** to con – *reinlegen* | **4** to cramp – *krampfen* | **5** calf – *Wade* | **6** drenched in sweat – *von Schweiß durchnässt* | **7** jersey – *Trikot*

I clicked the door open cautiously.

'Dad?'

'Bella?'

I felt the emotion that had been building up all day come out as I ran towards Dad, standing against the sink[8], hair messy and tired-looking, like even too tired for a hug. But I touched his arm, repeating, 'Where were you?'

'I'm sorry, I had to go buy a printer, so I went to Kmart this morning and I just couldn't work out which one to get.'

It sounded like an incomplete excuse as to where he had been all day, but I didn't press him any further.

We sat down at the kitchen table and I slowly rolled my socks off.

'I got so tired, I can't explain it,' Dad said. 'I really miss her, you know, and I end up getting myself in knots[9] because she was your mum You must miss her so much.'

'You're allowed to miss her, too, Dad.'

He tried to smile. 'How was the game? Did you score?'

'Yeah.' I didn't lift my head.

'I wish I could have seen it.'

'I had to play wing. It was a tough game, Dad. We lost. But we'll get there next time. I caught a train from the city, I passed through and posted—'

'You got the application in,' Dad interrupted, sighing with relief.

'Yeah. We'll be going to Canberra, Dad.'

I said it without knowing but feeling, feeling a determination in my feet. My hands brushed over the unpaid bills and the coffee rings stained into the table. 'I printed it at the State Library and I met a nice boy called Akachi who follows Real Madrid.'

Dad looked at me suspiciously.

'What?' I said.

'I thought you liked girls.'

I shrugged. 'It was 3—2. Donna scored the other one.'

'Tell me about your goal.'

'Yeah, I just got my body in the way.'

'Came off your eyebrow?'

'My knee!'

'Good one.'

'Totally intentional[10],' I said, and my mind started to wander to the next game I'd play, how Dad would be there to see my future goals.

---

8 sink – *Spüle* | **9** getting myself in knots – *völlig durcheinander sein* | **10** intentional – *absichtlich*

R 6 Choose ▶ Writing | p. 208

Choose either task A or B.

A Bella's day is full of challenges. Write about a challenging day that you have experienced, explaining the challenges you faced, how you dealt with them and what your feelings were.

B Write a story about a sports event. Include at least three of the following expressions from extract B. If you are not sure what the expressions mean, use a dictionary or look them up online.

defender by birth • *my team's biggest weapon* • *the girl I was playing* • *egging her on from the sideline* • *had it in her paws* • *we copped it* • *the coaches were subbing* • *the ref blew the whistle*

Was hast du alles gelernt? Diese Seite hilft dir dabei, das zu erkennen.
Falls du Hilfe benötigst, etwas nachlesen oder noch ein paar Übungen machen möchtest, findest du hier passende Hinweise.

WORTSCHATZ

Ich kann …	Aufgaben/Übungen/Hilfen
Wörter und Phrasen aus dem australischen Sprachgebrauch verstehen sowie Ortsnamen korrekt aussprechen *brekky • put a sock in it • Uluru • Mount Kosciuszko*	3 ▶ **DIFF** D2 ▶ **WB** 4
Zuhörerinnen und Zuhörer ansprechen *Today, I want to tell you about … • You may already know that … • Why is that? Well, …*	B7

SKILLS

Ich kann …	Aufgaben/Übungen/Hilfen
einem Videoclip Informationen entnehmen VIEWING	2, A1 ▶ **DIFF** D1, D5 ▶ Viewing | p. 212 ▶ **WB** 3, 6
einem Hörtext Informationen entnehmen LISTENING	3, A2, B6 ▶ **DIFF** D8 ▶ Listening | p. 202 ▶ **WB** 2, 19
einen Zeitungsartikel zusammenfassen WRITING	A8 ▶ T1, T2 | p. 19 ▶ **WB** 13
einen Blog lesen und verstehen READING	B2, B7 ▶ **DIFF** D13, D17 ▶ Reading | p. 203 ▶ **WB** 20
englischen Texten folgen und die wichtigsten Inhalte auf Deutsch wiedergeben MEDIATION	B6 ▶ **DIFF** D9 ▶ Mediation | p. 213 ▶ **WB** 16
eine dreiminütige Präsentation halten SPEAKING • MEDIA	B8 ▶ T1 | p. 25 ▶ Presentation | p. 206

GRAMMATIK

Ich kann …	Aufgaben/Übungen/Hilfen
verschiedene Zeitformen verwenden *Perth is the capital of the Australian state of Western Australia. • In 1829 Captain James Stirling founded Perth.*	▶ **DIFF** D3 ▶ G1R | p. 217 ▶ **WB** 5
Passivformen verwenden *The Cook statue was sprayed with red paint by two young men. • 26th January is officially known as Australia Day.*	A6 ▶ **DIFF** D11 ▶ G2R | p. 220 ▶ **WB** 12
***reported speech* verwenden** *Yini said that she would definitely come back to Australia sometime in the following year.*	▶ **DIFF** D14 ▶ G3R | p. 221 ▶ **WB** 14
***adverbial clauses* verwenden** *Before he goes to school, Theo showers and has breakfast. • Theo has started a blog because he wants to tell other students about his time in Australia.*	B5 ▶ G4R | p. 223 ▶ **WB** 18

On these pages you will learn how to present a picture for an oral exam.
First, there is an example task and a possible solution. Next, there is your task. You will learn how to present a picture, step by step. You can use the checklist on page 36 for other oral exams.

Example

1 Read the example task. Then listen to the solution. L 1/7 | S 4

EXAMPLE TASK

This photo was taken in Perth on 26th January 2020. Describe the photo in detail and explain which issue it illustrates. Use the elements of the photo as well as your knowledge of Aboriginal and Australian history.

SOLUTION

I am going to talk about a photo that was taken in Perth on 26th of January 2020. The photo shows many people protesting in a street.

I will now describe the photo in detail. In the background of the photo, you can see city buildings and trees. In the middle, there are people protesting. The photo is dominated by the many posters with messages written on them like 'invasion day' or 'We live on stolen land'. In the foreground, two men can be seen. If you take a closer look, you see that the men are holding a smoking metal basket. They seem to be burning something. The flags, posters, and the shirts of the two men all include the colours red, yellow, and black.

From what I have learned about the Australian flags, I know that the flags the protesters are holding are Australian Aboriginal flags. The two men in the foreground are wearing T-shirts with Australian Aboriginal flags on them as well. Considering what I know about Aboriginal and Australian history, I think that the people in the photo came together to protest against Australia Day, which celebrates the arrival of the British colonizers on 26th of January 1788.

The photo illustrates the strong opposition to this celebration. Many people in Australia think that it is wrong to celebrate the arrival of the British. They want people to remember the crimes that were committed by the British invaders after they had arrived in Australia. The protesters don't want to abolish Australia Day, but they say that the date of the celebration should be changed to acknowledge the crimes committed against the Aboriginal people and the hardships that they faced.

All in all, the general impression of the photo is that of a strong but peaceful call to action to acknowledge the crimes of the past.

Your task

2 Read your task, then follow the steps on page 35 to complete it.

Choose one of the photos. Describe the photo in detail and explain which topic it illustrates. Use the elements of the photo as well as what you have learned about the topic.

1

2

3

Step 1

Study the photo and take notes on ...
- what you can see,
- what the context might be and what you already know about the issue/topic,
- which issue/topic the photo illustrates.

Step 2

Start your presentation with one or two sentences and briefly describe what you can see.

I'm going to talk about a photo that ... • To start with, ... • Let me start by saying ... • The photo was taken in/on ... • The photo shows ...

Step 3

Now describe the photo in detail.
- Use the present progressive to describe what is happening.
- Make sure to cover all the relevant details in the photo.

Imagine you have to describe the photo to a person who cannot see it.

I will now describe the photo in detail. • Starting with the most prominent feature of the photo, ... • The photo is dominated by ...

In the foreground/background you can see ... • At the top/bottom of the photo there is ... • In the middle of the photo, ... can be seen. • In the upper/lower part ... • In the centre ...

It seems as if ... • As you can see from ..., the photo was taken in/on ... • There is/are ... on the photo who ... • The people in the photo ... • The central focus of the photo is ... • ... indicates/suggests that ... • It looks like ... • If you take a closer look at the photo, ...

Step 4

Consider the context of the photo. Think about what you already know about the issue/topic which the photo illustrates.

From what I know about ..., I think that ... • From what I've learned about ..., I'd guess that ... • As there is/are ... • I'd like to point out that ... • Considering what I know about ... • Keeping in mind what I have learned about ... I think ...

Step 5

Use your results from steps 1-4 to explain which issue the photo illustrates or which topic it relates to.

The photo illustrates the problem of ... • The photo highlights ... • In the photo you are confronted with ... • The photo conveys an idea of ... • The ... creates an atmosphere of ...

Step 6

Conclude your presentation with one or two sentences.

All in all, the photo is typical of ... • The general impression of the photo is that of ... • The ... represents/stands for ... • Considering the photo as a whole, it seems to depict ...

Tips:
- Use all of your given time to talk about the photo.
- Don't panic if you don't know all the words you would like to use. Paraphrase words.
- Don't get distracted. Focus on the photo.

Checklist: Speaking: Presenting pictures

Checklist

1. Study the picture and take notes on ...
   - what you can see,
   - what the context might be and what you already know about the issue/topic,
   - which issue/topic the picture illustrates.

2. Start your presentation with one or two sentences and briefly describe what you can see.

3. Now describe the picture in detail.
   Use the present progressive to describe what is happening.
   Make sure to cover all the relevant details.

4. Consider the context of the picture. Think about what you already know about the issue/topic which the picture illustrates.

5. Use your results from steps 1-4 to explain which issue the photo illustrates or which topic relates to.

6. Conclude with one or two sentences.
   Tips:
   - Use all of your given time to talk about the picture.
   - Don't panic if you don't know all the words you would like to use. Paraphrase words.
   - Don't get distracted. Focus on the picture.

2

Teenage life

In this Theme you will ...

- talk about teenagers of the past and the present
- hold a discussion
- exchange ideas on social media
- analyse a cartoon
- read a newspaper article
- write a report
- read a novel extract
- write a film review

2 Teens then and now

1: US teens with a driver's license

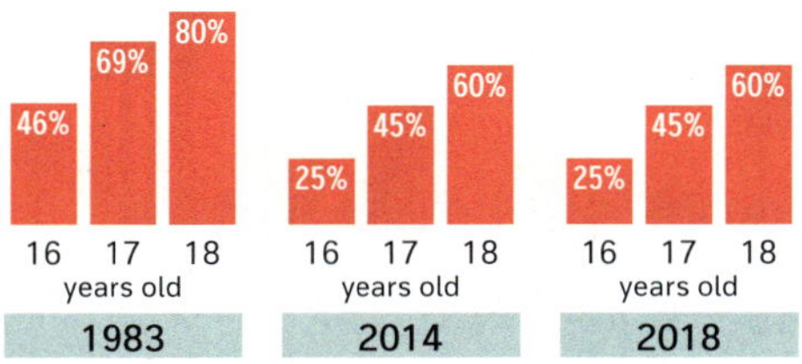

2: Americans who self-identified as LGBTQ+ in 2021

Gen Z (born 1997-2012) 20.8%

Millennials (born 1981-1996) 10.5%

Gen X (born 1965-1980) 4.2%

3: Mental health: Americans likely to be open about ...

... their mental health in 2019

Gen Z	27%
Millennials	15%
Gen X	13%

... receiving treatment / therapy from a professional in 2020

Gen Z	37%
Millennials	34%
Gen X	26%

1 Milling around ▶ Milling around | p. 214 ▶ WB 1 | p. 22

Milling around: What are the advantages/disadvantages of being a teenager? Collect your answers in class and save them for later.

Teenagers are more ... /are better at ... than adults.

While teenagers can ..., adults/children are supposed to ...

The best thing about being a teenager is ...

Being a teenager is sometimes hard because ...

2 Infographics ▶ Wordbank 7 | p. 242 ▶ WB 2 | p. 22

a) Study the six infographics and describe how the figures have changed over the years.

The first graphic highlights/shows ... • The second graphic is about/deals with ... • When you look at ..., you notice that ... • Over the years, the figure/percentage has increased/decreased by ... • The figures go up/down steadily/significantly from 1980 to ... • Compared to ... • Even though ... • While 80% of all 18-year-olds had a driver's licence in 1983, ... • Only 4.2% of Gen X identify as ... while 10.5% of all people who were born between ...

b) Explain which aspect you find most surprising and why.

c) In groups (3) speculate on the reasons for the changes. Talk about your ideas and save them for later.

3 8 things 80s teens did that you don't ▶ DIFF Training D1 | p. 151 ▶ WB 3 | p. 23

a) The title of this video is "8 things 80s teens did that you don't". Collect ideas about what might be presented in the clip.

b) Watch the video and note down which aspects are mentioned. Compare them to your ideas from a).

c) Imagine if one thing from the video came back, what would you like that to be? What wouldn't you want to come back? Give reasons.

4: US teens reading books & magazines nearly every day

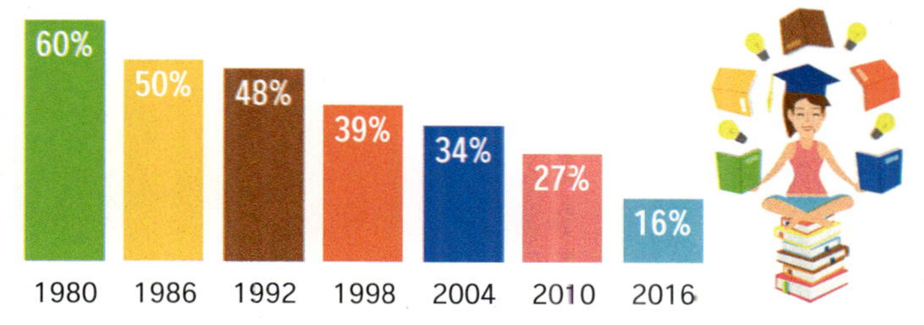

5: Daily smoking among American high school students

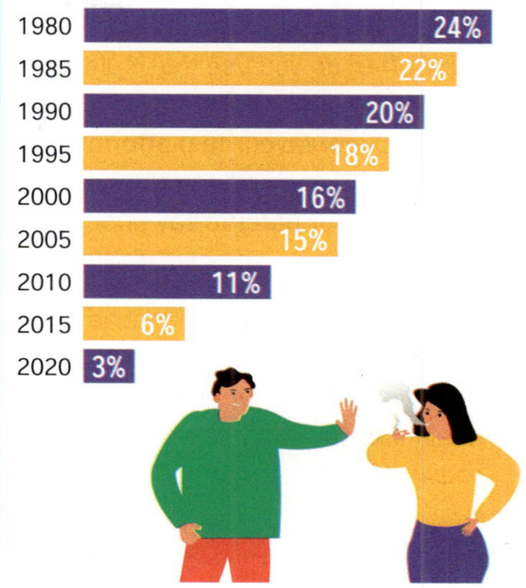

6: US high school students who have consumed alcohol

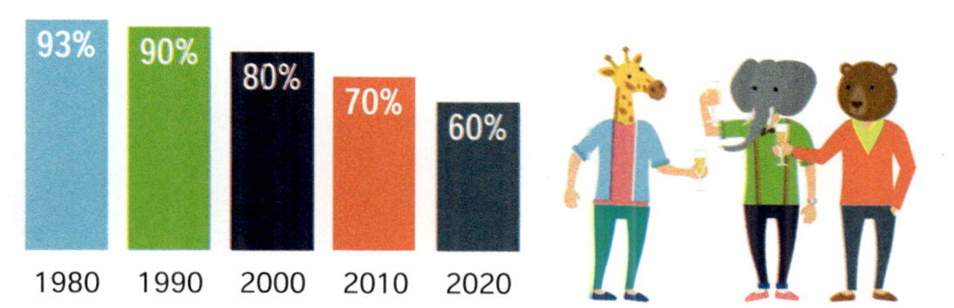

4 An interview

L 1/8 | S 5 ▸ Listening | p. 202

a) Listen to the interview and decide which statement fits the interview best.

- **A** Paula Tweedy claims that teenagers are more independent than they were in the 1980s.
- **B** Paula Tweedy explains why teenagers have become so dependent on modern technology.
- **C** Paula Tweedy talks about the characteristics of teenage life today compared to in the 1980s.

b) Group work (3). Each of you concentrates on two aspects of the infographics.

- Group member A focuses on "drinking" and "identifying as LGBTQ+".
- Group member B focuses on "smoking" and "being open about mental health".
- Group member C focuses on "driving" and "reading habits".

Listen again and note down why teenage life has changed over the years. ▸ **DIFF** Easy alternative D2 | p. 151

c) Compare your results with people from other groups who focused on the same aspects as you.

d) Share your results with your original group members, then decide if you were right in Intro 2c).

5 Teenage life in the future

▸ **DIFF** Training D3 | p. 152 ▸ **WB** 4 | p. 23

Think about teenage life in the future. What changes would you like to see? What would you be afraid of? Talk to a partner.

6 Discussion

▸ Speaking | p. 205 ▸ Wordbank 6 | p. 241 ▸ **WB** 5 | p. 23

Paula Tweedy claims: "Teenagers should be given more freedom and more power."
Discuss the statement. Find examples to support your opinion. Your ideas from Intro 1 can help you.

I think Paula Tweedy is right/wrong because … • If teens had more freedom and more power, … • I believe that … • Personally, I feel that … • I would say that … • When it comes down to it, … • For me, it's absolutely clear that … • As I see it, … • The point I would like to raise is … • As far as I'm concerned, … • I agree that … • Well, I don't think so because … • In contrast to what you have said, I … • I see what you mean but … • To be honest, I don't think that … • I would like to add that …

A1 Social media habits

▶ Wordbank 4 | p. 239 ▶ WB 6 | p. 24

a) Class survey: Find out how your class uses social media.
Collect feedback on these questions:

- Which platforms do you use?
- How often do you use these platforms? (e.g. once a day/week)
- What do you use them for? (e.g. communicating with friends)
- What is your favourite platform and why?
- If you don't use any social media platforms, what are the reasons for this?
- What do your parents say about your social media activity?

▶ DIFF Training D4 | p. 152 ▶ WB Media 4 ▶ WES-149226-2

Media
You can use a digital tool for your survey.

b) Write down positive and negative aspects of social media.
Use your results from A1a).
You can organize your ideas under umbrella terms (e.g. news, friendships, money, health). Example:

▶ DIFF Training D5 | p. 153

news/information

–	+
• *fake news*	• *easy to share*
• *overwhelming*	• *stay up to date*
• …	• …

A2 Cartoons

▶ DIFF Easy alternative D6 | p. 153 ▶ WB 7 | p. 24

Choose one of the cartoons and analyse it in detail.
Follow these steps:

1. Identify the topic.
2. Describe the situation, e.g. the setting, the characters, their body language, their facial expressions and what they are doing.
3. Explain what the characters are saying.
4. Explain the message of the cartoon.
5. Give your opinion on the cartoon.

▶ Wordbank 3 | p. 239

1. *The cartoon deals with/is concerned with the issue/topic of …*
2. *The cartoon shows two … who are …* • *The character on the left/right appears to be concerned/confused/angry/fearful/disgusted/…* • *… is looking at the floor/raising their eyebrows/widening their eyes/bowing their head/hunching their back/leaning forward/staring at …/pressing their lips together/frowning/…*
3. *The text suggests that …*
4. *You might conclude that the message of the cartoon is …*
5. *If you ask me, the cartoon is (not) funny/thought-provoking because …* • *I (don't) like the cartoon, especially …*

"I'm only liking her posts because I'm afraid if I don't, she won't like mine."

A3 What social media is doing to our brains ▶ Viewing | p. 212 ▶ WB 8 | p. 25

a) Before you watch the video, explain the meaning of each word or write a sentence using the word.

1 addicted
2 face-to-face
3 clickbait
4 self-centred
5 distraction
6 self-esteem

You can use a dictionary for help.

b) Watch the video and add any other positive and negative aspects of social media to your notes from A1b). ▶ DIFF Easy alternative D7 | p. 154

A4 A newspaper article ▶ Reading | p. 203 ▶ WB 9, 10 | p. 25

a) A newspaper headline is often used to attract the reader's attention. Look at the headline of the article and say what it might suggest about the author's point of view. ▶ DIFF Support D8 | p. 154

Social media is a bad feelings machine. Why can't we just turn it off for good?

by Sirin Kale

I have a fantasy and it goes like this: a political party is formed, running on an anti-social-media platform. It campaigns on a pledge[1] to ban social media. ("SWITCH IT OFF" is its [...] slogan.)

The party wins a general election[2] and at midnight, on what comes to be known as Social Media Freedom Day, the prime minister[3] pushes a giant button that blocks all access to social media. Crowds cheer. [...]

I write this as someone who owes her career and her partner to social media. I had no journalism qualifications, connections or experience when I began blogging [...] and through Twitter I was able to get a paid internship[4] that gave me my start in journalism. My boyfriend and I connected through Instagram after years of liking each other's posts. So much of my personal, and professional happiness has been made possible through social media.

But as time has gone on I have become more and more certain that the solution to many of the most pressing[5] issues of our time is simply to switch social media off.

I have spent much of 2021 reporting on the pandemic[6] – in particular how the spread of misinformation on social media has pushed people to reject lifesaving vaccinations[7]. I have listened to family members weep as they remember loved ones who would be alive today were it not for social media conspiracy theories. [...]

In October, Facebook whistleblower Frances Haugen testified before Congress about her experiences working at the social media giant. There, she saw evidence that its products were making teenagers anxious, depressed and suicidal →

1 pledge – *Versprechen* | 2 general election – *Parlamentswahlen* | 3 prime minister – *Premierminister/in* | 4 internship – *Praktikum* | 5 pressing – *dringend* | 6 pandemic – *Pandemie* | 7 lifesaving vaccinations – *lebensrettende Impfungen*

[...]. Facebook, Haugen concluded, was putting "astronomical profits before people". [...]

On social media [...] I see people radicalised into obsessive hatred of communities of people they've never even met. I see cases of a condition called "poster's brain" – in which [...] social media users feel compelled to[8] post offensive [...] content – so severe I fear there is no cure[9]. [...]

And you know what the tech overlords are doing while we are fighting on the internet all day? They are getting extremely rich. They're paddle-boarding in Hawaii. [...]

And of course, I am entirely complicit[10]. I use social media and even though I try hard not to be cruel on it, I'd be lying if I said I didn't enjoy watching someone I've formed a negative opinion about, despite having never met them in real life, get roasted by an internet horde. [...]

Of course I could delete all my social media accounts. [...] You think I don't want to do that? [...] But I'm a journalist. [...] I worry about disappearing. And besides, I'm addicted. I've checked Twitter eight times writing this piece.

I need a responsible adult to do it for me. I've had enough of the bad feelings machine. Won't somebody switch it off? Please? Can we switch it off?

---

8 to feel compelled to do sth – *sich gezwungen sehen, etw zu tun* | **9** cure – *Heilmittel, Lösung* | **10** to be complicit in sth – *(an etw) mitschuldig sein*

b) Read the article on pages 41/42 and decide whether the statements are true or false. Explain your decision by referring to specific lines from the article. ▶ **DIFF** Training D9 | p. 154

1. The author, Sirin Kale, has formed an anti-social-media party.
2. She does not have a university degree in journalism.
3. The author only associates negative things with social media.
4. She met her boyfriend when she worked for a newspaper as an intern.
5. Frances Haugen revealed some truths about a big social media company.
6. Haugen claimed that money is more important to social media companies than their users' well-being.
7. Tech companies are worried about online bullying.
8. As soon as Sirin Kale reads negative comments about somebody on social media, she logs off.

c) Explain in your own words what author Sirin Kale means by describing social media as "a bad feelings machine". Refer to your findings from A1b) and A3b).
▶ **DIFF** Training D10, D11 | p. 155 ▶ Wordbank 4, 6 | p. 239

A5 Zigzag debate

▶ Speaking | p. 205 ▶ Wordbank 4, 6 | p. 239 ▶ **DIFF** Training D12 | p. 156

Group work (6): Imagine you had the power to switch off social media for everyone for a month. Discuss if you would do it or not.

- Form two teams of three. One team is for, the other team is against it.
- Each team prepares arguments. Try to predict the others team's arguments and think of ways of responding to them.
- The team supporting the idea starts the debate with a short statement on their position.
- Then the teams take turns to argue their side. Make sure you refer to what the other team has said.
- After the debate, take a vote. Talk about what made you vote that way.

Listen to the others without interrupting.

A6 A room for my phone

▶ Reading | p. 203 ▶ WB 11 | p. 26

a) *Log Off* is an initiative for teenagers by teenagers. Read Olivia's contribution to the *Log Off* blog. Speculate on why she wrote this personal account and explain why you think so. Who did she write the text for? Give evidence from the text.

www.logoffmovement.org

About Us | Take Action | Design Challenge | **Blog** | Digital Challenge | More ...

A little over a year ago, I began to feel myself relying on my phone too much. Over time, I realized that my issue wasn't that I was addicted to my phone but it was how close my phone was to me at every moment of the day; the more I saw my phone, the more I felt the need to go on it. When walking around my house, my phone was always in my back pocket. When getting out of the shower, my phone was waiting for me on my sink. When doing my homework, it was always by my side.

[...]

I tried figuring out a system that would help me go on my phone less [...]. I decided the smartest way to do this was to find a room in my house where I would leave my phone for the majority of the day and not have to carry it around with me. [...] I chose the laundry room in my house to be the room that my phone would stay in. [...]

Every day after school, rather than bringing my phone with me to my room, I would stop by the laundry room and drop it off. While my phone was normally my source of distraction, I could finally feel myself focus more on the things I had to do when I didn't have my phone staring at me on my desk, waiting to be picked up. Throughout the day when walking up and down the stairs, I would sometimes check my phone to see the texts or calls I had received and quickly answer them, without ever leaving the room. [...] Already, after only a week [...] my screen time had gone down by half. [...] By noticing my actions and making the choice of building distance between myself and my phone, I've been able to enjoy my phone in a healthy way and not feel the attachment I always used to feel from it.

If you're anything like me and you feel the constant pressure to go on your phone just because it's in front of you, I highly recommend trying to find a room in your house that isn't your own and turning it into a room for your phone. By doing this, you might also be able to notice how often you normally are on your phone and begin to see the advantages of being away from it just like I did.

by Olivia Bancel

b) Read the text again and complete the sentences with modal verbs or their substitute forms.

▶ G6R | p. 225 ▶ DIFF Training D13 | p. 156

1 Olivia thought she **XXX** use her phone less.
2 With her phone on her desk, she **XXX** focus on her homework.
3 She decided that she **XXX** put her phone in a separate room.
4 She soon realized that she **XXX** check her messages non-stop.
5 Olivia **XXX** reduce her screen time after only a week.

c) Collect words and phrases from Olivia's personal account on page 43 that ...
- help structure a text, e.g. *a little over a year ago,*
- are used to describe her experience, e.g. *by noticing my actions.*

d) How do you feel about Olivia's experiment? Do you think it is realistic to keep your phone in a separate room for the majority of the day?
Discuss in class. ▶ Wordbank 6 | p. 241

A7 Challenge yourself!

▶ Buzz groups | p. 214 ▶ WB 12 | p. 27

Buzz groups (4-5):
Collect ideas to challenge yourself to reduce your screen time. This excludes time when you have to use digital devices for school.
Share your ideas in class.

A8 Target task Write a personal account

▶ Writing | p. 209 ▶ Wordbank 4 | p. 239 ▶ WB 13 | p. 27

Choose one of the ideas from A7 and try to reduce your screen time for a day (or longer).
Write a personal account of your experience for the *Log Off* blog.

1 Plan your text. Make notes on ...
- why you chose the idea,
- the challenges you faced while trying it out,
- how you felt during your experiment,
- the outcome.

2 Write your personal account. Use words and phrases from A6c). The checklist ▶ WES-149226-5 can help you.
- Start with a short introduction that describes your idea and your reasons for choosing it.
- In the main part of your account, describe in detail how your challenge went. Explain whether you succeeded in reducing your screen time or not.
- Write a conclusion in which you sum up your experience. Give at least one reason why you would recommend/not recommend trying it.
- Find a good heading for your text.

3 Peer editing: Swap your personal account with a partner's. Use the checklist to give each other feedback.

Remember ...
✓ who you are writing for (your audience),
✓ why you are writing (the purpose of your text),
✓ to structure your text clearly.

Need help? Look at page 45. T1 T2

Target task tools for A8: Write a personal account

T1 Words and phrases: Describing a challenge

Match the phrases and the German translations. There are more German phrases than you need.

1 The biggest challenge was ...
2 It felt like there was no end in sight.
3 It didn't bother me to ...
4 Although I ..., I missed ...
5 I made sure that ...
6 To achieve my goal ...
7 What I didn't expect was ...
8 I was surprised by ...
9 I didn't expect ... to be so difficult.
10 I was sure it was the right decision to ...
11 I doubted if it was a good idea to ...

A Es hat mich nicht gestört, ...
B Um mein Ziel zu erreichen, ...
C Ich war überrascht von ...
D Die größte Herausforderung war ...
E Ich habe nicht erwartet, dass ... so schwierig sein würde.
F Ich war mir sicher, dass es die richtige Entscheidung war ...
G Ich hatte Zweifel, ob es eine gute Idee war ...
H Es fühlte sich an, als sei kein Ende in Sicht.
I Ich war mir nicht sicher, ob ich ...
J Obwohl ich ..., habe ich ... vermisst.
K Mein Ziel habe ich nicht erreicht, aber ...
L Ich habe sichergestellt, dass ...
M Was ich nicht erwartet hatte, war ...

T2 Words: Adjectives

Expressive adjectives help to make your personal account more interesting.
Improve the personal account with the adjectives from the box. Sometimes there is more than one possibility.

amazing • enjoyable • horrible • intense • positive • satisfying • strange • terrible • useful

On the first day, it felt **1** not to be able to check my phone all the time. The biggest challenge was doing my homework without checking my messages constantly. I automatically wanted to grab my phone – and then I realized it wasn't on my desk, but in a box in the kitchen downstairs. To be honest, that was a **2** feeling!
There was this **3** need to see if I had any new messages and the **4** thought I might miss some important news from my friends. I still had five days of the experiment to go and it felt like there was no end in sight.
However, after a few days it didn't bother me anymore. It was **5** to see how much more quickly I was able to do my homework if I didn't look at my phone every few minutes, and I realized that the apps I spent most of my time on weren't that **6** .
When I saw how little time I was spending on my phone, I felt **7** . I'm glad some of my friends joined the experiment. Being with your friends is much more **8** when everyone isn't on their phone the whole time. Overall, the experiment was a **9** experience and I want to continue reducing my screen time.

B1 A book cover ▶WB 14 | p. 28

Look at the cover and speculate on what the book might be about. Consider the photo, the title and the subtitle "If you can't trust your mind, trust your heart."

B2 A book review ◀)) L 1/9

Listen to an extract from a book review to find out if your speculations from B1 were correct. Talk to a partner about whether you would like to read the book. Give reasons.

It would be quite exciting to find out ... • Personally, I find this subject ... • This book appeals to me because ... • Although I don't like the cover, I would like to read the book because ...

B3 *Words on Bathroom Walls* ▶WB 15, 16 | p. 28

16-year-old Adam Petrazelli writes about his daily life while taking part in a clinical study.

a) Read the extract. Describe your first impressions of Adam. Give reasons. ▶DIFF Training D14 | p. 157

aggressive • depressed • desperate • funny • humorous • loving • optimistic • pessimistic • sad • sarcastic • thoughtful • understanding

My first doctor said it was unusual for the symptoms to manifest in someone so young. Schizophrenic males are more commonly diagnosed in their early to late twenties.
I remember thinking, *Well, shit, that's awesome. I'm unusual.* [...]
In the beginning I thought it was my glasses. No, not glasses. Spectacles. I like that word better. I got them when I turned twelve because I couldn't stop squinting and it drove my mom nuts. Dr. Leung is the one doctor I actually like, because he fixed a problem by giving me something fairly simple. Spectacles.
Problem solved. I could see and my mom was happy.
But that was also when I realized I was seeing things other people couldn't see. I was the only one jerking my head or squinting my eyes to get a better look. Everyone else was looking at me, not the birds that flew through the open window or the strange people who sort of appeared in the living room. So I stopped wearing my spectacles and told my mom I'd lost them. For a while that worked and I could pretend, but eventually, she bought so many pairs there was no excuse. I was screwed.
I didn't tell her that I was seeing things for a long time. When I did finally tell her, it was because I didn't have a choice. The principal called, and when Mom hung up the phone, she looked at me as if she was seeing me for the first time.
"Mrs Brizeno said you looked up in the chemistry lab, started screaming, and fell to the floor."
I remember how calm she was. My mom has this Jedi voice that sort of washes over you when she's trying to get information. "What did you see?"
[...]
"Bats," I said, looking down at my shoes. "Huge black bats." [...] When she started crying, I wished that the bats had been real. That the creepy little bastards had eaten me in the chemistry lab and I'd never had to see the way my mom looked at me in that moment: like I was crazy.
My stepdad, Paul, is a nice guy. He's good for my mom. They dated for years before they got married, and he always made the effort to keep up with my life, ask me about school, etc. [...]
Now that he knows about me, about the *illness*, things are different. He doesn't know what to do with me anymore. We'll sit and watch TV, but I can almost hear him thinking when I'm in the

room. The weirdest feeling, aside from seeing things that aren't actually there, is sitting on the couch next to a grown man who is suddenly afraid of me. He didn't used to be afraid. It's hard not to take that personally. […]
I'd had friends back at my old school. I'd grown up with them. Ridden bikes with them. But when they found out what I was, they were afraid of me, just like Paul. After the incident at school and all the strange behavior, they stopped calling. I'd known Michael and Kevin since we were five. We'd been on the same T-ball team together. They'd at least sent "Get Well Soon" cards when I left school, no doubt forced into it by their mothers, but no one came around after that. My best friend, Todd, disappeared completely.

b) Note down what has happened to Adam so far in chronological order. ▶ **DIFF** Easy alternative D15 | p. 157
You can start like this: *1 Adam lives with his mother and his stepdad.*
2 He can't stop squinting so he gets glasses.
...

c) Note down what you find out about Adam, his mother, Paul, Michael, Kevin and Todd.

d) Draw a character map. Write down the names of the characters and use arrows and labels to indicate their relationships.

B4 Adam's friends

🔊 L 1/10-11 ▶ **DIFF** Support D16 | p. 157 ▶ **WB** 17 | p. 30

a) As Adam's new medication works well at first, he is able to hide his illness. At his new school, he makes friends with a boy called Dwight, and Maya, a girl Adam later falls in love with. He decides not to tell them about his illness. Comment on his decision.

> "Medication" can also be referred to as "drugs". In the US, a pharmacy is sometimes called a "drugstore".

b) For months, Adam continues to keep his illness a secret, but then his medication stops working. At the prom, he has another breakdown. He loses control and pushes Maya to the ground. While he is being treated in hospital, his mother tells his friends about his illness. Imagine what Dwight's and Maya's reactions might be, then listen to the two tracks to find out if you were right.

c) Explain ...
- how you interpret Dwight's behaviour,
- Maya's reaction.

d) Add Dwight and Maya to your character map from B3d).

B5 Mental well-being at school

Read the culture box.

In groups (3) discuss ...
- why mental well-being classes might be offered at US high schools,
- what you think about the health classes at Californian schools,
- if mental well-being classes should be introduced at German schools, too.

▶ Wordbank 6 | p. 241

Mental health education — Culture box

Most US high schools offer health education classes that not only cover topics like nutrition and exercise, but also teach students about mental well-being. For example, students learn how to manage stress and how to get help for themselves and others.
The state of California goes even further. All schools that offer health classes have to teach their students about depression, schizophrenia, bipolar disorder, obsessive-compulsive disorder, eating disorders and other mental health issues.

B6 Film trailer

▶ DIFF Support D17 | p. 158

Go online and watch the English trailer for *Words on Bathroom Walls*.
Explain which scene struck you the most and how you would interpret it.

B7 Working with film stills

▶ DIFF Support D18 | p. 158 ▶ WB 18, 19 | p. 30

a) Study the film stills and identify the main characters. Your character map from B4d) can help you.

1

2

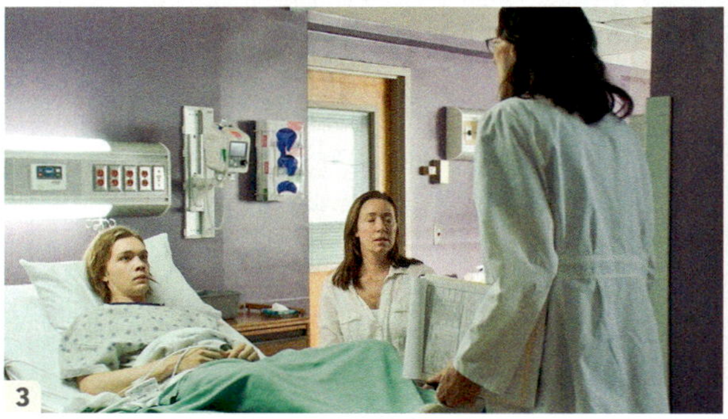
3

4

b) Work with a partner: Each of you chooses a film still to focus on.
Take notes on ... ▶ Wordbank 5 | p. 240 ▶ DIFF Easy alternative D19 | p. 159

- the setting:
  - What are the characters doing?
  - What is the situation?
- the atmosphere:
  - Which main colours are used?
  - Is the light used in the scene bright, dark, muted, ...?
  - Which effect do the colours and the light have?
- the camerawork:
  - Which field size was used and why? Check your results from D18 on page 158 for help.
- the overall impression:
  - What information does the scene give?
  - Which emotion(s) does the scene convey?

Present your results to each other. ▶ DIFF Extra D20 | p. 160

B8 Film review

▶ DIFF Training D21–D23 | p. 160 ▶ WB 20 | p. 31

a) Read the film review on page 49. How many stars (one to five) do you think the writer gave the film? Say why you think so.

b) A film review has three parts: introduction, main part and conclusion. Skim the review and identify the three parts.

Words on Bathroom Walls is an American romantic drama film from 2020. Directed by Thor Freudenthal and written by Nick Naveda, it is based on the novel by Julia Walton. The film stars Charlie Plummer, Taylor Russell, Molly Parker and Walton Goggins.

Adam is a high school student wanting to become a chef. After having a breakdown in his chemistry class, Adam finds out he has schizophrenia. When asked to leave the school, he starts a clinical trial for a new medication. He then transfers to a new school. At first, everything works well and Adam, for the first time, gets on well at school and at home He falls in love with Maya, an ambitious and clever girl. Hoping to lead a normal life, Adam decides to keep his illness a secret. To get the diploma needed to attend cooking school, Adam wants to finish high school without another incident. But gradually, his medication stops working and things take a turn for the worse.

I think it is important to have teenage romantic films that deal with mental health issues. I liked the film's message, which suggests that no one should be defined by an illness. The actors' performances, especially Charlie Plummer as Adam, really stood out for me, and I would definitely recommend listening to the film's soundtrack. But I also think the film's happy ending might not be very realistic, and there are some cheesy moments that reminded me of typical high school movies.

In conclusion, I would recommend the film because it is thought-provoking, dramatic and funny. Although it's sometimes a bit too much, all in all it is a touching story about growing up and about how, with the help of friends and family, you can get through anything.

c) Scan the film review and note down words and phrases that you can use to …

- give general information about a film *(… is an American romantic drama film from …; directed by …)*
- describe a film's plot *(Adam is a …; After …; When …)*
- comment on a film *(I think it is important to …; The actors' performances really stood out for me; …)*

B9 Grammar card **Participle constructions** ▶ G7 | p. 227 ▶ **DIFF** Training D24-D28 | p. 161 ▶ **WB** 21 | p. 32

To make a text more interesting to read, it is important to vary the sentence structures. One way to do this is by using participle constructions.

1 Copy the grid. Find the sentences with participle constructions in the film review and complete the grid. Highlight the differences between the longer and shorter sentences.

2 Check G7 to find out more about participle constructions.

Sentence …	Sentence with a participle construction
with a relative clause	
Adam is a high school student who wants to become a chef.	Adam is a high school student ***wanting*** to become a chef.
To get the diploma that is needed to attend cooking school, Adam wants to finish high school without another incident.	…
with an adverbial clause	
After he has had a breakdown in his chemistry class, Adam finds out he has schizophrenia.	…
When he is asked to leave the school, he starts a clinical trial for a new medication.	…
that combines two main clauses	
Adam decides to keep his illness a secret and he hopes he can lead a normal life.	…

B10 Using participle constructions ▶ G7 | p. 227 ▶ WB 22 | p. 32

Read the information about Julia Walton. Rewrite the sentences containing highlights using participle constructions.

Julia Walton was born in 1986 and lives in Huntington Beach, California, with her husband and children. When she realized that she was not happy in her job, she decided to become an author. She received a degree in Creative Writing after she had attended Chapman University in Los Angeles. Her first novel, which is called *Words on Bathroom Walls*, won several awards. After she had finished her first two books, she started writing her latest novel *On the Subject of Unmentionable Things*.

B11 Choose Working with films

Watch a film you like, then choose one of these tasks:

Write an interview with the main character.
- Write down at least five questions you would like to ask the character.
- Think about how they might answer.

OR

Imagine the events of the film happened in real life. Create a news report for TV about it.
- Take notes on the plot: what happened when and why? Who was involved?
- Write a script for your TV news report. You can record it, too. ▶ WB Media 6, 7 ▶ WES-149226-2

B12 Target task Write a film review ▶ Writing | p. 209 ▶ Wordbank 5 | p. 240

Choose a film you have recently watched and write a review of it.

1 Plan your review. Go online and find information on:
   - the genre (e.g. comedy, science fiction, drama, ...),
   - the year the film was released,
   - the actors,
   - the director.

   ▶ WB Media 5 ▶ WES-149226-2

2 Take notes on the plot.

3 Think about what you like/dislike about the film (e.g. the plot, the cast, the camerawork, the music, ...). Note down reasons for your opinion.

4 Write your review using the simple present. Checklist A ▶ WES-149226-5 can help you.
   - Introduction: Include the general information you collected in 1.
   - Main part: Describe the plot, but make sure it does not contain spoilers. Comment on the film and explain what you like/dislike about it.
   - Conclusion: Summarize your point of view and explain why you would/would not recommend the film.
   - Use adjectives and participle constructions to vary your sentences.
   - Check your spelling and grammar.

5 Peer editing: Swap your film review with a partner's. Use checklist B to give each other feedback.

Need help? Look at page 51. T1 T2

Target task tools for B12: Write a film review

T1 Words: Adjectives to describe films

a) The adjectives from the box can help you to make your film review more convincing.
Copy the grid and sort the adjectives into the categories. Some words fit into more than one category.

boring • captivating • catchy • clever • complex • confusing • (un)convincing • dramatic • dull • flat • powerful • moving • (un)predictable • (un)realistic • rich • slow • (un)spectacular • stereotypical • superb • surprising • (un)talented • thrilling • touching • tragic • two-dimensional • warm-hearted

You can use a dictionary for help.

story/plot	characters/acting/cast	music and sound/special effects
…	…	…

b) Complete the sentences using some of the adjectives from a). Sometimes there is more than one possible solution.

1 I think the cast is really disappointing as the two main actors are really XXX.
2 I was extremely surprised by the film's ending, the story is so XXX.
3 In my opinion, the plot is very XXX, which makes it difficult to follow the film.
4 Overall, it is an important story with a XXX message.
5 While the film's special effects are XXX, the soundtrack is rather XXX.
6 The acting is so XXX you will forget everything around you.

T2 Giving feedback: Film review

a) Download checklist B for film reviews. ▶ WES-149226-5
Then read the review and take notes on what should be changed to improve the text.

The Half of It is an American film. It was directed and written by Alice Wu. The film stars three young actors.

Ellie Chu lives in a small town called Squahamish. Ellie is shy and introverted. She doesn't really feel like she is a part of the popular crowd at her high school. Ellie is also a very good student and has her own business already. Ellie, whose mother is dead, wants to support her father, who moved with his family from China to America when she was five years old. Ellie secretly writes essays for other students to earn some extra money. One day, her classmate Paul Munsky asks Ellie for help. Paul wants Ellie to write a love letter to Aster Flores, the popular new girl he has a crush on. Ellie and Aster begin to connect via messages and letters over their similar hobbies and interests. Ellie slowly falls in love with Aster, but Aster thinks she is talking to Paul the whole time.

At first, *The Half of It* might look like any other film about teenagers falling in love. After the first few minutes of the film, I realised that this was not one of those stereotypical high school movies. However, I didn't like that Ellie and Aster don't become a couple at the end.

In conclusion, *The Half of It* is warm-hearted and funny. However, some parts of the plot are very predictable, and it does slow down in the middle of the movie. In contrast to that, the young, talented cast is fantastic. *The Half of It* is a moving story about friendship and self-acceptance.

b) Compare your feedback with a partner's.

2 Check, please!

In Ngozi Ukase's graphic novel Check, please!, *Eric Bittle is a freshman at Samwell University, a fictional university in Massachusetts.*
Eric was a successful figure skater when he was still in high school.
He also played in a mixed ice hockey team of boys and girls, which helped him get a scholarship.
In a vlog, Eric keeps his friends informed of how he settles in at university where his teammates call him "Bitty" or "Bits".

R 1

Read the information box and look at the examples below to help you talk about graphic novels.

Graphic novels
Graphic novels are novels mostly told in pictures. The difference between graphic novels and comic books is not always entirely clear. However, comic books are usually part of a series whereas graphic novels can also be stand-alone stories. This means that, just like a novel, they have a clear beginning, middle, and end. Graphic novels can tell stories of all kinds of genres: fiction or non-fiction, fantasy or history. Since the format differs from that of a novel, you can find some terms below that may help you when talking about graphic novels. These are just a few examples, as every graphic novel might use different design elements. If you want to learn more about how to work with graphic novels, take a look at the material under ▶ WES-149226-5 .

speech bubble a bubble that contains a character's direct speech

tail

gutter the space between two panels

frame the line which surrounds the panel

panel sequence a series of pictures

panel a single picture

R 2

Look at the section from Eric's vlog (extract A) and decide whether the statements are true or false. In each case say which of Eric's sentences gives you a clue.

Example: ***Statement 1 is true because Eric refers to a report in a magazine about universities in the US.***

1 Eric looked for detailed information before choosing his university.
2 Eric chose his university because of the quality of the teaching.
3 Eric's family situation has helped him be open about his sexual orientation.
4 Eric originally planned to tell his teammates that he is part of the LGBTQ+ community.
5 Eric regrets that he has not been open about his sexuality from the start.

A

ranking – *Platzierung*

R 3

a) Read extract B on pages 53-55 to find out what happens next with Eric and Shitty, one of his hockey teammates. Which sentence sums up the conversation best? Give reasons for your choice.

Eric's coming out ...

A went better than he had expected.
B wasn't something he worried about a lot.
C was something he didn't plan to do.
D was a big deal for both Eric and Shitty.

B

hoopla *(informal)* – *Rummel* | Winter Screw – *der jährliche Winterball der Samwell University* | to bring sth to a head – *etw zuspitzen; eine Entscheidung erzwingen* | judgment – *Urteil; Verurteilung* | were it not for ... – *wenn ... nicht wäre*

to come to terms with – *sich mit etw arrangieren; mit etw klarkommen* | like hens with their heads cut off – *kopflos; hier: gestresst* | casually – *beiläufig*

'ppreciate it (= to appreciate sth) – *etw zu schätzen wissen* | entire – *ganz*

to go at one's own pace – *etw im eigenen Tempo machen* | to beat sb up – *jdn zusammenschlagen*

Jesus Christ *(informal)* – *Du lieber Himmel!* | Ransom and Holster – *zwei von Erics Teamkollegen* | Jack – *Mannschaftskapitän des Eishockeyteams* | to have sb's back – *jdm den Rücken freihalten; für jdn da sein*

b) Choose two adjectives each for Eric and Shitty to describe how they behave in this situation and give reasons for your choice.

anxious • *arrogant* • *brave* • *calm* • *caring* • *cool* • *emotional* • *empathetic* • *kind* • *loyal* • *nervous* • *polite* • *relaxed* • *respectful* • *rude* • *serious* • *shy* • *understanding* • *worried* • ...

c) Compare your ideas with a partner.

In the end, Eric seems ... because Shitty ... and ...

From my perspective, Eric is ...

I think Shitty ... since Eric is probably ...

If you ask me, Eric behaves in a ... way as you can see that ... Shitty seems ...

In my opinion, Shitty behaves very ... in this situation because ...

R4

A few months later, the Samwell ice hockey team manages to reach the play-offs against Princeton. Read about what happens at the match (extract C). Then complete the sentences.

1 Eric hasn't updated his vlog for a while because ...
2 During the play-off against Princeton, he got hit hard by someone from the other team, so he ...
3 Unfortunately, Eric's team ...
4 Because Eric got hurt, he has to ...
5 Eric thinks he might be able to play again in August, but ...

C

concern – *Besorgnis, Interesse* | to get checked – *beim Eishockey von einem Gegner/einer Gegnerin angerempelt werden*

to eliminate – *ausscheiden* | nonsense – *Unsinn, Quatsch* | concussion – *Gehirnerschütterung*

R5

Write a comment to post under Eric's vlog. Make sure your comment includes ...
- whether you can understand why Eric and his team were so eager to win the match,
- how you would feel about winning/not winning a competition like the ice hockey championship,
- your hopes for Eric for the summer and his next semester at university.

▶ **WB** Media 2 ▶ WES-149226-2

R6

a) At the end of the season, a prize is given to the player who is really loyal to the team and therefore represents the team's spirit. Make notes on what a player should be like to fit this description.

b) Share your ideas in class.

R7

a) Read extract D to find out which player of the ice hockey team receives the "John Carlisle Award" for most devoted player.

D

senior rep speech – *Rede eines Vertreters/einer Vertreterin der Abschlussklasse* | devotion – *Treue, Aufopferung* | to exemplify – *als Beispiel für etw dienen*

b) Choose either task A or B.

A Eric has to give a short speech when he accepts the award. First write his speech, then present it in class.

B Continue the graphic novel. Think about what Eric might say in his speech and how his teammates might react. Draw at least four panels.

Was hast du alles gelernt? Diese Seite hilft dir dabei, das zu erkennen.
Falls du Hilfe benötigst, etwas nachlesen oder noch ein paar Übungen machen möchtest, findest du hier passende Hinweise.

WORTSCHATZ

Ich kann ...	Aufgaben/Übungen/Hilfen
Infografiken auswerten *The first graphic highlights/shows ... • Over the years, the figure/percentage has increased/decreased by ...*	2 ▶ **WB** 2
meine Meinung ausdrücken und begründen *I believe that ... • For me, it's absolutely clear that ... • It may be true that ..., however, ... • It seems to me that ...*	6, A5 ▶ **DIFF** D12 ▶ **WB** 5

SKILLS

Ich kann ...	Aufgaben/Übungen/Hilfen
einem Videoclip Informationen entnehmen VIEWING	3, A3 ▶ **DIFF** D1, D7 ▶ Viewing | p. 212 ▶ **WB** 3, 8
einem Hörtext Informationen entnehmen LISTENING	4, B2, B4 ▶ **DIFF** D2, D11 ▶ Listening | p. 202 ▶ **WB** 10, 17
eine Diskussion/Debatte führen SPEAKING	6, A5 ▶ **DIFF** D12 ▶ Speaking | p. 205
einen Cartoon analysieren SPEAKING/WRITING	A2 ▶ **DIFF** D6 ▶ **WB** 7
einem längeren Zeitungsartikel Informationen entnehmen READING	A4 ▶ **DIFF** D8, D9
einen Erfahrungsbericht schreiben WRITING	A8 ▶ T1, T2 | p. 45 ▶ Writing | p. 209 ▶ **WB** 13
einen Romanauszug lesen und verstehen READING	B3 ▶ **DIFF** D14, D15 ▶ **WB** 15, 16
Filmtrailer und Standbilder aus Filmen analysieren VIEWING • SPEAKING • MEDIA	B6, B7 ▶ **DIFF** D17-D21 ▶ **WB** 18
eine Filmkritik verfassen WRITING	B12 ▶ T1, T2 | p. 51 ▶ Writing | p. 209 ▶ **WB** 20

GRAMMATIK

Ich kann ...	Aufgaben/Übungen/Hilfen
verschiedene Zeitformen verwenden *I spend about two hours a day online. • When I started ...*	▶ **DIFF** D5 ▶ G1R | p. 217 ▶ **WB** 6
***Conditional clauses (type 2)* verwenden** *If teenagers had more power, they would probably change ...*	▶ **DIFF** D3 ▶ G5R | p. 224 ▶ **WB** 4
Modalverben und ihre Ersatzformen verwenden *She decided that she had to put her phone in a separate room.*	A6 ▶ **DIFF** D13 ▶ G6R | p. 225
Partizipialkonstruktionen verwenden *Born in 1986, Julia Walton lives in Huntington Beach, California, with her husband and her children.*	B9, B10 ▶ **DIFF** D24-D28 ▶ G7 | p. 227 ▶ **WB** 21, 22

Writing: Summary (literature)

Step by step

On these pages you will learn how to write a summary. First, there is an example task and a possible solution. Next, there is your task. You will learn how to write your own summary, step by step.

Example

1 Look at the example task and the solution.

EXAMPLE TASK

Read the extract of *Dare me* by Eric Devine, then summarize it.

There is no doubt that one of us will die. I'm not hoping for it, just considering the probability: three of us, ten stunts, each "death defying[1]". At least that's the plan: spend senior year completing one dare a month. Why? So we're legends by the end.

Ricky's driving and he looks at me, rocks his head to the music blaring, and says, "Ready, Ben?"

As if there's any answer I can give but yes. I know how it works. He looks in the rearview[2]. "John, ready?"

John gives a thumbs-up and gets the camera into position. "On you, Ben." He slides out of the rear window.

I turn and look. Nothing but cornstalks and pavement, blue sky and puffy white clouds. Perfection. I focus on that image and the stillness, the quiet. If I don't, I'll chicken out[3]. My mind's already filling with scenarios for how this will end badly. But school starts tomorrow, and I agreed to this, however it goes.

I pull the ski mask over my face and slide out the window.

The wind whips even though Ricky's only going like thirty miles per hour. I can't hear what John's saying. His mouth's moving, but it's like being in a dream, all background noise, nothing real. He jacks his thumb into the air, an obvious sign for me to get on the roof. I take a deep breath, steady my elbows, and push myself up.

My feet tingle[4] and my heart hammers, but I keep going. I grab the roof rack[5] and pull and am flat on top. The wind pours over me now, but the space around my face is calm. Unreal.

"Let's do it." John's words are faint, but they're enough to propel[6] me. I grip the rack and slide my feet beneath me. Ten seconds. All I have to do is stay on my feet and count.

I stand but wobble[7] and have to sit back down on my heels[8]. Shit, maybe I *can't* do this. No matter how much I convince

Three boys plan to complete a dare a month to become high school legends. The narrator is a boy called Ben, who is in a car with his two friends, Ricky and John. Ben has to complete the first dare. He is aware of potential risks but tries to focus on the peaceful landscape to keep calm because he agreed to follow through with the dare.

Ben puts on a ski mask and climbs onto the roof of the moving car. While Ricky is driving, John is filming the scene. At first Ben isn't sure if he can complete the task, but then he manages to stand on the roof. Even though he was very scared at first, he now starts to enjoy the experience.

1 death defying – *todesmutig* | **2** rearview (mirror) – *Rückspiegel* | **3** to chicken out – *kneifen* | **4** to tingle – *kribbeln* | **5** roof rack – *Dachgepäckträger* | **6** to propel – *antreiben* | **7** to wobble – *wackeln* | **8** heel – *Ferse*

myself. I look over at John for help, forgetting that the camera is on me. There's nothing he can do. This is all mine. I'd love nothing more than to crawl right back in the window, but it would be on film, and Ricky would never let me hear the end of it. Just like before.

I've decided that's not what *I* want, so I swallow, take another breath, and ease my way up.

I rock again, but only slightly. John raps[9] on the roof to let Ricky know I'm up, and Ricky lets out a scream. I spread my arms and yell along with him because this is fucking insane[10]. The road stretches before me, and one false move and I'm part of it. But Ricky's smooth, and it's like I'm on a skateboard without the rumble beneath my feet.

A car comes from the other direction and Ricky honks. The driver looks up and sees me and I look down at him and for a second our eyes meet. In his, pure panic. His mouth is dropped and his skin is paper-white. But then he's gone and my heart is racing and it's been ten seconds. I let out one more scream and tuck back to the roof rack.

A car comes from the other direction and the driver is shocked when he sees Ben. Ben, on the other hand, screams with excitement.

John smacks the car again to let Ricky know I'm done, and I hear muffled[11] cheering from within. I smile. It's big and hurts my cheeks and my eyes water from the wind, but this is the most alive I've felt in forever, exactly like Ricky said we would. One dare down, nine to go.

Safely back in the car, Ben feels very happy and thinks that he has never felt so alive.

9 to rap – *klopfen* | **10** insane – *wahnsinnig* | **11** muffled – *gedämpft*

SOLUTION

The extract of *Dare me* describes how three boys plan to complete one dare a month because they want to become high school legends.

The narrator, a boy called Ben, finds himself in a car with his two friends Ricky and John. Ben has to complete the first of ten dares. Despite being scared and aware of potential risks, Ben tries to overcome his fear and fulfil the dare because he has agreed to it.

Putting on a ski mask, he climbs onto the roof of the moving car. At first he isn't sure if he can complete the task. However, he then he manages to stand on the roof and enjoy the thrill of the experience while Ricky is driving and John is filming the scene. A car comes from the other direction and the driver is shocked when he sees Ben.

Safely back in the car, Ben is very happy and realizes that he has never felt so alive.

Your task

2 Read your task, then follow the steps on page 63 to complete it.

Read the next extract of *Dare me* and write a summary.

When I went to bed at 2:00 a.m., there were thirty-five views. I woke up at 7:00 and there were thirty-seven. I just checked my phone and we're up to a whopping[1] fifty. Ricky talked about these videos being "the best senior prank[2] ever" because they'll last all year. I had to agree to the brilliance of the uniqueness[3]. He also said that we'll be "larger than Jesse Holmes" and his crew. I don't know about that. One look at those guys, and it's obvious they own our school. Handsome, suave[4], athletic. Considering either hopeful outcome, fifty views aren't going to do jack.

John rolls up to my locker. "I'm still wrecked from yesterday. I kept dreaming about it. Woke up screaming."

I picture John in his bed, all wound up in his sheets, screaming into the night. Doesn't surprise me. He's always had nightmares. Scared the hell out of me the first time he slept over in fifth grade. "You've got a month before the next one. Try to relax."

He shakes his head and doesn't say anything, but I know what he means. This isn't our thing: trouble. That's Ricky's territory. But we're only visiting, right?

We walk toward the cafeteria and go as unnoticed as usual. I watch the clusters and wonder what the hot girls are discussing, the übergeeks, the Bible-thumpers. I remember Ricky's words: This is how we make our mark. You've seen all the stupid dares kids are doing. Cinnamon eating and vodka in the eye. Not us. We're going balls out and will leave here legends.

Yet day one of senior year feels like we never left. Classes have been exactly as I expected. I'm Mr./Mrs. so-and-so, and this class will be difficult. You are a senior, so I'm not holding your hand. Here's your first assignment[5]. And off we go.

John and I grab trays[6] and get served the miserable offerings and head to our table. Ricky's already there.

"Hey, John, don't trip[7]!"

Ricky laughs at his own joke and chews on a French fry.

"You hit that pothole[8] on purpose?" John sits but doesn't touch his food.

"That's one way of looking at it. Or maybe you wanted to end up on the windshield. Crying." Ricky smiles. "Guess we'll never know, huh?"

"I wasn't crying," John mumbles into his food.

He was totally crying, but who cares? It was good footage. Well, for our purposes.

---

1 whopping – *riesengroß* | **2** prank – *Streich* | **3** uniqueness – *Einzigartigkeit* | **4** suave – *weltmännisch* | **5** assignment – *Aufgabe* | **6** tray – *Tablett* | **7** to trip – *stolpern* | **8** pothole – *Schlagloch*

I take a bite of the hamburger. "You think maybe the low numbers are because of the distortion?"

Ricky takes a sip of his drink. He looks calm, like this is all part of his plan. "We need the masks and the blurring so we don't get in trouble. No faces, no identity match. We've been through this." He leans in. "Don't worry, I got this. Plan B, the old-fashioned route."

"What are you going to do?" I ask. I don't know how many times I've asked him this question. For all of high school, the answers didn't include me. Until now.

Ricky laughs. "Ben, don't worry, I'm going to make a PSA. You like those, don't you?" He climbs onto the table and I kind of hate him.

"Shit," John whispers.

Ricky looks around, smiling and waving. Some kids point. Others swear at him. But in a moment everyone is watching. He opens his mouth.

"Ladies and gentleman of the senior class, today is the beginning of our last year at this institution." His voice is steady and thick and he pauses for the cheers that accompany anything about seniors. "It could be just another year, the same as the last and the one before, where we hope for something exciting to actually happen, but it never does. Or, we can make a decision. We can decide to make that excitement a priority." He pauses dramatically and I wince. "That's what someone here has done."

The room murmurs and students look around at one another. I'm trying not to think of all the ways this could get us into trouble, but the infractions scramble my head.

"Do yourselves a favor," Ricky continues, "check out 'Brookwood High Senior Year Dare Number One' on YouTube. It seems like someone here has a plan for the year. Hopefully, you'll see it and feel like I did: pumped. Hopefully it will get you excited for this year. Hopefully it'll give you something fun to watch instead of just stalking one another on Twitter." Ricky thrusts his fist into the air and nods his head while looking around the room. He's gone too far. Most of the kids stare, while others start cracking jokes. A teacher motions for him to get off the table, and in a moment his big scene is over and people are back to their lunches. I'm quietly relieved.

"That was impressive," John says, as Ricky gets down from the table.

Ricky's jaw is set and his shoulders are pinned, and it seems he doesn't know where to look or what to say. His PSA failed, like the video. Maybe he's realizing that his ideas suck. This is nothing new, but the way he seems to feel about it is. I take another bite out of the hamburger, and it's like putting my mouth around a sponge.

Step 1	Download the text ▸ WES-149226-5. Read it carefully and highlight keywords and important details (like in the example task).
Step 2	Divide the text into meaningful parts. Usually, a new part begins with a different idea, different characters or a new action.
Step 3	Summarize each part (like in the example task). • The highlighted keywords can be useful, but you should use your own words as far as possible. • Leave out details that are not important. • Use the simple present.
Step 4	Think about what the extract as a whole is about. Then use this idea to write an introductory sentence. *In the extract, the narrator describes …* *The extract is about …* *In the first part of … the protagonist …* *The extract of … deals with …* *The story/extract presents …* *In the story/extract the reader gets to know …*
Step 5	Use your sentences from step 3 to write your summary. • Conjunctions and different sentence structures (e.g. participle constructions) make your summary more interesting to read. • Use other words for "say". • Don't use direct speech. *Although he …* *However, …* *Thinking that …, Ben …* *At school, Ben …* *Walking into the cafeteria, Ben …* *Ben thinks/believes/is convinced that …* *He feels that …* *When/After Ben …*
Step 6	Edit your summary. Check if … • you have used your own words, • you have left out any details that are not important, • your grammar and spelling are correct.

If you need help with a different summary task, you can use the checklist on page 64.

Checklist: Writing a summary (literature)

Checklist
1. Read the text carefully and highlight keywords and important details.
2. Divide the text into meaningful parts.
3. Summarize each part. • Use your own words as far as possible. • Leave out details that are not important. • Use the simple present.
4. Think about what the extract as a whole is about. Use this idea to write an introductory sentence.
5. Use your sentences from step 3 to write your summary. • Conjunctions and different sentence structures (e.g. participle constructions) make your summary more interesting to read. • Use other words for "say". • Don't use direct speech.
6. Edit your summary. Check if ... • you have used your own words, • you have left out any details that are not important, • your grammar and spelling are correct.

3

Human rights for all?

In this Theme you will ...

- talk about children's and young people's rights
- learn about young activists
- talk about different attitudes towards guns in the USA
- write a comment
- read a longer novel extract
- continue a story

3 Young people's rights

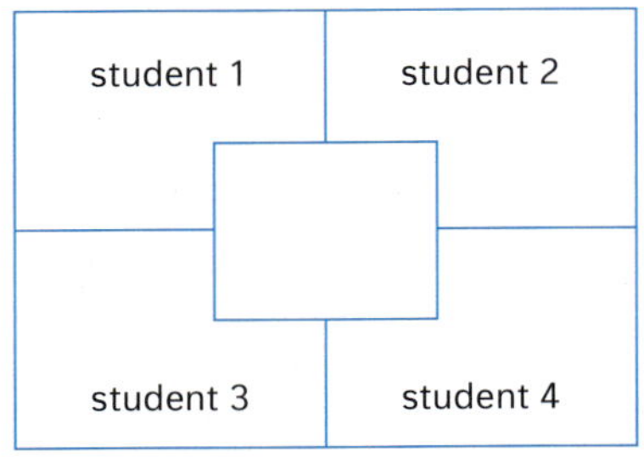

1 Placemat

▶ Placemat | p. 215 ▶ WB 1 | p. 40

Placemat (4): What are your rights as a teenager?

- Draw a rectangle in the middle of a sheet of paper.
- Each of you writes their ideas in their corner of the paper.
- Keep turning the paper until you have read each other's ideas.
- Edit your ideas and collect them in the middle.
- One of you presents your group's results in class.

2 Your rights

a) Below are some of the rights for children and young people that were agreed on by the United Nations in 1989. Read them, then look at the photos and match each photo to one right. Explain your choice.

b) Note down which rights you covered in Intro 1.
Example: *Right no. 5, 8, …*

c) Work with a partner. Find examples from your everyday lives for the rights that you did not cover in Intro 1. Then compare your ideas in class.
Example: *For me, "the right to have privacy" means that nobody is allowed to read my diary.*

3 Make a decision

▶ Speaking | p. 205 ▶ Wordbank 6 | p. 241 ▶ WB 2 | p. 40

a) Group work: Decide which right you think is the most important and which you think is the least important.
Consider how your life would be affected if these rights were not observed.

> I think the right to … is the most/least important. If I didn't have the right to …, …

b) In class, share your results and explain how and why you came to your decision.

c) Name any additional rights that you would include in the children's rights.
Explain why you think they are important and give examples.

1. The right to live
2. The right to develop and grow
3. The right to have an identity
4. The right to have parents
5. The right to have an adequate standard of living
6. The right to be protected from harm
7. The right to be informed and educated
8. The right to have thoughts and beliefs
9. The right to express feelings and opinions
10. The right to have privacy
11. The right to associate with others
12. The right to belong to a culture or religion
13. The right to be treated justly

A

D

4 Rights and responsibilities

a) Work with a partner. Talk about the difference between "right" and "responsibility".

b) Rights come with responsibilities. Think about which responsibilties come with ...

- the right to associate with others,
- the right to have privacy,
- the right to belong to a culture or a religion.

Share your results in class.

> Having the right to associate with others comes with the responsibility to allow others to choose if they want to associate with me.

5 Malala Yousafzai

▶ DIFF Training D1 | p. 164 ▶ WB 3 | p. 41

a) Watch the video clip and name the fact that you find the most surprising or impressive.

b) Name the rights Malala fights for. Explain the reasons for her activism.

c) Go online to find out what Malala does today.

▶ WB Media 5 ▶ WES-149226-2

6 Choose Young activists

▶ DIFF Training D2, Extra D3 | p. 164 ▶ WB 4 | p. 41

a) Research a young activist and note down ...

- main facts about the person,
- why this person chose to be an activist,
- what they do,
- what they have achieved so far.

▶ WB Media 5 ▶ WES-149226-2

b) Choose either task A or B.

A

- You are the activist you researched in a). Your partner asks you questions covering the points from a).
- Now swap roles and interview your partner.

B

- Use the information from a) to prepare a one-minute presentation.
- In groups of three, give your presentations.
- Check if each presentation has covered all the points from a). Give feedback.

B

C

E

F

3 "The right to be protected from harm"

A1 American gun culture ▶ WB 5 | p. 42

a) Round robin: Look at the photos and share your immediate reactions. ▶ Round robin | p. 215

b) Describe the photos and explain which aspects of gun culture they illustrate.

1

2

3

4

5

6

7

A2 News headlines ▶ WB 6 | p. 42

a) Read the headlines. Note down reasons why people in the US own guns and which problems arise from this. Keep your list for later.

1 Boston Boy Shoots to Protect Brother From Home Invaders

2 **Shooting: A Valuable Sport Or A Dangerous Hobby?**

3 **"My Rifle Isn't Just A Weapon. My Rifle Is A Part Of My Identity"**

4 Four-Year-Old Fires Fifteen Shots in Game at Kindergarten

5 Mass Shootings: More Guns Can Save Lives, Politician Claims

6 Girl Is Accidentally Shot By 5-Year-Old Brother With Gun From Father's Rifle Collection

b) Headlines often use stylistic devices to attract the reader's attention.
Study the headlines and find an example of each of the following:
- alliteration (two words that are close to each other in a sentence and start with the same letter),
- a quote,
- a rhetorical question (a question where you don't expect an answer),
- anaphora (words repeated at the beginning of a sentence/clause). ▶ DIFF Training D4 | p. 165

c) Use one or two of the stylistic devices from b) to create a headline about something that happened in your town or neighbourhood. You can also make something up (it doesn't have to be about guns!).

A3 Talking about statistics ▶ WB 7 | p. 43

In 2022, the US was the country with the highest number of privately owned guns.

a) Choose one chart each, study it and describe it to your partner.
- Point out what information is presented
- Explain what chart 1 shows about gun ownership and what chart 2 shows about child mortality. ▶ Wordbank 7 | p. 242

My chart deals with/lists ... • The main reason is ... while ... • ... is a reason that X percent named, while ... • When you look at ..., you notice that ... • X percent of all American children ... • The percentage of ... is significantly higher/lower in ... • In other countries such as ...

b) Add more reasons and problems to your list from A2a).

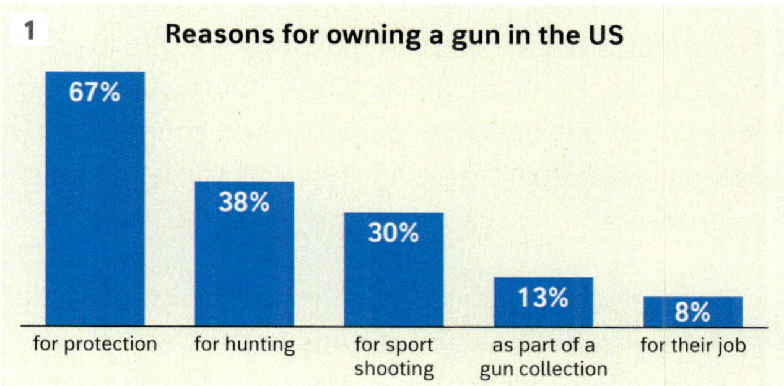

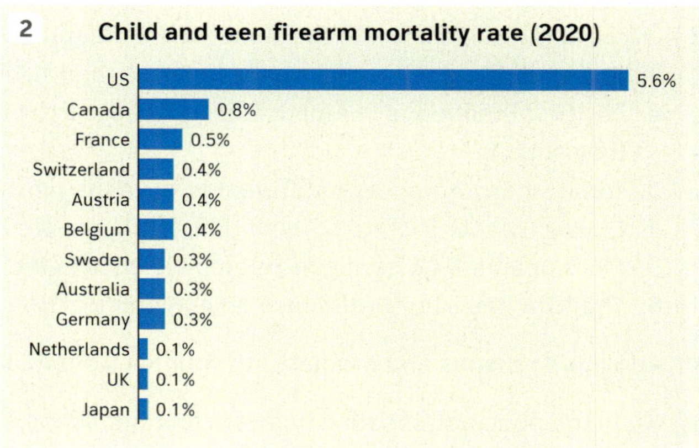

A4 **A cartoon** ▶ DIFF Extra D5 | p. 166

Study the cartoon and explain how it relates to the charts in A3a). ▶ Wordbank 3 | p. 239

"I know ... It's **so** nice to finally be able to leave the kids at home without a babysitter, now that they have the means to keep themselves safe."

A5 **Gun laws in the US** ▶ DIFF Easy alternative D6 | p. 166

Read the culture box and explain in your own words ...

- what rights the Second Amendment and the "Stand-your-ground" laws give to citizens in the US,
- why the "Stand-your-ground" laws are controversial.

Culture box

The Second Amendment and "Stand-your-ground" laws

The Second Amendment to the United States Constitution gives American citizens the right to keep and bear arms. This means that people can own and use weapons such as guns to protect themselves. There is, however, a lot of conflict surrounding the Second Amendment. Many Americans demand stricter gun laws, for example better background checks on people who wish to buy weapons.
In contrast, the National Rifle Association (NRA) is a strong supporter of gun rights.
Influenced by groups such as the NRA, many US states have passed "Stand-your-ground" laws, which allow people who believe their life to be in danger to use any means of self-defence, even if that involves gun-related violence such as shooting or killing another person.
Before the first "Stand-your-ground" law was passed in Florida in 2005, people were obliged to try to retreat from confrontation before responding by using a gun, for example. Evidence shows that "Stand-your-ground" laws do not prevent crime but are in fact connected to a rise in firearm homicides, which makes these laws highly controversial.

A6 **Four questions about guns in the US** L 1/13 | S 7 ▶ DIFF Training D7, D8 | p. 167 ▶ WB 8 | p. 43

a) Listen to the podcast and explain which fact about guns in the US is the most surprising to you.

b) Listen again and complete the sentences. Sometimes there is only one word missing.

1. In the US there are more private firearms than XXX.
2. The first Europeans in America used weapons to hunt animals and to XXX the places where they settled.
3. Today, many Americans still want to have the right to own a gun because XXX.
4. Buying weapons in the US isn't difficult. There are almost five times more XXX than grocery stores.
5. More people XXX from gun-related violence in the US than in any other industrialized country.
6. The NRA has a huge influence on gun politics. It uses its money to XXX.

c) Add more reasons and problems to your list from A2a)/A3b). ▶ WB Media 5 ▶ WES-149226-2

d) In the podcast, Christine answers four questions about guns in the US. Think of one more question. Research the answer online and present both the question and the answer to a partner.

A7 Comment ▶ DIFF Training D9-D11 | p. 168 ▶ WB 9-11 | p. 44

a) There is an ongoing debate in the US about stricter gun control laws.
Skim the comment and think of a headline that reflects the author's attitude towards this issue.

The US has the highest amount of gun owners in the world. Far too often we hear about incidents in the US involving a gun, or about horrifying mass shootings. Whereas most developed countries have some form of gun control measures (with Germany, the UK, Japan and Singapore having the strictest measures), the US has some of the least restrictive laws. I'm convinced that everyone would agree that living in a civilized society is a society without gun violence. Therefore stricter gun control laws are the only way forward for the US.

First of all, let's talk about the Second Amendment. Although many US citizens claim that the right to own a gun is protected by our Constitution, it is obvious to me that this idea is outdated. Having a potential army of citizens might have been necessary in the 18th century when the US gained independence from Britain and there was a threat that the British would invade again. However, today we have a military capable of protecting our country.

Secondly, some might say that there are enough restrictions on gun ownership already – quite a few states have background checks, which means people with a criminal record cannot buy guns. On the one hand, background checks are a step in the right direction. On the other hand, despite background checks, it is still relatively easy to buy a weapon. For example, in states like Florida people who sell weapons at gun shows are considered to be private sellers. They do not have to do an official background check on the buyer, which means that realistically anyone can still buy a gun. Statistics also show that in 63% of cases weapons used by criminals have often been stolen from people who owned them legally.

Finally, many Americans who are opposed to giving up their weapons claim that guns are an integral part of US culture. In certain states, shooting is indeed a popular sport and at weekends you can see families and their – sometimes quite young – children shooting "for fun". It is a fact that teaching children to point a real gun at something or someone is highly problematic. Furthermore, there is no guarantee that guns in private households are kept in a secure place. Guns in family homes often accidentally end up in the hands of children and lead to fatal accidents.

Taking everything into account, there can be no doubt that in order to reduce gun violence in the US, stronger gun control laws are needed across all states because every gun has the potential to harm or kill someone.

Ava Parker

b) A comment has three parts: **1** introduction **2** main part **3** conclusion
Study the comment and identify the three parts.

c) Copy the grid and note down arguments and counterarguments used in the main part.

	counterargument	argument
1	*constitutional right*	*outdated*
2		
3		

d) Scan the comment and note down words and phrases to …
- list your arguments (*First of all, …; …*),
- consider counterarguments (*Although many US citizens claim that …; …*),
- express your opinion (*I'm convinced that …; …*).

A8 A poem ▶ DIFF Extra D12 | p. 169 ▶ WB 12, 13 | p. 45

a) Read the poem by Amanda Gorman and describe your first impressions.

b) Read the poem again and ...
- name the topic,
- explain how the speaker describes the current situation.

c) Identify these stylistic devices:
- alliteration,
- personification (objects that are given human qualities),
- enjambement (a sentence that continues from one line to the next)

d) Is the poem effective in your opinion? Give reasons.

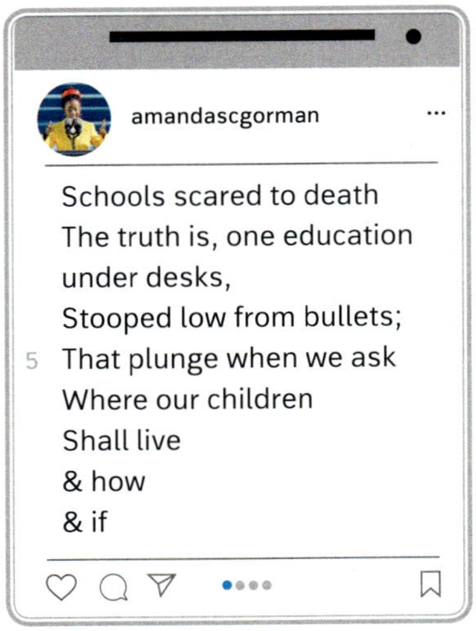
amandascgorman

Schools scared to death
The truth is, one education
under desks,
Stooped low from bullets;
That plunge when we ask
Where our children
Shall live
& how
& if

A9 School safety measures in the US ▶ WB 14 | p. 46

Due to the high number of school shootings, almost every school in the US has adopted lockdown drills.

a) Watch the video and explain how a lockdown drill works.
▶ DIFF Easy alternative D13 | p. 170

b) Collect pros and cons about lockdown drills at school.

c) Some US politicians say that schools would be safer if teachers carried guns at school. Discuss this idea. ▶ Wordbank 6 | p. 241

A10 Target task Write a comment ▶ Writing | p. 209 ▶ Wordbank 6 | p. 241 ▶ WB 15 | p. 47

Choose a statement and write a comment.

A *"Lockdown drills should be introduced at German schools, too."*
B *"There should be armed security guards at German schools, too."*

1. Think about the statement and collect arguments for and against it. Note them down in a grid.
2. Decide what you think of the statement. Find examples to support your opinion.
   Consider the counterarguments you collected in 1 and note down how you would argue against them.
3. Download the checklist ▶ WES-149226-5. Then start by writing a short paragraph to introduce the statement. State your opinion, but don't explain it yet.
4. In the main part of your comment, structure each paragraph by beginning with a counterargument to your opinion. Then write your argument which supports your opinion.
   Make your argumentation logical and convincing.
5. For the conclusion, sum up your opinion.
6. Use connectives to vary your sentence structure and use your list from A7d) to make your comment more interesting to read. Make sure that your grammar and spelling is correct.
7. Share your comments in groups of four. For each group, one member uses the checklist to check:
   - the structure,
   - the language,
   - the content.

   Use the checklist to give feedback.

Need help? Look at page 73. T1 T2

Target task tools for A10: Write a comment

T1 Words and phrases: Comment

A comment should include three parts: an introduction, a main part and a conclusion. There are many useful words and phrases that you can use in each part.
Copy the grid. Then read the words and phrases and sort them into the grid.

In my opinion ... • Statistics show that ... • All in all, there can be no doubt that ... • Some might say/suggest/... that ..., but ... • Furthermore ... • I believe ... • First of all ... • There is no guarantee that ... • Taking everything into account, I can only conclude that ... • On the one hand, ... On the other hand, ... • As far as I know, ... • In my view ... • It is a fact that ... • Finally ... • Because of ... • Secondly ... • All things considered, ... • I'm convinced that ... • Although ... claims/thinks/... that ..., I ... • It is obvious that ...

Introduction	
Stating your opinion	*In my opinion ...*
Main part	
Listing arguments and counterarguments	*First of all ...*
Presenting arguments to support your opinion	*Statistics show that...*
Considering counterarguments	*Some might say/suggest/... that ..., but ...*
Conclusion	
Concluding your statement	*All in all, there can be no doubt that ...*

T2 Writing: Connectives

Complete each sentence with a connective from the box.

although • and • as a result of • because • before • but • so • that • when

- Sometimes there is more than one possible solution.
- One of the connectives does not fit in any sentence.

1 Many people in the US own guns XXX the American constitution gives them the right to keep and bear arms.
2 The first Europeans needed weapons to hunt animals and defend themselves XXX they settled in America.
3 Many people use their guns for sport XXX enjoy going shooting or hunting.
4 The USA has some of the least restrictive gun laws in the world, XXX it is not difficult to buy weapons.
5 Every year, a large number of people die XXX mass shootings in the US.
6 Many critics say XXX there should be stricter gun laws in the US.
7 There is much opposition to current gun laws, XXX many people also defend their right to own a gun.

B1 Young adult literature ▶ WB 16, 17 | p. 48

a) Consider the title of Todd Strasser's young adult novel *No Place* and the title of Part B of this Theme. Speculate on what the novel might be about.

b) Read the plot summary of *No Place* and name three topics the book deals with.

Dan, who is a high school senior, seems to have it all: he is an excellent baseball player from a middle-class family, he hangs out with the in-crowd, dates the most popular girl in school, Talia, and hopes to get a baseball scholarship at college. But when his parents get into financial problems, Dan's life changes. Forced to leave their home, they first move in with Dan's uncle. But as resentment against his unemployed father increases, Dan and his parents leave the uncle's home to live in Dignityville, a tent town in the part of the city for homeless people. Struggling with his new life, Dan experiences both rejection and support from his friends and the community. Only after he has witnessed the unexpected decline of his own family does Dan realize how prejudiced society is against those whose ill fortune has turned them into social outcasts.

B2 No Place, extract 1 ▶ Reading | p. 203 ▶ WB 18, 19 | p. 49

a) Read the first extract from the novel and outline the situation that Dan, the main character, finds himself in. ▶ DIFF Training D14 | p. 170

Noah turned onto my street. When I spotted the U-Haul van backed into my driveway, my spirits plunged faster than a two-seam fastball. Stopping at the curb, Noah glanced at the van, but said nothing. I was pretty sure he knew what it meant, but it was something we'd never spoken about. And we'd spoken about practically everything.

"See you later?" he asked solemnly. I nodded, got out of the car, and pretended to walk up the driveway. The second Noah's taillights were out of sight, I stopped. A heavy sensation of dread had begun to mass in my chest. I'd known this day was coming sooner or later. Only I'd been clinging to the hope that it would be later. A *lot* later. Like, maybe, not in this lifetime.

"So this is the end?"

I slumped down while Mom got up and prepared a bowl of soup for me, adding boiled beef because she knew I needed extra protein in my diet. Both of my parents were vegetarians, but they were cool with me being a carnivore.

"*This is the end … buhm, buhm, buhm … beautiful friend, the end,*" Dad chanted as if even now he couldn't take it seriously. "I prefer to see it as a new beginning," Mom said. I shook my head. "Hard to believe."

"You don't have to," Dad said.

"It's just a temporary setback, Dan. We'll get things together. You'll see."

"We've got our health," added Mom. "Oh yeah, I forgot. Right." I pretended to agree. Like as long as we had our health it didn't matter that we were losing our home. […]

Neither of my parents had jobs. After being a stockbroker for a long time, Mom had been let go about five years ago when her firm went out of business. She'd looked for another job for almost four years before giving up. The longer you were out of work, she said, the more people believed there had to be something wrong with you, and the harder it was to find new employment.

For a while we managed to scrape by on Dad's salary as a supervisor for Burlington Inner City Youth Sports Program.

But then Dad had lost his job and now there was no way we could continue to live, eat, and keep up the payments on the house. The bank had started foreclosure proceedings – they were taking away our home so that they could resell it to someone else.

"When do we have to be out?" I asked, and took a sip of soup. Mom had grown most of the ingredients herself in the garden she tended in our backyard.
"Monday morning, seven a.m."
Since we'd known for months that this day was coming, my parents had sold a lot of their furniture and had put a few favourite pieces in storage, leaving only the bare essentials we needed to live. Over the weekend we would gather up that stuff and leave. Forever.

b) Quote from extract 1 to illustrate how differently Dan and his parents react to what is happening.

c) Read the info box and say who the narrator of the novel *No Place* is. Decide whether it is a first-person or third-person narrator. Give reasons for your decision.
Talk to a partner about what effect this has on the reader. ▶ **DIFF** Support D15 | p. 171

> **Narrative perspective**
> The author is the person who writes a story, the narrator tells the story.
> **A first-person narrator** tells a story from their perspective and is directly involved in the plot.
> **A third-person narrator** tells the story from an outside perspective.

B3 No Place, extract 2 ▶ WB 20 | p. 50

a) Read the next extract.
1. Say why Dan thinks the boy asks him to sign up for the march on Washington.
2. Explain what the boy means by "undivided attention" (l. 15).
3. Describe Dan's view on learning about former protest movements in class.
4. Illustrate the boy's motivation for asking students to take part in the march.

One day the following week I was leaving the cafeteria with Noah and some friends from the team, talking and laughing when the ratty-haired kid at the table in the hall called out, "Hey, Dan, ready to sign up?" I felt myself tense. All my friends, plus a couple of kids at the sign-up table, were watching and listening. "Why do you ask?"
"Seems like a good time," he said. Had he heard that we'd lost our home? Did he think that would make me more sympathetic to his cause? "Why's that?"
I gave him a hard look. Some kids will back down when you give them that look, but this kid kept his eyes steadily on mine. "Just figured for once I had your undivided attention." It took a second to realize that for the past few weeks I'd been with Talia every time I'd passed him, and he probably remembered that time she'd pulled me away before he had a chance to lay out his spiel. But Talia wasn't feeling well and had stayed home that day. Still, it had to take guts to stand up in front of senior athletes and call one out. I looked at the posters on the wall behind him.

> 400 AMERICANS HAVE MORE THAN HALF THE WEALTH IN THIS COUNTRY.
> WHY IS IT EASIER TO BELIEVE THAT 150,000,000 AMERICANS ARE BEING LAZY RATHER THAN THAT 400 AMERICANS ARE BEING GREEDY?
> STOP THE WAR ON THE POOR! [...]

"People are suffering," the kid said. "They can't find work, or get a decent education. You think it's fair that someone dies because he can't pay for adequate medical care while someone else with the same disease lives because he can?"
My friends started to drift away. Meanwhile, I thought of Meg's family living in Dignityville because her mom and brother had to practically spend everything they earned on medicine [...].
I used to think that life was like sports: Things were rarely fair. The other team cheated. Your best player got hurt. You threw a perfect strike and the ump called it a ball.

But that's a game, not life. In sports people don't die because they can't afford medicine. They don't become homeless because a company goes out of business or moves jobs overseas.

I gestured at the posters. "You really think marching's gonna make a difference?" The ratty-haired kid looked surprised. "You don't think protests changed the war in Vietnam or segregation in the South?" I couldn't say.

We may have studied those events in school, both those old protest movements were about as real to me as trigonometry.

You learned what you needed to ace the test. And not for an instant did it feel like it had any actual meaning in your life.

"If we don't do something, it's only going to get worse," the kid said. "And it's not the kind of thing one person can do. Marches show strength. They tell politicians that we have the numbers and the votes to change elections."

I was more than three years away from being able to drink legally, but only months from being able to vote. Sure, voting may have been way more important, but given the choice, I would have switched those two age requirements in a heartbeat.

The kid was still waiting for me to respond.

"Can I ask you something personal?" I said. "Why do you care? You homeless or something?"

The kid gave me a long, curious look, then said, "No, I care … because I'm *not* homeless."

b) The poster in extract 2 says "Stop the war on the poor!". Talk to a partner and speculate about what the kids at Dan's school meant by writing this statement on a poster.

B4 No Place, extract 3

Staying at Dan's uncle's house didn't work out for the family, so with hardly any money left, Dan's parents decide to live in Dignityville.

a) Think – pair – share: Imagine you were in Dan's situation. Speculate what problems Dan might have to face and how he might feel. ▸ Think – pair – share | p. 215

b) Read the next extract and analyse how Dan's family not having any money affects his life. Compare your results with your speculations from a).

At school Lisa, the lunch lady, made a habit of slipping me extra food, but I only took advantage of the offer when I'd missed breakfast or was really hungry. I guess we'd gotten a little lackadaisical about it, though, because the day came when I was in line and she said, "Need a little extra today, honey?"

"Yeah, thanks." I hadn't bought breakfast that morning because the weekend was coming and I wanted to hold on to whatever money I had for going out.

Lisa had just given me some extra chicken nuggets and tater tots when the next guy in line said, "Can I have some extra, too?"

"You can buy another main course if you want," Lisa told him. The guy pointed at me.

"How come he doesn't have to?"

"Are *you* homeless?" Lisa asked.

It was one of those moments when everything stops. I knew Lisa didn't intend anything mean by what she'd said, but it didn't matter. The guy scowled at me and I felt my face go hot and red. And it didn't end there. When I got to the lunch table where the usual suspects were huddled in conversation, Tory glanced up and saw me, then whispered something that caused them all to go silent. Stopping a few feet away from the table, I said, "Sorry. Didn't mean to interrupt. …"

Talia patted the spot beside her.
"Uh … it's Jen's birthday on Friday, and she wants us all to go to Wally's."
Wally's Wowza-Burger was a sort of imitation Planet Hollywood, and it wasn't cheap. Talia said, "We can go, right?" and gave me a look that I interpreted as, *Don't worry, I'll pay for everything.*

Unfortunately, I was pretty sure that everyone else at the table read that look as well. For the second time in less than two minutes, I felt my face go red with embarrassment.
Congratulations, Dan, you're now an official charity case. And everyone knows it.

They say timing is everything, but what they don't add is that it's true of bad timing as well. They also say that things come in threes. After being publicly humiliated twice in less time than it takes to lace up a pair of cleats, I couldn't wait for lunch to end. Food wasn't the only thing simmering in the cafeteria at that point. So was I. As soon as Talia and I left, I planned to ask her to be a little less obvious about the signals she sent in front of her friends.
"Yo, Dan." Out in the hall the scraggly-haired kid came around the sign-up table and planted himself in front of me, blocking my path, intruding in my space. Then he said, "I mean, come on."
That may have been what he said, but it wasn't what I heard. What I heard was, dude, now that the whole school knows you're living in Dignityville, how can you not sign up for the march?

I snapped. Grabbed his collar and yanked him toward me until our faces were so close that I could count the blackheads dotting his nose and forehead.
"Hey!" he cried, clamping his hands around my wrists and struggling to get out of my grip; but the only things clenched more tightly than my fistful of shirt collar were my teeth.
Everyone in the hall stopped and stared.
"Dan!" Talia gasped.
"Jeez, man, come on!" The kid squirmed. It was over in a flash. I'd made a mistake, and let go. Red-faced and breathing hard, the scraggly-haired kid scuttled back around the table. Feeling everyone's eyes, I raised my hands, palms out. "No harm, no foul." It must have sounded lame, but it was all that I could think of.
Talia tugged my arm and we started down the hall again.
"What was that about?" she hissed, as if she was the one who'd been embarrassed.
"Maybe my girlfriend freaking out because I'm temporarily homeless?" I spat angrily.
"I'm not the one who's freaking out. I just … wish it didn't have to be this way."
"And you think I don't?" I asked incredulously.

c) Make notes on how Dan, his friends and Talia deal with Dan's situation. Think about what their behaviour might suggest about their characters.
▶ **DIFF** Training D16-D18 | p. 171 ▶ **WB** 21 | p. 50

B5 Choose After the incident

When Dan grabbed the boy during lunch, he acted against the school rules. The boy reported Dan to a teacher and gave this account of the incident:

> I really can't explain what happened. I mean, I was just asking Dan to sign up for the march when he suddenly grabbed my collar. He didn't say anything. Then he let go. He held up his hands and said, "No harm, no foul." After that he walked off with his girlfriend.

Choose either task A or B:

A Now Dan has to explain what happened in a written statement. Write his statement.
Before you start, decide if Dan is going to tell the truth or if he is going to try to find an excuse for his behaviour. You can start your statement like this:
Let me explain what happened during lunch yesterday: ... The reason for ... is that ...

B Work with a partner. Dan is asked to see his guidance counselor and explain what happened. The school counselor is worried about his behaviour because Dan is usually a polite, popular boy.
- Before you start, decide if Dan is going to tell the truth or if he is going to try to find an excuse for his behaviour.
- Write role cards for Dan and the counselor and note down ideas for what they might say.
- Then do a role play.

B6 Target task Continue the story

▶ Writing | p. 209

Continue Dan's story.

1 Plan your text. Think about Dan's situation and what has happened.
Collect ideas on what might happen next ...
- between him and his friends, especially Talia,
- between him and his parents,
- between him and the boy organizing the march.

2 Write your story. Consider these aspects.

Plot and characters:
- Build on the plot that has been developed so far.
- Base your text on the information you have about the places and the characters in the story. Consider what you know about the way the characters speak, behave and relate to each other. Use your results from B2b) and B4c) to plan your text.
- Refer back to things that have already happened in the extracts you have read.

Narrative perspective:
Tell the story from the same point of view as the author (see B2c).

Style:
- Try to imitate the author's style. Use the past tense and direct speech. Use words and expressions that express how the narrator feels.
- Make sure your story is logical and easy to follow.

3 Peer editing: Swap your stories. Check if your partner has followed the tips from 2. Give feedback.

Need help? Look at page 79. T1 T2

Target task tools for B6: Continue the story

T1 Creative writing

Read the beginnings of three versions continuing Dan's story.
Copy the grid and note down whether they fulfil the criteria and give examples.

	version 1	version 2	version 3
the same narrative perspective Todd Strasser used	...	...	...
the same tense the author used	...	...	...
a style similar to the author's	...	...	...
a convincing presentation of the character	...	...	...

Version 1

Dan pulled away from Talia and ran out of the school. He was crying. He was so embarrassed about his situation but also disappointed in Talia. She just didn't understand. For her, big parties at expensive places were all that mattered. And yet he didn't want to lose her as well. He had lost too much already, his home, his dream, his dignity – he felt that his life was racing down a black tunnel that had no end.

Version 2

I had seen it coming. These past weeks had just been too much. The fact that I didn't have a proper home anymore, that I didn't have the money to buy food or to go to the places that Talia and her friends went to. Not that they meant that much to me, but they had been part of my life and my dream of becoming a baseball star. I was losing it completely. I was ruining my career, I might be expelled from school and I was losing Talia. "Wait!" someone was calling after me, as I raced out of school so that nobody could see my tears.

Version 3

All that stuff gets me. I don't want to go on. That idiot, what got into him? And Talia, I don't need her! Just leave me alone, all of you. I can make it on my own. I'll leave school, I'll get on the next plane to the West Coast, the surfers' paradise everyone is crazy about, and I'll show you, all of you, that you can't beat me.

T2 Words: Other words for 'say'

Todd Strasser uses a lot of direct speech to tell Dan's story. When you continue the story, you can use different verbs to express how someone says something.

a) Here are some verbs which Todd Strasser uses with direct speech. Write them down. Which feelings do they convey?
Example: *cry* → *sadness/anger*

cry • gasp • hiss • spit • whisper

b) Find more verbs that can be used instead of "say". You can use a dictionary for help.

3 Trell: Nothing But the Truth

The novel Trell: Nothing But the Truth *by Dick Lehr is set in Boston, USA, at the beginning of the 2010s. It deals with Trell, a young girl from a Black neighbourhood who is fighting for justice.*

R1 ▶ Reading | p. 203

a) Read extract A and outline what you learn about Trell and her family.

b) At first, Vinnie's bus service sounds like an enjoyable outing. Find passages in the text where the narrator suggests that this is not the case.

c) After reading extract A, start a list of legal terms that might help you with your tasks. Continue your list while you are reading the following extracts.

A The moment the door swung open, I grabbed the chrome bar and pulled myself up into the bus. Right behind me, I could hear Ma hit the steps hard. She didn't need the bar. I looked back: she even skipped steps.

"Don't say it," Ma ordered the driver.

Big Vinnie ignored her. "Mornin' Glory!" he hollered[1].

Ma and I both knew Vinnie would say that. He always did. *Mornin' Glory!* – the words radiating[2] from that big round sunshine of a smile.

The thing is, at the crack of dawn[3] on a Saturday, I was not in the mood for his singsong voice. [...]

I took a seat by the window a few rows back, while Vinnie laughed like he always did, even if no one joined in. I think Big Vinnie imagines himself piloting Ms. Frizzle's Magic School Bus[4], taking passengers on some kind of otherworldly joyride[5]. Otherworldly? Maybe. But joyride? No way. And if magic has anything to do with Big Vinnie's bus trips, it's more like the dark arts.

The truth is Big Vinnie had noticed a few years back that some of the mothers, wives, and girlfriends, and maybe their kids, from the neighborhoods of Roxbury and Mattapan were all needing to head out of the city on Saturday mornings, and Big Vinnie saw a way to make a buck[6].

He went and bought a mini school bus at an auction run by the city – a beat-up heap of yellow steel with more than two hundred thousand miles on it. Big Vinnie was handy[7], though, and he got the engine running okay, and he painted the body a sky blue. In cursive writing along one side he hand-painted *Vinnie's Van*, and right below drew a picture of a hula girl under a palm tree. I have no idea why Big Vinnie chose to add a hula girl, except he talked about one day, someday, going to Hawaii.

Big Vinnie's bus service has been running for six years now. Ma first heard about it from some of her friends at church – the AME Zion Church on the corner of Columbus Avenue and Northampton Street. Before that, when I was real little, every week Ma was either scrambling to find someone with a car that wasn't already filled or we'd rely on some combination of the subway, the commuter train line, and regular buses. Big Vinnie sometimes tries to claim his venture is a public service, but that's crazy talk. He's no nonprofit. He is doing just fine, smilin' that round sunshine smile of his, with a waiting list of people wanting a ride.

My name is Trell, by the way, and I'm fourteen. Van Trell is my real name, but no one calls me that except the teachers at the new school I went to this year. No matter how many times I

---

1 to holler *(AE)* – *brüllen* | **2** to radiate – *strahlen* | **3** at the crack of dawn – *in aller Frühe* | **4** Magic School Bus – *US-Kinderbuchserie, Ms. Frizzle ist die Hauptfigur* | **5** joyride – *Spritztour* | **6** to make a buck – *Geld verdienen* | **7** handy – *geschickt*

said my name is Trell, it was always, "Van Trell Taylor, would you please tell the class, blah blah blah." My ma's name is Shey, but really, it's Ma. Sometimes even her friends call her Ma. […]

Just about everybody who usually takes Big Vinnie's bus ride was on board. Ma was already talking to Marion Williams's mother, catching up on their week, with Ma asking if Marlon's great-aunt was feeling any better after the bad fall she'd taken down her cellar stairs. Terrance Jones's grandmother was in the front seat, and today she had brought along Terrance's three younger siblings. I overheard them talking about Terrance's birthday being next Tuesday. He was turning twenty-seven. My daddy's birthday was coming up, too, next month, in July. He'd be thirty-five.

The bus seated twenty passengers, and every seat was filled, with people like Ma and me, Marlon's mother, and Terrance's grandmother. We were like family because riding together these many months – years even – we'd all gotten to know one another pretty well. Where everyone lived, and who was who in their extended families, and certainly the reasons why we were Big Vinnie's regulars.

We were all taking the ninety-minute ride south of Boston to visit fathers and brothers and uncles in our lives – or, more accurately, missing from our lives. Walpole was our destination. It's the nickname for the state's maximum-security prison. It's where Marlon Williams is doing twelve for armed robbery. Where Terrance Jones is doing ten for drug dealing, or "possession with intent to distribute" – language I wish I didn't know.

My daddy? Romero Taylor?

Walpole is where he's in prison for murder.

Where he is sentenced for life.

Without the possibility for parole.

Except for one thing.

I know he didn't do it.

R 2

After Trell's father has asked Nora Walsh, a young lawyer, to look into his case again, Trell and Nora go through the documents to get a picture of the time when 13-year-old Ruby Graham was killed.

a) Read extract B and describe what Nora and Trell find out about the situation in Boston when the killing happened several years ago.

b) Study the headlines and explain Nora's criticism.

c) Explain why Nora compares the case of Trell's father to the historical situation of the Salem witch trials.

B Nora then began flipping through a stack of newspaper clippings to prove her point. "Ruby became an instant symbol for all that was wrong that summer – the drugs, the guns, the gang wars and violence. The city was rocked by this kind of lawlessness."

[…]

"The National Guard[1] – can you believe it? Soldiers in the streets of Boston?" Nora shook her head again. "The police were under a lot of pressure. Every day the story was all over TV and radio, and on the front pages of the newspaper – stories about the investigation and its lack[2] of progress, and about the community growing almost hysterical, demanding justice. The situation got strange fast, and dangerous – a feeling in the city something like the Salem witch trials. The police seemed obsessed with making an arrest no matter what."

I knew what Nora meant when she mentioned the witch trials. We had studied them in history class. The whole thing was so creepy, the fact that settlers in the 1690s in Salem, Massachusetts, got so freaked out that actual witches might be

---

1 National Guard – *US-Freiwilligen-Armee* | **2** lack – *Mangel*

around that they hanged a bunch of women and girls without any of them getting a fair trial. I learned that panic is a scary thing.

Nora pulled out another newspaper story tracking the investigation in the days after the murder. The headline read, "Police Net Closing In on Girl's Killer". The story opened: "An army of police working around the clock is closing in quickly on the killer of a 13-year-old girl who was hit by a stray bullet, officials said yesterday."

"See what I mean?" Nora said. "Pressure on police, the clock ticking." Nora put her hand on another newspaper in the pile and paused before pulling it out.

"Then there's this," she said, spreading open the paper and running her hand across the front page like she was smoothing a wrinkled sheet. The headline was the biggest yet on any of the papers Nora had shown me. "RUBY KILLER JAILED!" screamed the words in big block letters across the front page. Nora grumbled something about how awful the media could be. 'Ruby *killer* jailed,'" she repeated. "What a headline. What about innocent until proven guilty?" Nora let the question hang there and then shrugged. "But no one seemed to care. The cops had caught the shooter. It was like the city breathed a big sigh of relief[3]. People could sleep again at night."

3 to breathe a sigh of relief – *erleichtert aufatmen*

R 3

Nora's appeal to the judge to revise the court verdict is rejected.

a) Read extract C and describe how Trell and her mother react when they learn that Nora's appeal to reopen the case of Romero Taylor is not accepted.

b) Find passages in the text that support your view.

R 4

Outline Nora's plan and explain how it might help.

C I had never seen Nora look like this – defeated. Ma put her head down, and I could tell she was trying to hold it together and not cry. I grabbed at the ruling. I was mad. "It doesn't make sense, Nora!" I shouted. "It doesn't make sense. What does the judge mean, 'There is no reason to grant a new trial'? Nora, you gave him reasons, lots of reasons."

"You're right, Trell. We presented a lot of reasons why the judge should overturn your daddy's conviction."

I stood up. "There's got to be something more we can do."

"I've done as much as I can – as a lawyer, I mean. We filed an appeal, and the judge said no."

[...]

"But it's not fair," I said. "Daddy's trial was not fair."

"I agree, Trell," Nora said. "But what I'm saying is the system makes it really, really hard to reopen a finished case like your daddy's. It wants finality."

"There's got to be something," I insisted.

We sat there in silence for a few minutes. Then Nora slapped the floor and popped[1] up. "Maybe there is something."

I pulled Ma up.

Nora threw the judge's ruling onto the table, as if she were done with it. "We are right – the case is rotten, even if the judge doesn't agree. Maybe if we could get some help."

"What kind of help?" Ma asked.

[...]

"What if we got a reporter interested? What if a reporter knew what we know about your daddy's case – and what if the reporter was able to

1 to pop up – *sich aufrichten*

uncover some new evidence? What if the reporter wrote a story about this?"

I liked the idea.

"If people were to know what we know, that might put pressure on the police, the district attorney, the legal system – on all of them to take another look at the case. They might prefer finality, but with lots of publicity, they'd have to do something."

"I like this idea," I said, "a lot."

R 5

Clemens Bittner, a reporter from *The Boston Globe*, agrees to help uncover the truth. When he and Trell dig deeper into the case to find evidence that proves that her father is innocent, they find Juanda Tillery, one of the three witnesses whose statements were used against Trell's father.

a) Read extract D and outline what Juanda tells them that proves that their search for the truth is justified.

b) *'"Justice!" It was like Juanda spit the word out.'* Explain what this reaction reveals about Juanda's attitude and experience.

D

"I'm sayin' I don't recall Romero ever talking to Angelo about some business. In fact, they didn't talk about nothing, 'cause Angelo, he just passed us by."

"But it's what you said at the trial," I said. "It's in the transcript."

Juanda's hands went up. "I don't care what it says. I don't recall that." She was getting upset again. "Don't you get it? I was a weed smoker[1]. Smoked so much they called me See-weed, 'cause my friends, whenever they see me, I had weed.

"I was scared, is why I testified. They were threatening to lock me up. I was just a kid. The day I went to court, I'm waiting in a room and the guy starts up, yellin' and screamin' at me."

"What guy?" Clemens asked.

"I don't know that white man's name," she said. "The one who was askin' all the questions. That man, he could have got me to say anything the way he was sticking his face into mine and yellin'. Because I don't remember Romero or Angelo or anyone that night talking about taking care of any business."

Clemens's voice had gone calm and measured. "So, is it accurate to say you felt intimidated[2]? Like you had to say what they wanted or else?"

"I don't care what you want to call it." she said. "All I know is they told me in no uncertain terms that if I didn't testify, my ass was gonna end up in jail."

I started to take my notebook out, and Juanda pounced.

"Don't you start takin' notes," she ordered. "I told you, no story."

Clemens said, "Juanda, this is the help we're after. It's like a pattern[3]. It's what we're finding. Where witnesses – like you – were bullied into saying things that weren't true, but taken together, made Romero seem guilty."

"But he's not guilty," Juanda said. She spoke the words so casually, as if it was a matter of fact. "Everyone knows that."

"What do you mean everyone?" Clemens said.

"The street talks. The street knows Romero's no killer." I was ready to burst.

"With your help, maybe there'd be justice," I said. "Don't you see, Ms. Tillery?"

"Justice!" It was like Juanda spit the word out. "C'mon, girl."

1 weed smoker *(informal)* – *Haschischraucherin* | **2** to intimidate – *einschüchtern* | **3** pattern – *Muster*

R 6

After Bittner has sent his report of their findings to *The Boston Globe*, he and Trell have a meeting with the chief editor[1], Jack Morin.

a) Read extract E and describe the chief editor's reaction to Bittner's story.

b) What is Jack Morin's argument against publishing the article as the first part of a series to allow more time for further research?

E "You're on to something, no question," he said. "You've got good information – new information – to challenge the validity[2] of Romero Taylor's murder conviction. The new alibi information, for example, is real good. Two women saying they were with Romero when the little girl was shot – that's compelling." Jack Morin used his finger to run down the page. "Tracey Dailey and –"

"Boo," I said.

Jack Morin nodded slowly. "Yes, Boo. Tracey and Boo. But, reading the draft, it's not clear to me whether you plan to use their names. Can you?"

"We're working on it," Clemens said.

"We'll get them to go on the record," I said reassuringly.

[...]

"Now, in the section here where you summarize the heart of the prosecutor's case against Mr. Taylor – and, before I get to that, let me say, Clemens, the writing is terrific. Clear and concise – a truly readable account of a complicated case."

Clemens nodded his appreciation.

"In the summary then, you explain to the reader that it was testimony from three witnesses – all teenagers at the time, in 1989 – that proved crucial[3] to Frank Flanagan being able to win a murder conviction against Mr. Taylor." Jack Morin looked at the copy and read their names.

"Monique Catron, Juanda Tillery, and Travis Golson. Do I have that right?"

"That's right," Clemens said. He shifted in his seat.

"The new information about Monique Catron's brain cancer[4] is certainly revelatory," Jack Morin said. "Casts doubt on whether her testimony at the trial was reliable. The jury should have known her condition[5]. That's strong stuff."

Jack Morin put the copy down. "But my question for you: What about the other two? Why aren't they in the story? According to your reporting, you have determined that all three teenagers were crucial. So, Juanda Tillery, where's she?"

"We had a great interview with her," Clemens said.

Calmly, he described Juanda telling us about how she was pressured into saying things at the trial to make Daddy look guilty. "She said she lied, said she was so scared at the time she would have said anything the prosecutor and police wanted her to say."

Jack Morin looked straight at Clemens. "That's good, real good," he said. "But I don't see it here in the story, where it belongs. Why not?"

"Because she insisted everything she told us was off the record."

"It needs to be in the story," Jack Morin said, his voice flat and firm.

I was beginning to feel like I was in the principal's office getting bad news.

[...]

Clemens sat forward. "Okay, the draft's got some gaps – I get that. But hear me out. Of course we want to get Juanda Tillery to go on the record. Find Travis Golson. Sometimes, in stories like this, you get lucky and hit all the bases in a single shot. But here's my strategy for this story – we start off with a first installment[6] revealing[7] the alibi and Monique Catron's cancer as big new

1 chief editor – *Chefredakteur* | **2** validity – *Gültigkeit* | **3** crucial – *entscheidend* | **4** brain cancer – *Hirntumor* | **5** condition – *Zustand* | **6** installment – *Folge* | **7** to reveal – *enthüllen*

developments, and then we keep working to get Juanda and Travis, and we use them in follow-up stories."

Jack Morin listened. He was unmoved.

"Jack, it's strong stuff as it is – you already said so," Clemens argued. "We get the ball rolling, and then we leverage[8] the first story to spring loose[9] the rest."

"I hear you," the editor said, "and sometimes we do use an approach like that in an ongoing investigative story, publish each major piece of news as we get it."

"So?" Clemens said.

"But not on a story of this scale," the editor ruled.

"Ruby Graham's murder is one of the most notorious[10] in our lifetime, if not in Boston's history. She was so young, and it was a time of unprecedented[11] drugs and violence.

People thought the city was going to explode. When police arrested Romero Taylor, and when Frank Flanagan – the same Frank Flanagan who's running for mayor, I don't have to remind you – when Flanagan put Mr. Taylor away, people thought they'd saved the city and done God's work. My point is you don't challenge that legacy piecemeal[12]. It's got to be airtight, and, from what I see here, you don't have critical mass."

Jack Morin pushed his chair back and began to stand up.

"We're going to hold the presses on this one – for now," he said. "But Clemens – and you too, Van Trell – as disappointing as this news is, I want you back out there. This kid Travis, he seems huge. Find him and it's a new ballgame[13]."

---

8 to leverage – *benutzen* | **9** to spring loose – *ins Rollen bringen* | **10** notorious – *berüchtigt* | **11** unprecedented – *noch nie da gewesen* | **12** piecemeal – *stückchenweise* | **13** a new ballgame – *eine neue Situation*

R 7

a) After their visit to *The Boston Globe*, Bittner and Trell talk to Nora and Ma. Consider everyone's feelings, their hopes and worries and write the conversation they might have.

b) Group work (4): Read each other's texts and choose the most convincing one.

R 8 Choose

Choose either task A or B:

A *Trell: Nothing But the Truth* is based on a true story. The author, Dick Lehr, is a professor of journalism at Boston University and has written many non-fiction books for adults. In 2003, when he was a reporter for *The Boston Globe*, he helped to solve the case of a falsely convicted young Black American.
Why might a young adult novel today deal with a case like this? State your view.

B The story is told by Trell. Does she sound like a 14-year-old to you? Do you find her convincing? Do you think the author's choice of perspective works for the story?
State your view and give reasons.

3 I can ...

Was hast du alles gelernt? Diese Seite hilft dir dabei, das zu erkennen.
Falls du Hilfe benötigst, etwas nachlesen oder noch ein paar Übungen machen möchtest, findest du hier passende Hinweise.

WORTSCHATZ

Ich kann ...	Aufgaben/Übungen/Hilfen
meine Meinung ausdrücken und begründen *I think the right to ... is the most/least important. If I didn't have the right to ..., ... • If you ask me, the cartoon is (not) funny/thought-provoking because ...*	3 ▶ **DIFF** D5 ▶ **WB 15**
Statistiken auswerten *My chart deals with/lists ... • The percentage of ... is significantly higher in ...*	A3 ▶ **WB** 7

SKILLS

Ich kann ...	Aufgaben/Übungen/Hilfen
einem Videoclip Informationen entnehmen VIEWING	5, A9 ▶ Viewing | p. 212 ▶ **DIFF** D1, D13 ▶ **WB** 3, 13
Informationen im Internet recherchieren und auswerten MEDIA	6, A6
rhetorische Mittel erkennen und anwenden READING • WRITING	A2, A8 ▶ **DIFF** D4 ▶ **WB** 6, 12
einem Hörtext Informationen entnehmen LISTENING	A6 ▶ Listening | p. 202 ▶ **DIFF** D7 ▶ **WB** 2, 8
ein Gedicht analysieren SPEAKING	A8 ▶ **WB** 12
einen Kommentar verfassen WRITING	A10 ▶ T1, T2 | p. 73 ▶ Writing | p. 209 ▶ **WB** 15
einen längeren Romanauszug lesen, verstehen und analysieren READING	B2, B3, B4 ▶ **DIFF** D17 ▶ Reading | p. 203 ▶ **WB** 21
eine Geschichte fortschreiben WRITING	B6 ▶ T1, T2 | p. 79

GRAMMATIK

Ich kann ...	Aufgaben/Übungen/Hilfen
das *personal passive* verwenden *The students were given the books.*	▶ **DIFF** D8 ▶ G2R | p. 220 ▶ **WB** 10
***defining* und *non-defining relative clauses* verwenden** *There is a lot of controversy around the Second Amendment, which gives American citizens the right to bear arms.*	▶ **DIFF** D9 ▶ G8R | p. 230 ▶ **WB** 11
***contact clauses* verwenden** *Augusta in Maine was the place my parents chose for our summer vacation last year.*	▶ **DIFF** D10 ▶ G8R | p. 230
***relative clauses referring to a sentence* verwenden** *Theo won't make it to the party, which is very sad.*	▶ **DIFF** D11 ▶ G8R | p. 230
***reported speech* anwenden** *Esme said that there was going to be a science contest the next day.*	▶ **DIFF** D14 ▶ G3R | p. 221 ▶ **WB** 19

Reading: Analysing a speech

Step by step

On these pages you will learn how to analyse a speech, step by step.

There are different types of speeches.
- Informative speeches are meant to share information with the audience and to teach them about a topic (e.g. at the opening of a new museum).
- Persuasive speeches want to win over their audience by arguing a point (e.g. at a political event).
- Entertaining speeches are usually comical or dramatic to entertain the audience (e.g. at a wedding).

Malala Yousafzai gave a speech to the United Nations on her 16th birthday, after she had survived an attack by Taliban gunmen. Read her speech and analyse it, following steps 1-5 on page 89.

Today, it is an honour for me to be speaking again after a long time. Being here with such honourable people is a great moment in my life.

I don't know where to begin my speech. I don't know what people would be expecting me to say. But first of all, thank you to God for whom we all are equal and thank you to every person who has prayed[1] for my fast recovery[2] and a new life.

[...]

Dear Friends, on the 9th of October 2012, the Taliban shot me on the left side of my forehead. They shot my friends too. They thought that the bullets[3] would silence us. But they failed[4].

And then, out of that silence came thousands of voices. The terrorists thought that they would change our aims and stop our ambitions but nothing changed in my life except[5] this: Weakness, fear and hopelessness died. Strength, power and courage was born. I am the same Malala. My ambitions are the same. My hopes are the same. My dreams are the same.

[...]

Dear sisters and brothers, we realise the importance of light when we see darkness. We realise the importance of our voice when we are silenced. In the same way, when we were in Swat, the north of Pakistan, we realised the importance of pens and books when we saw the guns.

The wise saying, "The pen is mightier[6] than sword" was true. The extremists are afraid of books and pens. The power of education frightens them. They are afraid of women. The power of the voice of women frightens them. And that is why they killed 14 innocent[7] medical students in the recent attack in Quetta. And that is why they killed many female teachers and polio workers in Khyber Pakhtunkhwa and FATA. That is why they are blasting schools every day. Because they were and they are afraid of change, afraid of the equality that we will bring into our society.

[...]

Honourable Secretary General, peace is necessary for education. In many parts of the world, especially Pakistan and Afghanistan, terrorism, wars and conflicts stop children to go [stop children from going] to their schools. We are really tired of these wars. Women and

1 to pray – *beten* | **2** recovery – *Genesung* | **3** bullet – *Kugel* | **4** to fail – *scheitern* | **5** except – *außer* | **6** mighty – *mächtig* | **7** innocent – *unschuldig, unbeteiligt*

children are suffering in many parts of the world in many ways. In India, innocent and poor children are victims[8] of child labour. Many schools have been destroyed in Nigeria. People in Afghanistan have been affected by the hurdles of extremism for decades. Young girls have to do domestic child labour and are forced to get married at early age. Poverty, ignorance, injustice, racism and the deprivation[9] of basic rights are the main problems faced by both men and women.

Dear fellows, today I am focusing on women's rights and girls' education because they are suffering the most. There was a time when women social activists asked men to stand up for their rights. But, this time, we will do it by ourselves. I am not telling men to step away from speaking for women's rights rather I am focusing on women to be independent to fight for themselves.

Dear sisters and brothers, now it's time to speak up.

So today, we call upon[10] the world leaders to change their strategic policies in favour of peace and prosperity[11].

We call upon the world leaders that all the peace deals must protect women and children's rights. A deal that goes against the dignity[12] of women and their rights is unacceptable.

We call upon all governments to ensure free compulsory[13] education for every child all over the world.

We call upon all governments to fight against terrorism and violence, to protect children from brutality and harm.

We call upon the developed nations to support the expansion of educational opportunities for girls in the developing world.

We call upon all communities to be tolerant – to reject prejudice based on caste[14], creed[15], sect[16], religion or gender. To ensure freedom and equality for women so that they can flourish. We cannot all succeed when half of us are held back.

We call upon our sisters around the world to be brave – to embrace the strength within themselves and realise their full potential.

Dear brothers and sisters, we want schools and education for every child's bright future. We will continue our journey to our destination of peace and education for everyone. No one can stop us. We will speak for our rights and we will bring change through our voice. We must believe in the power and the strength of our words. Our words can change the world.

[…]

Dear brothers and sisters, we must not forget that millions of people are suffering from poverty, injustice and ignorance. We must not forget that millions of children are out of schools. We must not forget that our sisters and brothers are waiting for a bright peaceful future.

So let us wage a global struggle against[17] illiteracy[18], poverty and terrorism and let us pick up our books and pens. They are our most powerful weapons.

One child, one teacher, one pen and one book can change the world.

Education is the only solution. Education first.

8 victim – *Opfer* | **9** deprivation – *Beraubung* | **10** to call upon sb – *jdn aufrufen* | **11** prosperity *(no pl)* – *Wohlstand* | **12** dignity *(no pl)* – *Würde* | **13** compulsory – *obligatorisch* | **14** caste – *Kaste* (*Gesellschaftsschicht*) | **15** creed – *Glaubensbekenntnis* | **16** sect – *Religionsgemeinschaft* | **17** to wage a struggle against sb/sth – *den Kampf gegen etw/jdn aufnehmen* |**18** illiteracy *(no pl)* – *Analphabetismus*

Step 1

Download the speech ▶ WES-149226-5 and read it.
Look at the support box at the top of page 87 to decide what type of speech it is.

Step 2

A speech has three parts:

1 Introduction:
- The first part of a speech is used to attract the audience's attention.
- The speaker often starts with a short personal story, interesting facts or a joke.
- The first part of a speech also gives a general idea of what the speech is going to be about.

2 Main part:
- The main part focuses on the speaker's main ideas.
- In this part, the speaker tries to convince the audience of their point of view by including facts, statistics and arguments and by considering counterarguments.
- The use of stylistic devices (e.g. anaphora, direct address) helps the speaker to hold the audience's attention.

3 Conclusion:
- In the last part, the speaker summarizes their main ideas.
- In political speeches, speakers often end a speech by asking the audience to become involved in the matter.

Go through your copy of the speech and mark the three parts of Malala's speech.

Step 3

For each part of the speech, note down what Malala is talking about.
Explain what Malala wants to achieve with her speech.

To identify what Malala wants to achieve, you can ask yourself the following questions:
- **Who is the speaker?** What do you already know about Malala?
- **What kind of audience** is it?
- **When and where** does Malala give the speech?

Step 4

Identify the stylistic devices Malala uses to make her speech interesting and persuasive.
Use different colours to highlight the following elements on your copy:
- Personal references/Malala's own experiences
- Facts and examples to emphasize Malala's point
- Quotes
- Direct address (e.g. "Dear brothers and sisters")
- Anaphora (repeating the first words at the beginning of a sentence/clause)
- Enumeration (listing things/ideas, e.g. "weakness, fear and hopelessness")
- Antithesis (creating contrast, e.g. "out of that silence came thousands of voices")

Step 5

Say whether you consider Malala's speech effective. Give reasons.

If you need help with a different speech, you can use the checklist on page 90.

Checklist: Reading: Analysing a speech

Checklist

1. Read the speech and decide what type of speech it is.
   - informative speech (e.g. at the opening of a new museum)
   - persuasive speech (e.g. at a political event)
   - entertaining speech (e.g. at a wedding)
2. Identify the three parts of the speech (introduction, main part, conclusion).
3. For each part of the speech, note down what the speaker is talking about.
   Explain what the speaker wants to achieve with the speech.
   To identify what the speaker wants to achieve, you can ask yourself the following questions:
   - **Who is the speaker?** What do you already know about them or what can you find out?
   - **What kind of audience** is it?
   - **When and where** does the person give the speech?
4. Identify stylistic devices the speaker uses, e.g. personal references, facts and examples, quotes, direct address, anaphora, enumeration, antithesis, humour, ...
5. Say whether you consider the speech effective. Give reasons.

4

Chances and opportunities

In this Theme you will ...

- talk about summer jobs and part-time jobs for teenagers
- read advertisements for internships
- think about job requirements
- write a cover letter and a CV
- do a role-play job interview

4 Teen jobs

1 Teen jobs
▶ Think – pair – share | p. 215 ▶ DIFF Easy alternative D1 | p. 173 ▶ WB 1 | p. 58

Think – pair – share: What jobs for teenagers do you know? Collect ideas in class.
Tip: If you don't know the word, describe the job or use an online dictionary.

2 Different jobs
▶ DIFF Training D2, D3 | p. 173 ▶ WB 2, 3 | p. 58

a) Read the teenagers' reports on page 93.
Copy the grid and note down …
- their jobs,
- what they need to do (tasks),
- what skills/knowledge/personal qualities they need,
- the benefits,
- the disadvantages.

	Delan	Emma	Matt
job			
tasks			
skills etc.			
benefits			
disadvantages			

Compare your results with a partner's.

b) Look at your grid from a). Explain which of these jobs you would (not) like to do.

c) Start an ABC list for the word field "jobs". You can use words from page 93.

A *to assist sb*
B *benefits*
C *company, creative*
D *…*

3 Choose Advantages and disadvantages
▶ Wordbank 8 | p. 243

A With a partner choose situation 1 or 2 and prepare a role play. Find another pair and present your role plays, then give each other feedback (content, language, performance).

OR

B Choose situation 1 or 2 and write a dialogue. Swap your dialogue with a partner. Give each other feedback (content, spelling, grammar).

1 Your mother/father won't allow you to have a job. They want you to focus on school. You try to convince them that student jobs can prepare teens for working life.

2 You want more pocket money and your mother/father suggests that you find a job. You argue that there are disadvantages to teenagers having jobs.

4 Worst summer jobs
L 1/14 | S 8 ▶ Listening | p. 202 ▶ WB 4 | p. 59

a) Listen to a radio show about the worst summer jobs ever. Take notes on …
- what Mary's/Dustin's/Megan's/Patrick's jobs were or where they worked,
- what was bad about the jobs.

Compare your results with a partner's.
▶ DIFF Easy alternative D4 | p. 174

jam jar – *Marmeladenglas*
pipe – *Rohr*
fishing – *Fischerei, Angeln*
to shovel – *schaufeln*
sticky – *klebrig*
slippery – *rutschig*
pizza delivery boy – *Pizzabote*
smelly – *stinkend*
to lock sb out – *jd aussperren*

b) Tell each other which of the summer jobs you would have hated most and why.

disgusting • *embarrassing* • *exhausting* • *frustrating* • *hard* • *horrible* • *nasty* • *revolting*

c) What would be your idea of your worst summer job? Imagine taking part in a radio show. Note down what you would tell the listeners. Include these points:
- what you expected to gain from the job
- what you learned from the experience

d) In groups of four (three callers and one radio host) record your conversations with the host. Play your radio show to another group and listen to their show. ▶ WB Media 7 ▶ WES-149226-2

I make money in my spare time by finding free or cheap second-hand stuff, and then I sell it online. It's called "flipping"! Sometimes I can just sell the stuff as I find it, other times I have to repair or restyle things.

Anyone can get into flipping, but it helps if you're crafty, creative and confident about repairing things and if you have the right tools at home. It also helps if you're a good salesperson and know what something is worth.

The best thing about flipping is it's fun and doesn't really feel like a job, or at least that's how I see it. You find your DIY skills are always improving, and once you get good at it, you can make so much money! You also get to meet many interesting people.

There are disadvantages, too, of course. Sometimes you might invest a lot of time into something, like a piece of furniture, and you can't sell it. You then have to store it somewhere. I guess it helps to have a garage, too! Also it can be a lot of work, dealing with the online selling platforms. Sometimes people are rude and promise to collect something, but never turn up. I wonder why anyone would do that. It's so impolite!

Delan, 15

Two afternoons a week, I work for a company which gives tech support to elderly people. We help seniors with their devices, like smartphones and tablets. We also assist them with everyday digital tasks, like using video chat to speak to friends and family, streaming movies and TV, shopping online, sending messages and using any other apps you can think of. I also give classes about topics like social media, or taking and editing photos.

The most important quality for someone who does my job is patience. You have to be friendly and be able to explain complicated things in an easy-to-understand way. You also have to be trustworthy and discreet – people will often tell you their passwords when you are setting something up for them. And of course you need to be tech-savvy and know what you are talking about.

The benefits to my job are no two days are ever the same – there's always a new challenge. You always meet new people and it feels great helping them and making their lives easier.

But the people can also be the biggest disadvantage of the job at times, for example when they are impatient. Some people even ask whether our service is free, which is really annoying.

Emma, 15

I'm the team mascot for my local football team. My job is to go to all games on weekends and entertain the spectators. I walk around the field before the match and at half time and do funny things. I sometimes also take part in the choreography with the cheerleading team.

A lot of people think my job is easy, but it's actually quite hard. You need to be fit and healthy to be a mascot, and the costume is heavy, so you also need to be strong. It also helps if you are a creative and funny person. Don't forget you have to entertain people and make them laugh without speaking or them being able to see your face. That's not easy.

The best thing about my job is that all the fans love me and are always happy to see me. Many children ask if they can get a photo with me. I love meeting new people. I also love American football, and I get to watch every game of my team and hang out with the players!

The worst thing about my job is definitely the heavy costume: it can get hot and uncomfortable in there. It's also sometimes dangerous when you can't see very well and you fall over, like on stairs. And you can get a lot of nasty chants coming from the other team's fans – I don't enjoy that!

Matt, 16

4 Finding a job

A1 A good job
L 1/15 | S 9 ▶ WB 5 | p. 60

a) Listen to the podcast and say what it is about.

b) Listen again and note down what criteria are mentioned.
Example: *a good work-life balance, ...* ▶ DIFF Easy alternative D5 | p. 175

c) Collect more criteria in class and add them to your list from b).

A2 Being an influencer
▶ Wordbank 4 | p. 239 ▶ DIFF Training D6 | p. 175 ▶ WB 6, 7 | p. 60

a) Many young people dream of being an influencer on social media.
Collect positive and negative aspects of this job. Your results from A1c) can help you.

b) Watch the video clip to find out ...
- what Meghan does,
- what she likes/dislikes about her job.

Say if your results from a) match Meghan's experiences.

c) Meghan says that she can use social media to reach out to people offline and touch their lives. Explain what she means by that.

A3 Your future job
▶ Wordbank 8 | p. 243 ▶ WB 8-10 | p. 61

a) Think about your future job. Note down ...
- which aspects from A1c) would be important to you,
- which activities your job should involve,
- if and how you would like to interact with other people,
- where you would like to work (location),
- what things you wouldn't like to do at all.

b) Imagine what your work life might look like ten years from now. Use your notes from a) to talk to a partner about your future job. ▶ DIFF Training D7, D8 | p. 176

Ten years from now I will have found my dream job.

I will travel around the world and ...

I definitely won't ...

A4 Soft skills and hard skills
L 1/16 | S 10

a) Listen and explain what soft skills and hard skills are.

b) Listen again and list the soft skills and hard skills that are mentioned. ▶ DIFF Easy alternative D9 | p. 176

c) With a partner, find at least three more examples for soft skills and three more examples for hard skills. Share your ideas in class, then add them to your list from b).

A5 Job adverts
▶ DIFF Extra D10, Training D11 | p. 177 ▶ WB 11-13 | p. 62

a) Read the adverts on page 95. List the soft skills that are needed for each job.
Add them to your list from A4c).

b) Based on the soft skills that are needed for each job, think about which job would suit you most.
Find examples to support your decision, then tell a partner about your choice.

The internship would be the best job for me as I'm a well-organized and creative person. I always write to-do lists and I'm good at time management, for example when ...

c) Add more words and phrases to your word list from Intro 2c).

d)  Find an online career quiz and do it. Report to a partner what you think of the job that was suggested to you and ask your partner's opinion about it.

www.internationalworkexperience.com/internships_volunteers/global

Internship

Flickchat is an up-and-coming and fast-growing social media company. We want to connect people across the world and revolutionize the future of instant messaging.

FLICKCHAT

We are looking for an intern to work with us in our fabulous new office space. We are a small team and teamwork is essential. Everyone has their part to play in making Flickchat the best it can be. Potential applicants should be well-organized and creative – we like people who think outside the box to solve problems.

We are currently focusing on an exciting new feature for our platform. Experience in photo and/or video editing would be helpful for the role, but not essential. The most important thing for us is finding someone who is the right fit for the company – someone who understands our vision and can add their mark on whatever project they work on. We can't wait to hear from you!

Contact us:
Flickchat, Mr Tom Nuttall, 12 Blomfield Street
London, EC2M 7AJ, United Kingdom

Volunteer

Banff National Park is the oldest National Park in Canada. International volunteers will get to know the park through their involvement with group activities and special park events, as well as their daily responsibilities. They will also act as park representatives and will often be in contact with visitors. Hiking the trails to observe, record and report their conditions and any wildlife sightings is another important aspect of the job.

All volunteers will receive comprehensive training and an introduction to the park. They are expected to work five eight-hour shifts per week, usually between Wednesday and Sunday, as the weekends are the busiest times for us.

We are looking for candidates with the ability to work independently. Ideal volunteers have good problem-solving skills, are willing to work hard and remain flexible and positive regardless of ever-changing project work, locations and unpredictable weather. Volunteers must be energetic and physically capable of hiking in mountain areas.

Contact us:
Banff National Park, 224 Banff Avenue
Banff, AB T1L 1C3, Canada

Volunteer

Toucan Wildlife Center is an animal rescue shelter in Costa Rica. The center was set up by two biologists, and we look after wounded animals. Our goal is to try and release all animals who come to the center back into the wild. When that's not possible, we keep them with us and look after them.

TOUCAN WILDLIFE PARK

We are looking for volunteers to work at the center and help to care for the animals. This includes feeding the animals and cleaning cages etc. We are looking for highly motivated volunteers with a love of animals and nature conservation.

You need to be reliable and have excellent communication skills. Volunteers will also interact with visitors to the center, as we run daily tours to inform people about our work.

Your stay will be for a minimum of 12 weeks and you are expected to work eight hours a day spread across five days a week.

Contact us:
Toucan Wildlife Center, Reserva Conchal
Provincia de Guanacaste, 50308, Costa Rica

A6 Volunteering 🔊 L 1/17

a) Two of the job adverts in A5 are for volunteers. Come up with a definition of "volunteering".

b) Identify factors that make people want to volunteer.

c) Listen to the radio clip to find out if Laura's reasons for volunteering match your results from b).

d) Explain in English ...
- where Laura went and what she did,
- what was positive about her experience,
- what was negative about her experience.

e) Volunteering used to be seen in a very positive light. Today, there are more critical voices about volunteering. Speculate on the reasons.

A7 A CV

▶ Wordbank 8 | p. 243

A CV (= *curriculum vitae*) allows you to show the employer that you have the necessary skills to do the job.

a) Read Alex's CV and say which job from page 95 you think she is applying for. Give reasons.

b) Write your CV. Study the tips, then use Alex's CV as a model and follow its structure. ▶ WB 14 | p. 64 ▶ WB Media 3 ▶ WES-149226-2

www.career-tips-

Tips for your CV

- ✓ It is important to make your CV easy to read, so choose a clear layout.
- ✓ The content is more important than the layout/design.
- ✓ Grammar and spelling should be correct. Have your CV checked by someone who is good at editing.
- ✓ A clear and correct CV lets the employer know that you are serious about your application.
- ✓ Use formal language.

Alex Kaufmann

Tieckstr. 9, 22111 Hamburg, Germany | +49 1525 841 3756 | a.kaufmann@mail.com

Personal profile

I am hard-working and reliable. Being very organized, I like working independently, but I also have great communication skills. I love nature and animals and enjoy outdoor activities. I have always wanted to spend some time in a country with a warm climate. My hobbies are playing the piano, reading and walking my dog, Lupo.
References available on request.

Education

2018-present	Hoffmann-von-Fallersleben Gymnasium, Hamburg
2014-2018	Grundschule am Steinweg, Hamburg

Work experience

2023-present	Private tutor for younger students (subjects: English, German) Design my own worksheets online
07/2023-08/2023	Volunteered at an animal shelter during summer break Responsible for feeding the animals
07/2022-09/2022	Office job at ITX Support Solutions (Hamburg) Data entry for the company database Worked on the event team for a conference

Skills

IT Skills	Office software: word processing, spreadsheets, presentations, email Basic knowledge of HTML
Languages	German native speaker; English very good; Spanish basic

c) Read the culture box. Explain the advantages and disadvantages of different types of applications.

▶ DIFF Extra D12 | p. 178

International job applications

Culture box

In many countries, including Germany, it is common to include a photo (headshot) of yourself on your CV. This is not the case in the UK, USA or Ireland. In these countries, some people will also not include their age, their birthday, their marital status and their nationality.

A8 Grammar card *Let/make sb do sth, have sth done*

▶ DIFF Training D13 | p. 179 ▶ WB 15 | p. 65

- In the tips in A7b) you can find sentences which would need the verb *lassen* if translated into German (e.g. *Have your CV checked by someone who is good at editing.* → *Lass deinen Lebenslauf von jemandem prüfen, der gut redigieren kann.*).
- Start a grammar card. Check G11 on page 232 and note down when to use *to let somebody do something*, *to make somebody do something* or *to have something done*.

A9 Writing a cover letter

▶ DIFF Training D14 | p. 179 ▶ WB 16 | p. 65

a) Read Alex's first draft of her cover letter. Describe your first impression of her as an applicant.

What makes her a good candidate/only an average candidate is ... • She seems/doesn't seem to be well-suited to the project/job as she ... • Although she may ..., she lacks ... • I (don't) think she will attract the organization's attention because ... • The representatives of the organization/company will probably approve of ..., but might have a problem with ...

b) Read the checklist and compare it to the letter. Note down which parts of the letter should be changed.

c) Compare your results with a partner's. Together, rewrite Alex's cover letter. You can use Alex's CV from A7 for ideas. ▶ Wordbank 8 | p. 243

Alex Kaufmann
Hamburg, Germany

Toucan Wildlife Center
Reserva Conchal
Provincia de Guanacaste
50308
Costa Rica

Re: Application for volunteer position

Hi guys!

So I saw your volunteer advert online and I was so excited!

A bit about me – my name is Alex ☺ I absolutely luv animals and I've always wanted 2 go to the rainforest! I am organized and reliable. You can count on me! I have worked at an animal shelter and I'm good at explaining things.

It would be great if you could get back to me soon. I really would love to work for you guys!

Bye, see you soon!

- ✓ Use formal language and be polite.
- ✓ Make sure your grammar and spelling are correct.
- ✓ Keep the letter short and to the point.
- ✓ Write your full address in the top right.
- ✓ Next, on the left, write the name and the address of the person/organization you are writing to.
- ✓ Add the date on the right.
- ✓ Next, write a subject and say what your letter is about.
- ✓ Start the letter with *Dear Mr/Mrs/Ms ...* If you don't know the name of the person, write *Dear Sir/Madam*.
- ✓ In the first paragraph, explain why you are writing the letter (e.g. *I am writing in response to your advertisement.*).
- ✓ In the second paragraph, describe why you would be a good candidate for the job (e.g. *I have been studying English and Spanish for ... years/I believe I am a good candidate for this job because .../I am a ... person who likes ...*).
- ✓ When you come to the end of the letter, write one or two closing comments (e.g. *Thank you for considering my application. I look forward to hearing from you.*).
- ✓ Sign off your letter (e.g. *Yours faithfully, Alex Kaufmann*).

A10 A video CV

Some companies ask for a video CV so they can get to know applicants better.
Video CVs give candidates a chance to show off their communication skills and be creative.

a) Go online and find two examples of video CVs.
Watch them and note down ...
- what you like about them,
- what you don't like about them/what should be changed.

b) Share your results from a) with a partner.
Together, write a checklist for a video CV. These questions can help you:
- How should you greet your potential employer?
- How should you dress for the video?
- How can you show that you are the perfect candidate?
- How do you ensure a good video quality (sound and picture)?
- Which other aspects might be important to create a convincing video CV?

c) Choose one of the jobs from A5 or your future job from A3.
Use your checklists from b) to create a video CV.
▶ **WB** Media 6 ▶ WES-149226-2

d) Send your video to your partner. Ask them for feedback based on your checklist.

A11 Target task Write a cover letter ▶ Writing | p. 210

Write a cover letter for one of the jobs in A5.

1 Choose one of the jobs from A5. Check your results from A5a) to find out which soft skills are needed for the job and which of your characteristics could match them.

2 Think about which hard skills (qualifications/experience) you have.

3 Download the checklist and use the first part to plan and write your letter. ▶ WES-149226-5 ▶ Wordbank 8 | p. 243
▶ **WB** Media 3 ▶ WES-149226-2

4 Use the checklist from 3 to edit your letter.

5 Now make your letter anonymous (no name, no address) and print it out. In class, collect all the printed letters.
Form groups (3-4) for each job from A5.
Look at the applications for "your" job and choose the two applications that you think are the best.
Give reasons for your choice.

> To vary your sentence structure, you can use participle constructions and connectives (e. g. *although, however, but, ...*).

Need help? Look at page 99. T1 T2

Target task tools for A11: Write a cover letter

T1 Words: Soft skills

a) Decide which of the following skills are soft skills.

punctual • familiar with database software • reliable • good manners • confident • able to speak Spanish • familiar with computer systems • able to cope well with stress • tolerant • able to work well in a team • open to new challenges • good at logical thinking • diligent • detailed knowledge of modern literature • ambitious • flexible • able to play the piano

b) Match the following examples/situations/activities to a soft skill from a) that they illustrate. There is more than one correct answer.

Example: no problem speaking in front of a lot of people and expressing your opinion
→ ***confident***

1 taking part in a school exchange with a US high school
2 always doing your homework and doing extra homework, too
3 being sent to special maths and science events by your school
4 always being on time and doing the tasks you are supposed to do
5 helping your family business plan events, e.g. weddings and birthday parties
6 being a leader of a youth group

T2 Words: Register

a) It is important to use formal language in a cover letter. Identify the phrases that are formal language and that could be used in a cover letter. Note them down in a list.

A I look forward to hearing from you.
B Oh, and I've also added my references.
C You will find that I am ...
D I would love to gain experience by working for you.
E Don't worry, I never get stressed.
F I can't work Sundays, hope that's OK!
G One of my strengths is my ability to ...
H To be honest, I want this job so that I can learn something about computers.
I I would really appreciate the opportunity to tell you more about myself in an interview.
J Please write back soon!
K As described in the job advert, ...
L I would be very grateful if you could ...
M I have a strong interest in ...
N I'm a total maths genius!
O The guys at school say I'm always friendly.
P Please find my CV attached.
Q I am available during the summer, except for a two-week holiday.
R Having studied Spanish for four years, I am able to speak the language quite fluently.

b) Now look at the informal/inappropriate phrases from a). Think about formal/neutral expressions with the same meaning. You can use the formal phrases from a) to help you. Add them to your list.

Example: I'm a total maths genius!
→ ***Having studied maths for three years, I am very good with numbers.***

B1 Tips for a video job interview ▶ WB 17, 18 | p. 66

a) A lot of job interviews today are conducted via video. Close your books and collect ideas that can help someone to succeed in a video job interview.

b) Read the tips below and compare them to your results from a). Explain which would be the hardest tip for you to follow.

Preparation

1 Read the job advert again and think of reasons why you are the right fit for the job. You should also research the company/organization.
2 Practise your answers to common interview questions.
3 Dress appropriately.
4 Find a quiet space where nobody will disturb you.
5 Check that the microphone and camera on your device are working.
6 Check that the background is tidy or use a neutral background filter.

During the interview

7 Sit up straight and smile.
8 Listen carefully and give precise answers.
9 Be positive to show you are enthusiastic about the job.
10 Be relaxed, but remember that you are talking to your possible future employer and not to a friend.
11 It's OK to use hand gestures but don't fidget with your hair or touch your face.
12 Make sure you don't talk too fast.
13 Don't panic if you are asked a question that you cannot answer immediately.

After the interview

14 Send your interviewer a message thanking them for their time.
15 If you are rejected, ask for feedback. This can help you with future interviews.

c) Group work (3): Choose one or two aspects from the list in b) and make a short video clip about what applicants should do in a video job interview. It can also be a funny negative example of what not to do.

B2 Alex's job interview ▶ Viewing | p. 212 ▶ WB 19 | p. 67

a) Watch Alex's job interview. Use the list from B1b) and note down how well Alex follows the tips.

> Use symbols, abbrevations or keywords for your notes.

b) Discuss and decide whether you would give Alex the job.
▶ Wordbank 6 | p. 241

c) Give advice to Alex on what she could do differently next time.
▶ DIFF Support D15 | p. 180

d) Watch the interview again. Note down useful phrases you can use for a job interview. Compare your results with a partner's.
▶ DIFF Training D16 | p. 180

B3 Revision: Conditional clauses, type 3

▶ G5R | p. 224 ▶ DIFF Training D17 | p. 181 ▶ WB 20 | p. 67

Sometimes things can go wrong in a job interview.
Read the sentences and complete the verbs in the right tenses.

Example: It **XXX** (be) better if I **XXX** (know) more about the company.
It would have been better if I had known more about the company.

1 If I **XXX** (switch on) my computer earlier, I **XXX** (not be) late.
2 I **XXX** (be able to focus) better if my brother **XXX** (not practise) the piano in his room during the interview
3 My answers **XXX** (be) more convincing if I **XXX** (research) the company better.
4 If I **XXX** (listen) more carefully to the interviewer's questions, I **XXX** (have) a better chance.
5 The interviewer **XXX** (like) me better if I **XXX** (smile) more.
6 If the interviewer **XXX** (like) me better, I **XXX** (get) the job.

B4 Phrases for successful conversations

▶ DIFF Support D18 | p. 181 ▶ WB 21 | p. 68

a) It is useful to know phrases to make a conversation flow better. You can also use these phrases for a job interview. Copy the grid and sort the phrases. Some might fit into more than one category.

conversation openers	keeping the conversation going	buying time	ending a conversation
…	…	…	…

So what you are saying is …?
OK then, let's get started …
Right.
Sorry to have kept you waiting.
Don't worry about it.
When you say …, do you mean …?
I see.
Thank you so much for your time.
That's a good/an interesting question. Let me think.
I hope it's OK to ask: …?
I've never been asked that question before. Please give me a moment to think about it.
Have a good day!
How are you today?
Good! How are you?
Shall we start?
That sounds interesting/challenging/good/…
Pleased to meet you.
Likewise!
It's been great getting to know you.
So you are looking for an example of … Well, there are a few, but I think the most relevant is …

b) Find one more example for each category. Share your results in class and add them to your grid.

B5 Target task **Act out a video job interview** ▶ Speaking | p. 205

Imagine you sent an application for one of the adverts from page 95 and the company/organization has invited you for a video job interview. Prepare for and act out the job interview. ▶ Wordbank 8 | p. 243

1 Prepare for your role as an **applicant**:
- Study the job advert again carefully. Find out what the job requires and which qualifications you have for that job.
- Study the employer's questions below. Note down ideas for how you could respond in the interview.
- Make sure you bear in mind relevant tips from B1.
- Remember to use some of the phrases from B4 to make your conversation flow well.

Employer:	*Hi* (name of applicant), *how are you today?*
Applicant:	(Respond to the employer's greeting.)
Employer:	*Good! OK then, let's get started. You have applied to work as a/an* (add job title) *with us. What would make you successful in this job?*
Applicant:	(Answer the question.)
Employer:	*How do you cope with working under pressure?*
Applicant:	(Answer the question.)
Employer:	*Do you like working in a team or do you prefer working on your own?*
Applicant:	(Answer the question.)
Employer:	*How would you contribute to* (name of company/organization)*?*
Applicant:	(Answer the question.)
Employer:	*What are your general interests and hobbies?*
Applicant:	(Answer the question.)
Employer:	*Do you have any questions for me?*
Applicant:	(Ask a question about the job or the company/organization.)
Employer:	*That's a good question.* (Make up a short answer to the question). *It's been great getting to know you. We'll be in touch.*
Applicant:	(Thank the employer for their time and say that you look forward to hearing from them.)

2 Work with a partner. You are the applicant, your partner is the employer. Tell your partner which job you have applied for.
- Act out the video interview following the script in step 1.
- During the interview, your partner takes notes on the feedback checklist. ▶ WES-149226-5

3 After the interview, your partner gives you feedback on how convincing you were in your role as the applicant. They also tell you whether they would give you the job. They might also give you some advice on what you could do better next time.

4 Swap roles and do another video interview. Now you are the employer and your partner is the applicant (repeat steps 2 and 3).

Need help? Look at page 103. T1 T2

Target task tools for B5: Act out a video job interview

T1 Words: Prepositions

Here are some useful words and phrases for a job interview. Add the correct prepositions.

1 to be good XXX writing texts
2 to be in charge XXX a small project
3 to communicate easily XXX people
4 to be interested XXX new tasks
5 to gain insight XXX an international organization
6 to be good XXX people
7 to assist caring XXX the animals
8 to be capable XXX working independently
9 to be open XXX new experiences
10 to look XXX a challenge
11 to have experience XXX video editing
12 to be responsible XXX a small project

When you learn new words and phrases, it helps to memorize the correct prepositions.

in of with to for into at

T2 Speaking: Appropriate language for a job interview

a) Read the statements (A-F). Explain which statements are appropriate to use as an applicant in a job interview.

A Sorry I'm late ... Hope I'll be on time on my first day of work. Only joking. My mum will make sure I leave the house on time.

B As I wrote in my cover letter, I'm going to take my final exams next year and would like to make up my mind about what to do after school. There are different university courses and career options that seem attractive to me. In order to get a better idea of what might really suit me, I decided to apply for an internship at your company.

C Sorry, I don't understand what you mean. Why is this important? I have explained in my cover letter why I'm a great candidate for the job.

D What I expect from the job? Well, I'll do whatever. So yeah, I'm flexible as long as I get paid, I guess.

E A friend of mine, Sarah Holden, did an internship here last year. She recommended your company and said that you make sure your interns truly benefit from their work experience.

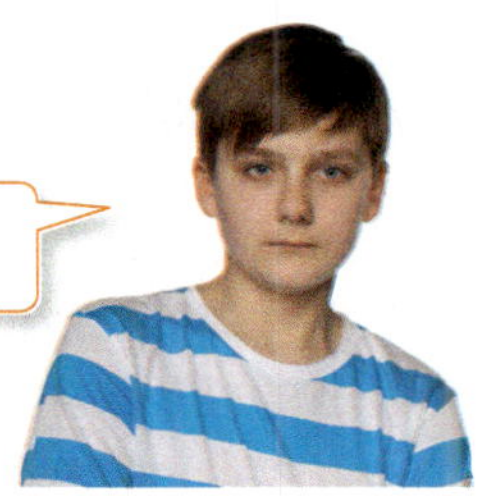

F Nope – no questions from me.

b) Choose two statements which are not appropriate and rephrase them so they can be used in a job interview.

4 English as a global language

Photo tour

P1

a) Look at the photos below. Say what they have in common.

1 Canada

2 Sri Lanka

3 Malta

4 India

5 South Africa

b) Why do you think the signs show information in more than one language?
Collect your ideas in class.

P2

a) The world map on page 105 shows where English is an official language or the first language.
Look at the map and name as many of the countries marked in orange as you can.

b) Work with a partner: Why do you think English is the first or an official language in those countries?
Note down your ideas.

P3 ▶ Viewing | p. 212

a) Watch the video to find out if you were right in P2b).

b) Read the statements below. Then watch the video again and decide if they are true or false.
Correct the false statements.

1. The colonization of the areas which are known today as the USA and the Caribbean marked the beginning of the British Empire.
2. English is the official language of the United States.
3. The English language became more important because of the worldwide influence of American companies after World War II.
4. Today, there are many different varieties of English but not all of them use correct grammar.
5. It is a positive development that English has almost reached the status of a global language.

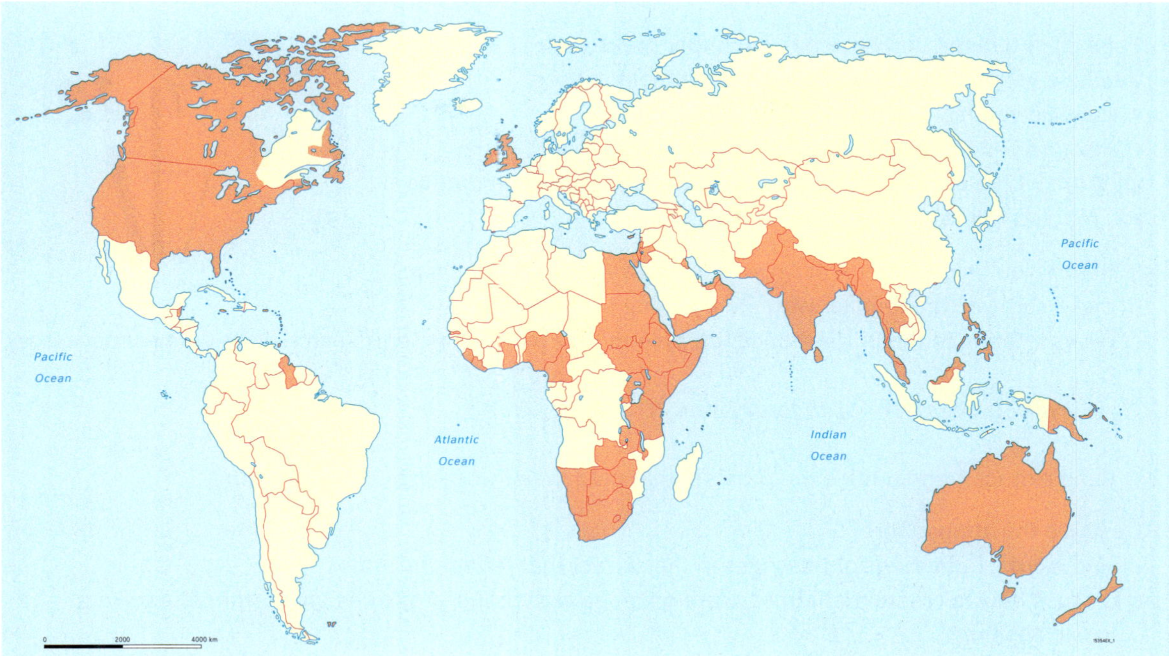

P4 ▶ Wordbank 7 | p. 242

a) Look at the statistics and describe them.

b) Consider the information from the video and the statistics. Say what you find most interesting or surprising.

Most common languages by number of total speakers

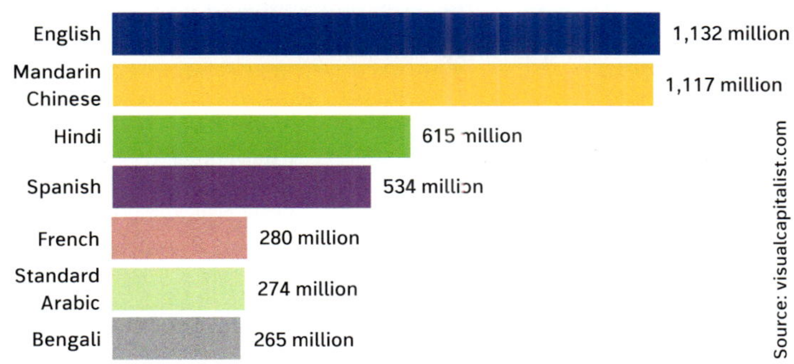

Most common languages by number of native speakers

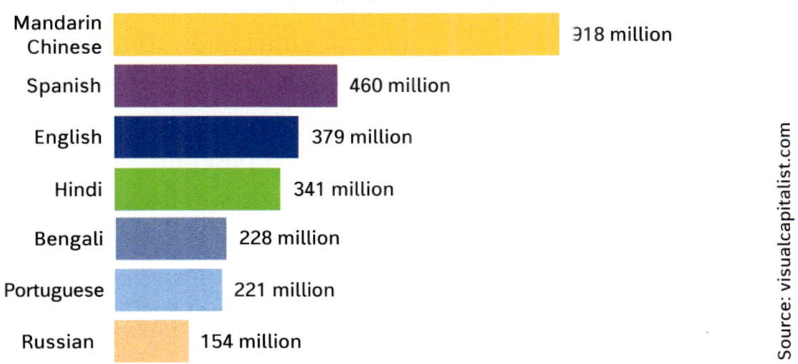

P5

Read the info box.
In class, talk about situations where you have used English (or another language) as a lingua franca.

The term *lingua franca* describes a language which is often used for communication by people who do not share a native language and don't speak each other's native languages. It can be a language also spoken by native speakers, but it can also be a new language which consists of elements from different languages. Sometimes the term "bridge language" is used.
Lingua franca originally described a language spoken in the 18th century based on Italian, Spanish, French, Arabic, Greek and Turkish.

R1

a) Think of situations that have put you under pressure, e.g. a tight deadline you had to meet, or a train you almost missed.
- How did you feel?
- How did you react to the pressure?

Work with a partner. Compare what you experienced and how you reacted to the situation.

b) 1 Before you read extract A of Anya Reiss' play *Forty-Five Minutes*, make sure you are familiar with the meaning of the following terms relating to the British education system. Use a dictionary or research them online if necessary.

A level • grades A-F • sixth form • Year 10 • GCSE • UCAS

2 Read extract A and outline the problem that puts the protagonists under pressure.

c) Describe the atmosphere.
- Find words, quotations or passages in the extract that reflect the atmosphere.
- Discuss how to create that atmosphere on stage with props, stage design or other effects (e.g. music, lighting).

d) Imagine you had to meet a deadline at school – e.g. to hand in project work, an essay, or a report – but you weren't able to finish the work on time. Make up plausible and convincing explanations or excuses as to why you couldn't possibly have met the deadline.
Milling around: Exchange your ideas with your classmates. ▸ Milling around | p. 214

Characters
Nathan, *sixth form*
Darrel, *sixth form*
Alex, *sixth form*
Georgie, *sixth form*
Trent, *sixth form*
Lara, *sixth form*
Louise, *year ten*

Setting
The school's computer room

A *Nathan and Darrel are sitting together at two computers, Alex separately on another.*

Nathan Read it out then.
Darrel All of it?
Nathan No the key points bit
Alex Can you please shut up?
Nathan It'll help you too
Alex I know what it says
Darrel Why can't you just read it to yourself?
Nathan Read it out loud
Alex Don't Darrel
Nathan Ignore her
Alex Oh fuck you
Nathan Read it out Darrel
Darrel 'Explain why you want to study the course you are applying for. If you mention your personal interests and hobbies, try to link them to the skills and experiences required for the course.'
Alex Oh 'cause you didn't know that?
Nathan Shut up. Go on
Darrel 'The personal statement could be used as the basis for an interview, so be prepared to answer questions on it. This may be your only written work that the course tutor sees before making a decision …'

Nathan Fuck
Darrel 'Make sure it is organized and literate.'
Alex Oh what a surprise
Nathan What is the matter with you?
Alex You're talking
Nathan About the form, we're talking about the form
Darrel 'Get the grammar, spelling and punctuation right.'
Alex Oh my God
Darrel That is a stupid thing to put up there
Nathan What?
Darrel That is a stupid thing to put up there, you're not going to try and get it wrong are you?
Nathan You got to do it on a computer anyway Darrel
Darrel So?
Nathan So obviously you're gonna get spelling and everything right
Darrel Not all words are on a computer
Nathan Yeah well not like swearing and names and stuff
Darrel They have swearing
Nathan No they don't
Darrel Yeah they do
Nathan No they don't, the red line comes up
Darrel No, they have it in the dictionary, they just don't offer it to you on spell-check suggestions
Nathan No they don't
Darrel Look, I'll show you
Alex We have forty-five minutes and you are doing that?
Nathan Why do you care? Just do your UCAS
Alex I'm doing my UCAS
Darrel *(about the computer)* Look, well they don't have 'shite' but they have everything else, see?
Nathan Someone must have added them
[…]
Alex Can you shut up!
Nathan Go to the library if we're annoying you
Alex It'll be full by now
Nathan You're Sixth Form
Alex They don't listen, the new kids
Nathan Course they will
Darrel Nah it's true Nath' this lot just don't give a fuck
Nathan Get Miss Barrett to chuck them off then
Alex I don't have time to go to the library, we've got forty-five minutes!
Darrel I swear it was next week
Nathan Darrel, if you say it again, if you say that again …
Darrel I told you, I'm sorry. I thought it was next week, I thought it was midnight next week!
Alex Oh my God please just be quiet
Nathan Go to the library!
Alex It's too loud in the library
Darrel What?
Alex Miss Barrett's always shouting at everyone to shut up, she's more annoying than you
Nathan If you care so much, why did you leave it till now?
Alex Because I've been off sick!
[…]
Georgie, **Lara** *and* **Trent** *come in.* **Lara**'s *in tears,* **Georgie** *slams down at a computer and turns it on.*
[…]
Georgie I thought the deadline was next week, she said she said didn't she, Lara?
Lara She said
Darrel I knew it! I told you it wasn't my fault
Nathan What? He did say the deadline was next week then?
Georgie They all said it was for next week, all of them, they said we should give it in at the end of this week and school would check them first then it was deadline next week
Darrel She told me I got it wrong and screamed at me for telling Nathan the wrong thing
Nathan And screamed at me for not checking
Darrel The bitch
Georgie I know she is such a bitch
Trent Yeah alright guys, alright but we still got forty-five minutes whoever's fault it is, we've all got to do it

Nathan I thought you guys weren't in today
Trent We were late for class, she said she'd let you lot off to do it too
Darrel Lara sit down and do the thing don't just stand there crying
Lara There's no point
Alex You can't miss the deadline Lara
[…]
Darrel Lara fucking open your UCAS
Lara There's no point! They read my statement said it was terrible, said I did it all wrong and Miss Hall would do it with me next week!
Alex You haven't finished your statement!
Nathan Yeah nor have me or Darrel
Trent Mine's still fucked up
Alex How can you not have done them!
Nathan I got some bullet points
Alex Oh my God
Nathan If you've done it, why are you here?
Alex To finish the form I hadn't put my results in and stuff. I'd done my statement!
Nathan They don't care really about statements, they know the teachers have done them
Lara They haven't done mine!
Georgie In Cambridge they throw them in the bin
Alex Yeah well lucky I'm not trying for Cambridge then isn't it?
Darrel Why didn't you fill in your results and stuff before, that's the easy bit
Alex Don't have internet at home
Nathan What?
Darrel What?
Trent You don't have internet at home!?
Georgie What the hell Alex? How do you do your homework?
Alex Er I dunno like every person before the millennium
Trent *(seeing she still hasn't started)* Lara!

R 2

a) Read extract B and explain the dispute between Nathan and Lara.

b) Collect information about the different characters from the first and second extracts. Choose quotations from or about the characters and write down how they can be interpreted in a grid. Explain what this reveals about the characters. Leave space to add more information later.

character	quotation	interpretation
Lara	*"It's no good" (l. 165), "I can't do it" (l. 167), "But it's all wrong" (l. 174)*	*is insecure, not very confident*
	"What! What why can't I say 'always'? What the hell, why can't I say 'always'?" (ll. 245/246)	*gets upset quickly when things don't go her way*
	…	*…*

B

Lara It's no good
Trent Be fine just stop crying and do it
Lara I can't do it
Georgie Alex why don't you help Lara?
Nathan She's helping me!
Trent Yeah but she's crying man
Nathan You want me to cry? I'll fucking cry if you want me to mate at least she's done hers, she's got words on a screen
Lara But it's all wrong she said it was all wrong
Alex I bet it's not

Lara No it's all wrong I didn't even get the pack I only just borrowed Beth's now

Georgie Her 'pack'?

Lara All the stuff with what you're not allowed to say, Miss Hall said I'd done everything you weren't supposed to

Darrel Then shut up and change it

Lara I can't! I don't know any words

Darrel Well I haven't done mine either

Lara Georgie?

Georgie I can't help you babe I'm shit with words as well

Lara *looks to* **Trent.**

Trent No I'm doing my statement too

Lara Please

Trent I'm applying for Sports Science I can't help you

Darrel Fuck off you are

Trent Yeah

Darrel Why you doing that?

Trent Because I want to be a Scientist of Sport

Darrel What?

Trent I want to be a sports teacher

Darrel Why?

Trent What are you doing?

Darrel Management and Leisure … what? What?

Trent Nothing man. You knock yourself out folding bed sheets

Darrel It's not like that

Lara Alex please

Nathan She's helping me!

Lara But she's the only one any good at English

Nathan She is helping me for fuck's sake. She is helping me!

Lara But like okay Alex, just tell me another word for 'and' okay?

Alex What?

Nathan She is helping me! I got like eighty words okay?

Lara Another word for 'and'?

Alex 'Also'

Lara I've used that

Alex 'In addition to'

Lara I used that like fifty times

Alex Oh um …

Louise 'Furthermore'

Lara What?

Louise 'Furthermore'

Georgie I thought you weren't going to speak

[…]

Louise Fine okay I won't help

Lara No please how do I say 'I've always had a passion for France and the language has always fascinated me'?

Georgie Why you talking about France?

Lara For background interest stuff

Louise What's wrong with that?

Lara Wrong with what?

Louise What you just said

Lara I'm not allowed to use the word 'passion' or 'fascinate'

Trent Or 'always'

Lara What!

Trent You're not allowed to say 'always' look at the list

Lara What! What why can't I say 'always'? What the hell, why can't I say 'always'?

Darrel Can you shut up Lara! Use the thesaurus on the computer

Lara But why can't I say it?

Darrel Just look it up man

Alex *is typing for* **Nathan** *by now and they have swapped seats.*

Nathan That's really good

Lara See Alex why won't you help me!

Nathan Lara look it up on the computer

Lara But I don't see why I can't say 'always'. What's wrong with 'always'?

Nathan *comes over to her computer and leans over using it.* **Lara** *is looking at the list.*

Lara And 'mistake'! I'm not allowed to say 'mistake' or 'hate' or 'nothing'! What the hell! What the hell! Why can't I say the word 'nothing'? What is wrong with the word 'nothing'?

She puts her head on her desk.

Nathan *(reading from the computer)* 'For ever, for all time, for eternity, for the end of time' …

Trent What you saying?

Nathan Other words for 'always'. Lara. Lara

Lara What?

Nathan Here are other words for always: 'for ever, for all time, for eternity, for the end of time' …

Lara I can't use them

Nathan Why not?

Lara 'I've for eternity had a passion for France and the language has for the end of time fascinated me'

Nathan Alright fine but I'm saying there's a thesaurus on the computer so stop trying to steal Alex

Lara I'm not trying to steal her! I just need some help okay, she's writing yours for you! She's not allowed to do that

Alex I'm not writing it for him

Nathan What are you doing then?

Alex I'm writing some bits you got to put it together yourself

Nathan Alex I don't have time for this, okay? You can't play jigsaw with it and test me

Alex Yeah but I don't know everything about you. I can't put all the personal stuff in

Nathan Like what?

Alex Like your GCSE grades

Nathan I can't put them down

Alex You had to in the form

Nathan Yeah but I'm not going to draw attention to them am I? They were all like Cs and Ds

R 3

a) Read extract C and describe what happens. Discuss Lara's reasons for choosing accountancy.

b) Add more information about the characters to your grid from R2.

C

Georgie You've not filled out your employment anyway

Darrel What?

Georgie On the form, you can't even send that

Darrel Why do I have to put that down? Why do they care where I've worked? I'm going to study, not work there

Alex *laughs, the others ignore.*

Trent It's so they can see what kind of person you are

Darrel What?

Trent Like hard working, 'done work experience' that kind of thing

Darrel It's none of their business!

Georgie Get over it Darrel

Darrel Nah 'cause I'm a kid okay and they're already judging me on everything I've done. What they're not going to take me because I haven't worked at Pizza Hut or something?

Georgie It's not like that

Lara I've never worked at Pizza Hut

Alex Oh God's sake shut up Lara and do your statement

Lara I never worked anywhere except at my mum's salon

Darrel Yeah well exactly

Lara And she didn't pay me so that doesn't count

Nathan You've worked Darrel

Darrel No. I'm not filling that bit out

Trent Don't be stupid man

Darrel No. I hate this shit it's none of their business where I've worked or if I have or haven't, makes no difference to whether I can do my course

Trent Well if you'd worked in a hotel or something –

Darrel Is that another crack about my course?

Trent No but I mean shows you want to do it, you know what I mean

Darrel No this is fucked! This is just like when you're little and the teachers make you draw pictures of your family and describe your bedroom and shit, they're just nosy

Alex Darrel I don't think they read the UCAS like it's *Heat* Magazine

[…]

Lara What do you want to be?

Alex Journalist

Nathan Yeah so you got to get your English degree, please stop screwing around and help me

Alex No, but I don't need a degree

Nathan Then why did you apply?

Alex Because my parents made me

Darrel Aw your parents made you

Trent Alex shut up

Alex Fine, okay do your work

Trent No I mean shut up about your parents made you and you don't want to go, you obviously do

Georgie Human resources officer, charity fundraiser, youth worker

Alex I don't

Georgie Probation officer

Alex But you know you want to be a sports coach?

Trent Yeah

Alex Exactly and you have to go to uni, you're fine it makes sense for you

Georgie Like loads of options

Alex Like Trent you're fine

Lara I don't know what I want to be

Alex That's probably why your personal statement is bad

Georgie What? Of course you know what you want to be

Lara No

Georgie Then why the hell are you applying for accountancy if you don't want to be an accountant?

Darrel You're applying for accountancy!

Lara Because I told Ted I want to make a lot of money and he said 'cause I got an A for maths I could take it for A level and then when I saw him again he said universities have really good employment graduate history for accountancy

Alex And that's why you picked it!

Lara Yeah

Alex But you don't want to be an accountant?

Lara I dunno, maybe

Louise And you are writing about France in your statement?

Nathan I know what I want to do Alex, does that mean you'll write my fucking statement please?

Alex What do you want to do?

Nathan Get into uni!

Alex Oh my God

Nathan *pushes her out of the way and starts on the computer himself.*

Alex Why did you apply?

Lara I dunno, everyone else was

Trent Right, done

Georgie Really?

Trent Whatever. Can't concentrate with all this, I'm going to send it

R4

What do you think will happen next? Continue the scene and write at least 200 words. Use the information you collected in your grid from R2.

R5

a) Group work: Choose one of the scenes and prepare a dramatic reading or a freeze-frame. Make clear how the different characters react to the crisis.

b) Perform your reading/your freeze-frame to another group and ask for feedback.

Use your grid from R2 to help you decide how to present a character.

c) Put the different scenes together and perform them in class.

Was hast du alles gelernt? Diese Seite hilft dir dabei, das zu erkennen.
Falls du Hilfe benötigst, etwas nachlesen oder noch ein paar Übungen machen möchtest, findest du hier passende Hinweise.

WORTSCHATZ

Ich kann ...	Aufgaben/Übungen/Hilfen
ein Gespräch beginnen und am Laufen halten *How are you today? • Shall we start? • That sounds interesting/challenging/ good. • So what you are saying is ...?*	B4 ▶ **DIFF** D18 ▶ **WB** 21
in einem Gespräch Zeit gewinnen *That's a good/an interesting question. Let me think.*	B4 ▶ **DIFF** D18
ein Gespräch beenden *It's been great getting to know you. • Thank you so much for your time.*	B4 ▶ **DIFF** D18 ▶ **WB** 21

SKILLS

Ich kann ...	Aufgaben/Übungen/Hilfen
einem Sachtext wesentliche Informationen entnehmen READING	2 ▶ Reading | p. 203 ▶ **DIFF** D2 ▶ **WB** 2
einem Hörtext Informationen entnehmen LISTENING	4, A1, A4 ▶ Listening | p. 202 ▶ **DIFF** D4, D5, D9 ▶ **WB** 3, 5
Informationen aus einem Videoclip entnehmen VIEWING	A2, B2 ▶ Viewing | p. 212 ▶ **DIFF** D6 ▶ **WB** 4, 6, 18, 19
Tipps für ein Videointerview sammeln und umsetzen SPEAKING • MEDIA	A10 ▶ **WB** 18
ein Anschreiben verfassen WRITING	A11 ▶ Writing | p. 210 ▶ T1, T2 | p. 99
Information aus einem deutschen Text auf Englisch wiedergeben MEDIA	▶ **DIFF** D10, D12 ▶ Mediation | p. 213
ein Bewerbungsgespräch führen SPEAKING	B5 ▶ T1, T2 | p. 103 ▶ **WB** 21

GRAMMATIK

Ich kann ...	Aufgaben/Übungen/Hilfen
verschiedene Futur-Formen verwenden *Ten years from now I will have found my dream job. • I will travel around the world and ... • I definitely won't ...*	A3 ▶ **DIFF** D7, D8 ▶ G10 | p. 231 ▶ **WB** 9, 10
Fragen in der indirekten Rede formulieren *I asked Emma if she enjoyed working with elderly people.*	▶ **DIFF** D3 ▶ G9 | p. 231
***let/make sb do sth* sowie *have sth done* verwenden** *On Monday, Laura's mother made her clean her room because it was not tidy.*	A8 ▶ **DIFF** D13 ▶ G11 | p. 232 ▶ **WB** 15
Bedingungssätze (Typ 3) verwenden *It would have been better if I had known more about the company.*	B3 ▶ G5R | p. 224 ▶ **WB** 20

Writing: Characterization

Step by step

On these pages you will learn how to write a characterization.
First, there is an example task and a possible solution.
Next, there is your task. You will learn how to write your own characterization, step by step.

Example

1 Look at the example task and the solution (page 116).

EXAMPLE TASK

Read the extract and write a characterization of Lucy.

"Lockwood & Co.: The Screaming Staircase" is a young adult supernatural thriller written by Jonathan Stroud. It is about an epidemic of ghosts ("Visitors") in Britain whose touch brings death. Children and young adults can fight them if they possess one of three "Talents": Touch, Sight or Listening. Lucy Carlyle is a young psychic investigator who desperately needs a new job after leaving her old ghosthunter agency in the north of England. She travels to London to find a new job, but has not been successful so far.

Number 35 Portland Row was a white-fronted residence of four floors, with faded green shutters and pink flowers in the window boxes. Even more than its neighbours it had a faint air of dilapidation[1]. Every surface looked as if it needed a lick of paint, or possibly just a clean. A small wooden sign clamped to the outside of the railing read:

A. J. LOCKWOOD & CO., INVESTIGATORS. AFTER DARK, RING BELL AND WAIT BEYOND THE IRON LINE.

[...]

Pushing open a wonky metal gate, I stepped onto a narrow path of broken tiles.

[...]

Ahead was a black-painted door. Ignoring the bell, I stepped over the line and knocked sharply on the door. After an interval a short, fat, tallow-haired youth wearing large round spectacles[2] looked out. 'Oh, another one,' he said. 'I thought we'd finished. Or are you Arif's new girl?' I gazed at him. 'Who's Arif?' 'Runs the corner store. He normally sends someone over with doughnuts about this time. You don't seem to have any doughnuts.' He looked disappointed. 'No. I have a rapier[3].' The youth sighed. 'So I guess you're another candidate. Name?' 'Lucy Carlyle. Are you Mr Lockwood?' 'Me? No.' 'Well, can I come in?' 'Yeah. The last girl's just gone down. From the look of her, she won't be very long.'

Even as he spoke, a scream of the utmost terror rang out from inside the house, and echoed off the ivy-clad walls of the yard below. Birds rose from trees up and down the street. I jerked back in shock, hands moving automatically to the hilt of my sword. The scream collapsed into a whimpering gargle and presently died away. I stared wide-eyed at the youth in the doorway, who hadn't stirred[4]. 'Ah, there we are,' he said. 'Didn't I say? Well, you're next up. Come in.'

Neither the boy nor the scream instilled[5] me with much confidence, and I was half inclined[6] to leave. But after two weeks in London,

1 dilapidation – *Verfall* | **2** spectacles *(pl.)* – *Brille* | **3** rapier – *Degen* | **4** to stir – *(sich) rühren* | **5** to instil – *einflößen* | **6** inclined – *geneigt*

I was almost out of options [...]. Besides, there was something in the manner of the youth, a subtle impudence[7] in the way he stood, that told me he half expected me to run. I wasn't having that. So I stepped swiftly past him, and entered a cool, wide hallway.

[...]

'Hold on a tick,' the boy said. He remained waiting by the open door. He was a little older than me, and not quite my height, though a good deal stockier[8]. He had podgy, rather bland features, nondescript except for a prominently squared jaw. Behind his glasses, his eyes were very blue. His sandy hair, which in texture reminded me of a horse's tail, flopped heavily across his brow. He wore white trainers, a pair of faded jeans, and a loosely tucked shirt, bulging around the midriff[9].

'Any minute now,' he said.

From deeper inside the house a murmur of voices rose to a crescendo. A side-door burst open: a well-dressed girl emerged at speed, eyes blazing[10], face chalk-white, scrunched coat dragging in her hand. She flashed me an expression of fury[11] and contempt[12], swore roundly at the fat boy, kicked the front door as she passed it, and was gone into the day. [...]

[The boy] led the way into a sunny living room, white-walled and cheery, decorated with [...] artefacts and totems. Two easy chairs and a sofa surrounded a low-lying coffee table. Also beside it, smiling broadly, was a tall, slim boy dressed in a dark suit. [...]

As I crossed to greet him, I used my senses, as I always do. The full range of senses, I mean – outer and inner. Just so I didn't miss anything. The most obvious thing to spot was a rounded, bulky object lying on the table, concealed[13] by a green-and-white spotted handkerchief. Did it have anything to do with the previous girl's discomfort? I thought it highly likely. There was the subtlest of noises too – something I could almost hear, but it kept its distance from my mind. I suppose if I'd concentrated I might have pinned it down ... but that would have meant standing like a plank with my eyes shut and my mouth open, which is never a great way to start an interview. So I just shook the boy's hand. 'Hello,' he said. 'I'm Anthony Lockwood.' 'Lucy Carlyle.'

He had very bright, dark eyes and a nice lopsided grin[14]. 'Very good to meet you. Tea? Or has George already offered you some?' The plump boy made a disparaging[15] gesture. 'I thought I'd wait until the first test was done,' he said. 'See if she was still here. I've wasted that many tea bags this morning.' 'Why not give her the benefit of the doubt,' Anthony Lockwood said, 'and go and put the kettle on?' The boy seemed unconvinced. 'All right – but I reckon she's a bolter[16].' He spun slowly on his heels and trudged out into the hall.

Anthony Lockwood waved me to a chair.

[...]

He settled himself on the couch opposite and smoothed out some papers before him. He had a very slender face, with a long nose and a dark mop of unruly hair. I realized almost with shock that he was scarcely older than me. His manner had been so assured, I hadn't noticed his age. I wondered for the first time why there were no supervisors present in the room.

'I see from your letter,' the boy said, 'that you're from the north of England. [...] OK, so you obviously knew from early on,' he continued, 'that you had a Talent. You had the Sight, of course, more than most of the other kids, and the bravery to use it. But according to your letter, that wasn't your real strength. You could listen too. And you had the power of Touch.' 'Well, Listening's my thing, really,' I said. 'As a kid in my cot[17] I used to hear voices whispering in the street – after curfew[18], when all the living were inside. But I've got good Touch too, though that often merges with what I hear. It's hard to separate them. For me, Touch sometimes triggers echoes of what's happened.'

7 impudence – *Dreistigkeit* | **8** stocky – *stämmig* | **9** midriff – *Taille* | **10** to blaze – *glühen* | **11** fury – *Wut* | **12** contempt – *Verachtung* | **13** to conceal – *verbergen* | **14** lopsided grin – *schiefes Grinsen* | **15** disparaging – *geringschätzig* | **16** bolter – *Ausreißer/in* | **17** cot – *Kinderbett* | **18** curfew – *Ausgangssperre*

'George can do a bit of that,' the boy said. 'Not me. I'm tone-deaf when it comes to Visitors. Sight's my thing. Death-glows and trails, and all the ghoulish residues[19] of death …' He grinned. 'Cheerful subject, isn't it? […]

'You know, I can't think what's keeping George. […] It's really time for the tests.' 'Yes, what tests are these?' I said hastily. 'If you don't mind my asking.'

'Not at all. It's what we use to assess the candidates. Frankly I don't set much store by people's letters or referrals, Ms Carlyle. I prefer to see their Talent with my own eyes …' […]

I wasn't going to mess it up. I sat forward on the sofa, making sure my back was straight, my hands neat in my lap. 'Who are your supervisors?' I asked. 'Do I get to meet them too?' A frown[20] flickered across the boy's forehead. 'No supervisors here. No adults. It's my company. I'm in charge. George Cubbins is deputy.' He looked at me. 'Some applicants had a problem with this set-up, so they didn't get very far. Does it bother you?'

'Oh no,' I said. 'No, I like the sound of it fine.' There was a brief silence.

The hall door opened and the plump boy's posterior backed through it, closely followed by the rest of him. He turned in a stately manner and advanced, carrying a tray with three steaming mugs and a plate of biscuits.

[…]

There was a polite interlude during which mugs were distributed, and sugar offered and declined. […]

'Right,' he said. 'Just a few tests, Ms Carlyle. Nothing to worry about at all. Are you ready?' 'Sure.' I could feel George's little eyes fixed upon me, and even Lockwood's casual tones could not disguise a certain eagerness[21]. But they were dealing with someone who'd survived the Wythburn Mill[22] alone. I wasn't going to fret[23] about this. Lockwood nodded. 'We might as well start here, then.'

He stretched out a languid hand to the spotted handkerchief and, after a ceremonial pause, flicked it away. Sitting on the table was a stocky cylinder of clear, thick glass, sealed at the top with a red plastic plug. […] it contained a greasy yellow smoke – not quite stationary, very slowly shifting. […]

With the nail of my middle finger I tapped the side of the glass; at once the smoke awoke, rippling outwards from the point of impact, becoming thicker, more granular, as it did so. As it separated, it revealed the object in the jar: a human skull, brown and stained, clamped to the bottom of the glass. The ripples of smoke contorted, twisted; they took on the horrid semblance of a face, with blankly rolling eyes and gaping mouth. For a moment the features were superimposed upon the skull beneath. I jerked back from the glass. The face devolved into stream-like ribbons of smoke that swirled about the cylinder, and presently became still.

I cleared my throat. 'Well, it's a ghost-jar,' I said. 'The skull's the Source, and that ghost is tied to it. Can't tell what sort. A Phantasm or a Spectre, maybe.' So saying, I sat back in a posture of nonchalant unconcern, as if Visitors in jars were something I dealt with every day of the week. In truth, I'd never seen one and the apparition[24] had shocked me. But not unduly so: after the previous girl's scream I'd expected something. Plus I'd heard of containers like this before. Lockwood's smile had momentarily frozen, as if uncertain whether to express surprise, pleasure or disappointment. In the end, pleasure won the day. 'Yes, that's right,' he said. 'Well done.' He put the handkerchief back on the cylinder and, with some effort, stowed it out of sight under the table. The plump boy sipped his tea loudly. 'She was shaken,' he said. 'You could see it.' I ignored the comment. […]

'Now, I'd like to test your Talent, if I may. I've got some items ready. Please tell me, if you

19 residue – *Rest* | **20** frown – *Stirnrunzeln* | **21** eagerness – *Eifer* | **22** *When working for another agency, Lucy and other children had to search the mill for ghosts. Lucy felt uneasy about the place and she tried to convince their supervisor to stop the mission, but he refused. A ghost then killed all the children, except for Lucy.* | **23** to fret – *sich Sorgen machen* | **24** apparition – *Erscheinung* can' – he opened the box and put an object on the table – 'what supernatural resonance you detect here.'

[…] I took it in my hand and closed my eyes, turning it this way and that, running my fingers lightly over the surface. I listened, waiting for echoes … Nothing came to me. This was no good. I shook my head, cleared my mind of distractions, shut out as best I could the occasional noise of traffic passing on the road, and the less occasional slurps of tea sounding from George's sofa. I tried again. No. Still nothing. After a few minutes I gave up. 'I'm sorry,' I said at last, 'I can't detect anything.'

Lockwood nodded. 'I should hope not. This is the cup George keeps his toothbrush in. Good. On to the next.' He picked up the cup and tossed it across to the plump boy, who caught it with a snort of mirth[25]. I felt myself go cold; I knew my cheeks were scarlet. I took hold of my rucksack, and stood abruptly. 'I'm not here to be made fun of,' I said. 'I'll find my own way out.' 'Ooh,' George said. 'Feisty[26].' I looked at him. His flop of hair, his glossy, shapeless face, his silly little glasses: everything about him made me livid[27]. 'That's right,' I said. 'Step over here and I'll show you exactly how feisty I am.' The boy blinked at me. 'I might just do that.' 'I don't see you moving.' 'Well, it's a deep sofa. It's taking me a while to get out of it.' 'Hold on, both of you,' Anthony Lockwood said. 'This is an interview, not a boxing match. George: shut up. Ms Carlyle: I apologize for upsetting you, but it was a serious test, which you passed with flying colours[28]. […]'

25 mirth – *Heiterkeit* | **26** feisty – *resolut; entschlossen* | **27** livid – *wütend* | **28** to pass with flying colours – *mit Bravour bestehen*

SOLUTION

Lucy Carlyle, who is the narrator of the story, is a girl from the north of England. In the extract, she has just arrived at the headquarters of Lockwood & Co. to apply for a job as a ghost hunter.
Even though she is younger than George Cubbins and Anthony Lockwood, who are both older children or teenagers, she is an experienced ghost hunter who can hear and feel ghosts.
She is a cautious person who usually uses all her senses to check her surroundings, but she is not easily scared. When the girl who entered the house before her flees in a panic, Lucy stands her ground and grips her sword. She is careful not to appear nervous or afraid, as she desperately needs the job.
Furthermore, she doesn't like to be underestimated. She is annoyed by George because she feels that he doesn't take her seriously. Instead of being intimidated by his behaviour, Lucy wants to demonstrate that she is a professional and very skilled person.
Lockwood and George are dealing "with someone who'd survived the Wythburn Mill alone" (ll.178/179), Lucy thinks when she is tested about her abilities and adds that she wasn't going "to fret about this" (ll. 179/180).
Although she tries her best to make a good impression, Lucy gets very angry when she feels that the boys are making fun of her. She is a proud person who would rather walk away from an important opportunity than to be treated badly. To make her point, she even considers a physical fight with George, who is older and heavier than her.
All in all, Lucy comes across as a skilled and talented person who knows her worth but tends to be hot-headed.

Your task

2 Read your task, then follow the steps below to complete it.

Write a characterization of George.

A character in a fictional text may be presented in different ways, for example ...
- through the narrator's description of a character's physical appearance,
- through direct comments on the character's personality by the narrator,
- by what the character does, says or thinks,
- by showing what other people think about the character.

Step 1

Download the extract ▶ WES-149226-5 and read it. Highlight facts about George.
- Name: What is his full name?
- Age: How old is he?
- Ability: What can he do?
- Job: What is his job?
- Physical appearance: What does he look like?

Step 2

To find out about a character's personality, you need to look at their behaviour and what they say. The narrator sometimes includes information about a character's personality as well.

Use different colours to highlight every passage in which ...
- George does something,
- George says something,
- the narrator (Lucy) comments on George's behaviour.

Step 3

Very often, it is not possible to use every passage about a character to find out about their personality.

George opens the door and looks disappointed when he sees Lucy. (ll. 20-27).
→ You can't draw any valuable conclusions about George's personality from this passage because the only reason for his disappointment is that he thought Lucy was there to deliver some doughnuts.

This is why you need to filter the passages you highlighted in step 2. Underline only those passages that you can use to draw conclusions about George's personality from.

Step 4

Go back to the passages you have underlined. Study them, then interpret them and write your results next to the underlined passages. For example:

'From the look of her she won't be very long.' (ll. 30/31)

George thinks he is a good judge of character.

'Ah, there we are,' he said. 'Didn't I say?' (l. 41)

He likes to be right about things.

Step 5	Write an introduction. Say who you are writing about and what the extract is about. Use the simple present. You can start like this: *George Cubbins is a boy who is deputy at Lockwood & Co. in London. In the extract, the narrator, Lucy Carlyle, describes …*
Step 6	Write the main part. Use your results from steps 1 and 4 to describe George. **Tips:** • You can use quotes to support your findings. • It is not necessary to present your findings in the order they appear in the text. *Another important fact is … • This shows that … • XXX comes across as … • It is quite apparent that … • Not only is …, but … • This is an example of … • XXX is portrayed as … • XXX seems to be … • This behaviour clearly shows that … • …*
Step 7	Write a conclusion. Briefly describe what you have found out about George and how he is presented. *All in all, George …*
Step 8	Edit your characterization: Check the grammar, spelling, language and content of your text.

Checklist: Writing a characterization

Checklist
1. Read the extract. Highlight facts about the character, e.g. name, age, physical appearance, hobbies, family, friends.
2. Highlight every passage in which the character acts, says something or the narrator comments on their behaviour.
3. Very often, it is not possible to use every passage about a character to find out about their personality. This is why you need to filter the passages you have highlighted. Underline only those passages that you can use to draw conclusions about the character's personality from.
4. Go back to the passages you have underlined. Study them and note down your interpretation.
5. Write an introduction. Say who you are writing about and what the extract is about. Use the simple present.
6. Write the main part. Use your results from steps 1 and 4 to describe the character. You can use quotes as well. It is not necessary to present your findings in the order they appear in the text.
7. Write a conclusion. Briefly describe what you have found out about the character and how the character is presented.
8. Edit your characterization: Check the grammar, spelling, language and content of your text.

5

The North of England

In this Theme you will ...

- plan a trip to the North of England
- make a timeline of Manchester's history
- analyse different types of newspaper articles
- talk about climate change activism
- hold a debate
- write a newspaper article

1

2

The architectually iconic **Museum of Liverpool** tells the story of the city and its people. Home to the Beatles and other world-famous musicians, Liverpool also has a vibrant music scene and is now a UNESCO city for music.

Each year on a weekend in August, one of the UK's most popular music festivals takes place in **Leeds**. With rock and pop acts, as well as house, drum 'n' bass, metal, techno and more, there is something for everyone!

1 The North of England

▶ **WB** 1 | p. 76

a) Look at the map at the back of your book.
What do you know about the North of England? Collect your ideas in class.

b) Look at the photos and read the texts. Note down in a list what cultural activities the four cities offer.

2 Four teenagers

L 2/1 | **S** 11 ▶ Listening | p. 202

a) Listen to the teenagers and say what they are talking about.

b) Listen again and use the grid to note down where the teens live and what they recommend.

▶ **DIFF** Training D1, Extra D2 | p. 182 ▶ **WB** 2 | p. 77

	city	recommendation
Bella		
Liam		
Muhammad		
Olivia		

c) Round robin: Explain which city seems the most attractive to you. ▶ Round robin | p. 215

I chose/picked ... because ... • *... appeals to me the most because ...* •
It wasn't easy to decide between ... and ... but I went for ... because ...

3 Cultural activities

▶ **DIFF** Support D3 | p. 184 ▶ **WB** 3 | p. 78

a) Talk to a partner about the cultural activities in your local area. Share ...
- what you have visited or tried,
- what you thought of it,
- what you wish you had in your local area.

b) Record tips for cultural free-time activities in your town or area (like the teenagers in Intro 2a).

▶ **WB** Media 7 ▶ WES-149226-2

3

4

Manchester does not only have great theatres, but there is also the recently developed MediaCity. Visitors can take a look behind the scenes of the studios where some of the most popular British TV shows are produced.

Sheffield celebrates the best new adventure and documentary films from around the world with an annual festival. There are exciting events and workshops on film-making throughout the year.

4 A class trip to the North of England

▶ Internet | p. 211 ▶ DIFF Extra D4, Support D5 | p. 184

Group work (4): Plan a 4-day class trip to the North of England and write an itinerary for your trip.

1 Choose two destinations. At least one of them should be Liverpool, Manchester, Leeds or Sheffield. To find out about other destinations in the North of England, you can use the map at the back of your book.

2 Plan how you will get there. You can use an online map to check travel times between locations.

3 Find out about accommodation. Choose a youth hostel or find some similar accommodation.

4 Do research online and note down the most famous sights in your destinations. Decide which you want to visit and why.

5 Include at least one cultural activity for each day. You can use your results from Intro 1 and 2 and check online for more information or activities. Write your itinerary. You can include a map or some photos.

> When you use photos, always name the source. **!**

Present your itineraries in class and vote for the trip most of you would like to go on.

▶ WB Media 5 ▶ WES-149226-2 ▶ WB 4, 5 | p. 78

DAY 1

9:10	Flight from Berlin to Manchester
13:00	Check-in YHA Manchester Hostel
16:00	Tour MediaCity
...	

DAY 2

...

DAY 3

...

5 Manchester

Part A

A1 Discover Manchester

▶ Reading | p. 203 ▶ Wordbank 2 | p. 238 ▶ WB 6-9 | p. 79

a) Read the texts on pages 122/123. Choose one photo for each text and write captions for the photos.

b) Read your captions to a partner. Can they guess which photo the caption refers to?

▶ **DIFF** Training D6 | p. 185

c) Watch the video. What can you find out about the Industrial Revolution? Take notes.

▶ Viewing | p. 212 ▶ **DIFF** Training D7 | p. 186

1

With nearly 200 languages spoken there, Manchester is one of the most diverse and multicultural cities in the UK. The city has attracted people since the Industrial Revolution, when a lot of Irish immigrants came to work in the cotton mills. Later, between 1951 and 1971, people from the Caribbean, South Africa, Kenya, India and Pakistan arrived in Manchester. Most had left their birth countries because of war, discrimination and, like the Irish a century before, poverty.

A

2

In the early 18th century, Manchester was a small market town with a population of less than 10,000 people. The invention of a machine called the "Spinning Jenny" in 1764 marked the beginning of the Industrial Revolution. Whereas before cotton thread was spun into cloth by hand, this machine could produce cloth at great speed. The Industrial Revolution changed people's lives dramatically. Manchester grew rapidly on the wealth created by the cotton industry. By 1840 it was referred to as "Cottonopolis". However, the cotton mills also employed children as young as ten years old. They had to work up to 14 hours a day for very little pay. It was dangerous work and many were injured or killed.

B

3

Emmeline Pankhurst was born in Manchester in 1858. She was the eldest daughter in a family of ten children. At age 14, she attended her first women's rights meeting with her mother. Emmeline worked relentlessly for 40 years to help women win the right to vote. Frustrated by the lack of progress, she and her daughter Christabel founded the Women's Social and Political Union (WSPU) in 1913. The WSPU's motto was "Deeds not words" and Emmeline sometimes turned to extreme measures in her fight for equal rights. She was jailed a number of times for breaking windows or setting fires to public buildings. The original WSPU banner is displayed in the People's History Museum.

C

A2 A timeline ▶ DIFF Training D8, Extra D9 | p. 187 ▶ WB 10 | p. 80

Manchester has developed over a long period of time to become the vibrant city it is today. Scan the texts for historical events and draw a timeline.

79 AD
Romans build "Mancunium"

1764

D

4 If a place name has 'chester', 'caster' or 'cester' in it, it's almost certainly Roman! What we now know as Manchester started as a Roman fort which was built in 79 AD. The Romans built "Mancunium" to guard strategically important roads to larger Roman forts at Chester and York. Like anywhere else in Britain, the Romans also introduced new plants, animals, words, ways of calculating and using money to pay for goods. Archaeologists found evidence of buildings such as temples, shops, bath houses and inns, which have been reconstructed and can be visited.

E

5 The Greater Manchester region lives and breathes football! It has four big football clubs, including two Premier League clubs: Manchester United (founded in 1878) and Manchester City (founded in 1880). With more than 75,000 seats, Manchester United's Old Trafford Stadium is the second biggest football stadium in the UK. Marcus Rashford is a famous football player from Manchester. He was born in 1997 and has four older siblings. His single parent mother worked multiple jobs to feed her children. Marcus Rashford is a role model to many young people, not just because he is a successful footballer. He has raised awareness of child hunger in the UK and has relentlessly campaigned for free school meals to support poorer families. His book *You Can Do It* instantly became a bestseller in 2022.

F

6 During the Second World War, Manchester was a centre for military production. Bombs, twin-engined bomber aircraft and barrage balloons were manufactured, mainly in the Trafford Park area. In December 1940, the city of Manchester was the target of heavy bombing by the German Luftwaffe. This is often referred to as "the Christmas Blitz".
Alan Turing was a brilliant mathematician. He created machines that helped crack the Germans' Enigma code in 1941. With his help, the allies were able to win the war in Europe. After the war, Turing worked at the University of Manchester. He laid the foundation for modern computing and artificial intelligence. A sculpture in memory of him can be found in Sackville Gardens.

A3 In the news ▶ WB 11, 12 | p. 81

Work with a partner. Look at the two newspaper articles. One article is from a tabloid (page 124) and one is from a quality newspaper (page 125). Which article would you prefer to read? Why?

The article from the quality newspaper/tabloid appeals to me more because ... • I'd prefer ... because ... • Although ... looks ..., I would choose to read ... • ... might provide more/better information. • ... wouldn't take as long to read. • ... the photo is more attractive. • ... the headline does/does not interest me.

CLIMATE CRAZIES CAUSE CHAOS!

Third gallery 'protest' this week, after oil terminal terror in April

by **Dale Winterbottom**
Friday 1 July 2022

After causing damage and disruption by spraying 'no new oil' onto the floor of the Manchester Art Gallery, two followers of the group Just Stop Oil glued their hands to a valuable Turner painting.

In a video taken by a visitor to the gallery, a hero gallery employee can be heard telling the gutless glue gangsters "I don't want to hear a word of what you've got to say!"

Yesterday's art attack has been the third this week by the group Just Stop Oil, with other protesters already having wreaked havoc in galleries in London and Glasgow. Don't they have any respect for our national treasures?

Just Stop Oil demand that the British government stop anything to do with fossil fuels and have threatened to continue with their protests until their demands are met.

The Manchester gallery was evacuated and closed while police and staff dealt with the incident. Two men have been arrested on suspicion of criminal damage.

A4 What happened? ▶ Reading | p. 203 ▶ WB 13 | p. 82

a) First read the article you have chosen in A3 and in one sentence say what it is about.

b) Copy the grid. Scan the article you have chosen in A3 and fill in the grid. Then read the other article and complete the grid. ▶ DIFF Support D10, Training D11 | p. 188

	who?	what?	when?	where?	why?
tabloid					
quality					

c) Collect other examples of protests you know or have heard of. ▶ DIFF Extra D12 | p. 189

Just Stop Oil activists protest in Manchester Art Gallery

Caroline Vance Fri 1 Jul 2022

On Thursday, two university students from the activist group Just Stop Oil glued themselves to the frame of a 19th-century Turner painting in the Manchester Art Gallery. It has been the third act of protest from the group this week, with two similar protests earlier in the week at art galleries in London and Glasgow.

Just Stop Oil is an environmental group that demands an end to oil, coal and gas projects. Through protest and other forms of direct action, it calls on the government to stop all exploration, development and production of fossil fuels in the UK. The group launched in February 2022 and made headlines in April with a month-long campaign of oil terminal disruptions across Southern England.

A video of the protest action was shared on social media by a gallery visitor and quickly gained millions of views. The video shows the men wearing Just Stop Oil T-shirts spray-painting "no new oil" onto the floor, before each applying glue to one of their hands and sticking themselves to the frame of the painting.

A gallery employee can be heard criticizing the two students for damaging private property and demanding that they make their protest a silent one. The comments on social media were mixed, with some criticizing the young men's lack of respect for an important work of art and causing a public nuisance, and others praising the form of protest and their message.

One of the protestors, a university student in his 20s, said: "I would like to say to anyone and everyone who is reading this, you may think this action is outrageous or scandalous but what choice do I have? The British Government is knowingly destroying the futures of young people and condemning billions of people all over the world to death by continuing to license new fossil fuel infrastructure."

The gallery was closed for a short period while the police dealt with the incident and the two men were arrested. Art experts are now evaluating the damage to the painting.

A5 Text analysis ▶ WB 14, 15 | p. 82

a) Work with a partner. Read the questions below and answer them for each of the newspaper articles on pages 124/125. ▶ DIFF Training D13 | p. 189

Layout

Headlines
- What is their size in relation to the text?
- What information is given?
- What effect does the choice of words create?

Photos
- What is their size in relation to the text?
- What do they show?
- What emotions do they evoke?

Text
- Which words and phrases does the author use to create the tone? Is the tone matter-of-fact or emotive?
- Does the author use stylistic devices (e.g. rhetorical questions, alliteration, direct address, exaggeration)? What is the effect?
- Look at your grid from A4b to find out how much factual information the author provides.

b) What are typical characteristics of quality newspapers and tabloids? Create a checklist for each type of newspaper. Consider the aspects from A5a). Keep your checklist for B9.

A6 Target task Prepare and hold a debate ▶ Speaking | p. 205

Group work (8): Debate the following statement:
"It is justified to damage property or cause disruption to raise awareness for a social or political cause."

1 Prepare your debate:
- Form two teams of four. One team is for, the other team is against the statement.
- Each team prepares arguments. Try to predict the other team's arguments and think of ways to respond to them. You can use examples from A4c) to support your arguments.

2 Hold your debate:
- The team supporting the idea starts the debate with a short statement on their position.
- Then the teams take turns to argue their side.
- Make sure you refer to what the other team has said.
- Use your strongest argument to conclude your position with a final statement.

3 After the debate:
- Take a vote on the statement. You are free to vote regardless of the side you argued for.
- Talk about what made you vote that way.

Listen to the others without interrupting. **!**

Need help? Look at page 127. T1 T2 T3

Target task tools for A6: Prepare and hold a debate

T1 Preparing arguments

Work with a partner. Choose one of these statements (A, B, C).
One of you notes down two arguments for and the other one two arguments against the statement. Now swap notes. Read your partner's arguments and write down how you could respond.

A "Violent video games should be banned."

B "PE should not be compulsory in school."

C "Everyone should learn three foreign languages at school."

T2 Words and phrases for a debate

Copy the grid and sort the phrases below into the grid. Add more phrases you know.

Expressing your opinion	Agreeing in part	Disagreeing	Adding an argument	Concluding your position
…	…	…	…	…

I have to disagree, because … • Although …, it doesn't necessarily mean that … • All in all, … • I would also like to add that … • As I see it, … • I strongly believe that … • Not only … but also … • To conclude, … • I'm sure … • I'm convinced that … • I'm against/for … • I can see your point but … • In addition to …, … • I have to admit that … , but … • I would also like to add that … • It may be true that …, however, … • To sum up, … • Maybe that is right, but … • … plus the fact that … • Perhaps I should also mention that … • The fact that … doesn't mean that … • Frankly, I don't believe …

T3 Responding to a statement

Read the statements. Respond to each sentence by writing a sentence that expresses your opinion. You can use phrases from your grid in T2.

1 Activists should pay for the damage they have caused.

2 People who don't protest against climate change are just lazy.

3 Politicians need to make stricter laws to protect the environment.

4 Disruptive climate protests just make people angry.

5 Activists who glue themselves onto streets are brave people.

6 Protests have always helped to change things.

B1 Conflicts at home ▶ WB 16 | p. 83

a) Think of possible causes for conflicts between teenagers and their parents. ▶ DIFF Easy alternative D14 | p. 190

b) Choose one of the causes for conflicts you collected in a). ▶ DIFF Support D15 | p. 190

- Make up a situation (e.g. a parent doesn't like the clothes the teen is wearing to school.)
- Partner A takes the role of a parent, partner B takes the role of a teen.
- Each of you collects arguments for "your" perspective.
- In your roles, talk about the conflict, exchange your arguments and find a way to solve your conflict.

B2 Scene one ▶ Reading | p. 203 ▶ DIFF Training D16, D17 | p. 191 ▶ WB 17, 18 | p. 84

a) Read the scene about a family conflict set in Manchester. Say what the conflict is about and who is involved.

Scene one

A bright and spacious kitchen. It's seven o'clock in the morning. 15-year-old Meryem is sitting at the kitchen table, silently reading her book. Her father, Tim, is also sitting at the table. Her mother, Priyanka, is leaning against the kitchen worktop, sipping coffee and checking her phone.

Mother: (*looking up from phone*) Tim, when will you be home tonight? Ben and Holly are asking if we would like to go out for dinner. Apparently there's a new wine bar on Blossom Street.

Father: (*sighing*) Hmm, I'm not sure. I have a meeting with a difficult client at 5pm.

Meryem's 17-year-old sister Amira enters the kitchen. She is already dressed for school. She flops onto a chair at the kitchen table.

Amira: (*to her father*) Ooh, is that the guy who wants everything for free?

Father: Yep, that's the one. He's just so much hard work.

Amira: He's the one who used to play for Manchester United, right? Why exactly does he want everything for free? He must have loads of money.

Father: That doesn't mean anything. It's often the richest people who are unbelievably tight.

Mother: (*laughing*) Well, look after the pennies and the pounds will look after themselves!

Father: (*laughing*) Well, he could at least give me some VIP tickets to a match. When I think what the tickets cost for the next game ...

Meryem: (*lowering her book*) What type of car is he looking for? Probably a huge SUV, right?

Father: (*unimpressed*) Of course, with the biggest engine possible and all the latest gadgets. Only the best!

Meryem: (*opening her mouth to say something ...*)

Amira: Uh-oh ... Here we go again!

Meryem: (*gives her sister a dirty look*) So let me sum up. This guy is rich and wants to keep as much of his money as possible for himself, all whilst driving around in some massive car which is terrible for the environment? Why do people have to be like that?

Mother: Meryem ...

Meryem: Ah, it just sucks! There are so many good causes people could support, if only they weren't so self-obsessed!

Amira: Don't look at me like that! I don't have time to be an activist. Sure, global warming isn't great, but do you know how much coursework I have for my A levels? And how good my marks need to be so I can go to university?

Meryem: Blah, blah, uni! You only want to become a doctor because mum's one! As if that's so important. Your future's going to look pretty bleak if nobody does anything about climate change now!

Mother: Meryem, you know we support your causes.

Meryem: Oh really? That's not at all the impression I get. Any of the suggestions I make here at home are always ignored.

Amira: (*shouting*) But I don't want to be vegan!

Meryem: I never said you should! You always twist what I say and ...

Mother: Stop it! I think we've all tried our best so far. We try to buy things with as little packaging as possible and we often cook vegetarian dishes. We only ever buy organic fruit and vegetables ...

Father: Which is extremely expensive by the way!

Meryem: Yeah, but that's not enough! You could all do so much more! You could get involved, you could donate money, you could ...

Mother: Excuse me. We *do* donate money to the local homeless shelter every year at Christmas and ...

Meryem: Yeah, but you could do more! Dad, the ton you spend on your stupid football matches could be better ...

Mother: (*angrily*) MERYEM! That's enough!

Father: Your mother and I have worked very hard to get to where we are today. We have a right to spend our hard-earned money on whatever we want to, don't you think?

Meryem: (*shrugging*) I think there should be a law that forces rich people to donate a portion of their money to good causes.

b) Collect information about Meryem and her family (names, relationship, jobs/what they do).

c) Create a character map.
- Use the information from b).
- Scan the scene to find out how the family members behave towards each other and what their feelings might be.

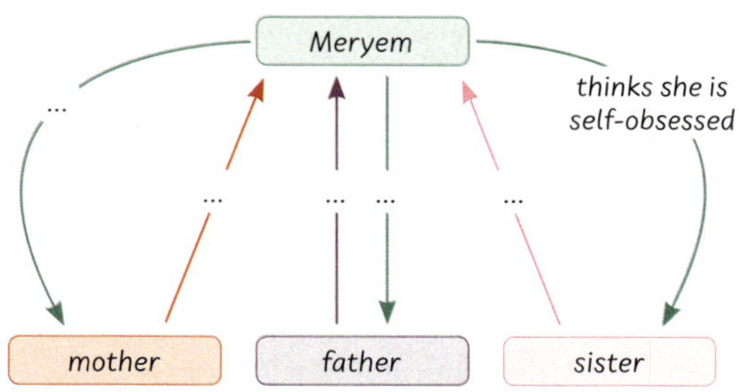

d) What could Meryem and her family do to solve their conflict?
Collect suggestions in class.
You can use your results from B1b).

One possible solution is ...

To solve their conflict, Meryem could ...

My suggestion would be to ...

To tackle this issue, they ...

e) Look at these formal phrases and find their informal equivalents in the scene.

1. It is not easy to be with him. → *He is just so much hard work.*
2. unwilling to spend money
3. If you concentrate on saving small amounts of money, at some point you will have a lot of money.
4. It is really annoying.
5. to use something somebody said but change the meaning
6. a lot of money

B3 Meryem's statement

Meryem says: "I think there should be a law that forces rich people to donate a portion of their money to good causes." Talk to a partner and say what you think about this statement.

B4 Scene two ▶ DIFF Training D18 | p. 191 ▶ WB 19 | p. 85

a) Read the scene and summarize what happens.

Scene two

A room in a youth club. Lottie and Orla are sitting on an old sofa. Lottie is flicking through a pile of printouts. Thomas is standing next to the sofa. Meryem rushes into the room.

Meryem: Sorry I'm late guys, I missed my bus.

Lottie: No worries, we haven't started yet.

Orla looks up from her phone and gives Meryem a friendly nod.

Thomas: So, if you missed your bus, how did you get here?

Meryem: (*blushing*) Erm, my parents gave me a lift in their car ...

Thomas raises his eyebrows, but doesn't say anything. Meryem sits down on a chair.

Lottie: OK, shall we start? We wanted to spend today thinking about how we can get more supporters. I've done some research and –

Meryem: But I thought we wanted to talk about what actions we are planning?

Lottie: But first we need more supporters. I read that it's better to do things in a sensible order if you want to be effective – get lots of supporters first, then plan what you want to do.

Meryem rolls her eyes and crosses her arms.

Thomas: Meryem, do you have a problem with that?

Meryem: No, but as I've already said, I think it's more important to plan what actions we are going to do.

Orla: We *are* already doing something. Every Saturday we collect signatures for our climate change petition.

Thomas: (*turning to Meryem*) Well, what's your suggestion, then?

Meryem: We need to open people's eyes! We need to motivate them to act! We need their attention! Have you read about the group in Bradford who went around slashing SUV tyres?

Lottie: You cannot be serious?!

Orla: That's a crime!

Meryem: Sure, but the newspapers report it and ...

Orla: I don't think activism should be at the cost of other people and their property.

Lottie: Erm, well ...

Thomas: (*looking at Meryem with disgust*) Interesting that you'd suggest something like that.

Meryem: Why?

Thomas: Come on, Meryem. Your father owns a car dealership and earns a living selling gas-guzzling tanks to money-obsessed snobs. You live in a big house, get chauffeured around by your parents in their big cars, and then *you* want to go round slashing tyres? It doesn't really fit together, does it?

Meryem: And what's that supposed to mean? Just because my parents happen to have a bit of money ...

Thomas: A bit?!

Meryem: That's not my fault, is it? What am I supposed to do about that?

Thomas: Well, you could start by keeping your good advice to yourself. I find it a bit problematic when privileged kids with rich parents try to be activists. I mean, what do you really know about the real world?

Orla: Come on, Thomas, that's not fair.

Thomas: Excuse me? What exactly do you think will happen when I get caught slashing tyres and my parents have to pay for the damage? Meryem's parents can maybe just break open their piggy bank, but ...

Meryem: (*standing up*) Fine. Then I don't want to bother you any longer.

Lottie: Meryem, wait ...

Meryem: No. No matter what I say, Thomas will tell me I'm wrong and criticize me because of my parents.

Orla: Are you bailing on us?

Meryem: (*walking towards the door*) Bye. I'll do my own thing.

b) Comment on Thomas's behaviour towards Meryem.

c) Speculate about ...
- Meryem's feelings,
- her future plans as an activist.

I imagine that ... | It's unlikely that ... | My guess is that ... | I wouldn't be surprised if ...

B5 Dramatic reading

Group work (4): Choose scene one (B2) or scene two (B4) and prepare a dramatic reading.

1. Decide who is going to read which role in the dialogue.
2. Go through the scene and practise reading your lines. Consider what you know about your character and express how they feel. Look up words you don't know how to pronounce.
3. Present your scene to another group. Download the checklist ▶ WES-149226-5 and give each other feedback.

> **Try to ...**
> - stress important words
> - use pauses
> - vary the volume of your voice
> - speak at an appropriate speed
> - sound natural

B6 Choose After the fight

Choose one of the tasks:

1. Thomas wants to tell a friend about the meeting with Meryem. Record Thomas's voice message for his friend. Talk about what happened and how you feel. ▶ WB Media 7 ▶ WES-149226-2

   OR

2. Continue the scene between Orla, Thomas and Lottie after Meryem has left. Write down what they are saying and doing and how they feel.

B7 Gerund or infinitive with *to*

▶ G15 | p. 234 ▶ DIFF Training D19, D20 | p. 192 ▶ WB 20 | p. 85

a) The verbs *remember, stop, mean, forget, try* and *go on* can be followed either by a **gerund** or by an **infinitive** with a difference in meaning.

Examples:

1. **A** Lottie stopped **talking** when Thomas interrupted her.
   B When Thomas sees the car, he stops **to stare** at Meryem and her parents.

2. **A** Being an activist means **supporting** a cause.
   B Lottie and Orla didn't mean **to offend** Meryem.

Say what the verbs *mean* and *stop* mean in German in each sentence.

b) Complete the sentences using the correct form of the verbs.

1 Orla: "Remember **XXX** (bring) the posters for the protest later!"
2 Thomas: "I meant **XXX** (tell) you earlier, but I forgot **XXX** (make) the posters."
3 Orla: "Oh no. People on the street won't stop **XXX** (listen) to us if we just stand there without posters!"
4 Thomas: "No problem. I can make the posters. I'll stop **XXX** (prepare) my speech for now. I'll try **XXX** (find) some boards and paint. What would be a good slogan to get people to stop **XXX** (ignore) climate change?"
5 Orla: "I'm not sure. But I've just remembered **XXX** (hear) something on a podcast last week that I liked. It was called 'Save the earth, save ourselves'. We could use that."

B8 A telephone conversation

L 2/2 | S 12 ▶ Listening | p. 202 ▶ WB 21 | p. 86

a) Listen to the dialogue between Meryem's father and his friend. Compare your ideas from B4c) with what has happened.

b) Listen again and take notes to answer these questions:
- Who was involved?
- What happened?
- When did it happen?
- Where did it happen?
- What were Meryem's reasons?

▶ DIFF Easy alternative D21 | p. 193

c) Talk to a partner about the incident. Say if you can understand Meryem and if her plan was effective.

pitch – *Spielfeld*
goalpost – *Torpfosten*
to chain sb to sth – *jdn an etw anketten*
lock – *Schloss*
zip tie – *Kabelbinder*
to boo – *ausbuhen*
to cancel – *abbrechen*

B9 Target task Write a newspaper article

▶ Writing | p. 210 ▶ WB 22 | p. 86

Write a newspaper article about the incident at the football match.

1 Plan your article by collecting all the facts.
- Use the information you collected in B8b): *who, what, when, where, why?*
- Add information from B2 and B4 that you want to use.
- Download this document ▶ WES-149226-5 to find quotes from people who were at the stadium.

2 Decide if you want to write an article for a quality newspaper or a tabloid newspaper.
Use your checklist from A5b). Depending on your choice, remember it will affect ...
- the tone (words and phrases that are matter-of-fact or emotive),
- how much/how little factual information you are going to include.

3 Write your article.
- To make your article interesting to read, vary your sentence structure: You can use participle constructions, the passive and connectives. ▶ G2R | p. 220, G7 | p. 227
- Use direct speech or reported speech to include at least one quote. ▶ G3R | p. 221

4 Create a headline that tells the reader what your article is about.
- You can also include a subheading to add extra information and stylistic devices (e.g. rhetorical question, alliteration, ...).
- Decide how big the headline should be in relation to the article.

5 Sketch or describe what kind of photos you would include and how big they should be in relation to the article.

6 Swap your article with a partner who has written an article for the other type of newspaper.
- Use your checklists from A5b) to check if your partner has included all the necessary features.
- Give each other feedback.

Need help? Look at page 133. T1 T2 T3

Target task tools for B9: Write a newspaper article

T1 Words: Writing a newspaper article

The following words and phrases can be useful when writing a newspaper article. Copy the grid and fill in the words and phrases from the box. You can use a dictionary if you need help.

~~especially~~ • ~~later~~ • ~~She claimed that ...~~ • ~~nevertheless~~ • Eyewitnesses say ... • Without a doubt, ... • A police officer stated/confirmed ... • in spite of • clearly • afterwards • hours later • obviously • later that day • in contrast to • He refused to comment. • although

order	emphasis	contrast	reporting what sb said
later	*especially*	*nevertheless*	*She claimed that ...*
...	...	...	...

T2 Expressing yourself in a different way

Rewrite the statements using a verb from the box.

~~take pride in~~ • recognize • regret • participate • speak out about • refuse • organize • support

Example: Thomas is very proud that he is an activist.
→ *Thomas takes pride in being an activist.*

1 Lottie and Orla don't want to be part of Meryem's plan.
2 Every week, Orla plans and prepares a meeting for the activists at the youth club.
3 Meryem's father is shocked when he sees his daughter on the football pitch.
4 Meryem is disappointed that her sister isn't interested in her ideas.
5 Meryem thinks it is important to express her opinion on climate action.
6 When a security guard tries to talk to Meryem, she doesn't answer.
7 After the incident, Amira is sad about not having listened to her sister.

T3 The passive ▶ G2R | p. 220

Newspaper headlines sometimes include passive constructions. Read these pieces of news and rewrite them as headlines using the passive:

- First, rewrite the sentence using a passive construction. You do not have to include all the information.
- Then turn your sentence into a headline by leaving out words that are not essential.

Example: Train driver falls ill and kills 200 people in an accident near Boston.
→ Passive sentence: *200 people are killed in a train accident near Boston.*
Headline: *200 people killed in train accident near Boston*

1 Grandmother saves little girl from crocodile attack.
2 Local people have planted 100 trees to celebrate the International Day of Forests.
3 Police have found the missing boy in a local park.
4 Scientists have discovered a deadly disease.
5 Astronauts are sent on a spacewalk to repair space shuttle.

1

2

4

5

P1 L 2/3 | S 13

a) Listen to a podcast about literature, films and TV programmes that are set in the North of England. Match the titles and the places. There is one more place than you need.

1 *Nowhere Boy* (The Beatles)
2 *Billy Elliot – I will dance*
3 *Coronation Street*
4 *All Creatures Great and Small*
5 *Wuthering Heights* (Emily Brontë)
6 *Daffodils* (William Wordsworth)

A Yorkshire Dales
B Lake District
C Liverpool
D West Yorkshire moors
E County Durham
F Manchester
G Whitby

b) Listen again and note down which part of the podcast is about ...

A a ballet-dancing boy from a 1980s mining village
B three sisters who produced masterpieces of literature
C the experiences of a vet who works in the countryside
D a poem that focuses on the beauty of nature
E one of the most famous bands in music history
F a famous soap opera about the lives of working-class people

c) Match the places (A-G) from a) with the photos (1-7).
Example: *1G, ...*

3

6

7

P2

a) Identify the photo that was not covered in the podcast in P1. Speculate on what it may show.

b) Read the questions. Then watch the video clip about *Dracula* and take notes.

1 When was the novel *Dracula* first published?
2 Why does Dracula come to England?
3 How does Dracula leave his boat and enter Whitby?
4 Why did Stoker choose Whitby as the setting for his story?
5 What happened at Whitby Abbey in May 2022?
6 How did people have to dress?

c) Use the information from the video to write a short text about Whitby and *Dracula* for the "Stories from the North" podcast.

P3

Choose one of the "Stories from the North" or look for another one. Prepare a short presentation about a novel, poem, film or TV programme from the North of England.
You can either choose one from the podcast or find a different one. Do some research online. Include details about what your chosen topic is about and what it shows about life in the North. Use pictures to support what you'd like to say.

▶ **WB** Media 5 ▶ WES-149226-2

5 The Summer We Turned Green

Reading tour

The novel The Summer We Turned Green *by William Sutcliffe deals with an attempt to stop a new airport runway*[1] *from being built. In order to protest, climate activists have moved into an empty house that will have to be demolished*[2].

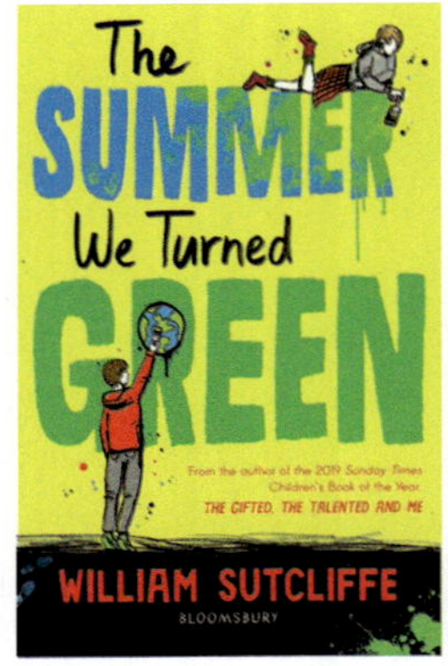

R1

a) Read extract A and describe how the novel starts.

b) Outline the situation in the suburban street where 17-year-old Rose and her younger brother Luke live, and explain why their parents don't want to accept that Rose has "gone over the road".

A It starts with a knock at my bedroom door.

Without waiting for an answer, my sister walks in, closing the door behind her as if she doesn't want anyone to hear what she's doing.

Rose never comes into my bedroom. She barely even speaks to me, but I suppose this is normal, since she's four years older and thinks that compared to her seventeen-year-old friends I'm about as interesting as a dust particle, so I have no idea what to say when she appears, says hi, then just stands there smiling at me.

There's a weird silence, because she doesn't seem to know what to say, either.

[…]

Then she says, 'You've got a sleeping bag, haven't you?'

'Yes.'

'Can I borrow it?'

'What for?'

'Sleeping in?' she replies, using the sarcastic statement-as-a-question intonation that drives our parents crazy.

'Are you going somewhere?'

'It's not important where I'm going, I'm just asking if you'll let me borrow it,' she says, with her eyes narrowing into a particular stare she has – the one that makes me wither and obey.

As always, it works, and next thing I know I'm rummaging[3] under my bed, hauling[4] out the sleeping bag and handing it over.

'Thanks, Luke. You're a star,' she says, already heading out of the room.

[…]

'Rose has gone,' says Mum.

'What?'

'Rose! She's gone!'

'Gone where?'

'I looked in her wardrobe and she's taken her clothes. We think she's gone over the road!' says Mum, with an air[5] of tragic climax[6] that Dad clearly can't make sense of.

'Er ...'

'With her stuff in a suitcase,' I say, translating Mum's panic into words Dad might actually understand.

'Oh!' says Dad. 'Right. So ... you're not saying she's popped out[7]. You're saying she's ...'

'Gone!'

'Over the road?'

'She borrowed my sleeping bag,' I point out.

Dad tends to need things explained to him very slowly, a bit like a small child but without fun.

'SHE TOOK YOUR SLEEPING BAG!?' yells Mum, which is when I realise I should have kept this to myself.

I nod.

'WHY DIDN'T YOU TELL US!?'

'I'm telling you now.' [...]

Why the big drama about a seventeen-year-old girl crossing the road with a suitcase and a sleeping bag? Well, the boring street in the boring suburb[8] where my boring home sits isn't as dull and safe as it used to be, because the house opposite, which used to be even more boring than ours, has become a magnet for every

1 runway – *Landebahn* | **2** to demolish – *abreißen* | **3** to rummage – *durchstöbern* | **4** to haul – *(mit viel Mühe) ziehen* | **5** air – *Ausstrahlung* | **6** climax – *Höhepunkt* | **7** to pop out – *kurz weg sein* | **8** suburb – *Vorort*

climate protester, anti-capitalist, extinction rebel, outcast and dropout in the country.

How?

Well, to explain this you have to go right back to when I was small. Nobody seems to know exactly when rumblings were first heard about a proposed[9] new runway for the airport near my home. For as long as I can remember the project was on, then off, then on again, and there was always talk of a never-ending round of meetings and consultations that sometimes sent the whole street into a panic about threats of demolition, and at other times seemed like an endless drone[10] of irrelevant background noise.

Then, roughly a year before the bizarre summer I'm going to tell you about, the project finally got a green light. On a morning that seemed like any other, the postman casually walked his usual route, unnoticed, delivering a small stack of dull looking brown envelopes which would change the street forever. Twenty letters landed on twenty doormats that day, telling every family who got one that their home was going to be bought from them, whether they wanted to sell or not, then demolished. Ours was spared. All the houses opposite were condemned.

Local outrage[11] ramped up[12] as the row of buildings emptied out and got boarded up, and the story even got some news coverage. Then gradually the abandoned house opposite ours filled up again with squatters[13]: anti-airport protesters, climate activists and, according to my parents, anyone else who thought it might be a laugh to hang out in a derelict[14] house all day instead of going out and getting a job.

9 propose – *vorschlagen* | **10** drone – *brummen* | **11** outrage – *Empörung* | **12** ramp up – *zunehmen* | **13** squatter – *Besetzer* | **14** derelict – *leer stehend*

R 2

Luke can't imagine why his sister has left home to live in the derelict house across the road, so he walks over himself.

a) Read extract B and describe the meeting between Luke and his sister. How has Rose changed and what are her motives for having moved in with the people across the road?

b) Explain how the relationship between Rose and her brother has changed.

B

It takes me a while to spot my sister. She looks different, but it takes me a moment to realise how. Then I twig[1] that it's her clothes, which, for the first time in ages, aren't black. But there's also something unfamiliar about her face. She hasn't been tattooed or pierced, yet she looks transformed. She looks happy. She's smiling, and not the weird, strained smile of the night she borrowed my sleeping bag, but a genuine one that actually fits with the rest of her face.

As soon as she spots me, this freakishly[2] contented[3] expression clouds over. She rearranges her features into a 'What the hell are you doing here?' look, and I respond with a shrug. She rolls her eyes, raises herself from the cushions she's curled up on and tiptoes[4] through the tangle of sprawled limbs[5] towards me.

'What do you want?' she says.

I probably should have thought of an answer to this question in advance. Bad planning on my part, there.

'Er ... I came to see you.'

'Why?'

'Because you're my sister.'

'Why are you behaving like a moron[6]?'

'I just wanted to say hi, and ... Mum and Dad have gone totally off the deep end about you moving in here, so I thought I'd come and take a look. See what it's all about.'

1 to twig – *kapieren* | **2** freakishly – *außergewöhnlich* | **3** contented – *zufrieden* | **4** to tiptoe – *auf Zehenspitzen gehen* | **5** tangle of sprawled limbs – *Gewirr ausgestreckter Gliedmaßen* | **6** moron – *Trottel*

'It's a climate protest. Why is that so hard to understand?'

'It's not.'

'I explained it to Mum, I explained it to Dad, now they've sent you. What's the problem?'

'They haven't sent me. I just came.'

'Why?'

'To see what you're doing.'

'I've told them what I'm doing. I'm taking a stand on the most important issue of our age.'

'OK. Right.'

'It's a global movement to face up to what's happening and actually change things, and I want to be part of it, instead of just ignoring the problem and distracting[7] myself by buying more and more stuff while we all wait for the planet to die. I know Mum and Dad are freaking out and they think this is crazy, but what's crazy is *not* doing it. What's crazy is carrying on as if nothing's wrong.'

'You're right.'

'Well, if you think I'm right, why won't you leave me alone?'

'Who says I'm on Mum and Dad's side?' I say. 'I agree with you. I went on all the school strike marches.'

'Big wow.'

'I want to help.'

'Really?'

'Yes.'

'Why?'

'Because you're right. And because our street has split in two, and it's pretty obvious which side of the road is the boring one.'

She looks me up and down assessingly[8], then says, 'Well, the best contribution you can make is to keep Mum and Dad off my back. Tell them you visit me regularly, and I'm really happy, and everyone here is really nice and normal.'

'Are they?'

'Well, they're nice. And you don't have to actually visit me. That's just what you have to tell them.'

7 distract – *ablenken* | **8** assessingly – *beurteilend*

R 3

Luke and Sky, the daughter of one of the protesters, move into a treehouse to keep an old tree from being cut down. After the first day the protest is in the media. Read extract C. Comment on the effect the protest has both on the protesters and the people in the street.

C

'WE'RE ON! WE'RE ON NOW!'

Everyone turns at the same time, and we see that she's staring at her mobile phone, on to which she's streaming the BBC news.

It's a while before I get to see it, because only so many people can look at one small screen at the same time, but her phone is passed around the room, with the same segment rewound and repeated, and when my turn comes I can barely believe my eyes. Everything I saw this morning from my perch in the treehouse is now in front of me again, but as part of a TV programme, as national news: the girl putting a flower into the bulldozer scoop and getting arrested; the police swarming over the barricade and struggling to drag away the protesters; the drumming and singing; then, most amazing of all, the interview with my dad. It's all there! Everything that happened in my little back-of-beyond[1] suburban street! On TV!

When I lift my eyes from the screen, Dad is at the centre of a huddle[2] of excited people, and I hear him say, 'Oh, it's only TV,' but his face is flushed and I can see that he's buzzing[3].

The strange thing is, TV is obviously less real than reality, but when you've seen something actually happen, then you get to see it in a news broadcast, it feels almost as if some higher authority has come along and stamped the events that took place in front of your eyes with a certification that makes them more real than they were before.

1 back-of-beyond – *am Ende der Welt* | **2** huddle – *Gruppe* | **3** he's buzzing – *er ist berauscht*

The verdict[4] on the news item from the commune members, who all try to play it cool but can't stop themselves squealing[5] if they see anyone they know on-screen, is that the protest comes out well. It's the police, not the demonstrators, who look violent, and it's clear from the reporter's slant[6] on events that the day represented a defeat for the demolition team and a victory for the climate rebels.

4 verdict – *Urteil* | **5** squeal – *kreischen* | **6** slant – *Tendenz*

R 4

Luke and Sky are asked to give an interview after the first day of the protest. Read extract D. Outline what they say and comment on their attitude.

D

'Well, we're recording,' he says. [...]

He goes still for a second, waits for some kind of signal off-camera, then turns away from us, gives an introduction about the protest and explains who we are. I try to listen to what he's saying but my mind goes blank, blurring into a fizz of panic, which only partially clears when I see him turn back to stare at us directly through the phone screen and ask a question which passes straight through my brain without me registering any sense of what he's asked.

Luckily Sky must have been managing to focus better than me, because she replies, in her usually chirpy voice, 'Fine! We're absolutely fine! What's being built here is an atrocity[1] and it shouldn't be allowed, and we're both very pleased to be taking a stand against it. My mum brought me up to believe that I shouldn't let people push me around, so that's what we're doing.'

'So do you really think that two kids up a tree can stop a multi-million-pound airport expansion going ahead?'

'I don't see what our age has to do with it. And no, we probably can't stop it, but we're already delaying[2] it, and also making people aware of what's going on. Not just us, but everyone who has come here to protest. This is a subject everyone should be thinking about and talking about – and here we are, talking to you, which is proof that what's happening here is already some kind of success.'

'Are you aware of how much protests like this cost the taxpayer[3]? Don't you think that now you've made your point you should come down?'

I feel I might be looking like an idiot, sitting here saying nothing, so I jump in with a quick answer. 'No! For years people having been asking politely for politicians to do something about climate change, and nothing ever happens. Until you get in the way of somebody making money, nobody even notices you're there.'

'For older people this whole thing is just an idea – a news story – but for us it's our lives,' says Sky, in a voice that reminds me of an engine shifting up a gear. 'Unless something drastic changes very soon, by the time we're your age, in maybe 2050 or 2070, the world as we know it will have been totally destroyed by people of your generation who didn't feel like giving up fast cars and weekends in Paris and plastic-wrapped fruit flown in from New Zealand. We're going to have to live with this. You can't understand how we feel.'

1 atrocity – *Grausamkeit* | **2** to delay – *verzögern* | **3** taxpayer – *Steuerzahler*

R 5

Choose an extract and rewrite it from another character's point of view.

Was hast du alles gelernt? Diese Seite hilft dir dabei, das zu erkennen.
Falls du Hilfe benötigst, etwas nachlesen oder noch ein paar Übungen machen möchtest, findest du hier passende Hinweise.

WORTSCHATZ

Ich kann ...	Aufgaben/Übungen/Hilfen
meine Meinung ausdrücken und begründen *I'm convinced that ..., because ... • As I see it, ... • I strongly believe that ... • I'm against/for ...*	A6 ▶ T2, T3 | p. 127
auf Gegenargumente eingehen *Although ..., it doesn't necessarily mean that ... • It may be true that ..., however ... • The fact that ... doesn't mean that ... • I can see your point but ... • In addition to ..., ... • I have to admit that ..., but ...*	A6 ▶ T2, T3 | p. 127
mögliche Gründe für Konflikte zwischen Eltern und Teenagern benennen *grades at school • hairstyle • homework • mobile phone use • noise • pocket money • smoking • taking care of pets*	B1 ▶ **DIFF** D14 ▶ **WB** 16

SKILLS

Ich kann ...	Aufgaben/Übungen/Hilfen
Informationen aus einem Videoclip entnehmen VIEWING	A1c ▶ Viewing | p. 212 ▶ **DIFF** D7 ▶ **WB** 8, 12
einen Zeitungsartikel schreiben WRITING	B9 ▶ Writing | p. 210 ▶ T1, T2 | p. 133
aus Sachtexten Informationen zu Veranstaltungen, Sehenswürdigkeiten, historischen Ereignissen und wichtigen Persönlichkeiten entnehmen READING	1, A1, A2 ▶ Reading | p. 203 ▶ **DIFF** D2, D4, D6 ▶ **WB** 1, 9
Zeitungsartikel analysieren und vergleichen READING	A4, A5 ▶ Reading | p. 203 ▶ **DIFF** D13 ▶ **WB** 14, 22
an einer Debatte teilnehmen SPEAKING	A6 ▶ Speaking | p. 205 ▶ T2, T3 | p. 127
einem Telefongespräch folgen LISTENING	B8 ▶ Listening | p. 202 ▶ **DIFF** D21

GRAMMATIK

Ich kann ...	Aufgaben/Übungen/Hilfen
entscheiden, ob ich den Infinitiv mit oder ohne *to* verwenden muss *My mum expects me to call her if I'm late. – My mum didn't hear the phone ring.*	▶ **DIFF** D8 ▶ G13R | p. 233 ▶ **WB** 10
adverbiale Bestimmungen an der richtigen Stelle im Satz platzieren *My younger brother was born in Berlin in 2019.*	▶ **DIFF** D11 ▶ G12 | p. 232 ▶ **WB** 13
Aussagen mit Hilfe des *emphatic do* Nachdruck verleihen *I do believe you are right.*	▶ **DIFF** D17 ▶ G14 | p. 234 ▶ **WB** 18
entscheiden, wann ich das Gerundium oder den Infinitiv verwenden muss *Being an activist means supporting a cause. • Lottie and Orla didn't mean to offend Meryem.*	B7 ▶ **DIFF** D19 ▶ G15 | p. 234 ▶ **WB** 20
das Gerundium nach Adjektiv mit Präposition/Verb mit Präposition verwenden *Charlotte is good at playing volleyball. • We look forward to going on holiday next month.*	▶ **DIFF** D20 ▶ G15 | p. 234

Writing: Letter to the editor

Step by step

Readers of newspapers sometimes write a letter to the editor to comment on an article they have read, usually in the hope that the letter will be published in the newspaper.

On these pages you will learn how to write a letter to the editor.
First, there is an example task and a possible solution.
Next, there is your task. You will learn how to write your own letter to the editor, step by step.

Example

1 Look at the example task and the solution.

EXAMPLE TASK

Read the newspaper article about the statue of Edward Colston that was toppled and pushed into Bristol Harbour in June 2020.
Write a letter to the editor in response to the article.

Why It Was Wrong To Topple The Colston Statue

By Simon Wood 08/06/2020

On 7th June, an angry mob tore down the statue of Edward Colston in Bristol and dumped it into the murky harbour waters. This was the final chapter in a long-running controversy surrounding the statue.

The city of Bristol has Edward Colston to thank for a number of things. Colston was born into a wealthy industrial family in 1736 and continued the family business once he was old enough. He was a generous philanthropist – he donated huge sums of money so that schools, churches and hospitals could be built in the city.

Because of this and other activities, city representatives at the time and ever since have rightly chosen to honour him by naming multiple streets and buildings after him. After his death in 1721, local business leaders dedicated a bronze statue to Colston, which, despite surviving for so many years, has since been toppled by this raging mob.

There is no doubt that Colston didn't only do good things. From the 1860s, he took part in and profited from the trade in enslaved African people – in fact, a large portion of his wealth came from this. During the course of the Atlantic slave trade, Colston was involved in the enslavement of over 84,000 people, 12,000 of whom were children. 19,000 people died aboard his ships. Survivors of the Atlantic crossing were sold into slavery, mostly to tobacco or sugar cane plantations in the Caribbean.

People have been demanding the removal of Colston's statue for a long time now. Back in the 1990s, more than 10,000 people signed a petition which protested the monument. In 2019, there was a failed attempt to add a plaque to the statue which was intended to inform people about Colston's involvement in the slave trade.

Of course, it is important to look at Colston's links to the slave trade. But it's wrong to get rid of the statue entirely. People can be both heroes and villains, and it's too simplistic to reduce his life down to the slave trade, considering the amount of good he also did for his hometown. Toppling his statue is an attempt to erase Edward Colston from the city's history.

Yet the angry mob involved in toppling the statue can't change history. The past is the past. If we don't want history to repeat itself, particularly events which are considered barbaric by today's standards, then it's important to create places and monuments which can remind us of the past.

Rather than removing the statue it would have been best to simply add a plaque with some additional information for passers-by. Edward Colston is and always will be a part of Bristol's rich history and toppling his statue can never change that.

SOLUTION

Dear Editor,

I am writing in response to the recent article "Why It Was Wrong To Topple The Colston Statue", which discusses the toppling of a statue of Edward Colston, a 17th-century trader in enslaved African people.

While the article acknowledges the controversy surrounding Colston and his involvement in the slave trade, it argues against the removal of his statue and suggests that the protesters were trying to erase him from history.

This argument misses the point entirely. Removing a statue of Colston does not erase him from history. Rather, it is a necessary step towards acknowledging what he did in his life. It is important to remember that Colston was not simply a philanthropist, but a man who profited from the slave trade and was responsible for the deaths of thousands of African people.

The article suggests that adding a plaque to the statue explaining Colston's involvement in the slave trade would have been a good solution. The author overlooks the fact that putting up a statue in someone's honour is a statement of power. It sends the message that Colston's contributions to Bristol are more important than the harm he caused as a slave trader. Adding a plaque would not change this message.

In short, the removal of Colston's statue was not an attempt to erase him from history, but a necessary step towards acknowledging the full extent of his life.

Kim Grayson, Bristol

Your task

2 Read your task, then follow the steps below to solve it.

YOUR TASK

Write a letter to the editor in response to the article "Climate Crazies Cause Chaos!" on page 124.

Step 1	Download the article ▸ WES-149226-5 and read it. Decide if you agree or disagree with the author.
Step 2	Highlight the passages you want to comment on (like in the example task).
Step 3	Think of arguments and examples to support your opinion and write them down. Arrange them in a logical order
Step 4	Before you begin writing your letter, keep in mind that you should use formal language.
Step 5	Write the introduction. • Start with *Dear Editor, …* • Name the article you are referring to at the beginning of your letter. *I am writing to you in response to the article … • In reference to your article … • I would like to respond to your article …*
Step 6	Write the main part. • Say why you are writing the letter, i.e. what you support/criticize/would like to comment on about the article. *I am writing to you to compliment the author on …/to express my concern about … • Having read your article about …, I would like to point out … • In the article …, the author claims that … • While the article acknowledges …, it argues for/against …* • Explain why you share or oppose the author's point of view. *I agree/disagree with the author's point of view on … • I personally believe that … • The article suggests that … • I would like to add some further aspects to the author's article. • What you need to keep in mind is … • I would like to support the author's argument that … because … • I think the author makes an important point by saying that … because … • As a supporter of … I totally agree/I see no reason why … • Although I understand why … I cannot accept the overall conclusion that … • I see the author's point but I still feel that … • I think the author is mistaken if … • The author fails to mention that … • I would question the argument that … because … • The author overlooks the fact that … • The argument misses the point.* • Follow a clear line of argument and stick to the most important point(s). • You can support your arguments with examples.

Step 7	Finish your letter. • End the letter with a strong statement that sums up your position. *The question can no longer be whether ..., but ...* • *All in all, there can be no doubt that ...* • *Ultimately, what matters is (that) ...* • *In short, ...* • *I urge you to provide more balanced and objective reporting in the future and avoid ...* • *Overall, the article ...* • *In closing, I would like to suggest ...* • Sign your name at the end. • State your place of residence. Do not use a sign-off phrase like *Yours faithfully/Yours sincerely* at the end of your letter.
Step 8	Edit your letter. Make sure that you use formal language and that your spelling, vocabulary and grammar are correct.

Checklist: Writing a letter to the editor

Checklist

1. Read the article and decide if you agree or disagree with the author.
2. Highlight the passages you want to comment on.
3. Think of arguments and examples to support your opinion and write them down. Arrange them in a logical order.
4. Before you begin writing your letter, keep in mind that you should use formal language.
5. Write the introduction.
   - Start with *Dear Editor, ...*
   - Name the article you are referring to at the beginning of your letter.
6. Write the main part.
   - Say why you are writing the letter, i.e. what you support/criticize/would like to comment on about the article.
   - Explain why you share or oppose the author's point of view.
   - Follow a clear line of argument and stick to the most important point(s).
   - You can support your arguments with examples.
7. Finish your letter.
   - End the letter with a strong statement that sums up your position.
   - Sign your name at the end.
   - State your place of residence.

   Do not use a sign-off phrase like *Yours faithfully/Yours sincerely* at the end of your letter.
8. Edit your letter. Make sure that you use formal language and that your spelling, vocabulary and grammar are correct.

Theme 1: Intro

D1 Training: Viewing

▶ After Intro 2 p. 12 ▶ Viewing | p. 212

Read the questions, then watch the video clip again and complete the sentences.

1 Australia is the **XXX** largest country in the world.
2 **XXX** was built because people couldn't agree whether Sydney or Melbourne should be Australia's capital.
3 Sydney is known for the Sydney Opera House and **XXX**.
4 The oldest and largest art gallery in the country is in **XXX**.
5 As most of Australia's inner parts are very dry with extreme weather conditions, more than 85% of Australians live on the **XXX**.
6 A train journey from Sydney to Perth takes 54 hours and runs through the **XXX**.
7 A sacred[1] and spiritual place in the Outback is **XXX**, a large ancient[2] rock.
8 One of the most popular sports in Australia is **XXX**, which is similar to rugby.

1 sacred – *heilig* | **2** ancient – *alt*

D2 Training: Pronunciation

L 1/4 | S 1 ▶ After Intro 2 | p.12 ▶ Listening | p. 202

a) What are the names of these places? Look at the map at the back of your book for help.
1 [pɜːθ] is the biggest city on the west coast.
2 Australia's largest city, with more than 5 million people, is ['sɪdni].
3 [ˌuːlə'ruː] is a sandstone formation in central Australia.
4 [ˌleɪk‿'eə] is in a desert in South Australia.
5 [ˌmaʊnt ˌkɒzi'ʌskəʊ] in New South Wales is 2,228 metres high.
6 [tæz'meɪniə] is an island in the south-east of Australia with a capital city called Hobart.

b) Listen and check.

D3 Training: Tenses (revision)

▶ After Intro 4 | p. 13 ▶ G1R | p. 217

Complete the text about Perth using the present perfect, simple past and simple present.

Perth **1** (be) the capital and largest city of the Australian state of Western Australia.
The first people who **2** (come) to live in the Perth area **3** (be) the Whadjuk Noongar people. Archaeological evidence **4** (show) that they **5** (stay) there for at least 45,000 years.
In 1829 Captain James Stirling founded Perth and **6** (name) it after the city of Perth in Scotland.
The city's population **7** (increase) in the late 19th century because of the Western Australia Gold Rushes. It **8** (grow) steadily since World War II as a result of a high immigration rate.
Perth's most famous buildings **9** (be) the Parliament House, the Government House and the Supreme Court Buildings. Today, more than two million people **10** (live) in Perth.

1 Diff and train

Theme 1: Part A

D4 Training: Paraphrasing ▶ After A1a | p. 14

Write definitions for these words. You can use a dictionary for help.

Example: to be in charge of → *When you are in charge of something, it means that you are the boss and you control how things are done.*

1 connection
2 disagree
3 to force sb to do sth
4 increase
5 one in five
6 percentage
7 population
8 poverty
9 to steal

D5 Easy alternative: Viewing ▶ Instead of A1b | p. 14 ▶ Viewing | p. 212

Copy the timeline. Watch the video, then match the dates with the information.

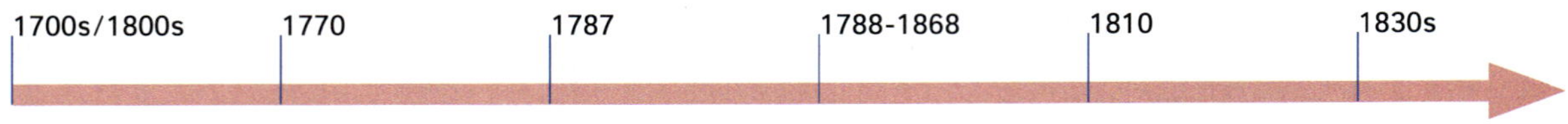

same rights for ex-prisoners, but not for Aboriginal population	the British sent their first ships to Australia	Industrial Revolution in the UK, much poverty, many crimes	free settlers founded new colonies in Australia	James Cook first arrived on the Australian continent	many British prisoners sent to Australia

D6 Training: Media research ▶ After A2a | p. 14

Australia is divided into six states and two territories. Each has its own flag. Choose one and research its flag. Write a description and explain the different parts of the flag.

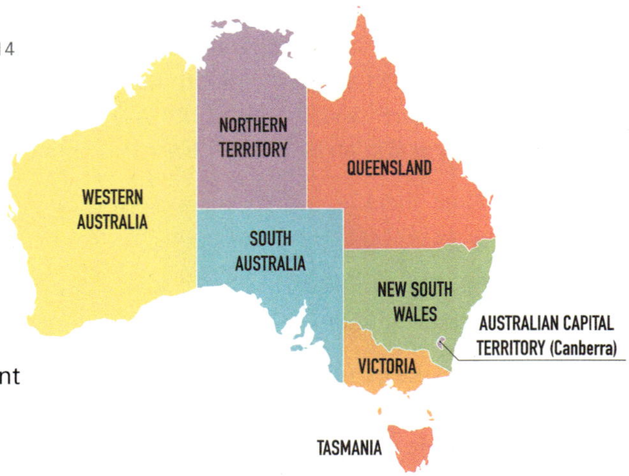

D7 Training: Statistics ▶ After A2 | p. 14

Today, Australia has a population of about 25 million. More than seven million people who live in Australia were not born there but came from almost 200 different countries.

Look at the pie chart. Decide whether the statements are true or false. Correct the false statements.

1 The majority of people living in Australia were not born there.
2 There are more immigrants from New Zealand than from China.
3 More immigrants come from Italy than from India.
4 There are more immigrants from Vietnam than from Malaysia.
5 Immigrants from the UK are the second largest group in the statistics.
6 About one third of the immigrants are from the UK, India and China.

Australian immigrants born in

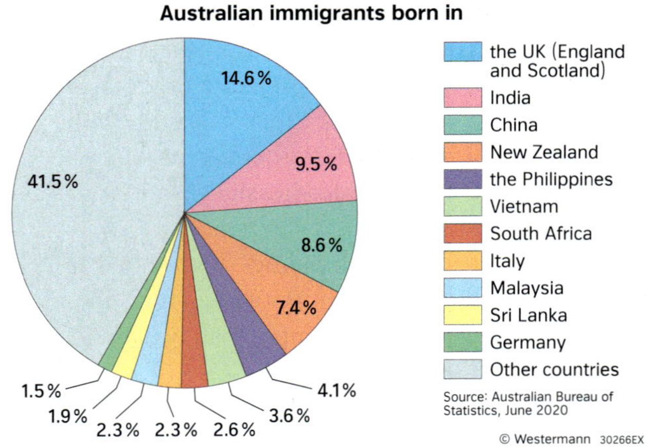

Source: Australian Bureau of Statistics, June 2020

D8 Training: Listening

L 1/5 | S 2 ▶ After A3 | p. 14 ▶ Listening | p. 202

Indigenous Australians use stories from the Dreaming to describe the "time before time", or the time of creation. Read the sentences (A–M), then listen to the Dreaming story and put the sentences in the right order. Start with D. One sentence does not fit.

A The kangaroo and the joey[1] could not find the wombat.
B The kangaroo put on the bag and it became a pouch[2] for her joey.
C The kangaroo could not find her joey.
D A mother kangaroo and her joey were looking for food.
E The kangaroo saw the hunter[3] and warned the wombat.
F The kangaroo took the wombat to where he could eat and drink.
G All mother kangaroos have pouches and they don't often lose their babies.
H The hunter tried to catch the kangaroo but he was too slow.
I She found her joey and left him sleeping.
J They met a wombat who needed help.
K The wombat cried for help when the hunter came.
L He left a special bag next to the kangaroo while she was sleeping.
M The spirit who had come to earth decided that the mother kangaroo was the kindest of all animals.

1 joey – *Kängurujunges* | **2** pouch – *Beutel* | **3** hunter – *Jäger*

D9 Training: Mediation

▶ After A4 | p. 16 ▶ Mediation | p. 213

Read Dylan Alcott's profile. Outline the main information in German.

In 2022 Paralympic medallist Dylan Alcott was named 'Australian of the year'. For more than a decade Alcott represented Australia at the Paralympics. After lots of hard work and discipline the athlete won several silver and gold medals in Paralympic tournaments such as wheelchair basketball and wheelchair tennis. He even won the 2018 Australian Open quad wheelchair title.
As a baby, Alcott had to have a major operation on his back, which left him fighting for his life for three years. But despite these challenges Dylan has made a success of himself, not only as an athlete, but also as a businessman and philanthropist. In 2017 the athlete created the Dylan Alcott Foundation to provide young disabled people with financial support for their education and to encourage paralympic sports. In addition, those who receive the foundation's scholarships benefit from regular mentoring. Alcott is a keen motivational speaker and feels strongly about supporting people with disabilities and changing the way society views them.

D10 Training: Reading

▶ After A5 | p. 17 ▶ Reading | p. 203

Read the text on page 17 again and complete the sentences.

1 On 26th January, Australia Day is celebrated but many people **XXX**.
2 In Brisbane, **XXX** through the business district to Musgrave Park.
3 **XXX** was damaged in Melbourne.
4 According to Deborah Sandy, Australia Day celebrations **XXX**.
5 The motto for Australia Day in Canberra was: **XXX**.
6 In his speech, Scott Morrison described Australia as the world's **XXX**.

D11 **Training: The passive (revision)** ▶ After A6 | p. 18 ▶ G2R | p. 220

Read the information about Baker Boy. Complete the sentences with the correct passive forms.

accept • hear • invite • know • give • recognize • release • remember

Danzal James Baker was born in Darwin, Australia on 10 October 1996. He is a successful Australian performance artist, who 1 *is known* as Baker Boy. He is a member of the Yolngu, a group of Indigenous Australian peoples who live in the Northern Territory. After college, he 2 at the Aboriginal Centre for the Performing Arts in Brisbane where he developed his love of dancing and acting. In 2017, his first single 3 . His first album followed in 2021. Baker Boy 4 for his musical contributions, receiving several prizes in the past few years. He 5 to perform both with national and international musicians. In Baker Boy's songs, elements of hip hop can 6 in combination with traditional indigenous music. He raps in Yolngu Matha, an indigenous language. He also plays the yidaki, which is the Yolngu name for the didgeridoo. Baker Boy 7 the Young Australian of the Year award in 2019. He wants to be an inspiration to Indigenous kids. He wants them to stay strong and positive and be proud of who they are and where they come from. He 8 by future generations as an inspiration.

Theme 1: Part B

D12 **Easy alternative: Words** ▶ Instead of B2c | p. 20

Match the definitions and synonyms with words from Theo's blog on pages 20/21. There is one more definition than you need.

1 *a person that lives in a place*
2 *knowledge about birds*
3 *a school for children between the ages of five and twelve*
4 *designing and building machines or structures*
5 *flying planes*
6 *one half of the earth*

A *hemisphere*
B *engineering*
C *aviation*
D *elementary school*
E *inhabitant*

D13 **Training: Reading** ▶ After B2 | p. 20 ▶ Reading | p. 203

Read Theo's blog on pages 20/21 and answer the questions.

1 Why did Theo decide to write a blog?
2 What is the best thing about Cairns?
3 What type of schools does Theo talk about in his blog?
4 What does Theo like about his Australian school?
5 What information does Theo give about marine science?
6 What does Theo write about the summer holidays?

D14 Training: Reported speech (revision) ▶ After B2 | p. 18 ▶ G3R | p. 221

Use reported speech to tell someone what the tourists at Sydney Airport said or asked.

Example: Yini: "I'll definitely come back here sometime next year!"
→ *Yini said that she would definitely come back to Australia sometime in the following year.*

Check the rules for backshift of tenses in ▶ G3R | p. 221

1 Youssef: "I loved our trip to Uluru last week."
2 Finn: "There are so many regions of Australia that I haven't seen yet."
3 Sophie: "The hot weather here is getting a bit too much for me."
4 Amira: "When can I board this plane?"
5 James: "Have you ever been to the Outback, Lucy?"
6 Anna: "Will the cricket season start again soon?"

D15 Easy alternative: Mediation ▶ Instead of B4c | p. 22 ▶ Mediation | p. 213

a) Read the article about the Royal Flying Doctor Service, then answer the questions in English.

Royal Flying Doctor Service

Wenn Menschen vor dem Jahr 1928 im Outback erkrankten, konnten sie oft nicht professionell medizinisch versorgt werden. Das änderte sich, als John Flynn den Aerial Medical Service (AMS) ins Leben rief.

Flynn war Pfarrer der Presbyterianischen Kirche und wurde 1912 beauftragt, über die Lebensbedingungen der Bewohner des Northern Territory zu berichten. Flynn fiel vor allem der Mangel an medizinischer Versorgung auf: Für das 2 Millionen km² große Outback gab es zum damaligen Zeitpunkt nur zwei Ärzte.

In den folgenden Jahren wurden daraufhin zwar fünfzehn Buschkrankenhäuser gegründet, doch die Entfernungen waren immer noch zu groß.

Flynn überlegte, wie man moderne Technik für die Lösung des Problems nutzen konnte, und begann Spenden zu sammeln, um Flugzeuge und Funkgeräte für die medizinische Versorgung einzusetzen. Im Mai 1928 nahm dann der erste Stützpunkt in Cloncurry (Queensland) seinen Dienst auf, zwei weitere Stützpunkte wurden in den 30er Jahren eingerichtet. 1942 wurde die Organisation in „Flying Doctor Service" umbenannt, und 1955 erteilte das englische Königshaus die Zustimmung, den Zusatz „Royal" verwenden zu dürfen.

Heute befindet sich der bekannteste Stützpunkt in Alice Springs. Der Royal Flying Doctor Service betreut fast alle gering besiedelten Gebiete und kann innerhalb von zwei Stunden jede Person in Australien erreichen und versorgen.

1 When did John Flynn found the Aerial Medical Service and why?
2 What happened after John Flynn had reported on the medical needs of people who lived in the Outback?
3 What happened between 1928 and 1955?
4 What further information is given about the Royal Flying Doctor Service?

Stützpunkt – *base*

b) Add relevant information to your class wall chart.

D16 Extra: Writing ▶ After B6 | p. 22

Read the tips that tourists have collected after travelling to Germany.
Choose three tips. For each tip find an example and write at least two sentences to explain it.
Example: *In Germany there are some shops, pubs and restaurants that don't accept credit cards. For example, when you buy …*

www.tipsfortourists.com/countries/Germany/more/.

Dos and Don'ts when travelling to Germany

1. Don't rely on your credit card, take cash as well.
2. Don't cross the street when the traffic lights are red.
3. Be aware that shops are closed on Sundays.
4. Use the person's last name when you meet a grown-up for the first time.
5. Don't be surprised to see naked people in a sauna.

D17 Training: Reading ▶ After B7 | p. 23 ▶ Reading | p. 203

Read Theo's blog on pages 23/24 again.
Decide if the statements are true or false. For each statement, find a sentence in the blog entry that supports your decision.

1 Fitzroy Island is a tropical island popular with tourists.
2 Theo's school always visits Fitzroy Island in the summer.
3 It is better to take a trip to Fitzroy Island when there aren't any storms.
4 Theo recommends visiting the turtle rehabilitation centre.
5 Many turtles are injured by stingers.
6 Baby corals build themselves a shell and attach themselves to jellyfish.
7 The Great Barrier Reef covers a huge area.
8 Many people help to prevent more coral bleaching.

D18 Training: Connectives ▶ After B7 | p. 23

Use connectives to combine the sentences halves.

1 *Theo chose marine science*
2 *You can visit the island anytime*
3 *The sea is calmer during dry season*
4 *There aren't too many stingers around Fitzroy Island*
5 *Dr Symmonds picked up the group*
6 *Theo was very impressed*
7 *Some turtles had been caught up in fishing nets*
8 *The corals lose their colour*

but
although
when
so
as a result of
after
so that
before

they had arrived.
they had been rescued by the centre.
tourists shouldn't take the risk.
he can take part on a trip to Fitzroy Island.
he visited the turtle rehabilitation centre.
the trip is more comfortable than in the wet season.
climate change and higher water temperatures.
it's better to go there during dry season.

Theme 2: Intro

D1 Training: Viewing

▶ After Intro 3 | p. 38 ▶ Viewing | p. 212

Read the sentences about the 80s. Then watch the video clip and complete the sentences.

1 Many cars had seat belts[1] but ...
2 It was more difficult to listen to your favourite music because ...
3 Everyone watched the same TV shows because ...
4 If you weren't at home and wanted to call a friend, you had to ...
5 In the 80s, teenagers had to spend more time in the library because ...
6 You really had to think about what you wanted to take a photo of because ...
7 Many high schools had special outdoor areas where ...
8 Teenagers had more freedom because ...

1 seat belt – *Sicherheitsgurt*

D2 Easy alternative: Listening

L 1/8 | S 5 ▶ Instead of Intro 4b | p. 39 ▶ Listening | p. 202

Group work (3). Each of you concentrates on two aspects of the infographics.

- Group member A focuses on "drinking" and "identifying as LGBTQ+".
- Group member B focuses on "smoking" and "being open about mental health".
- Group member C focuses on "driving" and "reading habits".

First, look at the possible reasons for why teenage life has changed. In each category, one reason is false. Then listen to the interview and identify the correct reasons. Note them down. Example: **Drinking: 1, ...**

Group member A

Drinking

1 Today there isn't as much social pressure to drink alcohol.
2 Young people know there's a chance a photo or video of them might appear online for anyone to see if they do something bad in public.
3 Today, drinking is illegal for teenagers and too expensive.
4 Teenagers today want to live a healthy lifestyle, and alcohol often doesn't fit into that.

Identifying as LGBTQ+

1 Nowadays many more people like to talk about their sexual orientation.
2 It is now considered cool to be LGBTQ.
3 There is more acceptance among young people for people to just be who they are.

Group member B

Smoking

1 Smoking is a lot more expensive than it used to be.
2 Because of social media teenagers don't have time to smoke anymore.
3 Smoking isn't considered cool anymore.
4 Today it's harder for tobacco companies to promote cigarettes.

Being open about mental health

1 Today it's more acceptable to talk about mental health and ask for help.
2 Teenagers in the 80s didn't have as many mental health issues.
3 People can share their experiences on the internet.

Group member C

Driving

1 Buying and using a car is more expensive than ever.
2 Nowadays, there are also more rules for young drivers.
3 There are a lot more travel options today, particularly in towns and cities.
4 Buses and trains have become less expensive.

Reading habits

1 Teenagers are no longer interested in reading novels.
2 You can get digital versions of books, newspapers and magazines.
3 Young people spend time online, so they have less time to read.

2 Diff and train

D 3 Training: Conditional clauses, type 2 (revision) ▶ **After Intro 5** | p. 39 ▶ G5R | p. 224

Complete the sentences with the correct forms of the verbs in brackets.

Example: If teenagers **XXX** (have) more power, they **XXX** probably **XXX** (change) many aspects of society.
→ *If teenagers had more power, they would probably change many aspects of society.*

1 The environment **XXX** (be) better protected if teenagers **XXX** (make) the laws.
2 If teenagers **XXX** (have) more power, society as a whole **XXX** (become) more open-minded.
3 Teenagers **XXX** probably **XXX** (be) more interested in politics if they **XXX** (be allowed to) vote from a younger age.
4 If young people **XXX** (have) more freedom, they **XXX** (be able to) decide what they want to do with their lives.
5 If there **XXX** (be) fewer rules for teenagers, teenagers **XXX** (not have to) fight against them anymore.

Theme 2: Part A

D 4 Training: Words and phrases ▶ **After A1a** | p. 40

a) Match the sentence halves.

1 What really matters to me
2 I wouldn't be the same if
3 It may not be for everyone,
4 I don't think I could
5 It means a lot to me that
6 I wouldn't know what to do

A but there is nothing better than going to the cinema or doing sport with your friends.
B survive even one day without the internet.
C without social media. You can connect with friends and share what's happening in your life – even if you're far away!
D I had to give up my phone! I can message people or post status and photos wherever I am.
E I can be in touch with people 24/7 thanks to modern technology.
F is meeting my friends in person and not just online.

b) Choose three of the statements from a).
Comment on them. These phrases may help you.

agree:
I completely agree that ... • That's what I think, too, because ... • It is absolutely right that ...

partly agree:
That might be the case if ..., but ... • It's right up to a point that ... but ... • I wouldn't quite say that ..., but ...

disagree:
I find it hard to believe that ... • It isn't as simple as that because ... • I can't imagine that ...

D5 Training: Tenses (revision)

▶ After A1b | p. 40 ▶ G1R | p. 217

Read what some high school students said in interviews about their use of social media. Fill in the verbs in the correct tenses. Watch out for signal words.

Kyla

I **1** (spend) about two hours a day online. Well, I often **2** (check) my profiles on my phone during the day as well. I **3** (not do) it in class, though. My best friend Tammy **4** (do) that last year and she **5** (get) into serious trouble for cheating in a test. I **6** (take) at least one photo for my favourite social media platform each day. I **7** (post) hundreds of photos since I started using it. What I **8** (like) about it is that it is so easy – I don't have to write long texts.

A few years ago, I **9** (use) social media all the time, but I **10** (take) down all my profiles a year or so ago. I **11** (not think) that my photos and personal information **12** (be) very safe out there. I guess that's why I **13** (not start) using social media again in the near future.

Zayne

Jennifer

I **14** (love) using social media. When I **15** (start) using it a few years ago, I just **16** (write) boring posts like "Hello from the school bathroom!" My messages **17** (change) a lot since then. I always **18** (try) to tell a little story, play with words or make the post interesting in some other way. Last year I **19** (delete) my old profile and **20** (create) a new one – "Stories of a girl geek". So far, my new profile **21** (attract) more than 900 followers. Maybe I **22** (reach) the 1,000 mark by the end of this month! That would be really cool!

D6 Easy alternative: Analysing cartoons

▶ Instead of A2 | p. 40 ▶ Wordbank 3 | p. 239

Analyse the cartoon. Follow steps 1-5:

Step 1 Identify the topic of the cartoon.
Choose the correct sentence.

A The cartoon deals with the impossible standards that are presented on social media.

B The cartoon deals with unfair standards that cute puppies have to live up to.

C The cartoon is concerned with unfair conditions for animal actors.

Step 2 Describe the situation. Complete the sentences.
The cartoon shows **1** who are **2** to each other.
The dog on the **3** has its **4** pointed towards the ground and is hunching its back. It seems to be **5** and **6**. The dog on the **7** is frowning at the other dog. It seems concerned about how the other dog is feeling.

Step 3 Explain what the characters are saying. Complete the sentence.
The dog on the left is saying that it is not fair that ...

➡

Step 4 Explain the message of the cartoon. Choose the correct ending.
You might conclude that the message of the cartoon is that ...
- **A** we need more realistic standards for dogs acting in videos.
- **B** the standards set on social media are unrealistic and cannot be reached.
- **C** pet videos on social media are all bad and should be banned.

Step 5 Choose a statement that best summarizes your opinion on the cartoon.

I find the cartoon quite funny because it makes fun of the impossible standards set on social media. It claims that even dogs feel the pressure of having to live up to them.

I don't find the cartoon funny because I've seen too many cartoons that criticize social media. I like social media anyway.

In my opinion, the cartoon is thought-provoking because it makes you think about the standards set on social media.

I don't like the cartoon, especially the boring colours and the pessimistic message.

If you ask me, the cartoon is ... because ...

D7 Easy alternative: Viewing

▶ Instead of A3b | p. 41 ▶ Viewing | p. 212

a) Read the notes.
Then watch the video about what social media is doing to our brains. Note down which of the points are mentioned in the video.

b) Add any positive or negative aspects of social media to your notes from A1b).

1 *very expensive for teenagers*
2 *non-verbal aspects of a conversation are missing*
3 *information is often outdated*
4 *makes us more self-centred*
5 *helps to connect people from all over the world*
6 *fear of missing out leads to problems*
7 *positive comments make you feel good*
8 *helps people with low self-esteem*
9 *negative comments upset you*
10 *most stories are positive and optimistic*

D8 Support: Words

▶ Before A4b | p. 41

Work with a partner. Make sure you know the meaning of these words before you read the article in A4 on pages 41/42. You can use a dictionary for help.

pledge • internship • to reject • vaccination • whistleblower • suicidal • to feel compelled to • cure • to be complicit • cruel • to disappear

D9 Training: Reading

▶ After A4b | p. 41 ▶ Reading | p. 203

Read the questions. Then read the article on pages 41/42 again and take notes for your answers. Use your notes to answer the questions in 2-3 sentences.

1 How has the author benefitted from social media?
2 What negative examples of using social media does she mention?

D10 Extra: Mediation ▶ After A4c | p. 41 ▶ Mediation | p. 213

Read the information about cyberbullying.
Then explain to a German-speaking person what cyberbullying is and what advice is given.
Give examples.

Cyberbullying

In a society that revolves increasingly around information technology, we can do so many things which we could not do before: working and studying from home, internet shopping, virtual communication … the list goes on. However, with greater opportunity comes greater risk. As the online world grows, so does the potential for problems such as cyberbullying.

Cyberbullying and its consequences

Cyberbullying is bullying which happens online, typically by means of the bully sending threatening or offensive messages to the victim on social media or digital forums. Although face-to-face bullying has significant consequences for the victim, cyberbullying sometimes damages the victim's physical and mental health even more. A cyberbully can send nasty messages anywhere and at any time and can be anonymous. This leaves the victim feeling powerless and isolated. Cyberbullying can lead to low self-esteem, depression and anxiety. This can result for example in sleeping difficulties, more frequent physical health issues and lower school exam results. Victims of cyberbullying may also avoid friends and social events.

What you can do

Young people suffer from the effects of cyberbullying not only while it is happening, but also for months and even years after it has been resolved, especially if it happens over a longer period of time. Therefore, it is really important to know how to deal with cyberbullying when it happens. First and foremost, if you are experiencing cyberbullying, it is essential that you let someone know – be it a family member, friend, teacher, or someone else you trust. It might not feel easy to do this, but it is so much easier to find a solution if you are not trying to deal with the problem alone. It is also very important not to react to the bully, however provocative the messages may be. You should block the bullies so that they can no longer send you messages. Bullies want to see that they are hurting you, so if you do not react, they may lose interest. Furthermore, make sure you take screenshots of the messages or images that you are sent. It is important that you have evidence, particularly if the situation does not improve or gets worse. There are professional organizations that can help you if you are not sure what to do. In some cases, it might even be necessary to call the police.

! Hier findest du Hilfe, falls du selbst von Cybermobbing betroffen bist:
Die „Nummer gegen Kummer“, ein kostenloses und anonymes Kinder- und Jugendtelefon, erreichst du unter der Telefonnummer 116111 (www.nummergegenkummer.de).

2 Diff and train

D11 Training: Listening/Speaking

L 1/12 | S 6 ▶ After A4c | p. 42

a) Explain the difference between bullying and cyberbullying. Listen to the first part of the podcast and check your answer.

b) Listen to the second part of the podcast. Explain why cyberbullying is so dangerous.

c) Listen to the third part of the podcast. Note down the suggestions which are mentioned in the podcast.

1 Treat the bully the way they treat you.
2 Talk to a friend, family member or teacher.
3 Contact a professional.
4 Block the bully.
5 Check your privacy settings.
6 Delete all your social media accounts.
7 Collect evidence so you can report the bully.

d) Ella says that some countries have passed laws against cyberbullying. How would you answer her questions to the listeners?
"Do you think that laws can stop cyberbullying?"
"What do you think the laws should say?"

Media
You can also record your answers as voice messages.
▶ WB Media 7 ▶ WES-149226-2

D12 Training: Speaking

▶ Before A5 | p. 42 ▶ Speaking | p. 205

Look at the phrases for expressing your opinion. Use them to react to the statements (1-4). Explain your opinion.

It may be true that ..., however, ... • It seems to me that ... • I have to admit that ..., but ... • In my opinion/view, ... • As I see it, ... • I'm against/for ... • As far as I'm concerned, ... • As far as I know, ... • I agree that ... • I have to disagree because ... • Frankly, I don't believe ... • It just isn't true that ... • In contrast to what they say, ... • I see their point but ... • To be honest, I don't think ... • Even if what they say is true, that doesn't mean that ...

1 Social media is completely useless.

2 You should never post pictures online because it is dangerous.

3 Only adults should be allowed to use social media.

4 Social media makes life a lot easier.

D13 Training: Modal verbs and their substitute forms (revision)

▶ After A6b | p. 43 ▶ G6R | p. 225

Write six rules about how to behave online.
Use different modal verbs or their substitute forms such as *should, can, must, may, might, be allowed to, ...*

Example: *You should not post anything that others might find offensive.*

Theme 2: Part B

D14 Training: Reading ▶ After B3a | p. 46

Read the definitions and find the correct words from the extract on pages 46/47.

1 something you wear to be able to see better
2 to move something suddenly, e.g. your head
3 someone who has a position of power in a school
4 a small animal with fur[1] and wings[2]
5 scary
6 to go out with each other

1 fur – *Fell, Pelz*
2 wing – *Flügel*

D15 Easy alternative: Reading ▶ Instead of B3b | p. 47 ▶ Reading | p. 203

Put the sentences in chronological order. Write down the numbers.

1 Adam lives with his mother and his stepdad.
2 Adam sees bats during chemistry class and starts screaming and falls to the floor.
3 His friends stop calling after the incident at school.
4 Adam can't stop squinting so he gets glasses.
5 His best friend Todd disappears completely.
6 The principal calls Adam's mother.
7 His stepdad doesn't know what to do with Adam anymore – he is suddenly afraid of him.
8 Adam can see better with the glasses but realizes that he sees things other people don't.
9 Adam stops wearing his glasses (and tells his mother he has lost them).
10 Adam has to tell his mother about the things he sees.

D16 Support: Speaking ▶ Before B4a | p. 47

Match the English and German sentences. There are more German sentences than you need.

1 I can understand Adam's decision because …
2 It seems to me that Adam is …
3 My personal view is that one should …
4 I must admit that …
5 If I were Adam, I would/wouldn't tell my new friends about the illness (either) because …
6 I have mixed opinions about this. On the one hand, … On the other hand, …
7 In my experience, it's always better to …
8 I'm sorry, but I have no opinion on this issue.

A Ich kann Adams Verhalten wirklich (nicht) nachvollziehen.
B Wenn ich Adam wäre, würde ich meinen neuen Freunden (auch nicht) von der Erkrankung erzählen, weil …
C Meine persönliche Meinung ist, dass man … sollte.
D Ich verstehe Adams Entscheidung, weil …
E Meiner Erfahrung nach ist es immer besser, …
F Es tut mir leid, aber ich habe keine Meinung zu diesem Thema.
G Es scheint mir, dass Adam …
H Ich muss zugeben, dass …
I Das ist eine wirklich schwierige Frage, weil …
J Ich bin unschlüssig bei diesem Thema. Einerseits … Andererseits …

D17 Support: Speaking

▶ Before B6 | p. 48 ▶ Wordbank 5 | p. 240

a) What is the function of a film trailer? Write down your ideas, then talk to a partner and agree on a list of criteria for a good film trailer.
b) Go online and watch the English trailer for *Shazam*.
c) Decide if the trailer meets your criteria from a).

D18 Training: Analysing films (field size)

▶ Before B7 | p. 48

The field size describes the distance between the camera and the object. Each type of camera shot gives the viewer different information about the plot and the characters.

Read the definitions of different field sizes and match them to the film stills.

1 Long shot:
gives a view of the setting, putting the action taking place in context

2 Medium long shot:
shows a person or people in interaction with their surroundings

3 Full shot:
shows a character's entire body, e.g. to show action or two or more characters together

4 Medium shot:
shows a person down to their waist. It is often used to make the audience feel included in the scene.

5 Close-up:
draws the viewer's attention to a person or a thing. It is often used to show emotions or to draw attention to something.

6 Extreme close-up:
focuses on a detail. It often creates suspense or a feeling of disorientation.

A

B

C

D

E
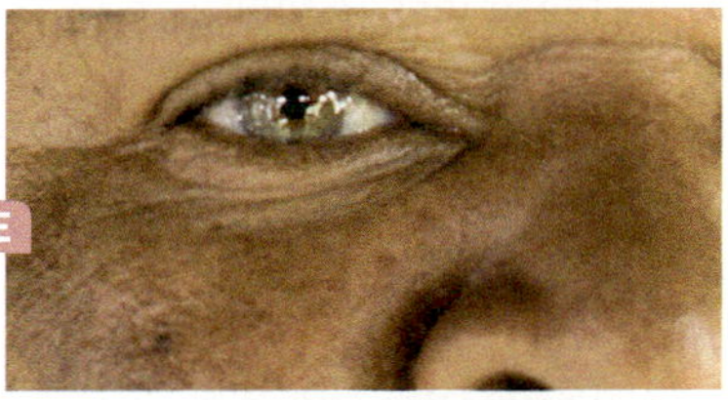

F

D19 Easy alternative: Working with film stills

▶ Instead of B7b | p. 48

Study the film still. Identify what you can find out about ...

- the setting,
- the atmosphere,
- the camerawork and
- the overall effect.

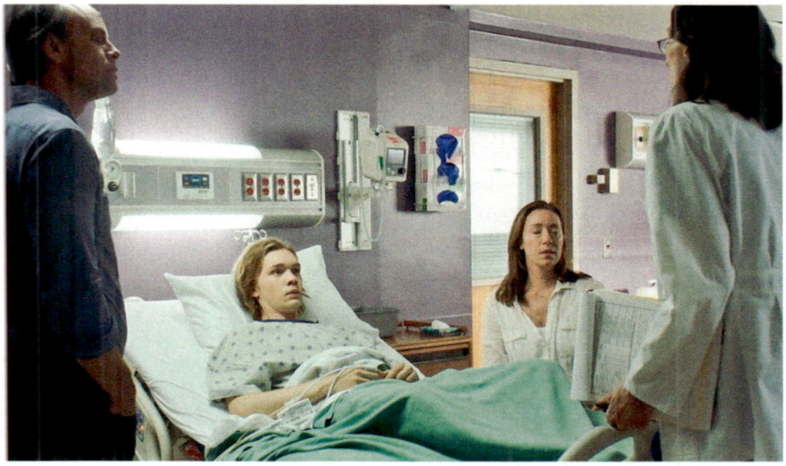

1. Describing the setting

- Use the present progressive to describe what the characters are doing.
  Example: *In the film still Adam is lying ... His mother and a doctor ... Adam and his mother are looking at ...*

- Use the simple present to describe the situation.
  - Where are Adam and his mother?
  - How might they feel in this moment?

This scene shows ... • Adam seems to be in a ... • The scene is situated/set in ... • He doesn't look injured so/but ... • He looks calm and/but ... • His mother seems to be ...

2. Describing the atmosphere

- Use the simple present to describe the atmosphere.
  - What main colours are used in this scene?
  - Which kind of light is used (bright/dark/muted)?
  - What is the effect?

When you look at the colours in this scene, you notice that ...
Because of the colours, the hospital room seems to be ...
The light in this scene is ...
The colours and the light used in this scene create an atmosphere that is ...

3. Describing the camerawork

- Use the simple present to describe the field size used in the scene and its effect.
- Check your results from D18 for help.

The fields size used in this scene is a ...
It gives a view of ...
I think it was used to show ...

4. Describing the overall impression

- Use the simple present to explain which overall impression is created in the still.
  - What information does the scene give?
  - Which emotion(s) does the scene convey?

In this scene, the viewer seems to learn about ...
The atmosphere in the scene is ...
The scene conveys a feeling of ...
For me, the scene feels ...
Due to the ..., the scene makes the viewer feel ...

D20 Extra: Working with film stills ▶ After B7 | p. 48

Work in groups (4). Study the film still closely, then use your imagination: what might have happened before? What might happen afterwards?

- Student A collects ideas about what might have happened the day before, student B about what might have happened five minutes before, student C about what might happen five minutes later, student D about what might happen the day after.
- Note down your ideas about what is happening in your timeslot and draw a sketch. Share your ideas.
- Together come up with a story and tell it to your classmates by showing them your sketches and the film still in chronological order.

D21 Training: Words ▶ After B8 | p. 48

Complete this short film review using the words in the box.

actress • audience • camerawork • cast • character • cinemagoers • director • plot • special effects

Many **1** have been enjoying the fantastic romantic comedy *Emma*, based on the famous novel by Jane Austen. The **2** centres around the beautiful and wealthy Emma Woodhouse, a young woman primarily interested in matchmaking who eventually finds true love. The **3** Anya Taylor-Joy plays the part brilliantly and, on the whole, the **4** was chosen well. I particularly enjoyed the way Johnny Flynn plays the **5** of George Knightley, the man Emma eventually falls in love with. The **6** , Autumn de Wilde, has succeeded in making an entertaining film, despite the fact that the story is not new and has been told many times. The **7** is skilful, and de Wilde does not need any computerized **8** to keep the **9** glued to the screen.

D22 Training: Mediation ▶ After B8 | p. 48 ▶ Mediation | p. 213

Your English friend is coming to Germany. You would like to watch the film *Catherine Called Birdy* with them having read this film review. Give your friend the main information about the film and tell them what this critic says about it.

www.filmkritiken_aktuell.de/aktuelle_filme-originale/XvbK/v00cT_N/b

Unbedingt ansehen: *Catherine, Lady wider Willen*

Catherine, Lady wider Willen (im Original *Catherine Called Birdy*) ist eine Komödie von Lena Dunham aus dem Jahr 2022 mit Bella Ramsey, Billie Piper und Andrew Scott. Der Film basiert auf dem gleichnamigen Roman von Karen Cushman. Er spielt im 13. Jahrhundert und erzählt die Geschichte eines 14-jährigen Mädchens namens Catherine, genannt Birdy. Birdy wohnt in einem Herrenhaus mit ihren Eltern und ihrem Bruder Robert. Ihr Vater will durchsetzen, dass sie baldmöglichst einen reichen Mann heiratet, um seine Finanzprobleme zu lösen. Allerdings ist Birdy sehr willensstark und möchte sich für keinen der interessierten Männer entscheiden. Der Film zeigt, wie sie dafür kämpft, ihre Freiheit zu bewahren. Obwohl der Film im Mittelalter spielt, greift er Themen wie Freiheit und Selbstbestimmung auf, die auch für heutige Teenager höchst relevant sind. Er überzeugt durch die humorvolle, aber trotzdem sensible Darstellung dieser Themen, ebenso wie durch die authentisch wirkende mittelalterliche Filmkulisse und die tolle Besetzung. ♥♥♥♥♥

D23 Training: Word formation ▶ After B8 | p. 48

In English, as in German, new words can be formed by adding suffixes.
For example, adding *-tic* to the noun *drama* forms the adjective *dramatic*.

a) Form new words by adding suffixes from the box.
You can use a dictionary for help.

-er • -tion • -ful • -ly/-ally

1 to broadcast → (noun)
2 sharp → (adverb)
3 to introduce → (noun)
4 dramatic → (adverb)
5 insight → (adjective)

b) Complete the text by adding the new words from a).

Dennis ran into the church shouting, "Stop the wedding!" He paused **1** .
"What the hell are you doing?" the vicar asked **2** .
– "But Vicar, she's already married!"

This is a typical scene from *EastEnders*, a programme that needs no **3** to the British public. Millions of Brits watch *EastEnders* four times a week on the BBC, Britain's biggest **4** . The plot is as **5** as it is dramatic, dealing with issues as diverse as divorce, drugs and racism.

D24 Training: Participles in place of relative clauses ▶ After B9 | p. 49 ▶ G7 | p. 227

Rewrite these sentences using a present or past participle to replace the relative clause.

Examples: I love watching the films which are shown at our local cinema.
→ *I love watching the films shown at our local cinema.*

I've been there so often that the guy who sells the tickets has become a friend of mine.
→ *I've been there so often that the guy selling the tickets has become a friend of mine.*

1 The popcorn which is sold at our cinema is also really good.
2 I try to read the film reviews which are published online before I go and watch a film.
3 The film which stars Bella Ramsey is called *Catherine Called Birdy*.
4 The actors who earn the most money live in Hollywood.
5 The film which is playing right now is really popular.

D25 Training: Participles in place of adverbial clauses

▶ After B9 | p. 49 ▶ G7 | p. 228

a) Rewrite these sentences using a present participle to replace the highlighted parts.

Example: Muhammad opened the door quietly because he knew that the baby was sleeping.
→ *Knowing that the baby was sleeping, Muhammad opened the door quietly.*

1 As Ava believed she was the only one in the house, she sang loudly in the shower.
2 Esme found her gloves while she was looking for her phone.
3 Harry began to cry when he heard the news.
4 As Ann thought that it was Monday, she started getting ready for school.

b) Rewrite these sentences using a perfect participle to replace the highlighted parts.

Example: After Lily said goodbye to her friend, she went back into the house.
→ *Having said goodbye to her friend, Lily went back into the house.*

1 After we finished eating, we washed up.
2 Now that I have spoken to my family, I feel better.
3 We were annoyed that the others were late because we had arrived early.
4 Ethan is excited about his trip to Asia because he has never left Europe before.

c) Rewrite these sentences using a present or perfect participle to replace the highlighted parts.

1 After he had visited the doctor, Adam was given glasses.
2 When Adam looked up during chemistry class, he saw bats.
3 After Adam had gone to hospital, he found out he had schizophrenia.
4 Adam's friends stopped calling because they found out about his illness.
5 When he was sitting next to him on the sofa, Adam could feel that his stepdad was afraid of him.
6 Adam needed a high school diploma because he wanted to become a chef.

D26 Training: Using participles to join two sentences

▶ After B9 | p. 49 ▶ G7 | p. 228

Rewrite the text by replacing the highlighted expressions with participle constructions.

The comedy *Catherine Called Birdy* was released in 2022. The film tells the story of Catherine, a 14-year-old Lady who lives in England in the 13th century.
1 Catherine is the youngest daughter of a rich family. She lives in a large house with her parents, brother and servants.
2 Catherine's father wants to solve his financial problems. He tries to marry her off to a rich husband.
3 Catherine is told to accept her role as a woman. She decides to fight for her freedom.
4 Catherine is faced with a number of possible husbands. She manages to scare them off in creative and funny ways.
5 The film brings up serious questions about women's rights. It is relevant to today's society.
6 The main characters are played by good actors. They are convincing and funny to watch.

Example: *1 Being the youngest daughter of a rich family, Catherine lives in a large house with her parents, brother and servants.*

D27 Training: Present participles after verbs of rest and motion ▶ After B9 | p. 49 ▶ G7 | p. 229

Rewrite the text using the present participle.

Example: *1 All day at school, I sat thinking about the film we were going to watch in the evening.*

Last night, my brother and I had a huge fight.
We were going to watch my favourite film together and I was really looking forward to it.
All day at school I **1** (sit/think) about the film we were going to watch in the evening.
I **2** (walk home/smile) because I was so excited.
But when I **3** (arrive/shout) hello, he was sitting listening to music and didn't even look up.
So rude of him!
To make things worse, my parents were standing there talking to each other and wouldn't leave the room, even though I asked them to.
After half an hour, we finally started watching the film. But you'll never guess what: then my sister **4** (come/run) into the living room, saying she wanted to watch a show on TV.
And my brother said that was OK!
After all that, we didn't even get to finish watching the film!
I couldn't believe it. I was really annoyed and we started arguing.
In the end, I **5** (leave the room/shout) that I would never watch a film with my brother again.
I **6** (run) to my room (cry) and went straight to bed.
I lay in bed, wishing that my family were not so annoying. What a night!

D28 Training: Present participles after verbs of perception ▶ After B9 | p. 49 ▶ G7 | p. 229

Complete the sentences using the present participle.

Example: *1 They could feel the wind blowing on their faces.*

In many US high schools there are health education classes in which students are taught how to manage stress and stressful situations. Some of the techniques are quite easy to learn.

For example, when feeling overwhelmed, students should try to focus on the present moment. They could for instance **1** (feel the wind/blow) on their faces or **2** (notice the smells/surround) them. It can also help to **3** (listen to the sounds/come and go).
Another technique is to imagine being in a place you really like, for instance on your favourite beach. Just imagine you can **4** (see the waves/roll) in and **5** (hear the seagulls/call). It can be relaxing to **6** (watch the ships/go by).
When students **7** (feel themselves/get stressed), they can use techniques such as these. Many students report that they **8** (notice their friends/calm down) when they use these techniques.

3 Diff and train

Theme 3: Intro

D1 Training: Viewing

▶ After Intro 5 | p. 67 ▶ Viewing | p. 212

Watch the video clip again. Answer the questions.

1 Name the person who taught Malala the importance of social justice and education.
2 After the TTP invaded, what were women not allowed to do?
3 What did the BBC do after Malala's first speech?
4 Where did Malala go after she was shot?
5 Who had a right to education after the bill[1] was changed in Pakistan?
6 With support from the *Malala Fund*, what did Malala do for refugees in Lebanon?

1 bill – *Gesetzentwurf*

D2 Training: Reading

▶ Before Intro 6a | p. 67

Read the texts about the two young activists. Then answer the questions about each of them.

1 Who are they and where are they from?
2 Why did they choose to be activists?
3 What do they do?
4 What have they achieved so far?

If you are not sure what a word means, the following tips can help you:
- Are there similar words in German or another language?
- Do you already know parts of the word or similar words?

If necessary, you can use a dictionary.

A

Thandiwe Abdullah is a *Black Lives Matter* activist from Los Angeles, USA. At the age of 15, she became the co-founder of the *Black Lives Matter Los Angeles Youth Vanguard* and helped to launch the *Black Lives Matter in Schools* campaign. One of her most important achievements so far has been winning the *Youth Vanguard* campaign to remove random police searches in schools. She is now working to remove police from school grounds completely. Abdullah comes from a family of activists and went to rallies and protests from a very young age with her mother, who is the co-founder of *Black Lives Matter Los Angeles*. Abdullah noticed that only few children were present at the protest events she attended. This is what inspired her to create a *Black Lives Matter* movement specifically for young people: she hopes to empower black youth to believe that they can create change. As part of her work with the *Youth Vanguard*, Abdullah has also successfully campaigned for more money to be given to schools in financial difficulties. She was also involved in *March for Our Lives*, a campaign for gun control.

B

Xiuhtezcatl ("X") Roske-Martinez is a climate activist and hip hop artist who lives in Colorado, USA. His father is from the Mashika people, one of the Indigenous populations in Mexico, and Indigenous traditions and experiences are an important background to Martinez' activism. Martinez argues that Indigenous people are disproportionally affected by the climate crisis and links the fight for climate action to wider issues of cultural oppression and inequality. His father raised him and his siblings according to the Mashika belief that all parts of the natural world are connected. This is an important reason why he feels so strongly about protecting the environment. Martinez has given TED talks and spoken several times about climate change at the United Nations, for example at the UN General Assembly at Rio+20, the UN summit in Rio de Janeiro. He is also the former Youth Director of Earth Guardians, an environmental activist organization. Furthermore, he and a group of other young people filed a lawsuit (Juliana v. United States) against the US government in 2015 for failing to act on climate change. As a musician, Martinez has released hip hop tracks about climate change, for example "Speak for the Trees", to raise awareness among young people about environmental issues.

D3 **Extra: Working with advertisements** ▶ After Intro 6 | p. 67

a) Study the advertisement and describe it.

> *The advertisement shows ... •*
> *At the bottom ... •*
> *In the foreground/background you can see ... •*
> *In the middle of the advert, ... can be seen. •*
> *The central focus is ...*

b) Say what the message is.

c) Say whether you consider the advertisement effective. Give reasons.

Theme 3: Part A

D4 **Training: Stylistic devices** ▶ After A2b | p. 69

Copy the grid. Match the examples (A-E) and functions (1-5) to the stylistic devices.

A Another day, another shooting: Man kills seven people in shopping mall
B Why don't we protect our kids? School shooting in Missouri leaves people in shock
C Our children learn to shoot before they learn how to walk
D Fatal fight on a farm in Florida: Woman fires at her own sister
E "Our hearts are broken": Community gathers after shooting in local gym

stylistic device	example	function
exaggeration	*C*	*3*
quote		
rhetorical question		
anaphora		
alliteration		

1 to make the reader think
2 to emphasize the beginning of a sentence/clause and make it easier to remember
3 to emphasize something by making it seem (even) more important or serious than it really is
4 to add rhythm to a sentence or clause
5 to make a headline more believable

D5 Extra: Analysing cartoons ▶ After A4 | p. 70 ▶ Wordbank 3 | p. 239

Analyse the cartoon.

You can use a dictionary for help.

1. Identify the topic of the cartoon.
   The cartoon deals with the issue/topic of …
2. Describe the situation.
   The cartoon shows a man who …
   His face looks …
   In the background, you can see …
   On one wall/On the other wall, there are …
   In the foreground, there is …
3. Explain the message of the cartoon.
   You might conclude that the message of the cartoon is that …
4. Give your opinion on the cartoon.
   If you ask me, the cartoon is quite/not/… funny/ thought-provoking/… because …
   I (don't) like the cartoon, especially …

D6 Easy alternative: Reading ▶ Instead of A5 | p. 70 ▶ Reading | p. 203

Read the culture box. Then choose the correct answers.

The Second Amendment and "Stand-your-ground" laws

Culture box

The Second Amendment to the United States Constitution gives American citizens the right to keep and bear arms. This means that people can own and use weapons such as guns to protect themselves. There is, however, a lot of conflict surrounding the Second Amendment. Many Americans demand stricter gun laws, for example better background checks on people who wish to buy weapons.
In contrast, the National Rifle Association (NRA) is a strong supporter of gun rights.
Influenced by groups such as the NRA, many US states have passed "Stand-your-ground" laws, which allow people who believe their life to be in danger to use any means of self-defence, even if that involves gun-related violence such as shooting or killing another person. Before the first "Stand-your-ground" law was passed in Florida in 2005, people were obliged to try to retreat from confrontation before responding by using a gun, for example. Evidence shows that "Stand-your-ground" laws do not prevent crime but are in fact connected to a rise in firearm homicides, which makes these laws highly controversial.

1. The Second Amendment gives US citizens the right to keep and bear arms, …
   - **A** which means they are only allowed to keep their weapons safely at home.
   - **B** which means they can own and use weapons to protect themselves.
   - **C** which means they can own weapons, but only use them for sport.
2. "Stand-your-ground" laws give people the right …
   - **A** to use any means of self-defence if they feel in danger.
   - **B** to use weapons in all conflicts with their neighbours.
   - **C** to use knives, but not guns to defend themselves.
3. The "Stand-your-ground" laws are controversial because …
   - **A** many people are afraid to use weapons to defend themselves.
   - **B** even more people than before have been shot dead since the laws were introduced.
   - **C** they do not allow citizens to use weapons to defend themselves.

D7 Training: Listening

L 1/13 | S 7 ▶ After A6 | p. 70 ▶ Listening | p. 202

Listen and match the correct sentence halves. There are two more endings than you need.

1 Shooting on ranges and hunting are
2 US gun culture is
3 The first European settlers who had weapons were
4 After the foundation of the USA, a list of basic rights was
5 It is not rare for children in the US
6 There hasn't been a fundamental gun law reform so far

A better able to survive.
B because many politicians always vote against new gun laws.
C when children find guns belonging to their parents.
D popular free-time activities in the US.
E drawn up for all citizens.
F to be taught how to shoot from an early age.
G deeply rooted in the country's history.
H they don't want to turn against the NRA.

D8 Training: Personal passive

▶ After A6b | p. 70 ▶ G2R | p. 220

Look at sentences 1-6, then rewrite them in the passive so that the indirect object is the subject. You can use the support box to help you.

There are some verbs in English that have two objects: a direct object and an indirect object, often a person. When these verbs are used in the passive, the indirect object usually becomes the subject of the sentence.

Active sentence:	The teacher *subject*	gave	**the students** *indirect object*	the books. *direct object*
Passive sentence:	**The students** *subject*	were given	the books. *direct object*	

1 The US constitution gave Americans the right to own guns after the War of Independence.
2 Even today, many parents teach their children a lot about how to use guns.
3 Some parents don't tell their children the truth about the dangers of guns.
4 President Joe Biden gave members of Congress his approval[1] for the introduction of stricter gun laws.
5 American citizens send the government a clear message in protests for stricter gun laws.
6 On the other hand, large numbers of the population show the NRA their support.

1 approval – *Zustimmung*

D9 Training: Defining and non-defining relative clauses (revision) ▶ After A7 | p. 71 ▶ G8R | p. 230

Complete the sentences using *which*, *that* or *who*. Add commas where necessary.

Example: There is a lot of controversy around the Second Amendment / **XXX** gives American citizens the right to bear arms.
→ *There is a lot of controversy around the Second Amendment, which gives American citizens the right to bear arms.*

> Check G8R on page 230 if you are unsure when to use commas.

1 The Second Amendment / **XXX** was introduced at the end of the 18th century / was based on an English law.
2 In the US, people can own weapons / **XXX** they use to protect themselves.
3 Many people / **XXX** demand stricter gun laws / support having background checks.
4 Changes / **XXX** supporters of stricter gun laws demand / include more limits on where people are allowed to carry guns.
5 The National Rifle Association / **XXX** is a strong supporter of gun rights / claims to have more than 5 million members.
6 In many US states, people / **XXX** believe their lives to be in danger / are legally allowed to use any means of self-defence.

D10 Training: Contact clauses (revision) ▶ After A7 | p. 71 ▶ G8R | p. 230

Read about Amelia's summer holidays. Rewrite the sentences that can be turned into contact clauses by leaving out the relative pronoun.

"Augusta in Maine was the place **1 that** my parents chose for our summer vacation last year. The journey there was very uncomfortable, as I was squashed between my little brother and sister in the back of the car, **2 which** also had all our luggage in it. To make things worse, my parents said that the house **3 that** they had rented only had two bedrooms, so my brother, sister and I would have to share. When we arrived, we were surprised to see that the driveway **4 that** belonged to the house already had a car on it. The people **5 who** owned the car were unpacking their luggage. My mum immediately phoned the travel agency **6 that** we had used to organize our holiday. The agent **7 who** she spoke to apologized and said that the house **8 that** the travel agency had found for us had accidentally been double-booked. The agent said she would give us our money back and offered to find a hotel **9 that** we could stay in instead. An hour later, we were all happy and settled into the hotel, **10 which** was very luxurious. And best of all – I had my own room!"

D11 Training: Relative clauses referring to a sentence

▶ After A7 | p. 71 ▶ G8R | p. 230

Combine the two sentences. The second sentence should be a relative clause referring to the first sentence. Look at the examples in the box to help you.

> Relative clauses with *which* can be used to comment on what has just been said.
> Examples: *Theo won't make it to the party, which is very sad.*
>
> *My cousin is getting married, which I find very exciting.*

1 Harper has decided to move to L.A. That was a big surprise for her parents.
2 When we finally got to the beach, it started to rain. We hadn't expected that.
3 The film we saw yesterday was extremely boring. That surprised me because I had found the trailer quite entertaining.
4 My friend is going to see the Grand Canyon during her holiday. This makes me very jealous.
5 Leo's little brother kept interrupting us while we were preparing for the exam. That was extremely annoying.
6 After the concert, Mason managed to go backstage and talk to the band. That was an unforgettable experience for him.
7 Olivia's parents spent $6,000 on a holiday trip to Florida. She cannot understand that.
8 Carl's friends came to visit him in hospital. He thought that was very nice.

D12 Extra: Mediation

▶ After A8 | p. 72 ▶ Mediation | p. 213

Your younger brother has heard of Amanda Gorman and wants to find out more about her. Read the article and answer his questions in German.

1 Wer ist Amanda Gorman und was macht sie?
2 Wodurch ist sie bekannt geworden?
3 Was steht da über ihr Leben?

Amanda Gorman – America's young lyrical voice

Amanda Gorman is a young American poet and activist. In her work, she addresses important subjects such as feminism, racism and oppression. She is best known for her poem *The Hill We Climb*, which she performed at the inauguration of President Joe Biden. This made her the youngest inaugural poet ever, at the age of 22. Parts of her poem were written on 6th January 2021, the day the Capitol building, the seat of the United States Congress, was stormed by Trump supporters. In light of so much conflict, Gorman states that this poem is a call for unity.

Gorman was raised by her mother, a single parent, in Los Angeles, and loved writing from an early age. She attended Harvard University, where she studied sociology. Since then, Gorman has gone on to become the first ever national youth poet laureate and has received praise from many other institutions.

3 Diff and train

D 13 Easy alternative: Viewing ▶ **Instead of A9a** | p. 72 ▶ Viewing | p. 212

Watch the video clip, then match the sentence parts.

1 Once a lockdown order has been issued,
2 When the teacher tells the class that there is a lockdown,
3 The students are reminded to stay quiet and
4 To make sure that all students at school are safe,
5 Before joining the students in the safe corner,
6 The teachers checks if all the students are in the classroom and
7 Students who are in a common area during a lockdown
8 Students who are outside during a lockdown

A all students should make their way to a safe corner in the classroom.
B to stay out of sight during the lockdown.
C reports missing students to the main office.
D the teacher repeats the lockdown order to the class.
E should go to the next classroom.
F the teacher locks the door, turns off the light and covers the windows.
G should stay outside.
H the teachers check the hallways and toilets.

Theme 3: Part B

D 14 Training: Reported speech (revision) ▶ **After B2a** | p. 74 ▶ G3R | p. 221

Use reported speech to tell a friend what some of the students and teachers in the school cafeteria said or asked.

Example: Esme: "There is going to be a science contest tomorrow."
→ *Esme said that there was going to be a science contest the next day.*

1 Mr Perez: "Zoe, stop running in the cafeteria."
2 Jamal: "I have an interview for a job at the library at 3 o'clock this afternoon."
3 Alice: "The cheerleading team is going on a trip to Daytona next week."
4 Hakan: "I can't find my calculator."
5 Amira: "I'm sure we'll win the basketball game."
6 Jenna: "Emily, have you prepared for the history test yet?" – Emily: "No, I haven't. I had choir practice yesterday."
7 Mrs Delgado: "What is on the menu today?"

D 15 Support: Narrative perspective ▶ Before B2c | p. 75

A story can be told from different narrative perspectives. What can you say about first-person and third-person narrators? Write down twelve sentences.

A A first-person narrator ...
B A third-person narrator ...

tells a story from their own perspective • *only knows about their own thoughts and feelings, and what others have told them* • *tells the story from an outside perspective* • *is directly involved in the plot* • *often knows details that the protagonists cannot know* • *has a limited and subjective perspective* • *is not directly involved in the plot* • *uses pronouns like* I, me *and* mine • *often has a more objective perspective* • *makes the reader feel (more) connected to the story* • *uses pronouns like* he, she, it *and* they • *makes the reader feel less connected to the story*

D 16 Training: Words ▶ After B4 | p. 77

Complete the sentences with the phrasal verbs from the box. Use the simple past.

clean up • *end up* • *find out* • *get on* • *get up* • *give up* • *hang out* • *look for* • *look out for* • *move out*

Look up the meaning of a phrasal verb in a dictionary if necessary.

My brother Ben and I **1** really well when we were kids. Ben is three years older than me and really **2** me when I was younger. We grew up with our father, who **3** very early every morning to go to work. Ben always made sure I was ready for school in the mornings and waited for me after school so that we could walk home together. I **4** with him and his friends most of the time and shared his favourite hobby, playing basketball.

All of this changed when my father lost his job. Ben wanted to help him and **5** a job to earn some money for our family. He **6** playing basketball and spent less time at home. Whenever Ben was at home, there were arguments because Ben never **7** the bathroom after using it. Ben just told Dad to calm down, which made Dad even angrier. They had a massive fight when Dad **8** that he had stopped going to school. In the end, Ben **9** and found a new flat. It makes me really sad that I hardly ever see him now. I don't understand how we **10** like this.

D17 Training: Reading

▶ After B4c | p. 77 ▶ Reading | p. 203

Read the statements about extract 3 on pages 76/77 and decide if they are true or false. Give evidence from the text. Correct the false statements.

1 Lisa, the lunch lady, offers Dan an extra helping of food because she knows he has very little money and is often hungry.
2 Dan is very embarrassed when Lisa explains why not everyone gets an extra portion.
3 Dan's friends go silent when he comes to their table because they are planning a surprise for him.
4 Dan's friends are planning to go to quite an expensive place, Wally's Wowza-Burger, but he says this is not a problem because he has saved some money.
5 Dan feels embarrassed because he thinks his girlfriend Talia makes it obvious to all their friends that she will pay for him.
6 Dan is happy that he has such an understanding girlfriend.
7 After these two incidents Dan feels furious and embarrassed at the same time.
8 When the boy stops Dan to ask him to sign up for the protest march, the boy says, "You live in Dignityville, how can you not sign up?", which makes Dan very angry.
9 Dan attacks the boy in a very violent way.
10 Dan finally lets go when his girlfriend pulls him away from the boy.

D18 Training: Words

▶ After B4c | p. 77

Skim extract 3 on pages 76/77 again and find verbs that match the definitions.

1 to look at someone with an angry and/or annoyed expression
2 to feel a negative emotion which becomes stronger
3 to become so angry that you suddenly cannot control your feelings any more
4 to make sb feel embarrassed
5 to pull somebody/something quickly and violently
6 to close or hold something tightly, often in anger
7 to breathe in quickly through your mouth when you are shocked or surprised
8 to say something quietly but angrily

Theme 4: Intro

D1 Easy alternative: Words ▶ Instead of Intro 1 | p. 92

a) Look at the photos and match them with the jobs. There are more jobs than photos.

babysitter • cleaner • gardener • lifeguard • newspaper deliverer • office help • pizza delivery person • receptionist • shop assistant • tour guide • tutor • waiter/waitress

1

2

3

4

5

6

b) Note down more jobs for teenagers. You can use an online dictionary for help.

D2 Training: Reading ▶ After Intro 2 | p. 92

Read the texts on page 93 again and complete the sentences.

1. "Flipping" means that you find free or cheap stuff and then ...
2. To get into flipping, you should be crafty, creative and ...
3. Not only can you make money and improve your DIY skills, but you also get to ...
4. Giving tech support to elderly people means that you help ...
5. To assist seniors with their devices, you should be patient, friendly and be able to ...
6. Being trustworthy and discreet is also very important because ...
7. As a team mascot you have to go to all the games and ...
8. Being a team mascot is a difficult job and you need to be ...
9. Matt gets to watch every game of his team and ...

D3 Training: Reported questions (revision)

▶ After Intro 2 | p. 92 ▶ G9 | p. 231

Use reported speech to tell a friend what you asked Emma about her job. Use different verbs to report your questions.

ask • inquire • want to know • wonder

> **!** To report a question without a question word, you can use *if* or *whether.*

Example: Emma, do you enjoy working with elderly people?
→ *I asked Emma if she enjoyed working with elderly people.*

1 How much money do you earn?
2 Do you like the other people you work with?
3 Who told you about the job?
4 What do you find most challenging?
5 Are there any special qualifications you need?
6 Would you recommend working for the company?
7 Do you have to work at weekends?
8 Are there more men or women among your customers?
9 How old is your oldest customer?

D4 Easy alternative: Listening

L 1/14 | S 8 ▶ Instead of Intro 4a | p. 92 ▶ Listening | p. 202

Listen to a radio programme about the worst summer jobs ever.
Choose the correct sentence parts.

1 Mary worked ...
A at a chocolate factory and had to put the chocolate into boxes.
B at a jam factory and had to put jam jars into boxes.
C on a strawberry farm and had to pick fruit.

2 The worst thing Mary had to do was ...
A put jam into jam jars.
B eat strawberry jam every day.
C shovel jam after a pipe burst.

3 Dustin worked ...
A as a pizza baker.
B as a waiter in a pizzeria.
C as a pizza delivery boy.

4 The worst thing about Dustin's job was that ...
A the customers were often unfriendly and one time he had an accident with his bike.
B he had to climb many stairs to a customer's apartment and one day his bike was stolen.
C a customer shouted at him and one day somebody stole his bike.

5 Megan worked ...
A in a fishing shop.
B at a fish factory.
C at a fish restaurant.

6 The worst thing about Megan's job was that ...
A it was cold in the shop.
B she had to sell fishing equipment.
C she had to touch worms and fish.

7 Patrick worked as a ...
A gardener.
B tutor.
C babysitter.

8 The worst thing about Patrick's job was that ...
A the children laughed at him.
B the children locked him out.
C the children were noisy.

Theme 4: Part A

D5 Easy alternative: Listening L 1/15 | **S** 9 ▶ **Instead of A1b** | p. 94 ▶ Listening | p. 202

Listen and note down which criteria are mentioned.

A *good work-life balance* • **B** *getting to know new people* • **C** *good job title* • **D** *safety* • **E** *travel* • **F** *having a good relationship with colleagues* • **G** *flexible hours* • **H** *being able to work from home* • **I** *modern workplace* • **J** *earning a lot of money* • **K** *making a difference and helping others* • **L** *career development* • **M** *learning something new* • **N** *doing something good for your local community* • **O** *being challenged* • **P** *workplace close to home*

D6 Training: Viewing ▶ **After A2** | p. 94

Read the questions, then watch the video. Choose the correct answers.

1 Why does the narrator say that Meghan's job doesn't look like a real job at first glance?
- A Because Meghan is paid to share photos about exciting outdoor adventures.
- B Because Meghan is paid to share photos of her beautiful house in Seattle.
- C Because Meghan only has to work one day a week.

2 What kind of products does Meghan promote in her posts?
- A She promotes all kinds of things, like cars, skiing gear or rucksacks.
- B She only promotes specific products like shoes and raincoats.
- C She promotes all kinds of things, like technical gear, snacks or travel destinations.

3 What percentage of her online feed is sponsored?
- A About five percent of her feed is sponsored.
- B About ten percent of her feed is sponsored.
- C About twenty percent of her feed is sponsored.

4 What did Meghan do before she became an influencer?
- A She worked in a shop selling mountaineering tents.
- B She went to law school, studying to become an attorney[1].
- C She stayed at home, looking after her two young children.

5 Why did Meghan start mountaineering again?
- A She went hiking again to look for geocaches.
- B She went hiking again to show her children the beautiful mountains.
- C She went hiking again to deal with the stresses of law school.

6 Why does Meghan put up with[2] the cold weather and often difficult conditions on her hikes?
- A Because she knows she will be paid well for her posts.
- B Because she loves the mountains and feels really happy when she is outdoors.
- C Because she just can't find a job in an office.

1 attorney – *Anwalt/Anwältin* | **2** to put up with – *ertragen*

D7 Training: Future progressive

▶ After A3 | p. 94 ▶ G10 | p. 231

a) Rebecca is a project manager at a company in London. Read what she says and complete each sentence using the future progressive.

Example: At half past seven I **XXX** (get ready) for work. I won't arrive at the office until half past eight.
→ *At half past seven I will be getting ready for work.*

1 Unfortunately, I won't be spending my coffee break with my colleague because she **XXX** (prepare) for a department meeting.
2 At 1 o'clock we **XXX** (not have) lunch in the canteen because we will be in a meeting.
3 I **XXX** (not speak) to any clients in the afternoon, so I will have time to work on my own projects.
4 We need to make sure our new business idea is finished. This time next week, we **XXX** (present) it to our boss.
5 I am normally still at the office at 4 pm, but today I **XXX** (travel) home from work at that time because from 5 pm I **XXX** (look after) my nephew.
6 On Thursday I **XXX** (work) from home, but my colleagues will be at the office.
7 This time next month I **XXX** (attend) a conference, so I **XXX** (not sit) at my desk.

b) Write your own sentences using the future progressive to describe what you will be doing ...
- at 4 pm tomorrow
- on Saturday morning
- this time next month
- soon

D8 Training: Future perfect

▶ After A3 | p. 94 ▶ G10 | p. 231

Complete the sentences using the future perfect.

Example: By the end of my time at school, I ...
→ *By the end of my time at school, I will have chosen my career.*

1 In three years' time, I ...
2 Soon it will be the summer holidays. By then, I ...
3 Ten years from now, I ...
4 By the time I am 18, I ...
5 In six months' time, ...

D9 Easy alternative: Listening

L 1/16 | S 10 ▶ Instead of A4b | p. 94

Copy the grid. Listen again and note down the soft and hard skills that are mentioned.
Tip: There are more skills than you need.

soft skills	hard skills
...	...

being able to drive a car • being creative • being open to new challenges • being well-organized • knowing how to use a computer • knowing how to do experiments • playing an instrument • speaking a foreign language

D10 Extra: Mediation ▶ After A5 | p. 94 ▶ Mediation | p. 213

Your friend from England would like a summer job in Germany. You have found this job advert. Write an email to your friend and let them know what the job is about and how to apply. You can use a dictionary.

www.weingut-trunkl-im-rheingau.de/Aktuelles/Sommerjob-in-einem-

Sommerjob in einem deutschen Weingut

Wolltest du schon immer einmal etwas Neues ausprobieren und dabei eine zauberhafte Region Deutschlands kennenlernen? Dann ist dieser Sommerjob genau das Richtige für dich.

Das Weingut Trunkl im Rheingau sucht eine engagierte junge Person, die sich nicht vor harter Arbeit scheut und sowohl selbstständig als auch im Team arbeiten kann. Zu deinem Job gehört es, unser Haus sauber zu machen, an drei Tagen pro Woche für unsere Gäste und das Team zu kochen, Gartenarbeit zu verrichten und dabei zu helfen, die Flaschen zu reinigen.

Du benötigst keine Vorkenntnisse. Wir bringen dir alles bei, was du für deine Arbeit bei uns wissen musst. Du solltest lediglich zeitlich flexibel und körperlich belastbar sein. Um unser Weingut zu erreichen, benötigst du einen PKW.

Hier die Konditionen:

- Teilzeit und flexible Dauer (Minimum vier Wochen)
- Freie Unterkunft und Verpflegung
- 100 Euro pro Tag

Bewerbungen bitte schriftlich und mit Lebenslauf per E-Mail an:
job@weinguttrunkl-rheingau.de

Hast du Interesse?
Dann bewirb dich bei uns!

D11 Training: Words ▶ After A5 | p. 94

a) Match the verbs on the left to the phrases on the right.

1 to practise for	**A** your reports and certificates
2 to put together	**B** a cover letter
3 to scan	**C** job adverts online
4 to choose	**D** your strengths and weaknesses
5 to become aware of	**E** an application
6 to look at	**F** the company you want to apply to
7 to contact	**G** a job interview
8 to write	**H** a suitable outfit for a job interview

b) Use your results from a) to write tips for a succesful application process.
Example: *Step 1: Look at job adverts online.*
Step 2: Scan your ...

D12 Extra: Mediation ▶ After A7 | p. 96 ▶ Mediation | p. 213

Read the article.

- Describe the experiment carried out by a scientist in 2016.
- Explain what the ADS said about anonymous application procedures in 2012.
- Explain why Ferda Ataman thinks that German companies would benefit from anonymous application procedures in times of labour shortage.

Write down your answers in English.

Die anonymisierte Bewerbung hat einen schweren Stand

Studien zeigen, dass anonymisierte Bewerbungen[1] für fairere Chancen sorgen. Im Ausland ist das Verfahren oft der Standard. Doch in Deutschland gibt es noch immer viele Bedenken.

Berlin – „Wenn Sie Yilmaz heißen, dann müssen Sie in Deutschland deutlich mehr Bewerbungen schreiben als mit dem Namen Schmidt – und das bei exakt gleicher Qualifikation. Studien zeigen das leider immer wieder“, sagt die Antidiskriminierungsbeauftragte des Bundes, Ferda Ataman. Etwa ein Viertel der Diskriminierungserfahrungen im Arbeitsleben würden in der ersten Phase, während der Arbeitssuche und Bewerbung, gemacht.

Ein Experiment erregte 2016 Aufsehen: Eine Wissenschaftlerin verschickt rund 1500 Bewerbungen – mal mit typisch deutschen Namen, mal mit typisch türkischen Namen und verschiedenen Fotos. Mit und ohne Kopftuch. Das Ergebnis: Eine Bewerberin ohne Kopftuch[2] und Migrationshintergrund[3] hatte die besten Chancen auf eine Stelle.

Eine Lösung können anonymisierte Bewerbungen sein, bei denen Personaler zum Beispiel nicht das Alter oder das Geschlecht des Bewerbers kennen. Heute steht zwar pflichttreu in Stellenausschreibungen „m/w/d“ (männlich/weiblich/divers), aber die anonymisierte Bewerbung hat sich in Deutschland nicht durchgesetzt. Anders sieht das im englischsprachigen Raum aus.

Arbeitgeber scheuen den Aufwand

„Die USA und Großbritannien haben schon in den 60ern einzelne Aspekte wie das Foto in Bewerbungen rausgenommen“, sagt Veronika Kneip, Professorin für Human Resource Management und Organisation an der Frankfurt University of Applied Sciences.

Für die schleppende Entwicklung bei diesem Thema in Deutschland gebe es verschiedene Gründe. „Die Arbeitgeber scheuen zum einen den Aufwand, den anonymisierte Verfahren bedeuten“, sagt Kneip.

Für das Verfahren, das Chancengleichheit ermöglichen soll, müssen etwa neue Formulare aufgesetzt oder Angaben geschwärzt werden. Bei Bewerberinnen und Bewerbern sowie Personalverantwortlichen kommt das laut Kneip nicht immer gut an: „Diejenigen, die auswählen, sind auch von ihrer Urteilskraft überzeugt.“ Viele Personaler glaubten, dass sogenannte Biases – unbewusste Vorurteile etwa durch Sozialisation und Erziehung – nicht in ihre Entscheidungen einfließen. Auf der Bewerberseite sei dagegen vieles einfach Gewohnheit. „Und diejenigen, die keine Diskriminierung erfahren haben, wollen unter Umständen mit Dingen wie einem Bewerbungsfoto punkten, über das sie sich selbst positiv inszenieren können“, sagt Kneip.

Die Antidiskriminierungsstelle des Bundes (ADS) testete das Verfahren der anonymisierten Bewerbung vor mehr als zehn Jahren zusammen mit mehreren Unternehmen und Verwaltungen. 2012 stellte die ADS im Abschlussbericht fest: „Bei Anonymisierung herrscht tendenziell Chancengleichheit für alle Bewerbendengruppen“. Der Versuch habe auch gezeigt, dass Frauen im Vergleich zum herkömmlichen Verfahren bessere Chancen auf eine Einladung zu einem Gespräch hätten.

Anonymisierte Bewerbungsverfahren international Standard

Peter Wald, Professor für Personalmanagement an der Hochschule für Technik, Wirtschaft und Kultur Leipzig, hält den Aufwand für die größte Hürde. „Gerade bei den KMU (Kleine und Mittlere Unternehmen) ist Recruiting oft kein professionelles Geschäft. Ein aufwendigeres Verfahren lehnen sie daher ab.“ Der Fachkräftemangel könnte aus seiner Sicht weitere Vorbehalte gegenüber dem Verfahren schüren. „Die Unternehmen glauben möglicherweise, dass sie wegen der Anonymisierung weniger Bewerbungen bekommen“, sagt Wald.

Deutsche Unternehmen setzen auf Freiwilligkeit

„International sind anonymisierte Bewerbungsverfahren eigentlich der Standard, sei es teilweise oder komplett anonymisiert“, sagt die Antidiskriminierungsbeauftragte Ataman. Deutschland hinke diesbezüglich hinterher. Ihrer Ansicht nach könnte das anonymisierte Verfahren für die Arbeitgeber einen „eindeutigen Wettbewerbsvorteil“ schaffen. „In Zeiten des Arbeitskräftemangels senden Unternehmen damit das Signal, offen für alle Gruppen zu sein und diskriminierungsbewusst auszuschreiben.“ […]

1 *anonymisierte Bewerbung* – anonymous job application | **2** *Kopftuch* – headscarf | **3** *Migrationshintergrund* – migrant background

D 13 Training: *let/make sb do sth, have sth done*

▶ After A8 | p. 97 ▶ G11 | p. 232

Last week, Laura was very busy. Complete the sentences with *let/make sb do sth* or *have sth done*. Often there is more than one solution.

1 On Monday, Laura's mother **XXX** her clean her room because it was not tidy.
2 On Tuesday, Laura **XXX** her hair cut.
3 On Wednesday, Laura's father **XXX** her repair her bike because it had been broken for a long time.
4 On Thursday, Laura's parents **XXX** her make the family lunch.
5 On Friday, Laura's brother **XXX** her use his computer to look for jobs.
6 On Saturday, Laura's mother **XXX** her call her grandma because it was her birthday.
7 On Sunday, Laura **XXX** her cover letter proofread by her brother.

D 14 Training: Words

▶ After A9 | p. 97

Copy and complete the sentences by filling in the most suitable words or phrases from the box.

complete tasks • develop emotionally • gain a new perspective on • gain experience • learn and build essential skills • offer a unique opportunity

1 Team sports help young people to **XXX** as well as physically.
2 The ability to **XXX** on time and provide customer support is essential for many jobs.
3 Exchange experience helps young people to **XXX** their understanding of other cultures.
4 By working abroad, young people can **XXX** and learn new skills without feeling like they are at school.
5 Experiencing daily working life is a good way to **XXX** and to discover what kind of work you enjoy.
6 Internships **XXX** to get to know a company.

4 Diff and train

Theme 4: Part B

D15 Support: Giving advice ▶ After B2c | p. 100

Study the different structures you can use to give advice.
Use different phrases to give advice to your partner about whether or not …

1 to buy a new mobile phone.
2 to skip school.
3 to apply for a summer job.
4 to go to the party at the weekend.

Should
This is probably the most common structure for giving advice.
You should …
We shouldn't …

It is common to use "I think …" and "I don't think …" with should:
I think you should/I don't think you should …

If I were you ▶ G5R | p. 224
Conditional clauses, type 2 are often used to give advice, especially in spoken English.
Note the use of *were* with *I* in the first clause.
In the second clause, we use *would* – contracted to *'d* – and *wouldn't*.
If I were you, I'd/I wouldn't …

Had better
This structure is common in spoken English and it is mainly used in the contracted form:
You'd better …

Ought to
This is the most formal structure used for giving advice, and so it isn't very common.
You ought to …/You ought not to …

D16 Training: Answering interview questions ▶ After B2d | p. 100

a) Read these questions from an interview for a fundraising job with a children's charity. Then choose the correct answers to the questions.

1 You're applying for a job in our fundraising team, is that correct?
2 Could you tell me a little bit about your educational background?
3 I'm impressed! Can you tell me about any job experience?
4 Tell me a bit more about your responsibilities at the bookshop.
5 How would these skills contribute to our fundraising team?
6 I see, good point! Just one last question. Why did you apply here? There are many other charities looking for support, too.

A One of my strengths is dealing with people. I usually take the first step and ask if I can help the customers. Besides, I also already have some experience in working with money and figures. This will be an advantage for handling donations responsibly.

B Sure! I've just completed four A levels in English, Maths, History, and French from the Royal Grammar School in Guildford. I got As in English, in Maths and History and a B in French.

C I really like the projects you support. Also, one of my cousins worked for you a few years ago and told me it was a great experience.

D Right now I'm working as an assistant in a local bookshop.

E Yes, that's right! I would very much like to support your fundraising team.

F My job is to help customers find what they are looking for and I also work at the cash desk. I often help with computer-related tasks behind the scenes, for example checking what needs to be ordered and making sure that the shop's database is up to date.

b) Look at the applicant's answers again and note down useful phrases you can use in an interview. You can add them to your list from B2d).

D17 **Training: Conditional clauses, type 3 (revision)** ▶ After B3 | p. 101 ▶ G5R | p. 224

Read the sentences and complete them. Use the correct tenses.

1 I would have applied for a volunteering job in Mexico if ...

2 If I hadn't made so many mistakes in my CV, ...

3 If I had tested my camera before the interview, ...

4 I wouldn't have talked about how much I hated my last boss if ...

5 I wouldn't have fidgeted with my hair so much if ...

6 I could have answered the interviewer's last question if ...

7 If I hadn't made a silly joke at the end of the interview, ...

8 I would have been less stressed if ...

D18 **Support: More phrases for conversations** ▶ After B4 | p. 101

Look at the phrases (1-10). Copy the grid and decide which function these phrases have in a conversation or an interview.

Asking the other person to say more about a certain topic	Introducing a different topic	Presenting yourself as polite and friendly
...	...	...

1 That sounds interesting. Please go on.
2 Can I ask you something about ...?
3 That is very kind of you.
4 Sure, no problem.
5 What I forgot to ask you earlier is: ...?
6 Something else that is very important to me is ...
7 If I have understood you correctly, you mean that ...
8 I didn't know that. Please tell me more.
9 That brings me to another point.
10 You're welcome.

5 Diff and train

Theme 5: Intro

D1 Training: Listening
L 2/1 | S 11 ▶ After Intro 2b | p. 120

Listen to the teenagers and choose the correct sentence endings.

1 Bella's secret tip for seeing art in Leeds is ...
A to book a private tour of a museum.
B to check out one of the many galleries.
C to walk around the city and discover some of the street art.

2 The big mural on the Athena Rising building shows ...
A a flying owl.
B a sleeping owl.
C a dancing owl.

3 Liam's recommendation for Liverpool is ...
A Bond Street.
B Bold Street.
C Bole Street.

4 Many people don't know about ...
A the art workshops in St Luke's Church.
B the two towers of St Luke's Church.
C the cool art installations in St Luke's Church.

5 The silent disco tour in Manchester costs ...
A fifteen pounds for an hour.
B fifty pounds for a day.
C fifteen pounds for two hours.

6 Muhammad wasn't sure about the tour because he ...
A already knows the city.
B thought the music would be bad.
C didn't like the idea of dancing in public with a group of strangers.

7 Olivia goes to John Street Kitchen in Sheffield ...
A for brunch and jazz music.
B for the best burgers and chips.
C for the weekly poetry night.

8 Olivia recommends the poetry night because ...
A there was an amazing jazz band.
B there were teenage poetry slammers.
C she writes her own poetry.

D2 Extra: Reading/Mediation
▶ After Intro 2b | p. 120 ▶ Reading | p. 203

a) Read the texts (1-8) and match them to the photos (A-J). There are two photos that do not match any text.

b) Work with a partner. Look at texts 1-8 again and choose three attractions you would like to visit. In German, tell your partner about them and why you chose them.

1 Located in Millennium Square, Leeds Civic Hall is a stunning building made of white stone. It has two towers, one on each side, and when you look closely, you can see a gold-covered owl on top of each tower. In the year 2000, a further four golden owl sculptures were erected in Millennium Square. The owl is the emblem of the city of Leeds, and you can find pictures and sculptures of owls all across the city.

2 Liverpool Cathedral is Britain's largest cathedral and the fifth largest in Europe! It is one of Liverpool's most treasured architectural gems. Climb the tower and enjoy the breathtaking 360-degree view of Liverpool from high above. On a clear day you can even see Blackpool Tower, which is 28 miles away!

A

B

C

3 When you visit Manchester, the National Football Museum is a must for all football fans. A range of exhibitions show how football became the favourite sport of millions of people around the world. The museum is home to the largest archive of football objects. Among the 2,500 football-related objects that are on display, visitors can see boots and shirts worn by world-famous football players, as well as medals and trophies.

4 Don't miss the Botanical Gardens when you visit Sheffield! You can explore 18 different areas of plants, as well as some stunning buildings. In the 19th century, the Botanical Gardens had a real-life black bear for the entertainment of visitors. Today, there is a sculpture of a bear to remind visitors of this past. In summer, you can relax in the shade among the many beautiful trees and in winter you can admire exotic plants in one of the pavilions.

5 Visit Leeds City Museum to find out about the fascinating history of Leeds and see incredible exhibits from around the world. In the Ancient Worlds Gallery, you can discover how Egyptians, Romans and Greeks lived. Nesyamun, the 3,000-year-old Egyptian priest, is one of the most popular exhibits among visitors. And the best thing: entry to the museum is free!

6 Discover Liverpool's seafaring past and visit the Maritime Museum. A guided tour of the nearby Old Dock will take you back in time. In the museum's galleries, you can learn about the fascinating stories of seafarers and passengers from the 1700s to the present day. There is also a Titanic exhibition about the disaster that happened in 1912. This includes many little-known aspects of what happened to the ship.

7 If you are looking for an interactive experience, make sure you go to the National Videogame Museum in Sheffield. You can learn about the creation of and the people behind popular video games, as well as learn about classic games. Workshops offer visitors the chance to create their own games!

8 The John Rylands Library in Manchester is a breathtaking masterpiece of Victorian Gothic architecture. In fact, it looks more like a castle or a cathedral. The library was built to remember John Rylands, who was one of Manchester's most successful businessmen. The library's collection includes many treasures, for example the St John fragment, which is the oldest known piece of the New Testament.

D

E

F

G

H

I

J

5 Diff and train

D3 Support: Words ▶ Before Intro 3 | p. 120

a) Match the words and write down phrases you can use to talk about art and culture. Add phrases that you already know.

b) If you want to say that you like something, you can use more expressive words than "great" or "good". Read the texts on pages 120/121 again and note down adjectives you can use instead. Add any other adjectives you know to your list.

	a concert/a festival/a musical
visit	*the cinema/the theatre*
go to	*a gallery/a museum*
take part in	*a new artist*
look at	*a tourist attraction*
discover	*a guided tour*
	a poetry slam/a workshop

D4 Extra: Reading ▶ Before Intro 4 | p. 121

Read the short article written in 2023 and the culture box. Then answer the questions.

Leeds 2023 is a cultural festival that will be taking place in Leeds for the whole of 2023. The motto of the festival, "letting culture loose", reflects how culture will be celebrated all over the city, not just in theatres and museums. The festival will also be a multicultural celebration of the city's diversity.

Leeds 2023 is a good example of turning bad news into good news. After ten years of preparing to be named European Capital of Culture 2023, Leeds missed out because of Brexit. Instead of being upset that their efforts had been wasted, the organizers decided to turn them into a fantastic celebration of Leeds culture.

175 languages are spoken in Leeds and the festival will include dancing, music, theatre and more from cultures across the globe. For example, there will be an exhibition about Indian fabrics, a Día de los Muertos (day of the dead) parade, and a series of talks by older members of the community about their lives in Leeds. Many events will be free and can be enjoyed by everyone.

The opening celebrations for Leeds 2023 took place on 7 January 2023. The show featured performances by many stars born and raised in Leeds, including singer Corinne Bailey Rae. As the child of an English mother and a Caribbean father, Rae is grateful for the opportunity to celebrate her home city. "I'd really like the city to feel it can stand up and be counted among some of the great creative cities in the UK," she says.

1. Name two examples of what makes this festival a multicultural celebration.
2. Sum up Corinne Bailey Rae's view of Leeds.
3. Explain in your own words how Leeds 2023 is an example of turning bad news into good news.

Culture box

Brexit

On 31st January 2020, the United Kingdom left the European Union, having been a member since 1973. Brexit (from "British exit") was the result of a UK-wide referendum in 2016. 51.89% of people voted to leave and 48.11% voted to remain in the EU. Both the referendum and the result divided opinion in the UK.

D5 **Support: Mediation** ▶ Before Intro 4 | p. 121 ▶ Mediation | p. 213

In order to plan a trip, you need to check how to get from one place to another. Read the instructions on how to use a navigation app on your phone or tablet. Summarize each step and the tips in German.

1. Turn on your GPS.
2. Open the navigation app.
3. Type the place you want to find in the SEARCH field. You can also tap it directly on the map.
4. Tap the button DIRECTIONS on the left. It will show you a car, a train, a person walking, a person waving for a taxi, a bike and a plane.
5. Choose how you want to travel from the options listed in 4. The app will now show your travel route on the map. It will also give you an estimated travel time.
6. Alternative routes will show in grey on the map. To follow an alternative route, tap the grey line.
7. To start navigation, tap the START button.
8. To stop or cancel navigation, tap the EXIT button.

TIPS:

- You can also follow voice directions to navigate to a place.
- Using a navigation app can drain your battery. Use a battery pack or turn off the screen. You will still be able to hear voice directions.
- Be careful when using headphones. Make sure you can still hear traffic noises around you.

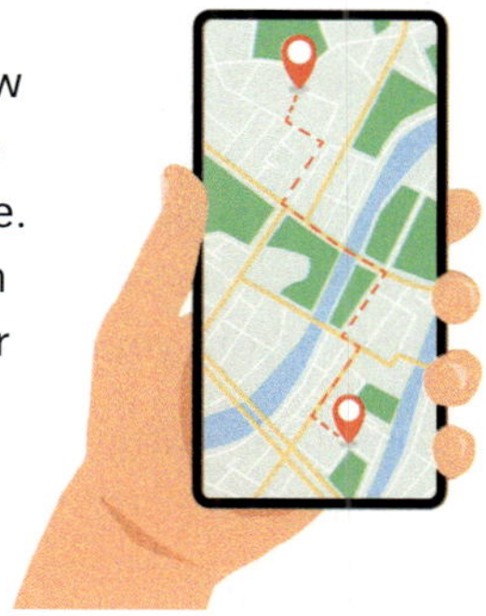

Theme 5: Part A

D6 **Training: Reading** ▶ After A1 b | p. 122

Read the texts on pages 122/123 again. Decide if each statement is true or false. Give evidence from the texts.

1 Many people from all over the world have been moving to Manchester for hundreds of years because of the city's interesting history.
2 The Industrial Revolution in Manchester began when a woman named Jenny figured out how to spin cloth really fast.
3 Even though the growth of the cotton industry brought a lot of wealth to the region, it also meant that many children had to work in the mills under horrible conditions.
4 When Emmeline Pankhurst was 40 years old, she went to her first Women's Rights meeting.
5 Pankhurst believed that sometimes radical action was necessary in the fight for equal rights for women.
6 The city we call "Manchester" today was originally built by the Romans about 1,000 years ago.
7 Marcus Rashford, who was born in Manchester, is admired by many because not only is he a great footballer but also someone who is involved with important charity work.
8 A memorial in Sackville Gardens commemorates the people who worked in the city's military production during the Second World War.

5 Diff and train

D7 Training: Viewing/Reading

▶ After A1c | p. 122

Listen to the song from A1c) again. Read the lyrics and answer the questions.

The Industrial Revolution Song
(by Jam Campus)

Before the mid-seventeen hundreds
Humans lived by where their food was growing
Life expectancy at thirty-five, limited education
Riding horses, simple weapons, every item you'd be owning
Made within your small community of family or companions

Then 1750 started in Great Britain
Clothing industry, weaving machines[1]
Increased the speed to build them
The Spinning Jenny[2], waterframe[3] improved the process
Water kept machines going
Then they made the steam engine[4]

And the steam engine, it changed everything
Railroads, steamboats, coal from mines, cotton dyes
In Britain, production, to pay humans, wages high
But coal was cheap and efficient for machines to mechanize

Chorus: *New manufacturing Industrial Revolution*
From small shops to factories
Changes and inventions, technology, transportation
Different way of life for many

Steam engines are working
More machines are turning
For an economic benefit
But the cities now overcrowded

From agricultural to industrial population
Meaning many people moved into the cities to work in
Couldn't support them, it's crowded, unsanitary[5]
And poor conditions within factories where people working

And steel everywhere, mass-produced
Replacing wood as the main building tool
Got that telegraph, send message, delivered the same night
New farming tools helped to increase the food supply

Profiting companies, efficient production lines […]
The times provided humans benefits economically
But damaged the environment negatively

Chorus

1 weaving machine – *Webmaschine* | **2** Spinning Jenny – *Name der ersten Spinnmaschine* | **3** waterframe – *erste durch ein Wasserrad betriebene Spinnmaschine* | **4** steam engine – *Dampfmaschine* | **5** unsanitary – *unhygienisch*

1. Where did most people live before the Industrial Revolution?
2. Name two negative aspects of life before the Industrial Revolution.
3. What was the impact of the steam engine?
4. How did the manufacturing of products change?
5. What were problems for people who moved to the cities to work in the new factories?

D8 Training: The infinitive with or without *to* (revision)

▶ After A2 | p. 123 ▶ G13R | p. 233

Lisa is on the phone with Robert to plan their trip to Manchester. Fill in the verbs from the box using the infinitive with or without *to*. You can look at G13R on page 233 for help.

(to) attend • (to) be • (to) book • (to) finish • (to) give • (to) go • (to) invite • (to) meet • (to) offer • (to) plan • (to) see • (to) try out • (to) visit • (to) walk around

> You can use some of the verbs more than once.

Robert: We need **1** planning our trip. When should we leave?

Lisa: My boss wants me **2** a meeting. She has refused **3** me a week off and expects me **4** back by Thursday. So we could **5** from Monday to Wednesday.

Robert: That's fine with me. Could I persuade you **6** the Science and Industry Museum?

Lisa: Why not? I have looked at the website, and the museum seems **7** a lot of fun activities and exhibits. At the moment, you can **8** over a hundred different retro games consoles. I would also like **9** the National Football Museum. Oh, and I've always wanted **10** on a tour of a stadium.

Robert: Wow, that might be a little too much football for a three-day trip. Maybe we should **11** the city instead. We could **12** a walking tour.

Lisa: Hmm, my friend advised me **13** our own route around the city instead. She says it is much more fun to decide for yourself what you see.

Robert: Yeah, she is right. On an organized tour you are forced **14** what they want to show you, so we can just plan **15** the sights we are interested in. Don't forget you promised we would **16** to a nice restaurant!

Lisa: I know, I know. We should **17** your friends from Manchester to come with us.

Robert: Great idea! But Simon will make us **18** to an Italian restaurant, that is his favourite.

Lisa: Italian food sounds great. If we plan **19** for a meal at 7 o'clock, it will still be quite early when we get back.

Robert: Great! I'll tell them **20** us there at 7!

D9 Extra: Pronunciation

▶ After A2 | p. 123

a) Watch part 1 of the video.
Sort the Mancunian words in the order they are introduced in the video. Write the Standard English word next to each Mancunian word.

> Mancunian =
> - sb or sth from Manchester
> - dialect spoken in Manchester

brew • buzzin' • chuddy • dead • gaggin' • hangin' • mint • mither • owt • sound

1. chuddy – chewing gum

b) Now watch part 2 of the video. Say these short Mancunian sentences out loud. Write down the words that sound different in Standard English. The list of English sounds on page 333 and the tip box can help you.

1 /ˌpliːz‿ˈelp mi/
2 /ˌsʊmtaɪmz ju ˌniːd ˈkʊrɪdʒ/
3 /aɪ ˌlʊv‿ə ˌglʌs‿əv ˈmɪlk/

> **Pronunciation**
> Standard English → Mancunian
> /ʌ/ → /ʊ/
> /aː/ → /ʌ/
> /h/ → not pronounced at the beginning of a word

D10 Support: Words ▶ After A4b | p. 125

a) Read the definitions for words from the articles on pages 124/125. Match the definitions to the words from the box. There are more words than you need.

1 to cause chaos
2 to consider carefully
3 very shocking
4 when sth is missing
5 to start
6 when there is no order
7 not quite the same
8 to move sb from a dangerous place
9 emotion experienced when someone is extremely scared
10 to tell sb you will hurt them if they do not do what you want
11 to be presented as an important news story

chaos
(to) evacuate
(to) evaluate
(to) make (the) headlines
lack
(to) launch
nuisance
outrageous
similar
suspicion
terror
(to) threaten
(to) wreak havoc

b) Find a definition for the two words which are left.
You can use a dictionary for help.

D11 Training: Sequence of adverbials ▶ After A4b | p. 125 ▶ G12 | p. 232

Put the words in the right order to form sentences. Look at G12 on page 232 if you need help with the sequence of adverbials.

Example: We / slowly / last week / walked / through the streets of Leeds
→ *We walked slowly through the streets of Leeds last week.*

1 Liz / later today / her brother / in Newcastle / is going to meet
2 We / during the summer holidays / visited / in Manchester / the Football Museum
3 The band / played / last week / fantastically / at their concert
4 We / this summer / are travelling / to York
5 Stanley's parents / in 2007 / got married / in Liverpool
6 Ada and Sebastian / at the cinema / agreed to meet / at 7 o'clock
7 Emilia / late at night / was dancing around / happily / in the street
8 Caleb / slowly / early in the morning / on the beach / is jogging

D12 Extra: Translation

▶ After A4c | p. 125

Read the newspaper article and translate it into English.

Verkehrschaos in Hamburger Innenstadt

Auf Hamburger Straßen kam es am Montagabend zu längeren Staus: Aktivisten der sogenannten „Letzten Generation" hatten sich an verschiedenen Stellen auf die Straßen der Hansestadt geklebt und dadurch den Feierabendverkehr blockiert. Es waren nicht die ersten Aktionen dieser Art in Hamburg. Immer wieder kam es in letzter Zeit zu Verkehrsbehinderungen, weil Aktivisten sich auf Brücken und Straßen geklebt hatten. Ziel dieser Aktionen ist es, auf die Gefahren des Klimawandels hinzuweisen.

! Translate the text staying as true to the original as possible. However, you might sometimes need to change the sentence structure (e.g. translate one long German sentence into two shorter English sentences).

D13 Training: Stylistic devices

▶ After A5a | p. 126 ▶ Reading | p. 204

a) Match the stylistic devices with their definitions.

1 something is described as much better or worse than it really is
2 a series of words beginning with the same sound
3 speaking to the reader directly
4 a question which expects no answer
5 two or more sentences/clauses that start with the same word(s)
6 objects or animals that have human characteristics

alliteration • anaphora • direct address • exaggeration • personification • rhetorical question

b) Read the sentences and name the stylistic device that is used in each one.

1 10 forever fashion favourites
2 Desperate times, desperate measures
3 The trees whispered to each other
4 This is why you haven't found love yet
5 Who wouldn't want a life without worry?
6 Spiderman is the best movie of the century
7 Ten teenage troublemakers arrested
8 Let's vote for a better future!
9 The sun smiled down on the gold medallist
10 First Olympic silver, then gold. Could it get any better?
11 You will cry, you will laugh, you will scream
12 I would die if anyone found out my secret

Theme 5: Part B

D14 Easy alternative: Conflicts at home ▶ Instead of B1a | p. 128

Copy the word web and add causes for conflicts between teenagers and their parents. You can add different ideas, too.

arguments with brothers/sisters • body piercings • boyfriend/girlfriend • clothes • church/religion • disrespectful behaviour • drinking alcohol • friends • getting up in the morning • grades at school • hairstyle • homework • mobile phone use • noise • not helping in the house • not tidying one's room • pocket money • smoking • taking care of pets • tattoos • type of music • volume of music • what (not) to eat • when to be home • ...

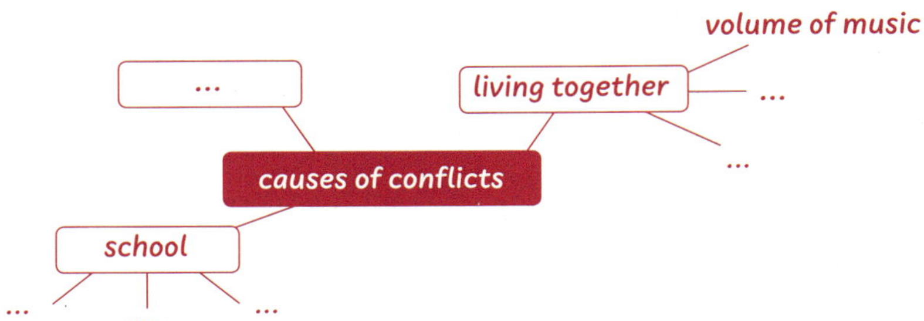

D15 Support: Words ▶ Before B1b | p. 128

Conflict happens in every relationship. Being respectful of each other usually helps solving a conflict. Here are some helpful phrases. Copy the grid and complete it.

Tell me why this is so important to you. • What would you say if ...? • I see what you mean. • I hear you, but I have a different view. • I agree with you that ... but ... • How would you feel about ...? • I understand why you feel that way. • Maybe we could ... • I can see your point but ... • I wasn't aware of this. • I want to understand why you feel that way. • How can we find a solution that works for both of us?

Showing respect	Disagreeing politely	Suggesting a compromise	Trying to understand the other person
I see what you mean.	*I hear you, but I have a different view.*	...	...

D16 Training: Reading ▶ After B2 | p. 128

Read the statements. Who says what? Scan the dialogue on pages 128/129 again and match the statements to the speakers.

A Meryem **B** Amira **C** mother, Priyanka **D** father, Tim

1 "You could all do so much more."
2 "We've all tried our best so far."
3 "It's often the richest people who are unbelievably tight."
4 "I don't have time to be an activist."
5 "We have a right to spend our hard-earned money on whatever we want to."
6 "You know we support your causes."
7 "I don't want to be vegan."
8 "Why do people have to be like that?"

D17 Training: Emphatic *do* ▶ After B2 | p. 128 ▶ G14 | p. 234

Use emphatic *do* to say these sentences in English.

Example: Ich glaube wirklich, dass du recht hast.
→ *I do believe you are right.*

1 Kleine Veränderungen machen doch einen großen Unterschied.
2 Ich hoffe wirklich, dass viele Leute an den Protesten teilnehmen werden.
3 Er hat tatsächlich versucht, weniger Fleisch zu essen.
4 Du hast doch bekommen, was du wolltest.
5 Ich habe wirklich das Licht ausgemacht. Ehrenwort!
6 Das stimmt nicht. Ich habe dir doch von dem Treffen erzählt!
7 Bitte trink doch noch eine Tasse Tee!

D18 Training: Reading ▶ After B4 p. 131

a) Read the statements about the scene on pages 130/131 and decide if they are true or false. Give evidence from the text.

1 Meryem took the bus to get to the youth club.
2 Thomas watches Meryem arrive at the youth club.
3 Lottie wants to use the meeting to plan a protest.
4 Meryem thinks that getting more supporters is very important.
5 Every Saturday the group collects signatures for their petition.
6 Lottie and Orla agree with what the group in Bradford did.
7 Thomas thinks that Meryem shouldn't be an activist.
8 Meryem is angry about being attacked by Thomas.

b) Correct the wrong statements.

D19 Training: Gerund or infinitive with *to*

▶ After B7 | p. 131 ▶ G15 | p. 234

The highlighted verbs in the sentences below can be followed by the gerund or the infinitive, depending on the meaning. Complete the sentences using the correct form of the verbs in brackets.

In this exercise, the verb followed by the gerund has a different meaning from the same verb followed by the infinitive.
You need to look at the context to decide whether the gerund or the infinitive is correct. You can look at G15 on page 234 for help.

1 Remember XXX (bring) some food and water to the protest on Friday!
I still remember XXX (go) to my first Fridays for Future protest a few years ago.
2 I have stopped XXX (eat) animal products to reduce my carbon footprint.
When Lily saw the graffiti on the wall, she stopped XXX (look at) it.
3 Leading an environmentally friendly life means XXX (travel) less by car.
Sorry, I meant XXX (tell) you that Said has left our activist group.
4 Oh no, I forgot XXX (text) Lucy about our meeting tomorrow!
He will never forget XXX (meet) the other activists for the first time.
5 My grandfather has really been trying XXX (eat) less meat, but I can see that it is difficult for him.
Rowan decided to try XXX (make) a podcast about climate change.
6 Nick went on XXX (talk) even though none of the other activists were listening to him.
After Isabelle had welcomed everyone to the group, she went on XXX (explain) which steps they wanted to take next.

D20 Training: Gerund after prepositions

▶ After B7 | p. 131 ▶ G15 | p. 234

Complete the sentences by adding the correct preposition from the box and the gerund of the verbs in brackets. You will need some of the prepositions more than once.

The gerund is used after adjectives that are followed by a preposition (e.g. *famous* ***for*** *doing sth*) and after some verbs that are followed by a preposition (e.g. *to worry* ***about*** *doing sth*).

about • at • in • of • on

Example: Amber likes parties very much, but she isn't keen XXX (go) to Felix's party.
→ *Amber likes parties very much, but she isn't keen on going to Felix's party.*

1 Although Eliah is crazy XXX (play) basketball, he has never dreamed XXX (become) a professional player.
2 Adam is extremely good XXX (play) the piano. However, he is afraid XXX (perform) on stage.
3 Martha is very fond XXX (tell) her little brother what to do.
4 Ibrahim likes acting very much. He is interested XXX (join) the drama club.
5 Jasmine goes everywhere by bike. She has never thought XXX (buy) a car.
6 After he had missed the bus, Ralph was worried XXX (arrive) late.
7 Shobika is excited XXX (go) to Spain next month. She is focusing XXX (improve) her Spanish before her trip.

D21 Easy alternative: Listening L 2/2 | S 12 ▶ Instead of B8b | p. 132

a) Listen and choose the correct answers.

1 Meryem's father ...
A went to a football match (Manchester United vs. Arsenal) last Saturday.
B watched a football match on TV last Saturday.
C went to a football match (Manchester United vs. Chelsea) last Saturday.

2 During the first half of the match, Meryem ...
A asked people to sign her petition.
B managed to get onto the pitch.
C recognized her father in the crowd.

3 Meryem then ...
A ran towards the goal and chained herself to a goalpost.
B ran onto the pitch and screamed at the football players.
C ran towards one of the players and chained him to the goalpost.

4 Meryem was wearing a T-shirt which said ...
A "No money for matches! Save the world!"
B "No money for football! Stop climate change!"
C "No money for football! Save the climate!"

5 Security guards tried to carry Meryem off the pitch but ...
A she screamed and kicked at them.
B it took them almost twenty minutes to carry her off.
C they couldn't get her off.

6 The people in the stadium ...
A were angry but stayed calm.
B were very angry and booed Meryem.
C were throwing things at Meryem.

7 At one point it looked like ...
A the security guards weren't going to be able to get Meryem off the goalpost.
B Meryem wanted to give up.
C the match was going to be cancelled.

8 After that Meryem was taken to an office and ...
A the police arrived.
B more security guards arrived.
C the Manchester coach wanted to speak with her.

9 At the moment, it is not clear ...
A what the consequences will be.
B if Meryem wants to come home.
C when the police will be in touch.

b) Use your results from a) to answer these questions about the incident:

1 What happened?
2 Who was involved?
3 When did it happen?
4 Where did it happen?
5 What were Meryem's reasons?

L Language training

In this Language training section you will find tips and exercises which will ...
- teach you how to adapt your language to best express your ideas,
- help you to make your written texts and spoken language more varied and therefore more interesting,
- help you to avoid common language and cultural mistakes when speaking English,
- teach you how to express yourself more concisely.

Assuming and speculating

Sometimes it is necessary to express yourself in a way that shows you are not 100% sure if what you are saying is a fact or if it will happen.
Situation: A friend asks you to play football next week but at the moment you are ill.
There are different ways of expressing your uncertainty.

A Use a modal auxiliary such as *might* or *may*.
Example: ***I might/may be able to play, but I'm not sure because ...***

B Use an introductory expression such as

I think ... • I suppose ... • I imagine ... • I assume ...
It could be ... • It seems likely/unlikely ...
Perhaps, ... • Possibly, ... • I will probably ...

Example: ***It seems unlikely that I'll feel better by then but who knows.***

C Use a conditional sentence.
Example: ***If I feel better, I'll come and play.***

L1

Write a sentence expressing uncertainty about these situations. Use each of the possibilities above.

1. You assume that you have passed the exam, but it was very difficult.
2. You hope that the weather will be good at the weekend so you can go swimming.
3. You assume that what your best friend tells you about another friend is true, but also that your best friend could be wrong.

L2 L 2/4 | S 14

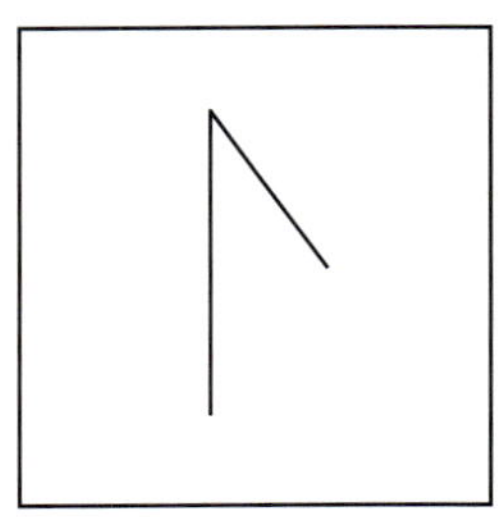

a) Work with a partner. Speculate on what the doodle on the right might be. Use some of the phrases from above.
b) Listen to some people talking about the doodle and see if you were right.
c) Listen again and note down additional phrases for speculating.
d) Use the phrases for assuming and speculating on this page and talk about the four doodles below with a partner.

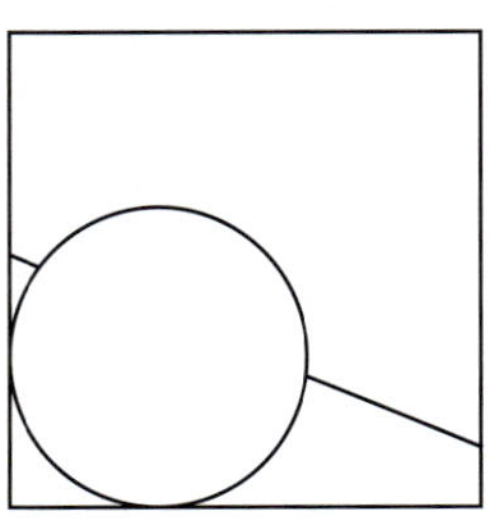
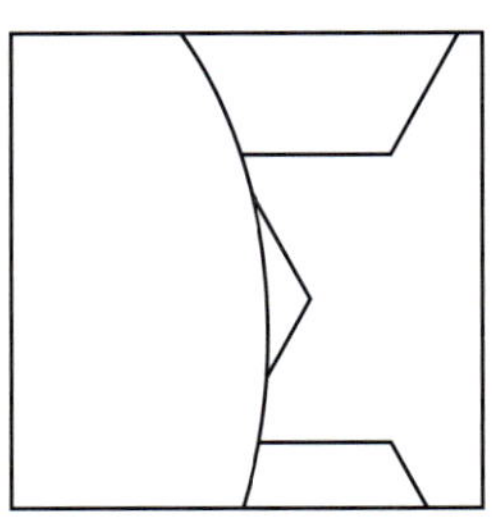
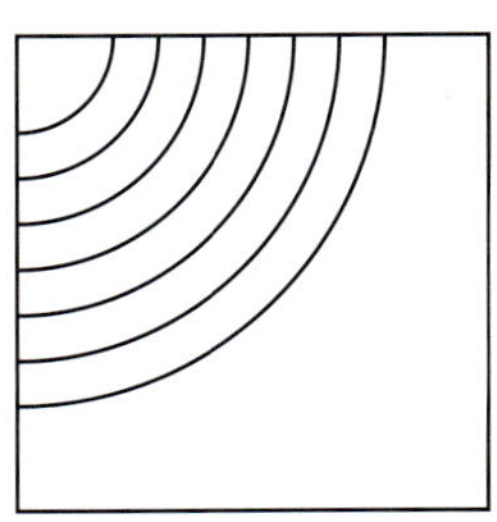

Varying sentence structure

Writing well is not just a question of putting good ideas into words and getting your grammar right. A good piece of writing will also use a variety of structures and vocabulary so that the reader will enjoy reading it.

Connectives/conjunctions and adverbs

L 3

a) Read both texts and describe what makes the second text more interesting.

A I have time in the morning. That morning I was late. I got up and then I cleaned my teeth. I got dressed and had breakfast. Then I put on my shoes and coat and I ran to the bus stop. The bus was late. I caught it and I met my friends and we went to school together.

B Generally I have enough time in the morning. That morning, however, I was late. After I had got up, I quickly cleaned my teeth. I actually had breakfast while I was getting dressed. As soon as I had put my shoes and coat on, I ran to the bus stop. I caught the bus just in time because, luckily for me, it was late. So I met my friends on the bus and we all went to school together.

b) Make a list of the connectives/conjunctions and adverbs that are used.

c) Read the blog entry. Use connectives/conjunctions and adverbs and rewrite it so that it sounds more interesting.

A night to remember

It's unbelievable what happened to me during my holiday in Ibiza. It was very hot and sunny. I went to the beach a lot. We met a lot of cool people. We played beach volleyball a lot. I went to dinner with my parents and my sister every evening. The food was amazing. One evening we were all having a good time. We went back to our rooms at about midnight. I discovered that I had left my hotel key in our room. My sister and I couldn't get in. We went into my parents' room, which was next door. We climbed onto the balcony outside our room. We had left a small window open. My sister is smaller than me. She had to climb in through the window. It was difficult. It was very dark. Then it was very light. The hotel manager was shining a torch at us. He said that he was going to call the police. We tried to explain. His English wasn't very good and our Spanish wasn't very good. We tried to convince him that we were the guests of this room. He believed us. We went to bed at 2 o'clock. We were very tired.

→ What are your most memorable holiday experiences?
→ Share them in the comments below.

L Language training

Participles

L4

a) Participles are often used in written English. Read the short text to see how participle constructions are used to vary the sentence structure.

Yesterday, on the coldest day of the year so far, Luna and Daisy, two dachshund sisters, went missing. The police found Luna in a bush straight away, but Daisy was not with her. Four police officers checked all the streets in the neighbourhood during their search, including the Beaumont Park area. Finally, having fetched[1] one of their police dogs for help, they found Daisy in the back garden of a house on Rosewood Road. Shivering from the cold, Daisy came running towards the police officers. Wagging her tail[2], she jumped into the police car to join her sister Luna. Safely squeezed[3] between two police officers, they were driven home. Tucked up under a blanket[4], the adventurous sisters fell asleep immediately. The overjoyed owners made a generous donation to the Retired Police Dogs Trust, a charity founded in 2019 and supported by celebrities like actress Dame Judi Dench.

1 to fetch – *holen* | **2** to wag one's tail – *mit dem Schwanz wedeln* | **3** to squeeze – *einzwängen* | **4** blanket – *Decke*

b) Look at the participles in the text and sort them according to their function.
You can use participles to:

A shorten adverbial clauses of time or reason
B shorten a relative clause in the active or passive voice
C combine information

c) Rewrite sentences from the text in L4a).

Example:

Four police officers checked all the streets in the neighbourhood during their search, including the Beaumont Park area.

→ *Four police officers checked all the streets in the neighbourhood during their search. They included the Beaumont Park area.*

L5

Use participles to combine or shorten these sentences:

1. When they spotted a good place for a picnic, they stopped the car.
2. The band which just played at a festival is going on a world tour next year.
3. When we heard our neighbours were missing their dog, we all went and looked for him.
4. Since he came home late yesterday, he decided to leave work early today.
5. Lou wore a fantastic jacket. The jacket belonged to her grandfather.
6. The man who is coming out of that shop is a famous actor.
7. He was cleaning his room and listening to music.
8. She was very angry because she had had to wait in the rain for nearly half an hour.

Varying expression

Using synonyms

When writing a text or talking to someone, it is important to vary your expression. Otherwise, you can sound vague and repetitive, as these examples illustrate:

A Holidays in California are nice. You can see a lot of nice places, go shopping and see the nice countryside. The weather is usually nice, too, with sunshine for most of the year. Last year my parents and I stayed in a very nice hotel in Ventura, not far from Los Angeles.

B I think that you are a bit young for an internship abroad when you are 15 or 16. I think that you should rather do that when you're older. It's easier, I think, to do an internship with a company here in Germany, in your home town. The best way to find an internship is to look online, I think.

L 6

You already know a number of synonyms (= words with similar meanings) for *nice* or *think*.
Copy the lists below and add more words. Use the words from your lists to rewrite texts A and B.

nice
great
wonderful
...

think
believe
suppose
...

Instead of a synonym, you can also use ...
- an opposite and negate it (e.g. *nice* – *not bad*)
- a phrase that means the same (e.g. *I think* ... – *In my opinion* ...)

L 7

Copy the word web and add more words to it.

Start a folder with words that are often used.
Find synonyms for each word and write them down.
You can organize your synonyms in a list or a word web, for example.

L 8

Some words can have different meanings depending on their context, for example the word *get*.
For these words you need to understand a text before using synonyms.

Look at the expressions containing the word *get* in the text below and rewrite the text by replacing the expressions with *get* with other verbs or expressions.

When I get up in the morning, I get my phone to see how many messages I have got. On the bus to school, I try to get a quiet place to sit so that I get the time and space to play a game on my phone. When I get to school, I have to turn my phone off. Sometimes I get it out of my bag during breaks and get up to date with social media.

L Language training

Paraphrasing

Paraphrasing means explaining an idea in other words, often in a simpler and clearer way. Situations in which you might have to paraphrase what you have said can include:

A When you are asked to repeat what you have said in other words because someone has not understood what you are trying to say.

B When you have to talk about an idea multiple times and do not want to repeat the same words again and again, e.g. in a presentation or an essay.

C When you cannot think of an English word or expression that sums up what you are trying to say, e.g. because you don't know the word or it is something typically German, for example, for which there is no English expression (e.g. *Fastnacht*, *Frühjahrsmüdigkeit*).

L 9

Look at the examples of situations in which paraphrasing is necessary.
Say which type of situation (A-C) they show.

1 "My brother can't come to the concert with us tonight. He's really busy right now at the moment applying for jobs and wants to finish his CV."
"His what?"

2 "It would be great to have you here that weekend, but I already have plans. I'm sorry. It's my sister's *Abi-Ball*."
"What's that? A sports match?"
"No, no. Well, an *Abi-Ball* is ..."

3 Internships can be a very rewarding experience. You get to find out more about a job that you might like to do in the future. If the company is happy with how your internship goes, they may invite you to come back – either for a holiday job, a proper job or additional training. And it's always good if you can include an internship on your CV.

4 "I really love dystopian novels. The *Hunger Games* books are my favourite. It's very interesting to think about what our world could look like in the future."
"Dysto-what?"
"Dystopian. Wait, let me explain ..."

L 10

Match the following example of paraphrasing to one of the examples (1-4) from L9.
Look closely at how the idea is explained in different words.

It means that the society in which the story takes place has developed in a negative way. People usually have no freedom to do what they want and are controlled by the state, often with the help of modern technology.

L 11

Use paraphrasing to complete the other dialogues from L9.

Style and register

You can express the same thing in many ways. Your choice of words, as well the style and register, will change how others interpret what you have said or written.

If you are annoyed at someone who will not stop talking, you could say "Please, be quiet!", or you could say "Shut up!" Both expressions mean a similar thing, but there is a clear difference in style and register. "Please, be quiet!" is polite and more formal than the colloquial and rude "Shut up!". "Shut up!" may be OK among friends (said jokingly), but it would not be OK if you said it to a stranger in a shop or on a train, for example.

L 12

a) Look at the examples below and find the sentences that are particularly informal. Use a dictionary if you are not sure what a phrase means.

b) Concentrate on the informal sentences and write a formal alternative that means the same.

1. "It came as quite a surprise when she invited me to stay at her place for the summer."
2. "Look at that shirt. I wouldn't be seen dead in it!"
3. "I'm gonna, like, ask my mum to give me some cash so that I can buy those cool shoes."
4. "I would tell her to leave me alone if she said anything like that to me."
5. "It's kinda boring hanging out with those kids all the time. My sis and her friends are only nine."

Unless you are writing an informal text (e.g. a diary entry, a dialogue), your texts in English lessons are supposed to be neutral or formal in style. Here are some important tips to remember:

Avoid short forms (e.g. *don't*, *wouldn't*, *he's*) in written texts.
Do not use colloquial expressions from spoken English (e.g. *wanna*, *kids*, *guys*).

L 13

a) Look at the following situations. Rank them from formal to informal.

1. You are in a shop and want to know if a T-shirt is available in a different size.
2. You meet a classmate and their parents, who you have met several times.
3. Your teacher wants to talk to you after class to discuss some details of your project.
4. You have been invited to a job interview at an international company with your future boss.

b) Choose one of the situations or invent a situation that you consider very formal or informal. Write a short dialogue using inappropriate register/language.

c) Work with a partner.
Swap your dialogues and rewrite them using the appropriate style and register.

L Language training

It is often not what you say but *how* you say it that can make a difference. Word choice and politeness are important. In English-speaking countries, people are often not direct when they speak. They prefer to modify criticism and not use any strong adjectives so as not to offend others.

Constructive criticism

L 14

a) Read this conversation and say why Adam reacts the way he does.

Adam: So, what did you think of the first chapter of my new book?
Joe: I suppose the storyline was OK, but the characters were rubbish – the main character was just dull, I didn't care about them at all. The setting was also weird. Why were there a load of teenagers alone on a desert island? I mean how did they get there? It was so unrealistic. I could have done it better myself!
Adam: So, you didn't like it?
Joe: That's not what I meant!
Adam: Really?! Well, I certainly won't get you to read any more chapters I write.

b) Listen to this second version. Note down the different ways of expressing criticism in the two conversations. Explain why Adam reacts differently. L 2/5 | S 15

Politeness

L 15

a) People are likely to react in an unfriendly way in English-speaking countries if you do not observe the rules of politeness. Read the conversation below. What impression do you get of the woman who is asking for help? What type of person do you think she is?

Woman 1: You must help me!
Woman 2: Why should I do that?
Woman 1: Because I've got a serious problem. My car won't start and I'm going to be late. You must drive me somewhere in your car.
Woman 2: What do you mean *must*. I don't have to do anything!
Woman 1: But I've got to be in Cambridge at three o'clock for a presentation. It's extremely important that I get there on time. I'm the one giving the presentation!
Woman 2: And it's extremely important that I go home and have a cup of tea! Goodbye.

b) Work with a partner: Rewrite the conversation convincingly so that the woman gets the help she needs. Then listen to a 'polite version' of the conversation. L 2/6 | S 16

False friends

Sometimes, there are English words that sound similar to German words, although their meaning is different. Words like these are called 'false friends'. Native English speakers who do not know German will not understand what you mean if you use these words in the wrong (German) context. Look at the table below with some common false friends.

If you are not absolutely sure, check your dictionary before using an English word which is similar in German, e.g. *Fitnessstudio* = 'gym' or 'fitness club'.
Beware of compound words. It is easy to make mistakes when translating them word for word, e.g. *Hochschule* is 'college' or 'university' in English (not 'high school'!).

German word	Correct English word ('good friend')	Incorrect English word ('false friend')	What the 'false friend' means in German
aktuell	topical, up-to-date	actual	*tatsächlich*
also	so	also	*auch*
bekommen	to get	to become	*werden*
sich blamieren	to make a fool of oneself	to blame sb	*jmd die Schuld geben*
brav	well-behaved, good	brave	*mutig*
Chance	opportunity	chance	*Zufall, Glück*
engagiert	committed, involved	engaged	*verlobt, besetzt (Telefon/WC)*
Gift	poison	gift	*Geschenk*
Grund	reason	ground	*(Erd)boden*
Handy	smartphone/(mobile) phone	handy	*nützlich*
Kritik	criticism	critic	*Kritiker/Kritikerin*
Marke	brand	mark	*Note, Zensur*
Meinung	opinion	meaning	*Bedeutung*
Note	mark	note	*Notiz*
Public Viewing	public screening	public viewing	*öffentliche Leichenaufbahrung*
Rat	advice	rat	*Ratte*
sensibel	sensitive	sensible	*vernünftig*
spenden	to donate	to spend	*ausgeben, verbringen*
sympathisch	nice, likeable	sympathetic	*mitfühlend*

L 16
Read the speech bubble and explain what went wrong in this conversation.

L 17
Work with a partner: Write a short dialogue in which false friends lead to a funny misunderstanding.

Listening Hören

Wenn du zum Beispiel Gespräche, Podcasts oder Berichte auf Englisch hörst, brauchst du nicht jedes Wort zu verstehen. Hier sind einige Tipps, die dir beim Verstehen helfen können.

1. Vor dem Hören

- Wie lautet die Aufgabe, die du bearbeiten sollst? Lies sie dir gründlich durch, damit du weißt, was genau du heraushören sollst.
- Überlege: Worum könnte es in dem Gespräch, dem Podcast oder dem Bericht gehen? Was weißt du schon über das Thema (z. B. Australien, soziale Medien, Klimawandel)?
- Sieh dir Überschriften und Bilder an: Vielleicht kannst du schon herausfinden, wer mit wem spricht oder wo sich die Personen befinden.
- Gibt es Hinweise, ob die Personen *British English, American English* oder eine andere Variante sprechen werden (z. B. *Australian English*)?

2. Während des Hörens

Konzentriere dich während des Hörens auf die Fragen, die du beantworten sollst. Folgende Strategien können dir dabei helfen:

Listening for the gist
- Um die Hauptgedanken des Gehörten (*gist*) zu verstehen, achte auf Wörter oder Begriffe, die häufiger genannt werden. Auf Details kommt es dabei nicht an.
- Stimmen und Tonfall der sprechenden Personen sowie Hintergrundgeräusche können dir helfen.

Listening for detail
- Um Einzelheiten (*details*) zu verstehen, musst du die Fragen in der Aufgabe genau verstanden haben. Überlege, auf welche Informationen du gezielt beim Hören achten musst.
- Notiere dir die Antworten zunächst in Stichwörtern, nicht in ganzen Sätzen.
- Wenn du die Aufgabe noch nicht gleich lösen konntest, dann höre das Gespräch, den Podcast oder den Bericht ein weiteres Mal an.

3. Nach dem Hören

- Wenn es möglich ist, vergleiche deine Ergebnisse mit jemandem aus deiner Klasse. Habt ihr das Gleiche herausgefunden?

Don't panic!
Du wirst nicht immer sofort verstehen, was jemand sagt:
- Wenn Personen einen Akzent haben, kann es ein wenig dauern, bis du dich daran gewöhnt hast. Nach einer Weile wirst du sie besser verstehen.
- Wenn du die sprechende Person siehst, kannst du häufig Rückschlüsse aus ihrer Körpersprache und Mimik ziehen.
- Wenn du mit jemandem sprichst und etwas nicht verstehst, kannst du die Person bitten, etwas zu wiederholen, zu erklären oder langsamer zu sprechen.

Reading Lesen

In *Camden Town 9* gibt es viele unterschiedliche Texte: Blogeinträge, Zeitungsartikel, Romanauszüge, ...
Hier sind einige Tipps, damit es dir leichter fällt, diese Texte zu verstehen.

1. Lesetechniken

- Versuche, beim ersten Lesen grob zu verstehen, worum es geht. Du musst nicht jedes Wort verstehen. Diese Lesetechnik nennt man ***skimming***.
- Beim ***scanning*** suchst du einen Text nach bestimmten Informationen ab, um z. B. eine Frage zu beantworten.
- Einen längeren Text kannst du leichter und schneller verstehen, indem du ihn in einzelne Abschnitte gliederst. Finde dann für jeden Abschnitt eine Überschrift, die in wenigen Worten zusammenfasst, worum es geht.
- In deinen eigenen Büchern oder auf Arbeitsblättern kannst du bereits während des Lesens wichtige Schlüsselwörter oder Informationen unterstreichen oder markieren. Du kannst mit verschiedenen Farben arbeiten. Anmerkungen zu Textstellen kannst du direkt am Rand notieren.

2. Umgang mit unbekannten Wörtern

Falls es unbekannte Wörter gibt, die du unbedingt verstehen musst, um eine Aufgabe zu lösen, hast du verschiedene Möglichkeiten, die Bedeutung herauszufinden.

Neue Wörter ohne Wörterbuch verstehen

- Kennst du **ähnliche Wörter im Deutschen** oder in einer anderen Sprache? Woran erinnert dich z. B. *atmosphere*?
- Vielleicht sind dir **einzelne Teile** eines englischen Wortes bekannt. Was könnte *agreement* heißen? Denk an *to agree.*
- Häufig kannst du die Bedeutung eines unbekannten Wortes aus dem **Textzusammenhang** verstehen. Sieh dir das folgende Beispiel an: *At our school students can compete in sports at different levels.* Kannst du aus dem Zusammenhang verstehen, was mit *to compete* gemeint ist?

Mit einem Wörterbuch arbeiten

- Wenn du ein englisches Wort nicht verstehst, kannst du es in einem Wörterbuch oder im *English-German dictionary* ab Seite 277 nachschlagen. Dort findest du Wörter und Redewendungen aus *Camden Town 5* bis *9*.
- Oft gibt es mehrere Bedeutungen für ein Wort. Sieh dir also immer alle Einträge zu einem Wort an, das du gerade nachschlägst, damit du die richtige Übersetzung findest.
- Die Einträge im *dictionary* zeigen auch, wie du ein Wort aussprichst. Eine Erklärung zu den Symbolen, die in der Lautschrift verwendet werden, findest du auf Seite 333.

Online-Wörterbuch

- Wörterbücher gibt es auch online oder als App. Sieh dir auch hier die Übersetzungsvorschläge genau an. Manchmal steht die passende Bedeutung nicht gleich an erster Stelle.
- Wenn du ein Online-Wörterbuch oder eine Wörterbuch-App verwendest, kannst du dir oft auch die Aussprache der Wörter anhören. Dazu gibt es meistens ein Lautsprecher-Symbol, das du auswählen musst.
- Kläre vorher, ob du ein Online-Wörterbuch oder eine App im Unterricht verwenden darfst.

3. Texte analysieren

Bei einer Textanalyse untersuchst du einen Text nach Aspekten wie Aufbau, Sprache, Stimmung, Erzählperspektive und Absicht der Autorin/des Autors.

Erzählperspektive (*narrative perspective*)

- Wenn du über fiktive Texte sprichst (z. B. Romane, Erzählungen, Gedichte), unterscheidest du zwischen Autorin/Autor (***author***) und Erzählerin/Erzähler (***narrator***). Die Person, die sich eine Geschichte ausdenkt und aufgeschrieben hat, ist die Autorin/der Autor. Die Person, aus deren Perspektive die Geschichte erzählt wird, ist die Erzählerin/der Erzähler.
  Beispiel: *Julia Walton is the author of the novel "Words on Bathroom Walls". Adam is the narrator of the story.*
- Bei den Erzählperspektiven unterscheidet man zwischen *first-person narrator* und *third-person narrator.*
- Ein ***first-person narrator*** erzählt die Geschichte aus ihrer/seiner Sicht und ist direkt an der Handlung beteiligt. Dadurch fühlt man sich beim Lesen nah an der Handlung. Ein *first-person narrator* kann nur über seine eigenen Gedanken und Gefühle berichten und hat dadurch eine begrenzte Pespektive. Es werden die Pronomen *I*, *me* und *mine* verwendet.
- Im Gegensatz dazu erzählt der ***third-person narrator*** eine Geschichte aus einer Außenperspektive. Er/sie berichtet über Dinge, welche die Figuren der Geschichte nicht wissen können. Ein *third-person narrator* nimmt häufig eine neutralere Perspektive ein. Es werden die Pronomen *he, she, it* und *they* verwendet.

Stilmittel (*stylistic devices*)

- In vielen Texten stehen die sprachliche Gestaltung und der Inhalt in einem Zusammenhang. Es gibt unterschiedliche Stilmittel, mit denen Aussagen betont, anschaulicher gemacht, Leserinnen/Leser direkt angesprochen oder Spannung erzeugt werden kann.

Stilmittel	Definition	Beispiel
alliteration (Alliteration)	aufeinanderfolgende Wörter, die mit dem gleichen Laut beginnen	*the sweet smell of success* *jump for joy*
anaphora (Anapher)	zwei oder mehrere Sätze/Satzteile, die mit einem oder mehreren gleichen Wörtern beginnen	*I spoke with Eliza Ramirez. I spoke with Reggie Banks.*
direct address (direkte Ansprache)	Leserin/Leser wird direkt angesprochen	*Let's do it now!*
enjambement (Zeilensprung)	Satz (z. B. in einem Gedicht), der über das Ende eines Verses fortgeführt wird	*We were running* *to find what happened* *beyond the hills.*
enumeration (Aufzählung)	Aufzählung von Wörtern	*She admired his hair, his eyes and his lips.*
exaggeration (Übertreibung)	übertriebene Darstellung oder Beschreibung	*They nearly died laughing.* *I have told you a thousand times.*
personification (Personifikation)	Übertragung von menschlichen Eigenschaften auf Tiere/Objekte	*The sun was smiling.*
quote (Zitat)	Zitat einer bekannten Persönlichkeit	*Like May Angelou said: "If you don't like something, change it."*
repetition (Wiederholung)	Wiederholung von Wörtern	*high, high above*
rhetorical question (rhetorische Frage)	Frage, auf die keine Antwort erwartet wird	*Can't you listen?*

Speaking with others
Sich mit anderen austauschen

1. Ein Gespräch führen

Im Unterricht tauschst du dich oft mit anderen zu vorgegebenen Themen oder Fragen aus. Es kann auch vorkommen, dass du in einem Rollenspiel ein formelles Gespräch führen sollst. Präge dir dazu einige nützliche Redewendungen ein.

Nützliche Redewendungen

So kannst du ein Gespräch beginnen:
Pleased to meet you. – Likewise.
OK then, let's get started ...

So kannst du ein Gespräch am Laufen halten:
That sound's interesting.
I see. / Right.
I hope it's OK to ask: ...?

So kannst du Zeit gewinnen, um kurz nachzudenken:
That's a good question. Let me think.
When you say ..., do you mean ...?

So kannst du ein Gespräch beenden:
Thank you so much for your time.
It's been great talking to you. / Have a good day.

2. Eine Debatte vorbereiten und durchführen

In einer Debatte arbeitet ihr unterschiedliche Positionen zu einem Thema heraus.
Damit eine Debatte gut funktioniert, gibt es einige Regeln.

Wählt eine kontroverse Frage oder ein Thema, das ihr debattieren wollt.

→ Bildet zwei Gruppen. Eine Gruppe argumentiert dafür, die andere dagegen.

↓ Jede Gruppe bereitet Argumente für ihre Seite vor.
Denkt auch an Argumente, die die Gegenseite vorbringen könnte und überlegt euch mögliche Antworten darauf.

↓ Beginnt die Debatte. Jede Seite trägt abwechselnd jeweils ein Argument vor. Hört den anderen zu, ohne sie zu unterbrechen.

↓ Nach der Debatte stimmt ihr über die Frage ab.
Unabhängig von eurer Gruppe könnt ihr frei abstimmen.

Be polite!
Sei im Gespräch mit anderen immer höflich und freundlich. Lass die anderen ausreden.
Verwende *sorry, please* und *thank you*.
Das gilt auch, wenn du anderer Meinung bist!

Giving a presentation Eine Präsentation halten

Manchmal musst du vor der Klasse etwas vortragen oder präsentieren. Hier sind ein paar Hilfen:

1. Bevor du etwas vorträgst

- Überlege: Was möchtest du zu deinem Thema sagen? Wie viel Zeit hast du für deinen Vortrag?
- Sammle deine Gedanken und schreibe sie in Stichpunkten auf, z. B. in einem *word web* oder in einer Liste. ▶Writing | p. 208
- Du kannst dir eine Karteikarte mit Notizen in Stichpunkten erstellen.
- Du kannst auch ein **Poster mit Bildern oder Fotos anfertigen**, um deine Präsentation interessanter zu gestalten. Wenn du Bilder aus dem Internet verwendest, dann vermerke, wo du sie gefunden hast.

So sieht ein gelungenes Poster aus:
✓ ansprechende Überschrift
✓ interessante Informationen, aber nicht zu viel Text
✓ lesbare Schrift
✓ passende Bilder mit Bildunterschriften (Quellenangabe nicht vergessen)

- Alternativ kannst du **Folien auf dem Computer oder Tablet erstellen.** Bei der Gestaltung ist wichtig, dass die Folien übersichtlich und leicht zu lesen sind. Auf die erste Folie schreibst du das Thema deiner Präsentation und deinen Namen. Auf die zweite Folie kommen die Punkte, über die du sprechen wirst. Diese führst du auf den nächsten Folien aus. Auf der vorletzten Folie fasst du die wichtigsten Informationen in ein bis zwei Sätzen zusammen. Auf der letzten Folie notierst du alle Quellen für Texte oder Bilder, die du verwendet hast.

So erstellst du übersichtliche Folien:
✓ Querformat
✓ Informationen in Stichpunkten
✓ nicht mehr als sieben Zeilen Text auf einer Folie
✓ lesbare Schrift (Text 28-32 pt, Überschrift 36-44 pt)
✓ nicht zu viele Farben
✓ keine Animationseffekte
✓ nur aussagekräftige Bilder

- Übe deinen Vortrag vor dem Spiegel, vor Freunden oder vor deiner Familie.
- Du kannst deinen Vortrag auch zur Probe mit einem Handy aufnehmen. Prüfe dann, ob du flüssig und verständlich gesprochen hast.
- Wenn du dir bei der Aussprache eines Wortes unsicher bist, kannst du die Lautschrift im Wörterbuch nachschlagen (siehe S. 277) oder dir das Wort in einem Online-Wörterbuch anhören.

Nützliche Redewendungen für deinen Vortrag
So kannst du deinen Vortrag strukturieren:
1 *Today I'd like to tell you about ... • My topic is ...*
2 *I'd like to begin with ... • First, I'm going to talk about ...*
3 *Secondly, I would like to show you ... • My next point is ...*
4 *Finally, let us take a look at ...*
5 *To sum up ... • That brings me to the end of my presentation. • Thank you for listening. • Are there any questions?*

So kannst du über Bilder/ein Poster/eine Folie sprechen:
This picture shows ...
On my poster/On this slide you can see ...

2. Während deines Vortrags

- Sprich langsam und deutlich.
- Sieh deine Zuhörerinnen und Zuhörer während des Sprechens an.
- Versuche, möglichst frei zu sprechen. Du kannst die wichtigsten Punkte von deinen Notizen oder deinem Poster ablesen.

Wenn du mal den Faden verlierst: Bleibe ruhig und versuche, dich an deinen Text zu erinnern. Du kannst dann sagen: *Just a moment, please.* oder *Wait a second.*

3. Nach dem Vortrag

- Wenn du zuhörst, wirst du manchmal aufgefordert, nach einem Vortrag Feedback zu geben. Folge dabei dieser Regel: Nenne zunächst eine Sache, die dir besonders gut gefallen hat. Mache dann einen Vorschlag, wie der Vortrag beim nächsten Mal noch besser werden kann. Das kannst du zum Beispiel so formulieren:

- Mache dir ein paar Notizen zum Feedback deiner Zuhörerinnen und Zuhörer. So kannst du dir merken, was du das nächste Mal noch besser machen kannst.

Writing Schreiben

Wenn du Texte schreibst, gehst du am besten Schritt für Schritt vor.

1. Planen

- Wie lautet die Aufgabe? Worüber sollst du schreiben?
  Was für eine Textsorte soll es sein: eine E-Mail, eine Filmkritik, ein Erfahrungsbericht, ...?
- Sammle Ideen und Wörter zu deinem Thema. Dafür gibt es verschiedene Möglichkeiten:

  Word web
  Du kannst ein *word web* entweder auf Papier schreiben oder ein Computer-Programm dazu verwenden. Mit dem Computer-Programm kannst du dein *word web* speichern und jederzeit bearbeiten.

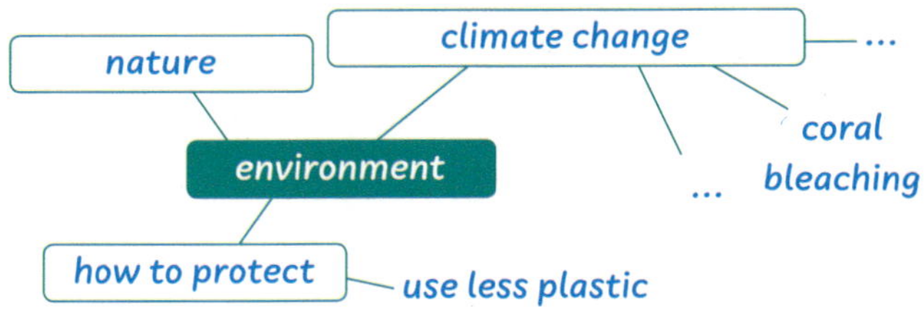

  Liste
  In einer Liste kannst du schnell und unkompliziert Ideen sammeln. Verwende Stichwörter und Abkürzungen, das spart Zeit. Am einfachsten geht das auf einem Blatt Papier. Es gibt aber auch Apps, die dir helfen, deine Notizen zu organisieren. Der Vorteil ist, dass du die Liste bearbeiten und beliebig erweitern kannst.

  Tabelle
  In einer Tabelle kannst du deine Ideen gleich in einer Struktur ordnen. Das bietet sich zum Beispiel an, wenn du darüber schreiben willst, was du magst und was nicht. Tabellen lassen sich auf Papier oder mit einem Textverarbeitungsprogramm auf dem Computer erstellen. Das ist praktisch, wenn du noch Zeilen oder Spalten ergänzen möchtest.

- Viele Texte lassen sich in Einleitung, Hauptteil und Schluss gliedern. Überlege dir vor dem Schreiben eine sinnvolle Reihenfolge: Was schreibst du zuerst, was folgt darauf und was kann am Ende stehen?

Auf den Seiten 209/210 stehen Hinweise, worauf du bei bestimmten Textsorten achten solltest. Informationen zum Erstellen von Texten am Computer/Tablet und zur Online-Kommunikation findest du unter:
- Writing and designing texts ▶ **WB** Media 3 ▶ WES-149226-2
- Writing comments online ▶ **WB** Media 2 ▶ WES-149226-2
- Writing a blog entry ▶ **WB** Media 1 ▶ WES-149226-2

2. Einen Entwurf verfassen

- Schau dir deine Planung noch einmal an und los geht's!
- Du kannst auch Texte im Buch als Muster benutzen: Übernimm passende Satzanfänge und Ausdrücke und ersetze die Wörter, die nicht zu deinem Thema passen.
- Unterteile deinen Text in Abschnitte: Beginne für jeden neuen Gedanken einen neuen Absatz.
- Verbinde Sätze mit Konjunktionen, damit sich dein Text flüssig liest.
- Verwende nicht immer das gleiche Wort: Verwende statt *say* z. B. *agree*, *wonder*, *ask* oder *answer*.
- Überlege dir eine passende Überschrift für deinen Text.
- Wenn du deinen Text am Computer oder auf einem Tablet schreibst, kannst du die Rechtschreib- und Grammatikkorrektur des Textverarbeitungsprogramms als zusätzliche Hilfe nutzen.

Eine Zusammenfassung schreiben (*summary*)
- Lies den ganzen Text aufmerksam durch, um dir einen Überblick zu verschaffen: Worum geht es?
- Teile den Text in sinnvolle Abschnitte ein.
- Notiere dir für jeden Abschnitt die wichtigsten Informationen. Wenn du eine Kopie des Textes hast, kennzeichne die Stellen, die wichtig sind.
- Beginne deine Zusammenfassung mit einer kurzen Einleitung, die beschreibt, worum es im Text geht.
- Verwende nun deine Notizen, um deine Zusammenfassung zu schreiben.
- Verzichte auf wörtliche Rede und ausschmückende Details.
- Deine Zusammenfassung darf keine eigene Meinung enthalten.
- Benutze die einfache Gegenwart (*simple present*).

Einen Erfahrungsbericht schreiben (*personal account*)
- Finde eine passende Überschrift, die das Interesse der Leserinnen und Leser weckt.
- Beginne mit einem Einleitungssatz. Er sollte kurz die Fragen *What? Where? Who? When?* und *Why?* beantworten.
- Im Hauptteil beschreibst du deine Erfahrung im Detail. Berichte der Reihe nach, was passiert ist und wie dich dabei gefühlt hast.
- Beende deinen Bericht mit einer kurzen Schlussfolgerung. War es eine gute oder eher eine schlechte Erfahrung für dich?

Eine Filmkritik schreiben (*film review*)
- Wähle einen Film und mache dir Notizen dazu: *What? Where? Who? When? Why?*
- Nenne Titel und Erscheinungsjahr und gib an, wer Regie geführt hat und wer die Hauptrollen spielt. Gib an, um welche Art von Film (*comedy, drama, ...*) es sich handelt.
- Gliedere deine Filmkritik in Einleitung, Hauptteil und Schluss.
- Beschreibe, worum es im Film geht, aber verrate nicht zu viel, wie z. B. das Ende. Erkläre, was dir an dem Film gefällt und was du nicht gelungen findest.
- Begründe abschließend in zwei bis drei Sätzen, warum du den Film empfiehlst oder nicht.

Eine Stellungnahme schreiben (*comment*)
- Notiere Ideen, die dir zum Thema oder zu der gestellten Frage einfallen. Eine Tabelle oder Liste mit Argumenten (dafür und dagegen), Begründungen und Beispielen hilft, deine Ideen zu ordnen.
- Entscheide dich, welche Position oder Meinung du vertrittst.
- Formuliere eine kurze Einleitung (ein bis zwei Sätze), die das Thema aufgreift und deine Meinung dazu wiedergibt.
- Strukturiere den Hauptteil, indem du jeden Absatz mit einem Gegenargument zu deiner Meinung beginnst. Anschließend setzt du dem ein Argument entgegen, das deine Position wiedergibt.
- Formuliere einen Schluss, der deine Meinung noch einmal klar zusammenfasst.

Eine Geschichte fortsetzen (*continuing a story*)
- Lies den oder die Textauschnitte genau durch und mache dir Notizen zu den einzelnen Figuren. Was erfährst du über die Figuren? Welche Eigenschaften haben sie? Was fühlen sie und warum? Wie ist das Verhältnis der Figuren zueinander?
- Verwende deine Notizen als Ausgangspunkt und denke dir eine Situation aus, die du beschreiben willst. Überlege dir, was passiert, welche Figuren beteiligt sind und was sie sagen könnten.
- Prüfe, ob das Verhalten der Figuren und das, was sie sagen, zu dem passt, was du dir im ersten Schritt notiert hast.
- Behalte die Erzählperspektive des Originaltextes bei und imitiere den Stil des Autors/der Autorin.

Einen Lebenslauf schreiben (*CV*)

- Ein Lebenslauf soll einen Überblick über deine Ausbildung, deine Qualifikationen, Fähigkeiten und Interessen geben.
- Gib deinen Namen, deine Adresse und deine Kontaktinformationen oben auf der Seite an.
- *Personal profile*: Fasse in einem kurzen Absatz die wichtigsten Informationen über dich zusammen.
- Darunter listest du *education* (Ausbildung), *work experience* (Arbeitserfahrung), *skills* (Fähigkeiten) und *languages* (Sprachkenntnisse). Beginne jeweils mit den aktuellsten Punkten.
- Achte darauf, dass dein Lebenslauf übersichtlich ist und nur relevante Informationen enthält.

Einen formellen Brief/ein Anschreiben verfassen (*formal letter/cover letter*)

- Rechts oben gibst du deinen Namen und deine Kontaktinformationen an.
- Darunter setzt du links Namen und Adresse des Empfängers.
- In der nächsten Zeile ergänzt du rechts das Datum.
- Danach kommt die Betreffzeile. Hier sagst du, worum es in deinem Brief geht.
- Beginne den Brief mit *Dear Mr/Mrs/Ms ...* oder *Dear Sir/Madam*, falls du den Namen nicht kennst.
- Im ersten Absatz erklärst du, weshalb du den Brief schreibst (z. B. *I am writing in response to your advertisement.*). Handelt es sich um ein Anschreiben, beschreibst du im zweiten Absatz, warum du gut für die Stelle geeignet bist (z. B. *I believe I am a good candidate for this job because ...*). Schließe deinen Brief mit ein bis zwei zusammenfassenden Sätzen ab.
- Verwende *Yours faithfully, ...* als Abschlussformel und unterschreibe mit deinem vollen Namen.
- Verwende formale Sprache.

Einen Zeitungsartikel schreiben (*newspaper article*)

- In einem Zeitungsartikel berichtest du über ein Ereignis, indem du so viele *wh*-Fragen wie möglich beantwortest: *Who? What? When? Where? Why?*
- Mit wörtlicher oder indirekter Rede kannst du Experten oder Augenzeugen zitieren.
- Zur besseren Lesbarkeit gliederst du deinen Artikel in sinnvolle Absätze.
- Finde eine passende Überschrift für deinen Artikel, die über das Thema des Artikels informiert und das Interesse der Lesenden weckt. In einer Unterüberschrift kannst du zusätzliche Informationen geben.
- Je nachdem, für welche Art von Zeitung (*quality newspaper* oder *tabloid*) du schreibst, wählst du den passenden Ton (*quality newspaper:* sachlich/informativ; *tabloid*: subjektiver/emotionaler).
- Verwende Passivformen, um den Fokus auf das Geschehene zu lenken.
- Verwende entsprechend der Art von Zeitung ein passendes Layout (Anordnung und Größe von Text, Bildern und Überschrift).

3. Überarbeiten und Fertigstellen

- Wenn es möglich ist, tauscht eure Texte untereinander aus. Markiert im fremden Text mit Bleistift oder mit der Korrekturfunktion des Textverarbeitungsprogramms, was euch besonders gefällt, was unverständlich ist, was noch ergänzt und was verbessert werden sollte.
- Schlage Wörter, bei denen du unsicher bist, im *dictionary* ab Seite 277 oder in einem Wörterbuch nach.
- Schau auch in der Grammatik ab Seite 216 nach, wenn du dir nicht ganz sicher bist.
- Dann kannst du deinen Text ins Reine schreiben.
- Sammle deine besten Texte in deiner Portfolio-Mappe.

Searching the internet Suchmaschinen benutzen

Es gibt verschiedene Möglichkeiten, im Internet zu einem Thema nach Informationen oder Bildern zu suchen.

1. Benutze eine Suchmaschine

- Formuliere möglichst genau, wonach du suchst. Je genauer deine Suchbegriffe sind, desto besser passende Suchergebnisse bekommst du.
- Gib die Suchbegriffe in eine Suchmaschine ein. Einfache Fragen (z. B. *Is Australia part of the Commonwealth?*) kannst du direkt ins Suchfeld eingeben.

2. Wähle passende Suchergebnisse aus

- Deine Aufgabe ist nun, aus der großen Anzahl von Treffern die besten Suchergebnisse auszuwählen.
- Sieh dir die Titel und Kurzbeschreibungen der Suchergebnisse an: Welche passen am besten zu deiner Suche?
- Wenn du etwas Passendes gefunden hast, öffne den Link in einem neuen Fenster und überfliege die Seite. Du musst nicht jedes Wort verstehen, entscheidend ist, ob du Informationen findest, die deine Frage beantworten.
- Prüfe, wer die Webseite erstellt hat. Handelt es sich um vertrauenswürdige Quellen (z. B. seriöse Medien oder ein Online-Lexikon) eine persönliche Meinung oder ist es eventuell sogar Werbung?
- Solltest du keine passenden Informationen finden, versuche es mit einer anderen Webseite oder beginne eine neue Suche mit anderen Suchbegriffen.

3. Halte nützliche Informationen fest

- Wenn du geeignete Webseiten gefunden hast, kannst du dir Notizen zu den Inhalten machen.
- Speichere die Internetadresse, damit du später noch weißt, wo du die Informationen gefunden hast.
- Wenn du Textausschnitte für deinen eigenen Text unverändert übernimmst, musst du diese mit Anführungszeichen als Zitat kenntlich machen und die Quelle (Internetadresse) angeben.
- Wenn du Bilder aus dem Internet verwenden willst, musst du ebenfalls die Quelle angeben.

4. Sei kritisch

- Informationen, die du im Internet findest, müssen nicht immer richtig sein. Sei deshalb kritisch und überprüfe die Informationen noch einmal auf anderen Seiten oder in einem Lexikon.

Set the alarm!
Setze dir am besten vor deiner Suche ein Zeitlimit. Es kann sonst schnell passieren, dass du von Link zu Link klickst und vergisst, wonach du eigentlich suchen wolltest.

Viewing Videos und Filme verstehen

Wenn du dir Videos oder Filme/Filmauschnitte auf Englisch ansiehst, brauchst du nicht jedes Wort zu verstehen. Hier sind einige Tipps, die dir beim Verstehen helfen können.

1. Vor dem Ansehen

- Wie lautet die Aufgabe, die du bearbeiten sollst? Lies sie dir gründlich durch, damit du weißt, was genau du herausfinden sollst.
- Überlege: Worum könnte es im Video oder Filmausschnitt gehen? Was weißt du schon über das Thema oder die Situation (z. B. Australien, soziale Medien, Klimawandel)?
- Gibt es ein Vorschaubild? Was ist darauf zu sehen? Vielleicht kannst du schon herausfinden, wer mit wem spricht oder wo sich die Personen befinden.

2. Während des Ansehens

- Während du das Video oder den Filmausschnitt ansiehst, konzentriere dich auf die Fragen, die du beantworten sollst.
- Bleibe entspannt, wenn schnell oder mit einem Akzent gesprochen wird und du nicht jedes Wort verstehst.
- Die Mimik, Gestik und Stimmlage der Personen können dir helfen zu verstehen, worum es geht. Achte darauf, wie die Personen sich verhalten. Wie fühlen sie sich? In welchem Verhältnis stehen die Personen zueinander?
- Achte bei Filmen auch darauf, welche Atmosphäre durch Hintergrundmusik, Kameraführung und Beleuchtung geschaffen wird.
- Mache dir Notizen. Notiere nur Stichwörter, keine ganzen Sätze.
- Wenn du die Aufgabe noch nicht gleich lösen konntest, dann sieh dir das Video oder den Filmausschnitt ein weiteres Mal an und achte auf Signalwörter. Ergänze deine Notizen.

3. Nach dem Ansehen

- Wenn es möglich ist, vergleiche deine Ergebnisse mit jemandem aus deiner Klasse. Habt ihr das Gleiche herausgefunden?

Nützliche Redewendungen, um über Filme zu sprechen
The characters' facial expressions show how frightened/scared/happy/... they are.
Their body language expresses fear/frustration/confidence/...
The lighting and the colours create an atmosphere of ...
The film's background music is used to emphasize ...
By shooting the scene in slow motion, the director focuses on ...
The camera is at a great distance from ... • *The camera is very close to ...*

Mediation Sprachmittlung

Wenn du zwischen zwei Sprachen vermittelst, nennt man das *mediation*. Damit kannst du Menschen helfen, die kaum Englisch oder Deutsch verstehen.

1. Analysiere die Aufgabe

Lies dir zuerst die Aufgabe genau durch und beantworte folgende Fragen:

- Welche „Rolle" wirst du einnehmen?
- In welcher Situation findet die Sprachmittlung statt?
- Auf welche Aspekte musst du dich konzentrieren?
- Wer ist dein Adressat?
- In welcher Art von Text (mündlich oder schriftlich) gibst du die Information wieder?

You take part in a school exchange with an Australian school. You are asked to give a short presentation on life at German schools in front of your Australian classmates. Your topic is how your school organizes work experience in year 10 and you take your school's info sheet below as a starting point.
Write down a script for your presentation. Focus on when and where you do your work experience, why you do it and what kinds of jobs you should look for.

2. Gib den Sinn wieder

Es kommt nicht darauf an, dass du alles Wort für Wort übersetzt. Wichtiger ist es, den Sinn wiederzugeben. Es muss nur klar werden, worum es geht. Unwichtige Einzelheiten kannst du weglassen.

3. Bilde kurze Sätze

Einen längeren Satz in eine andere Sprache zu übertragen, ist einfacher, wenn du kurze Sätze bildest. Zum Beispiel: „Im Film *Words on Bathroom Walls*, der auf einem Roman von Julia Walton basiert, spielen Charlie Plummer, Taylor Russell und Andy Garcia die Hauptrollen." → *The movie "Words on Bathroom Walls" is based on a novel by Julia Walton. The movie stars Charlie Plummer, Taylor Russell and Andy Garcia in the main roles.*

4. Umschreibe Wörter

Wenn dir ein bestimmtes Wort nicht einfällt, kannst du es umschreiben. Wenn du zum Beispiel nicht weißt, was „Praktikum" auf Englisch heißt. Dann kannst du sagen: *It's a job you do for a few weeks or months to get some work experience.*

Nützliche Redewendungen, um Wörter zu umschreiben

It's somebody who ...
It's something that you ... to ...
It's a place where ...
It's similar to ... • *It's the same as ...* • *It's the opposite of ...*
When you ..., you ...

5. Vorsicht bei Redewendungen

Jede Sprache hat ihre eigenen Redewendungen, die sich meistens nicht wortwörtlich übersetzen lassen. Beispiel: „Lisa hat einen Bärenhunger." → *Lisa is as hungry as a horse.* Falls du die Redewendung in der anderen Sprache nicht kennst oder es keine gibt, kannst du auch einfach den Sinn wiedergeben: *Lisa is very hungry.*

Working with others Mit anderen zusammenarbeiten

Buzz groups

In einer *buzz group* könnt ihr zu einem Thema Ideen sammeln oder eure Meinung austauschen.

1 Arbeitet in Gruppen (4-5 Personen).
2 Sprecht für ein paar Minuten über das Thema. Achtet darauf, mit leiser Stimme zu sprechen.
Einer/Eine von euch macht Notizen in Stichpunkten.
3 Wählt ein Gruppenmitglied, das der Klasse eure Ideen zum Thema kurz vorstellt.

Class wall chart

Eine *class wall chart* ist eine Wandzeitung in eurem Klassenzimmer, auf der ihr Informationen zu einem Thema (z. B. Australien) sammeln könnt.

1 Sammelt Informationen und Material zum Thema.
2 Legt gemeinsam fest, in welche Kategorien ihr eure Wandzeitung aufteilen wollt (z. B. *geography, sports, history, ...*).
3 Gestaltet für jede Kategorie ein Poster, das ihr anschließend aufhängt. Ordnet eure Materialien übersichtlich an. Probiert dabei verschiedene Möglichkeiten aus. Am besten ist eine Mischung aus Texten, Bildern und evtl. Diagrammen.
4 Bei längeren Unterrichtseinheiten könnt ihr auch weitere Kategorien zu eurer Wandzeitung hinzufügen.

Information relay

Mit dieser Methode könnt ihr Informationen aus längeren Texten erschließen und austauschen. Ihr könnt dabei in eurem eigenen Tempo arbeiten und müsst nicht darauf warten, bis die ganze Gruppe die Aufgabe erledigt hat.

1 Teilt die Klasse in zwei Gruppen (A und B).
2 Legt drei Punkte zum Austausch (*relay points*) im Klassenzimmer fest.
3 Gruppe A liest den Text und notiert sich Informationen zu einer bestimmten Frage. Gruppe B liest den Text und notiert sich Informationen zu einer anderen Frage.
4 Wer aus Gruppe A mit dem Lesen und Notieren fertig ist, begibt sich zum *relay point* A und vergleicht dort mit jemand anderem aus Gruppe A seine/ihre Notizen. Falls nötig, könnt ihr eure Notizen ergänzen oder korrigieren. Gruppe B verfährt genauso.
5 Anschließend geht ihr zum dritten *relay point* und wartet auf jemanden aus der anderen Gruppe. Tauscht die jeweiligen Informationen, die ihr gefunden habt, aus.

Milling around

Milling around bedeutet „Umherlaufen". Damit könnt ihr euch in der Klasse zu einem Thema austauschen.

1 Jede/Jeder in der Klasse geht mit Aufgabe und Stift durch den Raum, ohne dass dabei gesprochen wird.
2 Wenn deine Lehrerin/dein Lehrer ein Zeichen gibt, dann sprich mit der Person, vor der du gerade stehst. Tauscht euch über die Aufgabe aus und notiert die Ergebnisse.
3 Beim nächsten Zeichen gehst du weiter.

Placemat

Auf einer *placemat* sammelst du mit den anderen aus deiner Gruppe zu einem Thema gleichzeitig Ideen.

1 Jede/r von euch macht auf einem Teil eines großen Bogens Papier Notizen.
2 Anschließend dreht ihr die *placemat* so lange, bis jede/r alle Beiträge gelesen hat.
3 Einigt euch dann in der Gruppe auf die wichtigsten Punkte und notiert sie in der Mitte des Blattes.
4 Schließlich stellt ein Gruppenmitglied das Ergebnis in der Klasse vor.

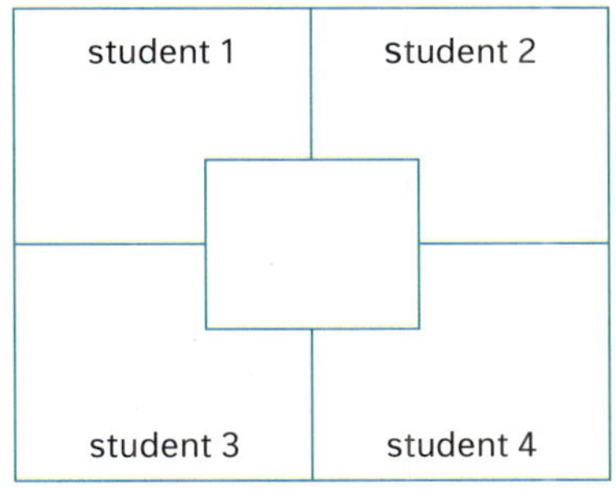

Round robin

Mit dieser Methode könnt ihr euch kurz zu einem Thema äußern.

1 Überlege dir zum vorgegebenen Thema eine kurze Stellungnahme aus ein oder zwei Sätzen.
2 Äußert euch reihum in der Klasse. Dabei sind keine Kommentare oder direkte Reaktionen erlaubt.
3 Wurde bereits vor dir etwas gesagt, was du sagen wolltest, dann überlege, ob dir noch ein weiterer Punkt einfällt oder ob du deine Stellungnahme etwas anders formulieren kannst.

Think – pair – share

Mit dieser Methode könnt ihr euch gemeinsam Gedanken zu einem Thema machen.

1 *Think:* Sammle deine Gedanken und mache dir Notizen.
2 *Pair:* Tausche dich mit jemandem aus. Ergänze deine Notizen.
3 *Share:* Teilt eure Gedanken mit einem anderen Paar.

think

pair

share

G Grammar

Inhalt

Theme 1

G1 R Die Zeitformen des Verbs 217
- **a)** Die einfache Gegenwart
- **b)** Die Verlaufsform der Gegenwart
- **c)** Die einfache Vergangenheit
- **d)** Die Verlaufsform der Vergangenheit
- **e)** Das Perfekt
- **f)** Die Verlaufsform des Perfekts
- **g)** Das Plusquamperfekt
- **h)** Die Verlaufsform des Plusquamperfekts
- **i)** Das Futur mit *going to*
- **j)** Das Futur mit *will*
- **k)** Die einfache Gegenwart mit Zukunftsbedeutung
- **l)** Die Verlaufsform der Gegenwart mit Zukunftsbedeutung

G2 R Das Passiv 220

G3 R Indirekte Rede 221

G4 R Adverbiale Nebensätze 223

Theme 2

G5 R Bedingungssätze, Typ 1–3 224

G6 R Modalverben und ihre Ersatzformen 225

G7 Partizipien und Partizipialkonstruktionen 227
- **a)** Partizipien anstelle von Relativsätzen
- **b)** Partizipien anstelle von adverbialen Nebensätzen
- **c)** Zwei Hauptsätze mit Partizipien verbinden
- **d)** Partizipien nach Verben der Ruhe oder Bewegung
- **e)** Partizipien nach Verben der Sinneswahrnehmung

Theme 3

G8 R Relativsätze 230
- **a)** Notwendige Relativsätze
- **b)** Notwendige Relativsätze ohne Relativpronomen
- **c)** Nicht-notwendige Relativsätze
- **d)** Nicht-notwendige Relativsätze, die sich auf einen Satz beziehen

Theme 4

G9 Besondere Satzstrukturen 231
- **a)** Indirekte Fragen
- **b)** Fragewort + Infinitiv mit *to*

G10 Weitere Futurformen 231
- **a)** Das *future perfect*
- **b)** Die Verlaufsform der Zukunft

G11 Ausdrucksmöglichkeiten für das deutsche ‚lassen' 232
- **a)** *Make/let* + Objekt + Infinitiv ohne *to*
- **b)** *Have something done*

Theme 5

G12 Adverbiale Bestimmungen im Satz 232

G13 R Der Infinitiv mit oder ohne *to* 233

G14 Das *emphatic 'do'* 234

G15 Das Gerundium oder der Infinitiv mit *to* 234

Grammatical terms 235

- Im folgenden Teil *Grammar* findest du die grammatischen Regeln. Wenn vorne im Buch zum Beispiel ▶ G5R | p. 224 steht, kannst du auf Seite 224 unter G5R die passenden Regeln nachschlagen. Das „R“ hinter der Nummer steht für *revision* (Wiederholung).
- Videos zu einzelnen Grammatikthemen findest du, indem du den Webcode WES-149226-4 auf www.westermann.de/webcode eingibst. Dort findest du auch den *Grammar*-Anhang aus Textbook 5 bis 8 zum Nachschlagen.

Theme 1

G1 R Die Zeitformen des Verbs ▶ D3 | p. 145, D5 | p. 153
Tenses

Die verschiedenen Zeitformen eines Verbs (*tenses*) helfen dir auszudrücken, wann etwas im Ablauf der Zeit (*time*) passiert. Außerdem sagen die verschiedenen Zeitformen etwas über Gewohnheiten und Zustände aus.

a) Die einfache Gegenwart The simple present

Das *simple present* verwendest du, ...

- um über Gewohnheiten oder regelmäßige Handlungen zu sprechen.

  They usually **eat** dinner at home.

- um über aufeinanderfolgende Handlungen zu sprechen.

  First you **change** into your sports clothes. Then you **warm up**. After that you **talk** to the coach.

- um über Zustände zu sprechen, die längere Zeit gültig sind oder längere Zeit andauern.

  My brother and his wife **live** in New York.

Signalwörter sind: *always, usually, often, sometimes, never, every day/week/..., on Mondays/...*

b) Die Verlaufsform der Gegenwart The present progressive

Das *present progressive* verwendest du, um Handlungen zu beschreiben, die im Augenblick des Sprechens ablaufen.

Laura **is doing** her homework at the moment.	My mother **is** just **talking** to her boss.

Signalwörter sind: *at the moment, right now, just, today.*

c) Die einfache Vergangenheit The simple past

Das *simple past* verwendest du, wenn du über Vorgänge und Handlungen sprichst, die abgeschlossen sind.

I **read** an article about social media yesterday.	We **went** to Spain in 2019.

Signalwörter sind: *yesterday, last week, last year, two years ago, in 2019.*

! Wie du weißt, gibt es im Englischen unregelmäßige Verben, die für das *simple past* eigene Formen haben. Eine Liste mit unregelmäßigen Verben findest du auf den Seiten 337–339.

d) Die Verlaufsform der Vergangenheit The past progressive

Das *past progressive* drückt aus, dass eine Handlung in der Vergangenheit im Gang war, als eine zweite Handlung einsetzte. Die zweite Handlung steht im *simple past*.

She **was searching** for her earring when the phone rang.
While she **was looking** everywhere for her earring, her son tried to call her.

e) Das Perfekt The present perfect

Das *present perfect* verwendest du, wenn du über Vorgänge und Handlungen sprichst, die ...

- in der Vergangenheit begonnen haben und bis in die Gegenwart andauern.

  He **has forgotten** to feed the cats for the third time. His dad is talking to him right now.

- zwar beendet sind, aber noch Auswirkungen auf die Gegenwart haben.

  Please wait a minute. I **haven't finished** my breakfast yet.

- gerade erst stattgefunden haben.

  I **have** just **finished** my homework.

Signalwörter sind: *ever, never, since, already, just, not yet.*

! Unregelmäßige Verben haben im *present perfect* eigene Formen.
Eine Liste mit unregelmäßigen Verben findest du auf den Seiten 337–339.

f) Die Verlaufsform des Perfekts The present perfect progressive

Du verwendest die Verlaufsform des Perfekts (*present perfect progressive*), um über eine Handlung zu sprechen, die in der Vergangenheit begonnen hat und immer noch andauert. Meistens handelt es sich um eine vorübergehende Handlung.
So bildest du das *present perfect progressive*: ***have/has* + *been* + *-ing*-Form des Verbs**.

She **has been watching** TV for over three hours.

g) Das Plusquamperfekt The past perfect

Das *past perfect* drückt aus, dass eine Handlung vor einer anderen Handlung in der Vergangenheit stattgefunden hat. Die zweite Handlung steht im *simple past*. Beide Handlungen sind abgeschlossen.

After the rain **had stopped**, they went to the park.
Claire ordered two hamburgers because she **hadn't eaten** since the day before.

! Unregelmäßige Verben haben ein unregelmäßiges Partizip Perfekt (*past participle*).
Eine Liste mit unregelmäßigen Verben findest du auf den Seiten 337–339.

h) Die Verlaufsform des Plusquamperfekts The past perfect progressive

Die Verlaufsform des Plusquamperfekts (*past perfect progressive*) verwendest du, um über eine Handlung zu sprechen, die vor einer anderen stattgefunden hat. Die neu eintretende Handlung steht im *simple past*.
Im Vergleich zum *past perfect* wird mit dem *past perfect progressive* die Dauer einer Handlung betont.
So wird das *past perfect progressive* gebildet: ***had* + *been* + *-ing*-Form des Verbs**.

When they finally arrived, their coach **had** already **been talking** about tactics for half an hour.

For, since, all day/week/month werden oft mit dem *past perfect progressive* verwendet.

i) Das Futur mit *going to* The *going to* future

Du verwendest das *going to future*, um über Absichten und Pläne für die Zukunft zu sprechen.

> We**'re going to fly** to Poland in July, but we haven't bought any tickets yet.
> She **isn't going to go** the party tomorrow.
> **Are** you **going to watch** the game tonight?

> *Tomorrow, soon, in January/February/March/..., in the future* sind Wörter, die oft zusammen mit dem *going to future* verwendet werden.

Mit dem *going to future* kannst du auch ausdrücken, dass du glaubst, dass etwas gleich passieren wird (weil es deutliche Hinweise darauf gibt).

> Look at the man with the dog! I think they are **going to get** very wet.

j) Das Futur mit *will* The *will* future

Du verwendest das *will future*, um über Vorhersagen, Versprechen und Vermutungen zu sprechen.

The weather **will be** great tomorrow.	I **won't tell** anyone about the surprise party.

> Diese Wörter bestimmen den zukünftigen Zeitpunkt näher, an dem etwas voraussichtlich stattfinden wird: *tonight, tomorrow, next year.*
> Mit diesen Wörtern kannst du eine Vermutung über ein zukünftiges Ereignis ausdrücken: *I think, I'm (not) sure, I hope, I guess, probably, maybe.*

k) Die einfache Gegenwart mit Zukunftsbedeutung
The simple present with future meaning

Sprichst du über feststehende Termine, die in der Zukunft liegen, kannst du dafür wie im Deutschen die einfache Gegenwart verwenden. Vor allem im Zusammenhang mit Fahrplänen, Programmen oder Öffnungszeiten wird das *simple present with future meaning* gebraucht.

> The train from Edinburgh **arrives** at seven o'clock.
> My work shift **finishes** at six o'clock.
> When **does** the museum **open**?

l) Die Verlaufsform der Gegenwart mit Zukunftsbedeutung
The present progressive with future meaning

Möchtest du über feste persönliche Pläne und Vorhaben sprechen, kannst du dazu das *present progressive* benutzen.

> I**'m** definitely **meeting** my friend tomorrow.
> **Are** you **spending** the day with Grandma?

> Aus dem Kontext oder durch Zeitangaben wie *tomorrow, next month, later today* etc. wird deutlich, dass es sich um die Zukunft und nicht die Gegenwart handelt.

G2 R Das Passiv
▶ p. 18 ▶ D11 | p. 148, D8 | p. 167

The passive

a) Bildung und Verwendung des Passivs How to form and use the passive

Aktivsätze sagen uns, wer oder was handelt. Wenn es aber nicht wichtig oder nicht klar ist, wer etwas tut oder getan hat, kannst du das Passiv (*passive*) verwenden. In diesen Fällen steht die Handlung im Vordergrund. Das Passiv bildest du aus einer **Form von *be* + *past participle***.

simple present (*am/is/are + past participle*)	Bags **are** often **stolen** at the market.
simple past (*was/were + past participle*)	A red bag **was stolen** at the market yesterday.
present perfect (*has/have been + past participle*)	The red bag **has been found**.
will future (*will be + past participle*)	The red bag **will be given** back to the owner.
going to future (*am/is/are going to be + past participle*)	The pickpocket **is going to be sent** to prison.
modal verbs (*can/must/may/... + be + past participle*)	The pickpocket **must be kept** in prison for a few days.

Verneinungen und Fragen werden im Passiv so gebildet:

Bags **aren't** often **stolen** at the market.
When and where **was** your bag **stolen**?

In Zeitungsüberschriften kommen häufig verkürzte Passivformen vor. Statt *A student from Atlanta **was accepted** to 40 universities* steht dann beispielsweise *Atlanta student **accepted** to 40 universities.*

Wenn du in einem Passiv-Satz die handelnde Person oder die Ursache für etwas nennen willst, hängst du sie mit ***by*** („von“, „durch“) an den Satz an.

The World Wide Web was invented **by** Tim Berners-Lee.	The house was damaged **by** a storm.

b) Persönliches Passiv Personal passive

Bei Verben mit zwei Objekten wird im Englischen häufig das ***personal passive*** verwendet. Dabei wird das indirekte Objekt eines Aktivsatzes zum Subjekt des Passivsatzes.

	Subjekt	Verb	Indirektes Objekt	Direktes Objekt
Aktivsatz:	Somebody	showed	Karl	the school rules.
Personal passive:	Karl	was shown		the school rules.

Im Deutschen verwenden wir andere Konstruktionen, z. B. einen Aktivsatz mit „man“ oder „jemand“:
***The students were given** one hour for the task.*
Man gab den Lernenden eine Stunde für die Aufgabe. / Die Lernenden hatten eine Stunde für die Aufgabe.

Man unterscheidet direkte und indirekte Objekte:
Das indirekte Objekt steht meistens für eine Person, das direkte Objekt für eine Sache.

G3 R Indirekte Rede
Reported speech

▶ D14 | p. 149, D14 | p. 170

Wenn du berichten willst, was jemand gesagt hat, verwendest du die indirekte Rede (*reported speech*). Die indirekte Rede besteht aus einem Begleitsatz und der wiedergegebenen Aussage. Beide Satzteile können durch *that* verbunden werden, man kann es aber meist auch weglassen.

a) Zeitverschiebung Backshift of tenses
Steht das Verb des Begleitsatzes in der Vergangenheit, erfolgt in der wiedergegebenen Aussage eine Zeitverschiebung (*backshift of tenses*): Die Zeitform der wiedergegebenen Aussage rückt gegenüber der direkten Rede sozusagen eine Stufe weiter in die Vergangenheit.

Direkte Rede (*direct speech*)	Indirekte Rede (*reported speech*)
simple present Alex to Mrs Sutcliffe: "The food **is** delicious."	➡ ***simple past*** Alex told Mrs Sutcliffe (that) the food **was** delicious.
present progressive Laura: "Noah, you **are getting** on my nerves!"	➡ ***past progressive*** Laura told Noah (that) he **was getting** on her nerves.
simple past Shelby: "I **messaged** Kim."	➡ ***past perfect*** Shelby said (that) she **had messaged** Kim.
past progressive Shelby: "I **was waiting** for you when Kim called."	➡ ***past perfect progressive*** Shelby said (that) she **had been waiting** for me when Kim called.
present perfect Ryan to Mrs Carson: "I'**ve** just **spoken** to my parents."	➡ ***past perfect*** Ryan told Mrs Carson (that) he **had** just **spoken** to his parents.
present perfect progressive Lisa: "I'**ve been baking** biscuits all day.	➡ ***past perfect progressive*** Lisa said (that) she **had been baking** biscuits all day.
past perfect Noah: "Ryan felt much better after he **had changed** his schedule."	➡ ***past perfect*** (no backshift) Noah said (that) Ryan had felt much better after he **had changed** his schedule.
past perfect progressive Tom: "By the time the bus arrived, I **had been waiting** for 20 minutes."	➡ ***past perfect progressive*** (no backshift) Tom said that by the time the bus had arrived, he **had been waiting** for 20 minutes.
will Ben to his girlfriend: "I **will** call you later."	➡ ***would*** Ben told his girlfriend (that) he **would** call her later.
is/are going to Ali to his friends: "I'**m going to** miss you."	➡ ***was/were going to*** Ali told his friends (that) he **was going to** miss them.
can/must/may Shelby to Ryan: "I **can** help you." Ali to Laura: "You **must** talk to Mrs Graham." Laura: "I **may** think about it."	➡ ***could/had to/might*** Shelby told Ryan (that) she **could** help him. Ali told Laura (that) she **had to** talk to Mrs Graham. Laura said (that) she **might** think about it.

Wenn die Aussage, die du wiedergibst, jetzt noch von Bedeutung oder allgemeingültig ist, wird kein *backshift of tenses* benötigt.
*Mrs Graham: "Phones **are** not allowed in the study hall."*
➡ *Mrs Graham **said** that phones **are** not allowed in the study hall.*

➡

b) Weitere Anpassungen in der indirekten Rede Further changes in reported speech
Personalpronomen (*personal pronouns*) und Possessivbegleiter (*possessive determiners*) müssen angepasst werden, damit der wiedergegebene Satz Sinn ergibt.

	direct speech	reported speech
I ➡ she/he	Mrs Graham: "**I** always work on Sundays."	Mrs Graham told me that **she** always worked on Sundays.
you ➡ I, me, we, us	Noah: "Tyler saw **you** at the supermarket."	Noah told us that Tyler had seen **us** at the supermarket.
we ➡ they	Vanessa and Kaito: "**We** had an amazing time at the beach."	Vanessa and Kaito said that **they** had had an amazing time at the beach.
my ➡ her, his	Ava: "**My** father has just left."	Ava said that **her** father had just left.
our ➡ their	Mr and Mrs Lin: "**Our** cat was ill."	The Lins said that **their** cat had been ill.
me ➡ him, her	Mateo: "Mira doesn't like **me**."	Mateo said that Mira didn't like **him**.
us ➡ them	Kim: "Joe took **us** to school."	Kim said that Joe had taken **them** to school.

So kannst du Orts- und Zeitangaben der Situation anpassen:

here	➡ there		
today	➡ that day	yesterday	➡ the day before
tomorrow	➡ the next day	three days ago	➡ three days before/earlier
next year	➡ the following year	last week/year	➡ the week/year before

c) Fragen in der indirekten Rede Reported questions
Wenn du eine **Entscheidungsfrage** (*yes/no question*) wiedergeben willst, benutzt du *if* oder *whether*.

Direkter Fragesatz *(direct question)*	Indirekter Fragesatz *(reported question)*
"Have I told you about my favourite book?"	She asked me **if** she had told me about her favourite book.
"Will you be home for Christmas?"	We wanted to know **whether** they would be home for Christmas.

Wenn die Frage mit einem **Fragewort** (*question word*) beginnt, übernimmst du das Fragewort:
*"**When** will the game start?"* ➡ *He asked her **when** the game would start.*

Die **Satzstellung** (*word order*) in indirekten Fragesätzen ist genauso wie in Aussagesätzen.

direct question	*reported question*	Aussagesatz zum Vergleich
"Where **is** **Aaron**?"	He asked her where **Aaron** **was**.	**Aaron** **was** at home.

Wie bei indirekten Aussagesätzen rückt auch bei indirekten Fragesätzen die Zeitform der wiedergegebenen Rede eine Stufe weiter in die Vergangenheit als die direkte Rede (*backshift of tenses*).

Wenn die Frage, die du wiedergibst, jetzt noch von Bedeutung oder allgemeingültig ist, wird kein *backshift of tenses* benötigt.
*Kayla: "How many types of snakes **live** in Asia?"* ➡ *Kayla asked how many types of snakes **live** in Asia.*

d) Bitten und Aufforderungen in der indirekten Rede Reported requests and commands

Wenn du eine Bitte (*request*) oder eine Aufforderung (*command*) im Imperativ wiedergeben möchtest, verwendest du den Infinitiv mit *to/not to*.

Direkte Rede *(direct speech)*	**Indirekte Bitte/Aufforderung *(reported request/command)***
"Please close the door."	He asked me **to close** the door.
"Don't wait until Monday."	Mr Wilkinson told Aisha **not to wait** until Monday.

Für Befehle und Aufforderungen verwendest du *tell somebody to do something*, für Bitten *ask somebody to do something*.

Da die Bitte bzw. Aufforderung mit einer Infinitivkonstruktion wiedergegeben wird, erfolgt kein *backshift of tenses*. Für weitere Verben im Satz gelten jedoch dieselben Regeln wie für indirekte Aussagesätze: *Karl's father: "**Be** polite to everybody you **meet**."* ➡ *Karl's father told him **to be** polite to everybody he **met**.*

G4 R Adverbiale Nebensätze Adverbial clauses ▶ p. 22

Adverbiale Nebensätze (*adverbial clauses*) werden durch eine Konjunktion wie *although, while* oder *because* eingeleitet. Durch adverbiale Nebensätze werden Texte flüssiger und interessanter. Du kennst das von den *connectives*.

! Adverbiale Nebensätze stehen vor oder nach dem Hauptsatz. Steht der adverbiale Nebensatz vor dem Hauptsatz, wird ein Komma gesetzt. Kommt er nach dem Hauptsatz, steht kein Komma.

Man unterscheidet folgende Arten von *adverbial clauses:*

Adverbiale Nebensätze ...	**Verwendete Konjunktionen**	
... der Zeit *(adverbial clauses of time)*	**when, whenever, while, as soon as, after, before, as, until**	**As soon as she had read the message**, she left the house.
... des Ortes/der Richtung *(adverbial clauses of place/direction)*	**where**	I told him **where we live**.
... des Vergleichs *(adverbial clauses of comparison)*	**as ... as, than**	Ben was nicer **than she had thought**.
... der Einräumung/des Gegensatzes *(adverbial clauses of concession/contrast)*	**although, even though, whereas, but**	**Although donuts are very popular**, they are not that easy to make.
... des Grundes *(adverbial clauses of reason)*	**because, as, since**	Amelia always walks to school **since she only lives one block away**.
... der Absicht/des Zwecks *(adverbial clauses of purpose)*	**so, so that**	Please pass me the orange juice **so that I can have something to drink**.
... der Art und Weise *(adverbial clauses of manner)*	**as if, as though**	He acted **as if he hadn't noticed**.

Bei einigen Konjunktionen kann man sowohl mit dem adverbialen Nebensatz als auch mit dem Hauptsatz beginnen. Es kommt darauf an, was man betonen möchte:

*Milan's cousin had lived in Ithaca **before he moved to Chicago**.* ➡ Der Fokus liegt auf der Information, dass Milans Cousin zuvor in Ithaca gelebt hat.

***Before he moved to Chicago**, Milan's cousin had lived in Ithaca.* ➡ Die Betonung liegt auf Chicago.

Theme 2

G5 R Bedingungssätze Conditional clauses ▶ D3 | p. 152

a) Bedingungssätze, Typ 1 Conditional clauses, type 1

Mit dem Bedingungssatz, Typ 1 (*conditional clause, type 1*) drückst du aus, was passiert, wenn eine Bedingung erfüllt wird. Im *if*-Satz steht das ***simple present***. Im Hauptsatz steht das ***will future***, ein Modalverb (z. B. *can, must*) oder der Imperativ.

If you **miss** the bus, you **will be** late.	**If** it **rains**, we **can go** inside.
If you **like** her, you **must call** her.	**If** you **need** help, **ask** Lara.

Bedingungssätze können mit dem *if*-Satz oder mit dem Hauptsatz beginnen.
Wenn sie mit dem *if*-Satz beginnen, werden sie mit einem Komma getrennt.
Wenn sie mit dem Hauptsatz beginnen, verwendest du kein Komma.

If you go to the cinema, I'**ll** come with you.	I'**ll** come with you **if** you go to the cinema.

b) Bedingungssätze, Typ 2 Conditional clauses, type 2

Der Bedingungssatz, Typ 2 (*conditional clause, type 2*) drückt aus, was unter einer nur gedachten Bedingung passieren würde oder könnte. Es geht um Ereignisse, die unwahrscheinlich oder unmöglich sind. Im *if*-Satz steht das ***simple past***. Im Hauptsatz steht z. B. ***would/could* + Infinitiv**.

If Ben **wasn't** so shy, he **would invite** Kayla to his party next week.
Teenagers **would make** the world a better place **if** they **had** more power.

Üblicherweise sagt man "If I were ...", aber auch "If I was ..." ist weit verbreitet:
*If I **were** rich, I could help a lot of people.*
*If I **was** better at climbing, I would like to take part in a competition.*

! Denke daran: *would* nur im Hauptsatz, nie im *if*-Satz!

c) Bedingungssätze, Typ 3 Conditional clauses, type 3

Mit dem Bedingungssatz, Typ 3 (*conditional clause, type 3*) spekulierst du, was in der Vergangenheit hätte passieren können, aber nicht passiert ist. Die Bedingung im *if*-Satz ist nicht mehr erfüllbar. Du kannst diese Art von Bedingungssatz verwenden, um über verpasste Möglichkeiten zu sprechen. Im *if*-Satz steht das ***past perfect***. Im Hauptsatz steht ***would/could/might* + *have* + *past participle***.

If I **had missed** the bus, I **would have been** late for school.
If it **had rained**, we **would have stayed** at home.
I **would have helped** you **if** you **had told** us about your problems.

G6 R Modalverben und ihre Ersatzformen
Modal verbs and their substitute forms

▶ p. 43 ▶ D13 | p. 156

Modalverben geben an, ob etwas erlaubt oder notwendig ist. Die meisten Modalverben haben nur Formen für das *simple present*. Im *simple past*, *present perfect*, *will future* und in anderen Zeitformen verwendest du deshalb die Ersatzformen (*substitute forms*).

a) Fähigkeit Ability

Wenn jemand in der Lage oder fähig ist, etwas zu tun, verwendest du ***can*** und die Ersatzform ***be able to***.

can – be able to (*können*)		
simple present	**can**	I **can** read.
simple past	**was/were able to**	She **was able to** play the piano at the age of 4.
present perfect	**have/has been able to**	Leo **has been able to** play the guitar since last year.
will future	**will be able to**	Her leg hurts. She **won't be able to** play football for four weeks.

❗ Im *simple past* kannst du auch ***could/couldn't*** verwenden: *I **couldn't** go to school because I was ill.*

b) Erlaubnis Permission

Mit ***may/may not, can/can't, mustn't*** und der Ersatzform ***be allowed to*** kannst du ausdrücken, dass etwas erlaubt oder verboten ist.

may, may not, can, can't, mustn't – (not) be allowed to (*dürfen, nicht dürfen*)		
simple present	**may/can** **may not** **can't** **mustn't**	**May/Can** I open the window? I'm sorry, but you **may not** leave your bike here. Craig **can't** eat milk products. You **mustn't** talk in class.
simple past	**was/were allowed to**	Students **were allowed to** use their phones in class.
present perfect	**have/has been allowed to**	My friend **has been allowed to** come on holiday with us.
will future	**will be allowed to**	Leyla **will be allowed to** go to her friends' party next week.

❗ Für ***may not*** gibt es keine Kurzform.

❗ ***Mustn't*** klingt wie „muss nicht“, heißt aber „etwas nicht dürfen“.
Wenn jemand etwas nicht zu tun braucht, verwendet man ***needn't***.

Mustn't ist strenger als *may not/can't*.

You are **not allowed** to play football in the park.

c) Notwendigkeit Necessity

Mit ***must*** und der Ersatzform ***have to*** kannst du ausdrücken, dass etwas getan werden muss.

must – have to (*müssen*)		
simple present	**must**	You **must** drive on the left in Britain.
simple past	**had to**	It was very late so she **had to** say goodbye and leave.
present perfect	**have/has had to**	Keira **has had to** apologize to her English teacher more than once.
will future	**will have to**	I'm afraid we **will have to** stay in Germany during the holidays.

Mit ***needn't*** und der Ersatzform ***don't have to*** kannst du ausdrücken, dass etwas nicht notwendig ist.

needn't – don't have to (*nicht müssen*)		
simple present	**needn't**	We **needn't** buy any milk. There's enough in the fridge.
simple past	**didn't have to**	I'm glad I **didn't have to** explain to my teacher why I was late.
present perfect	**haven't/hasn't had to**	Tom is lucky. He **hasn't had to** get up early since last summer.
will future	**won't have to**	I'm glad I **won't have to** spend any money on a new phone.

! ***Needn't*** hat die gleiche Bedeutung wie ***don't have to***, ist aber etwas förmlicher.

Du kannst die Ersatzformen der Modalverben auch im *simple present* verwenden.

*Leyla **is allowed to** go to her friend's party tonight.*

*I **have to** get up very early every morning.*

*We**'re not able to** accept your booking.*

*Don't worry. You **don't have to** help me.*

d) Empfehlung Advice

Mit ***should/shouldn't*** kannst du eine Empfehlung bzw. einen Rat aussprechen.

You **should** leave now if you want to catch the bus. | You **shouldn't** go to the party on your own.

Ought to/ought not to (Kurzform: ***oughtn't***) hat die gleiche Bedeutung wie ***should/shouldn't***, wirkt aber etwas strenger.

You **ought to** do more exercise. | You **ought not to** eat so much fast food.

e) Möglichkeit Possibility

Mit ***may/may not*** kannst du ausdrücken, dass etwas möglicherweise geschieht bzw. nicht geschieht.

It **may** rain today. | Kerima **may not** come to basketball practice today.

! ***May not*** ist nicht eindeutig. Es kann „wird möglicherweise nicht" und „darf nicht" heißen.

Statt ***may/may not*** kannst du auch ***might/might not*** verwenden.

Kim has been cycling all day long. She **might** be tired.

Ed has just called. He **might not** be able to go hiking with us this summer.

f) Vorschlag/Angebot Suggestion/offer

Wenn du einen Vorschlag oder ein Angebot machen möchtest, kannst du ***shall*** verwenden. Es taucht in Form einer Frage auf.

Shall I help you with the bags? | When **shall** we all meet for dinner?

g) Pflicht Obligation

Wenn du ausdrücken möchtest, dass es die Pflicht ist, etwas zu tun oder zu lassen, verwendest du ***be supposed to/not be supposed to***.

You **are supposed to** take off your shoes before you go into the gym.
Luke **was not supposed to** tell his father about the birthday surprise.

Wenn du dich besonders formell ausdrücken möchtest, kannst du ***be to*** verwenden. Die Konstruktion wird im gesprochenen Englisch nur selten verwendet, normalerweise nur für Regeln und Verordnungen.

Pupils **are to** arrive at school before eight o'clock.	We **are to** report to the headteacher if we are late.

h) Should/shouldn't, could/couldn't und die Perfektform des Infinitivs
should/shouldn't, could/couldn't and the perfect infinitive

Um auszudrücken, was hätte passieren oder getan werden sollen oder können, verwendest du ***should/shouldn't, could/couldn't + have + past participle***.

You **should have called** your parents to let them know you would be home late.
I'm sorry. I know I **shouldn't have talked** about you behind your back.

G7 Partizipien und Partizipialkonstruktionen

▶ p. 49 ▶ D24–D28 | p. 161

Participles and participle constructions

Das **Partizip Präsens** (*present participle*) wird für Verlaufsformen (*progressive forms*) verwendet.

She is **reading** a book at the moment.	We were **making** dinner when the phone rang.

Das **Partizip Perfekt** (*past participle*) wird für Zeitformen wie das *present perfect*, das *past perfect* und das Passiv verwendet.

He has not **finished** his homework yet.	The building was **destroyed** in the fire.

Du kannst Partizipien verwenden, um die Satzstruktur zu variieren.

a) Partizipien anstelle von Relativsätzen Participles in place of relative clauses

Du kannst mithilfe von Partizipien Relativsätze ersetzen. Voraussetzung ist, dass das Relativpronomen Subjekt des Relativsatzes ist. Ein *present participle* ersetzt einen Relativsatz im Aktiv, ein *past participle* einen Relativsatz im Passiv.

active sentence with a relative clause	sentence with present participle
The man who lives in the red house is my uncle.	The man **living** in the red house is my uncle.
My cousin who lives in Canada speaks perfect French.	My cousin **living** in Canada speaks perfect French.
Is there anybody who is listening to me?	Is there anybody **listening** to me?

passive sentence with a relative clause	sentence with past participle
Cars which are parked here will be reported.	Cars **parked** here will be reported.
Clothes which have been left in the gym can be picked up in room 221.	Clothes **left** in the gym can be picked up in room 221.
Have you posted all the photos which were taken on the trip?	Have you posted all the photos **taken** on the trip?

➡

b) Partizipien anstelle von adverbialen Nebensätzen Participles in place of adverbial clauses

Du kannst mithilfe von Partizipien auch einige adverbiale Nebensätze ersetzen. Dies betrifft vor allem adverbiale Nebensätze der Zeit (*when*) und des Grundes (*because*). Voraussetzung ist, dass das Subjekt des Hauptsatzes auch Subjekt des adverbialen Nebensatzes ist. Auch hier gilt: Ein *present participle* ersetzt einen Nebensatz im Aktiv, ein *past participle* ersetzt einen Nebensatz im Passiv.

sentence with adverbial clause	sentence with participle
Tim lost his phone when he was coming home from school.	Tim lost his phone **coming** home from school.
I fell in love with you when I saw you for the first time.	I fell in love with you **seeing** you for the first time.
She never goes to rock concerts because she hates loud music.	**Hating** loud music, she never goes to rock concerts.
As it was bought a week ago, the bread is now dry.	**Bought** a week ago, the bread is now dry.

Möchtest du ausdrücken, dass eine Handlung vor einer anderen geschehen ist, kannst du dafür das *perfect participle* verwenden. Es wird gebildet aus ***having + past participle***, ersetzt adverbiale Nebensätze im Aktiv und steht am Satzanfang.

sentence with adverbial clause	sentence with perfect participle
Lisa expected good results in her exam because she had worked really hard.	**Having worked** really hard, Lisa expected good results in her exam.
After I had moved, I had to make new friends.	**Having moved**, I had to make new friends.
Now that we have seen all the sights, we can go shopping.	**Having seen** all the sights, we can go shopping now.

Das *perfect participle* gibt es auch im Passiv. Es wird gebildet aus ***having + been + past participle***. Es ersetzt adverbiale Nebensätze, die im Passiv stehen. Auch hier beginnt der verkürzte Satz mit dem *perfect participle,* d. h. der früheren Handlung.

sentence with adverbial clause	sentence with perfect participle
After we had been attacked, we called the police at once.	**Having been attacked**, we called the police at once.
The shoes were cheap because they had been worn before.	**Having been worn** before, the shoes were cheap.

c) Zwei Hauptsätze mit Partizipien verbinden Using participles to join two sentences

Du kannst mithilfe von Partizipien auch zwei Hauptsätze verbinden, wenn beide Sätze das gleiche Subjekt haben und beide Handlungen zur gleichen Zeit ablaufen. Ein *present participle* ersetzt dann einen Satz im Aktiv, ein *past participle* einen Satz im Passiv.

two separate sentences	sentence with participle construction
The players left the field. They thought the match was over.	The players left the field **thinking** the match was over.
Jamie looked in the fridge. He hoped to find some milk.	Jamie looked in the fridge **hoping** to find some milk.
The students were encouraged by the good results. They decided to work even harder.	**Encouraged** by the good results, the students decided to work even harder.

d) Partizipien nach Verben der Ruhe oder Bewegung
Present participle after verbs of rest and motion

Nach Verben der Bewegung (z. B. *arrive, leave, come, go, run, walk*) und Verben der Ruhe (z. B. *sit, stand, lie, stay, remain*) wird häufig das *present participle* gebraucht. Diese Konstruktion wird benutzt, um zwei gleichzeitig ablaufende Handlungen zu beschreiben.

He **came running** out of his bedroom.
I **went looking** for our dog, but I couldn't find him.

e) Partizipien nach Verben der Sinneswahrnehmung Present participle after verbs of perception

Das *present participle* steht nach Verben der Sinneswahrnehmung (*verbs of perception*) wie z. B. *look, notice, see, hear, feel* und *smell*. Hierbei wird betont, dass der Handlungsablauf noch nicht abgeschlossen ist. Diese Partizipialkonstruktion wird gebildet aus **Verb + Objekt + *present participle***.

I **heard you talking** on the telephone.
My parents **saw the boy running** out of the shop.

Nach Verben der Sinneswahrnehmung kann auch der Infinitiv stehen, z. B. wenn betont werden soll, dass eine Handlung abgeschlossen ist.

The whole class **watched her get up and walk** to the blackboard.
I **saw our dog dig** a hole in the garden.

In short: Participle constructions

- You can use participle constructions to replace relative clauses and adverbial clauses if they have the same subject as the main clause.
  In addition, you can use participle constructions to link two main clauses if they share the subject and if the two actions are happening at the same time.
  For active clauses, you use the present participle (= *ing*-form).
  ***Going** home, she noticed that her purse was gone.*
  For passive clauses, you use the past participle.
  ***Founded** in 2018, the school still looked very new.*
- If one action happens before the other, you can use the perfect participle, in the active or in the passive voice.
  ***Having boarded** the plane, she suddenly felt scared that something might happen.*
  ***Having been awarded** to men for many years, the Oscar for best director went to a woman this year.*
- You can use the present participle after **verbs of rest and motion** and after **verbs of perception + object**:
  *Don't just **stand** there **waiting** for a reaction!*
  *I can **hear you** **talking** about my sister behind her back. That's not very nice.*

Having moved to a new neighbourhood last month, Sam often stops for a chat with his new next-door neighbour, Mr Black.

Theme 3

G8 R Relativsätze Relative clauses ▶ D9-D11 | p. 168

Um eine Person oder eine Sache genauer zu beschreiben, verwendest du Relativsätze (*relative clauses*). Es gibt zwei Arten von Relativsatzen: Notwendige Relativsätze (*defining relative clauses*) und nicht-notwendige Relativsätze (*non-defining relative clauses*).

a) Notwendige Relativsätze Defining relative clauses

Defining relative clauses beginnen in der Regel mit einem Relativpronomen (*relative pronoun*) – *who, which, that* oder *whose* – und bestimmen das Wort näher, auf das sie sich beziehen. Sie können nicht weggelassen werden, da der Hauptsatz sonst keinen Sinn ergäbe.

Lily is the girl **who is sitting next to your brother**.
I like Chicago but New York is the city **that I have always wanted to visit**.

b) Notwendige Relativsätze ohne Relativpronomen Contact clauses

Es gibt notwendige Relativsätze, bei denen du das Relativpronomen weglassen kannst. Sie heißen dann *contact clauses*, weil Hauptsatz und Relativsatz in direktem „Kontakt" stehen, also ohne ein Relativpronomen dazwischen.
Das Relativpronomen kannst du nur weglassen, wenn es Objekt des Relativsatzes ist.

Let me tell you about the book **I read in two days**.
I like Chicago but New York is the city **I have always wanted to visit**.

c) Nicht-notwendige Relativsätze Non-defining relative clauses

Non-defining relative clauses liefern zusätzliche Informationen über eine Person oder Sache im Hauptsatz. Sie könnten weggelassen werden, da der Hauptsatz auch ohne sie verständlich bliebe. *Non-defining relative clauses* sind vom Hauptsatz durch Kommas getrennt.

This is my friend Lewis, **who is on exchange from Dublin**.
This book, **which I bought yesterday**, is about New York.
Mia, **whose mother is our geography teacher**, is really nice.

! Das Relativpronomen *that* wird im nicht-notwendigen Relativsatz nicht verwendet.
Es kann nur im notwendigen Relativsatz stehen.

The book **that** I lost was about Native American history.

d) Nicht-notwendige Relativsätze, die sich auf einen Satz beziehen
Non-defining relative clauses referring to a sentence/an idea

Non-defining relative clauses können sich auch auf einen vorausgehenden ganzen Satz beziehen.

We had lunch at home, **which saved us a lot of time**.
Theo won't make it to the party, **which is a shame**.
My cousin is getting married, **which I find very exciting**.

Auch hier wird der Relativsatz vom Hauptsatz durch Komma getrennt.

Theme 4

G9 Besondere Satzstrukturen ▶ D3 | p. 174
Complex sentence structures

a) Indirekte Fragen   Indirect questions

Indirekte Fragen sind Fragen, die sich in einem Nebensatz verstecken. Du verwendest sie, wenn du höflich oder versteckt etwas in Erfahrung bringen möchtest.
Indirekte Fragen beginnen mit einem einleitenden Hauptsatz wie *I wonder, He wanted to know, …*

I would like to know what time the museum opens.
I often wonder what life was like before the invention of the internet.
He asked himself what he would have done if his friends hadn't helped him.

! Indirekte Fragen enden ohne Fragezeichen, da sie grammatisch gesehen keine Fragen sind.

b) Fragewort + Infinitiv mit *to*   Question word + infinitive with *to*

Auf ein Fragewort kann ein Nebensatz mit Modalverb folgen (*can, must, should, …*).
Allerdings ist es idiomatischer, an das Fragewort direkt den Infinitiv mit *to* anzuschließen.

subordinate clause: question word + modal verb	question word + infinitive with *to*
I need help. I don't know **what I should do**.	I need help. I don't know **what to do**.
We weren't sure **where we had to buy the tickets**.	We weren't sure **where to buy the tickets**.
My grandmother taught me **how I can make lasagne**.	My grandmother taught me **how to make lasagne**.

! Diese Konstruktion ist im Deutschen nicht möglich.

G10 Weitere Futurformen ▶ D7, D8 | p. 176
More ways to express the future

a) Das *future perfect*   The future perfect

Das *future perfect* wird aus ***will + have + past participle*** gebildet.
Du verwendest es, um auszudrücken, dass etwas zu einem bestimmten Zeitpunkt in der Zukunft abgeschlossen sein wird.

Hurry up! The others **will have eaten** all the food by the time we get to the party.
Our English test is next week. By then I **will have learnt** all of the irregular verbs by heart.

! Unregelmäßige Verben haben ein unregelmäßiges Partizip Perfekt (*past participle*).
Eine Liste mit unregelmäßigen Verben findest du auf den Seiten 337–339.

b) Die Verlaufsform der Zukunft   The future progressive

Du bildest das *future progressive* mit ***will + be + -ing*-Form des Verbs**.
Das *future progressive* verwendest du, um Dinge zu beschreiben, die zu einem bestimmten Zeitpunkt in der Zukunft gerade ablaufen werden.

At 10 o'clock tomorrow we **will be writing** an English exam.
I'**ll be having** coffee and cake with my grandparents on Tuesday.

G11 Ausdrucksmöglichkeiten für das deutsche ‚lassen' ▶ p. 97 ▶ D13 | p. 179
(English equivalents for 'lassen' in German)

a) *Make/let* + Objekt + Infinitiv ohne *to* *Make/let* + object + infinitive without *to*

Die Verben *let* und *make*, nach denen der Infinitiv ohne *to* und ein direktes Objekt steht, werden üblicherweise mit „lassen" übersetzt. Allerdings unterscheiden sie sich in ihrer Bedeutung: *let* meint zulassen/erlauben, während *make* veranlassen/zwingen bedeutet.

I **let him use** my phone.	*Ich habe ihn mein Handy benutzen lassen.* *Ich habe ihm erlaubt, mein Handy zu benutzen.*
My mother **made me buy** a new phone.	*Meine Mutter hat mich ein neues Handy kaufen lassen.* *Meine Mutter hat mich gezwungen, ein neues Handy zu kaufen.*

b) *Have something done*

Möchtest du ausdrücken, dass jemand etwas von jemand anderem machen lässt, verwendest du *have something done*.

Subjekt	Form von *have*	Objekt	Partizip Perfekt		
I	**had**	**my bike**	**repaired**	by a friend.	*Ich habe mein Fahrrad von einer Freundin reparieren lassen.*
My dad	**will have**	**his hair**	**cut**	next week.	*Nächste Woche lässt mein Vater sich die Haare schneiden.*

! Achte darauf, dass du *have something done* nicht mit dem *present perfect* oder *past perfect* verwechselst. Beim *present perfect* und *past perfect* steht das Objekt nach dem **Partizip Perfekt** (*past participle*), bei *have something done* davor:
Present perfect: I have **repaired my bike**. ➡ Ich habe mein Fahrrad repariert.
have something done: I want to have **my bike repaired**. ➡ Ich will mein Fahrrad reparieren lassen.

Theme 5

G12 Adverbiale Bestimmungen im Satz ▶ D11 | p. 188
Sequence of adverbials

Adverbien und adverbiale Bestimmungen können am Satzanfang, in der Mitte oder am Ende stehen, abhängig von ihrer Funktion (Häufigkeitsadverbien, Adverbien der Art und Weise, des Ortes und der Zeit).

Treffen mehrere adverbiale Bestimmungen am Satzende aufeinander, so gilt in der Regel **Art und Weise** + **Ort** + **Zeit**.

My younger brother was born **in Berlin** **in 2019**.
Three people were standing **quietly** **on the old bridge** **in the early morning**.
I hope to hang out with my best friend **in town** **after school tomorrow**.
Our team won the game and we celebrated **happily** **on the bus** **afterwards**.
The orchestra played **very well** **in Leeds** **on Monday night**.
Peter played **brilliantly** **on the pitch** **on Saturday**.

Bei Adverbien der bestimmten Häufigkeit *(once, twice, three times, many times, weekly, ...)* gilt:
Ort + **bestimmte Häufigkeit** + **Zeit**

My best friend and I met **at the cinema** **twice** **during the summer holidays**.
My parents stayed **in my grandparents' holiday flat** **three times** **last year**.

! Im Deutschen gelten bei adverbialen Bestimmungen andere Regeln: Zeit + Art und Weise + Ort.
Wir feierten am letzten Schultag ausgelassen im Schulhof.
Sie saßen nach dem Gespräch verärgert im Wohnzimmer.

G13 R Der Infinitiv mit oder ohne *to* ▶ D8 | p. 187
The infinitive with or without *to*

Es gibt den Infinitiv mit und ohne *to*. Meist wird der Infinitiv mit *to* gebraucht, z. B. nach den Verben *decide, hope, choose, offer, promise*.
Es gibt jedoch Fälle, in denen der Infinitiv ohne *to* verwendet werden muss.

a) Infinitiv mit *to* Infinitive with *to*

- Nach einem **Fragewort,** um einen Nebensatz mit Modalverb zu ersetzen (▶ G9):

My grandmother taught me how **to make** banana muffins.

- Nach ***expect, tell, ask, want, invite, force, teach, persuade, remind*** + **Objekt**:

My mum expects/wants me **to call** her if I'm late.	*Meine Mutter erwartet/will, dass ich sie anrufe, wenn ich mich verspäte.*
Why didn't you ask me **to help** you with your maths homework?	*Warum hast du mich nicht gebeten, dir bei den Mathehausaufgaben zu helfen?*
Lenn often tells his brother **to stop** shouting.	*Lenn sagt oft zu seinem Bruder, dass er aufhören soll zu schreien.*

! Auf *ask* und *expect* kann der Infinitiv mit *to* oder ein direktes Objekt und der Infinitiv mit *to* folgen:
I **asked to speak** to the boss. *Ich bat darum, mit der Chefin zu sprechen.*
I **asked** **you** **to speak** to the boss. *Ich bat dich, mit der Chefin zu sprechen.*
I **expect to be treated** fairly. *Ich erwarte, fair behandelt zu werden.*
I **expect** **him** **to be treated** fairly. *Ich erwarte, dass er fair behandelt wird.*

b) Infinitiv ohne *to* Infinitive without *to*

- Nach **Modalverben** wie z. B. *can, must, should* (▶ G6R):

I think you **should stop** playing the guitar. I'm afraid it sounds awful.

- Nach ***let/make*** + **Objekt** (▶ G11):

Why won't you **let** me **help** you with your maths homework?

- Nach **Verben der Sinneswahrnehmung** + **Objekt**:

My mum didn't **hear** the phone **ring**.	I'm very sorry I wasn't there to **see** you **score** the goal.

Verben der Sinneswahrnehmung sind: *watch, notice, hear, see, listen, feel.*

G14 Das *emphatic 'do'* Emphatic *do* ▶ D17 | p. 191

Möchtest du einer Aussage Nachdruck verleihen, kannst du das *emphatic 'do'* verwenden. Es wird aus ***do/does/did*** + **Infinitiv ohne *to*** gebildet und betont das Verb im Infinitiv. Im Deutschen benutzt du Wörter wie „doch", „ja", „wirklich", „tatsächlich". Beim Aussprechen betonst du ***do/does/did***.

I **do** hope she wasn't badly injured.	*Ich hoffe doch sehr, dass sie nicht schwer verletzt wurde.*
I **did** do my homework. I promise!	*Ich habe meine Hausaufgaben wirklich gemacht. Ehrenwort!*
Do have another piece of cake!	*Iss doch noch ein Stück Kuchen.*

G15 Das Gerundium oder der Infinitiv mit *to* ▶ p. 131 ▶ D19 | p. 192
Gerund or infinitive with *to*

Du bildest das Gerundium, indem du *-ing* an den Infinitiv des Verbs hängst.

- Das *gerund* kann Subjekt eines Satzes sein.

Walking is good for you.	**Eating cake** is my favourite hobby.

- Als Objekt eines Satzes steht das *gerund* häufig nach bestimmten Verben, z. B. *enjoy, keep, suggest, avoid, spend/waste time, imagine, recommend, consider*. Am besten merkst du dir diese Verben.

Jonah **enjoys swimming**.	Alicia **keeps talking** about poetry.

- Das *gerund* steht auch oft nach Adjektiv + Präposition oder Verb + Präposition.

Charlotte is **good at playing** volleyball.	We **look forward to going** on holiday next month.

- Das *gerund* kann ein eigenes Subjekt haben (Nomen oder Pronomen).

Our teacher doesn't like **us using** our phones in class.	I don't mind **Joe leaving** the party early.

! Im Deutschen gibt es diese Konstruktion nicht.

- Nach den Verben *begin, start, continue, like, love, hate, prefer* kannst du das *gerund* **oder** den Infinitiv mit *to* verwenden. Es gibt keinen Bedeutungsunterschied.

It **started raining** two hours ago. It **started to rain** two hours ago.	Es hat vor zwei Stunden angefangen zu regnen.

- Nach den Verben *remember, stop, try, mean, forget* und *go on* macht es einen Unterschied, ob du das *gerund* oder den Infinitiv mit *to* verwendest. Die Bedeutung verändert sich.

Remember to buy some milk, please. *(daran denken, etw zu tun)*	↔	I **remember going** to the market every Saturday when I was a child. *(sich an etw erinnern)*
He **stopped to think** about it. *(mit etw aufhören, um etw anderes zu tun)*	↔	He **stopped thinking** about it. *(aufhören, etw zu tun)*
She **tried to** find her key, but she couldn't. *(versuchen, etw zu tun)*	↔	She **tried playing** the piano, but she didn't like it. *(etw ausprobieren)*
He **meant to buy** some milk but then forgot. *(beabsichtigen, etw zu tun)*	↔	It **will mean coming** home late. *(etw bedeuten)*
She **forgot to turn** off the lights. *(vergessen, etw zu tun → man tut es nicht)*	↔	She will never **forget seeing** him for the first time. *(vergessen, etw getan zu haben → man hat es getan)*
She **went on to explain** the rules to us. *(etw als Nächstes tun)*	↔	She **went on talking** as if nothing had happened. *(fortfahren, etw zu tun)*

Grammatical terms

Englisch		Deutsch	Beispiel
adjective		Adjektiv	a **wonderful** book
adverb	G 12	Adverb	
adverb of degree		Gradadverb	**a little, very, extremely,** …
adverb of frequency		Häufigkeitsadverb	**sometimes, often, never, twice,** …
adverb of manner		Adverb der Art und Weise	He closed the door **angrily**.
adverbial		adverbiale Bestimmung	**in London, on the bed, during the night, after the game,** …
sentence adverb		Satzadverb	**firstly, after that, finally,** …
clause		Halbsatz, Satz	
adverbial clause	G 4R	adverbialer Nebensatz	My father didn't buy the apples **because they weren't fresh.**
clause of comparison		Vergleichssatz	**Mia can run as fast as Sophie.**
conditional clause, type 1	G 5Ra	Bedingungssatz, Typ 1	**If you miss the bus, you will be late.**
conditional clause, type 2	G 5Rb	Bedingungssatz, Typ 2	**If I were rich, I would help you.**
conditional clause, type 3	G 5Rc	Bedingungssatz, Typ 3	**If I hadn't walked the dog that day, I wouldn't have seen the poster.**
if-clause	G 5R	*If*-Satz	**If I had the money,** I would help you.
main clause	G 5R	Hauptsatz	If I could, **I would come with you.**
relative clause	G 8R	Relativsatz	This is the man **who helped me.**
emphatic 'do'	G 14		I **do** hope you're telling the truth.
future		Futur (Zukunft)	
going to future	G 1Ri	Futur mit *going to*	She**'s going to buy** a new skateboard.
will future	G 1Rj	Futur mit *will*	I'm sure he **will be** a pop star.
future perfect	G 10a		The bus **will have left** by then.
future progressive	G 10b	Verlaufsform der Zukunft	This time tomorrow we **will be sitting** at the airport.
simple present with future meaning	G 1Rk	einfache Gegenwart mit Zukunftsbedeutung	The museum **closes** at five o'clock.
present progressive with future meaning	G 1Rl	Verlaufsform der Gegenwart mit Zukunftsbedeutung	I**'m meeting** my friend in town tomorrow afternoon.
gerund	G 15	Gerundium	**Fighting** isn't fun. Everybody likes **going** on holiday.
infinitive		Infinitiv (Grundform)	(to) **walk**, (to) **go**, (to) **read**, …
infinitive with *to*	G 3Rd, G 9b, G 13Ra	Infinitiv mit *to*	Sam prefers **to go** by bus.
infinitive without *to*	G 11a, G 13Rb, G 14	Infinitiv ohne *to*	Please let me **go** to the party!
perfect infinitive	G 6Rh	Infinitiv Perfekt	You should **have come** with us.
modal verb	G 6R	Modalverb	**can, must, need, should,** …
noun		Nomen (Hauptwort, Substantiv)	
countable noun		zählbares Nomen	**song, child, car, dog,** …
uncountable noun		nicht zählbares Nomen	**milk, homework, information,** …
object		Objekt	
direct object	G 2R, G 11, G 13R	direktes Objekt	Leo wrote **an email**.
indirect object	G 2R	indirektes Objekt	Leo wrote **his aunt** an email.
participle		Partizip	
participle constructions	G 7	Partizipialkonstruktionen	The dog **sitting** over there is mine.
present participle	G 7	Partizip Präsens	**going, driving, drinking,** …
past participle	G 1R, G 2R, G 5R, G 6R, G 7, G 11	Partizip Perfekt	**eaten, gone, started,** …
perfect participle	G 7b		**having gone, having left,** …

G Grammar

Englisch		Deutsch	Beispiel
passive	G 2R	Passiv	The bag **was stolen**.
personal passive	G 2R	persönliches Passiv	The woman **was given** the bag.
past perfect	G 1Rg	Plusquamperfekt (Vorvergangenheit)	He didn't hand in his homework because his dog **had eaten** it.
past perfect progressive	G 1Rh	Verlaufsform des Plusquamperfekts	Hazel **had been sleeping** for two hours when Gianna messaged her.
past tense		Vergangenheitsform	
simple past	G 1Rc	einfache Vergangenheit	They **played** baseball yesterday.
past progressive	G 1Rd	Verlaufsform der Vergangenheit	Kate **was talking** to Tom when her mum called.
possessive determiner		Possessivbegleiter	**my, your, his, her, its, our, their**
preposition		Präposition	**at, in, of, for,** ...
present perfect	G 1Re	Perfekt	Kim **has written** a book about Utah.
present perfect progressive	G 1Rf	Verlaufsform des Perfekts	They **have been waiting** for the boat since six o'clock this morning.
present tense		Präsens (Gegenwart)	
simple present	G 1Ra	einfache Gegenwart	Leslie often **walks** to school.
simple present with future meaning	G 1Rk	einfache Gegenwart mit Zukunftsbedeutung	The lesson **starts** at 8 o'clock.
present progressive	G 1Rb	Verlaufsform der Gegenwart	Look, it**'s raining**.
present progressive with future meaning	G 1Rl	Verlaufsform der Gegenwart mit Zukunftsbedeutung	**I'm meeting** my friend in town tomorrow afternoon.
pronoun		Pronomen (Fürwort)	
indefinite pronoun		indefinites Pronomen	**somebody, anybody, something,** ...
personal pronoun		Personalpronomen	
object pronoun		Objektpronomen	**me, you, him, her, it, us, them**
subject pronoun		Subjektpronomen	**I, you, he, she, it, we, they**
possessive pronoun		Possessivpronomen	**mine, yours, hers,** ...
reciprocal pronoun		reziprokes Pronomen	**each other, one another**
reflexive pronoun		Reflexivpronomen	**myself, yourself, themselves,** ...
relative pronoun	G 8R	Relativpronomen	**who, which, that, whose**
question		Frage	
indirect question	G 3Rc, G 9	indirekte Frage	**I don't know what to do.**
question tag		Bestätigungsfrage	The book is great, **isn't it?**
question word	G 3Rc	Fragewort	**Where** did you go on holiday?
yes/no question	G 3Rc	Entscheidungsfrage	**Do you like chocolate?**
relative clause		Relativsatz	
contact clause	G 8Rb	Relativsatz ohne Relativpronomen	He is the boy **I met on holiday.**
defining relative clause	G 8Ra	notwendiger Relativsatz	This was the bag **that Alex had lost.**
non-defining relative clause	G 8Rc	nicht-notwendiger Relativsatz	Alex's bag, **which he had lost at the concert**, was red.
non-defining relative clause referring to sentence	G 8Rd	nicht-notwendiger Relativsatz, der sich auf einen Satz bezieht	We had lunch at home, **which saved us a lot of time.**
reported speech	G 3R	indirekte Rede	**She said that she had liked the film.**
substitute form	G 6R	Ersatzform	They **won't be able to** come.
tense	G 1R	Zeitform, Tempus	
verb		Verb	
dynamic verb		dynamisches Verb	(to) **help,** (to) **react**
regular / irregular verb		(un)regelmäßiges Verb	(to) **look**, (to) **walk** / (to) **give**, (to) **see**
stative verb		Zustandsverb	(to) **belong,** (to) **hate,** (to) **love,** ...
verb of perception	G 7e, G 13Rb	Verb der Sinneswahrnehmung	(to) **feel,** (to) **hear,** (to) **smell,** ...

In den Wordbanks sind nützliche Wörter und Redewendungen zu unterschiedlichen Themen zusammengefasst. Wenn bei einer Aufgabe vorne im Buch zum Beispiel ▶ Wordbank 2 | p. 238 steht, findest du auf Seite 238 passende Wörter zum Thema *History*.

1 Nature and environment

Native Australian animals

crocodile • dingo • emu • jellyfish • kangaroo • koala • platypus • possum • quokka • snake • spider • Tasmanian devil • turtle • wombat

platypus

Tasmanian devil

wombat

Landscape and nature in Australia

beach • coast • coral reef • desert • Great Barrier Reef • lake • mountain • ocean • Outback • river • sandstone formation • tropical island • tropical rainforest • Uluru

Climate change

bushfire • carbon footprint • coral bleaching • drought • extreme weather conditions • flooding • heatwave • higher water temperature • natural disaster • rising sea levels

You can ...

- grow heat-resistant corals
- observe pollution
- participate in beach cleaning
- volunteer for environmental projects
- conserve an ecosystem
- protect endangered/rare species
- reduce your carbon footprint
- join an environmental group
- protest against pollution
- reduce greenhouse gases
- take part in demonstrations

2 History

Talking about Australian history

ancestor • Aboriginal Australian • civilization • colony • Commonwealth • conflict • convict • danger • discrimination • disease • generation • gold rush • heritage • immigrant • immigration • indigenous • inequality • Invasion Day • mistreatment • National Reconciliation Week • National Sorry Day • prisoner • racism • settler • Stolen Generations • Torres Strait Islander

You can ...

- found a colony
- defend your land
- settle in a new area
- fight against the government/settlers
- fight for your rights
- have the same rights as sb else
- be discriminated against
- protest against mistreatment
- join a protest march
- strive for an equal society

Talking about Manchester and the Industrial Revolution

(child) labour • cloth • coal mine • cotton • Cottonopolis • industry • cotton mill • economy • factory • industrialization • invention • job opportunities • manufacturing • mass production • poverty • railroad • rapid growth • Spinning Jenny • steam engine • steel • telegraph • trade • warehouse • wealth • weaving machine

Talking about the women's rights movement

be arrested • be jailed • become an acitivist • collect signatures for a campaign • election • equal rights • extreme measures • find your voice • form a union • gain supporters • get involved • go on (hunger) strike • go to a march • hold a demonstration • leader • make a change • organize a protest • petition • poster • the right to vote • start a campaign • suffragette

3 Cartoons

Talking about cartoons

The cartoon deals/is concerned with …

The topic/issue addressed by the cartoon is …

The cartoon shows …

The … on the right/left appears to be/seems to be …

The text suggests that …

The cartoon claims that …

You might conclude the message of the cartoon is …

I (don't) like the cartoon because …

I find the cartoon funny/not funny/thought-provoking/… because …

4 Social media

You can …

- communicate with friends
- set up a profile
- check your profile
- take down/delete your profile
- share a post
- post a photo/comment
- create content
- (un)follow sb
- reach a certain number of followers
- attract followers
- get distracted on social media
- keep your personal information safe
- take a screenshot
- reduce your screen time
- block people online

anonymous • *app* • *blog* • *clickbait* • *comment* • *community* • *content* • *cyberbullying/online bullying* • *feed* • *follower* • *forum* • *hashtag* • *influencer* • *misinformation* • *platform* • *post*

W Wordbanks

5 Film

acting • atmosphere • camera angle • camerawork • cast • characters • cinematic device • directing • field size • lighting and colour • music and sound • setting • soundtrack • special effects

Genres

action • adventure • comedy • documentary • drama • fantasy • horror • mystery • romance • science fiction • thriller

Describing story and plot

action-packed • amusing • boring • captivating • clever • comical • complex • confusing • corny • dramatic • depressing • entertaining • fast-moving • funny • moving • powerful • romantic • sad • scary • slow • surprising • thought-provoking • thrilling • touching • tragic • (un)convincing • (un)predictable • (un)realistic • warm-hearted

Describing characters, acting and the cast

authentic • brilliant • flat • magnificent • spectacular • stereotypical • superb • two-dimensional • (un)convincing • (un)talented

Describing music, sound and special effects

catchy • clever • complex • convincing • dramatic • dull • entertaining • flat • powerful • rich • spectacular • (un)realistic

Talking about a film

... is a ... film from 2023.

The film was written by ...

The film is based on ...

The film stars ...

The main actors are ...

The leading actor is ...

It was released in ...

The film is about ...

The film deals with ...

The story is set in ...

The plot centres around ...

Giving your opinion on a film

- I was extremely surprised by ...
- In my opinion, the plot is very ...
- The film is difficult to follow because ...
- ... has succeeded in making an entertaining film.
- I liked the film's message, which ...
- I particularly enjoyed the way ... plays the role of ...
- I also think ... might not be very realistic because ...
- The camerawork is skilful.
- The film makes you forget everything around you.
- There are some cheesy moments.
- The film keeps the audience glued to the screen.
- The actor's performance really stood out for me.

6 Expressing your opinion

Stating your opinion in a discussion

As far as I know/I'm concerned, ... • As I see it ... • For me, it's absolutely clear that ... • I (strongly) believe that ... • I would say that ... • I'm against/for ... • I'm convinced that ... • In my opinion/view ... • It is a fact that ... • It is obvious to me that ... • Personally, I feel that ... • The point I would like to raise is ... • There can be no doubt that ... • When it comes down to it ...

Making a new point

I would like to add that ... • In addition to ..., you could also say ... • Perhaps I should also mention that ... • ... plus the fact that ...

Agreeing

I (completely) agree that ... • I couldn't agree more. • It is absolutely right that ... • That's what I think, too, because ... • You have a point there.

Disagreeing

Although ..., it doesn't necessarily mean that ... • I have to admit that ..., but ... • I see what you mean but ... • In contrast to what you said, I ... • It isn't as simple as that because ... • It may be true that ..., however ... • That might be the case if ..., but ... • The fact that ... doesn't mean that ... • To be honest, I don't think that ... • Well, I don't think so because ...

Summarizing your opinion

All in all ... • All things considered, ... • Finally, ... • Taking everything into account ... • To conclude ... • To sum up ...

7 Statistics

data • maximum/minimum • numbers • percentage • to grow/to decline • to increase/to decrease • turning point

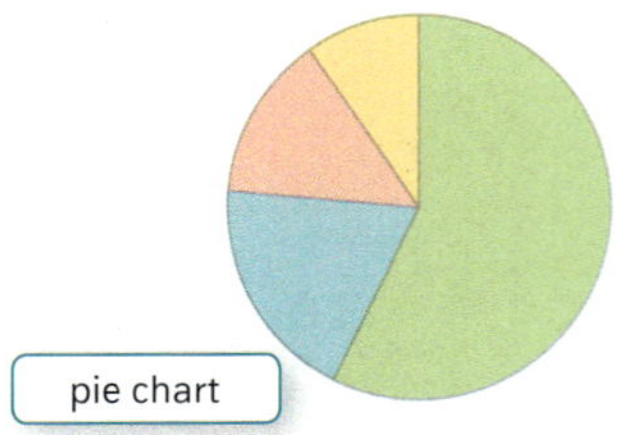

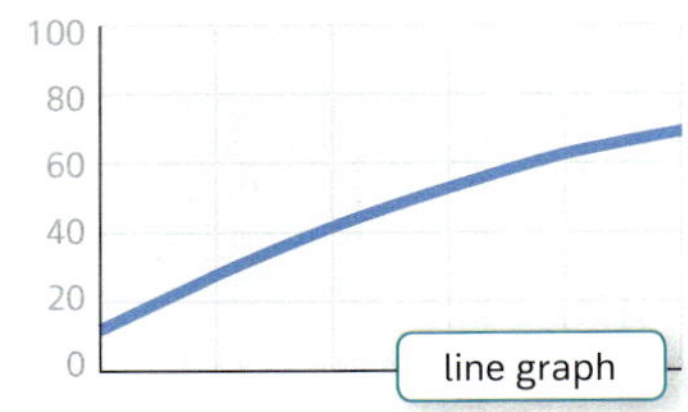

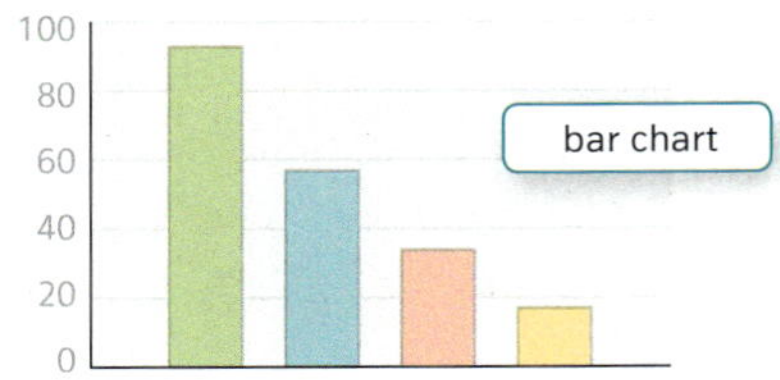

Describing charts

The chart shows …

The first graphic highlights/illustrates …

… % of all …

The biggest/smallest section is …

Only …% of … while …% of …

Over the years, the figure/percentage has increased/decreased by …

The proportion of … was much higher.

The graphic deals with …

If you compare the figures for X and Y, it becomes clear that …

When you look at …, you notice that …

In the pie chart/bar chart/ line graph you can see …

We can see a slight/sharp increase/decrease in …

It is clear that the figures differ siginificantly/are similar because …

The statistics are about …

The total number of … in … is …

The figures go up/down steadily …

The number of … has declined significantly after …

According to the figures …

The percentage of … is significantly higher/lower than …

By 2021 the … had almost …

Compared to …

By 2020, the … had almost doubled …

The … was twice as high as …

8 Jobs

application • cover letter • CV (curriculum vitae) • employee • employer • internship • job interview • personal profile • qualification • salary • volunteer • work experience

Hard skills

being familiar with computer systems/database software • experience in photo/video editing • knowledge of HTML • language skills • project management • writing skills

Soft skills

adaptability • ambition • commitment • communication skills • confidence • creativity • dedication • diligence • enthusiasm • flexibility • friendliness • logical thinking • patience • positivity • problem-solving skills • reliability • self-motivation • sensitivity • time management • trustworthiness

You can ...

- be the right fit for a company
- complete a task
- make a difference
- gain a new perspective on ...
- build skills to ...
- gain experience
- enjoy a challenge
- make money
- know what your work is worth
- invest a lot of time
- be responsible for a small project
- look for a challenge
- be capable of working independently
- be able to work well under pressure
- show commitment to ...
- be expected to work full-time/part-time

What you might be looking for in a job

ability to make a difference • ability to work from home • flexible hours • good salary • helping others/helping your local community • modern workplace • opportunity to develop new skills • opportunity to work abroad • positive company culture • safety • work-life balance • workplace close to home

W Wordbanks

Applying for a job

apply for a job as ... • apply for an internship • ask for feedback/a letter of recommendation • be invited to a job interview • get rejected • make a list of your skills • prepare for a job interview • research the company • write a CV/cover letter

Having a job interview

As I wrote in my cover letter ...

I believe I am the best candidate for this job because ...

One of my strengths is ...

I usually take the first step when it comes to ...

I've already gained some insight into ...

I have achieved ...

Right now, I'm working as ...

Something else that is very important to me is ...

I think the most valuable skill I have is ...

I enjoy working with ...

I'm good at ...

I prefer working in a team because ...

So you are looking for an example of .... Well, there are a few, but I think the most relevant is ...

That's a good and interesting question. Let me think.

... worked for you a few years ago.

In order to get a better idea of which career option might really interest me, I decided to apply for an internship at your company.

Can you tell me more about the team I would be working in?

I'd be very interested to know if it's possible to ...

Can I ask you something about ...?

What I forgot to ask you earlier is ...

May I contact you if I have any other questions?

Thank you for your time.

I look forward to hearing from you.

So funktionieren die Wortlisten

Es gibt Wortlisten nach *Themes* und eine alphabetische Wortliste *(dictionary)*.

Wortlisten nach *Themes*

In den Wortlisten nach *Themes* ab Seite 246 findest du die Wörter in der Reihenfolge, in der sie in den *Themes* vorkommen.
Am Ende der Wortliste zu jedem *Theme* steht *Say it in English*, eine Liste mit nützlichen Redewendungen.

Dictionary

Im *English-German dictionary* ab Seite 277 kannst du nachschlagen, wenn du die Bedeutung von einem englischen Wort aus dem Buch wissen möchtest.

So kannst du die Wortlisten nach *Themes* und das *dictionary* benutzen:

Fett gedruckte Wörter solltest du dir merken.	**heritage** /ˈherɪtɪdʒ/
Die / Lautschrift / zeigt an, wie man ein Wort ausspricht.	**precious** /ˈpreʃəs/
! weist auf wichtige Besonderheiten hin.	! **on** the **plane** – **im** Flugzeug
↔ bedeutet „ist das Gegenteil von".	**legal** ↔ illegal
In den gelb hinterlegten Kästen stehen Tipps und Hinweise.	**Längenmaße** 1 inch (= 2,54 cm) 12 inches = 1 foot (= 30,48 cm)
(irr) bedeutet: Dieses Verb ist unregelmäßig. Auf Seite 337–339 kannst du *irregular verbs* nachschlagen.	to **take a risk** *(irr)* /ˌteɪk‿ə ˈrɪsk/
(informal) bedeutet: Dieses Wort ist umgangssprachlich.	loads of *(informal)* /ˈləʊdz‿əv/
(*pl* **media**) bedeutet: Dieses Wort hat einen unregelmäßigen Plural (**media**).	**medium** (*pl* **media**) /ˈmiːdiəm, ˈmiːdiə/
(no pl) bedeutet: Dieses Wort hat keinen Plural.	**knowledge** *(no pl)* /ˈnɒlɪdʒ/
(pl) bedeutet: Dieses Wort wird nur oder gewöhnlich im Plural benutzt.	**stairs** *(pl)* /steəz/
° bedeutet: Dieses Wort ist nur für einen bestimmten Text wichtig. Du brauchst es nicht zu lernen.	° requirement /rɪˈkwaɪəmənt/
vacation (*AE* = **holiday** *BE*) bedeutet: Im *American English (AE)* verwendet man *vacation*, im *British English (BE) holiday*.	**internship** (*AE* = **placement** *BE*) /ˈɪntɜrnˌʃɪp/

AusE steht für *Australian English*.

Folgende Abkürzungen werden noch verwendet:

sb = somebody
sth = something
jdm/jdn = jemandem/jemanden
etw = etwas

Erfolgreich Vokabeln lernen

- Trainiere regelmäßig: Zehn Minuten pro Tag bringen dich ans Ziel!
- Lerne jeweils sechs oder sieben neue Vokabeln auf einmal. Wenn du diese sicher beherrschst, nimmst du dir die nächste Portion vor.
- Suche dir einen Platz zum Vokabellernen, an dem du dich wohlfühlst.
- Merke dir nicht nur einzelne Wörter, sondern auch ganze Redewendungen oder Sätze. Wie Wörter in Sätzen verwendet werden, siehst du in den Beispielsätzen in der rechten Spalte der Wortlisten. Außerdem findest du nützliche Redewendungen zu jedem *Theme* unter *Say it in English* (z. B. auf Seite 251).

Weitere Listen zum Nachschlagen:

1. *Names* (S. 330–332): Hier findest du die Namen, die in den *Themes* vorkommen, mit ihrer Lautschrift.
2. *Wörter, die im Deutschen und Englischen ähnlich sind* (S. 334/335)
3. *Class instructions* (S. 336): Hier findest du die häufigsten Arbeitsanweisungen in deinem Buch.
4. *Irregular verbs* (S. 337–339): Hier findest du die unregelmäßigen Verben.

Word lists

Theme 1: Australia

Wenn du ein englisches Wort aus dem Buch in den Wortlisten nach *Themes* nicht findest, kannst du es im *English-German dictionary* ab Seite 277 nachschlagen.
Anweisungen, die häufig im Buch vorkommen, kannst du in der Liste auf Seite 336 nachschlagen.

1	**Australia** /ɒˈstreɪliə/	Australien	It took Leah about 24 hours to get to **Australia** by plane.	p. 12
	the Outback /ðiˌˈaʊtbæk/	*der Busch Australiens*		
	separate /ˈsep(ə)rət/	getrennt, separat, einzeln	Koalas and kangaroos are **separate** species.	
	as /æz/	als, *hier:* während	**As** I got home, it started to rain.	
3	**Australian** /ɒˈstreɪliən/	Australier/in, australisch	My **Australian** friend comes from Canberra.	p. 13
A1	to **benefit** /ˈbenɪfɪt/	profitieren, Nutzen ziehen	I **benefit** from this decision.	p. 14
	to **profit (from/by)** /ˈprɒfɪt frɒm/baɪ/	profitieren (von), Nutzen ziehen (aus)	Jo does the hard work but Henry **profits** the most!	
	convict /ˈkɒnvɪkt/	Strafgefangene/r		
	guilty /ˈɡɪlti/	schuldig	He was **guilty** of the crime.	
	colony /ˈkɒləni/	Kolonie	Australia was a British **colony** until 1901.	
	control *(no pl)* /kənˈtrəʊl/	Kontrolle, Gewalt, Herrschaft	They were under British **control**.	
	to expire /ɪkˈspaɪə/	ablaufen, enden, auslaufen	Frz. *expirer*	
	to **found** /faʊnd/	gründen	Adelaide **was founded** in 1836.	
	indigenous /ɪnˈdɪdʒənəs/	(ein)heimisch		

Wenn *indigenous* eine Person oder Personengruppe bezeichnet, wird es häufig großgeschrieben.
Beispiele: *Indigenous Australians, Indigenous communities.*

	overcrowded /ˌəʊvəˈkraʊdɪd/	überfüllt, überlaufen	The restaurant was **overcrowded**: there were no seats left.	
	to **be related to** *(irr)* /ˌbiː rɪˈleɪtɪd‿tʊ/	verwandt sein (mit), in Beziehung stehen (zu)	We are **related** to each other. He is my uncle.	
	colonization *(no pl)* /ˌkɒlənaɪˈzeɪʃ(ə)n/	Kolonisation, Kolonisierung	The **colonization** of Australia began in 1788.	
A2	**official** /əˈfɪʃ(ə)l/	offiziell	Australia has no **official** language.	
	Aboriginal /ˌæbəˈrɪdʒ(ə)n(ə)l/	Aborigine *(australische/r Ureinwohner/in)*, der Aborigines, Aborigine-		

to **represent sb/sth** /ˌreprɪˈzent/	jdn/etw repräsentieren, jdn vertreten	They **represented** their country at the olympics.
stripe /straɪp/	Streifen	
A3 to impact /ˈɪmpækt/	beeinflussen, Auswirkungen haben auf	
unsure /ʌnˈʃʊə/	unsicher, ungewiss	Alicia was **unsure** of the answer.
to **be based on** *(irr)* /ˌbiː ˈbeɪst‿ɒn/	basieren auf, beruhen auf	This **is based on** a true story.
° the Dreaming /ðə ˈdriːmɪŋ/	*zentraler Begriff der Aborigine-Mythologie*	
foundation /faʊnˈdeɪʃ(ə)n/	Fundament, Basis, Grundlage, *hier:* Gründung	
religion /rɪˈlɪdʒ(ə)n/	Religion, Glaube	People often argue about **religion**.
creation /kriˈeɪʃ(ə)n/	(Er)schaffung, Produkt, Werk	The artist showed his new **creation**.
sacred /ˈseɪkrɪd/	heilig, geheiligt	
belief (*pl* **beliefs**) /bɪˈliːf, bɪˈliːfs/	Glaube, Überzeugung, Ansicht	Respecting others' **belief** is essential for a tolerant society.
connection /kəˈnekʃ(ə)n/	Verbindung, Beziehung, Zusammenhang	I feel a strong **connection** to my hometown.
to pass down /ˌpɑːs ˈdaʊn/	weitergeben, überliefern	
knowledge *(no pl)* /ˈnɒlɪdʒ/	Kenntnis(se), Wissen	Rebecca's **knowledge** of cats is impressive.
to **communicate** /kəˈmjuːnɪkeɪt/	kommunizieren, Kontakt haben	In a team it is important to **communicate**.
starvation *(no pl)* /stɑːˈveɪʃ(ə)n/	Hungertod, Verhungern, Unterernährung	
to abandon /əˈbændən/	verlassen, zurücklassen, aufgeben	Frz. *abandonner*, Sp. *abandonar*
will /wɪl/	Wille	
to **raise** /reɪz/	heben, *hier:* großziehen	Shadeene Evans **was raised** in an isolated community.
foster /ˈfɒstə/	Pflege-	
to **protest** /prəˈtest/	protestieren	They **protested** about their working conditions.
mistreatment *(no pl)* /mɪsˈtriːtmənt/	Misshandlung, schlechte Behandlung	
not until ... /nɒt‿ʌnˈtɪl/	erst ...	
widely /ˈwaɪdli/	weithin	
society /səˈsaɪəti/	Gesellschaft	We want a **society** that supports people who need help.
to **acknowledge** /əkˈnɒlɪdʒ/	zugeben, anerkennen, bestätigen	They should **acknowledge** their mistakes.
to **suffer (from)** /ˈsʌfə frɒm/	erleiden, ertragen, leiden (an/unter)	Many people **suffer** from a disease.
reconciliation *(no pl)* /ˌrekənsɪliˈeɪʃ(ə)n/	Aussöhnung, Versöhnung, Beilegung	When the war was over, they hoped for **reconciliation**.
prime minister /ˌpraɪm‿ˈmɪnɪstə/	Premierminister/in, Ministerpräsident/in	The **prime minister** is part of the government.
past /pɑːst/	vergangen, frühere(r, s)	We must learn from **past** mistakes.
rate /reɪt/	Maß, Menge, Rate, Quote	
A4 abuse /əˈbjuːs/	Missbrauch, Verletzung, Beschimpfung(en)	p. 16
mentoring *(no pl)* /ˈmentərɪŋ/	*Beratung und Unterstützung durch erfahrene Fach- oder Führungskräfte*	
according to /əˈkɔːdɪŋ tʊ/	nach, laut, gemäß	**According to** doctors, sweets are unhealthy.
capable /ˈkeɪpəb(ə)l/	fähig	Alex is **capable** of finishing this task.
worth *(no pl)* /wɜːθ/	Wert	The **worth** of the house decreased because of the broken windows.
cycle /ˈsaɪk(ə)l/	Kreislauf, Zyklus	This **cycle** must be broken for things to change.

tiny /ˈtaɪni/	winzig	**tiny** = very small
isolated /ˈaɪsəˌleɪtɪd/	abgelegen, isoliert	Frz. *isolé(e)*
to hunt /hʌnt/	jagen	
to adjust (to) /əˈdʒʌst‿tʊ/	einstellen, anpassen (an)	Frz. *ajuster*, Sp. *ajustar*
currently /ˈkʌrəntli/	zurzeit, gegenwärtig, momentan	We are **currently** waiting for an answer.
musician /mjuˈzɪʃ(ə)n/	Musiker/in	
pride *(no pl)* /praɪd/	Stolz	Holly takes **pride** in her work.
identity /aɪˈdentɪti/	Identität	Where you are from is part of your **identity**.
anger *(no pl)* /ˈæŋgə/	Ärger, Wut	Sam should learn to control his **anger**.
on a daily basis /ɒn‿ə ˌdeɪli ˈbeɪsɪs/	täglich, jeden Tag	
forearm /ˈfɔːrˌɑːm/	Unterarm	
heritage /ˈherɪtɪdʒ/	(Kultur)erbe	Family recipes are part of my **heritage**.
award /əˈwɔːd/	Preis, Auszeichnung	
creative /kriˈeɪtɪv/	kreativ, schöpferisch	Lizzy loves art and has always been very **creative**.
to **analyse** /ˈænəlaɪz/	analysieren, untersuchen	to **analyse** = to study in detail
to **overcome, overcame, overcome** /ˌəʊvəˈkʌm, ˌəʊvəˈkeɪm, ˌəʊvəˈkʌm/	bewältigen, meistern	Taylor **overcame** his past to become very successful.

Unregelmäßige Verben

Wie du weißt, haben unregelmäßige Verben unregelmäßige Formen: für das *simple past* und auch für das Partizip Perfekt. Diese Formen solltest du wie Vokabeln lernen, z. B. für *to grow*: *grew (simple past)* und *grown* (Partizip Perfekt). Du findest die Formen in der Liste der unregelmäßigen Verben (S. 337–339). Sie werden immer so angegeben: **to grow**, **grew**, **grown**.

Infinitiv **simple past** **Partizip Perfekt**

A5 Australia Day /ɒˈstreɪliə deɪ/	*Australiens offizieller Nationalfeiertag*	p. 17
protester /prəˈtestə/	Protestierende/r, Demonstrant/in	Many **protesters** against war marched through the streets.
across /əˈkrɒs/	über, *hier:* querdurch, über ... hinweg	I came all the way **across** town!
supporter /səˈpɔːtə/	Unterstützer/in, Anhänger/in, Verfechter/in	Sidney's **supporters** were happy she won.
despite /dɪˈspaɪt/	trotz	Toby walked to work, **despite** the rain.
march /mɑːtʃ/	Marsch	All of the soldiers were in the **march** through town.
central /ˈsentrəl/	zentral, Haupt-	The **central** train station is the biggest.
native /ˈneɪtɪv/	einheimisch, eingeboren	This plant is **native** to Australia: it only grows here.
speech /spiːtʃ/	Rede	Robert gave an emotional **speech** to the audience.
meanwhile /ˈmiːnˌwaɪl/	inzwischen, unterdessen, mittlerweile	My brother was being lazy, **meanwhile** I did all the work!
naval officer /ˌneɪv(ə)l‿ˈɒfɪsə/	Marineoffizier/in	
paint *(no pl)* /peɪnt/	Farbe, Lack	The **paint** on my walls is a nice colour.
to assess /əˈses/	(ein)schätzen, beurteilen	
to **abolish** /əˈbɒlɪʃ/	abschaffen, aufheben	The US **abolished** slavery in 1865.
suspect /ˈsʌspekt/	Verdächtige/r	
heated /ˈhiːtɪd/	hitzig, beheizt	
arrival /əˈraɪv(ə)l/	Ankunft	Frz. *arrivée*
forcefully /ˈfɔːsf(ə)li/	gewaltsam	
possibly /ˈpɒsəbli/	möglicherweise, gegebenenfalls	It could **possibly** rain, but I am not sure.

	elder /ˈeldə/	Ältere/r, ältere(r, s)		
	to **reflect** /rɪˈflekt/	spiegeln, zeigen, reflektieren	Ivy **reflected** for a moment and then made a suggestion.	
	to **mark** /mɑːk/	markieren, kennzeichnen	Today **marks** our tenth anniversary.	
	ceremony /ˈserəməni/	Zeremonie, Feier, Feierlichkeiten	There was a welcoming **ceremony** for new citizens.	
	citizenship *(no pl)* /ˈsɪtɪz(ə)nʃɪp/	Staatsangehörigkeit		
	multicultural /ˌmʌltiˈkʌltʃərəl/	multikulturell	This city is very **multicultural**: there are people here from all over the world.	
	faith /feɪθ/	Vertrauen, Glaube		
	to proclaim /prəˈkleɪm/	verkünden, erklären		
	deep /diːp/	tief	He was in a **deep** sleep and wouldn't wake up.	
	sense /sens/	Verstand, Sinn, *hier:* Gefühl	Tom felt a **sense** of pride as the crowd cheered.	
	gratitude *(no pl)* /ˈɡrætɪˌtjuːd/	Dankbarkeit		
	to span /spæn/	umfassen, umspannen		
	unmatched /ʌnˈmætʃt/	unerreicht, unübertroffen		
	beauty /ˈbjuːti/	Schönheit	I like hiking to see the **beauty** of nature.	
	wonder /ˈwʌndə/	Wunder	The Colosseum is one of the seven **wonders** of the world.	
	wrong /rɒŋ/	Unrecht		
	acknowledg(e)ment *(no pl)* /əkˈnɒlɪdʒmənt/	Eingeständnis, Anerkennung, Würdigung		
	hardship /ˈhɑːdʃɪp/	Not, Elend, Härte		
	to strive, strove, striven /straɪv, strəʊv, ˈstrɪv(ə)n/	sich bemühen, (an)streben		
	just /dʒʌst/	gerecht	**just** = fair	
	no matter … /nəʊ ˈmætə/	egal(,) …	They love their children, **no matter** what.	
A6	° First Nations /ˌfɜːst ˈneɪʃ(ə)nz/	Ureinwohner-, die einheimische Bevölkerung betreffend		p. 18
A8	to **publish** /ˈpʌblɪʃ/	veröffentlichen, herausgeben	The book **was published** in 2023.	
	to **vary** /ˈveəri/	variieren	My mood **varies** from day to day, sometimes I am happy but sometimes I am sad.	
B1	down under *(no pl, informal)* /ˌdaʊn‿ˈʌndə/	Australien, Neuseeland		p. 20
	abroad /əˈbrɔːd/	im/ins Ausland	I prefer going on holiday **abroad** to staying in this country.	
	to **gain** /ɡeɪn/	bekommen, erreichen, gewinnen	Australia **gained** independence from Britain.	
B2	loads of *(informal)* /ˈləʊdz‿əv/	jede Menge, massenhaft		
	personally /ˈpɜːs(ə)nəli/	persönlich, *hier:* ich für meinen Teil	I **personally** like chocolate but some people don't.	
	° cableway /ˈkeɪb(ə)lweɪ/	Seilbahn		
	to **run, ran, run** /rʌn, ræn, rʌn/	rennen, laufen, *hier:* verlaufen	The Amazon river **runs** through the middle of the rainforest.	
	tropical /ˈtrɒpɪk(ə)l/	Tropen-, tropisch	It is warm here because it is a **tropical** climate.	
	rainforest /ˈreɪnˌfɒrɪst/	Regenwald	The Amazon is the biggest **rainforest** on earth.	
	exception /ɪkˈsepʃ(ə)n/	Ausnahme	The rules must be followed, but I will make an **exception** for you.	
	to **sign up** /ˌsaɪn‿ˈʌp/	sich einschreiben, sich anmelden	Rory **signed up** for hockey club.	
	practical /ˈpræktɪk(ə)l/	praktisch, auf die Praxis bezogen	Wear **practical** shoes when hiking.	
	foreign /ˈfɒrɪn/	ausländisch, fremd, Fremd-	I am from Germany, so English is a **foreign** language.	

	range /reɪndʒ/	Reichweite, Bereich, Angebot		
	elective /ɪ'lektɪv/	Wahlfach		
	engineering *(no pl)* /ˌendʒɪ'nɪərɪŋ/	Technik, Ingenieurwissenschaft, Maschinenbau		
	aviation *(no pl)* /ˌeɪvi'eɪʃ(ə)n/	Fliegerei, Fliegen, Luftfahrt	Frz. *aviation*, Sp. *aviación*	
	psychology *(no pl)* /saɪ'kɒlədʒi/	Psychologie	! Achte auf die Aussprache.	
	° aquatic practices *(pl)* /əˌkwætɪk 'præktɪsɪz/	*Schulfach, das Gewässer unter ökologischen, kulturellen, wirtschaftlichen und Freizeitaspekten thematisiert*		
	° marine science /məˌriːn 'saɪəns/	Meereskunde		
	snorkelling *(no pl)* /'snɔːk(ə)lɪŋ/	Schnorcheln		
	licence /'laɪs(ə)ns/	Genehmigung, Erlaubnis, *hier:* Führerschein	Now that I have my **licence** I can drive the car.	
	coral reef /ˌkɒrəl 'riːf/	Korallenriff		
	coral /'kɒrəl/	Koralle(n-)		
	rowing *(no pl)* /'rəʊɪŋ/	Rudern	**Rowing** is a team sport.	
B5	just as ... (as) /'dʒʌst‿əz ... əz/	genauso ... (wie)		p. 22
B6	to **claim** /kleɪm/	behaupten, Anspruch erheben auf	Lucy **claimed** she didn't know about the homework.	
B7	to **get back, got back, got back** /ˌget 'bæk, ˌgɒt 'bæk, ˌgɒt 'bæk/	zurückkommen	Marc **got back** from his holiday yesterday.	p. 23
	turtle /'tɜːt(ə)l/	Schildkröte		
	rehabilitation *(no pl)* /ˌriəˌbɪlɪ'teɪʃ(ə)n/	Rehabilitation(s-), Wiedereingliederung		
	dry season /'draɪ ˌsiːz(ə)n/	Trockenzeit		
	wet season /'wet ˌsiːz(ə)n/	Regenzeit		
	stinger /'stɪŋə/	stechendes Insekt, brennende Pflanze		
	to **take a risk** *(irr)* /ˌteɪk‿ə 'rɪsk/	ein Risiko eingehen, etw riskieren	Lizzy **took the risk** and dived into the sea.	
	to nurse /nɜːs/	pflegen, fördern		
	to **get to do sth** *(irr)* /ˌget‿tə 'duː/	die Möglichkeit haben, etw zu tun	After a busy day, Oscar finally **got to bake** a cake.	
	jellyfish /'dʒeliˌfɪʃ/	Qualle		
	to **float** /fləʊt/	schwimmen, treiben, ziehen	Apples **float** in water.	
	to **attach** /ə'tætʃ/	anhängen, befestigen, anbringen	Sarah **attached** her keys to her rucksack so that she didn't lose them.	
	shell /ʃel/	Schale, Muschel, Panzer		
	° calcium carbonate *(no pl)* /ˌkælsiəm 'kɑːbəneɪt/	kohlensaures Kalzium *(z. B. Kalkstein)*		
	° limestone *(no pl)* /'laɪmˌstəʊn/	Kalkstein		
	° zooxanthellae *(pl)* /ˌzəʊəzæn'θeli/	*Algenart*		
	to **contain** /kən'teɪn/	enthalten	This letter **contains** all the important information. Lat. *continēre*	
	collection /kə'lekʃ(ə)n/	(An)sammlung, Auswahl	Max has a huge **collection** of video games – over 1,000!	
	harm *(no pl)* /hɑːm/	Schaden, Verletzung	Pollution does **harm** to the environment.	
	threat /θret/	(Be)drohung, Gefahr	The turtle population is under **threat**: there are fewer than before.	
	stressed /strest/	gestresst	Lucy has a lot of work to do. She is very **stressed**.	
	as a result (of sth) /æz‿ə rɪ'zʌlt‿əv/	als Folge (einer Sache)	My alarm clock didn't go off. **As a result**, I was late.	
	coral bleaching *(no pl)* /ˌkɒrəl 'bliːtʃɪŋ/	Korallenbleiche		

tragedy /ˈtrædʒədi/	Tragödie, Trauerspiel	His death was a **tragedy**.
precious /ˈpreʃəs/	wertvoll, kostbar	A **precious** ring is very expensive.
restoration /ˌrestəˈreɪʃ(ə)n/	Restaurierung(s-), Wiederherstellung	After the **restoration** the church looked much better.
to **specialize (in)** /ˈspeʃəlaɪz‿ɪn/	sich spezialisieren (auf)	Clara's company **specializes** in finding volunteers for environmental projects.
pollution *(no pl)* /pəˈluːʃ(ə)n/	Verschmutzung	**Pollution** is a problem for the environment.
pest /pest/	Schädling, Plage	
plate /pleɪt/	Teller	Plastic **plates** and **straws** are **banned** on the island.
straw /strɔː/	Stroh(-), Strohhalm	
to **ban** /bæn/	verbieten	
reader /ˈriːdə/	Leser/in	The newspaper has thousands of **readers** every day.

Say it in English – Theme 1

So kannst du ...

Aussagen und Meinungen eines Autors/einer Autorin wiedergeben	The author describes/points out/argues ... He moves on to explain ... She opens the article by describing ... At the end, the author expresses hope that ... According to the author, the main problem is ...
sagen, worum es in einem Artikel geht	Ben Miller's article ..., published in May 2023 in the Morning Sun, deals with ... In her article ..., which was published in ..., the author Julie Smith ...
deine Vorlieben ausdrücken	The best thing about Cairns is its location. My personal favourites are ... The best thing about marine science is that ...
sagen, worum es in einem Blog geht	I've been using my blog to share my experiences and adventures down under! Today's entry is about my school.
die Leserinnen und Leser eines Blogs direkt ansprechen	Today, I want to tell you about ... • You may already know that ... Why is that? Well, ... • Crazy, right? • Awesome, right? Let me know in the comments. • Check it out! If you ever have the chance to visit ..., you should definitely go to ... Did you know that ...? • As you probably know already ...
Vergleiche anstellen	In comparison with ... • While ... In contrast to ... • Unlike students in Germany, ...
über die Erfahrungen und Lebenswege junger Menschen sprechen	Isaiah grew up in 17 different foster homes. As a young adult, he founded a non-profit organization. Shadeene was born and raised in Borroloola. She grew up hunting and fishing with her dad. At age 12, she was given the chance to join the John Moriarty Football program. Although it was a great opportunity that would change her life, it also meant moving 3,000 km away from her family and adjusting to life in Sydney. Music helped him through difficult times at school, where he experienced discrimination and did not receive any support.

Theme 2: Teenage life

1	to **be supposed to do sth/be sth** *(irr)* /ˌbiː səˌpəʊzd‿tə ˈduː/ˈbiː/	etw tun sollen/etw sein sollen	I **am supposed to** visit my grandma at the weekend.	p. 38
2	**driver's license** (AE = **driving licence** BE) /ˈdraɪvərz ˌlaɪs(ə)ns/	Führerschein	Now that Jake has his **driver's license**, he can go to school by car.	
	LGBTQ+ /ˌel dʒiː biː tiː kjuː ˈplʌs/	*Abkürzung für Lesbian, Gay, Bisexual, Transgender and Queer and other kinds of identity*		
	mental health *(no pl)* /ˌment(ə)l ˈhelθ/	psychische Gesundheit		
	° therapy /ˈθerəpi/	Therapie, Behandlung		
	professional /prəˈfeʃ(ə)nəl/	Fachmann/Fachfrau, Profi	Marki is so good at golf; it is clear he is a **professional**.	
	daily /ˈdeɪli/	täglich, jeden Tag	A **daily** walk is very healthy.	
	smoking *(no pl)* /ˈsməʊkɪŋ/	Rauchen	**Smoking** is bad for your health.	
	among(st) /əˈmʌŋst/	unter, inmitten von	Is drinking alcohol common **among** high school students?	
	to **consume** /kənˈsjuːm/	konsumieren, verzehren	The cow **consumed** a lot of grass today.	
4	to **claim** /kleɪm/	behaupten, Anspruch erheben auf	Lucy **claimed** she didn't know about the homework.	p. 39
	habit /ˈhæbɪt/	Gewohnheit	Frz. *habitude*	
6	**personally** /ˈpɜːs(ə)nəli/	persönlich, *hier:* ich für meinen Teil	**Personally** I don't mind, but some people find it annoying.	
	to **come down to sth** *(irr)* /ˌkʌm ˈdaʊn tʊ/	auf etw ankommen, auf etw hinauslaufen	It **comes down to** the simple facts.	
	as I see it /æz‿ˈaɪ siː‿ɪt/	wie ich es sehe, meiner Meinung nach	**As I see it**, there is only one solution.	
	to **raise** /reɪz/	heben, *hier:* aufwerfen, vorbringen	My grandfather **raised** an interesting point yesterday.	
	as far as sb is concerned /əz ˌfɑːr‿əz‿ˈsʌmbədi‿ɪz kənˌsɜːnd/	was jdn anbelangt/betrifft	**As far as Phil is concerned**, his work is good enough.	
	to **be honest** *(irr)* /tə ˌbi‿ˈɒnɪst/	ehrlich gesagt, um die Wahrheit zu sagen	**To be honest**, I have no idea what you mean!	
A1	to **communicate** /kəˈmjuːnɪkeɪt/	kommunizieren, Kontakt haben	The **media** are important for **communicating** with the public.	p. 40
	medium (*pl* **media**) /ˈmiːdiəm, ˈmiːdiə/	(Informations)medium		
A2	to **analyse** /ˈænəlaɪz/	analysieren, untersuchen	Mark **analysed** the test results.	
	to **be concerned with sth** *(irr)* /ˌbiː kənˈsɜːnd wɪð/	sich um etw Gedanken machen, *hier:* etw behandeln	The programme **is concerned with** crime.	
	issue /ˈɪʃuː/	Thema, Angelegenheit, Problem, Streitfrage	There are more important **issues** than football.	
	setting /ˈsetɪŋ/	Einstellung, Umgebung, Schauplatz	The **setting** of this story is a hospital.	
	body language *(no pl)* /ˈbɒdi ˌlæŋgwɪdʒ/	Körpersprache	Katy said she was happy but her **body language** seemed angry.	
	facial expression /ˌfeɪʃ(ə)l‿ɪkˈspreʃ(ə)n/	Gesichtsausdruck	My **facial expression** shows my feelings.	
	to **appear** /əˈpɪə/	erscheinen, auftauchen, *hier:* scheinen	The patient **appeared** to be very unwell. Frz. *apparaître*, Sp. *aparecer*, Lat. *appārēre*	
	to **conclude** /kənˈkluːd/	enden, (ab)schließen, schlussfolgern	Tina **concluded** that it was time to go.	
A3	**brain** /breɪn/	Gehirn, Verstand	The **brain** is like the body's computer.	p. 41
	addicted (to) /əˈdɪktɪd‿tʊ/	süchtig (von/nach)	I am **addicted to** nuts: I eat them all the time.	
	distraction /dɪˈstrækʃ(ə)n/	Störung, Ablenkung, Zerstreuung	There were too many **distractions** for Connor to focus on his homework.	

face to face /ˌfeɪs tə ˈfeɪs/	persönlich	
self-centred /ˌselfˈsentəd/	selbstbezogen, egozentrisch	Only helping yourself is **self-centred**.
self-esteem *(no pl)* /ˌself‿ɪˈstiːm/	Selbstwertgefühl	My **self-esteem** has improved; I feel much happier.
A4 **reader** /ˈriːdə/	Leser/in	The **readers** were not happy with the storyline.
attention *(no pl)* /əˈtenʃ(ə)n/	Aufmerksamkeit, Achtung	The book's cover attracted Fred's **attention**.
to **turn off** /ˌtɜːn‿ˈɒf/	abschalten, ausmachen	**Turn off** the light and go to sleep!
for good /fə ˈɡʊd/	für immer, endgültig	
party /ˈpɑːti/	Partei, Gruppe	The two major political **parties** in the US are the Democratic Party and the Republican Party.
to campaign (for/against sth) /kæmˈpeɪn fɔː/əˌgenst/	(für etw) eintreten/(gegen etw) kämpfen	
to **ban** /bæn/	verbieten	Phones **have been banned** at my school!
giant /ˈdʒaɪənt/	Riese(n-), Gigant, riesig	I'm so hungry; I am going to order a **giant** ice cream.
button /ˈbʌt(ə)n/	Knopf	That **button** turns the computer on.
access *(no pl)* /ˈækses/	Zugang, Zutritt	John doesn't have **access** to that document, so he cannot read it.
to owe /əʊ/	schulden, verdanken	
connection /kəˈnekʃ(ə)n/	Verbindung, Beziehung, Zusammenhang	I have no **connection** to the sciences; I prefer history.
to **like** /laɪk/	mögen, *hier* liken	Sarah **liked** my post!
solution /səˈluːʃ(ə)n/	(Auf)lösung	Finally there is a **solution** for this problem!
in particular /ɪn pəˈtɪkjʊlə/	insbesondere, im Speziellen	Kimrun loves animals, **in particular** lions.
misinformation *(no pl)* /ˌmɪsɪnfəˈmeɪʃ(ə)n/	falsche Information, Fehlinformation(en)	There is lots of **misinformation** on social media: not everything is true!
to **push** /pʊʃ/	stoßen, schieben, drücken, *hier:* drängen	My dad **pushed** me to play football, but I don't really like it.
to **reject** /rɪˈdʒekt/	ablehnen, zurückweisen, abweisen	The school **rejected** my idea of a three-day weekend, but it would have been great!
to weep /wiːp/	weinen, schluchzen	
conspiracy theory /kənˈspɪrəsi ˌθɪəri/	Verschwörungstheorie	
to testify /ˈtestɪfaɪ/	als Zeuge/Zeugin aussagen	
Congress *(AE)* /ˈkɒŋɡrəs/	Kongress *(Parlament in den USA)*	
anxious /ˈæŋkʃəs/	besorgt, ängstlich	Francesca was **anxious** about the test.
depressed /dɪˈprest/	deprimiert, depressiv	He was extremely **depressed** when he heard the bad news.
obsessive /əbˈsesɪv/	zwanghaft, besessen	Kim is an **obsessive** reader: she always has a book.
case /keɪs/	Fall	Usually Mr Wallis would say no, but in this **case** he made an exception.
condition /kənˈdɪʃ(ə)n/	Zustand, Bedingung, *hier:* Leiden	I have a **condition** that makes it hard to walk.
offensive /əˈfensɪv/	anstößig	**Offensive** language must not be used here.
overlord /ˈəʊvəˌlɔːd/	Herrscher/in	
rich /rɪtʃ/	reich	Hollywood actors are usually **rich**, as they earn a lot of money.
entirely /ɪnˈtaɪəli/	ganz, total, völlig	That was **entirely** useless: it didn't work.
despite /dɪˈspaɪt/	trotz	**Despite** the bad weather, Nina and George still went for a walk.
to get roasted *(irr)* /ˌɡet ˈrəʊstɪd/	geröstet werden, *hier:* verrissen werden	
to **delete** /dɪˈliːt/	löschen, streichen	Oh no, I **deleted** my homework! Now I have to start again.

besides /bɪˈsaɪdz/	außerdem	I bought this shirt because I like it, and **besides**, it wasn't very expensive.	
responsible /rɪˈspɒnsəb(ə)l/	verantwortlich, zuständig	Tilly is **responsible** for taking out the rubbish today.	
specific /spəˈsɪfɪk/	genau, bestimmte(r, s), spezifisch	I don't want just any drink. I want that **specific** one.	
to **associate** /əˈsəʊsiˌeɪt/	in Verbindung bringen	Does you teacher only **associate** negative things with social media?	
intern /ˈɪntɜːn/	Praktikant/in	**Interns** help other people at work.	
to **reveal** /rɪˈviːl/	zeigen, enthüllen	Freja **revealed** that there was a surprise party.	
truth /truːθ/	Wahrheit	I know the **truth**, so stop lying!	
well-being *(no pl)* /ˌwelˈbiːɪŋ/	Wohl(ergehen), Wohlbefinden		
bullying *(no pl)* /ˈbʊliɪŋ/	Mobbing	**Bullying** can be a huge problem in schools.	
to log off /ˌlɒg‿ˈɒf/	sich ausloggen, sich abmelden		
A5 to predict /prɪˈdɪkt/	vorhersagen		p. 42
to **respond (to)** /rɪˈspɒnd‿tʊ/	reagieren (auf), antworten	Paul had lots of emails, but he **responded** to each one.	
A6 **account** /əˈkaʊnt/	Konto, Account, *hier:* Bericht	Luke's **account** of the incident was quite different to Rebecca's.	p. 43
to **rely on sb/sth** /rɪˈlaɪ‿ɒn/	sich auf jdn/etw verlassen	Frank **was relying on** Susie to take him to school. He couldn't get there without her.	
the … the /ðə ðə/	je …, desto …	**The** hungrier I am, **the** more I eat.	
shower /ˈʃaʊə/	Schauer, Regen, Dusche	Fred had to take a **shower** after football practice.	
sink /sɪŋk/	Waschbecken		
by /baɪ/	von, *hier:* an	My phone was alway **by** my side.	
to **figure out** /ˌfɪgər‿ˈaʊt/	herausfinden, begreifen	Peter finally **figured out** the answer to his maths question.	
smart /smɑːt/	schlau, clever	Lisa is very **smart** and gets good grades at school.	
majority /məˈdʒɒrəti/	Mehrheit, Großteil	The **majority** voted against it.	
laundry room /ˈlɔːndri ruːm/	Waschküche		
to drop off /ˌdrɒp‿ˈɒf/	absetzen, ablegen		
normally /ˈnɔːm(ə)li/	normalerweise	**Normally** I cycle to school but today I am walking.	
source /sɔːs/	Quelle, Informationsquelle	The internet is a great **source** of information.	
to **stare (at sb/sth)** /ˈsteər‿ət/	(jdn/etw an)starren	Robert **stared at** the stars because he thought they were pretty.	
throughout /θruːˈaʊt/	während, die ganze Zeit (über)	Rebecca has eaten three apples **throughout** the day.	
stairs *(pl)* /steəz/	Treppe	Liam went up the **stairs** to get to his English classroom.	
screen time *(no pl)* /ˈskriːn taɪm/	Bildschirmzeit		
by half /ˌbaɪ ˈhɑːf/	um die Hälfte	We reduced our costs **by half**. It is much cheaper now.	
distance /ˈdɪstəns/	Distanz, Strecke, Entfernung	The **distance** between Alex's house and school is three kilometres.	
attachment /əˈtætʃmənt/	Bindung, Anhang, Attachment	Tana still feels an **attachment** to her teddy bear.	

	realistic /ˌrɪəˈlɪstɪk/	realistisch	The horror film was so **realistic**; I was really scared.	
A7	**device** /dɪˈvaɪs/	Gerät, Vorrichtung, Apparat	Please leave mobile phones and other **devices** at home.	p. 44
A8	outcome /ˈaʊtˌkʌm/	Ergebnis, Resultat		
	purpose /ˈpɜːpəs/	Grund, Absicht, Ziel, Zweck	The **purpose** of her letter was to explain why she left for New York.	
B2	**extract** /ˈekstrækt/	Auszug	Peter thought they had to read the whole book, but it was only an **extract** of twenty pages.	p. 46
	subject /ˈsʌbdʒɪkt/	(Schul)fach, *hier:* Thema	The **subject** of my presentation is climate change.	
	to **appeal to sb/sth** /əˈpiːl tʊ/	jdn/etw reizen, jdn/etw ansprechen	The vampire book **appealed to** Kira because she loves scary stories.	
B3	**bathroom** *(AE)* /ˈbæθˌrum/	Toilette(n-)	Mark needs to go to the **bathroom** but he can't find one.	
	wall /wɔːl/	Wand	Hakim has lots of posters on his **wall**.	
	humorous /ˈhjuːmərəs/	humorvoll, lustig, witzig	My sister is so **humorous**: she always makes me laugh.	
	loving /ˈlʌvɪŋ/	liebevoll	Steven's grandparents are very **loving**. They always kiss him.	
	pessimistic /ˌpesəˈmɪstɪk/	pessimistisch	Jake was **pessimistic** about his test results. He kept saying that he had failed.	
	sarcastic /sɑːˈkæstɪk/	sarkastisch	**Sarcastic** people don't say what they mean, it is really confusing.	
	thoughtful /ˈθɔːtf(ə)l/	nachdenklich, wohl überlegt, aufmerksam	My friend is so **thoughtful**: she made me a cake for my birthday.	
	understanding /ˌʌndəˈstændɪŋ/	verständnisvoll	I forgot about my homework but the teacher was very **understanding**. She gave me an extra day to finish it.	

Words on Bathroom Walls

° unusual /ʌnˈjuːʒʊəl/	ungewöhnlich, untypisch
° to manifest /ˈmænɪfest/	(sich) zeigen
° schizophrenic /ˌskɪtsəʊˈfrenɪk/	Schizophrene/r, schizophren
° male /meɪl/	männlich
° commonly /ˈkɒmənli/	häufig, gemeinhin, gewöhnlich
° spectacles *(pl)* /ˈspektək(ə)lz/	Brille
° to turn /tɜːn/	(sich) (um)drehen, *hier:* werden
° to squint /skwɪnt/	blinzeln, schielen
° nuts *(informal)* /nʌts/	verrückt
° only /ˈəʊnli/	einzige(r, s)
° to jerk /dʒɜːk/	ruckartig bewegen
° sort of /ˈsɔːt‿əv/	irgendwie, sozusagen
° excuse /ɪkˈskjuːs/	Entschuldigung, Grund, Ausrede
° to be screwed *(informal)* *(irr)* /ˌbiː ˈskruːd/	geliefert sein, aufgeschmissen sein
° principal *(AE* = head teacher *BE)* /ˈprɪnsəp(ə)l/	Schulleiter/in, Direktor/in
° lab (= laboratory) /læb, ləˈbɒrət(ə)ri/	Labor
° to wash sb over /ˌwɒʃ ˌsʌmbədi‿ˈəʊvə/	über jdn (hinweg)spülen
° bat /bæt/	Fledermaus
° creepy *(informal)* /ˈkriːpi/	grus(e)lig, schaurig
° bastard *(informal)* /ˈbɑːstəd/	Dreckskerl, (Schweine)hund
° stepdad *(informal)* /ˈstepˌdæd/	Stiefpapa
° to date sb *(AE)* /ˈdeɪt/	mit jdm gehen
° effort /ˈefət/	Mühe, Anstrengung, Bemühung
° to keep up with sth *(irr)* /ˌkiːp‿ˈʌp wɪð/	bei etw auf dem Laufenden bleiben
° aside from /əˈsaɪd frəm/	abgesehen von
° grown /grəʊn/	erwachsen
° no doubt /ˌnəʊ ˈdaʊt/	zweifellos, ohne Zweifel

B4	medication /ˌmedɪˈkeɪʃ(ə)n/	Medikament(e)		p. 47
	illness /ˈɪlnəs/	Krankheit	If you have an **illness**, you don't feel well.	
	drug /drʌg/	Medikament, Droge, Rauschgift	"Medication" can also be referred to as "**drugs**".	
	pharmacy /ˈfɑːməsi/	Apotheke	Frz. *pharmacie*	
	drugstore (*AE*) /ˈdrʌgstɔːr/	Drogerie	**Drugstores** in the US sell medicines.	
	° to interpret /ɪnˈtɜːprɪt/	deuten, auslegen, wiedergeben		
B7	to **convey** /kənˈveɪ/	(r)überbringen, vermitteln	Deana finds it hard to **convey** her feelings.	
B8	**writer** /ˈraɪtə/	Verfasser/in, Autor/in	James really wants to be a **writer**. He will write lots of books.	p. 48
	to star in a film/play /ˌstɑːr‿ɪn‿ə ˈfɪlm/ˈpleɪ/	in einem Film/Theaterstück die Hauptrolle spielen		
	chef /ʃef/	Koch, Köchin		
	breakdown /ˈbreɪkˌdaʊn/	(Nerven)zusammenbruch, Scheitern	If you are too stressed, you might have a **breakdown**.	
	° schizophrenia *(no pl)* /ˌskɪtsəʊˈfriːniə/	Bewusstseinsspaltung, Schizophrenie		
	° clinical trial /ˌklɪnɪk(ə)l ˈtraɪəl/	klinische Studie		
	to transfer /trænsˈfɜː/	(über)wechseln, übertragen		
	to **get on (well) with sth** *(irr)* /ˌget‿ɒn ˈwel wɪð/	mit etw (gut) vorankommen	Corey **is getting on well with** his new hobby.	
	cooking *(no pl)* /ˈkʊkɪŋ/	Kochen, Koch-		
	gradually /ˈgrædʒuəli/	allmählich, sanft	At first high school was difficult, but Tara **gradually** got used to it.	
	to take a turn for the worse *(irr)* /ˌteɪk‿ə ˌtɜːn fə ðə ˈwɜːs/	sich zum Schlechten wenden		
	to **define** /dɪˈfaɪn/	definieren, festlegen	What does that word mean? Could you please **define** it?	
	to stand out, stood out, stood out /ˌstænd‿ˈaʊt, ˌstʊd‿ˈaʊt, ˌstʊd‿ˈaʊt/	hervorragen, sich abheben	My orange umbrella really **stands out**.	
	happy ending /ˌhæpi‿ˈendɪŋ/	Happy End	I'm glad when stories have a **happy ending**.	
	cheesy /ˈtʃiːzi/	käsig, kitschig		
	in conclusion /ɪn kənˈkluːʒ(ə)n/	zum Abschluss, abschließend	**In conclusion**, we should do more to stop bullying.	
	thought-provoking /ˈθɔːt prəˌvəʊkɪŋ/	nachdenklich stimmend		
	all in all /ˌɔːl‿ɪn‿ˈɔːl/	alles in allem	**All in all**, it was a good book.	
	touching /ˈtʌtʃɪŋ/	ergreifend, (be)rührend	It was such a **touching** book that it made me cry.	
	to **get through sth** *(irr)* /ˌget ˈθruː/	etw überstehen	Ola was having a bad day but she **got through** it.	
	plot /plɒt/	Handlung	The **plot** is a little complicated but it makes sense in the end.	
B9	to **vary** /ˈveəri/	variieren	Morgan **varied** the colours in his picture, so it was very bright.	
B10	to **contain** /kənˈteɪn/	enthalten	Be careful! That cake **contains** nuts and Isabelle is allergic.	p. 50

Say it in English – Theme 2

So kannst du …

über die Vor- und Nachteile sprechen, ein Teenager zu sein	Teenagers are more … Teenagers are better at … than adults. While teenagers can …, adults/children are supposed to … The best thing about being a teenager is … Being a teenager is sometimes hard because …
eine Grafik/ein Diagramm beschreiben	The first graphic highlights/shows … The second graphic is about/deals with … When you look at …, you notice that … Over the years, the figure has increased by … Over the years, the percentage has decreased by … The figures go up/down steadily/significantly from 1980 to … Compared to … Even though … While 80% of all 18-year-olds had a driver's licence in 1983, … Only 4.2% of Gen X identify as … while 10.5% of all people who were born between …
deine Meinung äußern	I think Paula Tweedy is right/wrong because … If teens had more freedom and more power, … I believe that … Personally, I feel that … I would say that … When it comes down to it, … For me, it's absolutely clear that … As I see it, … The point I would like to raise is … As far as I'm concerned, … I agree that …
dich äußern, wenn du anderer Meinung bist	Well, I don't think so because … In contrast to what you have said, I … I see what you mean but … To be honest, I don't think that …
in einer Diskussion einen Aspekt hinzufügen	I would like to add that …
einen Cartoon beschreiben	The cartoon deals with/is concerned with the issue/topic of … The cartoon shows two … who are … The character on the left/right appears to be …
Vermutungen über die Aussage eines Cartoons anstellen	The text suggests that … You might conclude that the message of the cartoon is …
deine Meinung zu einem Cartoon äußern	If you ask me, the cartoon is (not) funny/thought-provoking because … I (don't) like the cartoon, especially …
sagen, ob du ein Buch gerne lesen würdest	Although I don't like the cover, I would like to read the book because … This book appeals to me because … It would be quite exciting to find out … Personally, I find this subject …
Partizipialkonstruktionen verwenden, um Sätze kürzer zu formulieren	Adam is a high school student wanting to become a chef.

Theme 3: Human rights for all?

2	United Nations (UN) /juːˌnaɪtɪd ˈneɪʃ(ə)nz/	Vereinte Nationen		p. 66
	identity /aɪˈdentɪti/	Identität	The spy has a secret **identity**. Frz. *identité*, Sp. *identidad*	
	adequate /ˈædɪkwət/	ausreichend, angemessen	Tom's homework was **adequate**, but it wasn't great.	
	standard of living /ˌstændəd‿əv ˈlɪvɪŋ/	Lebensstandard		
	harm *(no pl)* /hɑːm/	Schaden, Verletzung	It is important to always be aware of the **harm** that our actions could cause.	
	to **educate** /ˈedjʊkeɪt/	unterrichten, ausbilden, erziehen	It is the responsibility of parents and schools to **educate** children on the importance of respecting other cultures.	
	belief (*pl* **beliefs**) /bɪˈliːf, bɪˈliːfs/	Glaube, Überzeugung, Ansicht	Respecting others' **belief** is essential for a tolerant society.	
	° privacy *(no pl)* /ˈprɪvəsi, ˈpraɪvəsi/	Privatsphäre, Intimsphäre		
	to **associate** /əˈsəʊsiˌeɪt/	in Verbindung bringen, *hier:* Kontakt haben/halten	Cara always tries to **associate** with people who share her interests.	
	religion /rɪˈlɪdʒ(ə)n/	Religion, Glaube	Hinduism and Islam are examples of **religions**.	
	just /dʒʌst/	gerecht	The judge's decision was **just**.	
3	**least** /liːst/	am wenigsten	That was my **least** favourite novel. It was extremely boring.	
	to **observe** /əbˈzɜːv/	beobachten, bemerken, *hier:* (be)achten	During the festival, we **observe** a moment of silence.	
5	**impressive** /ɪmˈpresɪv/	beeindruckend	Buckingham Palace is an **impressive** building.	p. 67
6	to **research** /rɪˈsɜːtʃ/	erforschen, recherchieren	Scientists **have been researching** this topic for years.	
	silence *(no pl)* /ˈsaɪləns/	Stille, Schweigen, Ruhe	The **silence** in the room made me feel uncomfortable.	
A1	**gun** /gʌn/	(Schuss)waffe, Pistole, Gewehr, *hier:* Waffen-	**Gun** control is an important topic in the US.	p. 68
	immediate /ɪˈmiːdiət/	umgehend, unmittelbar, direkt, augenblicklich	What was her **immediate** reaction?	
	elementary school (*AE* = **primary school** *BE*) /ˌeləˈment(ə)ri skul/	Grundschule	In **elementary school**, children learn basic skills.	
A2	to **arise, arose, arisen** /əˈraɪz, əˈrəʊz, əˈrɪz(ə)n/	aufkommen, sich ergeben	Unexpected problems can **arise** at any moment, so it's important to be prepared.	p. 69
	° invader /ɪnˈveɪdə/	Angreifer/in, Eindringling		
	shooting /ˈʃuːtɪŋ/	Schießerei, Schießen		
	valuable /ˈvæljʊb(ə)l/	wertvoll, kostbar	A ring can be very **valuable**.	
	rifle /ˈraɪf(ə)l/	Gewehr		
	weapon /ˈwepən/	Waffe	If you own a **weapon**, you need to think about health and safety.	
	shot /ʃɒt/	Schuss		
	politician /ˌpɒləˈtɪʃ(ə)n/	Politiker/in	The **politician** is talking to the press.	

	to **claim** /kleɪm/	behaupten, Anspruch erheben auf	Marcus **claimed** that the dog ate his homework.
	accidentally /ˌæksɪˈdent(ə)li/	versehentlich, zufällig	Michael was **accidentally** shot. He is in hospital now.
	to **shoot sb** *(irr)* /ʃuːt/	jdn anschießen, jdn erschießen	As he ran away, the thief **shot** a policeman.
	stylistic device /staɪˌlɪstɪk dɪˈvaɪs/	Stilmittel	The use of a **stylistic device** can be an effective tool for attracting the **reader**'s **attention**.
	reader /ˈriːdə/	Leser/in	
	attention *(no pl)* /əˈtenʃ(ə)n/	Aufmerksamkeit, Achtung	Frz. *attention*, Sp. *atención*
	quote /kwəʊt/	Zitat	The most famous **quotes** are from Shakespeare.
	rhetorical /rɪˈtɒrɪk(ə)l/	rhetorisch	The question is **rhetorical**: it doesn't need an answer.
	anaphora *(pl)* /əˈnæfərə/	Anapher *(Wiederholung eines Wortes oder mehrerer Wörter am Beginn aufeinanderfolgender Textteile)*	
	to **repeat** /rɪˈpiːt/	wiederholen	**Repeat** this phrase ten times until you can remember it.
A3	**chart** /tʃɑːt/	Diagramm, Schaubild	This **chart** deals with the reasons for owning a gun in the US.
	° mortality /mɔːˈtæləti/	Sterblichkeit(s-)	
	° protection /prəˈtekʃ(ə)n/	Schutz	
	° hunting *(no pl)* /ˈhʌntɪŋ/	Jagen, Jagd(-)	
	° rate /reɪt/	Maß, Menge, Rate, Quote	
A5	**law** /lɔː/	Gesetz, Recht	You're not allowed to do that! It is against the **law**. p. 70
	Second Amendment (to the United States Constitution) /ˌsekənd‿əˈmendmənt (tə ðə juːˌnaɪtɪd ˌsteɪts ˌkɒnstɪˈtjuːʃ(ə)n)/	*Zweiter Zusatzartikel (zur Verfassung der Vereinigten Staaten)*	
	citizen /ˈsɪtɪz(ə)n/	(Staats)bürger/in	Pierre is French, he is a **citizen** of France.
	controversial /ˌkɒntrəˈvɜːʃ(ə)l/	umstritten, kontrovers, strittig	The issue of gun control is a highly **controversial** topic.
	to bear, bore, borne /beə, bɔː, bɔːn/	(er)tragen	
	arms *(pl)* /ɑːmz/	Waffen	The right to bear **arms** is important to some Americans.
	such as /ˈsʌtʃ‿æz/	wie (zum Beispiel)	Richard and Joseph share lots of interests, **such as** sports, reading and animals.
	conflict /ˈkɒnflɪkt/	Konflikt, Kampf, Zusammenstoß	Harry solved the **conflict** and everyone was happy again.
	to **surround** /səˈraʊnd/	einkreisen, umgeben	The police **surrounded** the building.
	background check /ˈbækˌgraʊnd‿tʃek/	Nachforschungen, Screening	
	association /əˌsəʊsiˈeɪʃ(ə)n/	Vereinigung, Verband	There is a large **association** of football clubs.
	supporter /səˈpɔːtə/	Unterstützer/in, Anhänger/in, Verfechter/in	The politician's **supporters** cheered.
	to **pass** /pɑːs/	geben, (herüber)reichen, *hier:* verabschieden	The law **was passed** yesterday.
	means (of) /ˈmiːnz‿əv/	Weg, Mittel, Art	The **means of** transportation have improved over the years.

	self-defence *(no pl)* /ˌself dɪˈfens/	Selbstverteidigung	
	to **involve** /ɪnˈvɒlv/	beinhalten, umfassen, betreffen, beteiligen	This project **will involve** a lot of hard work.
	related /rɪˈleɪtɪd/	verbunden, verwandt, in Zusammenhang stehen	There was an increase in gun-**related** violence.
	to **be obliged to do sth** *(irr)* /ˌbi‿əˌblaɪdʒd‿tə ˈduː/	verpflichtet sein, etw zu tun	Students **are obliged to** go to school, even if they don't want to.
	to **retreat** /rɪˈtriːt/	sich zurückziehen, zurückweichen	The soldiers **retreated**, they went back.
	confrontation /ˌkɒnfrʌnˈteɪʃ(ə)n/	Auseinandersetzung, Konfrontation	The **confrontation** didn't last long, and soon they were friends.
	to **respond (to)** /rɪˈspɒnd‿tʊ/	reagieren (auf), antworten	Maya made sure she **responded to** all of her emails.
	in fact /ɪn ˈfækt/	genaugenommen	That is, **in fact**, true.
	rise /raɪz/	Steigen, Anstieg, Aufstieg	The **rise** in crime rates is worrying.
	homicide *(AE)* /ˈhɑmɪˌsaɪd/	Mord	
	control *(no pl)* /kənˈtrəʊl/	Kontrolle, Gewalt, Herrschaft	Paula has **control** over the design of her bedroom.
A6	to hunt /hʌnt/	jagen	
	grocery /ˈgrəʊsəri/	Lebensmittel-	
A7	to **reflect** /rɪˈflekt/	spiegeln, zeigen, reflektieren	The headline of the article **reflects** the authors **attitude** towards stricter gun control laws. p. 71
	attitude /ˈætɪˌtjuːd/	Haltung, Einstellung	
	issue /ˈɪʃuː/	Thema, Angelegenheit, Problem, Streitfrage	Gun control is an important **issue**.
	amount /əˈmaʊnt/	Menge, Betrag	James spent a huge **amount** of money on Christmas presents.
	horrifying /ˈhɒrɪˌfaɪɪŋ/	schrecklich, entsetzlich, grauenhaft	
	measure /ˈmeʒə/	Maßnahme, Maß, Messgerät	The UK has strict gun control **measures**.
	restrictive /rɪˈstrɪktɪv/	einschränkend, einengend	Frz. *restrictif (-ive)*
	convinced /kənˈvɪnst/	überzeugt	I am **convinced** we need to do more about climate change.
	society /səˈsaɪəti/	Gesellschaft	Lat. *societas*

Wenn ein Nomen allgemein verwendet wird, lässt man den bestimmten Artikel weg, z. B.:
***Society** has come a long way.*
Wenn das Nomen näher bestimmt wird, verwendet man dagegen den bestimmten Artikel, z. B.:
*The **society** of poets met up often.*

forward(s) /ˈfɔːwədz/	nach vorn(e), weiter, vorn(e)	I walked **forwards** when the traffic light was green.
first of all /ˌfɜːst‿əv‿ˈɔːl/	zu(aller)erst	Jack had a long to-do list. **First of all** he washed the dishes, then he cleaned his room.
constitution /ˌkɒnstɪˈtjuːʃ(ə)n/	Zusammensetzung, Konstitution, Verfassung, Satzung	While the US has a written **constitution**, the UK does not.
outdated /ˌaʊtˈdeɪtɪd/	veraltet, überholt	

to **gain** /geɪn/	bekommen, erreichen, gewinnen	Frank **gained** five new customers last month.
threat /θret/	(Be)drohung, Gefahr	The president received **threats** from people who did not agree with him.
to invade /ɪnˈveɪd/	einfallen (in), einmarschieren (in)	Lat. *invādere*
military /ˈmɪlɪt(ə)ri/	Militär(-), militärisch	The **military** had to assist the police.
capable /ˈkeɪpəb(ə)l/	fähig	Alex is **capable** of finishing this task.
restriction /rɪˈstrɪkʃ(ə)n/	Begrenzung, Einschränkung	We can't go by plane because of weather **restrictions**.
quite a few /ˌkwaɪt‿ə ˈfjuː/	eine ganze Menge	
record /ˈrekɔːd/	Aufzeichnungen, Akte, Vorgeschichte	Lisa has an excellent **record** at school. Her behaviour is very good and she has great grades.
direction /dɪˈrekʃ(ə)n/	Richtung	I realised I was going in the wrong **direction** when I looked at the map.
despite /dɪˈspaɪt/	trotz	**Despite** the bad weather, Freddie went for a walk.
official /əˈfɪʃ(ə)l/	offiziell	The US has no **official** language.
realistically /ˌrɪəˈlɪstɪkli/	realistisch (betrachtet)	Liam wants to go to space but **realistically** that won't happen.
legal /ˈliːg(ə)l/	legal, gesetzlich (vorgeschrieben)	**legal** ↔ illegal
to **be opposed to sth** *(irr)* /ˌbi‿əˈpəʊzd‿tə/	etw ablehnend gegenüberstehen, gegen etw sein	Dina and Ravi **are opposed to** the new rule about phones at school.
to **point (at/to)** /ˈpɔɪnt‿ət/tə/	deuten/zeigen (auf), *hier:* richten (auf)	The policewoman **pointed** her gun **at** the building.
furthermore /ˌfɜːðəˈmɔː/	außerdem, ferner	
guarantee /ˌgærənˈtiː/	Garantie, Zusicherung, Sicherheit	There is no **guarantee** that guns in private households are kept in a **secure** place.
secure /sɪˈkjʊə/	sicher, fest (verschlossen)	
to **take sth into account** *(irr)* /ˌteɪk ˌsʌmθɪŋ‿ˌɪntʊ‿əˈkaʊnt/	etw berücksichtigen	We have **to take** people's feelings **into account**.
doubt /daʊt/	Zweifel, Bedenken	No one had **doubts** about whether Nina would win the race.
across /əˈkrɒs/	über, *hier:* querdurch, über ... hinweg	There is a road **across** the whole country, from the east coast to the west coast.
to **harm** /hɑːm/	Schaden zufügen, schaden	Plastic **harms** the environment.
constitutional right /ˌkɒnstɪˌtjuːʃ(ə)n(ə)l ˈraɪt/	Grundrecht	
A8 **death** /deθ/	Tod, Ende	The **death** of his grandmother made Owen very sad. p. 72
truth /truːθ/	Wahrheit	I know the **truth**, so stop lying!
° to stoop /stuːp/	sich beugen, sich bücken	
° bullet /ˈbʊlɪt/	Kugel, Schuss-	
° to plunge /plʌndʒ/	(ab)stürzen	
current /ˈkʌrənt/	jetzig, gegenwärtig, aktuell	The **current** task is cleaning the kitchen; then we will clean the bathroom.

	° personification /pəˌsɒnɪfɪˈkeɪʃ(ə)n/	Personifikation, Personifizierung		
	° enjamb(e)ment /ɪnˈdʒæmmənt/	Enjambement *(Übergreifen des Satzes in den nächsten Vers)*		
A9	**safety** *(no pl)* /ˈseɪfti/	Sicherheit(s-)	**Safety** measures are taken to reduce risks.	
	to **adopt** /əˈdɒpt/	adoptieren, annehmen	The school **adopted** new school uniform rules.	
	drill /drɪl/	Übung, Probe(alarm)		
A10	**armed** /ɑːmd/	bewaffnet	In the US, police officers are **armed**: they carry guns.	
	to **state** /steɪt/	aussprechen, erklären, darlegen	Kim **stated** the facts but Dean didn't listen.	
B1	**plot** /plɒt/	Handlung	The **plot** of the film was interesting.	*p. 74*
	senior *(AE)* /ˈsinjər/	*Oberstufenschüler/in im letzten Jahr*		
	° middle-class /ˌmɪd(ə)l ˈklɑːs/	Mittelschicht-		
	° the in-crowd /ðiˌˈɪn kraʊd/	Insider-Clique		
	to **date sb** *(AE)* /ˈdeɪt/	mit jdm gehen	Emily and Chris **have been dating** for three months.	
	college /ˈkɒlɪdʒ/	College *(Eingangsstufe der Universität in den USA)*	She is studying history in **college**.	
	financial /faɪˈnænʃ(ə)l/	finanziell, Finanz-, Geld-	For financial reasons, we had to cancel our holiday.	
	resentment *(no pl)* /rɪˈzentmənt/	Verbitterung, Groll	Frz. *ressentiment*, Sp. *resentimiento*	
	unemployed /ˌʌnɪmˈplɔɪd/	arbeitslos	Sally **has been unemployed** for a month, but she is looking for a new job.	
	dignity *(no pl)* /ˈdɪgnəti/	Würde, Achtung		
	homeless /ˈhəʊmləs/	heimatlos, obdachlos	The city wants to end **homelessness**.	
	to **struggle** /ˈstrʌg(ə)l/	sich abmühen, kämpfen, ringen	Poppy **struggled** to do her homework.	
	rejection /rɪˈdʒekʃ(ə)n/	Ablehnung, Absage, Abweisung	Ben applied for six jobs but received five **rejections**.	
	to **witness** /ˈwɪtnəs/	beobachten, Zeuge/Zeugin sein, miterleben	Will **witnessed** the crime and told the police what happened.	
	unexpected /ˌʌnɪkˈspektɪd/	unerwartet	Sam's good grades were **unexpected**.	
	decline /dɪˈklaɪn/	Rückgang, Verschlechterung, Niedergang		
	prejudiced /ˈpredʒʊdɪst/	voreingenommen		
	ill fortune /ˌɪl ˈfɔːtʃən/	Pech		
	outcast /ˈaʊtˌkɑːst/	Ausgestoßene/r, Geächtete/r		
B2	**extract** /ˈekstrækt/	Auszug	Peter thought they had to read the whole book, but it was only an **extract** of twenty pages.	

No Place – extract 1

° driveway *(AE)* /ˈdraɪvˌweɪ/	Einfahrt	° salary /ˈsæləri/	Gehalt
° spirits *(pl)* /ˈspɪrɪts/	Gemütsverfassung, Mut, Stimmung	° payment /ˈpeɪmənt/	(Be)zahlung
° sensation /senˈseɪʃ(ə)n/	Gefühl, Sensation	° foreclosure proceedings *(pl)* /fɔːˈkləʊʒə prəˌsiːdɪŋz/	Zwangsvollstreckungsverfahren
° dread *(no pl)* /dred/	Furcht, (große) Angst	° to tend /tend/	sich kümmern um, pflegen
° to cling to sth /ˈklɪŋ tʊ/	sich an etw klammern	° backyard *(AE)* /ˌbækˈjɑrd/	Garten *(hinter einem Haus)*
° carnivore /ˈkɑːnɪvɔː/	Fleischfresser/in	° to put sth into storage *(irr)* /ˌpʊt ˌsʌmθɪŋ‿ˌɪntʊ ˈstɔːrɪdʒ/	etw (ein)lagern, etw unterstellen
° setback /ˈsetˌbæk/	Rückschlag	° the bare essentials /ðə ˌbeər‿ɪˈsenʃ(ə)lz/	das (Aller)nötigste
° stockbroker /ˈstɒkˌbrəʊkə/	Börsenmakler/in		
° to let go *(irr)* /ˌlet ˈgəʊ/	loslassen, *hier:* entlassen		
° employment *(no pl)* /ɪmˈplɔɪmənt/	Beschäftigung, Anstellung, Tätigkeit		
° to scrape by (on sth) /ˌskreɪp‿ˈbaɪ‿ɒn/	(mit etw) gerade so über die Runden kommen		

to **quote** /kwəʊt/	zitieren	The teacher began the class by **quoting** a famous writer.
first-person narrator /ˌfɜːst ˈpɜːs(ə)n‿nəˌreɪtə/	Icherzähler/in	
third-person narrator /ˌθɜːd ˈpɜːs(ə)n‿nəˌreɪtə/	personale/r Erzähler/in	
narrative /ˈnærətɪv/	Erzählung, Erzähl-, Schilderung	The **narrative** of the story was brilliant; I read for hours.
perspective /pəˈspektɪv/	Perspektive, Sicht, Blickwinkel	A third-person narrator tells the story from an outside **perspective**.
B3 to **sign up** /ˌsaɪn‿ˈʌp/	sich einschreiben, sich anmelden	Rory **signed up** for hockey club. p. 75
march /mɑːtʃ/	Marsch	Thousands of people joined the protest **march**.
undivided /ˌʌndɪˈvaɪdɪd/	uneingeschränkt, ungeteilt	
motivation *(no pl)* /ˌməʊtɪˈveɪʃ(ə)n/	Begründung, Motivation	**Motivation** is important for success.

No Place – extract 2

° tense /tens/	spannungsgeladen, angespannt	° segregation *(no pl)* /ˌsegrɪˈgeɪʃ(ə)n/	(Rassen)trennung
° cause /kɔːz/	Grund, Ursache, Anlass, *hier:* (gute) Sache	° to ace sth *(AE)* /eɪs/	etw mit Bravour bestehen
° to back down /ˌbæk‿ˈdaʊn/	nachgeben, einen Rückzieher machen	° actual /ˈæktʃuəl/	eigentlich, tatsächlich
° to figure *(informal)* /ˈfɪgə/	denken, annehmen	° strength /streŋθ/	Kraft, Stärke
° to lay out a spiel *(informal)* *(irr)* /ˌleɪ‿ˌaʊt‿ə ˈʃpiːl/	mit der alten Leier kommen	° vote /vəʊt/	Abstimmung, Wahl, Stimme
° It takes guts ... *(informal)* /ɪt‿ˌteɪks ˈgʌts/	Man braucht Mut ...	° election /ɪˈlekʃ(ə)n/	Wahl
° to suffer (from) /ˈsʌfə frɒm/	erleiden, ertragen, leiden (an/unter)	° requirement /rɪˈkwaɪəmənt/	Voraussetzung, Erfordernis

B4 to **analyse** /ˈænəlaɪz/	analysieren, untersuchen	I **analysed** the results to find out the answer. p. 76
speculation /ˌspekjʊˈleɪʃ(ə)n/	Spekulation, Vermutung	There has been lots of **speculation** about the crime, but no one is certain.

No Place – extract 3

° to make a habit of sth *(irr)* /ˌmeɪk‿ə ˈhæbɪt‿əv/	etw zur Gewohnheit werden lassen
° to slip /slɪp/	ausrutschen, abrutschen, *hier:* drauflegen
° main course /ˈmeɪn kɔːs/	Hauptgericht, Hauptgang
° to intend /ɪnˈtend/	beabsichtigen
° mean /miːn/	gemein, fies
° to scowl at sb /ˈskaʊl‿ət/	jdn mürrisch ansehen
° to huddle /ˈhʌd(ə)l/	sich zusammendrängen
° to cause sb to do sth /ˌkɔːz‿ˌsʌmbədi tə ˈduː/	jdn veranlassen, etw zu tun
° embarrassment /ɪmˈbærəsmənt/	Peinlichkeit, Verlegenheit
° charity /ˈtʃærəti/	Barmherzigkeit, Wohltätigkeits-organisation, *hier:* Sozialhilfe(-)
° case /keɪs/	Fall
° to humiliate /hjuːˈmɪlieɪt/	demütigen, erniedrigen, blamieren
° to simmer /ˈsɪmə/	sieden, köcheln
° to snap /snæp/	schnalzen, schnippen, *hier:* ausrasten
° to grab /græb/	schnappen, greifen, packen
° collar /ˈkɒlə/	Kragen
° to count /kaʊnt/	(ab)zählen, mitzählen, auszählen
° forehead / ˈfɔːhed, ˈfɒrɪd/	Stirn
° wrist /rɪst/	Handgelenk
° grip /grɪp/	Griff, Gewalt
° to clench /klentʃ/	umklammern, fest packen, *hier auch:* zusammenbeißen
° fistful /ˈfɪstfʊl/	Handvoll
° to breathe (in/out) /ˌbriːð‿ˈɪn/ˌbriːð‿ˈaʊt/	(ein/aus)atmen
° palms out /ˌpɑːmz‿ˈaʊt/	mit den Hand(innen)-flächen nach außen
° incredulous /ɪnˈkredjʊləs/	ungläubig, fassungslos

B6	to relate to /rɪˈleɪt‿tʊ/	sich beziehen auf, *hier:* in Beziehung stehen zu	p. 78
	to **imitate** /ˈɪmɪteɪt/	imitieren, nachahmen	Jade tried to **imitate** her favourite singer's voice.

Say it in English – Theme 3

So kannst du ...

über deine Rechte sprechen	I think the right to ... is the most/least important. If I didn't have the right to ..., ... Having the right to associate comes with the responsibility to allow others to choose if they want to associate with me. For me, "the right to have privacy" means that nobody is allowed to read my diary.
eine Grafik/ein Diagramm beschreiben	My chart deals with/lists ... The main reason is ... while ... ... is a reason that X percent named, while ... When you look at ..., you notice that ... ... percent of all American children ... The percentage of ... is significantly higher/lower in ...
deine Meinung ausdrücken	I'm convinced that everyone would agree that ... It is obvious to me that this idea is outdated.
Argumente aufzählen	First of all, let's talk about ... Secondly, some might say that ... Finally, ...
zwei gegensätzliche Positionen angeben	On the one hand, background checks are a step in the right direction. On the other hand, despite background checks, it is still relatively easy to buy a weapon.
eine abschließende Einschätzung formulieren	Taking everything into account, there can be no doubt that ...

Theme 4: Chances and opportunities

2 **knowledge** *(no pl)* /ˈnɒlɪdʒ/	Kenntnis(se), Wissen	Anna doesn't know much about animals, but she has lots of **knowledge** about flowers. p. 92
benefit /ˈbenɪfɪt/	Nutzen, Vorteil	
spare time *(no pl)* /ˌspeə ˈtaɪm/	Freizeit	Fred reads a lot in his **spare time**.
to **repair** /rɪˈpeə/	reparieren, (wieder) in Ordnung bringen	I **repaired** my bike instead of buying a new one.
to restyle /ˌriːˈstaɪl/	umgestalten, neu gestalten	
crafty /ˈkrɑːfti/	schlau, gerissen, *hier auch:* handwerklich begabt	
creative /kriˈeɪtɪv/	kreativ, schöpferisch	Mark is **creative**: he loves making music and writing his own songs.
salesperson (*pl* salespeople) /ˈseɪlzˌpɜːs(ə)n, ˈseɪlzˌpiːp(ə)l/	Verkäufer/in	
DIY (= do-it-yourself) *(no pl)* /ˌdiː‿aɪ ˈwaɪ, ˌduː‿ɪt jəˈself/	Heimwerken	
to **get to do sth** *(irr)* /ˌget‿tə ˈduː/	die Möglichkeit haben, etw zu tun	After a busy day, Oscar finally **got to bake** a cake.
to **invest** /ɪnˈvest/	investieren, anlegen	Gina **invests** a lot of time in her education. Frz. *investir*, Sp. *investir*
furniture *(no pl)* /ˈfɜːnɪtʃə/	Möbel	I don't have much **furniture** in my bedroom: just a bed and a desk.
to **store** /stɔː/	(auf)speichern, lagern, aufbewahren	Tara **stores** all her things in the wardrobe.
garage /ˈgærɪdʒ/	Garage, Tankstelle, (Kfz-)Werkstatt	Will parked the car in the **garage**.
also /ˈɔːlsəʊ/	auch, *hier:* darüber hinaus	Carrots are healthy. They **also** taste good.
rude /ruːd/	unhöflich	It is **rude** to point at people.
to **collect** /kəˈlekt/	(ein)sammeln, *hier:* abholen	Cara's mum **collects** her from school every day.
impolite /ˌɪmpəˈlaɪt/	unhöflich, frech, unverschämt	Don't talk with food in your mouth, it is **impolite**.
elderly /ˈeldəli/	ältere(r, s)	
device /dɪˈvaɪs/	Gerät, Vorrichtung, Apparat	Simrun uses her electronic **devices** to talk to her friends.
to **assist (in/with)** /əˈsɪst‿ɪn/wɪð/	(mit)helfen (bei)	The lady needed help, so Leah **assisted** her.
everyday /ˈevriˌdeɪ/	alltäglich	I would like to have more time to relax in my **everyday** life.
patience *(no pl)* /ˈpeɪʃ(ə)ns/	Geduld	Learning to play piano takes time, but Laura has a lot of **patience**, so she doesn't mind.
trustworthy /ˈtrʌstˌwɜːði/	vertrauenswürdig, zuverlässig	
discreet /dɪˈskriːt/	diskret, dezent, taktvoll	
to **set up, set up, set up** /ˌset‿ˈʌp/	errichten, einrichten	Polly **set up** a youth club in her hometown.
tech-savvy /ˈtekˌsævi/	technikaffin	
at times /ət ˈtaɪmz/	manchmal	School is difficult **at times**, but often it is fun.
impatient /ɪmˈpeɪʃ(ə)nt/	ungeduldig	Liam is so **impatient**: he hates waiting.
mascot /ˈmæskɒt/	Maskottchen	

	to **entertain** /ˌentəˈteɪn/	unterhalten	Will **entertained** his sister by dancing.
	spectator /spekˈteɪtə/	Zuschauer/in	
	field /fiːld/	Wiese, Feld, *hier AE*: Spielfeld	The **field** was empty before the players arrived.
	to **fall over, fell over, fallen over** /ˌfɔːl‿ˈəʊvə, ˌfel‿ˈəʊvə, ˌfɔːlən‿ˈəʊvə/	hinfallen, stürzen	Ivo **fell over** and hurt his foot.
	stairs *(pl)* /steəz/	Treppe	Bill walks up the **stairs** to get to his English class.
4	disgusting /dɪsˈɡʌstɪŋ/	empörend, widerlich, widerwärtig	
	revolting /rɪˈvəʊltɪŋ/	abstoßend, widerlich	
	to **gain** /ɡeɪn/	bekommen, erreichen, gewinnen	Ryan **gained** a lot of experience when he worked with his dad.
A1	to **mention** /ˈmenʃ(ə)n/	erwähnen	It is a secret: don't **mention** it to anyone else. p. 94
A3	to **involve** /ɪnˈvɒlv/	beinhalten, umfassen, betreffen, beteiligen	Which activities should your future job **involve**?
A5	**job ad(vert)/job advertisement** /ˈdʒɒb‿ˌædvɜːt/ ˈdʒɒb‿ədˌvɜːtɪsmənt/	Stellenanzeige	Jess saw the **job advertisement** online.
	internship (*AE* = **placement** *BE*) /ˈɪntɜrnˌʃɪp/	Praktikum	**Internships** are a good way of getting work experience.
	up-and-coming /ˌʌp‿ən ˈkʌmɪŋ/	aufstrebend	
	across /əˈkrɒs/	über, *hier:* querdurch, über ... hinweg	Lizzy ran **across** the whole school to find her classroom.
	intern /ˈɪntɜːn/	Praktikant/in	**Interns** help other people at work.
	fabulous /ˈfæbjʊləs/	fabelhaft, sagenhaft	I love your dress; it is **fabulous**!
	office space *(no pl)* /ˈɒfɪs‿speɪs/	Büroräume, Bürofläche(n)	
	essential /ɪˈsenʃ(ə)l/	unverzichtbar, wesentlich	Fruit and vegetables are **essential** for a healthy lifestyle.
	potential /pəˈtenʃ(ə)l/	Potenzial, potenziell, möglich	My **potential** employer wants to interview me.
	applicant /ˈæplɪkənt/	Bewerber/in	There are five **applicants** for this job.
	currently /ˈkʌrəntli/	zurzeit, gegenwärtig, momentan	Mara is **currently** studying, but later she will go out with her friends.
	feature /ˈfiːtʃə/	Merkmal, Kennzeichen, Besonderheit, *hier:* Feature	The robot has a special **feature**: it makes ice cream.
	editing *(no pl)* /ˈedɪtɪŋ/	Bearbeiten, Redigieren	The video was five minutes long, but after **editing** it is only three minutes.
	the right fit /ðə ˌraɪt ˈfɪt/	etwas Passendes, *hier:* die richtige Person	
	to add one's mark to sth /ˌæd‿wʌnz ˈmɑːk tʊ/	etw prägen, etw seinen Stempel aufdrücken	
	whatever /wɒtˈevə/	was auch immer, egal was	On Dan's birthday he can eat **whatever** he wants.
	involvement /ɪnˈvɒlvmənt/	Beteiligung	John was proud of his **involvement** with the youth club.
	daily /ˈdeɪli/	täglich, jeden Tag	Zoe brushes her teeth twice **daily**.
	to **act** /ækt/	handeln, vorgehen, *hier:* fungieren, tätig sein	Roger **was acting** as school principal for the week.

representative /ˌreprɪˈzentətɪv/	(Stell)vertreter/in, repräsentativ	Frz. *représentant(e)*, Sp. *representante*
to **hike** /haɪk/	wandern	Dani **hikes** through the mountains on weekends.
comprehensive /ˌkɒmprɪˈhensɪv/	umfassend	
training *(no pl)* /ˈtreɪnɪŋ/	Training, *hier:* Ausbildung, Schulung	You need **training** to become a teacher.
shift /ʃɪft/	Schicht	
candidate /ˈkændɪdeɪt/	Kandidat/in Bewerber/in	There are many good **candidates** for this job.
ability /əˈbɪləti/	Fähigkeit, Talent, Begabung	Tom has the **ability** to understand many languages.
willing /ˈwɪlɪŋ/	bereit, gewillt, willig	Sean is **willing** to work very hard to get good grades.
regardless of sth /rɪˈɡɑːdləs‿əv/	trotz etw, ungeachtet etw	
ever-changing /ˌevə ˈtʃeɪndʒɪŋ/	ständig wechselnd	
unpredictable /ˌʌnprɪˈdɪktəb(ə)l/	unvorhersehbar, unberechenbar	English weather is so **unpredictable**. Sometimes it is sunny then rainy again.
energetic /ˌenəˈdʒetɪk/	voller Energie	
capable /ˈkeɪpəb(ə)l/	fähig	Everyone is **capable** of good grades if they work hard.
animal rescue shelter /ˌænɪm(ə)l ˈreskjuː ˌʃeltə/	Tierauffangstation, Tierheim	
wounded /ˈwuːndɪd/	verletzt, verwundet	
the wild *(no pl)* /ðə ˈwaɪld/	die Wildnis	
to **care for** /ˈkeə fɔː/	sich kümmern um	Poppy **cared for** Alia's cat while she was on holiday.
to **feed, fed, fed** /fiːd, fed, fed/	(zu) essen geben, füttern	Elias **feeds** the dog every day.
motivated /ˈməʊtɪˌveɪtɪd/	motiviert	Sarah **was** very **motivated** to practise tennis because she really wanted to win.
conservation *(no pl)* /ˌkɒnsəˈveɪʃ(ə)n/	Schutz, Erhaltung	Bees help with the **conservation** of biodiversity.
reliable /rɪˈlaɪəb(ə)l/	verlässlich, zuverlässig	Peter is very **reliable**: you can trust him.
to **run, ran, run** /rʌn, ræn, rʌn/	rennen, laufen, *hier:* durchführen	The school **runs** a computing class every year.
to **spread, spread, spread** /spred/	(sich) ausbreiten, (sich) verbreiten, *hier:* verteilen	Aarav **spread** his homework tasks across the weekend, so he still had time for football practice.
to **suit sb/sth** /suːt/	zu jdm/etw passen	This shirt doesn't **suit** me; I need to find a new one.
A7 **CV (= curriculum vitae)** *(BE* = **résumé** *AE)* /ˌsiː ˈviː, kəˌrɪkjʊləm ˈviːtaɪ/	Lebenslauf	A clear and correct **CV** shows the **employer** that you are serious about your application. p. 96
employer /ɪmˈplɔɪə/	Arbeitgeber/in	
profile /ˈprəʊfaɪl/	Profil, Porträt	Thanks to James's volunteer work, he has an impressive **profile**.
hard-working /ˌhɑːdˈwɜːkɪŋ/	fleißig, hart arbeitend	Luke has done all his homework and cleaned the house; he is so **hard-working**.
reference /ˈref(ə)rəns/	(Arbeits)zeugnis, Referenz	Mia needs a **reference** from her employer.
on request /ɒn rɪˈkwest/	auf Anfrage, auf Wunsch	
present /ˈprez(ə)nt/	Gegenwart, jetzt, heute	Tom: "Forget the past and focus on the **present**."

	to **volunteer** /ˌvɒlən'tɪə/	sich freiwillig melden, *hier:* ehrenamtlich tätig sein	Diana **volunteers** at an animal shelter on weekends.	
	responsible /rɪ'spɒnsəb(ə)l/	verantwortlich, zuständig	Ola is **responsible** for getting her mum's birthday present.	
	data entry *(no pl)* /'deɪtə‿ˌentri/	Dateneingabe		
	database /'deɪtəˌbeɪs/	Datenbank(-)		
	word processing *(no pl)* /'wɜːd ˌprəʊsesɪŋ/	Textverarbeitung		
	spreadsheet /'spredˌʃiːt/	Tabellenkalkulation, Arbeitsblatt		
	native speaker /ˌneɪtɪv 'spiːkə/	Muttersprachler/in	Maria is from Spain: she is a **native speaker** of Spanish.	
	application /ˌæplɪ'keɪʃ(ə)n/	Bewerbung, Antrag, Anwendung	I checked my job **application** for mistakes before I sent it.	
	formal /'fɔːm(ə)l/	formell, förmlich, offiziell	I use **formal** language in a job application but informal language when chatting with my friends.	
	° marital status *(no pl)* /ˌmærɪt(ə)l 'steɪtəs/	Familienstand		
A9	**cover letter** /ˌkʌvə 'letə/	Anschreiben	In a **cover letter** you can tell the employer more about yourself.	*p. 97*
	average /'æv(ə)rɪdʒ/	(im) Durchschnitt, durchschnittlich	It is 25 degrees here on an **average** summer day.	
	suited (to) /'suːtɪd‿tʊ/	geeignet (für)	This job is **suited to** someone who loves being outside.	
	to **lack** /læk/	nicht haben, fehlen	Unfortunately, Tim **lacks** the skills for the job.	
	attention *(no pl)* /ə'tenʃ(ə)n/	Aufmerksamkeit, Achtung	Yasmine's application attracted the employer's **attention**.	
	to **approve of** /ə'pruːv‿əv/	genehmigen, billigen, *hier:* für gut halten	My mum **approves of** my new friend; she says he is nice and polite.	
	rainforest /'reɪnˌfɒrɪst/	Regenwald	The Amazon is the world's largest **rainforest**.	
	to **count on sb/sth** /'kaʊnt‿ɒn/	auf jdn/etw zählen	I can always **count on** Heather to be on time: she is never late.	
	to **get back to sb** *(irr)* /ˌget 'bæk tʊ/	sich (wieder) bei jdm melden	Will **never got back to** Lucy about her party. She doesn't know if he's coming.	
	to the point /tə ðə 'pɔɪnt/	griffig, prägnant, auf das Thema bezogen		
	subject /'sʌbdʒɪkt/	(Schul)fach, *hier:* Betreff	The **subject** line of an email should be short and relevant.	
	Dear Sir/Madam /ˌdɪə 'sɜː/'mædəm/	Sehr geehrte Damen und Herren		
	in response to /ɪn rɪ'spɒns tʊ/	in Erwiderung auf, als Antwort auf		
	closing /'kləʊzɪŋ/	End-, Schluss-, abschließend		
	Yours faithfully *(BE)* /ˌjɔːz 'feɪθf(ə)li/	*Schlussformel in einem nicht an eine bestimmte Person gerichteten formellen Brief*		
A11	**characteristic** /ˌkærɪktə'rɪstɪk/	(charakteristisches) Merkmal, typisch, charakteristisch	Think about which of your **characteristics** could match the skills that are needed.	*p. 98*
	qualification /ˌkwɒlɪfɪ'keɪʃ(ə)n/	Qualifikation, Ausbildung, Abschluss	To become a teacher, you need a teaching **qualification**.	
	anonymous /ə'nɒnɪməs/	anonym, ungenannt	The author is **anonymous**: no one knows who wrote the book.	

to **vary** /'veəri/	variieren	My mood **varies** from day to day: sometimes I am happy but sometimes I am sad.	
B1 to **research** /rɪ'sɜ:tʃ/	erforschen, recherchieren	Lily **researched** bears for her science homework.	p. 100
common /'kɒmən/	üblich, weit verbreitet, gemeinsam	It is **common** to feel nervous before an exam.	
to **work** /wɜ:k/	arbeiten, *hier:* funktionieren	Awiti's robot **works**! He doesn't need to work on it anymore.	
tidy /'taɪdi/	ordentlich, sauber	Ada is very organised and her room is very **tidy**.	
up straight /ˌʌp 'streɪt/	aufrecht		
enthusiastic /ɪnˌθju:zi'æstɪk/	enthusiastisch, begeistert	Callie wants to work in an animal shelter because she is **enthusiastic** about helping animals.	
relaxed /rɪ'lækst/	entspannt, locker	My parents are quite **relaxed**; I don't have a bed time.	
to gesture /'dʒestʃə/	deuten		
to fidget /'fɪdʒɪt/	(herum)zappeln, *hier:* herumspielen		
to **touch** /tʌtʃ/	berühren	A hot potato is something nobody wants to **touch**.	
to **panic** /'pænɪk/	in Panik geraten	Owen **panicked** when he couldn't find his phone.	
to **reject** /rɪ'dʒekt/	ablehnen, zurückweisen, abweisen	Unfortunately, my application was **rejected**.	
B3 to **go wrong** *(irr)* /ˌgəʊ 'rɒŋ/	schiefgehen	Something **went wrong** with Li's computer and she lost all her work.	p. 101
B4 to **flow** /fləʊ/	fließen	The river **flows** through the park.	
to **sort** /sɔ:t/	sortieren	Copy the grid and **sort** the phrases.	
opener /'əʊp(ə)nə/	Öffner, Anfang		
to keep sth going *(irr)* /ˌki:p ˌsʌmθɪŋ 'gəʊɪŋ/	etw in Gang halten		
to buy time *(irr)* /ˌbaɪ 'taɪm/	Zeit gewinnen/schinden		
to **get started** *(irr)* /ˌget 'stɑ:tɪd/	beginnen	James **got started** on cooking dinner as soon as he got home.	
challenging /'tʃælɪndʒɪŋ/	(heraus)fordernd	This task is **challenging**, but it will help you to learn.	
shall /ʃæl/	sollen, werden	I'm bored. **Shall** we leave?	
likewise /'laɪkwaɪz/	ebenfalls, gleichfalls, ebenso		
B5 to **require** /rɪ'kwaɪə/	brauchen, verlangen, benötigen	Thomas **required** help with his homework.	p. 102
to **respond (to)** /rɪ'spɒnd‿tʊ/	reagieren (auf), antworten	Jake never **responded to** Will's email.	
to **cope with** /'kəʊp wɪð/	zurechtkommen mit, bewältigen	David has lots of homework to do, but he **is coping with** the stress well.	
to **repeat** /rɪ'pi:t/	wiederholen	After the teacher **repeated** the question, Paul finally understood.	

Say it in English – Theme 4

So kannst du ...

über berufliche Pläne für die Zukunft sprechen	... years from now I will have found my dream job. I will travel around the world and ... I definitely won't ...
begründen, warum du für eine Stelle geeignet bist	The internship would be the best job for me as I'm a well-organized and creative person. I always write to do-lists and I'm good at time-management, for example when ...
dich in einem persönlichen Profil für eine Bewerbung präsentieren	I am hard-working and reliable. Being very organized, I like working independently, but I also have great communication skills. I love nature and animals and enjoy outdoor activities. I have always wanted to spend some time in a country with a warm climate. My hobbies are ...
über die Eignung einer Person für eine Stelle sprechen	What makes her a good candidate is ... What makes him only an average candidate is ... She seems/doesn't seem to be well-suited to the project/job, as she ... Although he may ..., he lacks ... I (don't) think she will attract the organization's attention because ... The representatives of the organization/company will probably approve of ..., but might have a problem with ...
ein Gespräch eröffnen	Pleased to meet you. Sorry to have kept you waiting. How are you today? OK then, let's get started ...
ein Gespräch am Laufen halten	That sounds interesting/challenging/good/... I hope it's OK to ask: ...?
in einem Gespräch Zeit gewinnen	I've never been asked that question before. Please give me a moment to think about it. So you are looking for an example of ... Well, there are a few, but I think the most relevant is ... When you say..., do you mean ...? So what you are saying is ...?
ein Gespräch beenden	It's been great getting to know you. Thank you so much for your time. Have a good day!
in einem Bewerbungsgespräch die Rolle einer Arbeitgeberin/eines Arbeitgebers einnehmen	How are you today? Good! OK then, let's get started. You have applied to work as a ... with us. What would make you successful in this job? How do you cope with working under pressure? Do you like working in a team or do you prefer working on your own? How would you contribute to ...? What are your general interests and hobbies? Do you have any questions for me? It's been great getting to know you. We'll be in touch.

Theme 5: The North of England

1	**architectural** /ˌɑːkɪˈtektʃ(ə)rəl/	architektonisch	Manchester Cathedral is one of the city's **architectural** highlights.	p. 120
	iconic /aɪˈkɒnɪk/	ikonisch, *hier:* kultig, Kult-		
	vibrant /ˈvaɪbrənt/	lebhaft, dynamisch, lebendig		
	medium (*pl* **media**) /ˈmiːdiəm, ˈmiːdiə/	(Informations)medium	The **media** are important for communicating with the public.	
	documentary /ˌdɒkjʊˈment(ə)ri/	Dokumentation, Dokumentarfilm	Callum enjoyed watching a **documentary** about his favourite band.	
2	to **appeal to sb/sth** /əˈpiːl tʊ/	jdn/etw reizen, jdn/etw ansprechen	This book **appeals to** teenagers; they love it.	
4	° itinerary /aɪˈtɪnərəri/	Reiseroute, Reiseplan	Frz. *itinéraire*, Sp. *itinerario*	p. 121
	accommodation *(no pl)* /əˌkɒməˈdeɪʃ(ə)n/	Unterkunft	We have booked our train tickets but we still have to find **accommodation**.	
	source /sɔːs/	Quelle, Informationsquelle	Anya always gets her information from good **sources**, like quality newspapers.	
	to **vote** /vəʊt/	wählen, *hier:* abstimmen	The Grey family **voted to** decide where their next holiday would be.	
	flight /flaɪt/	Flug	Ravi is scared of flying, but that **flight** from London to Barcelona wasn't so bad.	
A1	**multicultural** /ˌmʌltiˈkʌltʃərəl/	multikulturell	Birmingham is a very **multicultural** city: people from all over the world live there.	p. 122
	the Industrial Revolution /ðiˌɪnˌdʌstriəl revəˈluːʃ(ə)n/	die industrielle Revolution	The **Industrial Revolution** changed how we produce things.	
	° cotton mill /ˈkɒt(ə)n mɪl/	Baumwollspinnerei		
	birth /bɜːθ/	Geburt(s-), Abstammung, Herkunft		
	before /bɪˈfɔː/	zuvor, vorher, früher	Zola moved to Leeds in 2023. She had finished her studies the year **before**.	
	invention /ɪnˈvenʃ(ə)n/	Erfindung	The radio was a brilliant **invention**.	
	machine /məˈʃiːn/	Maschine, Apparat	**Machines** changed people's lives dramatically.	
	° to spin, spun, spun /spɪn, spʌn, spʌn/	rotieren, drehen, *hier:* spinnen		
	° thread /θred/	Garn, Zwirn, Faden		
	° cloth /klɒθ/	Tuch, Stoff		
	dramatically /drəˈmætɪkli/	dramatisch, beträchtlich, drastisch	The weather changed **dramatically**: it was sunny but now it is windy and rainy.	
	rapid /ˈræpɪd/	schnell, plötzlich, rasch	To fight climate change we must take **rapid** action.	
	wealth *(no pl)* /welθ/	Reichtum, Vermögen, Fülle	Lisa uses her **wealth** for good and gives money to charity.	
	to **refer (back) to** /rɪˌfɜː ˈbæk tʊ/	(zurück)verweisen auf, sich beziehen auf, *hier:* nennen, bezeichnen	Manchester is sometimes **referred to** as the capital of the North.	
	to employ /ɪmˈplɔɪ/	beschäftigen, einstellen, einsetzen		
	up to /ˈʌp tʊ/	bis (zu)	Children had to work **up to** 14 hours a day.	
	pay *(no pl)* /peɪ/	Lohn, Gehalt, Bezahlung		
	to **attend** /əˈtend/	besuchen, *hier:* teilnehmen an	Emily **attended** the meeting about school rules.	

relentless /rɪˈlentləs/	unnachgiebig, unablässig	
lack (of) *(no pl)* /ˈlæk‿əv/	Mangel (an)	Penelope's grades didn't improve because of her **lack of** work.
to **found** /faʊnd/	gründen	Manchester United was **founded** in 1878.
deed /diːd/	Tat	
to **turn** /tɜːn/	(sich) (um)drehen, *hier:* wenden	Amara **turned** to her mum for help.
measure /ˈmeʒə/	Maßnahme, Maß, Messgerät	The school had to improve safety **measures** after someone got hurt.
to jail /dʒeɪl/	einsperren, inhaftieren	
Roman /ˈrəʊmən/	Römer/in, römisch	
to guard /gɑːd/	bewachen	
goods *(pl)* /gʊdz/	Waren, Güter	
inn /ɪn/	Gasthaus	
to reconstruct /ˌriːkənˈstrʌkt/	rekonstruieren	
° Greater Manchester /ˌgreɪtə ˈmænˌtʃestə/	Großraum Manchester	
to **breathe (in/out)** /ˌbriːð‿ˈɪn/ˌbriːð‿ˈaʊt/	(ein/aus)atmen	When Tamir is nervous, he **breathes in**, holds it, and **breathes out**.
single parent /ˌsɪŋg(ə)l ˈpeərənt/	Alleinerziehende/r	
to **feed, fed, fed** /fiːd, fed, fed/	(zu) essen geben, füttern	Claire **feeds** her cat every morning.
role model /ˈrəʊl ˌmɒd(ə)l/	Vorbild, Rollenbild	
to **raise** /reɪz/	heben, *hier:* schärfen	The documentary **raised awareness** about climate change.
awareness *(no pl)* /əˈweənəs/	Bewusstsein	
to campaign (for/against sth) /kæmˈpeɪn fɔː/əˌgenst/	(für etw) eintreten/(gegen etw) kämpfen	
instantly /ˈɪnstəntli/	sofort	You can send messages over long distances almost **instantly** using the internet.
the Second World War /ðə ˌsekənd ˌwɜːld ˈwɔː/	der Zweite Weltkrieg	
military /ˈmɪlɪt(ə)ri/	Militär(-), militärisch	Victoria is interested in **military** history.

Als ***collective nouns*** (Sammelbegriffe) bezeichnet man Nomen, die mit einer Verbform im Singular oder im Plural verwendet werden können. Verwendet man die Verbform im Plural, stehen oft die einzelnen Gruppenmitglieder im Vordergrund und nicht die Gruppe als Ganzes.
*The team **are** playing well.*
*The military **are** controlling entry to the city.*

bomber /ˈbɒmə/	Bombenflugzeug	
aircraft (*pl* aircraft) /ˈeəˌkrɑːft/	Luftfahrzeug, Flugzeug	
barrage balloon /ˈbærɑːʒ bəˌluːn/	Sperrballon *(Ballon, der der Kriegsführung dient)*	
to **manufacture** /ˌmænjʊˈfæktʃə/	herstellen	The factory **manufactures** car parts.
mainly /ˈmeɪnli/	hauptsächlich, in erster Linie	David is not a vegetarian, but he **mainly** eats meals without meat.
the Blitz /ðə ˈblɪts/	*deutsche Luftangriffe auf britische Städte im Zweiten Weltkrieg*	
to crack /kræk/	(zer)brechen, *hier:* knacken	
the allies /ði‿ˈælaɪz/	die Alliierten	
to **lay, laid, laid** /leɪ, leɪd, leɪd/	legen	Priya **laid** the book on the table.
foundation /faʊnˈdeɪʃ(ə)n/	Fundament, Basis, Grundlage	

computing *(no pl)* /kəmˈpjuːtɪŋ/	EDV, Computing	
artificial intelligence (AI) *(no pl)* /ˌɑːtɪˌfɪʃ(ə)l‿ɪnˈtelɪdʒ(ə)ns, ˌeɪ‿ˈaɪ/	künstliche Intelligenz	**Artificial intelligence** is a very controversial topic.
A3 **tabloid** /ˈtæblɔɪd/	Boulevardzeitung, Klatschzeitung	**Tabloids** have very dramatic articles. p. 124
quality newspaper /ˈkwɒləti ˌnjuːzˌpeɪpə/	seriöse (Tages)zeitung	Will prefers reading a **quality newspaper** because the information is better.
disruption /dɪsˈrʌpʃ(ə)n/	Unterbrechung, Störung	
to **spray** /spreɪ/	(be)sprühen	Amelia **sprayed** her skateboard green.
oil /ɔɪl/	(Erd)öl	**Oil** is a kind of fossil fuel.
onto /ˈɒntə/	in, auf	We ran **onto** the beach when we saw the boat.
to **glue** /gluː/	kleben	Ryan **glued** his photographs into his book.
valuable /ˈvæljʊb(ə)l/	wertvoll, kostbar	A ring can be very **valuable**.
painting /ˈpeɪntɪŋ/	Bild, Gemälde, Malerei	Louise spent the day working on her **painting** of a horse.
employee /ɪmˈplɔɪiː/	Angestellte/r, Mitarbeiter/in, Beschäftigte/r	Poppy is the youngest **employee** at her company.
gutless *(informal)* /ˈgʌtləs/	feige, lahm	
attack /əˈtæk/	Angriff, Anfall	The army carried out an **attack** in the early morning hours.
protester /prəˈtestə/	Protestierende/r, Demonstrant/in	Many **protesters** against war marched through the streets.
to wreak havoc /ˌriːk ˈhævək/	schlimme Schäden anrichten	
treasure /ˈtreʒə/	Schatz	Pirates often hid their **treasure** to keep it safe.
fossil fuel /ˈfɒs(ə)l ˌfjuːəl/	fossiler Brennstoff	**Fossil fuels** are bad for the environment.
to **threaten** /ˈθret(ə)n/	(be)drohen	Richard **threatened** to find a new job if his employer didn't pay him more.
demand /dɪˈmɑːnd/	(An)forderung	The employer agreed to his employee's **demands**, so she stayed.
to **meet, met, met** /miːt, met, met/	(sich) treffen, *hier:* erfüllen, entsprechen	Sahar worked hard to **meet** his deadlines.
to **evacuate** /ɪˈvækjueɪt/	evakuieren, räumen	The town was **evacuated** because of extreme weather.
to **arrest sb (on suspicion of sth)** /əˌrest ˌsʌmbədi‿ɒn səˈspɪʃ(ə)n‿əv/	jdn (wegen des Verdachts auf etw) verhaften	The man was **arrested on suspicion of** stealing a car.
suspicion /səˈspɪʃ(ə)n/	Verdacht, Misstrauen	I don't know who did this, but I have my **suspicions**.
to **protest** /prəˈtest/	protestieren	People **protested** against the new rules.
frame /freɪm/	(Bilder)rahmen	
exploration /ˌekspləˈreɪʃ(ə)n/	Erforschung	Lat. *explōrātio*
to launch /lɔːntʃ/	starten, beginnen	
campaign /kæmˈpeɪn/	Kampagne, Aktion	Ross supports the **campaign** for a new library.
across /əˈkrɒs/	über, *hier:* querdurch, über ... hinweg	Ali walked all **across** town.
to **gain** /geɪn/	bekommen, erreichen, gewinnen	Diane wants to **gain** experience in teaching.
to spray-paint /ˈspreɪˌpeɪnt/	mit Farbe besprühen	

to **apply** /ə'plaɪ/	anwenden, gebrauchen, auftragen	Lucy **applied** glue to the back of the photos and **stuck** them in her book.
to **stick, stuck, stuck** /stɪk, stʌk, stʌk/	kleben, stecken	
to **criticize** /'krɪtɪsaɪz/	kritisch beurteilen, kritisieren	Many people **criticize** the government for not doing more to prevent climate change.
work of art /ˌwɜːk‿əv‿'ɑːt/	Kunstwerk	
public nuisance /ˌpʌblɪk 'njuːs(ə)ns/	öffentliches Ärgernis	
to praise /preɪz/	loben	
form /fɔːm/	Form, *hier:* Art	Painting and film are different **forms** of art.
outrageous /aʊt'reɪdʒəs/	empörend, unerhört	The cost of the food was **outrageous**: it was so expensive!
scandalous /'skænd(ə)ləs/	skandalös, unerhört	The story was so **scandalous** that it was in every newspaper.
to **condemn** /kən'dem/	verurteilen, verdammen	The government **condemned** the protests for being too violent.
death /deθ/	Tod, Ende	The **death** of his grandmother made Owen very sad.
to license /'laɪs(ə)ns/	die Lizenz erteilen, erlauben	
to evaluate /ɪ'væljueɪt/	beurteilen, bewerten	Frz. *évaluer*, Sp. *evaluar*
A5 **analysis** (*pl* **analyses**) /ə'næləsɪs, ə'næləsiːz/	Analyse, Beurteilung	The scientists conducted an **analysis** of their results. p. 126
size /saɪz/	Größe	The **size** of the house was surprisingly large.
to **evoke** /ɪ'vəʊk/	hervorrufen	The song **evoked** memories of my past.
tone /təʊn/	Klang, Ton, *hier:* Stimmung	The **tone** of the article is formal.
matter-of-fact /ˌmætər‿əv‿'fækt/	sachlich, nüchtern	Mia spoke in a **matter-of-fact** way, it was hard to know how she felt.
emotive /ɪ'məʊtɪv/	emotional, gefühlsbetont	The speech uses lots of **emotive** language.
stylistic device /staɪˌlɪstɪk dɪ'vaɪs/	Stilmittel	Alliteration is a **stylistic device**.
rhetorical /rɪ'tɒrɪk(ə)l/	rhetorisch	The question is **rhetorical**: it doesn't need an answer.
address /ə'dres/	Adresse, Anschrift, *hier:* Anrede	There are several examples of direct **address** in the article.
exaggeration /ɪgˌzædʒə'reɪʃ(ə)n/	Übertreibung	Toby says he saw a real dinosaur, but I think that was an **exaggeration**.
factual /'fæktʃuəl/	sachlich, auf Tatsachen beruhend	
characteristic /ˌkærɪktə'rɪstɪk/	(charakteristisches) Merkmal, typisch, charakteristisch	Rhyme is a **characteristic** feature of poetry.
A6 **cause** / kɔːz/	Grund, Ursache, Anlass; *hier:* (gute) Sache	Do you want to raise awareness for a political **cause**?

B1	**conflict** /ˈkɒnflɪkt/	Konflikt, Kampf, Zusammenstoß	Paul doesn't like **conflict** and tries not to argue with anyone. p. 128
B2	to **involve** /ɪnˈvɒlv/	beinhalten, umfassen, betreffen, beteiligen	This project **involves** working together.

Scene one

° client /ˈklaɪənt/	Kunde/Kundin, Klient/in, Auftraggeber/in
° rich /rɪtʃ/	reich
° tight *(informal)* /taɪt/	knausrig
° unimpressed /ˌʌnɪmˈprest/	unbeeindruckt
° engine /ˈendʒɪn/	Maschine, Motor
° dirty /ˈdɜːti/	dreckig, schmutzig, *hier:* böse
° whilst *(BE)* /waɪlst/	während, obwohl, wo(hin)gegen
° self-obsessed /ˌselfəbˈsest/	selbstsüchtig
global warming /ˌgləʊb(ə)l ˈwɔːmɪŋ/	Erwärmung der Erdatmosphäre
° mark *(BE)* /mɑːk/	Note, Zensur
° bleak /bliːk/	kahl, trostlos, düster
° to twist /twɪst/	(ver)drehen
° packaging *(no pl)* /ˈpækɪdʒɪŋ/	Verpackung(smaterial)
° dish /dɪʃ/	Schale, Schüssel, Gericht
° to donate /dəʊˈneɪt/	spenden
° homeless shelter /ˈhəʊmləs ʃeltə/	Notschlafstelle, Obdachlosenunterkunft
° law /lɔː/	Gesetz, Recht

B4 p. 130

Scene two

° to flick through sth /ˈflɪk θruː/	etw (schnell) durchblättern
° pile /paɪl/	Stapel, Haufen
° to rush /rʌʃ/	eilen, hetzen
° nod /nɒd/	Nicken
° to blush /blʌʃ/	erröten, rot werden
° to give sb a lift *(irr)* /ˌgɪv ˌsʌmbədi‿ə ˈlɪft/	jdn (im Auto) mitnehmen
° to raise one's eyebrows /ˌreɪz wʌnz‿ˈaɪˌbraʊz/	die Augenbrauen hochziehen
° sensible /ˈsensəb(ə)l/	vernünftig, angemessen, *hier:* sinnvoll
° to cross /krɒs/	überqueren, *hier:* verschränken
° to turn /tɜːn/	(sich) (um)drehen, *hier:* werden
° attention *(no pl)* /əˈtenʃ(ə)n/	Aufmerksamkeit, Achtung
° to slash /slæʃ/	aufschlitzen, aufschneiden
° tyre /ˈtaɪə/	Reifen
° disgust *(no pl)* /dɪsˈgʌst/	Abscheu, Ekel, Empörung
° car dealership /ˈkɑː ˌdiːləʃɪp/	Autohaus
° to earn a living /ˌɜːn‿ə ˈlɪvɪŋ/	seinen Lebensunterhalt verdienen
° gas-guzzling *(AE)* /ˈgæsˌgʌz(ə)lɪŋ/	spritfressend
° tank /tæŋk/	(Flüssigkeits)behälter, Tank, *hier:* Riesenauto
° to be obsessed (with sth) *(irr)* /ˌbi‿əbˈsest wɪð/	(von etw) besessen sein
° to be supposed to do sth/be sth *(irr)* /ˌbiː səˌpəʊzd‿tə ˈduː/ˈbiː/	etw tun sollen/ etw sein sollen
° to happen to do sth /ˌhæpən tə ˈduː/	zufällig etw tun
° piggy bank /ˈpɪgi bæŋk/	Sparschwein
° to bail on sb *(informal)* /ˈbeɪl‿ɒn/	jdn im Stich lassen

B5	**lines** *(pl)* /laɪnz/	Text *(für Schauspieler/innen)*	Sally learned all her **lines** for the play. p. 131
	to **stress** /stres/	betonen	Fred **stressed** the importance of waking up early.
	to **vary** /ˈveəri/	variieren	Omar **varies** what food he eats so he doesn't get bored.
	volume /ˈvɒljuːm/	Volumen, Umfang, Lautstärke	The **volume** is too high; it is so loud!
B7	to **stare (at sb/sth)** /ˈsteər‿ət/	(jdn/etw an)starren	The painting was so beautiful; Jade **stared at** it for hours.
	to **offend** /əˈfend/	beleidigen, kränken	Isabelle was **offended** by the joke.

speech /spiːtʃ/	Rede	The headmaster gave an extremely boring **speech**.
paint *(no pl)* /peɪnt/	Farbe, Lack	There's not much red **paint** left because Tom used most of it to paint his room.
B9 **quote** /kwəʊt/	Zitat	The most famous **quotes** are from Shakespeare.

Say it in English – Theme 5

So kannst du ...

über kulturelle Angebote sprechen	The Museum of Liverpool tells the story of the city and its people. Home to the Beatles and other world-famous musicians, Liverpool also has a vibrant music scene. Each year on a weekend in August, one of the UK's most popular music festivals takes place in Leeds. With rock and pop acts, as well as house, drum 'n' bass, metal, techno and more, there is something for everyone! Manchester does not only have great theatres, but there is also ... Visitors can take a look behind the scenes of ... Sheffield celebrates the best new adventure and documentary films from around the world with an annual festival. There are exciting events and workshops on film-making throughout the year.
eine Auswahl begründen	I chose ... because ... ... appeals to me the most because ... It wasn't easy to decide between ... and ... but I went for ... because ...
begründen, welchen Zeitungsartikel du lieber lesen würdest	The article from the quality newspaper/tabloid appeals to me more because ... I'd prefer ... because ... Although ... looks ..., I would choose to read ... ... might provide more/better information. ... wouldn't take as long to read. ... the photo is more attractive. ... the headline does/does not interest me.
in einem Zeitungsartikel über Protestaktionen berichten	It has been the third act of protest from the group this week, with two similar protests earlier in the week in London and Glasgow. Through protest and other forms of direct action, they demand that ... The group launched in ... and made headlines in April with ... A video of the protest action was shared on social media and quickly gained millions of views. The comments on social media were mixed, with some criticizing ..., and others praising the form of protest and their message. ... was closed for a short period while the police dealt with the incident and the two men were arrested.

English-German dictionary

Im *English-German dictionary* kannst du englische Wörter nachschlagen, die im Buch vorkommen.
- Die **fett gedruckten** Wörter solltest du dir merken.
- Wörter mit einem ° sind nur für einen bestimmten Text wichtig. Du brauchst sie nicht zu lernen.
- **1Intro 1** bedeutet: Dieses Wort kommt in *Theme* 1, Aufgabe 1 im Intro-Teil vor.
- **1B1** bedeutet: Dieses Wort kommt in *Theme* 1, Aufgabe B1 vor.
- **CT5** bedeutet: Dieses Wort kommt in *Camden Town 5* vor. **CT6, CT7** und **CT8** stehen für die Bände 6, 7 und 8.
- Folgende Abkürzungen werden noch verwendet:
  D = *Diff and train* R = *Reading tour* SBS = *Step by step*
  P = *Photo tour* T = *Target task tools*

3-D printer /ˌθriːˌdiː ˈprɪntə/ 3-D-Drucker **CT7**
° 24/7 (= twenty-four seven) /ˌtwenti ˌfɔː ˈsev(ə)n/ rund um die Uhr (und sieben Tage die Woche) **2D4**

A

° A /eɪ/ *beste Schulnote in Großbritannien und den USA* **4D16**
a/an /ə/ən/ ein(e) **CT5**
° a big deal /ə ˌbɪɡ ˈdiːl/ etwas Besonderes **2R3**
a bit /ə ˈbɪt/ ein bisschen; ein wenig **CT6**
° a bunch (of ...) *(informal, AE)* /ə ˈbʌntʃ‿əv/ einen Haufen (...) **3R2**
° a couple of ... /ə ˈkʌp(ə)l‿əv/ einige ...; ein paar ... **3B3**
° a dream come true /ə ˌdriːm ˌkʌm ˈtruː/ ein in Erfüllung gegangener Traum **2R2**
a few /ə ˈfjuː/ einige; wenige **CT6**
° a great/good deal (of sth) /ə ˌɡreɪt/ ˌɡʊd‿ˈdiːl‿əv/ eine Menge (...); ziemlich viel (...) **4SBS**
° A level /ˈeɪ ˌlev(ə)l/ *entspricht dem deutschen Abitur* **4D16**
° a lick of sth /ə ˈlɪk‿əv/ ein wenig von etw **4SBS**
a little /ə ˈlɪt(ə)l/ (ein) wenig; (ein) bisschen **CT6**
a lot (of) /ə ˈlɒt‿əv/ viel(e); eine Menge **CT6**
a must /ə ˈmʌst/ ein Muss **CT6**
° a number of /ə ˈnʌmbər‿əv/ einige; eine Reihe (von) **2D26, 5A1**
° a sort of /ə ˈsɔːt‿əv/ so etwas wie **3B4**
a year /ə ˈjɪə/ im Jahr **CT7**
to abandon /əˈbændən/ verlassen; zurücklassen; aufgeben **1A3**
° abbey /ˈæbi/ Abtei; Kloster **5P2**
° abbreviation /əˌbriːviˈeɪʃ(ə)n/ Abkürzung; Kürzel **4B2**
ability /əˈbɪləti/ Fähigkeit; Talent; Begabung **4A5**
be able to do sth /ˌbi‿ˌeɪbl tə ˈduː/ etw tun können **CT6**
° aboard /əˈbɔːd/ an Bord; im Zug **1B/T1, 5SBS**
to **abolish** /əˈbɒlɪʃ/ abschaffen; aufheben **1A5**
Aboriginal /ˌæbəˈrɪdʒ(ə)n(ə)l/ Aborigine *(australische/r Ureinwohner/in)*; der Aborigines; Aborigine- **1A2**
° Aboriginal Australian /ˌæbəˌrɪdʒ(ə)n(ə)l‿ɒ streɪliən/ australische/r Ureinwohner/in; die australischen Ureinwohner/innen betreffend **1A3**
about /əˈbaʊt/ über; von; wegen **CT5**; ungefähr **CT6**
above /əˈbʌv/ über **CT7**
° above /əˈbʌv/ oberhalb; darüber; oben; obige(r, s) **1R2, 5D2**
abroad /əˈbrɔːd/ im/ins Ausland **1B1**
° abrupt /əˈbrʌpt/ abrupt; plötzlich; schroff **4SBS**
absolutely /ˈæbsəluːtli/ absolut; völlig **CT8**
abuse /əˈbjuːs/ Missbrauch; Verletzung; Beschimpfung(en) **1A4**
to **accept** /əkˈsept/ annehmen; akzeptieren **CT7**
acceptable /əkˈseptəb(ə)l/ akzeptabel; hinnehmbar **CT8**
° acceptance *(no pl)* /əkˈseptəns/ Annahme; Zusage; Akzeptanz **2D2**
access *(no pl)* /ˈækses/ Zugang; Zutritt **2A4**
accident /ˈæksɪd(ə)nt/ Unfall **CT6**
accidentally /ˌæksɪˈdent(ə)li/ versehentlich; zufällig **3A2**
accommodation *(no pl)* /əˌkɒməˈdeɪʃ(ə)n/ Unterkunft **5Intro 4**
° to accompany /əˈkʌmp(ə)ni/ begleiten **2SBS**
according to /əˈkɔːdɪŋ tʊ/ nach; laut; gemäß **1A4**
account /əˈkaʊnt/ Konto; Account **CT7**; *hier:* Bericht **2A6**
° account /əˈkaʊnt/ *hier:* Schilderung **3B5**
° accountancy *(no pl)* /əˈkaʊntənsi/ Buchhaltung; Rechnungswesen **4R3**
° accountant /əˈkaʊntənt/ Buchhalter/in **4R3**
° accurate /ˈækjʊrət/ genau; akkurat; richtig **3R1**
to **take sth into account** /ˌteɪk ˌsʌmθɪŋ‿ˌɪntʊ‿əˈkaʊnt/ etw berücksichtigen **3A7**
° to ace sth *(AE)* /eɪs/ etw mit Bravour bestehen **3B3**
to **achieve** /əˈtʃiːv/ erreichen; erlangen; erzielen **CT8**
° achievement /əˈtʃiːvmənt/ Leistung; Errungenschaft **3D2**
to **acknowledge** /əkˈnɒlɪdʒ/ zugeben; anerkennen; bestätigen **1A3**
acknowledg(e)ment *(no pl)* /əkˈnɒlɪdʒmənt/ Eingeständnis; Anerkennung; Würdigung **1A5**
across /əˈkrɒs/ über **CT7**; *hier:* querdurch, über ... hinweg **1A5, 3A7, 4A5, 5A3**
° across /əˈkrɒs/ *hier:* gegenüber(liegend) **5R2**
act /ækt/ (Show)nummer; Akt **CT5**
° act /ækt/ *hier:* Band **5Intro 1**; Gesetz **1B/T1**
to **act** /ækt/ handeln; vorgehen; schauspiele(r)n; *hier:* sich verhalten **CT6**; fungieren, tätig sein **4A5**
° to act out /ˌækt‿ˈaʊt/ nachspielen **1R3, 4B5**
° acting *(no pl)* /ˈæktɪŋ/ Schauspielerei(-); Darstellung **1D11, 2B/T1, 5D18**
action /ˈækʃ(ə)n/ Handeln; Handlung; Tat **CT7**
° action-packed /ˈækʃ(ə)n pækt/ voller Action **Wordbank 5**
active /ˈæktɪv/ aktiv **CT5**
° activism *(no pl)* /ˈæktɪvɪs(ə)m/ Aktivismus **3Intro 5, 5B4**
activity /ækˈtɪvəti/ Aktivität; Tätigkeit **CT5**

actor /ˈæktə/ Schauspieler/in **CT6**
actress /ˈæktrəs/ Schauspielerin **CT6**
° actual /ˈæktʃuəl/ eigentlich; tatsächlich **3B3**
actually /ˈæktʃuəli/ eigentlich; wirklich; tatsächlich **CT6**
° AD (= Anno Domini) /ˌeɪ ˈdiː, ˌænəʊ ˈdɒmɪnaɪ/ nach Christus **5A1**
to **adapt (to)** /əˈdæpt‿tʊ/ (sich) anpassen (an) **CT8**
° adaptability *(no pl)* /əˌdæptəˈbɪləti/ Anpassungsfähigkeit **Wordbank 8**
to add one's mark to sth /ˌæd‿wʌnz ˈmɑːk tʊ/ etw prägen; etw seinen Stempel aufdrücken **4A5**
to **add (sth to sth)** /æd/ (etw etw) hinzufügen **CT6**
addicted (to) /əˈdɪktɪd‿tʊ/ süchtig (von/nach) **2A3**
in addition (to) /ɪn‿əˈdɪʃ(ə)n tʊ/ zusätzlich (zu); außerdem; darüber hinaus **CT8**
° additional /əˈdɪʃ(ə)nəl/ zusätzlich **3Intro 3, 5SBS**
address /əˈdres/ Adresse; Anschrift **CT6**; *hier:* Anrede **5A5**
to **address** /əˈdres/ adressieren; (sich) wenden an; ansprechen **CT7**
adequate /ˈædɪkwət/ ausreichend; angemessen **3Intro 2**
to adjust (to) /əˈdʒʌst‿tʊ/ einstellen; anpassen (an) **1A4**
° to admire /ədˈmaɪə/ bewundern **1R2, 5D2**
admiring /ədˈmaɪərɪŋ/ bewundernd **CT6**
admission /ədˈmɪʃ(ə)n/ Eintritt; Zutritt; Zulassung **CT8**
to **admit** /ədˈmɪt/ zugeben **CT7**
to **adopt** /əˈdɒpt/ adoptieren; annehmen **3A9**
adult /ˈædʌlt/ Erwachsene/r **CT6**
° to advance /ədˈvɑːns/ sich vorwärtsbewegen; näherkommen **4SBS**
advantage /ədˈvɑːntɪdʒ/ Vorteil **CT7**
adventure /ədˈventʃə/ Abenteuer; Erlebnis **CT6**
° adventurous /ədˈventʃ(ə)rəs/ abenteuerlustig; abenteuerlich **1A/T2**
job ad(vert)/job advertisement /ˈdʒɒb‿ˌædvɜːt/ˈdʒɒb‿ədˌvɜːtɪsmənt/ Stellenanzeige **4A5**
° advertisement /ədˈvɜːtɪsmənt/ Werbung; Reklame; Anzeige; Inserat **3D3**
advice *(no pl)* /ədˈvaɪs/ Rat(schlag); Ratschläge **CT7**
to **advise** /ədˈvaɪz/ (be)raten **CT8**
° aerial /ˈeəriəl/ aus der Luft; Luft- **1D15**
to **affect** /əˈfekt/ sich auswirken auf; beeinflussen **CT8**
° affected /əˈfektɪd/ betroffen **3D2**
° affection *(no pl)* /əˈfekʃ(ə)n/ Zuneigung; Liebe **1R2**
to **afford sth** /əˈfɔːd/ sich etw leisten; etw bieten **CT7**
° African /ˈæfrɪkən/ Afrikaner/in; afrikanisch **1R2, 5SBS**
African American /ˌæfrɪkən‿əˈmerɪkən/ Afroamerikaner/in; afroamerikanisch **CT8**
after /ˈɑːftə/ nach **CT5**; nachdem **CT7**
after all /ˌɑːftər‿ˈɔːl/ schließlich **CT8**
° after dark /ˌɑːftər ˈdɑːk/ nach Einbruch der Dunkelheit **4SBS**
after that /ˌɑːftə ˈðæt/ danach **CT6**
afternoon /ˌɑːftəˈnuːn/ Nachmittag **CT5**
in the afternoon /ˌɪn ðiˌ‿ɑːftəˈnuːn/ am Nachmittag **CT5**
afterward(s) /ˈɑːftəwədz/ später; danach; anschließend **CT8**
again /əˈgen/ wieder; noch einmal **CT5**
once again /ˌwʌns‿əˈgen/ wieder einmal; erneut **CT7**
against /əˈgenst/ gegen **CT5**
age /eɪdʒ/ Alter **CT6**
° age /eɪdʒ/ *hier:* Zeitalter, Ära **5R2**
aged ... /eɪdʒd/ im Alter von ... **CT7**
° agency /ˈeɪdʒ(ə)nsi/ Agentur; Behörde **4SBS**
° agent /ˈeɪdʒ(ə)nt/ Agent/in; *hier:* Reisebürokaufmann/frau **3D10**
° ages *(pl, informal)* /ˈeɪdʒɪz/ eine Ewigkeit; Ewigkeiten **5R2**
(a week) ago /ə ˌwiːk‿əˈgəʊ/ vor (einer Woche) **CT6**
to **agree** /əˈgriː/ zustimmen; sich einig sein **CT6**
to **agree (on sth)** /əˈgriː‿ɒn/ sich (auf etw) einigen; (über etw) einer Meinung sein **CT6**
agreement /əˈgriːmənt/ Übereinstimmung; Zustimmung; Vereinbarung **CT8**
° agricultural /ˌægrɪˈkʌltʃ(ə)rəl/ landwirtschaftlich; Agrar- **5D7**
° ahead /əˈhed/ vorn; voraus **4SBS**
aim /eɪm/ Ziel; Absicht **CT7**
to **aim** /eɪm/ zielen; anstreben; sich vornehmen **CT8**
air *(no pl)* /eə/ Luft **CT6**
° air *(no pl)* /eə/ *hier:* Ausstrahlung, Hauch **4SBS**
aircraft (*pl* aircraft) /ˈeəˌkrɑːft/ Luftfahrzeug; Flugzeug **5A1**
° airtight /ˈeətaɪt/ luftdicht; *hier:* wasserdicht **3R6**
alive /əˈlaɪv/ lebendig; lebend **CT8**
all /ɔːl/ alle(s) **CT5**; ganz; völlig **CT6**
all day /ˌɔːl ˈdeɪ/ den ganzen Tag **CT6**
all in all /ˌɔːl‿ɪn‿ˈɔːl/ alles in allem **2B8**
° all over the world /ˌɔːl‿ˌəʊvə ðə ˈwɜːld/ auf der ganzen Welt **3SBS, 5D4**
all the time /ˌɔːl ðə ˈtaɪm/ die ganze Zeit **CT7**
all the way /ˌɔːl ðə ˈweɪ/ den ganzen Weg **CT7**
all week /ˌɔːl ˈwiːk/ die ganze Woche über **CT6**
allergic (to) /əˈlɜːdʒɪk tʊ/ allergisch (auf/gegen) **CT7**
the allies /ðiˌ‿ˈælaɪz/ die Alliierten **5A1**
to **allow** /əˈlaʊ/ erlauben; ermöglichen **CT7**
be allowed to do sth /ˌbi‿əˌlaʊd‿tə ˈduː/ etw tun dürfen **CT6**
almost /ˈɔːlməʊst/ fast; beinahe **CT6**
alone /əˈləʊn/ allein **CT5**
to **leave sb alone** /ˌliːv ˌsʌmbədi‿əˈləʊn/ jdn in Ruhe lassen **CT7**
along /əˈlɒŋ/ entlang **CT6**
already /ɔːlˈredi/ schon; bereits **CT6**
° alright (= all right) /ɔːlˈraɪt/ in Ordnung **4R1**
also /ˈɔːlsəʊ/ auch **CT6**; *hier:* darüber hinaus **4Intro 2**
° alternatively /ɔːlˈtɜːnətɪvli/ als Alternative; stattdessen **1B8**
although /ɔːlˈðəʊ/ obwohl **CT7**
always /ˈɔːlweɪz/ immer **CT5**
am *(irr)* /æm/ bin, **CT5**
am (= ante meridiem) /ˌeɪ‿ˈem, ˌænti məˈrɪdiəm/ morgens; vormittags *(nur hinter Uhrzeit zwischen Mitternacht und 12 Uhr mittags)* **CT5**
amazed /əˈmeɪzd/ erstaunt; verblüfft **CT8**
amazing /əˈmeɪzɪŋ/ erstaunlich; toll **CT5**
° ambition /æmˈbɪʃ(ə)n/ Ehrgeiz; Ambition(en); (angestrebtes) Ziel **3SBS**
ambitious /æmˈbɪʃəs/ ehrgeizig **CT7**
° AME Zion Church /ˌeɪ‿em‿ˌiː ˈzaɪən tʃɜːtʃ/ *methodistische Kirche mit überwiegend afroamerikanischen Mitgliedern* **3R1**
Second Amendment (to the United States Constitution) /ˌsekənd‿əˈmendmənt (tə ðə juːˌnaɪtɪd ˌsteɪts ˌkɒnstɪˈtjuːʃ(ə)n)/ *Zweiter Zusatzartikel (zur Verfassung der Vereinigten Staaten)* **3A5**
American /əˈmerɪkən/ Amerikaner/in; amerikanisch **CT8**
Native American /ˌneɪtɪv‿əˈmerɪkən/ amerikanischer Ureinwohner/amerikanische Ureinwohnerin **CT8**
among(st) /əˈmʌŋst/ unter; inmitten von **2Intro 2**
amount /əˈmaʊnt/ Menge; Betrag **3A7**
amused /əˈmjuːzd/ amüsiert **CT7**

° amusing /əˈmjuːzɪŋ/ amüsant; unterhaltsam **Wordbank 5**
to **analyse** /ˈænəlaɪz/ analysieren; untersuchen **1A4, 2A2, 3B4**
analysis (*pl* **analyses**) /əˈnæləsɪs, əˈnæləsiːz/ Analyse; Beurteilung **5A5**
anaphora *(pl)* /əˈnæfərə/ Anapher *(Wiederholung eines Wortes oder mehrerer Wörter am Beginn aufeinanderfolgender Textteile)* **3A2**
ancestor /ˈænsestə/ Vorfahr(e)/ Vorfahrin; Ahn(e)/Ahnin **CT8**
° ancient world /ˌeɪnʃ(ə)nt ˈwɜːld/ (Welt der) Antike **5D2**
and /ænd/ und **CT5**
° ... and stuff (like that) *(informal)* /ən ˈstʌf laɪk ðæt/ ... und so; ... und dergleichen **4R1**
anger *(no pl)* /ˈæŋgə/ Ärger; Wut **1A4**
° angle /ˈæŋg(ə)l/ (Blick)winkel; Perspektive **Wordbank 5**
angry /ˈæŋgri/ verärgert; zornig; wütend **CT5**
animal /ˈænɪm(ə)l/ Tier **CT5**
animal rescue shelter /ˌænɪm(ə)l ˈreskjuː ˌʃeltə/ Tierauffangstation; Tierheim **4A5**
° animal shelter /ˈænɪm(ə)l ˌʃeltə/ Tierheim **4A7**
anniversary /ˌænɪˈvɜːs(ə)ri/ Jubiläum; Jahrestag **CT8**
to **announce** /əˈnaʊns/ bekanntgeben; verkünden **CT8**
announcement /əˈnaʊnsmənt/ Bekanntmachung; Mitteilung; Durchsage **CT8**
° to annoy sb /əˈnɔɪ/ jdn ärgern/nerven **4R1**
annoyed /əˈnɔɪd/ verärgert **CT6**
annoying /əˈnɔɪɪŋ/ ärgerlich; nervig **CT6**
annual /ˈænjuəl/ jährlich; Jahres- **CT7**
anonymous /əˈnɒnɪməs/ anonym; ungenannt **4A11**
another /əˈnʌðə/ noch eine(r, s); ein(e) andere(r) **CT7**
one another /ˌwʌn‿əˈnʌðə/ einander; gegenseitig **CT7**
answer /ˈɑːnsə/ Antwort; Lösung **CT5**
to **answer** /ˈɑːnsə/ (be)antworten **CT5**
to **answer the phone** /ˌɑːnsə ðə ˈfəʊn/ ans Telefon gehen **CT5**
° antithesis (*pl* antitheses) /ænˈtɪθəsɪs, ænˈtɪθəsiːz/ Gegenteil; Gegensatz **3SBS**
° anxiety /æŋˈzaɪəti/ Angst; Sorge; Besorgnis **2D10**
anxious /ˈæŋkʃəs/ besorgt; ängstlich **2A4**
any /ˈeni/ (irgend)ein(e); jede(r, s) **CT5**
anybody /ˈeniˌbɒdi/ jede(r, s); jemand **CT7**
anybody else /ˌeniˌbɒdi‿ˈels/ irgendjemand anders; noch jemand **CT7**
anyone /ˈeniˌwʌn/ (irgend)jemand **CT6**
anything /ˈeniθɪŋ/ (irgend)etwas; (irgend)was **CT7**
anything else /ˌeniθɪŋ‿ˈels/ alles andere; irgendetwas anderes **CT8**
° anytime /ˈeniˌtaɪm/ jederzeit **1D18**
anyway /ˈeniˌweɪ/ sowieso; jedenfalls; überhaupt; trotzdem **CT6**; *hier:* wie auch immer **CT8**
° anywhere /ˈeniˌweə/ überall; irgendwo **2D10**
° anywhere else /ˌeniˌweər‿ˈels/ irgendwo anders; *hier:* überall sonst **5A1**
not ... anywhere /nɒt ˈeniˌweə/ nirgendwo **CT6**
° apartment /əˈpɑːtmənt/ Wohnung; Apartment **4D4**
to **apologize (to/for)** /əˈpɒlədʒaɪz tʊ/ fɔː/ sich entschuldigen (bei/für) **CT6**
° apparent /əˈpærənt/ offensichtlich; scheinbar **4SBS**
° apparently /əˈpærəntli/ offensichtlich; anscheinend **5B2**
° appeal /əˈpiːl/ Appell; Einspruch; Berufung **3R3**
to **appeal to sb/sth** /əˈpiːl tʊ/ jdn/ etw reizen; jdn/etw ansprechen **2B2, 5Intro 2**
to **appear** /əˈpɪə/ erscheinen; auftauchen **CT7**
° to appear /əˈpɪə/ *hier:* scheinen **Wordbank 3**
appearance /əˈpɪərəns/ Erscheinen; Aussehen; Auftreten **CT7**
apple /ˈæp(ə)l/ Apfel **CT5**
applicant /ˈæplɪkənt/ Bewerber/in **4A5**
application /ˌæplɪˈkeɪʃ(ə)n/ Bewerbung; Antrag; Anwendung **4A7**
to **apply** /əˈplaɪ/ anwenden; gebrauchen; auftragen **5A3**
to **apply (for sth)** /əˈplaɪ fɔː/ (sich um etw) bewerben; (etw) beantragen **CT8**
° to appreciate /əˈpriːʃiˌeɪt/ schätzen; zu schätzen wissen **4A/T2**
° appreciation /əˌpriːʃiˈeɪʃ(ə)n/ Anerkennung; Verständnis; (Wert)steigerung **3R6**
° approach /əˈprəʊtʃ/ Ansatz; Herangehensweise **3R6**
appropriate /əˈprəʊpriət/ angemessen; angebracht; passend **CT7**
to **approve of** /əˈpruːv‿əv/ genehmigen; billigen; *hier:* für gut halten **4A9**
° approximately /əˈprɒksɪmətli/ ungefähr; etwa; circa **1P1**
April /ˈeɪprəl/ April **CT5**
° aquatic /əˈkwætɪk/ Wasser- **1B7**
° aquatic practices *(pl)* /əˌkwætɪk ˈpræktɪsɪz/ *Schulfach, das Gewässer unter ökologischen, kulturellen, wirtschaftlichen und Freizeitaspekten thematisiert* **1B2**
° aquatic safety *(no pl)* /əˌkwætɪk ˈseɪfti/ Sicherheit im Wasser **1B2**
° Arabic *(no pl)* /ˈærəbɪk/ Arabisch **4P4**
° archaeological /ˌɑːkiəˈlɒdʒɪk(ə)l/ archäologisch **1D3**
° archaeologist /ˌɑːkiˈɒlədʒɪst/ Archäologe/Archäologin **5A1**
architect /ˈɑːkɪˌtekt/ Architekt/in **CT6**
architectural /ˌɑːkɪˈtektʃ(ə)rəl/ architektonisch **5Intro 1**
are *(irr)* /ɑː/ bist; sind; seid **CT5**
aren't (= are not) /ɑːnt, ə nɒt/ bist nicht; seid nicht; sind nicht **CT5**
Are you serious? /ə jʊ ˈsɪəriəs/ Meinst du das ernst? **CT7**
area /ˈeəriə/ Gebiet; Region; Gegend **CT7**
to **argue** /ˈɑːgjuː/ argumentieren **CT8**
to **argue (about)** /ˈɑːgju‿əˌbaʊt/ sich streiten (wegen) **CT7**
argument /ˈɑːgjʊmənt/ Auseinandersetzung; Argument **CT7**
° argumentation *(no pl)* /ˌɑːgjumenˈteɪʃ(ə)n/ Argumentation; Beweisführung **3A10**
to **arise** *(irr)* /əˈraɪz/ aufkommen; sich ergeben **3A2**
arm /ɑːm/ Arm **CT6**
armed /ɑːmd/ bewaffnet **3A10**
arms *(pl)* /ɑːmz/ Waffen **3A5**
army /ˈɑːmi/ Armee; Heer **CT7**
around /əˈraʊnd/ umher; um; rund um; um ... herum **CT6**
to **be around** /ˌbi‿əˈraʊnd/ in der Nähe sein; da sein **CT6**
to **show sb (a)round** /ˌʃəʊ ˌsʌmbədi‿əˈraʊnd/ jdn herumführen **CT8**
to **turn (a)round** /ˌtɜːn‿əˈraʊnd/ sich umdrehen **CT6**
° to arrange /əˈreɪndʒ/ arrangieren; (an)ordnen **5SBS**
° arrest /əˈrest/ Verhaftung **3R2**
to **arrest sb (on suspicion of sth)** /əˌrest ˌsʌmbədi‿ɒn səˈspɪʃ(ə)n‿əv/ jdn (wegen des Verdachts auf etw) verhaften **5A3**
arrival /əˈraɪv(ə)l/ Ankunft **1A5**
to **arrive** /əˈraɪv/ ankommen; eintreffen **CT6**
arrogant /ˈærəgənt/ arrogant **CT6**
° arrow /ˈærəʊ/ Pfeil **2B3**
art /ɑːt/ Kunst(unterricht) **CT5**

° artefact /ˈɑːtɪˌfækt/ Artefakt *(von Menschen Geschaffenes)* **4SBS**
article /ˈɑːtɪk(ə)l/ Artikel **CT6**
artificial intelligence (AI) *(no pl)* /ˌɑːtɪˌfɪʃ(ə)l‿ɪnˈtelɪdʒ(ə)ns, ˌeɪ‿ˈaɪ/ künstliche Intelligenz **5A1**
artist /ˈɑːtɪst/ Künstler/in **CT6**
° artwork /ˈɑːtˌwɜːk/ Illustrationen; Kunstwerke **1A6**
° arvo *(informal, AusE)* /ˈɑːvəʊ/ Nachmittag **1 Intro 3**
as /æz/ als; wie **CT6**; weil; da **CT7**; *hier:* während **1 Intro 1**
as ... as /æz æz/ so ... wie **CT7**
as a result (of sth) /æz‿ə rɪˈzʌlt‿əv/ als Folge (einer Sache) **1B7**
as a whole /æz‿ə ˈhəʊl/ als Ganzes (betrachtet) **CT8**
° as far as /əz ˈfɑːr‿əz/ soweit **2D12, 3A/T1**
as far as sb is concerned /əz ˌfɑːr‿əz‿ˈsʌmbədi‿ɪz kənˌsɜːnd/ was jdn anbelangt/betrifft **2 Intro 6**
as I see it /æz‿ˈaɪ siː‿ɪt/ wie ich es sehe; meiner Meinung nach **2 Intro 6**
as if /æz‿ɪf/ als ob **CT7**
° as long as ... /əz ˈlɒŋ‿əz/ solange ...; sofern ... **4B/T2**
as opposed to /æz‿əˈpəʊzd‿tʊ/ im Gegensatz zu **CT8**
as soon as /əz‿ˈsuːn‿əz/ sobald **CT7**
° as to /ˈæz tʊ/ bezüglich; darüber **1R4, 4R1**
° as usual /æz ˈjuːʒʊəl/ wie üblich **2SBS**
as well /əz ˈwel/ auch **CT8**
as well as /əz ˈwel‿əz/ sowohl ... als auch ... **CT8**
Asia /ˈeɪʒə/ Asien **CT7**
Asian American /ˌeɪʒ(ə)n‿əˈmerɪkən/ US-Bürger/in asiatischer Abstammung; asiatisch-amerikanisch **CT8**
° aside from /əˈsaɪd frəm/ abgesehen von **1P1, 2B3**
to **ask** /ɑːsk/ fragen **CT5**; auffordern **CT7**
to **ask (for sth)** /ˈɑːsk fɔː/ (um etw) bitten **CT6**
to assess /əˈses/ (ein)schätzen; beurteilen **1A5**
to **assist (in/with)** /əˈsɪst‿ɪn/wɪð/ (mit)helfen (bei) **4 Intro 2**
° assistant /əˈsɪst(ə)nt/ Assistent/in; *hier:* Verkäufer/in **4D16**
shop assistant /ˈʃɒp‿əˌsɪst(ə)nt/ Verkäufer/in **CT5**
to **associate** /əˈsəʊsiˌeɪt/ in Verbindung bringen; *hier:* Kontakt haben/halten **3 Intro 2**
association /əˌsəʊsiˈeɪʃ(ə)n/ Vereinigung; Verband **3A5**
to **assume** /əˈsjuːm/ annehmen **CT7**

° assured /əˈʃɔːd/ (selbst)sicher **4SBS**
° astronaut /ˈæstrəˌnɔːt/ Astronaut/in **5B/T3**
° astronomical /ˌæstrəˈnɒmɪk(ə)l/ astronomisch; riesig **2A4**
at /æt/ auf; an; in; bei; um **CT5**
at all /ət‿ˈɔːl/ überhaupt **CT7**
at first /ət ˈfɜːst/ zuerst **CT6**
° at first sight/glance /ət ˌfɜːst ˈsaɪt/ ˈglɑːns/ auf den ersten Blick **4D6**
at home /ət ˈhəʊm/ zu Hause **CT5**
at last /ət ˈlɑːst/ endlich **CT6**
at least /ət ˈliːst/ mindestens; wenigstens; zumindest **CT6**
at night /ət‿ˈnaɪt/ nachts **CT6**
° at once /ət ˈwʌns/ sofort, auf einmal **4SBS**
at school /ət ˈskuːl/ in der Schule **CT5**
° at some point /ət ˈsʌm pɔɪnt/ irgendwann **5B2**
° at the back (of) /ət ðə ˈbæk‿əv/ hinten; am Ende (von) **1 Intro 2**
at the beginning /ət ðə bɪˈgɪnɪŋ/ am Anfang; zu Beginn **CT6**
at the bottom /ət ðə ˈbɒtəm/ unten; am Ende **CT8**
at the end /ət ði‿ˈend/ am Ende **CT6**
at the moment /ət ðə ˈməʊmənt/ im Augenblick; momentan **CT5**
° at the same time /ət ðə ˌseɪm ˈtaɪm/ gleichzeitig; zur gleichen Zeit; trotzdem **1R4**
° at the time /ət ðə ˈtaɪm/ zu dieser Zeit **1A/T2**
at the top /ət ðə ˈtɒp/ oben; an der Spitze **CT8**
at the weekend /ət ðə ˌwiːkˈend/ am Wochenende **CT5**
at times /ət ˈtaɪmz/ manchmal **4 Intro 2**
athlete /ˈæθliːt/ Athlet/in **CT7**
° athletic /æθˈletɪk/ sportlich; athletisch **2SBS**
athletics *(pl, AE)* /æθˈletɪks/ *Sport und andere Arten von körperlicher Betätigung* **CT8**
° Atlantic /ətˈlæntɪk/ Atlantik-; atlantisch **5SBS**
° Atlantic Ocean /ətˌlæntɪk‿ˈəʊʃ(ə)n/ Atlantischer Ozean **4P2**
° atmosphere /ˈætməsˌfɪə/ Atmosphäre; Stimmung **1SBS, 2D19, 4R1**
to **attach** /əˈtætʃ/ anhängen; befestigen; anbringen **1B7**
attachment /əˈtætʃmənt/ Bindung; Anhang; Attachment **2A6**
attack /əˈtæk/ Angriff; Anfall **5A3**
to **attack** /əˈtæk/ angreifen **CT7**
° attempt /əˈtempt/ Versuch **5R1, 5SBS**
to **attend** /əˈtend/ besuchen; *hier:* gehen auf **CT8**; teilnehmen an **5A1**

attention *(no pl)* /əˈtenʃ(ə)n/ Aufmerksamkeit; Achtung **2A4, 3A2, 4A9**
attitude /ˈætɪˌtjuːd/ Haltung; Einstellung **3A7**
to **attract** /əˈtrækt/ anziehen **CT7**
attraction /əˈtrækʃ(ə)n/ (Touristen)attraktion **CT6**
attractive /əˈtræktɪv/ attraktiv; verlockend **CT6**
° auction /ˈɔːkʃ(ə)n/ Auktion; Versteigerung **3R1**
audience /ˈɔːdiəns/ Publikum; Besucher; Zuschauer **CT5**
August /ˈɔːgəst/ August **CT5**
aunt /ɑːnt/ Tante **CT5**
Australia /ɒˈstreɪliə/ Australien **1 Intro 1**
Australia Day /ɒˈstreɪliə deɪ/ *Australiens offizieller Nationalfeiertag* **1A5**
Australian /ɒˈstreɪliən/ Australier/in; australisch **1 Intro 3**
° Australian Aboriginal /ɒˌstreɪliən‿ˌæbəˈrɪdʒ(ə)n(ə)l/ *die australischen Ureinwohner/innen betreffend* **1A2**
° Austria /ˈɒstriə/ Österreich **3A3**
° authentic /ɔːˈθentɪk/ authentisch; echt; glaubwürdig **Wordbank 5**
author /ˈɔːθə/ Schriftsteller/in; Verfasser/in; Autor/in **CT7**
° authority /ɔːˈθɒrəti/ Autorität; Befugnis; Behörde **5R3**
° automatically /ˌɔːtəˈmætɪkli/ automatisch; zwangsläufig **2A/T2, 4SBS**
autumn /ˈɔːtəm/ Herbst **CT5**
available /əˈveɪləb(ə)l/ verfügbar; erhältlich **CT8**
avenue /ˈævəˌnjuː/ Avenue; Boulevard; Allee **CT8**
average /ˈæv(ə)rɪdʒ/ (im) Durchschnitt; durchschnittlich **4A9**
aviation *(no pl)* /ˌeɪviˈeɪʃ(ə)n/ Fliegerei; Fliegen; Luftfahrt **1B2**
° to avoid /əˈvɔɪd/ (ver)meiden; ausweichen **2D10, 5SBS**
° to awake *(irr)* /əˈweɪk/ aufwachen; erwachen **4SBS**
award /əˈwɔːd/ Preis; Auszeichnung **1A4**
to **be aware of sth** /ˌbi‿əˈweər‿əv/ sich einer Sache bewusst sein **CT8**
awareness *(no pl)* /əˈweənəs/ Bewusstsein **5A1**
away /əˈweɪ/ weg **CT6**
to **turn away** /ˌtɜːn‿əˈweɪ/ sich abwenden; wegrücken **CT7**
awesome *(informal, AE)* /ˈɑːsəm/ spitze; super **CT8**

awful /ˈɔːf(ə)l/ furchtbar; schrecklich **CT6**
awkward /ˈɔːkwəd/ schwierig; unangenehm; peinlich **CT7**

B

° babe *(informal)* /beɪb/ Schatz; Baby; Süße/r **4R2**
back /bæk/ (wieder) zurück **CT5**; Rücken; Rückseite **CT6**
° back /bæk/ *hier:* der hintere Teil **3D10**
° to back /bæk/ rückwärts (ein)parken **3B2**
° to back down /ˌbæk‿ˈdaʊn/ nachgeben; einen Rückzieher machen **3B3**
° back pocket /ˌbæk ˈpɒkɪt/ Gesäßtasche **2A6**
background /ˈbækˌgraʊnd/ Hintergrund; Herkunft **CT8**
background check /ˈbækˌgraʊnd‿tʃek/ Nachforschungen; Screening **3A5**
° backpack *(AE)* /ˈbækˌpæk/ Rucksack(-) **1R2**
° backyard *(AE)* /ˌbækˈjard/ Garten *(hinter einem Haus)* **3B2**
bad /bæd/ schlecht; schlimm; böse **CT5**
bag /bæg/ Tasche **CT5**; Tüte **CT6**
° to bail on sb *(informal)* /ˈbeɪl‿ɒn/ jdn im Stich lassen **5B4**
to **bake** /ˈbeɪk/ backen **CT5**
° baker /ˈbeɪkə/ Bäcker/in **4D4**
° balanced /ˈbælənst/ ausgewogen; objektiv **5SBS**
° ball /bɔːl/ Ball; *hier: Baseball-Fachbegriff* **3B3**
° balls out *(informal)* /ˌbɔːlz‿ˈaʊt/ furchtlos; draufgängerisch **2SBS**
to **ban** /bæn/ verbieten **1B7, 2A4**
banana /bəˈnɑːnə/ Banane(n-) **CT5**
° banner /ˈbænə/ Transparent; Banner; Fahne **5A1**
° bar /bɑː/ Stange; Stab; Riegel **3R1**
bar chart /ˈbɑː tʃɑːt/ Säulendiagramm **CT8**
° barbaric /bɑːˈbærɪk/ barbarisch; grausam; unkultiviert **5SBS**
° barbecue /ˈbɑːbɪˌkjuː/ Grill; Grillparty **1R2, 4P1**
° barbie (= barbecue) *(informal, AusE)* /ˈbɑːbi, ˈbɑːbɪˌkjuː/ Grill(party) **1Intro 3**
° the bare essentials /ðə ˌbeər‿ɪˈsenʃ(ə)lz/ das (Aller)nötigste **3B2**
° barefoot /ˈbeəˌfʊt/ barfüßig; barfuß **1R4**
° barely /ˈbeəli/ kaum **5R1**
barrage balloon /ˈbærɑːʒ bəˌluːn/ Sperrballon *(Ballon, der der Kriegsführung dient)* **5A1**

° to base /beɪs/ basieren; beruhen; sich stützen auf **3B6, 4A10**
basic /ˈbeɪsɪk/ grundlegend; Grund-; (sehr) einfach **CT8**
° basic right /ˌbeɪsɪk ˈraɪt/ Grundrecht **3D7, 3SBS**
basically /ˈbeɪsɪkli/ im Wesentlichen; im Grunde; eigentlich **CT8**
° basket /ˈbɑːskɪt/ Korb; *hier:* Wanne **1SBS**
° bastard *(informal)* /ˈbɑːstəd/ Dreckskerl; (Schweine)hund **2B3**
° bat /bæt/ Fledermaus **2D15**
bath /bɑːθ/ (Bade)wanne; Bad(ezimmer) **CT5**
bathroom /ˈbɑːθˌruːm/ Bad(ezimmer) **CT5**
bathroom *(AE)* /ˈbæθˌrum/ Toilette(n-) **2B3**
° battery /ˈbæt(ə)ri/ Batterie; Akku **5D5**
° battery pack /ˈbæt(ə)ri pæk/ Zusatzakku; Powerbank **5D5**
battle /ˈbæt(ə)l/ Kampf; Gefecht; Schlacht **CT7**
° the BBC (= British Broadcasting Corporation) /ðə ˌbiː biː ˈsiː, ˌbrɪtɪʃ ˈbrɔːdkɑːstɪŋ ˌkɔːpəˌreɪʃ(ə)n/ *britische Rundfunkanstalt* **2D23, 3D1, 5R3**
to **be** *(irr)* /biː/ sein **CT5**
be able to do sth /ˌbi‿ˌeɪbl tə ˈduː/ etw tun können **CT6**
to **be about to do sth** /ˌbi‿əˌbaʊt‿tə ˈduː/ im Begriff sein, etw zu tun **CT8**
to **be afraid (of)** /ˌbi‿əˈfreɪd‿əv/ Angst haben/sich fürchten (vor) **CT8**
be allowed to do sth /ˌbi‿əˌlaʊd‿tə ˈduː/ etw tun dürfen **CT6**
to **be around** /ˌbi‿əˈraʊnd/ in der Nähe sein; da sein **CT6**
to **be aware of sth** /ˌbi‿əˈweər‿əv/ sich einer Sache bewusst sein **CT8**
to **be based on** /ˌbiː ˈbeɪst‿ɒn/ basieren auf; beruhen auf **1A3**
to **be called** /ˌbiː ˈkɔːld/ genannt werden; heißen **CT7**
° to be complicit (in sth) /ˌbiː kəmˈplɪsɪt‿ɪn/ (an etw) mitschuldig sein **2D8**
to **be concerned with sth** /ˌbiː kənˈsɜːnd wɪð/ sich um etw Gedanken machen; *hier:* etw behandeln **2A2**
° to be cool with sb/sth /ˌbiː ˈkuːl wɪð/ kein Problem mit jdm/etw haben **3B2**
° to be crazy about sb/sth /ˌbiː ˈkreɪzi‿əˌbaʊt/ nach jdm/etw verrückt sein **3B/T1, 5D18**
° to be done /ˌbiː ˈdʌn/ fertig sein **2SBS**
° to be eager to do sth /ˌbi‿ˌiːgə tə ˈduː/ etw unbedingt tun wollen **2R5**

° to be expected to do sth /ˌbi‿ɪkˌspektɪd‿tə ˈduː/ von jdm erwarten, dass er etw tut **Wordbank 8**
° to be fed up with sb/sth *(informal)* /ˌbiː ˌfed‿ˈʌp wɪð ˌsʌmbədi/ˌsʌmθɪŋ/ jdn/etw satthaben **1A/T2**
to **be fond of sb/sth** /ˌbiː ˈfɒnd‿əv/ jdn/etw gerne mögen **CT8**
to **be free** /ˌbiː ˈfriː/ frei haben/sein; Zeit für etw haben **CT8**
to **be friends (with sb)** /ˌbiː ˈfrendz wɪð/ (mit jdm) befreundet sein **CT7**
to **be fun** /ˌbiː ˈfʌn/ Spaß machen **CT5**
to **be honest** /tə ˌbi‿ˈɒnɪst/ ehrlich gesagt; um die Wahrheit zu sagen **2Intro 6**
° to be hooked into sth /ˌbi ˌhʊkt‿ˈɪntuː/ mit etw verbunden sein **1R2**
° to be in /ˌbi‿ˈɪn/ da sein **4R1**
° to be in charge (of) /ˌbi‿ɪn ˈtʃɑːdʒ‿əv/ verantwortlich/zuständig sein (für) **1D4, 4B/T1**
° to be in control (of sth) /ˌbi‿ɪn kənˈtrəʊl‿əv/ (etw) unter Kontrolle/im Griff haben **1P1**
to **be in touch (with sb)** /ˌbi‿ɪn ˈtʌtʃ wɪð/ (mit jdm) in Kontakt sein **CT6**
to **be into sb/sth** *(informal)* /ˌbi‿ˈɪntuː/ an jdm/etw interessiert sein **CT7**
to **be interested (in)** /ˌbi‿ˈɪntrəstɪd‿ɪn/ sich interessieren (für); interessiert sein (an) **CT6**
to **be keen on sb/sth** *(informal)* /ˌbiː ˈkiːn‿ɒn/ viel für jdn/etw übrig haben; auf jdn/etw scharf sein **CT7**
to **be located** /ˌbiː ləʊˈkeɪtɪd/ sich befinden; gelegen sein **CT8**
to **be mad about sb/sth** /ˌbiː ˈmæd‿əˌbaʊt/ nach jdm/etw verrückt sein **CT7**
° to be made of sth /ˌbiː ˈmeɪd‿əv/ aus etw bestehen **5D2**
° to be made up of /ˌbiː ˌmeɪd‿ˈʌp‿əv/ bestehen aus **1P1**
to **be missing** /ˌbiː ˈmɪsɪŋ/ fehlen **CT7**
° to be mistaken /ˌbiː mɪˈsteɪkən/ sich irren **5SBS**
° to be nowhere close/near to doing sth /ˌbiː ˌnəʊweə ˌkləʊs/ˌnɪə tə ˈduːɪŋ/ weit davon entfernt sein, etw zu tun **1R4**
to **be obliged to do sth** /ˌbi‿əˌblaɪdʒd‿tə ˈduː/ verpflichtet sein, etw zu tun **3A5**
° to be obsessed (with sth) /ˌbi‿əbˈsest wɪð/ (von etw) besessen sein **3R2, 5B4**
to **be on** /ˌbi‿ˈɒn/ auf dem Programm stehen; laufen **CT7**
to **be on one's way** /ˌbi‿ɒn wʌnz ˈweɪ/ auf dem Weg sein **CT6**

° to be on to sth /ˌbi‿ˈɒn tʊ/ einer Sache auf der Spur sein **3R6**
° to be one's turn /ˌbi wʌnz ˈtɜːn/ an der Reihe sein **5R3**
to **be opposed to sth** /ˌbi‿əˈpəʊzd‿tə/ etw ablehnend gegenüberstehen; gegen etw sein **3A7**
° to be out of sth /ˌbi‿ˈaʊt‿əv/ kein(e, en) ... (mehr) haben **4SBS**
° to be out of work /ˌbi‿ˌaʊt‿əv ˈwɜːk/ arbeitslos sein **3B2**
to **be over** /ˌbi‿ˈəʊvə/ vorbei sein **CT6**
to **be related to** /ˌbiː rɪˈleɪtɪd‿tʊ/ verwandt sein (mit); in Beziehung stehen (zu) **1A1**
to **be right** /ˌbiː ˈraɪt/ recht haben **CT5**
° to be screwed *(informal)* /ˌbiː ˈskruːd/ geliefert sein; aufgeschmissen sein **2B3**
to **be set** /ˌbiː ˈset/ liegen; spielen **CT8**
° to be situated /ˌbiː ˈsɪtʃueɪtɪd/ gelegen sein; liegen **1P1**; spielen **2D19**
° to be stoked *(informal, AusE)* /ˌbiː ˈstəʊkt/ glücklich sein; begeistert sein **1Intro 3**
to **be supposed to do sth/be sth** /ˌbiː səˌpəʊzd‿tə ˈduː/ˈbiː/ etw tun sollen/etw sein sollen **2Intro 1**
° to be tucked away (somewhere) /ˌbiː ˌtʌkt‿əˈweɪ ˌsʌmweə/ (irgendwo) versteckt liegen **1R2**
to **be up for sth** /ˌbi‿ˈʌp fɔː/ Lust auf etw haben **CT8**
to **be up to sth** /ˌbi‿ˈʌp tʊ/ etw vorhaben **CT6**
to **be used to (doing sth)** /ˌbiː ˈjuːst‿tuː ˌduːɪŋ/ gewohnt sein, (etw zu tun) **CT8**
to **be worth sth** /ˌbiː ˈwɜːθ/ etw wert sein **CT6**
to **be wrong** /ˌbiː ˈrɒŋ/ nicht stimmen; sich irren **CT5**
beach /biːtʃ/ Strand **CT6**
° bear /beə/ Bär **5D2**
to bear *(irr)* /beə/ (er)tragen **3A5**
° to bear sth in mind /ˌbeə ˌsʌmθɪŋ‿ɪn ˈmaɪnd/ etw (mit)berücksichtigen **4B5**
° beat /biːt/ Schlag; Takt; Beat **1R2**
° beat(en)-up *(informal)* /ˌbiːt(ən)‿ˈʌp/ ramponiert **3R1**
° to beat *(irr)* /biːt/ schlagen; besiegen; übertreffen **3B/T1**
beautiful /ˈbjuːtəf(ə)l/ schön **CT5**
beauty /ˈbjuːti/ Schönheit **1A5**
because /bɪˈkɒz/ weil; da **CT5**
because of /bɪˈkɒz‿əv/ wegen **CT6**
to **become** *(irr)* /bɪˈkʌm/ werden **CT6**
to **become friends (with)** /bɪˌkʌm ˈfrendz wɪð/ Freundschaft schließen (mit) **CT7**
bed /bed/ Bett **CT5**
bedroom /ˈbedruːm/ Schlafzimmer **CT5**
° beef *(no pl)* /biːf/ Rindfleisch **3B2**
° beehive /ˈbiːhaɪv/ Bienenstock; Bienenkorb **1P1**
before /bɪˈfɔː/ bevor; ehe **CT5**; vor **CT6**; zuvor; vorher; früher **5A1**
to **begin** *(irr)* /bɪˈɡɪn/ anfangen; beginnen **CT5**
beginning /bɪˈɡɪnɪŋ/ Anfang; Beginn **CT6**
at the beginning /ət ðə bɪˈɡɪnɪŋ/ am Anfang; zu Beginn **CT6**
in the beginning /ˌɪn ðə bɪˈɡɪnɪŋ/ am Anfang; zu Beginn **CT6**
to **behave** /bɪˈheɪv/ sich verhalten; sich benehmen **CT6**
behaviour /bɪˈheɪvjə/ Benehmen; Verhalten; Betragen **CT6**
behind /bɪˈhaɪnd/ hinter **CT5**
to **leave sb/sth behind** /ˌliːv bɪˈhaɪnd/ jdn/etw zurücklassen **CT8**
° behind the scenes /bɪˌhaɪnd ðə ˈsiːnz/ hinter den/die Kulissen **4D16**
° Belgium /ˈbeldʒəm/ Belgien **3A3**
belief (*pl* **beliefs**) /bɪˈliːf, bɪˈliːfs/ Glaube; Überzeugung; Ansicht **1A3, 3Intro 2**
° believable /bɪˈliːvəb(ə)l/ glaubwürdig; glaubhaft **3D4**
to **believe** /bɪˈliːv/ glauben **CT5**
° bell /bel/ Glocke; Türglocke **4SBS**
to **belong** /bɪˈlɒŋ/ (dazu)gehören **CT7**
to **belong to sb** /bɪˈlɒŋ tə/ jdm gehören **CT6**
below /bɪˈləʊ/ unten; darunter; unter(halb) **CT6**
° beneath /bɪˈniːθ/ unter; nach unten; darunter **2SBS, 4SBS**
to **benefit** /ˈbenɪfɪt/ profitieren; Nutzen ziehen **1A1**
benefit /ˈbenɪfɪt/ Nutzen; Vorteil **4Intro 2**
° Bengali /beŋˈɡɔːli/ Bengale/Bengalin; Bengali *(Sprache)*; bengalisch **4P4**
° beside /bɪˈsaɪd/ neben **3B4, 4SBS**
besides /bɪˈsaɪdz/ außerdem **2A4**
best /best/ beste(r, s) **CT5**; am besten; am liebsten; am meisten **CT6**
Best wishes /ˌbest ˈwɪʃɪz/ Herzliche Grüße **CT6**
to **bet** *(irr)* /bet/ wetten **CT7**
better /ˈbetə/ besser **CT5**
between /bɪˈtwiːn/ zwischen **CT5**
° beyond /bɪˈjɒnd/ jenseits (von); über **4SBS**
° Bible-thumper *(informal)* /ˈbaɪb(ə)l ˌθʌmpə/ *übertrieben bibeltreue Person* **2SBS**
big /bɪɡ/ groß, **CT5**
bike *(informal)* /baɪk/ (Fahr)rad **CT5**
° bill /bɪl/ Rechnung **1R4**
billionaire /ˌbɪljəˈneə/ Milliardär/in **CT8**
° bin /bɪn/ Mülleimer; Mülltonne **1SBS, 4R1**
biographical /ˌbaɪəˈɡræfɪk(ə)l/ biografisch **CT8**
° biography /baɪˈɒɡrəfi/ Biografie **1R1**
° biologist /baɪˈɒlədʒɪst/ Biologie/Biologin **4A5**
° bipolar disorder *(no pl)* /ˌbaɪˈpəʊlə dɪsˌɔːdə/ bipolare Störung *(psychische Erkrankung)* **2B5**
bird /bɜːd/ Vogel **CT5**
birth /bɜːθ/ Geburt(s-); Abstammung; Herkunft **5A1**
birthday /ˈbɜːθdeɪ/ Geburtstag(s-) **CT5**
biscuit *(BE)* /ˈbɪskɪt/ Keks; Biskuit **CT5**
° bit /bɪt/ Stück; Teil **4R1**
° bitch *(informal)* /bɪtʃ/ Hündin; *hier:* Miststück **4R1**
to **bite** *(irr)* /baɪt/ beißen **CT6**
° bizarre /bɪˈzɑː/ bizarr; seltsam **5R1**
black /blæk/ schwarz **CT5**
° Black /blæk/ afroamerikanisch **3R1**
° black bear /ˌblæk ˈbeə/ Schwarzbär **5D2**
° blackhead /ˈblækˌhed/ Mitesser **3B4**
° bland /blænd/ fade; nichtssagend **4SBS**
° blankly /ˈblæŋkli/ ausdruckslos **4SBS**
° to blare /bleə/ dröhnen **2SBS**
° to blast /blɑːst/ sprengen **3SBS**
° bleak /bliːk/ kahl; trostlos; düster **5B2**
the Blitz /ðə ˈblɪts/ *deutsche Luftangriffe auf britische Städte im Zweiten Weltkrieg* **5A1**
° to blink /blɪŋk/ zwinkern; zucken **4SBS**
to **block** /blɒk/ blockieren **CT7**
° to blog /blɒɡ/ bloggen; an einem Blog (mit)schreiben **2A4**
° to blow the whistle /ˌbləʊ ðə ˈwɪs(ə)l/ abpfeifen **1R4**
° to blow *(irr)* /bləʊ/ wehen; blasen; ertönen **2D28**
blue /bluː/ blau **CT5**
° to blur /blɜː/ verschwimmen (lassen) **2SBS, 5R4**
° to blush /blʌʃ/ erröten; rot werden **5B4**
board /bɔːd/ Brett; Tafel **CT5**
° board /bɔːd/ *hier:* stabiler (Plakat)karton **5B7**
° to board /bɔːd/ (ein Flugzeug oder Schiff) besteigen; an Bord gehen **1D14**
° to board up /ˌbɔːd‿ˈʌp/ mit Brettern vernageln **5R1**
boarder /ˈbɔːdə/ Internatsschüler/in **CT7**
boarding school /ˈbɔːdɪŋ skuːl/ Internat **CT7**

° to boast sth /bəʊst/ sich einer Sache rühmen **1P1**
boat /bəʊt/ Boot; Schiff **CT5**
body /'bɒdi/ Körper **CT7**
° body /'bɒdi/ *hier:* Karosserie **3R1**
body language *(no pl)* /'bɒdi ˌlæŋgwɪdʒ/ Körpersprache **2A2**
° to boil /bɔɪl/ kochen **3B2**
bomber /'bɒmə/ Bombenflugzeug **5A1**
° bombing /'bɒmɪŋ/ Bombardierung **5A1**
° to boo /buː/ ausbuhen **5D21**
book /bʊk/ Buch **CT5**
to **book** /bʊk/ reservieren; buchen **CT8**
° bookshop /'bʊkˌʃɒp/ Buchladen **4D16**
° boost /buːst/ Auftrieb **1A/T2**
° boot /buːt/ Stiefel **5D2**
bored /bɔːd/ gelangweilt **CT6**
to **get bored** /ˌget 'bɔːd/ sich (anfangen zu) langweilen **CT6**
boring /'bɔːrɪŋ/ langweilig **CT5**
born /bɔːn/ geboren **CT8**
° to borrow /'bɒrəʊ/ (aus)leihen **4R2, 5R1**
° boss /bɒs/ Chef/in; Boss **1D4, 4D7, 4D17, 5D8**
bossy /'bɒsi/ herrschsüchtig; herrisch **CT7**
° botanic(al) garden /bəˌtænɪk(ə)l 'gɑːd(ə)n/ botanischer Garten **5D2**
both /bəʊθ/ beide(s) **CT6**
both ... and ... /'bəʊθ ænd/ sowohl ... als auch ... **CT8**
° to bother /'bɒðə/ beunruhigen; stören **2A/T1, 4SBS, 5B4**
bottle /'bɒt(ə)l/ Flasche **CT6**
at the bottom /ət ðə 'bɒtəm/ unten; am Ende **CT8**
° bottom /'bɒtəm/ Boden; (unteres) Ende **4SBS**; untere(r, s) **Wordbank 3**
° to bounce off /ˌbaʊns‿'ɒf/ abprallen **1R4**
° to bow /baʊ/ sich verbeugen; nach vorn beugen **2A2**
° bowl /'bəʊl/ Schüssel; Schale **3B2**
box /bɒks/ Kiste; Schachtel; Kästchen **CT5**
° boxing *(no pl)* /'bɒksɪŋ/ Boxen; Box- **4SBS**
boy /bɔɪ/ Junge **CT5**
boyfriend /'bɔɪˌfrend/ Freund **CT6**
brain /breɪn/ Gehirn; Verstand **2A3**
brave /breɪv/ tapfer; mutig **CT7**
° bravery *(no pl)* /'breɪvəri/ Tapferkeit; Mut **4SBS**
break /breɪk/ Pause **CT6**
to **break** *(irr)* /breɪk/ (zer)brechen; verstoßen gegen **CT6**
to **break down** *(irr)* /ˌbreɪk 'daʊn/ stehen bleiben; versagen; zusammenbrechen **CT7**
breakdown /'breɪkˌdaʊn/ (Nerven)zusammenbruch; Scheitern **2B8**
breakfast /'brekfəst/ Frühstück(s-) **CT6**
to **take a deep breath** /ˌteɪk‿ə ˌdiːp‿'breθ/ tief Luft holen **CT7**
to **breathe (in/out)** /ˌbriːð‿'ɪn/ ˌbriːð‿'aʊt/ (ein/aus)atmen **5A1**
° breathtaking /'breθˌteɪkɪŋ/ atemberaubend **1P1, 5D2**
° breeze /briːz/ Brise; (leichter) Wind **1R2**
° brekky *(informal, AusE)* /'breki/ Frühstück **1Intro 3**
bridge /brɪdʒ/ Brücke **CT7**
° brief /briːf/ kurz; knapp **1A4, 4SBS**
bright /braɪt/ hell; grell; leuchtend **CT8**
° bright /braɪt/ *hier:* glücklich **3SBS**
° brightly coloured /ˌbraɪtli 'kʌləd/ knallbunt **1P1**
° brilliance *(no pl)* /'brɪljəns/ Genialität **2SBS**
brilliant *(informal, BE)* /'brɪljənt/ brillant; strahlend; toll, klasse **CT5**
to **bring** *(irr)* /brɪŋ/ (mit)bringen **CT5**
to **bring along** *(irr)* /ˌbrɪŋ‿ə'lɒŋ/ mitbringen **CT8**
° to bring up *(irr)* /ˌbrɪŋ‿'ʌp/ zur Sprache bringen **2D26**; *hier:* großziehen **5R4**
Brit *(informal)* /brɪt/ Brite; Britin **CT7**
Britain /'brɪt(ə)n/ Großbritannien **CT6**
British /'brɪtɪʃ/ britisch **CT7**
° the British Empire /ðə ˌbrɪtɪʃ‿'empaɪə/ *das frühere britische Weltreich* **4P3**
° bro (= brother) *(informal)* /brəʊ/ Bruder(herz) **2R3**
° broad /brɔːd/ breit **4SBS**
° broadcast /'brɔːdˌkɑːst/ Übertragung; Sendung **5R3**
° to broadcast *(irr)* /'brɔːdˌkɑːst/ senden; übertragen **1B4**
° broadcaster /'brɔːdˌkɑːstə/ Sprecher/in; Moderator/in; *hier:* Rundfunkanstalt **2D23**
° broken /'brəʊkən/ zerbrochen; kaputt; gebrochen **4D13**
brother /'brʌðə/ Bruder **CT5**
° brow /braʊ/ Stirn; Augenbraue **4SBS**
brown /braʊn/ braun **CT5**
° to brush /brʌʃ/ (be)streichen; streifen; (ab)bürsten **1R4**
° brutality /bruː'tæləti/ Brutalität; Gewalt(tätigkeit) **3SBS**
° bud /bʌd/ Knospe; *hier:* Ohrstöpsel **1R2**
budgie (= budgerigar) *(informal)* /'bʌdʒi, 'bʌdʒəriˌgɑː/ Wellensittich **CT5**
° bugle /'bjuːg(ə)l/ Horn *(Musikinstrument)* **1A5**
to **build** *(irr)* /bɪld/ bauen **CT7**
builder /'bɪldə/ Bauarbeiter/in **CT6**
building /'bɪldɪŋ/ Gebäude **CT6**
° to bulge /bʌldʒ/ sich wölben **4SBS**
° bulky /'bʌlki/ massig; sperrig **4SBS**
° bulldozer /'bʊldəʊzə/ Bulldozer; Planierraupe **5R3**
° bullet /'bʊlɪt/ Kugel; Schuss- **3A8**
° bullet point /'bʊlɪt pɔɪnt/ Aufzählungspunkt **4R1**
° bully /'bʊli/ Rüpel; Schläger; *hier:* jemand, der mobbt **2D10**
° to bully sb into doing sth /ˌbʊli ˌsʌmbədi‿ˌɪntə 'duːɪŋ/ jdn so weit einschüchtern, dass er etw tut **3R5**
bullying *(no pl)* /'bʊliɪŋ/ Mobbing **2A4**
° bureau /'bjʊərəʊ/ Amt; Behörde **1D7**
to **burn** *(irr)* /bɜːn/ (ab)brennen; verbrennen **CT7**
° to burst *(irr)* /bɜːst/ platzen; brechen **3R5, 4D4**
bus /bʌs/ Bus **CT5**
° bushfire /'bʊʃˌfaɪə/ Buschfeuer **1Intro 1**
business /'bɪznəs/ Handel; Geschäft(s-); Unternehmen; Firma; Betrieb **CT7**
That's none of your business. *(informal)* /ðæts ˌnʌn‿əv jə 'bɪznəs/ Das geht dich/euch/Sie nichts an. **CT7**
° business district /'bɪznəs ˌdɪstrɪkt/ Geschäftsviertel **1A5**
° businessman /'bɪznəsmæn/ Geschäftsmann; Manager; Unternehmer **5D2**
busy /'bɪzi/ beschäftigt; arbeitsreich; stark besucht **CT6**
but /bʌt/ aber **CT5**
° but /bʌt/ außer; als **3R1**
button /'bʌt(ə)n/ Knopf **2A4**
to **buy** *(irr)* /baɪ/ kaufen **CT5**
° to buy sth *(informal)* /baɪ/ etw glauben; etw abkaufen **1R2**
to buy time /ˌbaɪ 'taɪm/ Zeit gewinnen/schinden **4B4**
° buyer /'baɪə/ Käufer/in **3A7**
by /baɪ/ von; per **CT6**; indem; bis (spätestens) **CT8**; *hier:* an **2A6**
° by bike /ˌbaɪ 'baɪk/ mit dem (Fahr)rad **5D18**
° by birth /ˌbaɪ 'bɜːθ/ von Geburt; *hier:* geboren, Naturtalent **1R4**
by half /ˌbaɪ 'hɑːf/ um die Hälfte **2A6**
° by means of sth /ˌbaɪ 'miːnz‿əv/ durch etw; mit etw; mithilfe einer Sache **2D10**
° by now /baɪ 'naʊ/ mittlerweile **4R1**
° by the time /ˌbaɪ ðə 'taɪm/ bis **4D8, 5R4**
by the way /ˌbaɪ ðə 'weɪ/ übrigens **CT8**
° by then /ˌbaɪ 'ðen/ bis dahin **4D8**

Bye! (= **Goodbye!**) *(informal)* /baɪ, ɡʊdˈbaɪ/ Tschüss! **CT5**
Bye for now. *(informal)* /ˈbaɪ fə naʊ/ Bis bald. **CT5**

C

° cable car /ˈkeɪb(ə)l kɑː/ Seilbahn **1P1**
° cableway /ˈkeɪb(ə)lweɪ/ Seilbahn **1B2**
cage /keɪdʒ/ Käfig **CT5**
cake /keɪk/ Kuchen **CT5**
° calcium carbonate *(no pl)* /ˌkælsiəm ˈkɑːbəneɪt/ kohlensaures Kalzium *(z. B. Kalkstein)* **1B7**
° to calculate /ˈkælkjʊleɪt/ (be)rechnen **5A1**
calculator /ˈkælkjʊˌleɪtə/ (Taschen)rechner **CT5**
calendar /ˈkælɪndə/ Kalender **CT5**
Californian /ˌkæləˈfɔːniən/ Kalifornier/in; kalifornisch **CT8**
call /kɔːl/ (Telefon)anruf; Ruf **CT6**
phone call (= **telephone call**) /ˈfəʊn kɔːl, ˈtelɪˌfəʊn kɔːl/ Anruf; Telefongespräch **CT5**
to **call** /kɔːl/ (an)rufen; nennen **CT6**
° call /kɔːl/ *hier:* Aufruf **1SBS**
° to call on sb /ˈkɔːl‿ɒn/ jdn aufrufen **5A3**
° to call out /ˌkɔːl‿ˈaʊt/ (aus)rufen; aufschreien **3B3**
to **be called** /ˌbiː ˈkɔːld/ genannt werden; heißen **CT7**
° caller /ˈkɔːlə/ Anrufer/in **4Intro 4**
calm /kɑːm/ ruhig; gelassen **CT5**
to **calm down** /ˌkɑːm ˈdaʊn/ sich beruhigen **CT5**
° camerawork *(no pl)* /ˈkæmrəˌwɜːk/ Kameraführung **2D19**
campaign /kæmˈpeɪn/ Kampagne; Aktion **5A3**
to campaign (for/against sth) /kæmˈpeɪn fɔː/əˌɡenst/ (für etw) eintreten/(gegen etw) kämpfen **2A4, 5A1**
° campus /ˈkæmpəs/ Universität; Campus **2R1**
can't (= **cannot**) /kɑːnt, ˈkænɒt/ nicht können; *hier auch:* nicht dürfen **CT5**
° to cancel /ˈkæns(ə)l/ absagen; *hier:* abbrechen **5D5**
candidate /ˈkændɪdeɪt/ Kandidat/in; Bewerber/in **4A5**
candle /ˈkænd(ə)l/ Kerze **CT6**
canteen /kænˈtiːn/ Kantine; Mensa **CT5**
can /kæn/ können **CT5**
capable /ˈkeɪpəb(ə)l/ fähig **1A4, 3A7, 4A5**
capital (city) /ˌkæpɪt(ə)l ˈsɪti/ Hauptstadt **CT7**
° capitalist /ˈkæpɪt(ə)lɪst/ Kapitalist/in; Ausbeuter/in **5R1**
° Capitol /ˈkæpɪt(ə)l/ Kapitol *(Kongresspalast in Washington)* **3D12**
captain /ˈkæptɪn/ (Mannschafts)kapitän/in **CT7**
caption /ˈkæpʃ(ə)n/ Überschrift; Titel; Bildunterschrift **CT8**
° captivating /ˈkæptɪˌveɪtɪŋ/ faszinierend; bezaubernd **2B/T1**; fesselnd **Wordbank 5**
to **capture** /ˈkæptʃə/ gefangen nehmen; festnehmen **CT7**; auf Film festhalten **CT8**
car /kɑː/ Auto **CT5**
° car dealership /ˈkɑː ˌdiːləʃɪp/ Autohaus **5B4**
° carbon footprint /ˌkɑːbən ˈfʊtˌprɪnt/ CO_2-Fußabdruck *(Maß für individuell verursachten CO_2-Ausstoß)* **5D17**
card /kɑːd/ Karte **CT5**
care /keə/ Betreuung; Aufsicht; Pflege **CT5**
to **take care** /ˌteɪk‿ˈkeə/ aufpassen; achten auf **CT7**
to **care (about)** /ˈkeər‿əˌbaʊt/ sich etw machen (aus) **CT7**
to **care for** /ˈkeə fɔː/ sich kümmern um **4A5**
career /kəˈrɪə/ Beruf; Karriere; Werdegang **CT7**
careful /ˈkeəf(ə)l/ vorsichtig; sorgfältig **CT6**
° Caribbean /ˌkærɪˈbiən/ Karibik; karibisch **5D4**
° caring /ˈkeərɪŋ/ warmherzig; mitfühlend; fürsorglich **2R3**
° carnivore /ˈkɑːnɪvɔː/ Fleischfresser/in **3B2**
to **carry** /ˈkæri/ tragen; bei sich haben **CT8**
° to carry on (with sth) /ˌkæri‿ˈɒn wɪð/ etw fortsetzen; etw weiterhin tun **5R2**
° to carry out /ˌkæri‿ˈaʊt/ durchführen; ausführen **4D12**
case /keɪs/ Koffer; Hülle **CT5**; Fall **2A4**
° case /keɪs/ *hier:* Argument(e) **3R6**
° cash /kæʃ/ Bargeld **1D16**
° cash desk *(BE)* /ˈkæʃ desk/ Kasse; Kassenschalter **4D16**
° casserole /ˈkæsərəʊl/ Schmortopf; Kasserolle **1R2**
° cast /kɑːst/ Besetzung; Ensemble **2D21, 3B12**
° to cast doubt on sth /ˌkɑːst‿ˈdaʊt‿ɒn/ etw in Zweifel ziehen **3R6**
castle /ˈkɑːs(ə)l/ Burg; Schloss **CT6**
° casual /ˈkæʒuəl/ zufällig; gelegentlich; beiläufig; lässig **4SBS**
° casually /ˈkæʒuəli/ beiläufig; zufällig; lässig **2R2, 3R5, 5R1**
cat /kæt/ Katze **CT5**
to **catch** *(irr)* /kætʃ/ (auf)fangen; einfangen; ergreifen **CT6**
° to catch up *(irr)* /ˌkætʃ‿ˈʌp/ einholen; aufarbeiten; nachholen **1R4, 3R1**
° catchy /ˈkætʃi/ eingängig; einprägsam **2B/T1**
° cathedral /kəˈθiːdrəl/ Kathedrale; Dom; Münster **5D2**
° 'cause (= because) *(informal)* /kʌz, bɪˈkɒz/ weil **3R5, 4R1, 4R3**
cause /kɔːz/ Grund; Ursache; Anlass **CT8**; (gute) Sache **5A6**
to **cause** /kɔːz/ verursachen **CT8**
° to cause sb to do sth /ˌkɔːz‿ˌsʌmbədi tə ˈduː/ jdn veranlassen, etw zu tun **3B4**
° cautious /ˈkɔːʃəs/ vorsichtig; achtsam; ängstlich **1R4, 4SBS**
to **celebrate** /ˈseləˌbreɪt/ feiern **CT5**
celebration /ˌseləˈbreɪʃ(ə)n/ Feier; Fest **CT6**
celebrity /səˈlebrəti/ Berühmtheit; Star **CT7**
° cellar /ˈselə/ (Wein)keller **3R1**
central /ˈsentrəl/ zentral; Haupt- **1A5**
° central /ˈsentrəl/ *hier:* Mittel- **1D2**
centre /ˈsentə/ Zentrum; Mitte **CT6**
° to centre on/(a)round /ˈsentər‿ɒn/‿əˌraʊnd/ sich drehen um **2D21**
century /ˈsentʃəri/ Jahrhundert **CT8**
° ceremonial /ˌserəˈməʊniəl/ zeremoniell **1P1, 4SBS**
ceremony /ˈserəməni/ Zeremonie; Feier; Feierlichkeiten **1A5**
certain /ˈsɜːt(ə)n/ sicher; gewiss; bestimmt **CT6**
° certificate /səˈtɪfɪkət/ Urkunde; Bescheinigung **4D11**
° certification /ˌsɜːtɪfɪˈkeɪʃ(ə)n/ Zertifikat; Bestätigung; Qualifikation **5R3**
° to chain sb/sth to sth /ˈtʃeɪn tʊ/ jdn/etw an etw (an)ketten **5D21**
chair /tʃeə/ Stuhl **CT5**
° chalk /tʃɔːk/ Kalkstein; Kreide **4SBS**
challenge /ˈtʃælɪndʒ/ Herausforderung **CT6**
° to challenge /ˈtʃælɪndʒ/ (heraus)fordern **2A7**; *hier:* infrage stellen **3R6**
challenging /ˈtʃælɪndʒɪŋ/ (heraus)fordernd **4B4**
° championship /ˈtʃæmpiənʃɪp/ Meisterschaft **2R5**
chance /tʃɑːns/ Möglichkeit; Gelegenheit; Chance **CT5**
change /tʃeɪndʒ/ (Ver)änderung; Wechsel; Umstellung **CT7**

climate change *(no pl)* /ˈklaɪmət‿tʃeɪndʒ/ Klimawandel **CT8**
to **change** /ˈtʃeɪndʒ/ (ver)ändern; (aus)wechseln **CT5**
the Channel /ðə ˈtʃæn(ə)l/ der Ärmelkanal **CT7**
° chant /tʃɑːnt/ (Sprech)gesang; Sprechchor **1A5, 4Intro 2**
° to chant /tʃɑːnt/ singen; im Sprechchor rufen **1P1, 3B2**
° chapter /ˈtʃæptə/ Kapitel **5SBS**
character /ˈkærɪktə/ Charakter; Figur **CT5**
characteristic /ˌkærɪktəˈrɪstɪk/ (charakteristisches) Merkmal; typisch; charakteristisch **4A11, 5A5**
° characterization /ˌkærɪktəraɪˈzeɪʃ(ə)n/ (Personen)beschreibung **4SBS**
to **charge** /tʃɑːdʒ/ aufladen **CT7**
° charity /ˈtʃærəti/ Barmherzigkeit; Wohltätigkeitsorganisation; *hier:* Sozialhilfe(-) **3B4, 4D16, 5D6**
° charity fundraiser /ˈtʃærəti ˌfʌndˌreɪzə/ *Spendenbeschaffer/in für wohltätige Zwecke* **4R3**
chart /tʃɑːt/ Diagramm; Schaubild **3A3**
bar chart /ˈbɑː tʃɑːt/ Säulendiagramm **CT8**
pie chart /ˈpaɪ tʃɑːt/ Tortendiagramm; Kuchendiagramm **CT8**
to **chase** /tʃeɪs/ hinterherlaufen; verfolgen **CT8**
chat /tʃæt/ Unterhaltung; Chat(-) **CT7**
to **chat** /tʃæt/ plaudern; chatten **CT7**
° to chauffeur /ˈʃəʊfə/ herumchauffieren **5B4**
cheap /tʃiːp/ billig; preiswert **CT5**
° to cheat /tʃiːt/ täuschen; betrügen **2D5**
background check /ˈbækˌgraʊnd‿tʃek/ Nachforschungen; Screening **3A5**
to **check** /tʃek/ überprüfen; nachsehen **CT5**
° to check out /ˌtʃek‿ˈaʊt/ untersuchen; überprüfen; *hier:* ansehen **2SBS**
° cheek /tʃiːk/ Wange; Backe **2SBS, 4SBS**
to **cheer** /tʃɪə/ jubeln **CT8**
° cheer /tʃɪə/ Beifallsruf; Jubel(-) **1R4, 2SBS**
to **cheer up** /ˌtʃɪər‿ˈʌp/ aufmuntern **CT6**
cheerful /ˈtʃɪəf(ə)l/ fröhlich; vergnügt; heiter **CT8**
cheerleading *(no pl, AE)* /ˈtʃɪrˌlidɪŋ/ *Anfeuern des Publikums bei Sportveranstaltungen* **CT8**
° cheery /ˈtʃɪəri/ fröhlich; lustig **4SBS**
cheese /tʃiːz/ Käse **CT5**
cheesy /ˈtʃiːzi/ käsig; kitschig **2B8**
chef /ʃef/ Koch; Köchin **2B8**
° chemistry *(no pl)* /ˈkemɪstri/ Chemie(-) **2D15**
° chest /tʃest/ Brust(korb) **1R4, 3B2**
° to chew /tʃuː/ kauen **2SBS**
° chewing gum *(no pl)* /ˈtʃuːɪŋ‿ˌgʌm/ Kaugummi **5D9**
chicken /ˈtʃɪkɪn/ Huhn; Hähnchen; Hühnchen **CT5**
° child labour *(no pl)* /ˈtʃaɪld ˌleɪbə/ Kinderarbeit **3SBS**
child *(pl* **children)** /tʃaɪld, ˈtʃɪldrən/ Kind **CT5**
childish /ˈtʃaɪldɪʃ/ kindisch **CT7**
° Chinese /ˌtʃaɪˈniːz/ Chinese/Chinesin; Chinesisch *(Sprache)*; chinesisch **4P4**
chips *(pl. BE)* /tʃɪps/ Pommes frites **CT5**
° chirpy /ˈtʃɜːpi/ quietschfidel; aufgekratzt **5R4**
chocolate /ˈtʃɒklət/ Schokolade **CT5**
choice /tʃɔɪs/ (Aus)wahl **CT7**
choir /ˈkwaɪə/ Chor **CT7**
to **choose** *(irr)* /tʃuːz/ (aus)wählen **CT6**
° choreography *(no pl)* /ˌkɒriˈɒgrəfi/ Choreografie(-) **4Intro 2**
° chorus /ˈkɔːrəs/ Refrain; Chor **5D7**
Christmas /ˈkrɪsməs/ Weihnachten; Weihnachts- **CT6**
° chrome /krəʊm/ Chrom(-) **3R1**
° chronological /ˌkrɒnəˈlɒdʒɪk(ə)l/ chronologisch **2D15**
° to chuck *(informal)* /tʃʌk/ schmeißen **1R2, 4R1**
church /tʃɜːtʃ/ Kirche **CT6**
cinema /ˈsɪnəmə/ Kino **CT6**
° cinemagoer (*BE* = moviegoer *AE*) /ˈsɪnəməˌgəʊə/ Kinogänger/in **2D21**
° cinematic device /ˌsɪnəˌmætɪk dɪˈvaɪs/ filmisches Stilmittel **Wordbank 5**
° cinnamon /ˈsɪnəmən/ Zimt **2SBS**
circle /ˈsɜːk(ə)l/ Kreis **CT8**
° circumstance /ˈsɜːkəmstəns/ Umstand; Lage **1R2**
citizen /ˈsɪtɪz(ə)n/ (Staats)bürger/in **3A5**
citizenship *(no pl)* /ˈsɪtɪz(ə)nʃɪp/ Staatsangehörigkeit **1A5**
city /ˈsɪti/ (Groß)stadt(-); städtisch **CT6**
civil rights *(pl)* /ˌsɪvəl ˈraɪts/ Bürgerrechte **CT8**
° civilized /ˈsɪvəˌlaɪzd/ zivilisiert; höflich; kultiviert **3A7**
to **claim** /kleɪm/ behaupten; Anspruch erheben auf **1B6, 2Intro 4, 3A2**
° to clamp /klæmp/ fest halten; klammern **3B4, 4SBS**
° clan /klæn/ Clan; Sippe; Sippschaft **1B/T1**
to **clap** /klæp/ klatschen **CT6**
° clarity *(no pl)* /ˈklærəti/ Klarheit; Schärfe **1R2**
class /klɑːs/ (Schul)klasse; Unterricht, Kurs **CT5**
° classic /ˈklæsɪk/ klassisch; typisch **5D2**
classmate /ˈklɑːsˌmeɪt/ Klassenkamerad/in; Mitschüler/in **CT5**
classroom /ˈklɑːsˌruːm/ Klassenzimmer **CT5**
° clause /klɔːz/ Satz(glied); Satzteil; Klausel **3A2**
clean /kliːn/ sauber; rein **CT5**
to **clean** /kliːn/ sauber machen; reinigen; putzen **CT5**
to **clean up** /ˌkliːn‿ˈʌp/ sauber machen; reinigen; putzen; wegräumen **CT8**
° cleaner /ˈkliːnə/ Raumpfleger/in; Reinigungskraft **4D1**
clear /klɪə/ klar; deutlich **CT5**
° to clear /klɪə/ klären; räumen; reinigen **4SBS**; *hier:* verschwinden **5R4**
° to clear one's throat /ˌklɪə wʌnz ˈθrəʊt/ sich räuspern **4SBS**
° cleats *(AE)* /kliːts/ *Sportschuhe mit Stollen* **3B4**
° to clench /klentʃ/ umklammern; fest packen; *hier auch:* zusammenbeißen **3B4**
° clickbait *(no pl)* /ˈklɪkˌbeɪt/ Klickfang; Klickköder **2A3**
° client /ˈklaɪənt/ Kunde/Kundin; Klient/in; Auftraggeber/in **4D7, 5B2**
climate /ˈklaɪmət/ Klima **CT8**
climate change *(no pl)* /ˈklaɪmət‿tʃeɪndʒ/ Klimawandel **CT8**
° climate crazies *(pl)* /ˈklaɪmət ˌkreɪziz/ *abwertend verwendete Bezeichnung für Klimaaktivisten/aktivistinnen* **5A3**
to **climb (up)** /ˌklaɪm‿ˈʌp/ (hinauf)steigen; klettern (auf); besteigen **CT6**
climbing *(no pl)* /ˈklaɪmɪŋ/ Bergsteigen; Klettern **CT7**
° to cling to sth /ˈklɪŋ tʊ/ sich an etw klammern **3B2**
° clinical study /ˌklɪnɪk(ə)l ˈstʌdi/ klinische Studie **2B3**
° clinical trial /ˌklɪnɪk(ə)l ˈtraɪəl/ klinische Studie **2B8**
° clipping /klɪp/ Zeitungsausschnitt; Pressebeleg **3R2**
close /kləʊs/ nah(e) **CT6**; eng **CT7**
to **close** /kləʊz/ schließen; zumachen **CT5**
closely /ˈkləʊsli/ eng; sorgfältig; genau **CT8**
closing /ˈkləʊzɪŋ/ End-; Schluss-; abschließend **4A9**

° cloth /klɒθ/ Tuch; Stoff **5A1**
clothes *(pl)* /kləʊðz/ Kleider; Kleidung **CT5**
° clothing *(no pl)* /ˈkləʊðɪŋ/ (Be)kleidung **5D7**
° cloud /klaʊd/ Wolke **2SBS**
° to cloud over /ˌklaʊd‿ˈəʊvə/ sich verdüstern; sich verfinstern **5R2**
cloudy /ˈklaʊdi/ bewölkt; bedeckt **CT6**
club /klʌb/ Klub; Verein; Arbeitsgemeinschaft **CT5**
° clubhouse /ˈklʌbˌhaʊs/ Klubhaus; Vereinshaus **2R7**
° clue /kluː/ Hinweis; Tipp; Spur **2R1**
clumsy /ˈklʌmzi/ ungeschickt **CT7**
° cluster /ˈklʌstə/ Bündel; *hier:* (Menschen)traube **2SBS**
° co-founder /ˈkəʊˌfaʊndə/ Mit(be)gründer/in **3D2**
coach /kəʊtʃ/ Trainer/in; Coach, Sportlehrer/in **CT7**
° coal /kəʊl/ Kohle(-) **5A3**
° coal mine /ˈkəʊl maɪn/ Kohlenbergwerk; Kohlengrube **5D7**
coast /kəʊst/ Küste **CT6**
° coastline /ˈkəʊstˌlaɪn/ Küste(nlinie) **1P1**
coat /kəʊt/ Mantel **CT5**
coffee /ˈkɒfi/ Kaffee **CT7**
° coffee table /ˈkɒfi ˌteɪb(ə)l/ Couchtisch; Beistelltisch **4SBS**
cold /kəʊld/ kalt **CT5**
° to collapse /kəˈlæps/ zusammenbrechen; einstürzen **4SBS**
° collar /ˈkɒlə/ Kragen **3B4**
° colleague /ˈkɒliːg/ (Arbeits)kollege/-kollegin **4D5**
to **collect** /kəˈlekt/ (ein)sammeln **CT7**; *hier:* abholen **4Intro 2**
collection /kəˈlekʃ(ə)n/ (An)sammlung; Auswahl **1B7**
college /ˈkɒlɪdʒ/ College *(Eingangsstufe der Universität in den USA)* **3B1**
° college /ˈkɒlɪdʒ/ Gymnasium; Hochschule **1D11**
° colonialist /kəˈləʊniəlɪst/ Kolonialist/in **1A5**
colonization *(no pl)* /ˌkɒlənaɪˈzeɪʃ(ə)n/ Kolonisation; Kolonisierung **1A1**
° colonizer /ˈkɒlənaɪzə/ *jemand, der kolonialisiert* **1SBS**
colony /ˈkɒləni/ Kolonie **1A1**
colour /ˈkʌlə/ Farbe **CT5**
° colourful /ˈkʌləf(ə)l/ farbenfroh **1A6**
combination /ˌkɒmbɪˈneɪʃ(ə)n/ Kombination; Verbindung **CT8**
° to combine /kəmˈbaɪn/ verbinden; kombinieren **1D18, 3D11**
to **come** *(irr)* /kʌm/ kommen; mitkommen **CT5**
Come on! *(informal)* /ˌkʌm‿ˈɒn/ Komm(t) jetzt!; Mach(t) schon! **CT5**
° to come across *(irr)* /ˌkʌm‿əˈkrɒs/ begegnen; stoßen auf; *hier:* herüberkommen, wirken **4SBS**
° to come along *(irr)* /ˌkʌm‿əˈlɒŋ/ mitgehen; (mit)kommen **5R3**
to **come down to sth** /ˌkʌm ˈdaʊn tʊ/ auf etw ankommen; auf etw hinauslaufen **2Intro 6**
to **come in** *(irr)* /ˌkʌm‿ˈɪn/ hereinkommen **CT5**
to **come out** *(irr)* /ˌkʌm‿ˈaʊt/ herauskommen **CT6**
° to come out *(irr)* /ˌkʌm‿ˈaʊt/ *hier:* sich outen **2R1**
° to come up *(irr)* /ˌkʌm‿ˈʌp/ hochkommen; *hier:* näher rücken, bevorstehen **3R1**; *hier:* angezeigt werden **4R1**
to **come up with sth** /ˌkʌm‿ˈʌp wɪð/ auf etw kommen; sich etw einfallen lassen **CT8**
° to come with *(irr)* /ˈkʌm wɪð/ enthalten; beinhalten; mit sich bringen **3Intro 4**
° to come/spring to (sb's) mind /ˌkʌm/ˌsprɪŋ tʊ (ˌsʌmbədiz) ˈmaɪnd/ (jdm) einfallen **1Intro 1**
comedy /ˈkɒmədi/ Comedy(show); Komödie **CT8**
° comfortable /ˈkʌmftəb(ə)l/ behaglich; bequem; komfortabel **1D18**
° comic book /ˈkɒmɪk bʊk/ Comicbuch **2R2**
° comical /ˈkɒmɪk(ə)l/ komisch; lustig **3SBS**
command /kəˈmɑːnd/ Befehl; Kommando; Kontrolle **CT8**
to **commemorate sb/sth** /kəˈmeməreɪt/ einer Person/Sache gedenken **CT8**
comment /ˈkɒment/ Kommentar; Bemerkung **CT6**
to **comment (on)** /ˈkɒment‿ɒn/ kommentieren **CT7**
to **commit** /kəˈmɪt/ begehen **CT8**
° commitment /kəˈmɪtmənt/ Engagement; Verpflichtung **Wordbank 8**
common /ˈkɒmən/ üblich; weit verbreitet; gemeinsam **4B1**
° common /ˈkɒmən/ *hier:* gemeinschaftlich (genutzt) **3D13**
to **have sth in common (with sb)** /ˌhæv ˌsʌmθɪŋ‿ɪn ˈkɒmən wɪð/ etw (mit jdm) gemein(sam) haben **CT7**
° commonly /ˈkɒmənli/ häufig; gemeinhin; gewöhnlich **2B3**
° commune /ˈkɒmjuːn/ Kommune **5R3**
° the Commonwealth /ðə ˈkɒmənˌwelθ/ das Commonwealth *(Staatenbund)* **1A2**
to **communicate** /kəˈmjuːnɪkeɪt/ kommunizieren; Kontakt haben **1A3, 2A1**
community /kəˈmjuːnəti/ Gemeinde; Gemeinschaft **CT8**
° commuter train /kəˈmjuːtə treɪn/ Pendlerzug **3R1**
° companion /kəmˈpænjən/ Begleiter/in; Gefährte/Gefährtin **5D7**
company /ˈkʌmp(ə)ni/ Firma; Unternehmen **CT6**
to **compare** /kəmˈpeə/ vergleichen **CT6**
compared with/to /kəmˈpeəd wɪð/tə/ verglichen mit **CT8**
comparison /kəmˈpærɪs(ə)n/ Vergleich **CT8**
° compelling /kəmˈpelɪŋ/ zwingend; fesselnd **3R6**
to **compete** /kəmˈpiːt/ wetteifern; antreten; kämpfen **CT8**
competition /ˌkɒmpəˈtɪʃ(ə)n/ Wettbewerb **CT6**
to **complain (about)** /kəmˈpleɪn‿əˌbaʊt/ sich beklagen (über) **CT8**
complete /kəmˈpliːt/ vollständig; komplett; völlig **CT7**
to **complete** /kəmˈpliːt/ vervollständigen; ausfüllen **CT6**; zu Ende bringen, absolvieren **CT8**
completely /kəmˈpliːtli/ völlig **CT7**
° complex /ˈkɒmpleks/ komplex; kompliziert **2B/T1**
complicated /ˈkɒmplɪˌkeɪtɪd/ kompliziert; schwierig **CT7**
° to compliment /ˈkɒmplɪment/ ein Kompliment machen **5SBS**
comprehensive /ˌkɒmprɪˈhensɪv/ umfassend **4A5**
° compromise /ˈkɒmprəmaɪz/ Kompromiss **5D15**
° compulsory /kəmˈpʌlsəri/ vorgeschrieben; obligatorisch; Pflicht- **5A/T1**
° computerized /kəmˈpjuːtəraɪzd/ mit Computern erstellt **2D21**
computing *(no pl)* /kəmˈpjuːtɪŋ/ EDV; Computing **5A1**
to **concentrate** /ˈkɒns(ə)nˌtreɪt/ (sich) konzentrieren **CT7**
° concern /kənˈsɜːn/ Anliegen; Sorge; Besorgnis **2R4, 5SBS**
concerned /kənˈsɜːnd/ betroffen; besorgt; beunruhigt **CT8**
as far as sb is concerned /əz ˌfɑːr‿əz‿ˈsʌmbədi‿ɪz kənˌsɜːnd/ was jdn anbelangt/betrifft **2Intro 6**
to **be concerned with sth** /ˌbiː kənˈsɜːnd wɪð/ sich um etw Gedanken machen; *hier:* etw behandeln **2A2**
° concert /ˈkɒnsət/ Konzert **3D11, 5D3, 5D11**

° concise /kən'saɪs/ prägnant; exakt; kurz und bündig **3R6**
to **conclude** /kən'klu:d/ enden; (ab)schließen; schlussfolgern **2A2**
conclusion /kən'klu:ʒ(ə)n/ Abschluss; Schluss; Schlussfolgerung **CT7**
in conclusion /ɪn kən'klu:ʒ(ə)n/ zum Abschluss; abschließend **2B8**
to **condemn** /kən'dem/ verurteilen; verdammen **5A3**
condition /kən'dɪʃ(ə)n/ Zustand; Bedingung **CT8**; *hier:* Leiden **2A4**
to **conduct** /kən'dʌkt/ (durch)führen; leiten **CT8**
° confidence *(no pl)* /'kɒnfɪd(ə)ns/ (Selbst)vertrauen; Zuversicht **4SBS, Wordbank 8**
confident /'kɒnfɪd(ə)nt/ zuversichtlich; selbstsicher; selbstbewusst **CT6**
° to confirm /kən'fɜ:m/ bestätigen **5B/T1**
conflict /'kɒnflɪkt/ Konflikt; Kampf; Zusammenstoß **3A5, 5B1**
° to confront /kən'frʌnt/ begegnen; konfrontieren **1SBS**
confrontation /ˌkɒnfrʌn'teɪʃ(ə)n/ Auseinandersetzung; Konfrontation **3A5**
confused /kən'fju:zd/ verwirrt; durcheinander; verworren **CT7**
° confusing /kən'fju:zɪŋ/ verwirrend **2B/T1**
° Congratulations! /kənˌgrætʃʊ'leɪʃ(ə)nz/ Gratuliere!; (Herzlichen) Glückwunsch! **3B4**
Congress *(AE)* /'kɒŋgrəs/ Kongress *(Parlament in den USA)* **2A4**
to **connect** /kə'nekt/ verbinden; anschließen **CT8**
connection /kə'nekʃ(ə)n/ Verbindung; Beziehung; Zusammenhang **1A3, 2A4**
to **conquer** /'kɒŋkə/ erobern; besiegen; bezwingen **CT7**
° consequence /'kɒnsɪkwəns/ Folge; Konsequenz **2D10, 5D21**
conservation *(no pl)* /ˌkɒnsə'veɪʃ(ə)n/ Schutz; Erhaltung **4A5**
° to conserve /kən'sɜ:v/ sparen; erhalten; schützen **Wordbank 1**
to **consider** /kən'sɪdə/ nachdenken; betrachten; berücksichtigen; *hier:* ansehen (als) **CT8**
° to consider /kən'sɪdə/ *hier:* in Betracht ziehen **4SBS**
° considering sth /kən'sɪdərɪŋ/ wenn man etw bedenkt **1SBS, 2SBS, 5SBS**
° to consist of sth /kən'sɪst‿əv/ aus etw bestehen **4P5**
conspiracy theory /kən'spɪrəsi ˌθɪəri/ Verschwörungstheorie **2A4**
° constant /'kɒnstənt/ dauernd; ständig; permanent **2A6**
° constantly /'kɒnstəntli/ ständig **2A/T2**
constitution /ˌkɒnstɪ'tju:ʃ(ə)n/ Zusammensetzung; Konstitution; Verfassung; Satzung **3A7**
constitutional right /ˌkɒnstɪˌtju:ʃ(ə)nəl 'raɪt/ Grundrecht **3A7**
° consultation /ˌkɒns(ə)l'teɪʃ(ə)n/ Beratung; Besprechung **5R1**
to **consume** /kən'sju:m/ konsumieren; verzehren **2Intro 2**
to **contact sb** /'kɒntækt/ sich mit jdm in Verbindung setzen **CT6**
to **contain** /kən'teɪn/ enthalten **1B7, 2B10**
° container /kən'teɪnə/ Behälter; Gefäß; Container **4SBS**
content /'kɒntent/ Inhalt **CT8**
contest /'kɒntest/ Wettbewerb; Wettkampf; Wettstreit **CT8**
to **continue** /kən'tɪnju:/ weitermachen; fortfahren **CT7**
° to contort /kən'tɔ:t/ sich verzerren; sich verziehen **4SBS**
° to contract /kən'trækt/ schrumpfen; verkürzen; zusammenziehen **4D15**
° contrast /'kɒntrɑ:st/ Gegensatz; Kontrast **3SBS, 5B/T1**
to **contribute** /kən'trɪbju:t/ beisteuern; beitragen **CT8**
contribution /ˌkɒntrɪ'bju:ʃ(ə)n/ Beitrag; Spende **CT8**
to **control** /kən'trəʊl/ kontrollieren; steuern; beherrschen **CT7**
control *(no pl)* /kən'trəʊl/ Kontrolle; Gewalt; Herrschaft **1A1, 3A5**
controversial /ˌkɒntrə'vɜ:ʃ(ə)l/ umstritten; kontrovers; strittig **3A5**
° controversy /'kɒntrəvɜ:si/kən'trɒvəsi/ Kontroverse; Auseinandersetzungen **5SBS**
° convenience /kən'vi:niəns/ Zweckmäßigkeit; Annehmlichkeit; *hier:* Toilette **4P1**
conversation /ˌkɒnvə'seɪʃ(ə)n/ Gespräch; Unterhaltung **CT7**
to **convey** /kən'veɪ/ (r)überbringen; vermitteln **2B7**
convict /'kɒnvɪkt/ Strafgefangene/r **1A1**
° to convict /kən'vɪkt/ verurteilen **3R8**
° conviction /kən'vɪkʃ(ə)n/ Verurteilung; Überzeugung **3R3**
° to convince /kən'vɪns/ überzeugen **2SBS, 3SBS, 4Intro 3**
convinced /kən'vɪnst/ überzeugt **3A7**
convincing /kən'vɪnsɪŋ/ überzeugend **CT7**
cook /kʊk/ Koch/Köchin **CT6**
to **cook** /kʊk/ kochen **CT6**
cooking *(no pl)* /'kʊkɪŋ/ Kochen; Koch- **2B8**
to **keep cool** /ˌki:p 'ku:l/ ruhig bleiben; cool bleiben **CT7**
° cool /ku:l/ kühl; kalt **4SBS**
to **cooperate** /kəʊ'ɒpəreɪt/ kooperieren; mitmachen **CT8**
° cop *(informal, AE)* /kɒp/ *umgangssprachliche Bezeichnung für Polizist* **3R2**
° to cop it *(informal, BE)* /'kɒp‿ɪt/ dran sein; gekillt werden **1R4**
to **cope with** /'kəʊp wɪð/ zurechtkommen mit; bewältigen **4B5**
° copy /'kɒpi/ Kopie, Exemplar, Ausgabe **3SBS**
to **copy** /'kɒpi/ abschreiben; kopieren **CT6**
coral /'kɒrəl/ Koralle(n-) **1B2**
coral bleaching *(no pl)* /ˌkɒrəl 'bli:tʃɪŋ/ Korallenbleiche **1B7**
coral reef /ˌkɒrəl 'ri:f/ Korallenriff **1B2**
corner /'kɔ:nə/ Ecke **CT6**
° corner store /'kɔ:nə stɔ:/ Eckladen **4SBS**
° cornstalk /'kɔ:nˌstɔ:k/ Maisstengel **2SBS**
° corny /'kɔ:ni/ kitschig; abgedroschen **Wordbank 5**
° coronation /ˌkɒrə'neɪʃ(ə)n/ Krönung(szeremonie) **5P1**
to **correct** /kə'rekt/ korrigieren **CT6**
° cost /kɒst/ Preis; Kosten **5B4**
° to cost *(irr)* /kɒst/ kosten **5D1**
costume /'kɒstju:m/ Kostüm **CT7**
° cotton /'kɒt(ə)n/ Baumwolle **5A1**
° cotton mill /'kɒt(ə)n mɪl/ Baumwollspinnerei **5A1**
to **cough** /kɒf/ husten; sich räuspern **CT7**
couldn't (= could not) /'kʊdnt, kʊd 'nɒt/ *Vergangenheitsform von "can't"* **CT6**
° to count /kaʊnt/ (ab)zählen; mitzählen; auszählen **2SBS, 3B4, 4R3, 5D4**
to **count on sb/sth** /'kaʊnt‿ɒn/ auf jdn/etw zählen **4A9**
° counterargument /'kaʊntəˌɑ:gjʊmənt/ Gegenargument **3A7**
country /'kʌntri/ Land **CT7**
countryside *(no pl)* /'kʌntriˌsaɪd/ Land(schaft) **CT7**
county /'kaʊnti/ Grafschaft; (Verwaltungs)bezirk **CT8**
° couple /'kʌp(ə)l/ Paar **2B/T2**
courage /'kʌrɪdʒ/ Mut **CT8**
° courageous /kə'reɪdʒəs/ mutig; tapfer **1A/T2**
course /kɔ:s/ Kurs **CT8**
of course /əv 'kɔ:s/ natürlich **CT5**
° course /kɔ:s/ *hier:* (Ver)lauf **5SBS**
° coursework *(no pl)* /'kɔ:sˌwɜ:k/ *schriftliche Arbeit, die bei der Prüfung in die Wertung eingeht* **5B2**

° court /kɔ:t/ Gericht **3R5**; *hier:* Platz **1B2**
° court verdict /ˈkɔ:t ˌvɜ:dɪkt/ Gerichtsurteil **3R3**
to **cover** /ˈkʌvə/ bedecken; behandeln **CT8**
° to cover /ˈkʌvə/ *hier:* sich erstrecken über **1B4**; *hier:* abdecken **3D13**
° coverage /ˈkʌv(ə)rɪdʒ/ Berichterstattung **5R1**
cover letter /ˌkʌvə ˈletə/ Anschreiben **4A9**
cow /kaʊ/ Kuh **CT5**
to crack /kræk/ (zer)brechen; *hier:* knacken **5A1**
° crack /kræk/ Riss; *hier:* Witz **4R3**
° to crack a joke *(informal)* /ˌkræk‿ə ˈdʒəʊk/ einen Witz reißen **2SBS**
crafty /ˈkrɑ:fti/ schlau; gerissen; *hier auch:* handwerklich begabt **4Intro 2**
to **crash** /kræʃ/ (ab)stürzen; knallen **CT8**
° to crawl /krɔ:l/ krabbeln; kriechen **2SBS**
crazy /ˈkreɪzi/ verrückt **CT8**
to **create** /kriˈeɪt/ erschaffen; erstellen **CT7**
creation /kriˈeɪʃ(ə)n/ (Er)schaffung; Produkt; Werk **1A3**
creative /kriˈeɪtɪv/ kreativ; schöpferisch **1A4, 4Intro 2**
° creative writing *(no pl)* /kriˌeɪtɪv ˈraɪtɪŋ/ kreatives Schreiben **2B10**
° creativity *(no pl)* /ˌkri:eɪˈtɪvəti/ Kreativität **Wordbank 8**
° creature /ˈkri:tʃə/ Kreatur; Lebewesen; Geschöpf **5P1**
° credit card /ˈkredɪt kɑ:d/ Kreditkarte **1D16**
° creek /kri:k/ kleine Bucht; Bach **1R2**
° creepy *(informal)* /ˈkri:pi/ grus(e)lig; schaurig **2B3, 3R2**
° crew *(informal)* /kru:/ Besatzung; *hier:* Bande **2SBS**
crime /kraɪm/ Verbrechen **CT8**
criminal /ˈkrɪmɪn(ə)l/ Verbrecher/in; verbrecherisch; kriminell **CT7**
° crisis (*pl* crises) /ˈkraɪsɪs, ˈkraɪsi:z/ Krise **3D2, 4R5**
° criterion (*pl* criteria) /kraɪˈtɪəriən, kraɪˈtɪəriə/ Kriterium **2D17, 3B/T1, 4A1**
° critic /ˈkrɪtɪk/ Kritiker/in; Rezensent/in **3A/T2**
critical /ˈkrɪtɪk(ə)l/ kritisch **CT8**
° criticism *(no pl)* /ˈkrɪtɪˌsɪz(ə)m/ Kritik; kritische Anmerkung(en) **3R2**
to **criticize** /ˈkrɪtɪsaɪz/ kritisch beurteilen; kritisieren **5A3**
to **cross** /krɒs/ überqueren **CT6**
° to cross /krɒs/ *hier:* verschränken **5B4**
° crossing /ˈkrɒsɪŋ/ Überfahrt **5SBS**
crowd /kraʊd/ (Menschen)menge; Zuschauermenge **CT7**
crowded /ˈkraʊdɪd/ überfüllt **CT8**
crown /kraʊn/ Krone **CT7**
cruel /ˈkru:əl/ grausam; gemein **CT6**
to **cry** /kraɪ/ weinen; schreien **CT6**
° cue card /ˈkju: kɑ:d/ Stichwortkarte **1B8**
cultural /ˈkʌltʃ(ə)rəl/ kulturell; Kultur- **CT8**
culture /ˈkʌltʃə/ Kultur **CT7**
cup /kʌp/ Tasse; Becher **CT7**
cupboard /ˈkʌbəd/ Schrank **CT6**
° curb /kɜrb/ Randstein **3B2**
° cure /kjʊə/ (Heil)mittel; Lösung **2D8**
curious /ˈkjʊəriəs/ neugierig; wissbegierig **CT7**
° curious /ˈkjʊəriəs/ *hier:* seltsam **3B3**
° to curl up /ˌkɜ:l‿ˈʌp/ sich einrollen; sich kuscheln **5R2**
current /ˈkʌrənt/ jetzig; gegenwärtig; aktuell **3A8**
currently /ˈkʌrəntli/ zurzeit; gegenwärtig; momentan **1A4, 4A5**
° cursive writing *(no pl)* /ˌkɜ:sɪv ˈraɪtɪŋ/ Schreibschrift **3R1**
° cushion /ˈkʊʃ(ə)n/ Kissen; Polster **5R2**
customer /ˈkʌstəmə/ Kunde/Kundin **CT5**
to **cut** *(irr)* /kʌt/ schneiden **CT7**
° to cut down *(irr)* /ˌkʌt‿ˈdaʊn/ fällen; kürzen **5R3**
° (to cut/make a) long story short /ˌkʌt/ˌmeɪk‿ə ˌlɒŋ ˌstɔ:ri ˈʃɔ:t/ um es kurz zu machen **2R4**
cute /kju:t/ süß; niedlich **CT7**
CV (= curriculum vitae) (*BE* = **résumé** *AE*) /ˌsi: ˈvi:, kəˌrɪkjʊləm ˈvi:taɪ/ Lebenslauf **4A7**
° cyberbullying *(no pl)* /ˈsaɪbəˌbʊliɪŋ/ Cybermobbing **2D10**
cycle /ˈsaɪk(ə)l/ Kreislauf; Zyklus **1A4**
cyclist /ˈsaɪklɪst/ Radfahrer/in **CT7**
° cylinder /ˈsɪlɪndə/ Zylinder; Walze; Flasche **4SBS**

D

dad *(informal)* /dæd/ Papa; Vati **CT5**
° daffodil /ˈdæfədɪl/ Osterglocke; (gelbe) Narzisse **5P1**
daily /ˈdeɪli/ täglich; jeden Tag **2Intro 2, 4A5**
on a daily basis /ˌɒn‿ə ˌdeɪli ˈbeɪsɪs/ täglich; jeden Tag **1A4**
° daily life /ˌdeɪli ˈlaɪf/ Alltag(sleben) **2B3**
to **damage** /ˈdæmɪdʒ/ schaden; beschädigen **CT8**
damage *(no pl)* /ˈdæmɪdʒ/ Schaden; (Be)schädigung **CT8**
dance /dɑ:ns/ Tanz **CT5**; Ball **CT8**
to **dance** /dɑ:ns/ tanzen **CT5**
dancer /ˈdɑ:nsə/ Tänzer/in **CT5**
dancing *(no pl)* /ˈdɑ:nsɪŋ/ Tanzen **CT5**
danger /ˈdeɪndʒə/ Gefahr **CT7**
dangerous /ˈdeɪndʒərəs/ gefährlich **CT5**
° dare /deə/ Mutprobe **2SBS**
° Dare me /ˈdeə mi:/ Stell(t) mich auf die (Mut)probe **2SBS**
° dark /dɑ:k/ dunkel **3R1, 2B7, 4SBS**
° darkness *(no pl)* /ˈdɑ:knəs/ Dunkelheit **3SBS**
° data /ˈdeɪtə/ Daten **Wordbank 7**
data entry *(no pl)* /ˈdeɪtə‿ˌentri/ Dateneingabe **4A7**
database /ˈdeɪtəˌbeɪs/ Datenbank(-) **4A7**
date /deɪt/ Datum **CT5**; Verabredung; Rendezvous; Date; Partner/in **CT8**
to **date sb** *(AE)* /ˈdeɪt/ mit jdm gehen **3B1**
daughter /ˈdɔ:tə/ Tochter **CT5**
day /deɪ/ Tag **CT5**
all day /ˌɔ:l ˈdeɪ/ den ganzen Tag **CT6**
Australia Day /ɒˈstreɪliə deɪ/ *Australiens offizieller Nationalfeiertag* **1A5**
dead /ded/ tot **CT7**
° deadly /ˈdedli/ tödlich **5B/T3**
to **deal with** *(irr)* /ˈdi:l wɪð/ sich befassen mit **CT8**
° to deal with *(irr)* /ˈdi:l wɪð/ *hier:* umgehen **1R4, 3B4**; *hier:* bewältigen **1R6, 4D6**
° dealing /ˈdi:lɪŋ/ Handeln; Dealen **3R1**
Dear ..., /dɪə/ Sehr geehrte(r) ...; Liebe(r, s) ... **CT6**
Dear Sir/Madam /ˌdɪə ˈsɜ:/ˈmædəm/ Sehr geehrte Damen und Herren **4A9**
death /deθ/ Tod; Ende **3A8, 5A3**
debate /dɪˈbeɪt/ Debatte; Diskussion **CT8**
° to debate /dɪˈbeɪt/ diskutieren; debattieren **5A6**
° decade /ˈdekeɪd/ Jahrzehnt **1D9, 3SBS**
December /dɪˈsembə/ Dezember **CT5**
° decent /ˈdi:s(ə)nt/ anständig; ordentlich; nett **3B3**
to **decide** /dɪˈsaɪd/ entscheiden; bestimmen **CT5**
decision /dɪˈsɪʒ(ə)n/ Entscheidung; Entschluss **CT7**
decline /dɪˈklaɪn/ Rückgang; Verschlechterung; Niedergang **3B1**
° to decline /dɪˈklaɪn/ sinken; (ab)fallen; zurückgehen **Wordbank 7**; *hier:* ablehnen **4SBS,**
° to decorate /ˈdekəreɪt/ dekorieren; verzieren **4SBS**
decoration /ˌdekəˈreɪʃ(ə)n/ Dekoration; Verzierung **CT6**
decrease /ˈdi:kri:s/ Abnahme; Rückgang **CT8**

to **decrease** /diːˈkriːs/ abnehmen; zurückgehen **CT8**
° to dedicate /ˈdedɪkeɪt/ (sich) widmen **5SBS**
° dedication *(no pl)* /ˌdedɪˈkeɪʃ(ə)n/ Engagement; Einsatz **Wordbank 8**
deed /diːd/ Tat **5A1**
deep /diːp/ tief **1A5**
to **take a deep breath** /ˌteɪk‿ə ˌdiːp‿ˈbreθ/ tief Luft holen **CT7**
° deeply rooted /ˌdiːpli ˈruːtɪd/ tief verwurzelt **3D7**
to **defeat** /dɪˈfiːt/ besiegen; schlagen **CT7**
° defeat /dɪˈfiːt/ Niederlage **5R3**
to **defend** /dɪˈfend/ verteidigen **CT7**
° defender /dɪˈfendə/ Beschützer/in; Verteidiger/in **1R2, 3D3**
to **define** /dɪˈfaɪn/ definieren; festlegen **2B8**
definitely /ˈdef(ə)nətli/ eindeutig; definitiv **CT6**
degree /dɪˈgriː/ Grad **CT8**
° degree /dɪˈgriː/ *hier:* Abschluss **2B10, 4R3**
° dehydration *(no pl)* /ˌdiːhaɪˈdreɪʃ(ə)n/ (Aus)trocknung **1R2**
to **delete** /dɪˈliːt/ löschen; streichen **2A4**
delicious /dɪˈlɪʃəs/ köstlich; lecker **CT5**
to **deliver** /dɪˈlɪvə/ liefern; zustellen **CT8**
° deliverer /dɪˈlɪv(ə)rə/ Austräger/in; *hier:* Fahrer/in **4D1**
° delivery boy/girl /dɪˈlɪv(ə)ri bɔɪ/gɜːl/ Austräger/in; *hier:* Fahrer/in **4D4**
° delivery person /dɪˈlɪv(ə)ri ˌpɜːs(ə)n/ Lieferant/in; Lieferer/-in **4D1**
demand /dɪˈmɑːnd/ (An)forderung **5A3**
to **demand** /dɪˈmɑːnd/ verlangen; fordern **CT8**
° democracy /dɪˈmɒkrəsi/ Demokratie **1P1**
° demolition /ˌdeməˈlɪʃ(ə)n/ Abriss **5R1**
° to demonstrate /ˈdemənˌstreɪt/ zeigen; demonstrieren; nachweisen **4SBS**
° demonstrator /ˈdemənˌstreɪtə/ Demonstrant/in **5R3**
° department /dɪˈpɑːtmənt/ Institut; Abteilung **4D7**
° depending on ... /dɪˈpendɪŋ‿ɒn/ je nach ...; je nachdem, ... **5B9**
to depict /dɪˈpɪkt/ darstellen; beschreiben **1SBS**
depressed /dɪˈprest/ deprimiert; depressiv **2A4**
° depressing /dɪˈpresɪŋ/ deprimierend **Wordbank 5**
° deputy /ˈdepjʊti/ Stellvertreter/in **4SBS**

to **describe** /dɪˈskraɪb/ beschreiben **CT6**
description /dɪˈskrɪpʃ(ə)n/ Beschreibung **CT5**
desert /ˈdezət/ Wüste **CT8**
to **design** /dɪˈzaɪn/ entwerfen; gestalten **CT7**
designer /dɪˈzaɪnə/ Designer/in; Entwickler/in **CT8**
desk /desk/ Schreibtisch **CT5**
despair *(no pl)* /dɪˈspeə/ Verzweiflung **CT8**
desperate /ˈdesp(ə)rət/ verzweifelt **CT7**
despite /dɪˈspaɪt/ trotz **1A5, 2A4, 3A7**
dessert /dɪˈzɜːt/ Nachtisch **CT5**
destination /ˌdestɪˈneɪʃ(ə)n/ (Reise)ziel; Bestimmungsort **CT8**
to **destroy** /dɪˈstrɔɪ/ zerstören; vernichten **CT8**
destruction *(no pl)* /dɪˈstrʌkʃ(ə)n/ Zerstörung **CT8**
° detailed /ˈdiːteɪld/ detailliert; genau; ausführlich **2R1, 4A/T1**
° to detect /dɪˈtekt/ wahrnehmen; bemerken **4SBS**
° determination *(no pl)* /dɪˌtɜːmɪˈneɪʃ(ə)n/ Entschlossenheit; Entschiedenheit; Bestimmung **1R4**
° to determine /dɪˈtɜːmɪn/ entscheiden; ermitteln; bestimmen **3R6**
° determined /dɪˈtɜːmɪnd/ entschlossen **1R2**
to **develop** /dɪˈveləp/ entwickeln; entstehen; erarbeiten **CT8**
° developed /dɪˈveləpt/ entwickelt; Industrie- **3A7**
development /dɪˈveləpmənt/ Entwicklung **CT8**
device /dɪˈvaɪs/ Gerät; Vorrichtung; Apparat **2A7, 4Intro 2**
stylistic device /staɪˌlɪstɪk dɪˈvaɪs/ Stilmittel **3A2**
° to devolve /dɪˈvɒlv/ übergehen; übertragen werden **4SBS**
° devoted /dɪˈvəʊtɪd/ treu; aufrichtig; *hier:* aufopfernd **2R7**
° Día de los Muertos /ˌdiːəʊ də lɒs ˈmweətɒs/ *mexikanischer Feiertag* **5D4**
° to diagnose /ˈdaɪəgnəʊz/ diagnostizieren; erkennen **2B3**
dialogue /ˈdaɪəlɒg/ Gespräch; Dialog **CT6**
diary /ˈdaɪəri/ Tagebuch; (Termin)kalender **CT6**
to **keep a diary** /ˌkiːp‿ə ˈdaɪəri/ ein Tagebuch führen **CT6**
dictionary /ˈdɪkʃən(ə)ri/ Wörterbuch **CT7**

° didgeridoo /ˌdɪdʒəriˈduː/ *röhrenförmiges Blasinstrument australischer Ureinwohner* **1D11**
didn't (= did not) /ˈdɪdnt, dɪd nɒt/ *Vergangenheitsform von "don't/doesn't"* **CT6**
° to die away /ˌdaɪ‿əˈweɪ/ nachlassen; verstummen **4SBS**
to **die (of)** /ˈdaɪ‿əv/ sterben (an) **CT7**
diet /ˈdaɪət/ Nahrung; Ernährung; Diät **CT7**
to **differ (from/in)** /ˈdɪfə frɒm/ɪn/ sich unterscheiden (von/in) **CT8**
difference /ˈdɪfrəns/ Unterschied; Verschiedenheit; Abweichung **CT7**
different /ˈdɪfrənt/ anders; andere(r, s); verschieden **CT5**
difficult /ˈdɪfɪk(ə)lt/ schwierig; schwer **CT5**
° difficulty /ˈdɪfɪk(ə)lti/ Mühe; Schwierigkeit; Problem **1A4**
° to dig *(irr)* /dɪg/ graben; wühlen **3R5**
° digger /ˈdɪgə/ Goldgräber/in **1A/T2**
dignity *(no pl)* /ˈdɪgnəti/ Würde; Achtung **3B1**
° diligence *(no pl)* /ˈdɪlɪdʒəns/ Sorgfalt; Eifer; Fleiß **Wordbank 8**
° diligent /ˈdɪlɪdʒ(ə)nt/ fleißig; sorgfältig; gewissenhaft **4A/T1**
° dingo /ˈdɪŋgəʊ/ Dingo *(australischer Wildhund)* **Wordbank 1**
dining room /ˈdaɪnɪŋ ruːm/ Esszimmer; Speisesaal **CT5**
dinner /ˈdɪnə/ Abendessen; Mittagessen **CT6**
° diploma /dɪˈpləʊmə/ Diplom **2B8**
° diplomatic /ˌdɪpləˈmætɪk/ diplomatisch; taktvoll **1R2**
to **direct** /daɪˈrekt/ Regie führen **CT8**
° direct /dɪˈrekt/ direkt; unmittelbar **3SBS, 4SBS, 5A3**
direction /dɪˈrekʃ(ə)n/ Richtung **3A7**
° directions *(pl)* /dɪˈrekʃ(ə)nz/ Anweisungen; Instruktionen; *hier:* Wegbeschreibung **5D5**
directly /dɪˈrektli/ direkt; genau; sofort **CT7**
director /daɪˈrektə/ Direktor/in; Regisseur/in **CT8**
dirty /ˈdɜːti/ dreckig; schmutzig **CT6**
° dirty /ˈdɜːti/ *hier:* böse **5B2**
° disability /ˌdɪsəˈbɪləti/ Unfähigkeit; Behinderung; Benachteiligung **1D9**
° disabled /dɪsˈeɪb(ə)ld/ mit Behinderung **1D9**
disadvantage /ˌdɪsədˈvɑːntɪdʒ/ Nachteil **CT7**
to **disagree** /ˌdɪsəˈgriː/ nicht übereinstimmen; nicht einverstanden sein **CT6**
to **disappear** /ˌdɪsəˈpɪə/ verschwinden **CT7**

disappointed /ˌdɪsəˈpɔɪntɪd/ enttäuscht **CT5**
disappointing /ˌdɪsəˈpɔɪntɪŋ/ enttäuschend **CT6**
° disappointment /ˌdɪsəˈpɔɪntmənt/ Enttäuschung **1R4, 4SBS**
° disaster /dɪˈzɑːstə/ Katastrophe; Unglück **5D2**
natural disaster /ˌnætʃ(ə)rəl dɪˈzɑːstə(ə)ri/ Naturkatastrophe **CT8**
° discipline /ˈdɪsəplɪn/ Disziplin; Sport(art) **1D9**
° discomfort /dɪsˈkʌmfət/ Unbehagen; Unannehmlichkeit **4SBS**
to **discover** /dɪˈskʌvə/ herausfinden; entdecken **CT7**
° discovery /dɪˈskʌv(ə)ri/ (Neu)entdeckung **1A/T2**
discreet /dɪˈskriːt/ diskret; dezent; taktvoll **4Intro 2**
to **discriminate against sb** /dɪˈskrɪmɪneɪt‿əˌgenst/ jdn diskriminieren **CT8**
discrimination *(no pl)* /dɪˌskrɪmɪˈneɪʃ(ə)n/ Diskriminierung; Benachteiligung **CT8**
to **discuss** /dɪˈskʌs/ besprechen; diskutieren **CT6**
disease /dɪˈziːz/ Krankheit; Leiden; Gebrechen **CT8**
° to disguise /dɪsˈgaɪz/ (sich) verkleiden; verbergen **4SBS**
° disgust *(no pl)* /dɪsˈgʌst/ Abscheu; Ekel; Empörung **5B4**
° disgusted /dɪsˈgʌstɪd/ angeekelt; angewidert; empört **2A2**
disgusting /dɪsˈgʌstɪŋ/ empörend; widerlich; widerwärtig **4Intro 4**
° dish /dɪʃ/ Schale; Schüssel; Gericht **5B2**
dishwasher /ˈdɪʃˌwɒʃə/ Geschirrspülmaschine **CT5**
to **dislike** /dɪsˈlaɪk/ nicht mögen **CT8**
° disorientation *(no pl)* /dɪsˌɔːriənˈteɪʃ(ə)n/ Desorientierung **2D18**
° to display /dɪˈspleɪ/ aushängen; (an)zeigen **5A1**
° disproportionally /ˌdɪsprəˈpɔːʃ(ə)nəli/ überproportional; unverhältnismäßig hoch **3D2**
° dispute /ˈdɪspjuːt/ Debatte; Streit **4R2**
° disrespectful /ˌdɪsrɪˈspektf(ə)l/ respektlos **5D14**
disruption /dɪsˈrʌpʃ(ə)n/ Unterbrechung; Störung **5A3**
° disruptive /dɪsˈrʌptɪv/ störend **5A/T3**

distance /ˈdɪstəns/ Distanz; Strecke; Entfernung **2A6**
° distinctive /dɪˈstɪŋktɪv/ charakteristisch; unverwechselbar **1P1**
° distortion /dɪˈstɔːʃ(ə)n/ Verzerrung; Verdrehung **2SBS**
° distracted /dɪˈstræktɪd/ abgelenkt; verwirrt; zerstreut **1SBS**
distraction /dɪˈstrækʃ(ə)n/ Störung; Ablenkung; Zerstreuung **2A3**
° to distribute /dɪˈstrɪbjuːt/ verteilen; vertreiben; verbreiten **3R1, 4SBS**
° district attorney *(AE)* /ˌdɪstrɪkt əˈtɜːrni/ Staatsanwalt/-anwältin **3R3**
° to disturb /dɪˈstɜːb/ stören; beunruhigen **4B1**
diverse /daɪˈvɜːs/ vielfältig; divers; unterschiedlich **CT8**
diversity *(no pl)* /daɪˈvɜːsəti/ Vielfalt **CT8**
° to divide /dɪˈvaɪd/ (auf)teilen; spalten **5D4**
to **divide into** /dɪˈvaɪd‿ˌɪntʊ/ (auf)teilen in **CT7**
° divorce /dɪˈvɔːs/ Scheidung **2D23**
divorced /dɪˈvɔːst/ geschieden **CT7**
DIY (= do-it-yourself) *(no pl)* /ˌdiː‿aɪ ˈwaɪ, ˌduː‿ɪt jəˈself/ Heimwerken **4Intro 2**
to **do** *(irr)* /duː/ machen; tun **CT5**
to **do research** /ˌduː ˈriːsɜːtʃ/ (er)forschen; recherchieren **CT7**
to **get to do sth** /ˌget‿tə ˈduː/ die Möglichkeit haben, etw zu tun **4Intro 2**
to **make sb do sth** /ˌmeɪk ˌsʌmbədi ˈduː/ jdn zu etwas bringen; jdn etwas tun lassen **CT7**
to **tell sb to do sth** /ˌtel ˌsʌmbədi tə ˈduː/ jdm sagen, dass er/sie etw tun soll **CT8**
doctor /ˈdɒktə/ Arzt/Ärztin **CT5**
documentary /ˌdɒkjʊˈment(ə)ri/ Dokumentation; Dokumentarfilm **5Intro 1**
dog /dɒg/ Hund **CT5**
to **walk the dog** /ˌwɔːk ðə ˈdɒg/ den Hund ausführen **CT5**
° domestic /dəˈmestɪk/ häuslich; Haus-; in der Familie **3SBS**
° to dominate /ˈdɒmɪneɪt/ beherrschen; dominieren **1SBS**
don't (= do not) /dəʊnt, duː ˈnɒt/ nicht tun; nicht machen **CT5**
° to donate /dəʊˈneɪt/ spenden **5B2**
° donation /dəʊˈneɪʃ(ə)n/ (Geld)spende; Zuwendung **4D16**

to **have sth done** /ˌhæv ˌsʌmθɪŋ ˈdʌn/ etw tun lassen **CT8**
door /dɔː/ Tür **CT5**
to **slam the door shut** /ˌslæm ðə ˈdɔː ʃʌt/ die Tür zuschlagen **CT7**
° doormat /ˈdɔːˌmæt/ Fußmatte; Fußabstreifer **5R1**
° doorway /ˈdɔːˌweɪ/ (Tür)eingang **4SBS**
dorm (= dormitory) *(informal)* /dɔːm, ˈdɔːmɪtri/ Schlafsaal **CT7**
° dos and don'ts *(pl)* /ˌduːz‿ən ˈdəʊnts/ *Verhaltensregeln* **1D16**
° to dot /dɒt/ mit einem Punkt versehen; *hier:* übersäen **3B4**
° to double /ˈdʌb(ə)l/ (sich) verdoppeln **Wordbank 7**
° to double-book /ˌdʌb(ə)l ˈbʊk/ doppelt reservieren **3D10**
doubt /daʊt/ Zweifel; Bedenken **3A7**
° to doubt /daʊt/ misstrauen; (be)zweifeln **2D4**
down /daʊn/ hinunter; herunter **CT6**
to **come down to sth** /ˌkʌm ˈdaʊn tʊ/ auf etw ankommen; auf etw hinauslaufen **2Intro 6**
up and down /ˌʌp‿ən ˈdaʊn/ auf und ab **CT8**
down under *(no pl, informal)* /ˌdaʊn‿ˈʌndə/ Australien; Neuseeland **1B1**
downstairs /ˌdaʊnˈsteəz/ (nach) unten **CT5**
downtown *(AE)* /ˈdaʊnˌtaʊn/ Innenstadt(-); Stadtmitte **CT8**
draft /drɑːft/ Entwurf **CT7**
° to draft /drɑːft/ entwerfen **2R3**
° to drag /dræg/ ziehen; schleifen **4SBS, 5R3**
° to drain /dreɪn/ leeren; erschöpfen **5D5**
drama *(no pl)* /ˈdrɑːmə/ Schauspielerei; Drama; Theater(-) **CT5**
dramatic /drəˈmætɪk/ dramatisch **CT7**
dramatically /drəˈmætɪkli/ dramatisch; beträchtlich; drastisch **5A1**
° drastic /ˈdræstɪk/ drastisch **5R4**
to **draw** *(irr)* /drɔː/ zeichnen **CT6**
° to draw *(irr)* /drɔː/ *hier:* (an)ziehen, lenken **4R2**
° to draw up *(irr)* /ˌdrɔː‿ˈʌp/ aufsetzen; verfassen **3D7**
° dread *(no pl)* /dred/ Furcht; (große) Angst **3B2**
dream /driːm/ Traum(-) **CT5**
to **dream (of)** *(irr)* /ˈdriːm‿əv/ träumen (von) **CT8**

° the Dreaming /ðə ˈdriːmɪŋ/ *zentraler Begriff der Aborigine-Mythologie* **1A3**
fancy dress party *(BE)* /ˌfænsi ˈdres ˌpɑːti/ Kostümfest **CT5**
to **dress** /dres/ sich anziehen; sich (ver)kleiden **CT7**
to **get dressed** /ˌget‿ˈdrest/ sich anziehen **CT7**
° to drift away /ˌdrɪft‿əˈweɪ/ wegtreiben; davonziehen **3B3**
drill /drɪl/ Übung; Probe(alarm) **3A9**
drink /drɪŋk/ Getränk; Trinken **CT6**
to **drink** *(irr)* /drɪŋk/ trinken **CT5**
° drinking *(no pl)* /ˈdrɪŋkɪŋ/ Trinken; Alkoholtrinken **2D2**
to **drive** *(irr)* /draɪv/ fahren **CT7**
° to drive sb crazy /ˌdraɪv ˌsʌmbədi ˈkreɪzi/ jdn zum Wahnsinn treiben **5R1**
driver /ˈdraɪvə/ Fahrer/in **CT8**
driver's license (*AE* = **driving licence** *BE*) /ˈdraɪvərz ˌlaɪs(ə)ns/ Führerschein **2Intro 2**
° driveway *(AE)* /ˈdraɪvˌweɪ/ Einfahrt **3D10**
° driving *(no pl)* /ˈdraɪvɪŋ/ Fahren **2D2**
to **drop** /drɒp/ fallen (lassen) **CT8**
to drop off /ˌdrɒp‿ˈɒf/ absetzen; ablegen **2A6**
° dropout /ˈdrɒpaʊt/ (Studien)abbrecher/in; Schulabbrecher/in **5R1**
drought /draʊt/ Trockenheit; Dürre **CT8**
drug /drʌg/ Medikament; Droge; Rauschgift **2B4**
drugstore (*AE*) /ˈdrʌgstɔːr/ Drogerie **2B4**
° drumming *(no pl)* /ˈdrʌmɪŋ/ Getrommel; Trommeln **5R3**
dry /draɪ/ trocken **CT6**
dry season /ˈdraɪ ˌsiːz(ə)n/ Trockenzeit **1B7**
duck /dʌk/ Ente **CT5**
° dude *(informal, AE)* /dud/ Typ; Kerl; Mann **2R3, 3B4**
° due /djuː/ fällig; erwartet **1R2**
° due to /ˈdjuː tu/ wegen **3A9**
° dull /dʌl/ langweilig; eintönig; matt; trüb(e) **2B/T1, 5R1**
° to dump /dʌmp/ abladen; wegwerfen; loswerden **5SBS**
° dunno (= don't know) *(informal)* /dəˈnəʊ/ weiß nicht **4R1**
during /ˈdjʊərɪŋ/ während **CT6**
° dust particle /ˈdʌst ˌpɑːtɪk(ə)l/ Staubpartikel **5R1**
° dye /daɪ/ Färbemittel **5D7**

E

each /iːtʃ/ jede(r, s) **CT6**
each other /ˌiːtʃ‿ˈʌðə/ einander; gegenseitig **CT6**
eager /ˈiːgə/ begierig; eifrig; einsatzfreudig **CT7**
ear /ɪə/ Ohr **CT5**
° earlier /ˈɜːliə/ früher; vorhin **4D18**
early /ˈɜːli/ früh; zeitig **CT6**
to **earn** /ɜːn/ verdienen; einbringen **CT7**
° to earn a living /ˌɜːn‿ə ˈlɪvɪŋ/ seinen Lebensunterhalt verdienen **5B4**
° earphones *(pl)* /ˈɪəfəʊnz/ Kopfhörer **1R2**
earth *(no pl)* /ɜːθ/ Erde **CT7**
° to ease one's way /ˌiːz wʌnz ˈweɪ/ sich langsam und vorsichtig bewegen **2SBS**
east /iːst/ Osten; östlich; Ost- **CT7**
Easter /ˈiːstə/ Ostern; Oster- **CT6**
easy /ˈiːzi/ leicht; einfach **CT5**
° easy chair /ˈiːzi tʃeə/ Sessel **4SBS**
to **eat** *(irr)* /iːt/ essen; fressen **CT5**
° eating disorder /ˈiːtɪŋ dɪsˌɔːdə/ Essstörung **2B5**
° to echo /ˈekəʊ/ (wider)hallen **4SBS**
economic /ˌiːkəˈnɒmɪk/ ökonomisch; Wirtschafts-; wirtschaftlich **CT8**
° economical /ˌiːkəˈnɒmɪk(ə)l/ ˌekəˈnɒmɪk(ə)l/ wirtschaftlich; ökonomisch; sparsam **1A/T2, 5D7**
economy /ɪˈkɒnəmi/ Wirtschaft **CT8**
° ecosystem /ˈiːkəʊˌsɪstəm/ Ökosystem **Wordbank 1**
to **edit** /ˈedɪt/ redigieren; bearbeiten **CT6**
editing *(no pl)* /ˈedɪtɪŋ/ Bearbeiten; Redigieren **4A5**
° editor /ˈedɪtə/ Herausgeber/in; Redakteur/in **1R1, 5SBS**
to **educate** /ˈedjʊkeɪt/ unterrichten; ausbilden; erziehen **3Intro 2**
education *(no pl)* /ˌedjʊˈkeɪʃ(ə)n/ Bildung; Ausbildung **CT7**
° education *(no pl)* /ˌedjʊˈkeɪʃ(ə)n/ *hier:* Erziehung **2B5**
° educational /ˌedjʊˈkeɪʃ(ə)nəl/ schulisch; Bildungs-; pädagogisch **3SBS, 4D16**
effect /ɪˈfekt/ Wirkung; Effekt; Auswirkung **CT8**
effective /ɪˈfektɪv/ fähig; wirksam; wirkungsvoll **CT7**
° efficient /ɪˈfɪʃ(ə)nt/ leistungsstark; effizient **5D7**
° effort /ˈefət/ Mühe; Anstrengung; Bemühung **1R2, 2B3, 4SBS, 5D4**
e.g. /ˌiː ˈdʒiː/ z. B. *(zum Beispiel)* **CT7**
egg /eg/ Ei **CT6**
° to egg sb on /ˌeg‿ˈɒn/ jdn anstacheln **1R4**
° Egyptian /iˈdʒɪpʃ(ə)n/ Ägypter/in; ägyptisch **5D2**
eight /eɪt/ acht **CT5**
either ... or ... /ˌaɪðə ˈɔː/ entweder ... oder ... **CT7**
° either of /ˈaɪðər‿əv/ einer/eine/eines von **2SBS**
° elbow /ˈelbəʊ/ Ell(en)bogen **2SBS**
elder /ˈeldə/ Ältere/r; ältere(r, s) **1A5**
elderly /ˈeldəli/ ältere(r, s) **4Intro 2**
° eldest /ˈeldəst/ älteste(r, s) **5A1**
° election /ɪˈlekʃ(ə)n/ Wahl **3B3**
elective /ɪˈlektɪv/ Wahlfach **1B2**
electricity *(no pl)* /ɪˌlekˈtrɪsəti/ Elektrizität **CT7**
elementary school (*AE* = **primary school** *BE*) /ˌeləˈment(ə)ri skul/ Grundschule **3A1**
elephant /ˈelɪfənt/ Elefant **CT5**
eleven /ɪˈlev(ə)n/ elf **CT5**
else /els/ sonst (noch) **CT8**
anything else /ˌeniθɪŋ‿ˈels/ alles andere; irgendetwas anderes **CT8**
someone else /ˌsʌmwʌn‿ˈels/ jemand anders **CT6**
embarrassed /ɪmˈbærəst/ verlegen; peinlich berührt **CT7**
embarrassing /ɪmˈbærəsɪŋ/ peinlich; unangenehm **CT6**
° embarrassment /ɪmˈbærəsmənt/ Peinlichkeit; Verlegenheit **3B4**
° emblem /ˈembləm/ Emblem; Symbol; Wahrzeichen **5D2**
° to embrace /ɪmˈbreɪs/ umarmen; aufgreifen; sich zu eigen machen **3SBS**
° to emerge /ɪˈmɜːdʒ/ herauskommen; auftauchen **4SBS**
to **emigrate** /ˈemɪgreɪt/ auswandern; emigrieren **CT7**
emotion /ɪˈməʊʃ(ə)n/ Gefühl; Emotion **CT6**
emotional /ɪˈməʊʃ(ə)nəl/ emotional; gefühlvoll **CT7**
emotive /ɪˈməʊtɪv/ emotional; gefühlsbetont **5A5**
° empathetic /ˌempəˈθetɪk/ einfühlsam; empathisch **2R3**
° emphasis /ˈemfəsɪs/ Betonung; Schwerpunkt **5B/T1**
to **emphasize** /ˈemfəsaɪz/ betonen; hervorheben **CT8**
° emphatic /ɪmˈfætɪk/ nachdrücklich; emphatisch; bestimmt **5D16**
to **employ** /ɪmˈplɔɪ/ beschäftigen; einstellen; einsetzen **5A1**
employee /ɪmˈplɔɪiː/ Angestellte/r; Mitarbeiter/in; Beschäftigte/r **5A3**
employer /ɪmˈplɔɪə/ Arbeitgeber/in **4A7**

° employment *(no pl)* /ɪmˈplɔɪmənt/ Beschäftigung; Anstellung; Tätigkeit **3B2, 4R3**
° to empower /ɪmˈpaʊə/ stärken; befähigen **3D2**
empty /ˈempti/ leer **CT7**
to **empty** /ˈempti/ (ent)leeren; ausräumen **CT5**
° to encourage /ɪnˈkʌrɪdʒ/ ermutigen, ermuntern; *hier:* fördern **1D9**
end /end/ Ende; Schluss **CT6**
at the end /ət ðiˈend/ am Ende **CT6**
in the end /ˌɪn ðiˈend/ letzten Endes; schließlich; zum Schluss **CT6**
to **end** /end/ beenden; zu Ende bringen; enden **CT5**
to **end up** /ˌendˈʌp/ enden **CT6**
° endangered /ɪnˈdeɪndʒəd/ vom Aussterben bedroht **Wordbank 1**
ending /ˈendɪŋ/ Ende; Schluss **CT6**
° endless /ˈendləs/ endlos; unzählig; unendlich **5R1**
enemy /ˈenəmi/ Feind/in **CT7**
energetic /ˌenəˈdʒetɪk/ voller Energie **4A5**
energy *(no pl)* /ˈenədʒi/ Energie; Kraft **CT6**
° engine /ˈendʒɪn/ Maschine; Motor **3R1, 5B2**
engineering *(no pl)* /ˌendʒɪˈnɪərɪŋ/ Technik; Ingenieurwissenschaft; Maschinenbau **1B2**
England /ˈɪŋglənd/ England **CT7**
English /ˈɪŋglɪʃ/ Englisch(-); englisch **CT5**
° enigma /ɪˈnɪgmə/ Rätsel; *hier:* Name des wichtigsten deutschen Verschlüsselungsgeräts im Zweiten Weltkrieg **5A1**
° enjamb(e)ment /ɪnˈdʒæmmənt/ Enjambement *(Übergreifen des Satzes in den nächsten Vers)* **3A8**
to **enjoy** /ˈɪndʒɔɪ/ genießen **CT5**
to **enjoy yourself** /ˈɪndʒɔɪ jəˌself/ sich amüsieren **CT7**
° enjoyable /ɪnˈdʒɔɪəb(ə)l/ angenehm; nett; unterhaltsam **2A/T2, 3R1**
° enormous /ɪˈnɔːməs/ enorm; riesig; gewaltig **1A/T2**
enough /ɪˈnʌf/ genügend; ausreichend; genug **CT5**
° to enslave /ɪnˈsleɪv/ versklaven **5SBS**
° enslavement *(no pl)* /ɪnˈsleɪvmənt/ Versklavung **5SBS**
° to ensure /ɪnˈʃɔː/ sicherstellen; garantieren **3A6, 4A10**
to **enter** /ˈentə/ eingeben; eintragen; (herein)kommen **CT8**
to **entertain** /ˌentəˈteɪn/ unterhalten **4Intro 2**
entertaining /ˌentəˈteɪnɪŋ/ unterhaltsam **CT8**
entertainment /ˌentəˈteɪnmənt/ Unterhaltung **CT8**
° enthusiasm *(no pl)* /ɪnˈθjuːziˌæzəm/ Enthusiasmus; Begeisterung **2R7, Wordbank 8**
enthusiastic /ɪnˌθjuːziˈæstɪk/ enthusiastisch; begeistert **4B1**
° entire /ɪnˈtaɪə/ gesamt; ganz; vollständig **2D18**
entirely /ɪnˈtaɪəli/ ganz; total; völlig **2A4**
entry /ˈentri/ Eintrag; Eintritt **CT7**
° enumeration *(no pl)* /ɪˌnjuːməˈreɪʃ(ə)n/ Aufzählung **3SBS**
° envelope /ˈenvələʊp/ (Brief)umschlag; Kuvert **5R1**
environment /ɪnˈvaɪrənmənt/ Umwelt; Umgebung **CT6**
environmental /ɪnˌvaɪrənˈment(ə)l/ Umwelt-; die Umwelt betreffend; ökologisch **CT6**
environmentally friendly /ɪnˌvaɪrənˌment(ə)li ˈfrendli/ umweltfreundlich **CT8**
to **envy sb (sth)** /ˈenvi/ jdn (um etw) beneiden **CT7**
° epidemic /ˌepɪˈdemɪk/ Epidemie; Seuche; seuchenartig **4SBS**
equal /ˈiːkwəl/ gleich(berechtigt) **CT8**
° equality *(no pl)* /ɪˈkwɒləti/ Gleichberechtigung; Gleichheit **3SBS**
° equipment *(no pl)* /ɪˈkwɪpmənt/ Ausrüstung; Ausstattung; Equipment **4D4**
° equivalent /ɪˈkwɪvələnt/ Entsprechung; Gegenstück **1Intro 3, 5B2**
° to erase /ɪˈreɪz/ entfernen; (aus)löschen **5SBS**
to erect /ɪˈrekt/ errichten; aufstellen **5D2**
to **escape** /ɪˈskeɪp/ fliehen; flüchten **CT8**
especially /ɪˈspeʃ(ə)li/ besonders; insbesondere **CT5**
essay /ˈeseɪ/ Aufsatz **CT7**
essential /ɪˈsenʃ(ə)l/ unverzichtbar; wesentlich **4A5**
° estimated /ˈestɪmeɪtɪd/ geschätzt; voraussichtlich **5D5**
etc (= et cetera) /et ˈset(ə)rə/ usw.; etc. **CT7**
° eternity *(no pl)* /ɪˈtɜːnəti/ Ewigkeit **4R2**
Europe /ˈjʊərəp/ Europa **CT8**
European /ˌjʊərəˈpiːən/ Europäer/in; europäisch **CT7**
° the European Union /ðə ˌjʊərəˌpiːən ˈjuːniən/ die Europäische Union **5D4**
to **evacuate** /ɪˈvækjueɪt/ evakuieren; räumen **5A3**
to evaluate /ɪˈvæljueɪt/ beurteilen; bewerten **5A3**
even /ˈiːv(ə)n/ selbst; sogar; noch, überhaupt **CT6**
even if /ˈiːv(ə)nˌɪf/ selbst wenn **CT7**
even though /ˌiːv(ə)n ˈðəʊ/ obwohl **CT8**
not even /ˈnɒtˌiːvn/ noch nicht einmal **CT7**
evening /ˈiːvnɪŋ/ Abend **CT5**
in the evening /ˌɪn ðiˈiːvnɪŋ/ am Abend **CT6**
event /ɪˈvent/ Ereignis; Veranstaltung; Event **CT6**
eventually /ɪˈventʃuəli/ schließlich **CT8**
ever /ˈevə/ jemals; schon (ein)mal **CT6**
° ever since /ˌevə ˈsɪns/ seitdem **5SBS**
ever-changing /ˌevə ˈtʃeɪndʒɪŋ/ ständig wechselnd **4A5**
every /ˈevri/ jede(r, s) **CT6**
everybody /ˈevriˌbɒdi/ alle; jede/r **CT5**
everyday /ˈevriˌdeɪ/ alltäglich **4Intro 2**
° everyday life /ˌevriˌdeɪ ˈlaɪf/ Alltagsleben **3Intro 2**
everyone /ˈevriˌwʌn/ jede/r **CT5**
everything /ˈevriθɪŋ/ alles **CT6**
everywhere /ˈevriˌweə/ überall **CT7**
evidence *(no pl)* /ˈevɪd(ə)ns/ Beweis(e) **CT7**
to **evoke** /ɪˈvəʊk/ hervorrufen **5A5**
exactly /ɪgˈzæktli/ genau **CT6**
exaggeration /ɪgˌzædʒəˈreɪʃ(ə)n/ Übertreibung **5A5**
exam /ɪgˈzæm/ Prüfung **CT8**
to **examine** /ɪgˈzæmɪn/ prüfen; untersuchen **CT8**
example /ɪgˈzɑːmp(ə)l/ Beispiel **CT5**
excellent /ˈeksələnt/ ausgezeichnet **CT5**
° except /ɪkˈsept/ außer **3SBS**; *hier:* aber **1R4, 3R1, 4R3**
° except for ... /ɪkˈsept fɔː/ außer ...; bis auf ... **4A/T2**
exception /ɪkˈsepʃ(ə)n/ Ausnahme **1B2**
° excerpt /ˈeksɜːpt/ Auszug; Exzerpt **2A/T2**
exchange /ɪksˈtʃeɪndʒ/ (Aus)tausch(-) **CT7**
to **exchange** /ɪksˈtʃeɪndʒ/ austauschen; umtauschen; wechseln **CT8**
excited /ɪkˈsaɪtɪd/ aufgeregt **CT5**
° excitement /ɪkˈsaɪtmənt/ Aufregung; Erregung **2SBS**
exciting /ɪkˈsaɪtɪŋ/ aufregend; spannend **CT5**
exclamation /ˌekskləˈmeɪʃ(ə)n/ Ausruf **CT7**
° to exclude /ɪkˈskluːd/ ausschließen **2A7**
° excuse /ɪkˈskjuːs/ Entschuldigung; Grund; Ausrede **1R4, 2B3, 3B5, 4R1**

Excuse me! /ɪk'skju:s mi/ Entschuldigen Sie bitte!; Entschuldigung! CT5
to **execute** /'eksɪˌkju:t/ hinrichten CT7
exercise /'eksəsaɪz/ Übung; Aufgabe CT5
° exercise /'eksəsaɪz/ *hier:* Bewegung 2B5
exercise book /'eksəsaɪz bʊk/ Heft CT5
exhausting /ɪg'zɔ:stɪŋ/ anstrengend CT7
° exhibit /ɪg'zɪbɪt/ Ausstellungsstück; Exponat 5D2
exhibit (*AE* = **exhibition** *BE*) /ɪg'zɪbɪt/ Ausstellung CT8
exhibition /ˌeksɪ'bɪʃ(ə)n/ Ausstellung; Vorführung CT6
to **exist** /ɪg'zɪst/ existieren; bestehen; leben; vorkommen CT8
° exit /'eksɪt/ Ausgang; Weggehen; Ausfahrt 5D4
° exotic /ɪg'zɒtɪk/ exotisch 5D2
° expansion /ɪk'spænʃ(ə)n/ Expansion; Erweiterung; Ausdehnung 3SBS, 5R4
to **expect** /ɪk'spekt/ erwarten; rechnen CT7
expectation /ˌekspek'teɪʃ(ə)n/ Erwartung CT8
° to expel sb from sth /ɪk'spel ˌsʌmbədi frɒm/ jdn von etw verweisen 3B/T1
expensive /ɪk'spensɪv/ teuer CT5
experience /ɪk'spɪəriəns/ Erfahrung; Erlebnis CT7
to **experience** /ɪk'spɪəriəns/ erleben; erfahren CT8
° experienced /ɪk'spɪəriənst/ erfahren; geschult 4SBS
to expire /ɪk'spaɪə/ ablaufen; enden; auslaufen 1A1
to **explain (sth to sb)** /ɪk'spleɪn ˌsʌmθɪŋ tʊ ˌsʌmbədi/ (jdm etw) erklären CT5
° explanation /ˌeksplə'neɪʃ(ə)n/ Erklärung; Erläuterung 4R1
° to explode /ɪk'spləʊd/ explodieren; sprengen 3R6
exploration /ˌeksplə'reɪʃ(ə)n/ Erforschung 5A3
° to explore /ɪk'splɔ:/ erforschen; untersuchen 1P1, 5D2
to **express** /ɪk'spres/ ausdrücken; aussprechen CT7
expression /ɪk'spreʃ(ə)n/ Ausdruck; Äußerung CT7
facial expression /ˌfeɪʃ(ə)l‿ɪk'spreʃ(ə)n/ Gesichtsausdruck 2A2
° expressive /ɪk'spresɪv/ ausdrucksstark; ausdrucksvoll 2A/T2, 5D3
° extended family /ɪkˌstendɪd 'fæm(ə)li/ Großfamilie 3R1
° extent (*no pl*) /ɪk'stent/ Größe; Ausdehnung; Umfang; Ausmaß 5SBS
° extinction rebel /ɪk'stɪŋkʃ(ə)n ˌreb(ə)l/ *Anhänger/in der Umweltschutzbewegung Extinction Rebellion* 5R1
extract /'ekstrækt/ Auszug 2B2, 3B2
extremely /ɪk'stri:mli/ äußerst; höchst CT8
° extremism (*no pl*) /ɪk'stri:mɪz(ə)m/ Extremismus 3SBS
eye /aɪ/ Auge CT5
° eyebrow /'aɪˌbraʊ/ Augenbraue 1R4
° eyewitness /'aɪˌwɪtnəs/ Augenzeuge/-zeugin 5B/T1

F

F (= Fahrenheit) (*no pl*) /'færənhaɪt/ Fahrenheit *(in den USA verwendete Temperatureinheit)* CT8
° fabric /'fæbrɪk/ Stoff(-) 5D4
fabulous /'fæbjʊləs/ fabelhaft; sagenhaft 4A5
face /feɪs/ Gesicht CT5
face to face /ˌfeɪs tə 'feɪs/ persönlich 2A3
to **face sth** /feɪs/ sich etw gegenübersehen; etw gegenüberstehen CT8
° to face up to sth /ˌfeɪs‿'ʌp tʊ/ etw ins Auge sehen 5R2
facial expression /ˌfeɪʃ(ə)l‿ɪk'spreʃ(ə)n/ Gesichtsausdruck 2A2
facilities (*pl*) /fə'sɪlətiz/ Einrichtungen; Anlagen CT8
fact /fækt/ Wirklichkeit; Tatsache CT7
° factor /'fæktə/ Faktor; Umstand 4A6
factory /'fækt(ə)ri/ Fabrik(-) CT8
factual /'fæktʃuəl/ sachlich; auf Tatsachen beruhend 5A5
° faded /'feɪdɪd/ ausgeblichen; verblichen 4SBS
° to fail /feɪl/ versagen; scheitern; missglücken 2SBS, 5SBS
° to fail to do sth /ˌfeɪl tə 'du:/ etw versäumen/nicht tun 3D2, 5SBS
° faint /feɪnt/ leise; schwach 2SBS, 4SBS
fairly /'feəli/ ziemlich; recht CT8
faith /feɪθ/ Vertrauen; Glaube 1A5
Yours faithfully (*BE*) /ˌjɔ:z 'feɪθf(ə)li/ *Schlussformel in einem nicht an eine bestimmte Person gerichteten formellen Brief* 4A9
° fake news (*pl*) /ˌfeɪk 'nju:z/ Fake News *(in den Medien, insbesondere in Social Media, in manipulativer Absicht verbreitete Falschmeldungen)* 2A1
fall (*AE* = **autumn** *BE*) /fɔ:l/ Herbst CT8
to **fall** (*irr*) /fɔ:l/ (um)fallen; stürzen CT6
° to fall ill /ˌfɔ:l‿'ɪl/ krank werden 5B/T3
to **fall in love (with sb)** /ˌfɔ:l‿ɪn 'lʌv wɪð/ sich (in jdn) verlieben CT7
to **fall over** (*irr*) /ˌfɔ:l‿'əʊvə/ hinfallen; stürzen 4Intro 2
false /fɔ:ls/ falsch CT6
fame (*no pl*) /feɪm/ Ruhm CT8
° familiar /fə'mɪliə/ vertraut; vertraulich 4A/T1
family /'fæm(ə)li/ Familie CT5
famous /'feɪməs/ berühmt CT5
fancy dress party (*BE*) /ˌfænsi 'dres ˌpɑ:ti/ Kostümfest CT5
fantastic (*informal*) /fæn'tæstɪk/ fantastisch CT5
° fantasy /'fæntəsi/ Vorstellung; Fantasie(-) 1P1, 2A4
far /fɑ:/ weit CT6
° far /fɑ:/ *hier:* viel 3A7
so far /'səʊ fɑ:/ bisher CT8
farm /fɑ:m/ Bauernhof CT6
farmer /'fɑ:mə/ Bauer/Bäuerin CT6
farming (*no pl*) /'fɑ:mɪŋ/ Ackerbau und Viehzucht CT8
° to fascinate /'fæsɪneɪt/ faszinieren 4R2
fascinated (by/with) /'fæsɪneɪtɪd baɪ/wɪð/ fasziniert (von) CT8
fascinating /'fæsɪneɪtɪŋ/ faszinierend CT6
fashion /'fæʃ(ə)n/ Mode(-) CT7
fast /fɑ:st/ schnell CT6
° fast-moving /ˌfɑ:st 'mu:vɪŋ/ spannend Wordbank 5
fat /fæt/ dick; fett CT5
° FATA /'fɑ:tə/ *ehemals unabhängiges Stammesgebiet (in Pakistan) unter Bundesverwaltung* 3SBS
° fatal /'feɪt(ə)l/ tödlich; fatal; verhängnisvoll 3A7
father /'fɑ:ðə/ Vater CT5
fault /fɔ:lt/ Schuld; Fehler CT7
° favor (*AE* = favour *BE*) /'feɪvər/ Gefallen 2SBS
favourite /'feɪv(ə)rət/ Liebling(s-); Favorit/in CT5
to **fear** /fɪə/ (be)fürchten CT8
° fear /fɪə/ Angst; Furcht; Befürchtung 2D7, 2SBS, 3B/T2, 3SBS
° fearful /'fɪəf(ə)l/ ängstlich 2A2
° feather /'feðə/ Feder 1P1
feature /'fi:tʃə/ Merkmal; Kennzeichen; Besonderheit; *hier:* Feature 4A5
° to feature /'fi:tʃə/ aufweisen; erscheinen; *hier:* bieten 5D4
February /'februəri/ Februar CT5
fee /fi:/ Gebühr; Beitrag; Entgelt CT7
to **feed** (*irr*) /fi:d/ (zu) essen geben; füttern 4A5, 5A1
to **feel** (*irr*) /fi:l/ (sich) fühlen; denken CT5

° to feel compelled to do sth /ˌfiːl kəmˌpeld tə ˈduː/ sich gezwungen sehen, etw zu tun **2D8**
to **feel like doing sth** /ˌfiːl‿laɪk ˈduːɪŋ/ Lust haben, etw zu tun **CT7**
to **feel sorry** /ˌfiːl ˈsɒri/ bedauern; leidtun **CT6**
feeling /ˈfiːlɪŋ/ Gefühl **CT5**
° fella *(informal)* /ˈfelə/ Typ **1R2**
° fellow /ˈfeləʊ/ Kollege/Kollegin; Mit...; ...genosse/genossin **3SBS**
felt tip /ˈfelt‿tɪp/ Filzstift **CT5**
° female /ˈfiːmeɪl/ Weibchen; Frau; weiblich **3SBS**
° feminism *(no pl)* /ˈfemənɪz(ə)m/ Feminismus **3D12**
festival /ˈfestɪv(ə)l/ Fest **CT6**
° few /fjuː/ einige; wenige **2D3, 3D2**
quite a few /ˌkwaɪt‿ə ˈfjuː/ eine ganze Menge **3A7**
° fiction /ˈfɪkʃ(ə)n/ Erfindung; Fiktion **2R2**
° fictional /ˈfɪkʃ(ə)nəl/ erfunden; fiktiv **2R1, 4SBS**
to fidget /ˈfɪdʒɪt/ (herum)zappeln; *hier:* herumspielen **4B1**
field /fiːld/ Wiese; Feld; hier *AE*: Spielfeld **4Intro 2**
° field /fiːld/ *hier:* Fundort **1A/T2**
° field size /ˈfiːld saɪz/ Einstellungsgröße **2D18**
fifth /fɪfθ/ fünfte(r, s) **CT5**
fight /faɪt/ Kampf; Streit **CT7**
to **fight** *(irr)* /faɪt/ (be)kämpfen **CT6**
figure /ˈfɪɡə/ Gestalt; Figur; Zahl, Wert **CT8**
° to figure *(informal)* /ˈfɪɡə/ denken; annehmen **3B3**
to **figure out** /ˌfɪɡər‿ˈaʊt/ herausfinden; begreifen **2A6**
° figure skater /ˈfɪɡə ˌskeɪtə/ Eiskunstläufer/in **2R1**
° to file a lawsuit /ˌfaɪl‿ə ˈlɔːˌsuːt/ Klage erheben **3D2**
to **fill in** /ˌfɪl‿ˈɪn/ (aus)füllen; eintragen **CT6**
° to film /fɪlm/ filmen; drehen **1P1, 2SBS**
° film set /ˈfɪlm set/ Filmkulisse; Drehort **1P1**
° film-making *(no pl)* /ˈfɪlmˌmeɪkɪŋ/ Filmproduktion **5Intro 1**
° filming location /ˈfɪlmɪŋ ləʊˌkeɪʃ(ə)n/ Drehort **1P1**
° to filter /ˈfɪltə/ (heraus)filtern **4SBS**
° to filter through /ˌfɪltə ˈθruː/ durchscheinen; durchsickern; *hier:* wehen (durch) **1R2**
final /ˈfaɪn(ə)l/ letzte(r, s); End-; entscheidend; endgültig **CT7**
° finality *(no pl)* /faɪˈnæləti/ Endgültigkeit; Entschiedenheit **3R3**
finally /ˈfaɪn(ə)li/ schließlich; endlich; abschließend, zum Schluss **CT6**
financial /faɪˈnænʃ(ə)l/ finanziell; Finanz-; Geld- **3B1**
° find /faɪnd/ Fund; Entdeckung **1A/T2**
to **find** *(irr)* /faɪnd/ finden **CT5**
° to find one's way around sth /ˌfaɪnd wʌnz ˈweɪ‿əˌraʊnd/ sich in etw zurechtfinden **2B1**
to **find out** *(irr)* /ˌfaɪnd‿ˈaʊt/ herausfinden **CT5**
finding /ˈfaɪndɪŋ/ Entdeckung; Ergebnis **CT7**
fine /faɪn/ in Ordnung; gut; schön **CT6**
to **finish** /ˈfɪnɪʃ/ (be)enden; aufhören **CT6**
finished /ˈfɪnɪʃt/ fertig; beendet **CT7**
to **fire** /ˈfaɪə/ (ab)feuern; schießen **CT8**
firearm /ˈfaɪərˌɑːm/ Schusswaffe **CT8**
fireworks *(pl)* /ˈfaɪəˌwɜːks/ Feuerwerk **CT6**
° firm /fɜːm/ Firma; Unternehmen **3B2**
° firm /fɜːm/ stabil; fest; entschieden **3R6**
first /fɜːst/ zuerst; als Erstes; erste(r, s) **CT5**
° first aid *(no pl)* /ˌfɜːst‿ˈeɪd/ Erste Hilfe **4P1**
° first and foremost /ˌfɜːst‿ən ˈfɔːməʊst/ zuallererst **2D10**
° First Nations /ˌfɜːst ˈneɪʃ(ə)nz/ Ureinwohner-; die einheimische Bevölkerung betreffend **1A6**
first of all /ˌfɜːst‿əv‿ˈɔːl/ zu(aller)erst **3A7**
° first off *(informal)* /ˌfɜːst‿ˈɒf/ erst (einmal) **2R4**
first-person narrator /ˌfɜːst ˈpɜːs(ə)n‿nəˌreɪtə/ Icherzähler/in **3B2**
° to fish /fɪʃ/ fischen; angeln **1A4**
fish and chips *(no pl, BE)* /ˌfɪʃ‿ən ˈtʃɪps/ *frittierter Fisch mit Pommes frites* **CT5**
fish (*pl* **fish** *or* **fishes**) /fɪʃ, fɪʃ, fɪʃɪz/ Fisch **CT5**
° fishing net /ˈfɪʃɪŋ net/ Fisch(er)netz **1B7**
° fishing *(no pl)* /ˈfɪʃɪŋ/ Fischerei; Fischen; Angeln **1B2**
° fist /fɪst/ Faust **2SBS**
° fistful /ˈfɪstfʊl/ Handvoll **3B4**
the right fit /ðə ˌraɪt ˈfɪt/ etwas Passendes; *hier:* die richtige Person **4A5**
to **fit** /fɪt/ passen (zu) **CT6**
to **fit in** /ˌfɪt‿ˈɪn/ dazupassen **CT7**
five /faɪv/ fünf **CT5**
to **fix** /fɪks/ festmachen; reparieren; in Ordnung bringen **CT7**
° to fix /fɪks/ *hier:* fixieren **4SBS**
° fizz *(no pl)* /fɪz/ Sprudel(n); Zischen **5R4**
flag /flæɡ/ Fahne; Flagge **CT8**
° in a flash /ɪn‿ə ˈflæʃ/ in Sekundenschnelle **3B4**
° to flash /flæʃ/ blitzen; aufleuchten **4SBS**
flat /flæt/ flach; eben; emotionslos **CT7**
flat *(BE)* /flæt/ (Etagen)wohnung; Mietwohnung **CT7**
to **flee** *(irr)* /fliː/ fliehen; flüchten **CT7**
° flexibility *(no pl)* /ˌfleksəˈbɪləti/ Flexibilität; Beweglichkeit **Wordbank 8**
° to flick /flɪk/ sich schnell (und ruckartig) bewegen **4SBS**
° to flick through sth /ˈflɪk θruː/ etw (schnell) durchblättern **5B4**
° to flicker /ˈflɪkə/ (auf)flackern; aufkommen **4SBS**
flight /flaɪt/ Flug **5Intro 4**
° to flip through sth /ˌflɪp ˈθruː/ etw (schnell) durchblättern **3R2**
° flipping *(no pl)* /ˈflɪpɪŋ/ *Aufkaufen und Aufwerten gebrauchter Gegenstände, die anschließend mit Gewinn weiterverkauft werden* **4Intro 2**
to **float** /fləʊt/ schwimmen; treiben; ziehen **1B7**
flood /flʌd/ Überschwemmung; Hochwasser; Flut **CT8**
flooding *(no pl)* /ˈflʌdɪŋ/ Überflutung; Überschwemmung **CT8**
floor /flɔː/ Boden **CT5**; Stock(werk) **CT7**
° flop /flɒp/ Flop; Reinfall; *hier:* Fallen **4SBS**
° to flop /flɒp/ fallen; sich fallen lassen **4SBS, 5B2**
° to flourish /ˈflʌrɪʃ/ (auf)blühen; florieren **3SBS**
to **flow** /fləʊ/ fließen **4B4**
flower /ˈflaʊə/ Blume **CT6**
fluently /ˈfluːəntli/ flüssig; fließend **CT7**
° to flush /flʌʃ/ erröten; rot werden **5R3**
to **fly** *(irr)* /flaɪ/ fliegen **CT5**
° flying lesson /ˈflaɪɪŋ ˌles(ə)n/ Flugstunde **1B2**
to **focus** /ˈfəʊkəs/ sich konzentrieren; fokussieren **CT7**
° focus /ˈfəʊkəs/ Mittelpunkt; Brennpunkt; Schwerpunkt **1SBS, 3D3**
° focus(s)ed /ˈfəʊkəst/ fokussiert; konzentriert **1R2**
° to fold /fəʊld/ (zusammen)falten **3Intro 1, 4R2**
folder /ˈfəʊldə/ Mappe; Schnellhefter; Ordner **CT5**
to **follow** /ˈfɒləʊ/ (be)folgen **CT6**
° to follow sth through /ˌfɒləʊ ˌsʌmθɪŋ ˈθruː/ etw durchziehen **2SBS**
° follow-up /ˈfɒləʊ‿ʌp/ Fortsetzung(s-); Nach-; Anschluss- **3R6**

following /ˈfɒləʊɪŋ/ folgende(r, s) CT7
food /fuːd/ Essen; Nahrung; Futter CT5
° foolish /ˈfuːlɪʃ/ töricht; unklug 1R4
foot /fʊt/ Fuß *(= 0,3048 Meter)* CT8
foot (*pl* **feet**) /fʊt, fiːt/ Fuß CT5
° footage *(no pl)* /ˈfʊtɪdʒ/ Filmmaterial 2SBS
football /ˈfʊtˌbɔːl/ Fußball CT5
football (= American football) *(AE)* /ˈfʊtˌbɔl, əˌmerɪkən ˈfʊtˌbɔl/ Football *(in Amerika aus dem Rugby entwickelte Ballsportart)* CT8
° footballer *(BE)* /ˈfʊtˌbɔːlə/ Fußballspieler/in 5A1
° footy/footie *(informal, AusE)* /ˈfʊti/ Australian Rules Football *(in Australien verbreitete Sportart)* 1Intro 3
for /fɔː/ für CT5; seit CT6
for a long time /fər‿ə ˌlɒŋ ˈtaɪm/ lange Zeit CT7
° for a while /fər‿ə ˈwaɪl/ eine ganze Weile 2R3, 3B2
for example /fər‿ɪɡˈzɑːmp(ə)l/ zum Beispiel CT5
° for God's sake *(informal)* /fə ˌɡɒdz‿ˈseɪk/ um Himmels willen 4R3
for good /fə ˈɡʊd/ für immer; endgültig 2A4
° for instance /fər‿ˈɪnstəns/ zum Beispiel 2D28
° for life /fə ˈlaɪf/ lebenslang 3R1
° for once /fə ˈwʌns/ ausnahmsweise 3B3
to **force** /fɔːs/ zwingen CT8
forcefully /ˈfɔːsf(ə)li/ gewaltsam 1A5
forearm /ˈfɔːrˌɑːm/ Unterarm 1A4
forecast /ˈfɔːkɑːst/ Prognose; Vorhersage CT8
° foreclosure proceedings *(pl)* /fɔːˈkləʊʒə prəˌsiːdɪŋz/ Zwangsvollstreckungsverfahren 3B2
foreground /ˈfɔːˌɡraʊnd/ Vordergrund; Mittelpunkt CT8
° forehead /ˈfɔːhed, ˈfɒrɪd/ Stirn 3B4, 3SBS, 4SBS
foreign /ˈfɒrɪn/ ausländisch; fremd; Fremd- 1B2
forest /ˈfɒrɪst/ Wald CT8
forever /fərˈevə/ ewig; ständig CT6
° forever /fərˈevə/ *hier:* für immer 3B2
to **forget** *(irr)* /fəˈɡet/ vergessen CT5
form /fɔːm/ Form; Art 5A3
° form /fɔːm/ *hier:* Formular 4R1
to **form** /fɔːm/ formen; bilden CT6
formal /ˈfɔːm(ə)l/ formell; förmlich; offiziell 4A7
° formation /fɔːˈmeɪʃ(ə)n/ Bildung; Formation 1D2
former /fɔːmə/ ehemalige(r, s); frühere(r, s) CT8
° fort /fɔːt/ Fort; Festung 5A1
forward(s) /ˈfɔːwədz/ nach vorn(e); weiter; vorn(e) 3A7
to **look forward to sth** /ˌlʊk ˈfɔːwəd‿tə/ sich auf etw freuen CT6
fossil fuel /ˈfɒs(ə)l ˌfjuːəl/ fossiler Brennstoff 5A3
foster /ˈfɒstə/ Pflege- 1A3
to **found** /faʊnd/ gründen 1A1, 5A1
foundation /faʊnˈdeɪʃ(ə)n/ Fundament; Basis; Grundlage; *hier:* Gründung 1A3, 5A1
° foundation /faʊnˈdeɪʃ(ə)n/ *hier:* Stiftung 1D9
four /fɔː/ vier CT5
fourth /fɔːθ/ vierte(r, s) CT5
frame /freɪm/ (Bilder)rahmen 5A3
France /frɑːns/ Frankreich CT7
° frankly /ˈfræŋkli/ offen (gesagt) 2D12, 4SBS, 5A/T2
° to freak out *(informal)* /ˌfriːk‿ˈaʊt/ ausflippen; ausrasten 3B4, 5R2
free /friː/ frei; gratis CT5
to **be free** /ˌbiː ˈfriː/ frei haben/sein; Zeit für etw haben CT8
free time /ˌfriː ˈtaɪm/ Freizeit CT5
freedom *(no pl)* /ˈfriːdəm/ Freiheit CT8
° to freeze *(irr)* /friːz/ gefrieren; *hier:* erstarren 4SBS
French /frentʃ/ Französisch(-); französisch CT5
° French fries (*pl, AE* = chips *BE*) /ˌfrentʃ ˈfraɪz/ Pommes frites 2SBS
° frequent /ˈfriːkwənt/ häufig; regelmäßig 2D10
fresh /freʃ/ neu; ungebraucht; frisch CT5
° freshman (*pl* freshmen, *AE*) /ˈfreʃmən, ˈfreʃmən/ *Schüler/in einer Highschool im ersten Jahr* 2R1
Friday /ˈfraɪdeɪ/ Freitag CT5
friend /frend/ Freund/in CT5
° friendliness *(no pl)* /ˈfrendlinəs/ Freundlichkeit Wordbank 8
friendly /ˈfrendli/ freundlich CT5
to **be friends (with sb)** /ˌbiː ˈfrendz wɪð/ (mit jdm) befreundet sein CT7
to **become friends (with)** /bɪˌkʌm ˈfrendz wɪð/ Freundschaft schließen (mit) CT7
to **make friends (with sb)** /ˌmeɪk ˈfrendz wɪð/ (mit jdm) Freundschaft schließen CT7
friendship /ˈfrendʃɪp/ Freundschaft CT7
° to frighten /ˈfraɪt(ə)n/ erschrecken; Angst machen 3SBS
frightened /ˈfraɪt(ə)nd/ verängstigt CT8
° fringe /frɪndʒ/ Franse; Rand(-); hier *BE*: Pony 1R2
from /frɒm/ von; aus CT5
° from within /frɒm wɪðˈɪn/ von innen (heraus) 2SBS
° front /frʌnt/ Vorder- 3R1
° front door /ˌfrʌnt‿ˈdɔː/ Vordertür; Haustür 4SBS
° front page /ˌfrʌnt ˈpeɪdʒ/ Titelseite 3R2
° to frown /fraʊn/ die Stirn runzeln; *hier:* nachdenklich ansehen 2D6
fruit (*pl* **fruit** *or* **fruits**) /fruːt, fruːts/ Frucht; Obst CT5
frustrated /frʌˈstreɪtɪd/ frustriert CT6
frustrating /ˌfrʌˈstreɪtɪŋ/ frustrierend CT8
fossil fuel /ˈfɒs(ə)l ˌfjuːəl/ fossiler Brennstoff 5A3
° to fulfil /fʊlˈfɪl/ erfüllen; nachkommen; verwirklichen 2SBS
to **fulfill** (*AE* = **fulfil** *BE*) /fʊlˈfɪl/ erfüllen; nachkommen; verwirklichen CT8
full /fʊl/ voll(ständig) CT6
fun *(no pl)* /fʌn/ Spaß CT6; lustig, Spaß machend CT8
to **be fun** /ˌbiː ˈfʌn/ Spaß machen CT5
to **make fun of sb** /ˌmeɪk ˈfʌn‿əv/ sich über jdn lustig machen CT7
function /ˈfʌŋkʃ(ə)n/ Aufgabe; Pflicht; Funktion CT7
° fund /fʌnd/ Fonds 3D1
° fundamental /ˌfʌndəˈment(ə)l/ grundlegend 3D7
° fundraising /ˈfʌndreɪzɪŋ/ Fundraising; Geldbeschaffung; Benefiz- 4D16
funny /ˈfʌni/ lustig; witzig; komisch; merkwürdig CT5
° furious /ˈfjʊəriəs/ (sehr) wütend; heftig; stürmisch 3D17
furniture *(no pl)* /ˈfɜːnɪtʃə/ Möbel 4Intro 2
further /ˈfɜːðə/ weiter(e, er, es); noch mehr; (noch) weiter CT8
furthermore /ˌfɜːðəˈmɔː/ außerdem; ferner 3A7
future /ˈfjuːtʃə/ Zukunft CT6
° future /ˈfjuːtʃə/ zukünftig; für die Zukunft 1D11, 4A10, 5B4
° future perfect /ˌfjuːtʃə ˈpɜːfɪkt/ vollendetes Futur; Futur II 4D8
° future progressive /ˌfjuːtʃə prəʊˈɡresɪv/ Verlaufsform der Zukunft 4D7

G

° g'day *(informal, AusE)* /ɡəˈdeɪ/ Tag; hi; hallo *(in Australien)* 1Intro 1
° gadget /ˈɡædʒɪt/ *kleiner, raffinierter technischer Gegenstand* 5B2
to **gain** /ɡeɪn/ bekommen; erreichen; gewinnen 1B1, 3A7, 4Intro 4, 5A3
gallery /ˈɡæləri/ Galerie CT7
game /ɡeɪm/ Spiel CT5
° gang war /ˈɡæŋ wɔː/ Bandenkrieg 3R2

° gap /gæp/ Lücke **3R6**
° gaping /ˈgeɪpɪŋ/ weit geöffnet; klaffend **4SBS**
garage /ˈgærɪdʒ/ Garage; Tankstelle; (Kfz-)Werkstatt **4Intro 2**
garden /ˈgɑːd(ə)n/ Garten **CT5**
° gardener /ˈgɑːd(ə)nə/ Gärtner/in; Gartenarbeiter/in **4D1**
° gargle /ˈgɑːg(ə)l/ Gurgeln **4SBS**
gas station (*AE* = **petrol station** *BE*) /ˈgæs‿steɪʃ(ə)n/ Tankstelle **CT8**
° gas-guzzling *(AE)* /ˈgæs,gʌz(ə)lɪŋ/ spritfressend **5B4**
° to gasp /gɑːsp/ keuchen; nach Luft ringen **3B4**
° gate /geɪt/ Tor; Pforte; Flugsteig **4SBS**
to **gather** /ˈgæðə/ (sich ver)sammeln **CT8**
° to gather up /ˌgæðər‿ˈʌp/ aufsammeln; zusammensammeln **3B2**
° gay /geɪ/ Homosexuelle(r); Schwule(r); homosexuell; schwul **2R3**
° to gaze /geɪz/ starren **4SBS**
° GCSE (= General Certificate of Secondary Education) /ˌdʒiː siː‿es‿ˈiː/ *Abschlussprüfung der Sekundarstufe 1* **4R1**
° gear *(no pl)* /gɪə/ Ausrüstung; Sachen; Kleidung **4D6**
° geek *(informal)* /giːk/ (Computer)freak **2D5, 2SBS**
° gem /dʒem/ Edelstein; Juwel; Meisterwerk **5D2**
° gender /ˈdʒendə/ Geschlecht(sidentität) **3SBS**
general /ˈdʒen(ə)rəl/ allgemein; generell **CT8**
° Gen(eration) X /ˌdʒen(əˌreɪʃ[ə]n)‿ˈeks/ *bezeichnet die Generation der zwischen 1965 und 1980 Geborenen* **2Intro 2**
° Gen(eration) Z /ˌdʒen(əˌreɪʃ[ə]n) ˈzed/ *bezeichnet die Generation der zwischen 1997 und 2012 Geborenen* **2Intro 2**
generous /ˈdʒenərəs/ großzügig; freigebig **CT7**
° genius /ˈdʒiːniəs/ Genie; Genialität **4A/T2**
° genocide /ˈdʒenəsaɪd/ Völkermord **1SBS**
° genuine /ˈdʒenjuɪn/ echt; ehrlich **5R2**
° geocache /ˈdʒiːəʊˌkæʃ/ *beim Geocaching zu suchender Behälter* **4D6**
geography /dʒiːˈɒgrəfi/ Erdkunde; Geografie **CT5**
German /ˈdʒɜːmən/ Deutsche/r; deutsch; Deutsch(unterricht) **CT5**
° gesture /ˈdʒestʃə/ Handbewegung; Geste **4B1**
° to gesture /ˈdʒestʃə/ deuten **3B3**
to **get** *(irr)* /get/ erhalten; bekommen; holen; werden **CT5**; (hin)kommen **CT6**
to **get along (with sb)** /ˌget‿əˈlɒŋ wɪð/ sich (mit jdm) verstehen **CT8**
to **get back** *(irr)* /ˌget ˈbæk/ zurückkommen **1B7**
to **get back to sb** /ˌget ˈbæk tʊ/ sich (wieder) bei jdm melden **4A9**
to **get bored** /ˌget ˈbɔːd/ sich (anfangen zu) langweilen **CT6**
° to get changed /ˌget‿ˈtʃeɪndʒd/ sich umziehen **1R2**
to **get divorced** /ˌget‿dɪˈvɔːst/ geschieden werden **CT7**
to **get dressed** /ˌget‿ˈdrest/ sich anziehen **CT7**
to **get into trouble** /ˌget‿ˌɪntʊ ˈtrʌb(ə)l/ in Schwierigkeiten geraten **CT8**
° to get involved /ˌget‿ɪnˈvɒlvd/ verwickelt werden; *hier:* tätig werden **3SBS**
to **get lost** /ˌget ˈlɒst/ sich verirren; sich verlaufen **CT6**
to **get married** /ˌget ˈmærid/ heiraten **CT7**
to **get off** *(irr)* /ˌget‿ˈɒf/ aussteigen **CT6**
° to get off *(irr)* /ˌget‿ˈɒf/ *hier:* runterkommen **2SBS**
to **get on sb's nerves** /ˌget‿ɒn ˌsʌmbədiz ˈnɜːvz/ jdm auf die Nerven gehen **CT7**
to **get on sth** /ˈget‿ɒn/ in etw einsteigen **CT6**
to **get on (well) with sth** /ˌget‿ɒn ˈwel wɪð/ mit etw (gut) vorankommen **2B8**
to **get on (with sb)** /ˌget‿ˈɒn wɪð/ sich (mit jdm) verstehen **CT7**
° to get out of sth /ˌget‿ˈaʊt‿əv/ aus etw herauskommen **2A6**
° to get over /ˌget‿ˈəʊvə/ hinter sich bringen **4R3**
to **get over sb/sth** /ˌget‿ˈəʊvə/ über jdn/etw hinwegkommen **CT7**
to **get ready (for sth)** /ˌget ˈredi fɔː/ sich (für etw) fertig machen **CT6**
° to get rid of sb/sth /ˌget ˈrɪd‿əv/ jdn/etw loswerden **5SBS**
to get roasted /ˌget ˈrəʊstɪd/ geröstet werden; *hier:* verrissen werden **2A4**
to **get started** /ˌget ˈstɑːtɪd/ beginnen **4B4**
° to get the ball rolling /ˌget ðə ˌbɔːl ˈrəʊlɪŋ/ eine Sache in Gang bringen **3R6**
to **get to do sth** /ˌget‿tə ˈduː/ die Möglichkeit haben, etw zu tun **1B7, 4Intro 2**
° to get to do sth /ˌget‿tə ˈduː/ *hier:* zu etw kommen **2D27**
to **get to know sb/sth** /ˌget‿tə ˈnəʊ/ jdn/etw kennenlernen **CT7**
to **get through sth** /ˌget ˈθruː/ etw überstehen **2B8**
to **get together** /ˌget‿təˈgeðə/ sich treffen; wieder zusammenkommen **CT7**
to **get up** *(irr)* /ˌget‿ˈʌp/ aufstehen **CT6**
to **get used to** /ˌget ˈjuːst‿tʊ/ sich gewöhnen an **CT7**
° Get well soon! /ˌget ˌwel ˈsuːn/ Gute Besserung! **2B3**
° geyser /ˈgiːzə/ˈgaɪzə/ Geysir **1P1**
° ghost /gəʊst/ Geist; Gespenst **4SBS**
° ghoulish /ˈguːlɪʃ/ schaurig **4SBS**
giant /ˈdʒaɪənt/ Riese(n-); Gigant; riesig **2A4**
gift /gɪft/ Geschenk; Spende **CT8**
girl /gɜːl/ Mädchen **CT5**
° girlfriend /ˈgɜːlˌfrend/ Freundin **3B4**
to **give** *(irr)* /gɪv/ geben **CT5**
to **give/make a speech** /ˌgɪv/ˌmeɪk‿ə ˈspiːtʃ/ eine Rede halten **CT7**
° to give sb a day/week off /ˌgɪv ˌsʌmbədi‿ə ˌdeɪ/ˌwiːk‿ˈɒf/ jdm einen Tag/eine Woche freigeben **5D8**
° to give sb a hard look /ˌgɪv ˌsʌmbədi‿ə ˌhɑːd ˈlʊk/ jdm fest in die Augen sehen **3B3**
to **give sb a hug** /ˌgɪv ˌsʌmbədi‿ə ˈhʌg/ jdn umarmen **CT7**
° to give sb a lift /ˌgɪv ˌsʌmbədi‿ə ˈlɪft/ jdn (im Auto) mitnehmen **5B4**
to **give sth to sb** /ˈgɪv ˌsʌmθɪŋ tʊ ˌsʌmbədi/ jdm etw geben **CT5**
to **give up** *(irr)* /ˌgɪv‿ˈʌp/ aufgeben; resignieren **CT7**
° to give up *(irr)* /ˌgɪv‿ˈʌp/ *hier:* sich trennen von **2D4, 5R4**
° given /ˈgɪv(ə)n/ angesichts; *hier:* angenommen, man hätte ... **3B3**
glad /glæd/ glücklich; dankbar; froh **CT5**
° to glance /glɑːns/ (flüchtig) schauen **3B2**
glass /glɑːs/ Glas **CT7**
glasses *(pl)* /ˈglɑːsɪz/ Brille **CT6**
global warming /ˌgləʊb(ə)l ˈwɔːmɪŋ/ Erwärmung der Erdatmosphäre **5B2**
° globe /gləʊb/ Erde; Globus **5D4**
° glossy /ˈglɒsi/ glänzend **4SBS**
glove /glʌv/ Handschuh **CT5**
° glow /gləʊ/ Leuchten; Schein(en); Glühen; Licht **4SBS**
glue /gluː/ Klebstoff; Kleber **CT5**
to **glue** /gluː/ kleben **5A3**
° to glue /gluː/ *hier:* fesseln **2D21**
to **go** *(irr)* /gəʊ/ gehen; fahren **CT5**
° ... to go /tə ˈgəʊ/ noch ... **2SBS**

What's going on? /ˌwɒts ˌɡəʊɪŋ‿ˈɒn/ Was geht hier vor?; Was ist los? **CT7**
° to go ahead /ˌɡəʊ‿əˈhed/ vor(aus)gehen; vorangehen **5R4**
° to go blank /ˌɡəʊ ˈblæŋk/ eine Mattscheibe haben; nicht mehr klar denken können **5R4**
° to go by /ˌɡəʊ ˈbaɪ/ vorbeigehen; vergehen **1R2**
to **go for a walk** /ˌɡəʊ fər‿ə ˈwɔːk/ einen Spaziergang machen **CT5**
° to go for sth /ˈɡəʊ fɔː/ sich für etw entscheiden **5Intro 2**
to **go in** *(irr)* /ˌɡəʊ‿ˈɪn/ hineingehen **CT6**
° to go off the deep end about sth /ˌɡəʊ‿ˌɒf ðə ˈdiːp‿end‿əˌbaʊt/ sich maßlos über etw aufregen **5R2**
to **go on** *(irr)* /ˌɡəʊ‿ˈɒn/ weitergehen; weitermachen; weiterreden **CT6**; passieren **CT8**
° to go on *(irr)* /ˌɡəʊ‿ˈɒn/ *hier:* (be)nutzen **2A6**
to **go on a tour** /ˌɡəʊ‿ɒn‿ə ˈtʊə/ eine Tour machen **CT6**
to **go on a trip** /ˌɡəʊ‿ɒn‿ə ˈtrɪp/ einen Ausflug/eine Reise machen **CT6**
° to go on (hunger) strike /ˌɡəʊ‿ɒn‿ˈhʌŋɡə straɪk/ in den (Hunger)streik treten **Wordbank 2**
° to go on the record /ˌɡəʊ‿ɒn ðə ˈrekɔːd/ etw zu Protokoll geben **3R6**
to **go online** /ˌɡəʊ‿ˌɒnˈlaɪn/ online gehen **CT6**
° to go out *(irr)* /ˌɡəʊ‿ˈaʊt/ ausgehen; ausfallen **3B4, 5B2**; hier: miteinander (aus)gehen **2D14**
° to go out of business /ˌɡəʊ‿ˌaʊt‿əv ˈbɪznəs/ das Geschäft aufgeben **3B2**
° to go red /ˌɡəʊ ˈred/ rot werden **3B4**
to **go shopping** /ˌɡəʊ ˈʃɒpɪŋ/ einkaufen gehen **CT6**
° to go silent /ˌɡəʊ ˈsaɪlənt/ verstummen **3D17**
to **go to sleep** /ˌɡəʊ tə ˈsliːp/ (ein)schlafen **CT7**
to **go swimming** /ˌɡəʊ ˈswɪmɪŋ/ schwimmen gehen **CT6**
to **go through** *(irr)* /ˌɡəʊ ˈθruː/ durchgehen **CT7**
to **go together** *(irr)* /ˌɡəʊ təˈɡeðə/ zusammengehören; passen **CT7**
to **go with** /ˈɡəʊ wɪð/ zu ... gehören; zu ... passen **CT6**
to **go wrong** /ˌɡəʊ ˈrɒŋ/ schiefgehen **4B3**
goal /ɡəʊl/ Ziel; Tor **CT5**
to **score (a goal)** /ˌskɔːr‿ə ˈɡəʊl/ (ein Tor) schießen **CT5**
° goalpost /ˈɡəʊlˌpəʊst/ Torpfosten **1R4, 5D21**
God /ɡɒd/ Gott **CT8**

to keep sth going /ˌkiːp ˌsʌmθɪŋ ˈɡəʊɪŋ/ etw in Gang halten **4B4**
° gold medal /ˌɡəʊld ˈmed(ə)l/ Goldmedaille(n-) **1A3**
° gold rush /ˈɡəʊld rʌʃ/ Goldrausch **1D3**
° golf course /ˈɡɒlf kɔːs/ Golfplatz **2R7**
° gonna (= going to) *(informal)* /ˈɡʌnə, ˈɡəʊɪŋ tʊ/ werden **3B3, 4R1**
good /ɡʊd/ gut **CT5**
for good /fə ˈɡʊd/ für immer; endgültig **2A4**
(good) luck /ˌɡʊd ˈlʌk/ Glück **CT6**
Good luck! /ˌɡʊd ˈlʌk/ Viel Glück! **CT7**
goodbye /ˌɡʊdˈbaɪ/ Abschied(s-) **CT7**
goods *(pl)* /ɡʊdz/ Waren; Güter **5A1**
gorgeous /ˈɡɔːdʒəs/ herrlich; großartig **CT7**
° gotten (= got) *(AE)* /ˈɡɑt(ə)n/ werden **3B4**
government /ˈɡʌvənmənt/ Regierung(s-) **CT8**
° GPS (= global positioning system) /ˌdʒiː piː‿ˈes, ˌɡləʊb(ə)l pəˈzɪʃ(ə)nɪŋ ˌsɪstəm/ *satellitengestütztes Navigationssystem* **5D5**
° to grab /ɡræb/ schnappen; greifen; packen **2A/T2, 3B4**
grade /ɡreɪd/ Note **CT8**
grade *(AE)* /ɡreɪd/ Klasse **CT8**
gradually /ˈɡrædʒuəli/ allmählich; sanft **2B8**
° graduate /ˈɡrædʒuət/ Absolvent/in *(einer [Hoch]schule)* **4R3**
° grammar school *(BE)* /ˈɡræmə skuːl/ *entspricht dem deutschen Gymnasium* **4D16**
grandchild (*pl* **grandchildren**) /ˈɡrænˌtʃaɪld, ˈɡrænˌtʃɪldrən/ Enkelkind **CT7**
grandfather /ˈɡrænˌfɑːðə/ Großvater **CT5**
grandma *(informal)* /ˈɡrænˌmɑː/ Oma; Omi **CT5**
grandmother /ˈɡrænˌmʌðə/ Großmutter **CT5**
grandpa *(informal)* /ˈɡrænˌpɑː/ Opa; Opi **CT5**
grandparents *(pl)* /ˈɡrænˌpeərənts/ Großeltern **CT5**
° to grant /ɡrɑːnt/ gewähren; billigen **3R3**
° granular /ˈɡrænjələ/ körnig; gekörnt **4SBS**
line graph /ˈlaɪn ɡrɑːf/ Liniendiagramm **CT8**
° graphic novel /ˌɡræfɪk ˈnɒvl/ Graphic Novel; Bildergeschichte **2R1**
graphics *(pl)* /ˈɡræfɪks/ Grafik(en) **CT8**
grateful /ˈɡreɪtf(ə)l/ dankbar **CT6**
gratitude *(no pl)* /ˈɡrætɪˌtjuːd/ Dankbarkeit **1A5**

° greasy /ˈɡriːsi/ fett(ig); schmierig; glitschig **4SBS**
great /ɡreɪt/ groß; riesig; großartig; wunderbar **CT5**
Great Britain /ˌɡreɪt ˈbrɪt(ə)n/ Großbritannien **CT6**
° Greater Manchester /ˌɡreɪtə ˈmænˌtʃestə/ Großraum Manchester **5A1**
° greedy /ˈɡriːdi/ (hab)gierig; raffsüchtig **3B3**
° Greek /ɡriːk/ Grieche/Griechin; griechisch **4P5, 5D2**
green /ɡriːn/ grün **CT5**
° greenhouse gas /ˈɡriːnˌhaʊs ɡæs/ Treibhausgas **Wordbank 1**
to **greet** /ɡriːt/ (be)grüßen **CT8**
° greeting /ˈɡriːtɪŋ/ Begrüßung; Anrede **4B5**
grey /ɡreɪ/ grau **CT5**
grid /ɡrɪd/ Gitter(netz); Tabelle **CT6**
° to grin /ɡrɪn/ grinsen **4SBS**
° grip /ɡrɪp/ Griff; Gewalt **3B4**
° to grip /ɡrɪp/ packen; ergreifen **2SBS, 4SBS**
grocery /ˈɡrəʊsəri/ Lebensmittel- **3A6**
ground /ɡraʊnd/ (Erd)boden; Erde **CT7**
° ground /ɡraʊnd/ *hier:* Gelände **3D2**
sports ground /ˈspɔːts ˌɡraʊnd/ Sportplatz **CT7**
group /ɡruːp/ Gruppe(n-) **CT6**
to **grow up** *(irr)* /ˌɡrəʊ‿ˈʌp/ erwachsen werden; aufwachsen **CT8**
° grown /ɡrəʊn/ erwachsen **2B3**
° grown-up /ˈɡrəʊn‿ʌp/ Erwachsene/r **1D16**
° growth *(no pl)* /ɡrəʊθ/ Wachstum **1A/T2, 5D6**
to **grow** *(irr)* /ɡrəʊ/ wachsen; gedeihen; anbauen **CT8**
° to grow *(irr)* /ɡrəʊ/ *hier:* werden **1R2, 3R2**
° gruffly /ˈɡrʌfli/ barsch; schroff **1R2**
° to grumble /ˈɡrʌmb(ə)l/ knurren **3R2**
guarantee /ˌɡærənˈtiː/ Garantie; Zusicherung; Sicherheit **3A7**
guard /ɡɑːd/ Wache **CT7**
to guard /ɡɑːd/ bewachen **5A1**
° guarded /ˈɡɑːdɪd/ zurückhaltend; vorsichtig **1R2**
° guardian /ˈɡɑːdiən/ Hüter/in; Wächter/in **3D2**
to **guess** /ɡes/ (er)raten; annehmen; schätzen **CT6**
° guess /ɡes/ Vermutung; Annahme **5B4**
guest /ɡest/ Gast; Gäste- **CT6**
° guidance counselor *(AE)* /ˈɡaɪd(ə)ns ˌkaʊnsələr/ Studien-/Fachberater/in **3B5**

guide /gaɪd/ (Reise)führer/in; Führer/in im Museum etc. **CT7**
° guided tour /ˌgaɪdɪd‿ˈtʊə/ Führung **5D2**
guilty /ˈgɪlti/ schuldig **1A1**
guitar /gɪˈtɑː/ Gitarre(n-) **CT6**
° to gulp /gʌlp/ (hinunter)schlucken; *hier:* hinunterstürzen **1R2**
gun /gʌn/ (Schuss)waffe; Pistole; Gewehr **CT8**; *hier:* Waffen- **3A1**
° gunman (*pl* gunmen) /ˈgʌnmən, ˈgʌnmən/ Bewaffnete/r **3SBS**
gutless *(informal)* /ˈgʌtləs/ feige; lahm **5A3**
° gutter /ˈgʌtə/ Gosse; Dachrinne; *hier: Zwischenraum zwischen zwei Panels* **2R1**
guy *(informal)* /gaɪ/ Kerl; Typ; Bursche **CT7**
guys *(pl, informal)* /gaɪz/ Leute **CT7**
gym /dʒɪm/ Turnhalle **CT6**
gym (= **gymnastics**, *pl*) /dʒɪm, dʒɪmˈnæstɪks/ Turnen **CT5**

H

habit /ˈhæbɪt/ Gewohnheit **2Intro 4**
° had better do sth /həd ˌbetə ˈduː/ *drückt aus, dass jd etw tun soll* **4D15**
hair *(no pl)* /heə/ Haare **CT5**
° hair tie /ˈheə taɪ/ Haargummi **1R2**
hairdresser /ˈheəˌdresə/ Friseur; Friseurin **CT6**
° hairstyle /ˈheəˌstaɪl/ Frisur **5D14**
half (*pl* **halves**) /hɑːf, hɑːvz/ Hälfte **CT6**
by half /ˌbaɪ ˈhɑːf/ um die Hälfte **2A6**
half past (seven) /ˌhɑːf pɑːst ˈsev(e)n/ halb (acht) **CT5**
° half time /ˌhɑːf ˈtaɪm/ Halbzeit **1R4, 4Intro 2**
hall /hɔːl/ Korridor; Halle; Aula **CT8**
° hallway /ˈhɔːlˌweɪ/ Korridor; Diele; Flur **3D13, 4SBS**
° to hammer /ˈhæmə/ hämmern **2SBS**
hand /hænd/ Hand **CT5**
on the one hand /ˌɒn ðə ˈwʌn hænd/ einerseits; auf der einen Seite **CT7**
on the other hand /ˌɒn ði‿ˈʌðə hænd/ andererseits; auf der anderen Seite **CT7**
° to hand in /ˌhænd‿ˈɪn/ einreichen; abgeben **4R1**
° to hand (over) /ˌhænd‿ˈəʊvə/ (über)geben; (über)reichen **1R2, 5R1**
° handkerchief /ˈhæŋkəˌtʃɪf/ Taschentuch **4SBS**
° to handle /ˈhænd(ə)l/ anfassen; regeln; umgehen mit **4D16**
° handshake /ˈhændʃeɪk/ Händeschütteln; Händedruck **1R2**
° handsome /ˈhæns(ə)m/ gut aussehend **2SBS**

° to hang out *(irr)* /ˌhæŋ‿ˈaʊt/ sich (irgendwo zum Zeitvertreib) aufhalten; sich herumtreiben **5R1**
to **hang out with sb** *(informal)* /ˌhæŋ‿ˈaʊt wɪð/ Zeit mit jdm verbringen **CT8**
° to hang sb /hæŋ/ jdn (er)hängen **3R2**
to **hang up** *(irr)* /ˌhæŋ‿ˈʌp/ aufhängen **CT7**
° to hang up *(irr)* /ˌhæŋ‿ˈʌp/ *hier:* auflegen **2B3**
to **happen** /ˈhæpən/ geschehen; passieren **CT5**
° to happen to do sth /ˌhæpən tə ˈduː/ zufällig etw tun **5B4**
° happiness *(no pl)* /ˈhæpinəs/ Glück; Zufriedenheit; Fröhlichkeit **2A4**
happy /ˈhæpi/ glücklich; zufrieden; fröhlich **CT5**
happy ending /ˌhæpi‿ˈendɪŋ/ Happy End **2B8**
harbor (*AE* = **harbour** *BE*) /ˈharbər/ **CT8**
hard /hɑːd/ hart; schwer; schwierig; fest; kräftig **CT6**
° hard skills *(pl)* /ˈhɑːd skɪlz/ Hard Skills *(rein fachliche Qualifikation)* **4D9**
hard-working /ˌhɑːdˈwɜːkɪŋ/ fleißig; hart arbeitend **4A7**
hardly /ˈhɑːdli/ kaum; schwerlich **CT8**
hardly ever /ˌhɑːdli‿ˈevə/ fast nie; so gut wie nie **CT8**
hardship /ˈhɑːdʃɪp/ Not; Elend; Härte **1A5**
to **harm** /hɑːm/ Schaden zufügen; schaden **3A7**
harm *(no pl)* /hɑːm/ Schaden; Verletzung **1B7, 3Intro 2**
° hastily /ˈheɪstɪli/ eilig; hastig; übereilt **4SBS**
hat /hæt/ Hut; Mütze **CT6**
to **hate** /heɪt/ hassen; verabscheuen **CT5**
hate *(no pl)* /heɪt/ Hass **CT8**
° hatred *(no pl)* /ˈheɪtrɪd/ Hass; Abscheu **2A4**
to **have** *(irr)* /hæv/ haben; trinken, zu sich nehmen **CT5**
° to have a crush on /ˌhæv‿ə ˈkrʌʃ‿ɒn/ verknallt sein in **2B/T2**
° Have a good day! /ˌhæv‿ə ˌgʊd‿ˈdeɪ/ Einen schönen Tag noch! **4B4**
to **have a look at ...** /ˌhæv‿ə ˈlʊk‿ət/ sich ... ansehen; bei ... nachsehen **CT8**
to **have got** *(irr)* /ˌhæv ˈgɒt/ haben **CT5**
to **have lunch** /ˌhæv ˈlʌntʃ/ zu Mittag essen **CT5**
to **have sth done** /ˌhæv ˌsʌmθɪŋ ˈdʌn/ etw tun lassen **CT8**

to **have sth in common (with sb)** /ˌhæv ˌsʌmθɪŋ‿ɪn ˈkɒmən wɪð/ etw (mit jdm) gemein(sam) haben **CT7**
have to *(irr)* /ˈhæv tə/ müssen **CT6**
to **have/take a shower** /ˌhæv/ˌteɪk‿ə ˈʃaʊə/ sich duschen **CT6**
to wreak havoc /ˌriːk ˈhævək/ schlimme Schäden anrichten **5A3**
he /hiː/ er, **CT5**
he's (= he is) /hiːz, ˈhi‿ɪz/ er ist **CT5**
head /hed/ Kopf **CT5**
° to head (for/to) /ˈhed fɔː/tʊ/ zusteuern (auf); gehen (zu) **1A/T2, 2SBS, 3R1, 5R1**
° head of state /ˌhed‿əv ˈsteɪt/ Staatsoberhaupt **1P1**
heading /ˈhedɪŋ/ Überschrift; Titel **CT7**
headline /ˈhedˌlaɪn/ Schlagzeile; Überschrift **CT8**
headphones *(pl)* /ˈhedˌfəʊnz/ Kopfhörer **CT7**
° headquarters *(pl)* /hedˈkwɔːtəz/ Hauptsitz; Zentrale **4SBS**
° headshot /ˈhedˌʃɒt/ *auf Kopf und Gesicht zentriertes Foto* **4A7**
health *(no pl)* /helθ/ Gesundheit(s-) **CT8**
healthy /ˈhelθi/ gesund **CT5**
° heap /hiːp/ Haufen **3R1**
to hear *(irr)* /hɪə/ hören **CT5**
° to hear sb out /ˌhɪə ˌsʌmbədi‿ˈaʊt/ jdn ausreden lassen **3R6**
heart /hɑːt/ Herz **CT7**
° heart /hɑːt/ *hier:* Kern **3R6**
° to heat /hiːt/ erhitzen; aufwärmen **1R2**
° heat-resistant /ˈhiːt rɪˌzɪst(ə)nt/ hitzebeständig **1B7**
heated /ˈhiːtɪd/ hitzig; beheizt **1A5**
° heatwave /ˈhiːtˌweɪv/ Hitzewelle **Wordbank 1**
heavily /ˈhevɪli/ stark; schwer **CT8**
heavy /ˈhevi/ schwer **CT7**
° heel /hiːl/ Ferse **4SBS**
height /haɪt/ Höhe; (Körper)größe **CT8**
Hello! /həˈləʊ/ Hallo! **CT5**
to **help** /help/ helfen **CT5**
help *(no pl)* /help/ Hilfe **CT5**
to **help yourself (to sth)** /ˈhelp jəˌself tʊ/ sich (an etw) bedienen **CT7**
helpful /ˈhelpf(ə)l/ hilfsbereit; hilfreich; nützlich **CT7**
° helping /ˈhelpɪŋ/ (Essens)portion **3D17**
helpless /ˈhelpləs/ hilflos; machtlos **CT7**
° hemisphere /ˈhemɪˌsfɪə/ (Erd)halbkugel; Hemisphäre **1D12**
her /hɜː/ ihr(e); ihr; sie **CT5**
here /hɪə/ hier **CT5**

° Here we go again! *(informal)* /ˌhɪə wi ˌɡəʊ‿əˈɡen/ Jetzt geht das schon wieder los! **5B2**
° Here we go! /ˌhɪə wi ˈɡəʊ/ Jetzt geht's los! **1R4**
Here you are. /ˌhɪə ju‿ˈɑː/ Hier, bitte.; Bitte schön. **CT5**
heritage /ˈherɪtɪdʒ/ (Kultur)erbe **1A4**
hero (*pl* **heroes**) /ˈhɪərəʊ, ˈhɪərəʊz/ Held/in **CT8**
hers /hɜːz/ ihre(r, s); ihrs **CT6**
herself /həˈself/ sich; (sich) selbst **CT7**
Hi! *(informal)* /haɪ/ Hi! **CT5**
to **hide** *(irr)* /haɪd/ (sich) verstecken **CT7**
high /haɪ/ hoch **CT6**
to **highlight** /ˈhaɪˌlaɪt/ hervorheben; markieren **CT8**
highly /ˈhaɪli/ hoch-; ausgesprochen; äußerst **CT8**
highway *(AE)* /ˈhaɪˌweɪ/ Bundesstraße; Highway **CT8**
to **hike** /haɪk/ wandern **4A5**
° hike /haɪk/ Wanderung **4D6**
hiking *(no pl)* /ˈhaɪkɪŋ/ Wandern; Wander- **CT7**
° hill /hɪl/ Hügel; Berg **1P1, 3D12**
° hilt /hɪlt/ Griff **4SBS**
him /hɪm/ ihm; ihn **CT5**
himself /hɪmˈself/ sich; (sich) selbst **CT7**
° Hindi *(no pl)* /ˈhɪndi/ Hindi *(Amtssprache in Indien)* **4P4**
to **hire** /ˈhaɪə/ einstellen; beauftragen **CT8**
his /hɪz/ sein(e) **CT5**; seine(r, s); seins **CT6**
° His mouth is dropped. /hɪz ˌmaʊθ‿ɪz ˈdrɒpt/ Ihm ist die Kinnlade heruntergefallen. **2SBS**
° to hiss /hɪs/ zischen; fauchen **3B4**
historic /hɪˈstɒrɪk/ historisch **CT7**
historical /hɪˈstɒrɪk(ə)l/ geschichtlich; historisch **CT7**
history /ˈhɪst(ə)ri/ Geschichte **CT5**
° to hit all the bases with a single shot /ˌhɪt‿ɔːl ðə ˌbeɪsɪz wɪð‿ə ˌsɪŋɡ(ə)l ˈʃɒt/ zwei Fliegen mit einer Klappe schlagen **3R6**
to **hit** *(irr)* /hɪt/ schlagen; treffen; stoßen (gegen) **CT8**
to **hold** *(irr)* /həʊld/ halten **CT6**; veranstalten **CT8**
° to hold on *(irr)* /ˌhəʊld‿ˈɒn/ warten **4SBS**
° to hold on to /ˌhəʊld‿ˈɒn tʊ/ (sich) festhalten (an); behalten **3B4**
° to hold the press(es) /ˌhəʊld ðə ˈpresɪz/ den Druck verzögern **3R6**
to **hold up** *(irr)* /ˌhəʊld‿ˈʌp/ hochhalten **CT6**
° hole /həʊl/ Loch **1R4**

holiday /ˈhɒlədeɪ/ Urlaub; Ferien **CT5**; Feiertag **CT8**
on holiday /ɒn ˈhɒlədeɪ/ im Urlaub; in den Ferien **CT5**
home /həʊm/ Zuhause; Haus; Wohnung; zu Hause; nach Hause; Heim **CT5**
at home /ət ˈhəʊm/ zu Hause **CT5**
home-made /ˌhəʊmˈmeɪd/ hausgemacht; selbst gemacht **CT8**
homecoming *(no pl, AE)* /ˈhoʊmˌkʌmɪŋ/ Ehemaligentreffen **CT8**
homeland /ˈhəʊmˌlænd/ Heimat(land) **CT8**
homeless /ˈhəʊmləs/ heimatlos; obdachlos **3B1**
° homeless shelter /ˈhəʊmləs ˌʃeltə/ Notschlafstelle; Obdachlosenunterkunft **5B2**
hometown /ˈhəʊmˌtaʊn/ Heimatstadt **CT8**
homework *(no pl)* /ˈhəʊmˌwɜːk/ Hausaufgabe(n) **CT5**
homicide *(AE)* /ˈhɑmɪˌsaɪd/ Mord **3A5**
honest /ˈɒnɪst/ ehrlich **CT7**
to **be honest** /tə ˌbi‿ˈɒnɪst/ ehrlich gesagt; um die Wahrheit zu sagen **2Intro 6**
° honey *(informal)* /ˈhʌni/ Honig; *hier:* Schatz, Süße/r **3B4**
° to honk /hɒŋk/ hupen **2SBS**
° honour /ˈɒnə/ Ehre **3SBS, 5SBS**
° to honour /ˈɒnə/ ehren; in Ehren halten **5SBS**
° honourable /ˈɒn(ə)rəb(ə)l/ ehrenhaft; ehrenwert; verehrt **3SBS**
to **hoover** /ˈhuːvə/ staubsaugen **CT5**
hope /həʊp/ Hoffnung **CT6**
to **hope** /həʊp/ hoffen **CT5**
hopeful /ˈhəʊpf(ə)l/ zuversichtlich **CT8**
° hopefully /ˈhəʊpf(ə)li/ hoffnungsvoll; hoffentlich **2SBS**
° hopelessness *(no pl)* /ˈhəʊpləsnəs/ Hoffnungslosigkeit **3SBS**
horrible /ˈhɒrəb(ə)l/ schrecklich **CT5**
° horrid /ˈhɒrɪd/ entsetzlich; grauenhaft **4SBS**
horrifying /ˈhɒrɪˌfaɪɪŋ/ schrecklich; entsetzlich; grauenhaft **3A7**
horse /hɔːs/ Pferd **CT5**
hospital /ˈhɒspɪt(ə)l/ Krankenhaus **CT6**
host /həʊst/ Gastgeber/in; Gast- **CT8**
° host /həʊst/ *hier:* Moderator/in **4Intro 4**
hot /hɒt/ heiß; warm **CT5**
° hot /hɒt/ *hier:* scharf **2SBS**
° hot springs *(pl)* /ˌhɒt ˈsprɪŋz/ heiße Quellen; Thermalquellen **1P1**
° hot-headed /ˌhɒtˈhedɪd/ hitzköpfig **4SBS**
hour /ˈaʊə/ Stunde **CT5**

house /haʊs/ Haus **CT5**
terraced house *(BE)* /ˈterəst haʊs/ Reihenhaus **CT7**
° household /ˈhaʊsˌhəʊld/ Haushalt(s-) **3A7**
how /haʊ/ wie **CT5**
° how to ... /ˈhaʊ tə/ wie man ... **1SBS, 2SBS, 3SBS, 4D10, 5D5**
How about ...? /ˈhaʊ‿əˌbaʊt/ Wie wäre es mit ...? **CT5**
How are you? /ˌhaʊ‿ˈɑː jʊ/ Wie geht es dir/Ihnen/euch? **CT5**
° How come (...)? /ˌhaʊ ˈkʌm/ Wie das?; Wieso (...)? **3B4**
How many ...? /ˌhaʊ ˈmeni/ Wie viele ...? **CT5**
how much /ˌhaʊ ˈmʌtʃ/ wie viel **CT6**
How much is/are ...? /ˈhaʊ mʌtʃ‿ɪz/ə/ Was kostet/kosten ...? **CT5**
How old are you? /ˌhaʊ‿ˈəʊld‿ə jʊ/ Wie alt bist du?; Wie alt seid ihr? **CT5**
however /haʊˈevə/ jedoch; aber **CT7**
° however /haʊˈevə/ *hier:* egal wie **2D10**
° to huddle /ˈhʌd(ə)l/ sich zusammendrängen **3B4**
to **give sb a hug** /ˌɡɪv ˌsʌmbədi‿ə ˈhʌɡ/ jdn umarmen **CT7**
to **hug** /hʌɡ/ umarmen **CT7**
° hug /hʌɡ/ Umarmung **1R4**
huge /hjuːdʒ/ riesig; riesengroß **CT7**
° hula /ˈhuːlə/ Hula(-) *(traditioneller Tanz auf Hawaii)* **3R1**
human /ˈhjuːmən/ Mensch; menschlich **CT7**
° human resources officer /ˌhjuːmən rɪˈzɔːsɪz‿ˌɒfɪsə/ Personalleiter/in **4R3**
° human rights *(pl)* /ˌhjuːmən ˈraɪts/ Menschenrechte **3D3**
° to humiliate /hjuːˈmɪlieɪt/ demütigen; erniedrigen; blamieren **3B4**
humorous /ˈhjuːmərəs/ humorvoll; lustig; witzig **2B3**
° to hunch one's back /ˌhʌntʃ wʌnz ˈbæk/ einen Buckel machen **2D6**
hungry /ˈhʌŋɡri/ hungrig **CT5**
to hunt /hʌnt/ jagen **1A4, 3A6**
° hunter /ˈhʌntə/ Jäger/in **4SBS**
° hunting *(no pl)* /ˈhʌntɪŋ/ Jagen; Jagd(-) **3A3**
° hurdle /ˈhɜːd(ə)l/ Hürde; Hindernis **3SBS**
° hurried /ˈhʌrid/ hastig; überstürzt **1R2**
to **hurry** /ˈhʌri/ sich beeilen **CT7**
Hurry up! /ˌhʌri‿ˈʌp/ Beeil dich!; Beeilt euch! **CT6**
hurt /hɜːt/ verletzt; verwundet **CT6**
to **hurt (sb)** *(irr)* /ˈhɜːt ˌsʌmbədi/ (jdm) wehtun; (jdn) verletzen **CT6**
° husband /ˈhʌzbənd/ (Ehe)mann **2D26**
° hut /hʌt/ Hütte **1B/T1**

I

I /aɪ/ ich **CT5**
° I don't care. /ˌaɪ dəʊn ˈkeə/ Es ist mir egal. **3R5**
I don't like ... /aɪ ˈdəʊnt laɪk/ Ich mag ... nicht. **CT5**
I don't mind ... /ˌaɪ dəʊn ˈmaɪnd/ ... ist mir egal; ... macht mir nichts aus **CT7**
° I hear you. /aɪ ˈhɪə jʊ/ Ich verstehe dich. **3R6, 5D15**
I like ... /aɪ ˈlaɪk/ Ich mag ... **CT5**
I see. /aɪ ˈsiː/ Ich verstehe. **CT8**
I see what you mean. /aɪ ˌsiː wɒt jʊ ˈmiːn/ Ich weiß, was du meinst. **CT7**
° I see your point. /aɪ ˌsiː jə ˈpɔɪnt/ Ich verstehe, was du sagst. **2D12, 5A/T2**
I'd like to (= I would like to) /ˌaɪd ˈlaɪk tʊ/ ich würde gern **CT6**
I'd love to have /ˌaɪd ˈlʌv tə hæv/ ich hätte gerne **CT5**
I'd rather (= I would rather) /aɪd ˈrɑːðə/ ich würde lieber **CT7**
I'm (= I am) /aɪm, ˈaɪ‿əm/ ich bin; *auch:* ich heiße, **CT5**
I'm afraid ... /ˌaɪm‿əˈfreɪd/ Leider ...; Ich fürchte ... **CT5**
I'm from ... /ˈaɪm frəm/ Ich komme aus ... **CT5**
I'm sorry. /ˌaɪm ˈsɒri/ Entschuldigung.; Tut mir leid. **CT5**
ice /aɪs/ Eis **CT5**
ice cream /ˌaɪs ˈkriːm/ Eiscreme; Eis **CT5**
iconic /aɪˈkɒnɪk/ ikonisch; *hier:* kultig, Kult- **5Intro 1**
ID (= identity) (card) /ˌaɪˈdiː kɑːd, aɪˈdentɪti kɑːd/ (Personal)ausweis **CT8**
idea /aɪˈdɪə/ Idee; Einfall **CT5**; Vorstellung **CT6**; Ahnung **CT7**
ideal /aɪˈdɪəl/ Ideal(bild); ideal **CT7**
to **identify** /aɪˈdentɪfaɪ/ identifizieren; feststellen **CT8**
identity /aɪˈdentɪti/ Identität **1A4, 3Intro 2**
° i.e. /ˌaɪ‿ˈiː/ d. h. **5SBS**
if /ɪf/ wenn; falls; ob **CT6**
even if /ˈiːv(ə)n‿ɪf/ selbst wenn **CT7**
° ignorance *(no pl)* /ˈɪɡnərəns/ Ignoranz; Unwissenheit **3SBS**
to **ignore** /ɪɡˈnɔː/ ignorieren; nicht beachten **CT7**
ill fortune /ˌɪl ˈfɔːtʃən/ Pech **3B1**
° illegal /ɪˈliːɡ(ə)l/ ungesetzlich; rechtswidrig; illegal **2D2**
illness /ˈɪlnəs/ Krankheit **2B4**
to **illustrate** /ˈɪləstreɪt/ illustrieren **CT7**
image /ˈɪmɪdʒ/ (Eben)bild; Abbild; Vorstellung **CT8**
° imagination /ɪˌmædʒɪˈneɪʃ(ə)n/ Fantasie; Vorstellungskraft **2D20**
to **imagine** /ɪˈmædʒɪn/ sich vorstellen **CT5**
to **imitate** /ˈɪmɪteɪt/ imitieren; nachahmen **3B6**
° imitation /ˌɪmɪˈteɪʃ(ə)n/ Nachahmung; Kopie **3B4**
immediate /ɪˈmiːdiət/ umgehend; unmittelbar; direkt; augenblicklich **3A1**
immediately /ɪˈmiːdiətli/ sofort; gleich; direkt **CT7**
immigrant /ˈɪmɪɡrənt/ Einwanderer/in; Immigrant/in **CT7**
immigration *(no pl)* /ˌɪmɪˈɡreɪʃ(ə)n/ Einwanderung(s-); Immigration **CT8**
IMO (= in my opinion) /ˌaɪ‿ˌem‿ˈəʊ, ɪn ˈmaɪ‿əˌpɪnjən/ meiner Meinung nach **CT8**
impact /ˈɪmpækt/ Auswirkung; Einfluss **CT8**
° impact /ˈɪmpækt/ hier: Einschlag **4SBS**
to impact /ˈɪmpækt/ beeinflussen; Auswirkungen haben auf **1A3**
impatient /ɪmˈpeɪʃ(ə)nt/ ungeduldig **4Intro 2**
impolite /ˌɪmpəˈlaɪt/ unhöflich; frech; unverschämt **4Intro 2**
importance *(no pl)* /ɪmˈpɔːt(ə)ns/ Bedeutung; Wichtigkeit **CT8**
important /ɪmˈpɔːt(ə)nt/ wichtig; wesentlich; bedeutend **CT5**
impossible /ɪmˈpɒsəb(ə)l/ unmöglich **CT6**
to **impress** /ɪmˈpres/ beeindrucken; imponieren **CT7**
impression /ɪmˈpreʃ(ə)n/ Eindruck **CT7**
impressive /ɪmˈpresɪv/ beeindruckend **3Intro 5**
to **improve** /ɪmˈpruːv/ (sich) verbessern; besser werden **CT7**
in /ɪn/ in **CT5**
° in a flash /ɪn‿ə ˈflæʃ/ in Sekundenschnelle **3B4**
° in a heartbeat /ɪn‿ə ˈhɑːtˌbiːt/ sofort; ohne zu zögern **3B3**
in addition (to) /ɪn‿əˈdɪʃ(ə)n tʊ/ zusätzlich (zu); außerdem; darüber hinaus **CT8**
° in advance /ɪn‿ədˈvɑːns/ im Voraus **5R2**
° in brackets /ɪn ˈbrækɪts/ eingeklammert; in Klammern **2D3, 5D17**
in class /ɪn ˈklɑːs/ im Unterricht **CT5**
° in closing /ɪn ˈkləʊzɪŋ/ abschließend; zum Schluss **5SBS**
in comparison with/to /ɪn kəmˈpærɪs(ə)n wɪð/tʊ/ im Vergleich zu; verglichen mit **CT8**
in conclusion /ɪn kənˈkluːʒ(ə)n/ zum Abschluss; abschließend **2B8**
in contrast to /ɪn ˈkɒntrɑːst‿tʊ/ im Gegensatz zu **CT8**
in fact /ɪn ˈfækt/ genaugenommen **3A5**
° in favour of /ɪn ˈfeɪvər‿əv/ für; zugunsten (von) **3SBS**
° in forever /ɪn fərˈevə/ je(mals) **2SBS**
in front of /ɪn ˈfrʌnt‿əv/ vor **CT5**
in general /ɪn ˈdʒen(ə)rəl/ im Allgemeinen; generell **CT8**
in German /ɪn ˈdʒɜːmən/ auf Deutsch **CT5**
° in memory of sb/sth /ɪn ˈmem(ə)ri‿əv/ zum Gedenken an jdn/etw **5A1**
in my opinion /ɪn ˈmaɪ‿əˌpɪnjən/ meiner Meinung nach **CT7**
° in my view /ɪn ˈmaɪ vjuː/ meiner Meinung nach **2D12, 3A/T1**
° in no uncertain terms /ɪn‿ˌnəʊ‿ʌnˌsɜːt(ə)n ˈtɜːmz/ klar und deutlich **3R5**
° in one's twenties /ˌɪn wʌnz ˈtwentiz/ zwischen 20 und 29 Jahre alt **2B3**
in order to do sth /ɪn‿ˌɔːdə tə ˈduː/ um etw zu tun **CT8**
° in part /ɪn ˈpɑːt/ teilweise; zum Teil **5A/T2**
in particular /ɪn pəˈtɪkjʊlə/ insbesondere; im Speziellen **2A4**
° in person /ɪn ˈpɜːs(ə)n/ persönlich **2D4**
° in public /ɪn ˈpʌblɪk/ in der Öffentlichkeit; öffentlich **2D2, 5D1**
° in reference to /ɪn ˈref(ə)rəns tʊ/ mit Bezug auf **5SBS**
° in relation to /ɪn rɪˈleɪʃ(ə)n tʊ/ in Bezug auf **5A5**
in response to /ɪn rɪˈspɒns tʊ/ in Erwiderung auf; als Antwort auf **4A9**
° in short /ɪn ˈʃɔːt/ kurz gesagt **5SBS**
° in sight /ɪn ˈsaɪt/ in Sicht **2A/T1**
° in spite of /ɪn ˈspaɪt‿əv/ trotz **5B/T1**
in the afternoon /ˌɪn ði‿ɑːftəˈnuːn/ am Nachmittag **CT5**
in the beginning /ˌɪn ðə bɪˈɡɪnɪŋ/ am Anfang; zu Beginn **CT6**
in the end /ˌɪn ði‿ˈend/ letzten Endes; schließlich; zum Schluss **CT6**
in the evening /ˌɪn ði‿ˈiːvnɪŋ/ am Abend **CT6**
° in (the) light of sth /ˌɪn (ðə) ˈlaɪt‿əv/ angesichts einer Sache **3D12**
in the morning /ˌɪn ðə ˈmɔːnɪŋ/ morgens; am Morgen; am Vormittag **CT6**
in-line skating *(no pl)* /ˌɪnˌlaɪn ˈskeɪtɪŋ/ Inlineskaten **CT5**
° inappropriate /ˌɪnəˈprəʊpriət/ ungeeignet; unangebracht; unangemessen **4A/T2**
° inaugural /ɪˈnɔːɡjʊrəl/ Antritts- **3D12**
° inauguration /ɪˌnɔːɡjʊˈreɪʃ(ə)n/ Amtseinführung **3D12**

inch /ɪntʃ/ Zoll *(2,54 cm)* CT8
incident /ˈɪnsɪd(ə)nt/ (Vor)fall; Zwischenfall; Ereignis CT8
to **include** /ɪnˈkluːd/ beinhalten; mit einschließen; aufnehmen CT6
° including /ɪnˈkluːdɪŋ/ einschließlich 1P1, 4A7, 5A1
incomplete /ˌɪnkəmˈpliːt/ unvollständig; unfertig CT7
increase /ˈɪŋkriːs/ Anstieg; Zunahme CT8
to **increase** /ɪnˈkriːs/ (an)steigen; zunehmen; wachsen CT8
° increasingly /ɪnˈkriːsɪŋli/ zunehmend 2D10
incredible /ɪnˈkredəb(ə)l/ unglaublich CT8
° incredulous /ɪnˈkredjʊləs/ ungläubig; fassungslos 3B4
° the in-crowd /ðiˈɪn kraʊd/ Insider-Clique 3B1
independence *(no pl)* /ˌɪndɪˈpendəns/ Unabhängigkeit CT8
independent /ˌɪndɪˈpendənt/ unabhängig; selbstständig CT7
° index card /ˈɪndeks kɑːd/ Karteikarte 2R3
India /ˈɪndiə/ Indien CT7
Indian /ˈɪndiən/ Inder/in; indisch CT7
° Indian Ocean /ˌɪndiən ˈəʊʃ(ə)n/ Indischer Ozean 4P2
° to indicate /ˈɪndɪkeɪt/ (an)zeigen; hindeuten 1SBS
indigenous /ɪnˈdɪdʒənəs/ (ein)heimisch 1A1
° Indigenous Australian /ɪnˌdɪdʒənəs ɒˈstreɪliən/ australische/r Ureinwohner/in 1A5
individual /ˌɪndɪˈvɪdʒuəl/ Einzelne/r; Individuum; einzeln; individuell CT8
industrial /ɪnˈdʌstriəl/ industriell; Industrie- CT8
the Industrial Revolution /ðiˌɪnˌdʌstriəl revəˈluːʃ(ə)n/ die industrielle Revolution 5A1
° industrialization *(no pl)* /ɪnˌdʌstriəlaɪˈzeɪʃ(ə)n/ Industrialisierung Wordbank 2
° industrialized /ɪnˈdʌstriəlaɪzd/ industrialisiert; Industrie- 3A6
industry /ˈɪndəstri/ Industrie; Branche CT8
° inequality /ˌɪnɪˈkwɒləti/ Ungleichheit 3D2
to **influence** /ˈɪnfluəns/ beeinflussen CT8
° influence /ˈɪnfluəns/ Einfluss 3A6, 4P3
° influencer /ˈɪnfluənsə/ *jemand, der in sozialen Netzwerken besonders einflussreich ist* 4A2

to **inform** /ɪnˈfɔːm/ informieren; benachrichtigen; mitteilen CT7
informal /ɪnˈfɔːm(ə)l/ informell; locker; zwanglos CT7
information *(no pl)* /ˌɪnfəˈmeɪʃ(ə)n/ Information(en); Auskunft CT5
informative /ɪnˈfɔːmətɪv/ informativ CT8
° infraction /ɪnˈfrækʃ(ə)n/ Verstoß 2SBS
° ingredient /ɪnˈgriːdiənt/ Zutat; Bestandteil 3B2
° to inhabit /ɪnˈhæbɪt/ bewohnen 1B/T1
inhabitant /ɪnˈhæbɪtənt/ Einwohner/in; Bewohner/in CT8
to **injure** /ˈɪndʒə/ verletzen; schaden CT8
injured /ˈɪndʒəd/ verletzt CT7
° injustice *(no pl)* /ɪnˈdʒʌstɪs/ Ungerechtigkeit; Unrecht 3SBS
° inland /ɪnˈlænd/ ins Landesinnere; im Landesinneren 1A/T2
inn /ɪn/ Gasthaus 5A1
° inner /ˈɪnə/ Innen-; innere(r, s) 1D1, 4SBS
° inner city /ˌɪnə ˈsɪti/ Innenstadt; (Stadt)zentrum 3B2
° innocent /ˈɪnəs(ə)nt/ unschuldig; unbeteiligt; harmlos 3R2
° to inquire /ɪnˈkwaɪə/ sich erkundigen 4D3
° insecure /ˌɪnsɪˈkjʊə/ unsicher; instabil; nicht sicher 1R2, 4R2
inside /ˈɪnˌsaɪd/ innen, in(nerhalb), (nach) drinnen CT6
° insight /ˈɪnsaɪt/ Einsicht; Einblick 4B/T1
° to insist /ɪnˈsɪst/ (darauf) bestehen 3R3
° to inspire /ɪnˈspaɪə/ inspirieren 3D2
° instant /ˈɪnstənt/ Moment; Augenblick 3B3
° instant messaging *(no pl)* /ˌɪnstənt ˈmesɪdʒɪŋ/ Instant Messaging *(sofortige Nachrichtenübermittlung im Chat)* 4A5
instantly /ˈɪnstəntli/ sofort 5A1
instead /ɪnˈsted/ stattdessen CT8
instead of /ɪnˈsted əv/ (an)statt CT8
° instruction /ɪnˈstrʌkʃ(ə)n/ Anweisung; Instruktion 1B4
° integral /ˈɪntɪgrəl/ɪnˈtegrəl/ wesentlich 3A7
artificial intelligence (AI) *(no pl)* /ˌɑːtɪˌfɪʃ(ə)l ɪnˈtelɪdʒ(ə)ns, ˌeɪˈaɪ/ künstliche Intelligenz 5A1
intelligent /ɪnˈtelɪdʒ(ə)nt/ klug; intelligent CT5
° to intend /ɪnˈtend/ beabsichtigen 3B4, 5SBS
° intense /ɪnˈtens/ intensiv 2A/T2
° intent *(no pl)* /ɪnˈtent/ Absicht; Vorsatz 3R1

intention /ɪnˈtenʃ(ə)n/ Absicht CT8
° to interact /ˌɪntərˈækt/ interagieren 1B4, 4A3, 4A5
interest /ˈɪntrəst/ Interesse CT8
° to interest sb /ˈɪntrəst/ jdn interessieren Wordbank 8
interesting /ˈɪntrəstɪŋ/ interessant CT6
° interlude /ˈɪntəluːd/ Periode; Abschnitt; Pause 4SBS
intern /ˈɪntɜːn/ Praktikant/in 2A4, 4A5
on the internet /ˌɒn ðiˈɪntəˌnet/ im Internet CT5
internship (*AE* = **placement** *BE*) /ˈɪntɜrnˌʃɪp/ Praktikum 4A5
° to interpret /ɪnˈtɜːprɪt/ deuten; auslegen; wiedergeben 2B4, 3B4, 4R2
to **interrupt** /ˌɪntəˈrʌpt/ unterbrechen CT8
° intersection /ˈɪntəˌsekʃ(ə)n/ (Straßen)kreuzung 1R1
° interval /ˈɪntəv(ə)l/ (zeitlicher) Abstand; Intervall 4SBS
interview /ˈɪntəˌvjuː/ Interview; Vorstellungsgespräch CT7
job interview /ˈdʒɒb ˌɪntəˌvjuː/ Bewerbungsgespräch; Vorstellungsgespräch CT8
to **interview** /ˈɪntəˌvjuː/ interviewen; befragen CT7
° interviewer /ˈɪntəˌvjuːə/ *hier: jemand, der mit jemandem ein Vorstellungsgespräch führt* 4B1
° to intimidate /ɪnˈtɪmɪdeɪt/ einschüchtern 4SBS
into /ˈɪntuː/ in CT5
to **be into sb/sth** *(informal)* /ˌbi ˈɪntuː/ an jdm/etw interessiert sein CT7
to **introduce** /ˌɪntrəˈdjuːs/ vorstellen CT7; einführen; näherbringen CT8
introduction /ˌɪntrəˈdʌkʃ(ə)n/ Vorstellung; Einleitung; Einführung CT7
° introductory /ˌɪntrəˈdʌkt(ə)ri/ vorbereitend; einleitend 2SBS
° introverted /ˈɪntrəʊˌvɜːtɪd/ introvertiert 2B/T2
° to intrude /ɪnˈtruːd/ stören; eindringen 3B4
to invade /ɪnˈveɪd/ einfallen (in); einmarschieren (in) 3A7
° invader /ɪnˈveɪdə/ Angreifer/in; Eindringling 1SBS, 3A2
to **invent** /ɪnˈvent/ erfinden CT7
invention /ɪnˈvenʃ(ə)n/ Erfindung 5A1
to **invest** /ɪnˈvest/ investieren; anlegen 4Intro 2
° investigation /ɪnˌvestɪˈgeɪʃ(ə)n/ Untersuchung; (Über)prüfung; Ermittlung 3R2

° investigative /ɪnˈvestɪgətɪv/ Forschungs-; Untersuchungs-; Ermittlungs- **3R6**
° investigator /ɪnˈvestɪˌgeɪtə/ Ermittler/in **4SBS**
invitation /ˌɪnvɪˈteɪʃ(ə)n/ Einladung(s-) **CT5**
to **invite** /ɪnˈvaɪt/ einladen **CT6**
to **involve** /ɪnˈvɒlv/ beinhalten; umfassen; betreffen; beteiligen **3A5, 4A3, 5B2**
involvement /ɪnˈvɒlvmənt/ Beteiligung **4A5**
Ireland /ˈaɪələnd/ Irland **CT8**
° Irish /ˈaɪrɪʃ/ irisch **5A1**
° iron /ˈaɪən/ Eisen; eisern **4SBS**
° irrelevant /ɪˈreləvənt/ belanglos; unerheblich; unwichtig **5R1**
is *(irr)* /ɪz/ ist **CT5**
isn't (= is not) /ˈɪznt, ɪz ˈnɒt/ ist nicht **CT5**
island /ˈaɪlənd/ Insel **CT7**
isolated /ˈaɪsəˌleɪtɪd/ abgelegen; isoliert **1A4**
issue /ˈɪʃuː/ Thema; Angelegenheit; Problem; Streitfrage **2A2, 3A7**
° to issue /ˈɪʃ(j)uː/ ausstellen; erteilen; *hier:* veröffentlichen **1B/T1**; *hier:* erlassen **3D13**
it /ɪt/ er; sie; es; ihm; ihr; ihn **CT5**
It doesn't matter. /ɪt‿ˌdʌz(ə)nt ˈmætə/ Das ist nicht wichtig.; Es spielt keine Rolle. **CT7**
° it gets me *(informal)* /ɪt ˈgets miː/ es geht mir auf die Nerven **3B/T1**
IT *(no pl)* **(= information technology)** /ˌaɪ ˈtiː, ˌɪnfəˈmeɪʃ(ə)n tekˌnɒlədʒi/ Informationstechnologie **CT7**
° It takes guts ... *(informal)* /ɪt‿ˌteɪks ˈgʌts/ Man braucht Mut ... **3B3**
it's (= it is) /ɪts, ˈɪt‿ɪz/ es ist; hier spricht; es kostet **CT5**
° It's no good /ɪts ˌnəʊ ˈgʊd/ Es hat keinen Zweck; Es bringt nichts **4R2**
Italian /ɪˈtæliən/ Italiener/in; Italienisch; italienisch **CT8**
° italics *(pl)* /ɪˈtælɪks/ Kursivschrift/-druck **2D23**
Italy /ˈɪtəli/ Italien **CT8**
° item /ˈaɪtəm/ Artikel; Gegenstand **4SBS, 5D7**
° itinerary /aɪˈtɪnərəri/ Reiseroute; Reiseplan **5Intro 4**
its /ɪts/ sein(e); ihr(e) **CT5**
itself /ɪtˈself/ sich; (sich) selbst **CT7**
° ivy-clad /ˈaɪvi klæd/ mit Efeu bewachsen **4SBS**

J

° jack *(informal, AE)* /dʒæk/ rein gar nichts **2SBS**
° to jack (up) /ˌdʒæk‿ˈʌp/ (hoch)heben **2SBS**
jacket /ˈdʒækɪt/ Jacke **CT8**
to jail /dʒeɪl/ einsperren; inhaftieren **5A1**
° jail /dʒeɪl/ Gefängnis **3R5**
° jam /dʒæm/ Marmelade(n-) **4D4**
January /ˈdʒænjuəri/ Januar **CT5**
° Japan /dʒəˈpæn/ Japan **3A3**
° Japanese /ˌdʒæpəˈniːz/ Japaner/in; Japanisch; japanisch **1B2**
° jar /dʒɑː/ Glas; Topf; Krug **4D4**
° jaw /dʒɔː/ Kiefer **2SBS, 4SBS**
jealous /ˈdʒeləs/ eifersüchtig; neidisch **CT7**
° jeez! *(informal, AE)* /dʒiz/ du meine Güte! **3B4**
jellyfish /ˈdʒeliˌfɪʃ/ Qualle **1B7**
° to jerk /dʒɜːk/ ruckartig bewegen **2B3, 4SBS**
° jigsaw /ˈdʒɪgsɔː/ Puzzle(spiel) **4R2**
job /dʒɒb/ Stelle; Job; Arbeit **CT5**
job ad(vert)/job advertisement /ˈdʒɒb‿ˌædvɜːt/ˈdʒɒb‿ədˌvɜːtɪsmənt/ Stellenanzeige **4A5**
job interview /ˈdʒɒb‿ˌɪntəˌvjuː/ Bewerbungsgespräch; Vorstellungsgespräch **CT8**
° job title /ˈdʒɒb ˌtaɪt(ə)l/ Berufsbezeichnung **4B5**
° to jog /dʒɒg/ joggen **5D11**
to **join** /dʒɔɪn/ verbinden; sich anschließen **CT7**
to **join in** /ˌdʒɔɪn‿ˈɪn/ mitmachen **CT6**
joke /dʒəʊk/ Spaß; Streich; Witz **CT7**
to **joke** /dʒəʊk/ scherzen; witzeln; Spaß machen **CT8**
° journalism *(no pl)* /ˈdʒɜːnəˌlɪz(ə)m/ Journalismus **2A4, 3R8**
journey /ˈdʒɜːni/ Reise **CT8**
judge /dʒʌdʒ/ Richter/in; Mitglied einer Jury **CT7**
° to judge /dʒʌdʒ/ (be)urteilen; schätzen **4R3**
° judge of character /ˌdʒʌdʒ‿əv ˈkærɪktə/ Menschenkenner/in **4SBS**
juice /dʒuːs/ Saft **CT5**
July /dʒʊˈlaɪ/ Juli **CT5**
jump /dʒʌmp/ Sprung; Satz **CT6**
to **jump** /dʒʌmp/ springen **CT6**
° to jump in /ˌdʒʌmp‿ˈɪn/ hineinspringen; *hier:* dazwischenreden **5R4**
jumper *(BE)* /ˈdʒʌmpə/ Pullover; Pulli **CT5**
June /dʒuːn/ Juni **CT5**
° jury /ˈdʒʊəri/ Jury; Preisgericht; *hier:* die Geschworenen **3R6**
just /dʒʌst/ nur; bloß; einfach; gerade **CT5**; genau **CT6**; gerecht **1A5, 3Intro 2**
just as ... (as) /ˈdʒʌst‿əz ... əz/ genauso ... (wie) **1B5**
° Just joking/Only joking *(informal)* /ˌdʒʌst ˈdʒəʊkɪŋ/ˌəʊnli ˈdʒəʊkɪŋ/ War (nur) 'n Scherz **4B/T2**
justice *(no pl)* /ˈdʒʌstɪs/ Gerechtigkeit; Justiz **CT8**
° justified /ˈdʒʌstɪfaɪd/ gerechtfertigt; berechtigt **3R2, 5A6**

K

° kangaroo /ˌkæŋgəˈruː/ Känguru **1D8**
° Kaurna /ˈgɑːnə/ *Stamm der Aborigines* **1B/T1**
kayaking *(no pl)* /ˈkaɪækɪŋ/ Kajakfahren **CT5**
° keen /kiːn/ begeistert; leidenschaftlich **1D9**
to **keep** *(irr)* /kiːp/ (bei)behalten; aufbewahren; halten **CT5**
to **keep a diary** /ˌkiːp‿ə ˈdaɪəri/ ein Tagebuch führen **CT6**
° to keep calm /ˌkiːp ˈkɑːm/ die Ruhe bewahren **2SBS**
to **keep cool** /ˌkiːp ˈkuːl/ ruhig bleiben; cool bleiben **CT7**
to **keep doing sth** /ˌkiːp ˈduːɪŋ/ etw (immer) weiter tun **CT7**
° to keep going /ˌkiːp ˈgəʊɪŋ/ weitermachen; weitergehen **2SBS**
° to keep in mind /ˌkiːp‿ɪn ˈmaɪnd/ nicht vergessen **5SBS**; *hier:* berücksichtigen **1SBS**
° to keep sb informed /ˌkiːp ˌsʌmbədi‿ɪnˈfɔːmd/ jdn auf dem Laufenden halten **2R1**
° to keep sb off one's back /ˌkiːp ˌsʌmbədi‿ˌɒf wʌnz ˈbæk/ (sich) jdn vom Leib halten **5R2**
° to keep sb waiting /ˌkiːp ˌsʌmbədi ˈweɪtɪŋ/ jdn warten lassen **4B4**
to keep sth going /ˌkiːp ˌsʌmθɪŋ ˈgəʊɪŋ/ etw in Gang halten **4B4**
to **keep up** *(irr)* /ˌkiːp‿ˈʌp/ hochhalten; aufrechterhalten **CT8**
to **keep up with sb** /ˌkiːp‿ˈʌp wɪð/ mit jdm Schritt halten **CT7**
° to keep up with sth /ˌkiːp‿ˈʌp wɪð/ bei etw auf dem Laufenden bleiben **2B3**
° keeper *(informal, BE)* /ˈkiːpə/ Torhüter/in **1R4**
° key /kiː/ wesentlich; wichtig **4R1**
keyword /ˈkiːˌwɜːd/ Schlüsselwort; Stichwort **CT8**
kid *(informal)* /kɪd/ Kind; Jugendliche/r **CT6**
to **kidnap** /ˈkɪdnæp/ entführen **CT7**
to **kill** /kɪl/ töten; umbringen **CT7**
° killer /ˈkɪlə/ Mörder/in; Killer/in **3R2**
kilometre /kɪˈlɒmɪtə/ Kilometer **CT7**

kind /kaɪnd/ nett; freundlich; liebenswürdig **CT6**; Art; Sorte **CT7**
° kind of /'kaɪnd‿əv/ irgendwie **2SBS**
° kinda (= kind of) *(informal, AE)* /'kaɪndə, 'kaɪnd‿əv/ irgendwie **2R3**
° kindergarten /'kɪndəˌgɑ:t(ə)n/ Kindergarten *(BE)*; Vorschule *(AE)* **3A2**
king /kɪŋ/ König **CT6**
kingdom /'kɪŋdəm/ Königreich **CT7**
to **kiss** /kɪs/ küssen **CT7**
° kiss /kɪs/ Kuss **1R2**
kitchen /'kɪtʃən/ Küche **CT5**
° kiwi /'ki:wi:/ Kiwi *(Frucht oder Vogelart)*; Neuseeländer/in *(umgangssprachlich)* **1P1**
knee /ni:/ Knie **CT7**
° knife (*pl* knives) /naɪf, naɪvz/ Messer **3D6**
pocket knife (*pl* **pocket knives**) /'pɒkɪt naɪf, 'pɒkɪt naɪvz/ Taschenmesser **CT6**
to **knock** /nɒk/ klopfen; stoßen **CT7**
° knock /nɒk/ Klopfen; Schlag **5R1**
° to knock out /ˌnɒk‿'aʊt/ herausschlagen; ausschalten; außer Gefecht setzen **4R2**
to **know** *(irr)* /nəʊ/ wissen; kennen **CT5**
to **get to know sb/sth** /ˌget‿tə 'nəʊ/ jdn/etw kennenlernen **CT7**
° knowingly /'nəʊɪŋli/ wissentlich; bewusst **5A3**
knowledge *(no pl)* /'nɒlɪdʒ/ Kenntnis(se); Wissen **1A3, 4Intro 2**
known /nəʊn/ bekannt **CT8**
Korean American /kəˌriən‿ə'merɪkən/ US-Bürger/in koreanischer Abstammung; koreanisch-amerikanisch **CT8**

L

° lab (= laboratory) /læb, lə'bɒrət(ə)ri/ Labor **2B3**
° label /'leɪb(ə)l/ Etikett; Bezeichnung **2B3**
° labour shortage /'leɪbə ˌʃɔ:tɪdʒ/ Arbeitskräftemangel **4D12**
° to lace (up) /ˌleɪs‿'ʌp/ (zu)schnüren **3B4**
to **lack** /læk/ nicht haben; fehlen **4A9**
lack (of) *(no pl)* /'læk‿əv/ Mangel (an) **5A1**
° lackadaisical /ˌlækə'deɪzɪk(ə)l/ desinteressiert; lustlos **3B4**
° Ladies and gentlemen /ˌleɪdiz‿ən 'dʒent(ə)lmən/ Meine Damen und Herren **2SBS**
° lady /'leɪdi/ Frau; Dame **2D26, 3D17**
° laid-back *(informal)* /ˌleɪd 'bæk/ locker; gelassen **1R2**
lake /leɪk/ See **CT7**
° lame /leɪm/ lahm; schwach **3B4**
lamp /læmp/ Lampe **CT5**
° landscape /'lændˌskeɪp/ Landschaft(s-) **1P1, 2SBS**
language /'læŋgwɪdʒ/ Sprache **CT5**
body language *(no pl)* /'bɒdi ˌlæŋgwɪdʒ/ Körpersprache **2A2**
° languid /'læŋgwɪd/ träge; matt; *hier:* lässig **4SBS**
° lap /læp/ Schoß **4SBS**
large /lɑ:dʒ/ groß **CT8**
last /lɑ:st/ letzte(r, s) **CT6**
° to last /lɑ:st/ (an)dauern; überstehen **2SBS**
° last name /'lɑ:st neɪm/ Familienname **1D16**
late /leɪt/ (zu) spät **CT5**
later /'leɪtə/ später **CT5**
latest /'leɪtɪst/ jüngste(r, s); letzte(r, s); neueste(r, s) **CT7**
Latin /'lætɪn/ Latein(-); lateinisch **CT8**
to **laugh (at sb/sth)** /'lɑ:f‿ət/ lachen (über jdn/etw) **CT5**
to launch /lɔ:ntʃ/ starten; beginnen **5A3**
laundry room /'lɔ:ndri ru:m/ Waschküche **2A6**
law /lɔ:/ Gesetz; Recht **3A5**
° law school *(AE)* /'lɔ: skul/ juristische Fakultät **4D6**
° lawlessness *(no pl)* /'lɔ:ləsnəs/ Gesetzlosigkeit **3R2**
lawyer /'lɔ:jə/ Anwalt/Anwältin **CT8**
to **lay** *(irr)* /leɪ/ legen **5A1**
° to lay out a spiel *(informal)* /ˌleɪ‿ˌaʊt‿ə 'ʃpi:l/ mit der alten Leier kommen **3B3**
to **lay the table** *(BE)* /ˌleɪ ðə 'teɪb(ə)l/ den Tisch decken **CT5**
lazy /'leɪzi/ faul; träge **CT5**
to **lead** *(irr)* /li:d/ führen **CT7**
° leader /'li:də/ Leiter/in; Führer/in **3SBS, 4A/T1, 5SBS**
° leading /'li:dɪŋ/ führend; Haupt- **Wordbank 5**
leaflet /'li:flət/ Flyer; Prospekt **CT6**
° to lean *(irr)* /li:n/ sich beugen; sich lehnen **2A2, 4R1, 5B2**
to **learn** *(irr)* /lɜ:n/ lernen **CT5**; erfahren **CT6**
learning *(no pl)* /'lɜ:(r)nɪŋ/ Lernen; Lern- **CT8**
least /li:st/ am wenigsten **3Intro 3**
to **leave** *(irr)* /li:v/ verlassen; weggehen; (zurück)lassen **CT6**
° to leave *(irr)* /li:v/ *hier:* austreten (aus) **1A2**
to **leave for** *(irr)* /'li:v‿fɔ:/ gehen nach/zu/auf **CT7**
to **leave out** *(irr)* /ˌli:v‿'aʊt/ auslassen; weglassen **CT7**
to **leave sb alone** /ˌli:v ˌsʌmbədi‿ə'ləʊn/ jdn in Ruhe lassen **CT7**
to **leave sb/sth behind** /ˌli:v bɪ'haɪnd/ jdn/etw zurücklassen **CT8**
° Lebanon /'lebənən/ Libanon **3D1**
left /left/ übrig **CT7**
on the left /ˌɒn ðə 'left/ links; auf der linken Seite **CT6**
to **turn right/left** /ˌtɜ:n 'raɪt/'left/ rechts/links abbiegen **CT6**
° left-hand /ˌleft 'hænd/ linke(r, s) **1P1, Wordbank 3**
leg /leg/ Bein **CT5**
° legacy /'legəsi/ Vermächtnis; Erbe **3R6**
legal /'li:g(ə)l/ legal; gesetzlich (vorgeschrieben) **3A7**
° legal system /ˌli:g(ə)l 'sɪstəm/ Rechtssystem **3R3**
° legal term /ˌli:g(ə)l 'tɜ:m/ Rechtsbegriff **3R1**
legend /'ledʒ(ə)nd/ Sage; Legende **CT8**
° leisure *(no pl)* /'leʒə/ Freizeit(-) **4R2**
lemonade /ˌlemə'neɪd/ Limonade **CT5**
length /leŋθ/ Länge **CT8**
less /les/ weniger **CT8**
lesson /'les(ə)n/ (Unterrichts)stunde **CT5**
to **let** *(irr)* /let/ lassen **CT5**
let's (= let us) /lets, 'let‿ʌs/ Lass(t) uns **CT5**
° to let go /ˌlet 'gəʊ/ loslassen; *hier:* entlassen **3B2**
° to let loose /ˌlet 'lu:s/ loslassen; freien Lauf lassen **5D4**
° to let sb know sth /ˌlet ˌsʌmbədi 'nəʊ/ jdn etw wissen lassen; jdn über etw informieren **4D10**
letter /'letə/ Brief; Buchstabe **CT6**
cover letter /ˌkʌvə 'letə/ Anschreiben **4A9**
° letter of recommendation /ˌletər‿əv ˌrekəmen'deɪʃ(ə)n/ Empfehlungsschreiben **Wordbank 8**
° letter to the editor /ˌletə tə ði‿'edɪtə/ Leserbrief **5SBS**
LGBTQ+ /ˌel dʒi: bi: ti: 'kju: 'plʌs/ *Abkürzung für Lesbian, Gay, Bisexual, Transgender and Queer and other kinds of identity* **2Intro 2**
° LGBTQIA+ /ˌel dʒi: bi: ti: kju‿aɪ‿eɪ 'plʌs/ *Abkürzung für Lesbian, Gay, Bisexual, Transgender and Queer (or Questioning), Intersex, Asexual (or Allies) and other kinds of identity* **1R1**
liar /'laɪə/ Lügner/in **CT5**
liberty /'lɪbəti/ Freiheit **CT8**
library /'laɪbrəri/ Bibliothek; Bücherei **CT5**

licence /ˈlaɪs(ə)ns/ Genehmigung; Erlaubnis; *hier:* Führerschein **1B2**
driver's license (*AE* = **driving licence** *BE*) /ˈdraɪvərz ˌlaɪs(ə)ns/ Führerschein **2Intro 2**
to license /ˈlaɪs(ə)ns/ die Lizenz erteilen; erlauben **5A3**
° to lick /lɪk/ (ab)lecken; (ab)schlecken **1R2**
° to lie *(irr)* /laɪ/ liegen; sich hinlegen **1R2, 2D27, 4SBS**
to **lie (to sb)** /ˈlaɪ tʊ/ (jdn be)lügen **CT6**
° life expectancy /ˈlaɪf‿ɪkˌspektənsi/ Lebenserwartung **5D7**
life (*pl* **lives**) /laɪf, laɪvz/ Leben **CT5**
° lifeguard /ˈlaɪfˌgɑːd/ Bademeister/in; Rettungsschwimmer/in **4D1**
° lifestyle /ˈlaɪfˌstaɪl/ Lebensstil **2D2**
° lifetime /ˈlaɪfˌtaɪm/ Leben(szeit) **3B2**
° to lift /lɪft/ (auf)heben **1R4, 5R3**
light /laɪt/ Licht; Lichtquelle; Lampe **CT6**
° to light up *(irr)* /ˌlaɪt‿ˈʌp/ erhellen; aufleuchten **1A6**
° lighting *(no pl)* /ˈlaɪtɪŋ/ Beleuchtung(sanlage) **4R1, Wordbank 5**
° lightly /ˈlaɪtli/ leicht; wenig **4SBS**
traffic lights *(pl)* /ˈtræfɪk laɪts/ Ampel **CT6**
like /laɪk/ wie; als ob **CT6**
to **like** /laɪk/ mögen **CT5**; liken **2A4**
° like this /ˌlaɪk ˈðɪs/ so; auf diese Weise **3B5**
likely /ˈlaɪkli/ wahrscheinlich **CT8**
likewise /ˈlaɪkwaɪz/ ebenfalls; gleichfalls; ebenso **4B4**
° limestone *(no pl)* /ˈlaɪmˌstəʊn/ Kalkstein **1B7**
limit /ˈlɪmɪt/ (Höchst)grenze; Limit **CT8**
to **limit** /ˈlɪmɪt/ einschränken; beschränken; begrenzen **CT8**
° limit /ˈlɪmɪt/ *hier:* Beschränkung **3D9**
° limited /ˈlɪmɪtɪd/ begrenzt; eingeschränkt **3D15, 5D7**
line /laɪn/ Linie; Zeile **CT5**; *hier:* Reihe **CT7**
° line /laɪn/ *hier:* Spruch **1R2**; *hier:* (Warte)schlange **3B4**
line graph /ˈlaɪn grɑːf/ Liniendiagramm **CT8**
lines *(pl)* /laɪnz/ Text *(für Schauspieler/innen)* **5B5**
° link /lɪŋk/ Verbindung; Beziehung; Link **5SBS**
° to link /lɪŋk/ verbinden **3D2, 4R1**
lion /ˈlaɪən/ Löwe **CT5**
° lip /lɪp/ Lippe **1R2, 2A2**
list /lɪst/ Liste **CT6**
to **list** /lɪst/ auflisten **CT8**
to **listen to** /ˈlɪs(ə)n tə/ zuhören; (an)hören **CT5**
° listener /ˈlɪs(ə)nə/ Zuhörer/in **2D11, Intro 4**
° listening *(no pl)* /ˈlɪs(ə)nɪŋ/ Zuhören; *hier:* Hörvermögen **4SBS**
° literally /ˈlɪt(ə)rəli/ buchstäblich; wortwörtlich; wirklich **2R3**
° literate /ˈlɪt(ə)rət/ gebildet **4R1**
literature *(no pl)* /ˈlɪtrətʃə/ (Fach)literatur **CT7**
° to litter /ˈlɪtə/ Müll wegwerfen **1SBS**
little /ˈlɪt(ə)l/ klein(e, er, es) **CT6**
° little /ˈlɪt(ə)l/ wenig **2A/T2, 5D2**
to **live** /lɪv/ leben; wohnen **CT5**
° to live up to sth /ˌlɪv‿ˈʌp tʊ/ etw gerecht werden; etw erfüllen **2D6**
living room /ˈlɪvɪŋ ruːm/ Wohnzimmer **CT5**
to **load** /ləʊd/ (auf)laden; einräumen **CT5**
loads of *(informal)* /ˈləʊdz‿əv/ jede Menge; massenhaft **1B2, 4R3**
local /ˈləʊk(ə)l/ hiesig; örtlich; Ortsansässige/r; Einheimische/r **CT7**
to **be located** /ˌbiː ləʊˈkeɪtɪd/ sich befinden; gelegen sein **CT8**
location /ləʊˈkeɪʃ(ə)n/ Lage; (Stand)ort **CT8**
° to lock /lɒk/ (ab)schließen **3D13**
° to lock sb out /ˌlɒk ˌsʌmbədi‿ˈaʊt/ jdn aussperren **4D4**
° to lock up /ˌlɒk‿ˈʌp/ einsperren **3R5**
° lockdown *(AE)* /ˈlakˌdaʊn/ *Anordnung, den derzeitigen Aufenthaltsort nicht zu verlassen oder sich an einen sichereren Ort zu begeben* **3D13**
° lockdown drill *(AE)* /ˈlakˌdaʊn drɪl/ Abriegelungsübung **3A9**
locker /ˈlɒkə/ Schließfach; Spind **CT8**
° locker room /ˈlɒkə ruːm/ Umkleideraum (mit Schließfächern) **2R3**
to log off /ˌlɒg‿ˈɒf/ sich ausloggen; sich abmelden **2A4**
° logical /ˈlɒdʒɪk(ə)l/ logisch; vernünftig **1B5, 3A10, 5SBS**
lonely /ˈləʊnli/ einsam **CT5**
long /lɒŋ/ lang **CT5**
° look /lʊk/ Blick; Gesichtsausdruck **2SBS, 4SBS**
to **have a look at ...** /ˌhæv‿ə ˈlʊk‿ət/ sich ... ansehen; bei ... nachsehen **CT8**
to **look** /lʊk/ sehen; aussehen; schauen **CT5**
to **look after** /ˌlʊk‿ˈɑːftə/ sich kümmern um **CT6**
to **look at** /ˈlʊk‿ət/ (sich) ansehen; anschauen **CT5**
to **look for** /ˈlʊk fɔː/ suchen nach **CT5**
to **look forward to sth** /ˌlʊk ˈfɔːwəd‿tə/ sich auf etw freuen **CT6**
to **look out for sb/sth** /ˌlʊk‿ˈaʊt fɔː/ nach jdm/etw ausschauen **CT8**
° to look out for sb/sth /ˌlʊk‿ˈaʊt fɔː/ *hier:* auf jdn/etw aufpassen **3D16**
to **look up sth** /ˌlʊk‿ˈʌp/ etw nachschlagen; etw heraussuchen **CT7**
° loosely tucked /ˌluːsli ˈtʌkt/ locker sitzend **4SBS**
to **lose** *(irr)* /luːz/ verlieren; aus den Augen verlieren **CT6**
° to lose it *(informal)* /ˈluːz‿ɪt/ durchdrehen **3B/T1**
to **lose one's way** /ˌluːz wʌnz ˈweɪ/ sich verirren **CT6**
lost /lɒst/ verlaufen; verloren **CT7**
to **get lost** /ˌget ˈlɒst/ sich verirren; sich verlaufen **CT6**
° lot *(informal, BE)* /lɒt/ Trupp; Haufen; Pack **4R1**
lots of *(informal)* /ˈlɒts‿əv/ viel(e); eine Menge **CT5**
loud /laʊd/ laut **CT6**
love /lʌv/ Liebe **CT6**
to **love** /lʌv/ lieben; sehr mögen **CT5**
° loved ones /ˈlʌvd wʌnz/ die Liebsten; die Angehörigen **2A4**
lovely /ˈlʌvli/ schön; hübsch; lecker **CT6**
lover /ˈlʌvə/ Liebende/r; Liebhaber/in **CT7**
loving /ˈlʌvɪŋ/ liebevoll **2B3**
low /ləʊ/ niedrig; gering; tief **CT6**
° lower /ˈləʊə/ niedriger; untere(r, s) **1SBS**
° to lower /ˈləʊə/ senken; verringern **5B2**
(good) luck /ˌgʊd ˈlʌk/ Glück **CT6**
Good luck! /ˌgʊd ˈlʌk/ Viel Glück! **CT7**
° luckily /ˈlʌkɪli/ glücklicherweise; zum Glück **5R4**
luggage *(no pl)* /ˈlʌgɪdʒ/ (Reise)gepäck **CT8**
lunch /lʌntʃ/ Mittagessen **CT5**
to **have lunch** /ˌhæv ˈlʌntʃ/ zu Mittag essen **CT5**
° lush /lʌʃ/ saftig (grün) **1P1**
° luxurious /lʌgˈʒʊəriəs/ luxuriös; Luxus- **3D10**
° lyrical /ˈlɪrɪk(ə)l/ lyrisch **3D12**
lyrics *(pl)* /ˈlɪrɪks/ (Lied)text **CT6**

M

° ma *(informal)* /mɑː/ Mama; Mutti **3R1**
machine /məˈʃiːn/ Maschine; Apparat **5A1**
to **be mad about sb/sth** /ˌbiː ˈmæd‿əˌbaʊt/ nach jdm/etw verrückt sein **CT7**
° mad /mæd/ wahnsinnig; verrückt; *hier:* wütend **3R3**

magazine /ˌmægəˈziːn/ Zeitschrift; Magazin **CT7**
° magic *(no pl)* /ˈmædʒɪk/ Magie; Zauber **3R1**
° magnificent /mægˈnɪfɪs(ə)nt/ wunderbar; großartig; hervorragend **Wordbank 5**
main /meɪn/ Haupt- **CT6**
° main course /ˈmeɪn kɔːs/ Hauptgericht; Hauptgang **3B4**
° main office /ˌmeɪn‿ˈɒfɪs/ Hauptverwaltung **3D13**
mainly /ˈmeɪnli/ hauptsächlich; in erster Linie **5A1**
majesty /ˈmædʒəsti/ Majestät **CT7**
major /ˈmeɪdʒə/ bedeutend; wichtig; schwer **CT8**
majority /məˈdʒɒrəti/ Mehrheit(s-) **CT8**; Großteil **2A6**
to **make** *(irr)* /meɪk/ machen; erstellen **CT5**
° to make a habit of sth /ˌmeɪk‿ə ˈhæbɪt‿əv/ etw zur Gewohnheit werden lassen **3B4**
° to make a/your point /ˌmeɪk‿ə/jə ˈpɔɪnt/ etw ansprechen; (s)ein Argument einbringen; *hier:* (s)einen Standpunkt deutlich machen **4SBS, 5R4, 5SBS**; mit etw recht haben **Wordbank 6**
° to make eye contact /ˌmeɪk‿ˈaɪ ˌkɒntækt/ Blickkontakt aufnehmen **1B8**
to **make friends (with sb)** /ˌmeɪk ˈfrendz wɪð/ (mit jdm) Freundschaft schließen **CT7**
to **make fun of sb** /ˌmeɪk ˈfʌn‿əv/ sich über jdn lustig machen **CT7**
° to make one's mark /ˌmeɪk wʌnz ˈmɑːk/ auffallen; Aufsehen erregen **2SBS**
to **make sb do sth** /ˌmeɪk ˌsʌmbədi ˈduː/ jdn zu etwas bringen; jdn etwas tun lassen **CT7**
° to make sense /ˌmeɪk ˈsens/ (einen) Sinn ergeben **3R3, 4R3**
° to make sense of sth /ˌmeɪk ˈsens‿əv/ sich auf etw einen Reim machen **5R1**
to **make sth** /ˈmeɪk ˌsʌmθɪŋ/ etw schaffen; in etw reinkommen **CT7**
to **make sure (that)** /ˌmeɪk ˈʃɔː ðət/ darauf achten, (dass) **CT5**; sicherstellen, (dass) **CT6**
to **make up** /ˌmeɪk‿ˈʌp/ erfinden; (sich) ausdenken **CT7**
° to make up one's mind /ˌmeɪk‿ˌʌp wʌnz ˈmaɪnd/ sich entscheiden **4B/T2**
° male /meɪl/ männlich **2B3**
° man *(informal)* /mæn/ Mann; Mensch **5B7**
man (*pl* **men**) /mæn, men/ Mann **CT5**

° to manage /ˈmænɪdʒ/ leiten; führen; managen; *hier:* umgehen **2D28**
to **manage sth** /ˈmænɪdʒ/ etw schaffen **CT8**
° manager /ˈmænɪdʒə/ Manager/in; Leiter/in **4D7**
° Mancunian /mænˈkjuːniən/ Einwohner/in der Stadt Manchester; aus Manchester **5D9**
° Mandarin /ˈmændərɪn/ Mandarin *(chinesische Hochsprache)* **4P4**
° to manifest /ˈmænɪfest/ (sich) zeigen **2B3**
° manner /ˈmænə/ Weise; Art **4SBS**
° manners *(pl)* /ˈmænəz/ Manieren; (gutes) Benehmen **4A/T1**
to **manufacture** /ˌmænjʊˈfæktʃə/ herstellen **5A1**
° manufacturing *(no pl)* /ˌmænjʊˈfæktʃərɪŋ/ Herstellung(s-); Fertigung **5D7**
many /ˈmeni/ viele **CT5**
° Maori /ˈmaʊri/ Maori(-); maorisch **1P1**
map /mæp/ (Land)karte; (Stadt)plan **CT6**
March /mɑːtʃ/ März **CT5**
march /mɑːtʃ/ Marsch **1A5, 3B3**
to **march** /mɑːtʃ/ marschieren **CT7**
° marine /məˈriːn/ Meeres-; Schiffs-; Marine- **1B2**
° marine biologist /məˌriːn baɪˈɒlədʒɪst/ Meeresbiologie/Meeresbiologin **1B7**
° marine science /məˌriːn ˈsaɪəns/ Meereskunde **1B2**
° marital status *(no pl)* /ˌmærɪt(ə)l ˈsteɪtəs/ Familienstand **4A7**
to **mark** /mɑːk/ markieren; kennzeichnen **1A5**
° mark /mɑːk/ Fleck; (Kenn)zeichen; Marke **2D5**
to add one's mark to sth /ˌæd‿wʌnz ˈmɑːk tʊ/ etw prägen; etw seinen Stempel aufdrücken **4A5**
° mark *(BE)* /mɑːk/ Note; Zensur **5B2**
market /ˈmɑːkɪt/ Markt **CT6**
° marriage /ˈmærɪdʒ/ Heirat; Trauung; Ehe **2D23**
married /ˈmærid/ verheiratet **CT7**
to **get married** /ˌget ˈmærid/ heiraten **CT7**
to **marry** /ˈmæri/ heiraten **CT7**
° to marry sb off (to sb) /ˌmæri ˌsʌmbədi‿ˈɒf tʊ/ jdn (mit jdm) verheiraten **2D26**
mascot /ˈmæskɒt/ Maskottchen **4Intro 2**
° mask /mɑːsk/ Maske; Fassade **2SBS**
mass /mæs/ Masse; Massen-; Menge **CT7**
° to mass /mæs/ sich ansammeln; anwachsen **3B2**

° mass-produced /ˌmæs prəˈdjuːst/ in Massenproduktion hergestellt **5D7**
° massive /ˈmæsɪv/ riesig; enorm; massiv **3D16**
° masterpiece /ˈmɑːstəˌpiːs/ Meisterwerk; Meisterstück **5D2**
match /mætʃ/ Spiel; Partie **CT7**
to **match** /mætʃ/ zuordnen **CT6**
° match /mætʃ/ Treffer; Zuordnung **2SBS**
to **match sth** /ˈmætʃ/ zu etw passen **CT8**
° matchmaking *(no pl)* /ˈmætʃˌmeɪkɪŋ/ (Ver)kuppeln **2D21**
° mate *(informal, BE)* /meɪt/ Freund/in; Kumpel **4R2**
° mathematician /ˌmæθ(ə)məˈtɪʃ(ə)n/ Mathematiker/in **5A1**
maths *(informal, pl)* /mæθs/ Mathe(unterricht) **CT5**
° matter /ˈmætə/ Angelegenheit; Sache **3SBS**
° to matter /ˈmætə/ von Bedeutung sein **2D4, 5SBS**
It doesn't matter. /ɪt‿ˌdʌz(ə)nt ˈmætə/ Das ist nicht wichtig.; Es spielt keine Rolle. **CT7**
matter-of-fact /ˌmætər‿əv‿ˈfækt/ sachlich; nüchtern **5A5**
° maximum-security prison /ˌmæksɪməm sɪˌkjʊərəti ˈprɪz(ə)n/ Hochsicherheitsgefängnis **3R1**
May /meɪ/ Mai **CT5**
may /meɪ/ können; dürfen **CT6**
maybe /ˈmeɪbi/ vielleicht; möglicherweise **CT5**
mayor /meə/ Bürgermeister/in **CT8**
me /miː/ mir; mich **CT5**
meal /miːl/ Mahlzeit; Essen **CT6**
to **mean** *(irr)* /miːn/ bedeuten; meinen **CT6**
I see what you mean. /aɪ ˌsiː wɒt jʊ ˈmiːn/ Ich weiß, was du meinst. **CT7**
to **mean to do sth** /ˌmiːn tə ˈduː/ etw tun wollen; etw beabsichtigen **CT7**
° mean /miːn/ gemein; fies **3B4**
meaning /ˈmiːnɪŋ/ Bedeutung **CT7**
° meaningful /ˈmiːnɪŋf(ə)l/ bedeutsam; wichtig; bedeutungsvoll; *hier:* sinnvoll **1A7**
means (of) /ˈmiːnz‿əv/ Weg; Mittel; Art **3A5**
meanwhile /ˈmiːnˌwaɪl/ inzwischen; unterdessen; mittlerweile **1A5**
measure /ˈmeʒə/ Maßnahme; Maß; Messgerät **3A7, 5A1**
° measured /ˈmeʒəd/ gemäßigt; bedächtig; wohl überlegt **3R5**
° meat /miːt/ Fleisch **5D17**
° to mechanize /ˈmekənaɪz/ mechanisieren **5D7**
° medal /ˈmed(ə)l/ Medaille **5D2**

° medallist /ˈmed(ə)lɪst/ Medaillengewinner/in **1D9, 5D13**
medical /ˈmedɪk(ə)l/ medizinisch; ärztlich **CT7**
° medical /ˈmedɪk(ə)l/ *hier:* Medizin- **3SBS**
medication /ˌmedɪˈkeɪʃ(ə)n/ Medikament(e) **2B4**
medicine *(no pl)* /ˈmed(ə)s(ə)n/ Medizin; Medikamente **CT6**
medium (*pl* media) /ˈmiːdiəm, ˈmiːdiə/ (Informations)medium **2A1, 5Intro 1**
to **meet** *(irr)* /miːt/ (sich) treffen **CT5**; kennenlernen **CT7**; *hier:* erfüllen, entsprechen **5A3**
to **meet up (with sb)** /ˌmiːt‿ˈʌp wɪð/ (jdn) treffen **CT8**
melody /ˈmelədi/ Melodie **CT6**
member /ˈmembə/ Mitglied **CT7**
° memoirs *(pl)* /ˈmemˌwɑːz/ (Lebens)erinnerungen; Memoiren **1R1**
° memorial /məˈmɔːriəl/ Denkmal **5D6**
° to memorize /ˈmeməraɪz/ sich einprägen; auswendig lernen **4B/T1**
memory /ˈmem(ə)ri/ Gedächtnis; Andenken; Erinnerung **CT8**
° mental /ˈment(ə)l/ geistig; mental; psychisch **2B5**
mental health *(no pl)* /ˌment(ə)l ˈhelθ/ psychische Gesundheit **2Intro 2**
to **mention** /ˈmenʃ(ə)n/ erwähnen **4A1**
mentoring *(no pl)* /ˈmentərɪŋ/ *Beratung und Unterstützung durch erfahrene Fach- oder Führungskräfte* **1A4**
menu /ˈmenjuː/ Speisekarte **CT5**
° to merge /mɜːdʒ/ verschmelzen; zusammenkommen **4SBS**
° to mess sth up *(informal)* /ˌmes‿sʌmθɪŋ‿ˈʌp/ etw vermasseln; etw in Unordnung bringen **4SBS**
message /ˈmesɪdʒ/ Nachricht; Botschaft **CT6**
voice message /ˈvɔɪs ˌmesɪdʒ/ Sprachnachricht **CT7**
to **message sb** /ˈmesɪdʒ/ jdm eine (elektronische) Nachricht schicken **CT6**
messaging *(no pl)* /ˈmesɪdʒɪŋ/ (Text)nachrichtenversand **CT7**
° messy /ˈmesi/ unordentlich; schlampig **1R4**
° metre /ˈmiːtə/ Meter **1D2**
° microphone /ˈmaɪkrəˌfəʊn/ Mikrofon **4B1**
° microplastics *(pl)* /ˈmaɪkrəʊˌplæstɪks/ Mikroplastik *(sehr kleine Kunststoffteilchen)* **1B7**
° mid(-) /mɪd/ Mitte (der) **5D7**
middle /ˈmɪd(ə)l/ Mitte **CT6**
° middle-class /ˌmɪd(ə)l ˈklɑːs/ Mittelschicht- **3B1**
midnight *(no pl)* /ˈmɪdˌnaɪt/ Mitternacht **CT6**
° midterms *(pl, AE)* /ˈmɪdtɜːrmz/ Halbjahresprüfungen **2R3**
might /maɪt/ könnte; vielleicht **CT7**
mile /maɪl/ Meile *(= 1,609 km)* **CT7**
military /ˈmɪlɪt(ə)ri/ Militär(-); militärisch **3A7, 5A1**
° milk *(no pl)* /mɪlk/ Milch **5D9**
° Millennials *(pl)* /mɪˈleniəlz/ *auch Gen(eration) Y genannt, bezeichnet die Generation der zwischen 1981 und 1996 Geborenen* **2Intro 2**
° millennium /mɪˈleniəm/ Jahrtausend; *hier:* Jahrtausendwende **4R1**
° mind /maɪnd/ Geist; Verstand; Kopf **2B1, 4SBS, 5R4**; *hier:* Gedanken **1R4**
I don't mind ... /ˌaɪ dəʊn ˈmaɪnd/ ... ist mir egal; ... macht mir nichts aus **CT7**
mine /maɪn/ meine(r, s); meins **CT6**
° mining *(no pl)* /ˈmaɪnɪŋ/ Bergbau(-) **5P1**
prime minister /ˌpraɪm‿ˈmɪnɪstə/ Premierminister/in; Ministerpräsident/in **1A3**
minority /maɪˈnɒrəti/ Minderheit **CT8**
minute /ˈmɪnɪt/ Minute **CT5**
mirror /ˈmɪrə/ Spiegel **CT7**
miserable /ˈmɪz(ə)rəb(ə)l/ unglücklich; elend; armselig **CT6**
misinformation *(no pl)* /ˌmɪsɪnfəˈmeɪʃ(ə)n/ falsche Information; Fehlinformation(en) **2A4**
to **miss** /mɪs/ verpassen; verfehlen; vermissen **CT6**
Miss *(BE)* /mɪs/ *hier:* Frau Lehrerin *(Anrede)* **CT6**
° to miss out /ˌmɪs‿ˈaʊt/ verpassen; sich entgehen lassen **2D7**; *hier:* das Nachsehen haben **5D4**
° to miss the point /ˌmɪs ðə ˈpɔɪnt/ an der Sache vorbeigehen **5SBS**
missing /ˈmɪsɪŋ/ verschwunden; fehlend **CT6**
mistake /mɪˈsteɪk/ Fehler; Irrtum; Versehen **CT5**
mistreatment *(no pl)* /mɪsˈtriːtmənt/ Misshandlung; schlechte Behandlung **1A3**
mixed /mɪkst/ gemischt; zweideutig **CT7**
(mobile) phone /ˌməʊbaɪl ˈfəʊn/ (Mobil)telefon; Handy **CT5**
model /ˈmɒd(ə)l/ Modell; Muster; Vorlage **CT7**
mom *(informal, AE)* /mɑm/ Mama **CT8**
moment /ˈməʊmənt/ Moment; Augenblick **CT7**
at the moment /ət ðə ˈməʊmənt/ im Augenblick; momentan **CT5**
° momentarily /ˈməʊmənt(ə)r(ə)li/ kurz; eine Weile; momentan **4SBS**
monarch /ˈmɒnək/ Monarch/in; Herrscher/in **CT7**
Monday /ˈmʌndeɪ/ Montag **CT5**
money *(no pl)* /ˈmʌni/ Geld **CT5**
pocket money /ˈpɒkɪt mʌni/ Taschengeld **CT6**
month /mʌnθ/ Monat **CT5**
° monument /ˈmɒnjʊmənt/ Denkmal; Monument **5SBS**
mood /muːd/ Laune; Stimmung **CT7**
moon /muːn/ Mond **CT7**
° moor /mʊə/ Heideland; (Hoch)moor **5P1**
° mop /mɒp/ Mopp; Wischer; *hier:* Haarbüschel **4SBS**
more /mɔː/ (noch) mehr; weitere(r, s) **CT5**
morning /ˈmɔːnɪŋ/ Morgen; Vormittag **CT5**
in the morning /ˌɪn ðə ˈmɔːnɪŋ/ morgens; am Morgen; am Vormittag **CT6**
° mortality /mɔːˈtæləti/ Sterblichkeit(s-) **3A3**
most /məʊst/ (die) meisten **CT6**
mostly /ˈməʊstli/ meistens; größtenteils; hauptsächlich **CT8**
mother /ˈmʌðə/ Mutter **CT5**
° motion /ˈməʊʃ(ə)n/ Bewegung **2D27**
° to motion (for) sb to do sth /ˌməʊʃ(ə)n fə ˌsʌmbədi tə ˈduː/ jdn durch einen Wink auffordern, etw zu tun **2SBS**
° to motivate /ˈməʊtɪveɪt/ motivieren; veranlassen **5B4**
motivated /ˈməʊtɪˌveɪtɪd/ motiviert **4A5**
motivation *(no pl)* /ˌməʊtɪˈveɪʃ(ə)n/ Begründung; Motivation **3B3**
° motivational speaker /ˌməʊtɪˌveɪʃ(ə)nəl ˈspiːkə/ *Vortragsredner/in, der/die es versteht, das Publikum für ein bestimmtes Thema zu motivieren* **1D9**
° motive /ˈməʊtɪv/ Motiv; Beweggrund **5R2**
motorway *(BE)* /ˈməʊtəˌweɪ/ Autobahn **CT7**
° mound settlement /ˈmaʊnd ˌset(ə)lmənt/ (Erd)hügelsiedlung **1B/T1**
mountain /ˈmaʊntɪn/ Berg **CT7**
° mountain range /ˈmaʊntɪn reɪndʒ/ Gebirgszug **1P1**
° mountaineering *(no pl)* /ˌmaʊntɪˈnɪərɪŋ/ Bergsteigen **4D6**
mouse (*pl* mice) /maʊs, maɪs/ Maus **CT5**
mouth /maʊθ/ Mund **CT5**

to **move** /mu:v/ (sich) bewegen **CT5**; (um)ziehen **CT7**
° move /mu:v/ Bewegung **2SBS**
° to move along /ˌmu:v‿əˈlɒŋ/ weitergehen; *hier:* weitermachen **2R7**
° to move in with sb /ˌmu:v‿ˈɪn wɪð/ bei jdm einziehen **3B1, 5R2**
° to move on to sth /ˌmu:v‿ˈɒn tʊ/ zu etw übergehen **1A/T1**
° to move out /ˌmu:v‿ˈaʊt/ ausziehen; wegräumen **3D16**
moved /mu:vd/ bewegt; gerührt **CT7**
movement /ˈmu:vmənt/ Bewegung **CT8**
movie *(AE)* /ˈmuvi/ (Kino)film **CT8**
° moving /ˈmu:vɪŋ/ beweglich; (sich) bewegend **2B/T1**
mph (= miles per hour) /ˌem pi‿ˈeɪtʃ, ˌmaɪlz pər‿ˈaʊə/ *Meilen pro Stunde* **CT8**
Mr (= Mister) /ˈmɪstə/ Herr *(Anrede)* **CT5**
Mrs /ˈmɪsɪz/ Frau *(Anrede)* **CT5**
Ms /məz/ Fr.; Frau *(Alternativbezeichnung zu Mrs und Miss, die sowohl für verheiratete wie unverheiratete Frauen zutrifft)* **CT6**
much /mʌtʃ/ viel **CT5**
How much is/are ...? /ˈhaʊ mʌtʃ‿ɪz/ə/ Was kostet/kosten ...? **CT5**
° mug /mʌg/ Becher *(mit Henkel)*; Tasse **4SBS**
° multi- /ˈmʌlti/ Multi-; Viel- **1A5, 5R4**
multicultural /ˌmʌltiˈkʌltʃərəl/ multikulturell **1A5, 5A1**
° multiple /ˈmʌltɪp(ə)l/ vielfach; mehrere **5A1**
mum *(informal)* /mʌm/ Mama; Mutti **CT5**
° to mumble /ˈmʌmb(ə)l/ murmeln; nuscheln **1R2, 2SBS**
° mural /ˈmjʊərəl/ Wandgemälde **5D1**
murder /ˈmɜ:də/ Mord; Ermordung **CT8**
° murky /ˈmɜ:ki/ trüb; düster **5SBS**
° murmur /ˈmɜ:mə/ Gemurmel **4SBS**
° to murmur /ˈmɜ:mə/ murmeln; raunen **2SBS**
° Murri (people) /ˈmʌri ˌpi:p(ə)l/ *Bezeichnung für die indigenen Einwohner in Queensland* **1A5**
muscle /ˈmʌs(ə)l/ Muskel **CT7**
music /ˈmju:zɪk/ Musik(unterricht) **CT5**
musician /mjuˈzɪʃ(ə)n/ Musiker/in **1A4**
a must /ə ˈmʌst/ ein Muss **CT6**
must /mʌst/ müssen **CT5**
mustn't (= must not) /ˈmʌsnt, mʌst ˈnɒt/ nicht dürfen **CT5**
° muted /ˈmju:tɪd/ gedämpft; stumm; gedeckt **2D19**
my /maɪ/ mein(e) **CT5**
° (my) goodness *(informal)* /maɪ ˈgʊdnəs/ du meine Güte; du liebe Zeit **2R2**
to **my mind** /tə ˈmaɪ maɪnd/ meiner Meinung nach **CT8**
My name is ... /ˈmaɪ neɪm‿ɪz/ Ich heiße ... **CT5**
myself /maɪˈself/ mir; mich; ich (selbst) **CT7**
mystery /ˈmɪst(ə)ri/ Geheimnis; Rätsel **CT7**
° mystery /ˈmɪst(ə)ri/ *hier:* Mystery *(Film, Roman o. Ä., in dem es um schaurige, übernatürliche Ereignisse geht)* **Wordbank 5**

N

° nail /neɪl/ (Finger)nagel **4SBS**
° naked /ˈneɪkɪd/ nackt **1D16**
name /neɪm/ Name **CT5**
to **name** /neɪm/ (be)nennen **CT7**
° to name /neɪm/ *hier:* ernennen, wählen **1D9**
narrative /ˈnærətɪv/ Erzählung; Erzähl-; Schilderung **3B2**
narrator /nəˈreɪtə/ Erzähler/in **CT7**
° narrow /ˈnærəʊ/ eng; schmal **4SBS**
° to narrow /ˈnærəʊ/ (sich) verengen **5R1**
nasty /ˈnɑ:sti/ scheußlich; schlimm; ekelhaft; übel **CT6**
national /ˈnæʃ(ə)nəl/ national **CT7**
° National Rifle Association (NRA) /ˌnæʃ(ə)nəl ˈraɪf(ə)l‿əˌsəʊsiˌeɪʃ(ə)n (ˌen‿ɑ:r‿ˈeɪ)/ *US-Waffenverband und Lobbyorganisation* **3D6**
° nationality /ˌnæʃəˈnæləti/ Nationalität; Staatsangehörigkeit **4A7**
native /ˈneɪtɪv/ einheimisch; eingeboren **1A5**
Native American /ˌneɪtɪv‿əˈmerɪkən/ amerikanischer Ureinwohner/ amerikanische Ureinwohnerin **CT8**
° native language /ˌneɪtɪv ˈlæŋgwɪdʒ/ Muttersprache **4P5**
native speaker /ˌneɪtɪv ˈspi:kə/ Muttersprachler/in **4A7**
natural /ˈnætʃ(ə)rəl/ natürlich; angeboren; Natur- **CT7**
natural disaster /ˌnætʃ(ə)rəl dɪˈzɑ:stə(ə)ri/ Naturkatastrophe **CT8**
nature *(no pl)* /ˈneɪtʃə/ Natur **CT6**
naval officer /ˌneɪv(ə)l‿ˈɒfɪsə/ Marineoffizier/in **1A5**
° to navigate /ˈnævɪgeɪt/ navigieren; steuern **5D5**
° navigation /ˌnævɪˈgeɪʃ(ə)n/ Navigation(skunde) **1B2**
navy /ˈneɪvi/ Marine(-); (See)flotte; marineblau **CT7**
near /nɪə/ nahe; in der Nähe **CT5**
° nearby /ˌnɪəˈbaɪ/ in der Nähe (gelegen); nahe gelegen **1B2**
nearly /ˈnɪəli/ fast; beinahe **CT8**
° neat /ni:t/ ordentlich; sauber **4SBS**
necessary /ˈnesəs(ə)ri/ nötig; notwendig; erforderlich **CT6**
need /ni:d/ Bedarf; Notwendigkeit; Bedürfnis **CT7**
to **need** /ni:d/ müssen; brauchen **CT5**
needn't (= need not) /ˈni:dnt, ni:d ˈnɒt/ nicht müssen; nicht brauchen **CT5**
negative /ˈnegətɪv/ negativ; ablehnend **CT6**
neighbour /ˈneɪbə/ Nachbar/in **CT5**
neighbourhood /ˈneɪbəˌhʊd/ Nachbarschaft; (Wohn)viertel; Gegend **CT7**
° neither ... nor ... /ˌnaɪðə ˈnɔ:/ weder ... noch **4SBS**
° neither of ... /ˈnaɪðər‿əv/ keine(r)/ kein(e)s von ... beiden **3B2**
° nephew /ˈnefju:/ˈnevju:/ Neffe **4D7**
to **get on sb's nerves** /ˌget‿ɒn ˌsʌmbədiz ˈnɜ:vz/ jdm auf die Nerven gehen **CT7**
nervous /ˈnɜ:vəs/ nervös **CT5**
° net /net/ Netz **1R4, 3R2**
° the Netherlands /ðə ˈneðələndz/ die Niederlande **3A3**
never /ˈnevə/ nie(mals) **CT5**
° to never hear the end of it /ˌnevə hɪə ði‿ˈend‿əv‿ɪt/ ewig davon sprechen **2SBS**
° never-ending /ˌnevərˈendɪŋ/ endlos; unaufhörlich **5R1**
° nevertheless /ˌnevəðəˈles/ trotzdem; dennoch; nichtsdestoweniger **5B/T1**
new /nju:/ neu **CT5**
° the New Testament /ðə ˌnju: ˈtestəmənt/ das Neue Testament **5D2**
New Year's Eve /ˌnju: jɪəz‿ˈi:v/ Silvester **CT6**
° New Zealand /nju ˈzi:lənd/ Neuseeland **1D7, 5R4**
° New Zealander /nju ˈzi:ləndə/ Neuseeländer/in **1P1**
news *(pl)* /nju:z/ Neuigkeit; Nachricht **CT6**
° news report /ˈnju:z rɪˌpɔ:t/ Nachrichtenbeitrag; Meldung **2B11**
newspaper /ˈnju:zˌpeɪpə/ Zeitung(s-) **CT6**
quality newspaper /ˈkwɒləti ˌnju:zˌpeɪpə/ seriöse (Tages)zeitung **5A3**
next /nekst/ nächste(r, s) **CT5**; als Nächste(r, s) **CT6**
next door /ˌnekst‿ˈdɔ:/ nebenan; benachbart **CT7**
next to /ˈnekst‿tə/ neben **CT5**

nice /naɪs/ schön; angenehm; nett; freundlich; gut **CT5**
° nickname /ˈnɪkˌneɪm/ Spitzname; Kosename **3R1**
night /naɪt/ Nacht; Abend **CT5**
at night /ət‿ˈnaɪt/ nachts **CT6**
nightmare /ˈnaɪtˌmeə/ Albtraum **CT6**
nine /naɪn/ neun **CT5**
no /nəʊ/ nein; kein/e **CT5**
no. (= number) /ˈnʌmbə/ Nummer **CT7**
° no doubt /ˌnəʊ ˈdaʊt/ zweifellos; ohne Zweifel **2B3**
° no longer /nəʊ ˈlɒŋgə/ nicht mehr **1R4, 2D2, 5SBS**
no matter ... /ˌnəʊ ˈmætə/ egal(,) ... **1A5**
° no matter what /ˌnəʊ ˌmætə ˈwɒt/ egal wie **3R2**
no one /ˈnəʊ wʌn/ niemand **CT6**
No way! *(informal)* /ˌnəʊ ˈweɪ/ Ausgeschlossen! **CT7**
° no worries *(informal, AusE)* /ˌnəʊ ˈwʌriz/ kein Problem; gern geschehen **1Intro 3, 5B4**
nobody /ˈnəʊbɒdi/ niemand; keiner **CT7**
° nod /nɒd/ Nicken **5B4**
° to nod /nɒd/ nicken **1R2, 2SBS, 4SBS, 3B2, 5R1**
noise /nɔɪz/ Lärm; Krach; Geräusch **CT8**
noisy /ˈnɔɪzi/ laut **CT5**
° non- /nɒn/ Nicht(-); nicht **1A3**
° non-fiction *(no pl)* /ˌnɒn ˈfɪkʃ(ə)n/ Sachliteratur(-) **2R2, 3R8**
° non-profit /ˌnɒn ˈprɒfɪt/ gemeinnützig; nicht gewinnorientiert **1A4, 3R1**
° non-verbal /ˌnɒnˈvɜːb(ə)l/ nonverbal **2D7**
° nonchalant /ˈnɒnʃələnt/ nonchalant; gleichgültig **4SBS**
° nondescript /ˈnɒndɪˌskrɪpt/ unscheinbar; undefinierbar **4SBS**
° none /nʌn/ keine(r, s); niemand; nichts **5D17**
° nope *(informal)* /nəʊp/ nö **4B/T2**
° nor /nɔː/ und auch nicht; noch **4R1**
normal /ˈnɔːm(ə)l/ normal; üblich **CT7**
normally /ˈnɔːm(ə)li/ normalerweise **2A6**
north /nɔːθ/ Norden; nördlich; Nord- **CT7**
° North Island /ˈnɔːθ‿ˌaɪlənd/ neuseeländische Nordinsel **1P1**
northern /ˈnɔːðən/ nördlich; Nord- **CT8**

Northern Ireland /ˌnɔːðən‿ˈaɪələnd/ Nordirland **CT7**
nose /nəʊz/ Nase **CT5**
° nosy /ˈnəʊzi/ neugierig **4R3**
not /nɒt/ nicht **CT5**
not ... any /nɒt‿ˈeni/ kein; keine(r, s) **CT5**
not ... anymore /nɒt ˌeniˈmɔː/ nicht mehr **CT7**
not ... anyone /nɒt ˈeniˌwʌn/ niemand **CT6**
not ... anything /nɒt ˈeniθɪŋ/ gar nichts **CT7**
not ... anything else /nɒt ˌeniθɪŋ‿ˈels/ gar nichts anderes **CT7**
not ... anywhere /nɒt ˈeniˌweə/ nirgendwo **CT6**
not ... either /nɒt ˈaɪðə/ auch nicht **CT7**
° not any longer /nɒt‿ˌeni ˈlɒŋgə/ nicht mehr; nicht länger **5B4**
not even /ˈnɒt‿iːvn/ noch nicht einmal **CT7**
° not necessarily /nɒt ˌnesəˈserəli/ nicht unbedingt **5A/T2**
° to not set much store by sth /nɒt ˌset mʌtʃ ˈstɔː baɪ/ von etw wenig halten **4SBS**
not until ... /nɒt‿ʌnˈtɪl/ erst ... **1A3**
note /nəʊt/ Notiz; Mitteilung **CT7**
° to note /nəʊt/ beachten **4D15**
to **note down** /ˌnəʊt‿ˈdaʊn/ (sich) notieren **CT6**
° notebook /ˈnəʊtˌbʊk/ Notizbuch; Notebook(-Computer) **3R5**
nothing /ˈnʌθɪŋ/ nichts **CT5**
to **notice** /ˈnəʊtɪs/ bemerken; beachten **CT6**
novel /ˈnɒv(ə)l/ Roman **CT8**
November /nəʊˈvembə/ November **CT5**
now /naʊ/ jetzt; nun **CT5**
Bye for now. *(informal)* /ˈbaɪ fə naʊ/ Bis bald. **CT5**
° now that ... /ˈnaʊ ðæt/ jetzt, wo ... **3A4**
° nowadays /ˈnaʊəˌdeɪz/ heutzutage **2D2**
nowhere /ˈnəʊweə/ nirgends; nirgendwo **CT8**
public nuisance /ˌpʌblɪk ˈnjuːs(ə)ns/ öffentliches Ärgernis **5A3**
number /ˈnʌmbə/ Nummer; Zahl; Ziffer, **CT5**
to **number** /ˈnʌmbə/ nummerieren; (ab)zählen **CT8**
nurse /nɜːs/ (Kranken)schwester; Krankenpfleger **CT6**
to nurse /nɜːs/ pflegen; fördern **1B7**
nut /nʌt/ Nuss **CT7**
° nutrition *(no pl)* /njuːˈtrɪʃ(ə)n/ Ernährung **2B5**
° nuts *(informal)* /nʌts/ verrückt **2B3**

O

° to obey /əˈbeɪ/ gehorchen; (be)folgen **5R1**
object /ˈɒbdʒekt/ Objekt; Gegenstand **CT8**
° objective /əbˈdʒektɪv/ objektiv **3D15, 5SBS**
to **be obliged to do sth** /ˌbi‿əˌblaɪdʒd‿tə ˈduː/ verpflichtet sein, etw zu tun **3A5**
to **observe** /əbˈzɜːv/ beobachten; bemerken **CT8**; *hier:* (be)achten **3Intro 3**
obsessive /əbˈsesɪv/ zwanghaft; besessen **2A4**
° obsessive-compulsive disorder *(no pl)* /əbˌsesɪv kəmˈpʌlsɪv dɪsˌɔːdə/ Zwangsstörung **2B5**
obvious /ˈɒbviəs/ deutlich; offensichtlich **CT7**
obviously /ˈɒbviəsli/ offensichtlich; deutlich **CT7**
° occasional /əˈkeɪʒ(ə)nəl/ gelegentlich **4SBS**
ocean /ˈəʊʃ(ə)n/ Ozean; (Welt)meer **CT8**
(one) o'clock /ˌwʌn‿əˈklɒk/ (ein) Uhr **CT5**
October /ɒkˈtəʊbə/ Oktober **CT5**
of /əv/ von **CT5**
of course /əv ˈkɔːs/ natürlich **CT5**
off /ɒf/ weg(-) **CT7**
° off sick *(BE)* /ˌɒf ˈsɪk/ krank(gemeldet) **4R1**
° off the record /ˌɒf ˈlɪmɪts/ inoffiziell; nicht für die Öffentlichkeit bestimmt **3R6**
° Off we go! *(informal)* /ˌɒf wi ˈgəʊ/ Los geht's! **2SBS**
to **offend** /əˈfend/ beleidigen; kränken **5B7**
offensive /əˈfensɪv/ anstößig **2A4**
offer /ˈɒfə/ Angebot **CT7**
to **offer** /ˈɒfə/ (an)bieten **CT5**
° offering /ˈɒf(ə)rɪŋ/ Angebot **2SBS**
office /ˈɒfɪs/ Büro; Amt **CT8**
office space *(no pl)* /ˈɒfɪs‿speɪs/ Büroräume; Bürofläche(n) **4A5**
naval officer /ˌneɪv(ə)l‿ˈɒfɪsə/ Marineoffizier/in **1A5**
official /əˈfɪʃ(ə)l/ offiziell **1A2, 3A7**
often /ˈɒf(ə)n/ oft **CT5**
oil /ɔɪl/ (Erd)öl **5A3**
° oil terminal /ˈɔɪl ˌtɜːmɪn(ə)l/ Tanklager **5A3**
old /əʊld/ alt **CT5**
old-fashioned /ˌəʊld ˈfæʃ(ə)nd/ altmodisch; traditionsverbunden **CT7**
° Olympic /əˈlɪmpɪk/ olympisch **1A3**

OMG (= oh my God) /ˌəʊ‿em ˈdʒiː, ˌəʊ maɪ ˈɡɒd/ Oh (mein) Gott!; Großer Gott! **CT7**
on /ɒn/ auf; an **CT5**; in **CT6**; zu **CT7**
° on /ɒn/ *hier:* nach, auf ... zu **3B3**
on a daily basis /ɒn‿ə ˌdeɪli ˈbeɪsɪs/ täglich; jeden Tag **1A4**
° on board /ˌɒn ˈbɔːd/ an Bord **3R1**
° on display /ˌɒn dɪˈspleɪ/ ausgestellt **1B/T1, 5D2**
° on foot /ɒn ˈfʊt/ zu Fuß **5D8**
on holiday /ɒn ˈhɒlədeɪ/ im Urlaub; in den Ferien **CT5**
on one's own /ˌɒn wʌnz‿ˈəʊn/ (ganz) allein(e) **CT7**
° on purpose /ɒn ˈpɜːpəs/ absichtlich **2SBS**
on request /ɒn rɪˈkwest/ auf Anfrage; auf Wunsch **4A7**
on stage /ɒn ˈsteɪdʒ/ auf der/die Bühne **CT6**
on the internet /ˌɒn ði‿ˈɪntəˌnet/ im Internet **CT5**
on the left /ˌɒn ðə ˈleft/ links; auf der linken Seite **CT6**
on the one hand /ˌɒn ðə ˈwʌn hænd/ einerseits; auf der einen Seite **CT7**
on the other hand /ˌɒn ði‿ˈʌðə hænd/ andererseits; auf der anderen Seite **CT7**
on the right /ˌɒn ðə ˈraɪt/ rechts; auf der rechten Seite **CT6**
° on the subject of sb/sth /ˌɒn ðə ˈsʌbdʒɪkt‿əv/ über jdn/etw **2B10**
° on the whole /ˌɒn ðə ˈhəʊl/ im Ganzen; insgesamt **2D21**
on time /ɒn ˈtaɪm/ pünktlich **CT8**
° on top /ɒn ˈtɒp/ obendrauf **2SBS**
on TV /ˌɒn ˌtiː ˈviː/ im Fernsehen **CT5**
° On you! /ˌɒn ˈjuː/ Auf dich!; Wohl bekomms! **2SBS**
once /wʌns/ einmal **CT7**; sobald **CT8**
° once /wʌns/ früher; einst **1R2, 3D3**
once again /ˌwʌns‿əˈɡen/ wieder einmal; erneut **CT7**
one /wʌn/ eins; ein(e, er, es) **CT5**
one another /ˌwʌn‿əˈnʌðə/ einander; gegenseitig **CT7**
° one day /ˈwʌn deɪ/ eines Tages **1R2, 2B/T2, 4D4**
° one in five /ˌwʌn‿ɪn ˈfaɪv/ jede/r Fünfte **1D4**
(one) o'clock /ˌwʌn‿əˈklɒk/ (ein) Uhr **CT5**
° ongoing /ˈɒnˌɡəʊɪŋ/ laufend; anhaltend **3A7**
only /ˈəʊnli/ nur **CT5**
° only /ˈəʊnli/ einzige(r, s) **2B3**
onto /ˈɒntə/ in; auf **5A3**
° Oops! /uːps/ Ups!; Hoppla! **2R1**
to **open** /ˈəʊpən/ öffnen; aufschlagen **CT5**
open (from ... to ...) /ˈəʊpən frəm tʊ/ offen; geöffnet (von ... bis ...) **CT5**
° open-minded /ˌəʊpən ˈmaɪndɪd/ aufgeschlossen; unvoreingenommen **2D3**
opener /ˈəʊp(ə)nə/ Öffner; Anfang **4B4**
opening /ˈəʊp(ə)nɪŋ/ Öffnen; Öffnung; Eröffnung(s-); Anfang(s-) **CT6**
° opera house /ˈɒp(ə)rə haʊs/ Opernhaus **1A6**
° to operate /ˈɒpəreɪt/ operieren; arbeiten; bedienen; betreiben **1B4**
opinion /əˈpɪnjən/ Meinung; Ansicht; Standpunkt **CT6**
in my opinion /ɪn ˈmaɪ‿əˌpɪnjən/ meiner Meinung nach **CT7**
opportunity /ˌɒpəˈtjuːnəti/ Gelegenheit; Chance; Möglichkeit **CT8**
° to oppose /əˈpəʊz/ ablehnen; sich widersetzen **5SBS**
to **be opposed to sth** /ˌbi‿əˈpəʊzd‿tə/ etw ablehnend gegenüberstehen; gegen etw sein **3A7**
° opposite /ˈɒpəzɪt/ gegenüber(liegend) **4SBS, 5R1**
° opposition /ˌɒpəˈzɪʃ(ə)n/ Widerstand; Opposition; Gegensatz **1SBS, 3A/T2**
° oppression *(no pl)* /əˈpreʃ(ə)n/ Unterdrückung; Druck; Bedrängnis **3D2**
optimistic /ˌɒptɪˈmɪstɪk/ optimistisch **CT7**
° option /ˈɒpʃ(ə)n/ Wahl; Möglichkeit; Option **1R4, 2D2, 4B/T2, 5D5**
or /ɔː/ oder **CT5**
° or anything *(informal)* /ɔːr‿ˈeniθɪŋ/ oder so was **1R4**
° oral /ˈɔːrəl/ mündlich **1SBS**
orange /ˈɒrɪndʒ/ orange; orange(farben) **CT5**
order /ˈɔːdə/ Ordnung; Reihenfolge **CT8**
in order to do sth /ɪn‿ˌɔːdə tə ˈduː/ um etw zu tun **CT8**
to **order** /ˈɔːdə/ (an)ordnen; bestellen **CT7**
° order /ˈɔːdə/ Befehl; Anordnung **3D13**
organic /ɔːˈɡænɪk/ organisch; Bio- **CT6**
° organism /ˈɔːɡəˌnɪz(ə)m/ Organismus; Lebewesen **1B2**
to **organize** /ˈɔːɡənaɪz/ organisieren **CT7**
organizer /ˈɔːɡəˌnaɪzə/ Organisator/in **CT8**
original /əˈrɪdʒ(ə)nəl/ ursprünglich; Original- **CT8**
originally /əˈrɪdʒ(ə)nəli/ ursprünglich **CT7**
other /ˈʌðə/ andere(r, s) **CT5**
the other one /ði‿ˈʌðə wʌn/ der/die andere **CT7**
° other-worldly /ˌʌðəˈwɜːldli/ übernatürlich; jenseits; nicht von dieser Welt **3R1**
others *(pl)* /ˈʌðəz/ andere **CT7**
ought to do sth /ˌɔːtə ˈduː/ etw tun sollen **CT7**
our /aʊə/ unser(e) **CT5**
ours /aʊəz/ unsere(r, s) **CT6**
ourselves /aʊəˈselvz/ uns (selbst); wir (selbst) **CT7**
out /aʊt/ außen; draußen **CT6**
° out loud /ˌaʊt ˈlaʊd/ laut **2R3, 4R1, 5D9**
out of /ˈaʊt‿əv/ aus **CT7**
° out of sight /ˌaʊt‿əv ˈsaɪt/ außer Sichtweite **3D13, 4SBS**
the Outback /ði‿ˈaʊtbæk/ *der Busch Australiens* **1Intro 1**
outcast /ˈaʊtˌkɑːst/ Ausgestoßene/r; Geächtete/r **3B1**
outcome /ˈaʊtˌkʌm/ Ergebnis; Resultat **2A8**
outdated /ˌaʊtˈdeɪtɪd/ veraltet; überholt **3A7**
° outdoors /ˌaʊtˈdɔːz/ draußen; im Freien **4D6**
° outer /ˈaʊtə/ äußere(r, s); Außen- **4SBS**
° outgoing /ˌaʊtˈɡəʊɪŋ/ kontaktfreudig; (aus)scheidend; ausgehend **1R2**
° outing /ˈaʊtɪŋ/ Ausflug; Outing **3R1**
to **outline** /ˈaʊtlaɪn/ (kurz) umreißen; skizzieren **CT8**
outrageous /aʊtˈreɪdʒəs/ empörend; unerhört **5A3**
outside /ˌaʊtˈsaɪd/ (dr)außen; außerhalb; nach draußen **CT5**
° outward(s) /ˈaʊtwədz/ nach außen **4SBS**
over /ˈəʊvə/ hinüber; herüber; drüben; herüben; über **CT7**
to **be over** /ˌbi‿ˈəʊvə/ vorbei sein **CT6**
to **get over sb/sth** /ˌɡet‿ˈəʊvə/ über jdn/etw hinwegkommen **CT7**
° overall /ˌəʊvərˈɔːl/ Gesamt-; allgemein; insgesamt **2A/T2, 5SBS**
to **overcome** *(irr)* /ˌəʊvəˈkʌm/ bewältigen; meistern **1A4**
° to overcome *(irr)* /ˌəʊvəˈkʌm/ bewältigen; meistern; *hier:* überwinden **2SBS**
overcrowded /ˌəʊvəˈkraʊdɪd/ überfüllt; überlaufen **1A1**
° to overhear *(irr)* /ˌəʊvəˈhɪə/ zufällig mithören; unabsichtlich belauschen **3R1**
° to overlook /ˌəʊvəˈlʊk/ übersehen; überblicken **5SBS**
overlord /ˈəʊvəˌlɔːd/ Herrscher/in **2A4**
° overseas /ˌəʊvəˈsiːz/ im/ins Ausland **3B3**

° to overturn /ˌəʊvəˈtɜːn/ revidieren; (um)stürzen; umkippen **3R3**
° overwhelmed /ˌəʊvəˈwelmd/ überwältigt; überfordert **2D28**
° overwhelming /ˌəʊvəˈwelmɪŋ/ überwältigend; riesig **2A1**
to owe /əʊ/ schulden; verdanken **2A4**
° owl /aʊl/ Eule **5D1**
own /əʊn/ eigene(r, s) **CT6**
on one's own /ˌɒn wʌnz‿ˈəʊn/ (ganz) allein(e) **CT7**
to **own** /əʊn/ besitzen **CT8**
owner /ˈəʊnə/ Besitzer/in; Eigentümer/in **CT5**
° ownership /ˈəʊnəʃɪp/ Besitz; Eigentum **3A3**

P

° Pacific Ocean /pəˌsɪfɪk‿ˈəʊʃ(ə)n/ Pazifischer Ozean; Pazifik **4P2**
to pack /pæk/ (ein)packen **CT7**
° pack /pæk/ Pack(ung); Paket; *hier:* Infomappe **4R2**
° to pack up /ˌpæk‿ˈʌp/ zusammenpacken; *hier:* Feierabend machen **1R2**
° packaging *(no pl)* /ˈpækɪdʒɪŋ/ Verpackung(smaterial) **5B2**
° paddleboarding *(no pl)* /ˈpæd(ə)lˌbɔːdɪŋ/ *kniend oder liegend auf einem Brett rudern* **2A4**
page /peɪdʒ/ Seite **CT5**
° to paint /peɪnt/ malen; (an)streichen **3R1, 4SBS**
paint *(no pl)* /peɪnt/ Farbe; Lack **1A5, 5B7**
painting /ˈpeɪntɪŋ/ Bild; Gemälde; Malerei **5A3**
pair /peə/ Paar **CT7**
° palm (tree) /ˈpɑːm triː/ Palme **3R1**
° palms out /ˌpɑːmz‿ˈaʊt/ mit den Hand(innen)flächen nach außen **3B4**
pancake /ˈpænˌkeɪk/ Pfannkuchen; Omelette **CT7**
° panel /ˈpæn(ə)l/ (Schalt)tafel; *hier:* Panel *(Einzelbild in einer Sequenz)* **2R1**
to **panic** /ˈpænɪk/ in Panik geraten **4B1**
° panic *(no pl)* /ˈpænɪk/ Panik **2SBS, 3R2, 4SBS, 5R1**
paper *(no pl)* /ˈpeɪpə/ Papier(-) **CT6**
piece of paper /ˌpiːs‿əv ˈpeɪpə/ Blatt Papier **CT5**
parade /pəˈreɪd/ Parade; Umzug **CT8**
° paradise /ˈpærədaɪs/ Paradies **3B/T1**
paragraph /ˈpærəˌgrɑːf/ Absatz; Abschnitt **CT7**
° Paralympic /ˌpærəˈlɪmpɪk/ paralympisch *(die Paralympischen Spiele betreffend)* **1D9**
° Paralympics *(pl)* /ˌpærəˈlɪmpɪks/ *Olympische Spiele für Menschen mit Behinderungen* **1D9**
to **paraphrase** /ˈpærəˌfreɪz/ umschreiben; (mit anderen Worten) wiedergeben **CT8**
single parent /ˌsɪŋg(ə)l ˈpeərənt/ Alleinerziehende/r **5A1**
parents *(pl)* /ˈpeərənts/ Eltern **CT5**
° parliament /ˈpɑːləmənt/ Parlament **1B/T1**
° parliamentary /ˌpɑːləˈment(ə)ri/ parlamentarisch; Parlaments- **1P1**
° to parody /ˈpærədi/ parodieren **2D6**
° parole *(no pl)* /pəˈrəʊl/ bedingte Haftentlassung; Hafturlaub **3R1**
part /pɑːt/ Teil **CT5**; Part, Rolle **CT6**
° partially /ˈpɑːʃəli/ teilweise **5R4**
participant /pɑːˈtɪsɪpənt/ Teilnehmer/in **CT8**
to **participate (in)** /pɑːˈtɪsɪpeɪt‿ɪn/ (an etw) teilnehmen; sich (an etw) beteiligen **CT8**
particular /pəˈtɪkjʊlə/ bestimmt; besondere(r, s); speziell **CT7**
particularly /pəˈtɪkjʊləli/ besonders; vor allem **CT8**
° partly /ˈpɑːtli/ zum Teil; teils; teilweise **2D4**
party /ˈpɑːti/ Partei; Gruppe **2A4**
to **pass** /pɑːs/ geben; (herüber)reichen; verabschieden **3A5**
° to pass /pɑːs/ vorbeigehen an **3B3, 4SBS**
° to pass around /ˌpɑːs‿əˈraʊnd/ herumreichen **5R3**
to pass down /ˌpɑːs ˈdaʊn/ weitergeben; überliefern **1A3**
° to pass (sb) by /ˌpɑːs ˈbaɪ/ (an jdm) vorbeigehen **3R5**
° to pass through /ˌpɑːs ˈθruː/ durchlaufen; passieren **1R4, 5R4**
° passage /ˈpæsɪdʒ/ (Text)passage; Abschnitt **3R1, 4R1, 4SBS, 5SBS**
° passenger /ˈpæsɪndʒə/ Fahrgast; Passagier/in **3R1, 5D2**
° passer-by /ˌpɑːsə ˈbaɪ/ Passant/in; Vorübergehende/r **5SBS**
° passion /ˈpæʃ(ə)n/ Passion; Vorliebe; Leidenschaft **4R2**
° passionate /ˈpæʃ(ə)nət/ leidenschaftlich; mitreißend **1D9**
password /ˈpɑːsˌwɜːd/ Kennwort; Passwort **CT7**
past /pɑːst/ nach **CT5**; Vergangenheit **CT6**; an ... vorbei; hinter, **CT7**; vergangen; frühere(r, s) **1A3**
° to pat /pæt/ tätscheln; *hier:* (mit der Handfläche) schlagen (auf) **3B4**
path /pɑːθ/ Weg; Pfad; Bahn; *hier:* Schneise **CT8**
patience *(no pl)* /ˈpeɪʃ(ə)ns/ Geduld **4Intro 2**
patient /ˈpeɪʃ(ə)nt/ geduldig **CT7**
° to pause /pɔːz/ eine (kurze) Pause machen; innehalten **2SBS, 3R2**
° pavement *(AE)* /ˈpeɪvmənt/ Asphalt **2SBS**
° paw /pɔː/ Pfote; Tatze; Pranke **1R4**
to **pay** *(irr)* /peɪ/ (be)zahlen **CT5**
° payment /ˈpeɪmənt/ (Be)zahlung **3B2**
PE (= physical education) /ˌpiː‿ˈiː, ˌfɪzɪk(ə)l‿ˌedjʊˈkeɪʃ(ə)n/ Sport *(als Schulfach)* **CT5**
° peace *(no pl)* /piːs/ Frieden; Ruhe **3SBS**
peaceful /ˈpiːsf(ə)l/ friedlich; ruhig **CT8**
pen /pen/ Stift **CT5**
pencil /ˈpensl/ Bleistift **CT5**
pencil case /ˈpensl keɪs/ Federmäppchen **CT5**
pencil sharpener /ˈpensl ˌʃɑːp(ə)nə/ (Bleistift)spitzer **CT5**
penguin /ˈpeŋgwɪn/ Pinguin **CT5**
° penny (*pl* pence *or* pennies) /ˈpeni, pens, ˈpeniz/ Penny *(Untereinheit des brit. Pfunds)* **5B2**
people /ˈpiːp(ə)l/ Volk **CT6**
people *(no pl)* /ˈpiːp(ə)l/ Leute; Menschen **CT5**
per /pɜː/ pro **CT8**
percent (*no pl, AE* = **per cent** *BE*) /pərˈsent/ Prozent **CT8**
percentage /pəˈsentɪdʒ/ Prozentsatz **CT8**
° perception *(no pl)* /pəˈsepʃ(ə)n/ Wahrnehmung; Empfinden **2D28**
° perch /pɜːtʃ/ Sitzstange; Hochsitz **5R3**
perfect /ˈpɜːfɪkt/ perfekt **CT5**
to **perform** /pəˈfɔːm/ vorführen; aufführen; auftreten **CT6**
performance /pəˈfɔːməns/ Vorführung; Darbietung; Vorstellung **CT7**; *hier:* Leistung, Abschneiden **CT8**
° performing arts *(pl)* /pəˌfɔːmɪŋ‿ˈɑːts/ darstellende Künste **1D11**
perhaps /pəˈhæps/ vielleicht **CT5**
period /ˈpɪəriəd/ Zeitspanne; Zeitraum; Periode; (Unterrichts)stunde **CT8**
person /ˈpɜːs(ə)n/ Person **CT6**
personal /ˈpɜːs(ə)nəl/ persönlich; privat **CT7**
° personality /ˌpɜːsəˈnæləti/ Persönlichkeit; Charakter **4SBS**
personally /ˈpɜːs(ə)nəli/ persönlich **CT8**; *hier:* ich für meinen Teil **1B2, 2Intro 6**
° personification /pəˌsɒnɪfɪˈkeɪʃ(ə)n/ Personifikation; Personifizierung **3A8, 5D13**

perspective /pəˈspektɪv/ Perspektive; Sicht; Blickwinkel **3B2**
to **persuade** /pəˈsweɪd/ überreden; überzeugen **CT7**
° persuasive /pəˈsweɪsɪv/ überzeugend **3SBS**
pessimistic /ˌpesəˈmɪstɪk/ pessimistisch **2B3**
pest /pest/ Schädling; Plage **1B7**
pet /pet/ Haustier **CT5**
° phantasm /ˈfæntæzəm/ Trugbild; Geistererscheinung **4SBS**
pharmacy /ˈfɑːməsi/ Apotheke **2B4**
° philanthropist /fɪˈlænθrəpɪst/ Philanthrop/in; Menschenfreund/in **1D9, 5SBS**
photo (= photograph) /ˈfəʊtəʊ, ˈfəʊtəˌgrɑːf/ Foto **CT5**
to **answer the phone** /ˌɑːnsə ðə ˈfəʊn/ ans Telefon gehen **CT5**
phone call (= telephone call) /ˈfəʊn kɔːl, ˈtelɪˌfəʊn kɔːl/ Anruf; Telefongespräch **CT5**
to **phone** /fəʊn/ anrufen; telefonieren **CT6**
° photography *(no pl)* /fəˈtɒgrəfi/ Fotografie; Foto- **3D3**
° phrasal verb /ˌfreɪz(ə)l vɜːb/ Phrasal Verb *(Partikelverb)* **3D16**
phrase /freɪz/ Satz; Ausdruck **CT5**
physical /ˈfɪzɪk(ə)l/ körperlich; physisch **CT7**
piano /piˈænəʊ/ Klavier; Piano **CT5**
° to pick /pɪk/ aussuchen; auswählen; *hier:* pflücken **4D4**
to **pick up** /ˌpɪk‿ˈʌp/ aufheben; abholen **CT6**; abheben **CT7**
picture /ˈpɪktʃə/ Bild **CT5**
° to picture /ˈpɪktʃə/ sich vorstellen **2SBS**
pie /paɪ/ Pastete; Kuchen **CT6**
pie chart /ˈpaɪ tʃɑːt/ Tortendiagramm; Kuchendiagramm **CT8**
piece /piːs/ Stück **CT6**
piece of paper /ˌpiːs‿əv ˈpeɪpə/ Blatt Papier **CT5**
° to pierce /pɪəs/ durchstechen; piercen **5R2**
pig /pɪg/ Schwein **CT5**
° piggy bank /ˈpɪgi bæŋk/ Sparschwein **5B4**
° pile /paɪl/ Stapel; Haufen **3R2, 5B4**
pilot /ˈpaɪlət/ Pilot/in **CT6**
° to pilot /ˈpaɪlət/ fliegen **3R1**
° to pin down /ˌpɪn ˈdaʊn/ genau definieren; festnageln **4SBS**
pink /pɪŋk/ rosa; pink **CT5**
° pinned /pɪnd/ angespannt **2SBS**
° pipe /paɪp/ Rohr **4D4**
° pitch *(BE)* /pɪtʃ/ (Spiel)feld; Platz **5B/T2**
place /pleɪs/ Ort; Platz; Stelle **CT5**
to **plan** /plæn/ planen **CT6**
plane /pleɪn/ Flugzeug **CT6**
planet /ˈplænɪt/ Planet **CT7**
° plank /plæŋk/ Brett; Latte; Pfeiler **4SBS**
° planning *(no pl)* /ˈplænɪŋ/ Planung; Planungs- **5R2**
plant /plɑːnt/ Pflanze **CT5**
° to plant /plɑːnt/ pflanzen; *hier:* sich setzen **3B4**
° plantation /plɑːnˈteɪʃ(ə)n/ Plantage; Pflanzung **5SBS**
° plaque /plæk/ Tafel; Schild; Plakette **5SBS**
plastic /ˈplæstɪk/ Plastik(-); Kunststoff(-) **CT6**
plate /pleɪt/ Teller **1B7**
° platypus /ˈplætɪpəs/ Schnabeltier **Wordbank 1**
play /pleɪ/ Spiel; (Theater)stück **CT7**
to **play** /pleɪ/ spielen **CT5**
° to play /pleɪ/ *hier:* kommen, gezeigt werden **2D24**
° play *(AE)* /pleɪ/ Spielzug **2R4**
° play-offs *(pl)* /ˈpleɪɒfs/ *System von Ausscheidungsspielen* **2R4**
player /ˈpleɪə/ Spieler/in **CT7**
please /pliːz/ bitte, **CT5**
pleased /pliːzd/ froh; zufrieden **CT5**
° Pleased to meet you. /ˌpliːzd‿tə ˈmiːt juː/ Freut mich, Sie kennenzulernen. **4B4**
° pleasure /ˈpleʒə/ Freude; Vergnügen **4SBS**
° pledge /pledʒ/ Versprechen; Zusicherung **2D8**
plot /plɒt/ Handlung **2B8, 3B1**
° plug /plʌg/ Stöpsel; Stecker; Pfropfen **4SBS**
° plump /plʌmp/ rund(lich); füllig **4SBS**
° to plunge /plʌndʒ/ (ab)stürzen **3A8**
pm (= post meridiem) /ˌpiː‿ˈem, ˌpəʊst məˈrɪd‿əm/ nachmittags; abends *(nur hinter Uhrzeit zwischen 12 Uhr mittags und Mitternacht)* **CT5**
pocket knife (*pl* pocket knives) /ˈpɒkɪt naɪf, ˈpɒkɪt naɪvz/ Taschenmesser **CT6**
pocket money /ˈpɒkɪt mʌni/ Taschengeld **CT6**
° podgy *(informal, BE)* /ˈpɒdʒi/ dick; fett **4SBS**
poem /ˈpəʊɪm/ Gedicht **CT7**
poet /ˈpəʊɪt/ Dichter/in **CT8**
° poet laureate /ˌpəʊɪt ˈlɔːriət/ *hohe Auszeichnung für einen Dichter/eine Dichterin* **3D12**
poetry *(no pl)* /ˈpəʊɪtri/ Dichtung; Lyrik; Gedichte **CT7**
° poetry slam /ˈpəʊɪtri slæm/ Poetry-Slam *(öffentlicher „Dichterwettstreit", bei dem die Teilnehmer/innen selbst verfasste Texte vortragen)* **5D3**
° poetry slammer /ˈpəʊɪtri ˌslæmə/ *Teilnehmer/in bei einem Poetry-Slam* **5D1**
point /pɔɪnt/ Punkt **CT7**
to the point /tə ðə ˈpɔɪnt/ griffig; prägnant; auf das Thema bezogen **4A9**
starting point /ˈstɑːtɪŋ pɔɪnt/ Ausgangspunkt; Ansatzpunkt **CT8**
point of view /ˌpɔɪnt‿əv‿ˈvjuː/ Ansicht; Einstellung; Sicht **CT7**
to **point (at/to)** /ˈpɔɪnt‿ət/tə/ deuten/zeigen (auf); richten (auf) **3A7**
to **point out** /ˌpɔɪnt‿ˈaʊt/ hinweisen; deuten; aufmerksam machen; verdeutlichen **CT8**
° to polarize /ˈpəʊləraɪz/ polarisieren **1A5**
police /pəˈliːs/ Polizei(-) **CT6**
° police officer /pəˈliːs‿ɒfɪsə/ Polizeibeamte(r)/-beamtin **5B/T1**
policeman (*pl* policemen) /pəˈliːsmən/ Polizist **CT6**
policewoman (*pl* policewomen) /pəˈliːsˌwʊmən, pəˈliːsˌwɪmɪn/ Polizistin **CT6**
° policy /ˈpɒləsi/ Programm; Strategie; Grundsatz; Politik **3SBS**
° polio *(no pl)* /ˈpəʊliəʊ/ Kinderlähmung **3SBS**
polite /pəˈlaɪt/ höflich **CT7**
political /pəˈlɪtɪk(ə)l/ politisch **CT7**
politician /ˌpɒləˈtɪʃ(ə)n/ Politiker/in **3A2**
° politics *(pl)* /ˈpɒlətɪks/ Politik **2D3**
pollution *(no pl)* /pəˈluːʃ(ə)n/ Verschmutzung **1B7**
° pool /puːl/ Tümpel; kleiner See; Lache **1P1**
poor /pɔː/ arm **CT6**; schlecht **CT8**
popular /ˈpɒpjʊlə/ beliebt; populär **CT6**
population *(no pl)* /ˌpɒpjʊˈleɪʃ(ə)n/ Bevölkerung; Einwohnerzahl **CT7**
pork /pɔːk/ Schweinefleisch **CT7**
° portion /ˈpɔːʃ(ə)n/ (An)teil; Portion **3D17, 5SBS**
° to portray /pɔːˈtreɪ/ porträtieren; darstellen **4SBS**
° Portuguese /ˌpɔːtʃʊˈgiːz/ Portugiese/Portugiesin; Portugiesisch; portugiesisch **4P4**
position /pəˈzɪʃ(ə)n/ Platz; Stelle; Position; Standpunkt **CT8**
positive /ˈpɒzətɪv/ positiv **CT6**

° positivity *(no pl)* /ˌpɒzəˈtɪvəti/ positive Einstellung **Wordbank 8**
° to possess /pəˈzes/ besitzen **4SBS**
° possession /pəˈzeʃn/ Besitz(ungen) **3R1**
° possibility /ˌpɒsəˈbɪləti/ Möglichkeit **3R1, 2A/T2**
possible /ˈpɒsəb(ə)l/ möglich **CT5**
possibly /ˈpɒsəbli/ möglicherweise; gegebenenfalls **1A5**
° possum /ˈpɒsəm/ *Beuteltierart* **Wordbank 1**
post /pəʊst/ *online veröffentlichter Beitrag/Artikel/Eintrag* **CT5**
to **post** /pəʊst/ posten *(einen Beitrag/Artikel online stellen)* **CT5**
° to post /pəʊst/ *hier:* (per Post) schicken **1R4**
° post office /ˈpəʊst‿ˌɒfɪs/ Post(amt) **1R2**
postcard /ˈpəʊstˌkɑːd/ Postkarte **CT6**
° posterior /pɒˈstɪəriə/ Hinterteil; Hintern **4SBS**
° postman (*pl* postmen) /ˈpəʊstmən/ Postbote; Briefträger **5R1**
° posture /ˈpɒstʃə/ (Körper)haltung; Stellung; Pose **4SBS**
potato (*pl* **potatoes**) /pəˈteɪtəʊ, pəˈteɪtəʊz/ Kartoffel **CT5**
potential /pəˈtenʃ(ə)l/ Potenzial; potenziell; möglich **4A5**
° to pounce /paʊns/ losspringen; einen Satz machen **3R5**
° pound /paʊnd/ Pfund *(britische Währung)* **5D1**
° to pour /pɔː/ gießen; schütten; *hier:* strömen **2SBS**
poverty *(no pl)* /ˈpɒvəti/ Armut **CT8**
power /ˈpaʊə/ Macht; Kraft; Stärke **CT6**
powerful /ˈpaʊəf(ə)l/ mächtig; stark; druckvoll **CT7**
° powerless /ˈpaʊələs/ machtlos; unfähig **2D10**
practical /ˈpræktɪk(ə)l/ praktisch; auf die Praxis bezogen **1B2**
practically /ˈpræktɪkli/ praktisch; quasi **CT8**
° practice *(no pl)* /ˈpræktɪs/ Übung; Training **2R3**; *hier:* Probe **3D15**
to **practise** /ˈpræktɪs/ üben **CT5**
to praise /preɪz/ loben **5A3**
° praise *(no pl)* /preɪz/ Lob **3D12**
° pre- /priː/ Vor- **1P1**
precious /ˈpreʃəs/ wertvoll; kostbar **1B7**
to predict /prɪˈdɪkt/ vorhersagen **2A5**
° predictable /prɪˈdɪktəb(ə)l/ vorhersehbar; berechenbar **2B/T1**
to **prefer** /prɪˈfɜː/ vorziehen; bevorzugen **CT7**
° prejudice /ˈpredʒʊdɪs/ Vorurteil **3SBS**
prejudiced /ˈpredʒʊdɪst/ voreingenommen **3B1**
° Premier League *(BE)* /ˌpremiə ˈliːg/ *(Erste Fußballliga in England)* **5A1**
premiere /ˈpremieə/ Premiere; Uraufführung **CT6**
preparation /ˌprepəˈreɪʃ(ə)n/ Vorbereitung; Zubereitung **CT8**
to **prepare** /prɪˈpeə/ vorbereiten; erstellen **CT6**
° presence *(no pl)* /ˈprez(ə)ns/ Präsenz; Anwesenheit; Gegenwart **1P1**
present /ˈprez(ə)nt/ Geschenk **CT6**; Gegenwart; jetzt; heute **4A7**
° present /ˈprez(ə)nt/ derzeitig; jetzig; gegenwärtig **2D28**; anwesend **4SBS**; vorhanden **3D2, 5D2**
to **present (sth to sb)** /prɪˈzent/ (jdm etw) präsentieren **CT6**
° to present (sth to sb) /prɪˈzent/ *hier:* (jdm etw) überreichen **2R7**
° present-day /ˌprez(ə)nt‿ˈdeɪ/ heutig **1A5**
presentation /ˌprez(ə)nˈteɪʃ(ə)n/ Präsentation **CT6**
° presently /ˈprez(ə)ntli/ bald; gleich; nach kurzer Zeit **4SBS**
president /ˈprezɪdənt/ Präsident/in; Vorsitzende/r **CT8**
° to press /pres/ (zusammen)drücken; (aus)pressen; *hier:* bedrängen **1R4**; *hier:* zusammenpressen **2A2**
pressure /ˈpreʃə/ Druck; Stress; Belastung **CT8**
° to pressure sb into doing sth /ˌpreʃə ˌsʌmbədi‿ɪntə ˈduːɪŋ/ jdn dazu drängen, etw zu tun **3R6**
to **pretend** /prɪˈtend/ vorgeben; vortäuschen **CT7**
pretty /ˈprɪti/ hübsch; nett **CT5**
pretty *(informal)* /ˈprɪti/ ziemlich **CT7**
to **prevent** /prɪˈvent/ verhindern **CT7**
° previous /ˈpriːviəs/ vor(her)ig; vorhergehend **4SBS**
price /praɪs/ Preis **CT5**
pride *(no pl)* /praɪd/ Stolz **1A4**
° priest /priːst/ Priester; Geistlicher **5D2**
° primarily /ˈpraɪm(ə)rəli/praɪˈmerəli/ hauptsächlich; in erster Linie **2D21**
° primary school *(BE)* /ˈpraɪməri skuːl/ Grundschule **1B2**
prime minister /ˌpraɪm‿ˈmɪnɪstə/ Premierminister/in; Ministerpräsident/in **1A3**
° principal (*AE* = head teacher *BE*) /ˈprɪnsəp(ə)l/ Schulleiter/in; Direktor/in **2D15, 3R6**
to **print out** /ˌprɪnt‿ˈaʊt/ ausdrucken **CT7**
° printer /ˈprɪntə/ Drucker **1R2**
° printing press /ˈprɪntɪŋ pres/ Druckerpresse **1B/T1**
° printout /ˈprɪntˌaʊt/ Ausdruck **3SBS**
° priority /praɪˈɒrəti/ Priorität **2SBS**
prison /ˈprɪz(ə)n/ Gefängnis(-); Haft **CT7**
prisoner /ˈprɪz(ə)nə/ Gefangene/r; Häftling **CT7**
privacy *(no pl)* /ˈprɪvəsi, ˈpraɪvəsi/ Privatsphäre; Intimsphäre **3Intro 2**
° privately /ˈpraɪvətli/ privat; insgeheim; persönlich **3A3**
° privileged /ˈprɪvəlɪdʒd/ privilegiert; bevorrechtigt **5B4**
prize /praɪz/ (Sieg)preis; Gewinn **CT5**
° probability /ˌprɒbəˈbɪləti/ Wahrscheinlichkeit **2SBS**
probably /ˈprɒbəbli/ wahrscheinlich **CT6**
° probation officer /prəˈbeɪʃ(ə)n‿ˌɒfɪsə/ Bewährungshelfer/in **4R3**
problem /ˈprɒbləm/ Schwierigkeit; Problem **CT5**
° problem-solving *(no pl)* /ˈprɒbləm ˌsɒlvɪŋ/ Problemlöse(n) **4A5**
problematic(al) /ˌprɒbləˈmætɪk(ə)l/ problematisch; schwierig **CT7**
° procedure /prəˈsiːdʒə/ Verfahren; Vorgehensweise; Prozess **4D12**
° process /ˈprəʊses/ Prozess; Verfahren **4D11, 5D7**
to proclaim /prəˈkleɪm/ verkünden; erklären **1A5**
° proclamation /ˌprɒkləˈmeɪʃ(ə)n/ Verkündigung; öffentliche Bekanntmachung **1B/T1**
° Proclamation Day /ˌprɒkləˈmeɪʃ(ə)n deɪ/ *regionaler Feiertag in Australien* **1B/T1**
to **produce** /prəˈdjuːs/ herstellen; produzieren **CT8**
° product /ˈprɒdʌkt/ Produkt; Erzeugnis **2A4**
professional /prəˈfeʃ(ə)nəl/ beruflich; Berufs-; professionell; berufstätig **CT7**; Fachmann/Fachfrau; Profi **2Intro 2**
profile /ˈprəʊfaɪl/ Profil; Porträt **4A7**
to **profit (from/by)** /ˈprɒfɪt frɒm/baɪ/ profitieren (von); Nutzen ziehen (aus) **1A1**
programme /ˈprəʊgræm/ Programm; Sendung; Programmheft **CT7**
progress *(no pl)* /ˈprəʊgres/ Vorwärtskommen; Fortschritt **CT8**
° prom *(AE)* /prɑm/ *Ball am Ende des Jahres in einer amerikanischen Highschool* **2B4**
° prominent /ˈprɒmɪnənt/ auffällig; vorstehend **1SBS, 4SBS**
to **promise** /ˈprɒmɪs/ versprechen **CT6**
to **promote** /prəˈməʊt/ (be)fördern; aufsteigen **CT8**

° to promote /prəˈməʊt/ *hier:* bewerben **2D2, 4D6**
° to pronounce /prəˈnaʊns/ aussprechen; verkünden **1R2, 5D9**
pronunciation *(no pl)* /prəˌnʌnsiˈeɪʃ(ə)n/ Aussprache **CT8**
° proof /pruːf/ Beweis **5R4**
° to proofread *(irr)* /ˈpruːfriːd/ Korrektur lesen **4D13**
° prop /prɒp/ Requisit *(für eine Theater- oder Filmszene verwendeter Gegenstand)* **4R1**
° to prop /prɒp/ lehnen; stützen; halten **1R2**
° proper /ˈprɒpə/ echt; richtig; anständig **3B/T1**
properly /ˈprɒpəli/ richtig; korrekt; anständig **CT8**
property *(no pl)* /ˈprɒpəti/ Eigentum; (Immobilien)besitz **CT8**
° proportion /prəˈpɔːʃ(ə)n/ Anteil; Verhältnis **1P1, Wordbank 7**
° pros and cons *(pl)* /ˌprəʊz‿ən ˈkɒnz/ Für und Wider; Pro und Kontra **3A9**
° prosecutor /ˈprɒsɪkjuːtə/ Ankläger/in **3R6**
to **protect** /prəˈtekt/ (be)schützen **CT7**
° protection /prəˈtekʃ(ə)n/ Schutz **3A3**
° protein /ˈprəʊtiːn/ Eiweiß(-); Protein **3B2**
to **protest** /prəˈtest/ protestieren **1A3, 5A3**
protester /prəˈtestə/ Protestie-rende/r; Demonstrant/in **1A5, 5A3**
proud /praʊd/ stolz **CT7**
° to prove /pruːv/ beweisen; sich erweisen **1R4, 3R5, 3R6**
° to prove one's point /ˌpruːv wʌnz ˈpɔɪnt/ beweisen, dass jmd recht hat **3R2**
° to prove sb guilty /ˌpruːv ˌsʌmbədi ˈɡɪlti/ jds Schuld beweisen **3R2**
to **provide sb/sth with sth** /prəˈvaɪd ˌsʌmbədi/ˌsʌmθɪŋ wɪð/ jdn/etw mit etw versorgen; jdm/etw etw bieten **CT8**
° province /ˈprɒvɪns/ Provinz **1B/T1**
° provocative /prəˈvɒkətɪv/ provozierend **2D10**
° PSA (= public service announcement) /ˌpiː‿es‿ˈeɪ/ öffentliche Mitteilung **2SBS**
° psychic /ˈsaɪkɪk/ übersinnlich; psychisch **4SBS**
psychology *(no pl)* /saɪˈkɒlədʒi/ Psychologie **1B2**
° pub /pʌb/ Kneipe **1D16**
public /ˈpʌblɪk/ öffentlich **CT8**
° the public /ðə ˈpʌblɪk/ die Öffentlichkeit; die Allgemeinheit **2D23**

public nuisance /ˌpʌblɪk ˈnjuːs(ə)ns/ öffentliches Ärgernis **5A3**
publication /ˌpʌblɪˈkeɪʃ(ə)n/ Veröffentlichung **CT8**
° publicity *(no pl)* /pʌbˈlɪsəti/ Publicity; Reklame; Werbung **3R3**
to **publish** /ˈpʌblɪʃ/ veröffentlichen; herausgeben **1A8**
° puffy /ˈpʌfi/ verquollen; *hier:* bauschig **2SBS**
to **pull** /pʊl/ ziehen **CT6**
° to pull away from sb/sth /ˌpʊl‿əˈweɪ frɒm/ sich von jdm/etw wegbewegen **3D17**
° pumped *(informal)* /pʌmpt/ begeistert **2SBS**
pumpkin /ˈpʌmpkɪn/ Kürbis(-) **CT8**
° punctual /ˈpʌŋktʃuəl/ pünktlich **4A/T1**
° punctuation *(no pl)* /ˌpʌŋktʃuˈeɪʃ(ə)n/ Zeichensetzung; Interpunktion **4R1**
to **punish** /ˈpʌnɪʃ/ (be)strafen **CT6**
pupil /ˈpjuːp(ə)l/ Schüler/in **CT5**
° puppy /ˈpʌpi/ junger Hund; Welpe **2D6**
° pure /pjʊə/ rein; pur **2SBS**
purple /ˈpɜːpl/ violett; lila **CT5**
purpose /ˈpɜːpəs/ Grund; Absicht; Ziel; Zweck **2A8**
to **push** /pʊʃ/ stoßen; schieben; drücken **CT6**; *hier:* drängen **2A4**
to **put** *(irr)* /pʊt/ setzen; legen; stellen **CT5**
° to push around /ˌpʊʃ‿əˈraʊnd/ herumschubsen **5R4**
° Put a sock in it! *(informal, AusE)* /ˌpʊt‿ə ˈsɒk‿ɪn‿ɪt/ Halt den Mund! **1Intro 3**
to **put away** *(irr)* /ˌpʊt‿əˈweɪ/ wegräumen; beiseitelegen **CT6**
° to put down *(irr)* /ˌpʊt‿ˈdaʊn/ ablegen; abstellen; aus der Hand legen; *hier:* eintragen **4R2**
to **put on** *(irr)* /ˌpʊt‿ˈɒn/ anziehen; aufführen **CT8**
° to put sth into storage /ˌpʊt ˌsʌmθɪŋ‿ˌɪntʊ ˈstɔːrɪdʒ/ etw (ein)lagern; etw unterstellen **3B2**
° to put the kettle on /ˌpʊt ðə ˈketl‿ɒn/ Wasser aufsetzen **4SBS**
° to put together *(irr)* /ˌpʊt‿təˈɡeðə/ zusammensetzen; zusammenbauen; zusammenstellen **4D11**
° to put up *(irr)* /ˌpʊt‿ˈʌp/ aufhängen; hochheben **1Intro 1**; *hier:* aufstellen **5SBS**
puzzled /ˈpʌz(ə)ld/ ratlos; verwirrt; (sehr) überrascht **CT7**

Q

° quad /ˈkwɒd/ Quad(-) *(vierrädriges Motorrad)* **1D9**
qualification /ˌkwɒlɪfɪˈkeɪʃ(ə)n/ Qualifikation; Ausbildung; Abschluss **4A11**
quality /ˈkwɒləti/ Qualität; Art; Eigenschaft; Merkmal **CT8**
quality newspaper /ˈkwɒləti ˌnjuːzˌpeɪpə/ seriöse (Tages)zeitung **5A3**
quarter (past/to) /ˈkwɔːtə pɑːst/tə/ Viertel (nach/vor) **CT5**
queen /kwiːn/ Königin **CT6**
question /ˈkwestʃ(ə)n/ Frage **CT5**
° to question /ˈkwestʃ(ə)n/ befragen; bezweifeln **5SBS**
quick /kwɪk/ schnell **CT6**
quiet /ˈkwaɪət/ leise; ruhig **CT5**
° quiet /ˈkwaɪət/ Stille; Ruhe **2SBS**
quite /kwaɪt/ ziemlich; ganz **CT7**
quite a few /ˌkwaɪt‿ə ˈfjuː/ eine ganze Menge **3A7**
° quokka /ˈkwɒkə/ *Beuteltierart* **1Intro 1**
° quotation /kwəʊˈteɪʃ(ə)n/ Zitat **4R1**
quote /kwəʊt/ Zitat **3A2, 5B9**
to **quote** /kwəʊt/ zitieren **3B2**

R

race /reɪs/ Rasse; Spezies; Rennen; Lauf **CT7**
° to race /reɪs/ rennen; rasen **2SBS, 3B/T1**
racism *(no pl)* /ˈreɪˌsɪz(ə)m/ Rassismus **CT8**
° radical /ˈrædɪk(ə)l/ radikal **5D6**
° to radicalize /ˈrædɪkəlaɪz/ radikalisieren **2A4**
° to rage /reɪdʒ/ toben; wüten **5SBS**
° railing /ˈreɪlɪŋ/ Geländer **4SBS**
° railroad (*AE* = railway *BE*) /ˈreɪlˌrəʊd/ Gleise; Schienen; *hier:* (Eisen)bahn **5D7**
railway /ˈreɪlweɪ/ Gleise; Schienen; (Eisen)bahn **CT7**
to **rain** /reɪn/ regnen **CT6**
° raincoat /ˈreɪnˌkəʊt/ Regenmantel **4D6**
rainforest /ˈreɪnˌfɒrɪst/ Regenwald **1B2, 4A9**
rainy /ˈreɪni/ regnerisch **CT6**
to **raise** /reɪz/ heben; *hier:* großziehen **1A3**; *hier:* aufwerfen, vorbringen **2Intro 6**; *hier:* schärfen **5A1**
° to raise /reɪz/ *hier:* sich erheben **5R2**
° to raise one's eyebrows /ˌreɪz wʌnz‿ˈaɪˌbraʊz/ die Augenbrauen hochziehen **2A2**
° rally /ˈræli/ Versammlung; Kundgebung; Treffen **3D2**

rancher /ˈrɑːntʃə/ Viehzüchter/in **CT8**
° random /ˈrændəm/ zufällig; wahllos **3D2**
range /reɪndʒ/ Reichweite; Bereich; Angebot **1B2**
° to rap /ræp/ rappen **1D11**
rapid /ˈræpɪd/ schnell; plötzlich; rasch **5A1**
° rare /reə/ rar; selten **3D7**
° rarely /ˈreəli/ selten; nicht oft **1R2, 3B3**
rate /reɪt/ Maß; Menge; Rate; Quote **1A3**
rather /ˈrɑːðə/ ziemlich; recht **CT7**
° rather /ˈrɑːðə/ *hier:* sondern **3SBS**; *hier:* eher **4SBS**; *hier:* vielmehr **5SBS**
I'd rather (= I would rather) /aɪd ˈrɑːðə/ ich würde lieber **CT7**
rather than /ˈrɑːðə ðæn/ anstelle; (und) nicht **CT8**
° ratty /ˈræti/ verlottert; verknotet **3B3**
° re (= regarding) /riː, rɪˈgɑːdɪŋ/ bezüglich **4A9**
RE (= religious education) /ˌɑːr‿ˈiː, rəˌlɪdʒəs‿edjʊˈkeɪʃ(ə)n/ Religionslehre **CT5**
to **reach** /riːtʃ/ erreichen **CT7**
to **reach out** /ˌriːtʃ‿ˈaʊt/ ausstrecken; sich einsetzen **CT8**
° to reach out to sb /ˌriːtʃ‿ˈaʊt‿tʊ/ jdn erreichen; sich (hilfesuchend) an jdn wenden **4A2**
to **react (to sb/sth)** /riˈækt‿tə/ (auf jdn/etw) reagieren **CT5**
reaction (to) /riˈækʃ(ə)n tʊ/ Reaktion (auf) **CT7**
to **read** *(irr)* /riːd/ lesen **CT5**
to **read out** *(irr)* /ˌriːd‿ˈaʊt/ laut vorlesen **CT6**
reader /ˈriːdə/ Leser/in **1B7, 2A4, 3A2**
reading *(no pl)* /ˈriːdɪŋ/ Lesen **CT5**
ready /ˈredi/ fertig; bereit **CT6**
real /rɪəl/ wirklich; echt **CT6**
° real-life /ˌrɪəlˈlaɪf/ real; echt **5D2**
realistic /ˌrɪəˈlɪstɪk/ realistisch **2A6**
realistically /ˌrɪəˈlɪstɪkli/ realistisch (betrachtet) **3A7**
° reality /riˈæləti/ Realität; Wirklichkeit **5R3**
to **realize** /ˈrɪəlaɪz/ sich einer Sache bewusst sein/werden; bemerken **CT8**
° to realize /ˈrɪəlaɪz/ *hier:* verwirklichen **3SBS**
really /ˈrɪəli/ wirklich; tatsächlich; echt **CT5**
° rear /rɪə/ hintere(r, s); *hier:* Heck- **2SBS**
° to rearrange /ˌriːəˈreɪndʒ/ umstellen; umräumen; verlegen **5R2**
reason /ˈriːz(ə)n/ Grund **CT5**
° reassuring /ˌriːəˈʃɔːrɪŋ/ beruhigend **3R6**
° to recall /rɪˈkɔːl/ sich erinnern; zurückrufen **3R5**
to **receive** /rɪˈsiːv/ erhalten; bekommen **CT8**
° recent /ˈriːs(ə)nt/ kürzlich; *hier:* jüngst.../letzt... **1A6, 5SBS**
recently /ˈriːs(ə)ntli/ kürzlich; vor Kurzem; neulich **CT8**
° receptionist /rɪˈsepʃ(ə)nɪst/ *jemand, der in der Rezeption arbeitet* **4D1**
recipe /ˈresəpi/ Rezept **CT5**
° to reckon /ˈrekən/ (be)rechnen; denken **1R2, 4SBS**
to **recognize** /ˈrekəgnaɪz/ (wieder)erkennen; anerkennen **CT8**
to **recommend** /ˌrekəˈmend/ empfehlen **CT8**
recommendation /ˌrekəmenˈdeɪʃ(ə)n/ Empfehlung **CT8**
reconciliation *(no pl)* /ˌrekənsɪliˈeɪʃ(ə)n/ Aussöhnung; Versöhnung; Beilegung **1A3**
to reconstruct /ˌriːkənˈstrʌkt/ rekonstruieren **5A1**
record /ˈrekɔːd/ Aufzeichnungen; Akte; Vorgeschichte **3A7**
to **record** /rɪˈkɔːd/ aufzeichnen; aufnehmen **CT6**
° rectangle /ˈrekˌtæŋg(ə)l/ Rechteck **3Intro 1**
red /red/ rot **CT5**
° red-faced /ˌred ˈfeɪst/ mit (hoch)rotem Kopf **3B4**
to **reduce** /rɪˈdjuːs/ verringern; reduzieren **CT6**
° ref (= referee) *(informal)* /ref, ˌrefəˈriː/ Schiri **1R4**
to **refer (back) to** /rɪˌfɜː ˈbæk tʊ/ (zurück)verweisen auf; sich beziehen auf **CT7**; *hier:* nennen, bezeichnen **5A1**
reference /ˈref(ə)rəns/ (Arbeits)zeugnis; Referenz **4A7**
° reference /ˈref(ə)rəns/ Verweis; Anspielung; Bezugnahme **1R2, SBS**
° referendum (*pl* referendums *or* referenda) /ˌrefəˈrendəm, ˌrefəˈrendəmz, ˌrefəˈrendə/ Referendum; Volksabstimmung **5D4**
° referral /rɪˈfɜːrəl/ Überweisung; Einweisung; *hier:* Empfehlung **4SBS**
to **reflect** /rɪˈflekt/ spiegeln; zeigen; reflektieren **1A5, 3A7**
to **refuse** /rɪˈfjuːz/ ablehnen; verweigern **CT8**
regardless of sth /rɪˈgɑːdləs‿əv/ trotz etw; ungeachtet etw **4A5**
region /ˈriːdʒn/ Region; Gegend **CT8**
° register /ˈredʒɪstə/ Register; Verzeichnis; *hier:* Sprachebene **4A/T2**
° to register /ˈredʒɪstə/ registrieren **5R4**
to **regret** /rɪˈgret/ bedauern; bereuen **CT7**
regular /ˈregjʊlə/ regelmäßig **CT7**; normal **CT8**
° regular /ˈregjʊlə/ Stammgast **3R1**
rehabilitation *(no pl)* /ˌriəˌbɪlɪˈteɪʃ(ə)n/ Rehabilitation(s-); Wiedereingliederung **1B7**
to **reject** /rɪˈdʒekt/ ablehnen; zurückweisen; abweisen **2A4, 4B1**
rejection /rɪˈdʒekʃ(ə)n/ Ablehnung; Absage; Abweisung **3B1**
to relate to /rɪˈleɪt‿tʊ/ sich beziehen auf; *hier:* in Beziehung stehen zu **3B6**
related /rɪˈleɪtɪd/ verbunden; verwandt; in Zusammenhang stehen **3A5**
to **be related to** /ˌbiː rɪˈleɪtɪd‿tʊ/ verwandt sein (mit); in Beziehung stehen (zu) **1A1**
relationship /rɪˈleɪʃ(ə)nʃɪp/ Beziehung **CT7**
relative /ˈrelətɪv/ Verwandte/r **CT8**
° relatively /ˈrelətɪvli/ relativ **1A/T2**
to **relax** /rɪˈlæks/ entspannen **CT6**
relaxed /rɪˈlækst/ entspannt; locker **4B1**
° relaxing /rɪˈlæksɪŋ/ entspannend; erholsam **2D28**
° relay /ˈriːleɪ/ Staffellauf **1A3**
to **release** /rɪˈliːs/ freilassen; entlassen; veröffentlichen **CT8**
relentless /rɪˈlentləs/ unnachgiebig; unablässig **5A1**
° reliability *(no pl)* /rɪˌlaɪəˈbɪləti/ Zuverlässigkeit; Vertrauenswürdigkeit **Wordbank 8**
reliable /rɪˈlaɪəb(ə)l/ verlässlich; zuverlässig **4A5**
° reliable /rɪˈlaɪəb(ə)l/ *hier:* glaubwürdig **3R6**
° relief *(no pl)* /rɪˈliːf/ Erleichterung; Entlastung **1R4**
relieved /rɪˈliːvd/ erleichtert **CT6**
religion /rɪˈlɪdʒ(ə)n/ Religion; Glaube **1A3, 3Intro 2**
religious education /rəˌlɪdʒəs‿edjʊˈkeɪʃ(ə)n/ Religionslehre **CT5**
to **rely on sb/sth** /rɪˈlaɪ‿ɒn/ sich auf jdn/etw verlassen **2A6**
to **remain** /rɪˈmeɪn/ (übrig) bleiben **CT8**
to **remember** /rɪˈmembə/ sich erinnern; daran denken **CT6**
to **remind** /rɪˈmaɪnd/ erinnern **CT8**
° remote /rɪˈməʊt/ fern; (weit) entfernt; abgelegen **1B4**
° removal /rɪˈmuːv(ə)l/ Beseitigung; Entfernung; Umzug **5SBS**
° to remove /rɪˈmuːv/ entfernen **5SBS**; *hier:* abschaffen **3D2**

° to rent /rent/ (ver)mieten **3D10**
° to reopen /ˌriːˈəʊpən/ wieder aufnehmen; wieder eröffnen **3R3**
to **repair** /rɪˈpeə/ reparieren; (wieder) in Ordnung bringen **4Intro 2**
to **repeat** /rɪˈpiːt/ wiederholen **3A2, 4B5**
° to rephrase /ˌriːˈfreɪz/ neu formulieren **4B/T2**
° to replace (with) /rɪˈpleɪs wɪð/ ersetzen (durch) **2D25, 5D7**
° to reply /rɪˈplaɪ/ antworten; erwidern **1R4, 5R1, 5R4**
report /rɪˈpɔːt/ (Zeitungs-)Bericht; (Zeitungs-)Meldung; Zeugnis **CT7**
to **report** /rɪˈpɔːt/ berichten; melden; wiedergeben **CT8**
° to report /rɪˈpɔːt/ *hier:* anzeigen **2D11**
° reported question /rɪˌpɔːtɪd ˈkwestʃ(ə)n/ indirekte Frage **4D3**
° reporting *(no pl)* /rɪˈpɔːtɪŋ/ Berichterstattung **5SBS**
to **represent sb/sth** /ˌreprɪˈzent/ jdn/etw repräsentieren; jdn vertreten **1A2**
representative /ˌreprɪˈzentətɪv/ (Stell)vertreter/in; repräsentativ **4A5**
on request /ɒn rɪˈkwest/ auf Anfrage; auf Wunsch **4A7**
to **require** /rɪˈkwaɪə/ brauchen; verlangen; benötigen **4B5**
° requirement /rɪˈkwaɪəmənt/ Voraussetzung; Erfordernis **3B3**
to **rescue** /ˈreskjuː/ retten; befreien **CT7**
research /ˈriːsɜːtʃ/ (Er)forschung; Untersuchung; Recherche **CT8**
to **do research** /ˌduː ˈriːsɜːtʃ/ (er)forschen; recherchieren **CT7**
to **research** /rɪˈsɜːtʃ/ erforschen; recherchieren **3Intro 6, 4B1**
° to resell *(irr)* /ˌriːˈsel/ weiterverkaufen **3B2**
resentment *(no pl)* /rɪˈzentmənt/ Verbitterung; Groll **3B1**
reservation /ˌrezəˈveɪʃ(ə)n/ Reservierung; Reservation *(den amerikanischen Ureinwohnern/Ureinwohnerinnen vorbehaltenes Gebiet in Nordamerika)* **CT8**
° residence /ˈrezɪd(ə)ns/ Wohngebäude; Wohnsitz **4SBS, 5SBS**
resident /ˈrezɪd(ə)nt/ Bewohner/in **CT8**
resistance *(no pl)* /rɪˈzɪst(ə)ns/ Widerstand **CT8**
° to resolve /rɪˈzɒlv/ (auf)lösen; klären; beschließen **2D10**
° resonance /ˈrezənəns/ (Nach)hall; Resonanz **4SBS**
° resourceful /rɪˈzɔːsf(ə)l/ ideenreich; einfallsreich **1R2**
to **respect** /rɪˈspekt/ respektieren **CT7**
° respectful /rɪˈspektf(ə)l/ respektvoll **2R3, 5D15**
to **respond (to)** /rɪˈspɒnd‿tʊ/ reagieren (auf); antworten **2A5, 3A5, 4B5**
responsibility /rɪˌspɒnsəˈbɪləti/ Verantwortung; Verantwortlichkeit; Zuständigkeit **CT8**
responsible /rɪˈspɒnsəb(ə)l/ verantwortlich; zuständig **2A4, 4A7**
° rest /rest/ (Ruhe)pause; Erholung **2D27**
° to rest /rest/ (aus)ruhen; *hier:* lehnen **1R2, 2R4**
° restaurant /ˈrestrɒnt/ Restaurant; Gaststätte **4D4, 5D8**
restoration /ˌrestəˈreɪʃ(ə)n/ Restaurierung(s-); Wiederherstellung **1B7**
restriction /rɪˈstrɪkʃ(ə)n/ Begrenzung; Einschränkung **3A7**
restrictive /rɪˈstrɪktɪv/ einschränkend; einengend **3A7**
to restyle /ˌriːˈstaɪl/ umgestalten; neu gestalten **4Intro 2**
result /rɪˈzʌlt/ Folge; Ergebnis **CT6**
° to result in sth /rɪˈzʌlt‿ɪn/ etw zur Folge haben; zu etw führen **2D10**
to **retreat** /rɪˈtriːt/ sich zurückziehen; zurückweichen **3A5**
to **return** /rɪˈtɜːn/ zurückkehren; zurückkommen **CT7**
to **reveal** /rɪˈviːl/ zeigen; enthüllen **2A4**
° revelatory /ˌrevəˈleɪt(ə)ri/ aufschlussreich **3R6**
review /rɪˈvjuː/ Überprüfung; Kritik; Rezension; Bewertung **CT6**
° to revise /rɪˈvaɪz/ überarbeiten; überdenken; korrigieren **3R3**
revolting /rɪˈvəʊltɪŋ/ abstoßend; widerlich **4Intro 4**
° revolution /ˌrevəˈluːʃ(ə)n/ Revolution; (umwälzende) Neuerung **1D5**
° to revolutionize /ˌrevəˈluːʃəˌnaɪz/ revolutionieren **4A5**
° to revolve around sth /rɪˈvɒlv‿əˌraʊnd/ sich um etw drehen **2D10**
° reward /rɪˈwɔːd/ Belohnung; Anerkennung **1A/T2**
° to rewind *(irr)* /ˌriːˈwaɪnd/ zurückspulen **5R3**
to **rewrite** *(irr)* /ˌriːˈraɪt/ neu schreiben; überarbeiten; umschreiben **CT7**
rhetorical /rɪˈtɒrɪk(ə)l/ rhetorisch **3A2, 5A5**
to **rhyme** /raɪm/ (sich) reimen **CT7**
rhyming /ˈraɪmɪŋ/ Reim- **CT7**
rhythm /ˈrɪðəm/ Rhythmus; Takt **CT6**
° ribbon /ˈrɪbən/ Band; Streifen; *hier:* Schwade **4SBS**
rice *(no pl)* /raɪs/ Reis **CT5**
rich /rɪtʃ/ reich **2A4**
° rich /rɪtʃ/ *hier:* gehaltvoll, schwer **2B/T1**
ride /raɪd/ Fahrt; Fahrgeschäft **CT8**
to **ride** *(irr)* /raɪd/ fahren (mit); reiten **CT5**
rifle /ˈraɪf(ə)l/ Gewehr **3A2**
right /raɪt/ richtig **CT5**; Recht **CT7**
on the right /ˌɒn ðə ˈraɪt/ rechts; auf der rechten Seite **CT6**
constitutional right /ˌkɒnstɪˌtjuːʃ(ə)nəl ˈraɪt/ Grundrecht **3A7**
civil rights *(pl)* /ˌsɪvəl ˈraɪts/ Bürgerrechte **CT8**
° right *(informal)* /raɪt/ also **4B4**
the right fit /ðə ˌraɪt ˈfɪt/ etwas Passendes; *hier:* die richtige Person **4A5**
° right-hand /ˌraɪt ˈhænd/ rechte(r, s) **Wordbank 3**
° right now /ˌraɪt ˈnaʊ/ jetzt (gerade); sofort; gleich **2D24**; *hier:* zurzeit **4D16**
to **ring (up)** *(irr)* /ˌrɪŋ‿ˈʌp/ anrufen; klingeln; läuten **CT5**
° to ring out *(irr)* /ˌrɪŋ‿ˈaʊt/ ertönen **4SBS**
° Rio+20 /ˌriːəʊ ˌplʌs ˈtwenti/ *UN-Konferenz in Rio über nachhaltige Entwicklung* **3D2**
riot /ˈraɪət/ Krawall; Unruhen; Ausschreitungen **CT8**
° ripple /ˈrɪp(ə)l/ leichte Welle; Kräuselung; *hier:* Schwaden **4SBS**
° to ripple /ˈrɪp(ə)l/ (sich) kräuseln **4SBS**
rise /raɪz/ Steigen; Anstieg; Aufstieg **3A5**
° to rise *(irr)* /raɪz/ steigen; aufgehen; sich erheben **4SBS, Wordbank 1**
° risk /rɪsk/ Risiko **2D10**
to **take a risk** /ˌteɪk‿ə ˈrɪsk/ ein Risiko eingehen; etw riskieren **1B7**
° risky /ˈrɪski/ riskant **2R4**
rival /ˈraɪv(ə)l/ Rivale/Rivalin; Konkurrent/in **CT7**
river /ˈrɪvə/ Fluss **CT6**
road /rəʊd/ Straße **CT6**
° robbery /ˈrɒbəri/ Raub(überfall) **3R1**
robot /ˈrəʊbɒt/ Roboter **CT7**
rock /rɒk/ Stein; Fels(en) **CT6**
° to rock /rɒk/ schaukeln; auf und ab bewegen **2SBS**; *hier:* erschüttern **3R2**
role /rəʊl/ Rolle **CT6**
role model /ˈrəʊl ˌmɒd(ə)l/ Vorbild; Rollenbild **5A1**
role play /ˈrəʊl pleɪ/ Rollenspiel **CT7**
° to roll /rəʊl/ (auf)rollen; drehen **1R2, 2SBS**
° to roll off /ˌrəʊl‿ˈɒf/ herunterrollen; *hier:* ausziehen **1R4**

° to roll one's eyes /ˌrəʊl wʌnz‿ˈaɪz/ die Augen verdrehen **1R2, 5B4**
Roman /ˈrəʊmən/ Römer/in; römisch **5A1**
° romance /rəʊˈmæns/ Romantik; Romanze; *hier:* Liebesfilm **Wordbank 5**
romantic /rəʊˈmæntɪk/ Romantiker/in; romantisch **CT7**
° roo *(informal, AusE)* /ruː, ˌkæŋgəˈruː/ Känguru **1Intro 3**
° roof /ruːf/ Dach **2SBS**
room /ruːm/ Zimmer; Raum **CT5**; Platz **CT6**
laundry room /ˈlɔːndri ruːm/ Waschküche **2A6**
rose /rəʊz/ Rose **CT7**
° rotten /ˈrɒt(ə)n/ korrupt; verfault; verdorben **3R3**
rough /rʌf/ rau; hart **CT8**
° roughly /ˈrʌfli/ grob; ungefähr; schätzungsweise **5R1**
° round /raʊnd/ rund **3R1, 4SBS**; Runde; Folge **5R1**
° to round /raʊnd/ umrunden; umgehen **1R4**
round (= around) /raʊnd, əˈraʊnd/ (her)um; umher **CT6**
° rounded /ˈraʊndɪd/ rund; gerundet **4SBS**
° roundly /ˈraʊndli/ gründlich; gehörig **4SBS**
route /ruːt/ Strecke; Route **CT6**
routine /ruːˈtiːn/ Routine; Gewohnheit(en); Nummer **CT8**
° row /rəʊ/ Reihe **3R1, 5R1**
rowing *(no pl)* /ˈrəʊɪŋ/ Rudern **1B2**
royal /ˈrɔɪəl/ Angehörige/r der Königsfamilie; königlich; Königs- **CT7**
rubber *(BE)* /ˈrʌbə/ Radiergummi **CT5**
to **take out the rubbish** /ˌteɪk‿ˌaʊt ðə ˈrʌbɪʃ/ den Müll hinausbringen **CT5**
rude /ruːd/ unhöflich **4Intro 2**
° to ruin /ˈruːɪn/ zerstören; verderben; kaputtmachen **3B/T1**
rule /ruːl/ Regel **CT5**
to **rule** /ruːl/ regieren; (be)herrschen **CT7**
° to rule /ruːl/ *hier:* entscheiden **3R6**
ruler /ˈruːlə/ Lineal **CT5**
° ruling /ˈruːlɪŋ/ (Gerichts)entscheidung **3R3**
° rumble /ˈrʌmb(ə)l/ Grollen **2SBS**
° rumblings *(pl)* /ˈrʌmblɪŋz/ Grollen; Donnern; (erste) Anzeichen **5R1**
rumour /ˈruːmə/ Gerücht **CT7**
to **run** *(irr)* /rʌn/ rennen; laufen **CT5**; *hier:* verlaufen **1B2**; *hier:* durchführen **4A5**
° to run *(irr)* /rʌn/ *hier:* betreiben, führen **4SBS**
° to run for sth /ˈrʌn fɔː/ für etw kandidieren **3R6**
to **run into sb** /ˌrʌn‿ˈɪntuː/ jdm über den Weg laufen **CT8**
° rush /rʌʃ/ Eile **2R3**
° to rush /rʌʃ/ eilen; hetzen **5B4**
Russian /ˈrʌʃ(ə)n/ Russe/Russin; Russisch; russisch **CT8**

S

sacred /ˈseɪkrɪd/ heilig; geheiligt **1A3**
sad /sæd/ traurig **CT5**
° sadness *(no pl)* /ˈsædnəs/ Traurigkeit; Trauer **3B/T2**
safe /seɪf/ sicher **CT5**; in Sicherheit **CT6**
safety *(no pl)* /ˈseɪfti/ Sicherheit(s-) **3A9**
to **sail** /seɪl/ (auf dem Wasser) fahren/reisen; segeln **CT7**
sailor /ˈseɪlə/ Matrose; Seemann; Segler/in **CT7**
salad /ˈsæləd/ Salat **CT5**
° salary /ˈsæləri/ Gehalt **3B2**
° sale /seɪl/ (Aus)verkauf; Absatz **3D5**
salesperson (*pl* salespeople) /ˈseɪlzˌpɜːs(ə)n, ˈseɪlzˌpiːp(ə)l/ Verkäufer/in **4Intro 2**
° salon /ˈsælɒn/ Salon; Geschäft **4R3**
° sandstone /ˈsændˌstəʊn/ Sandstein **1D2**
° sandy /ˈsændi/ sandig; *hier:* sandfarben **4SBS**
the same /ðə ˈseɪm/ der-/die-/dasselbe; der/die/das Gleiche **CT6**
° sanger *(informal, AusE)* /ˈsæŋgə/ Sandwich **1Intro 3**
sarcastic /sɑːˈkæstɪk/ sarkastisch **2B3**
satisfied /ˈsætɪsfaɪd/ zufrieden **CT6**
° satisfying /ˈsætɪsˌfaɪɪŋ/ zufriedenstellend **2A/T2**
Saturday /ˈsætədeɪ/ Samstag **CT5**
sauce /sɔːs/ Soße; Sauce **CT5**
to **save** /seɪv/ retten; (be)wahren; sparen **CT6**
to **say** *(irr)* /seɪ/ sagen **CT5**
to **say goodbye (to sb)** /ˌseɪ ˌgʊdˈbaɪ tʊ/ (jdm) Auf Wiedersehen sagen; sich (von jdm) verabschieden **CT6**
to **say hello (to sb)** /ˌseɪ həˈləʊ tə ˌsʌmbədi/ (jdn) (be)grüßen **CT6**
to **say sorry** /ˌseɪ ˈsɒri/ sich entschuldigen **CT5**
° saying /ˈseɪɪŋ/ Sprichwort **3SBS**
° scale /skeɪl/ Skala; Maßstab; Ausmaß; Umfang **3R6**
to **scan (for)** /ˈskæn fə/ absuchen (nach); überfliegen; (ein)scannen **CT7**
scandalous /ˈskænd(ə)ləs/ skandalös; unerhört **5A3**
° scarcely /ˈskeəsli/ kaum **4SBS**
to **scare** /skeə/ Angst machen; erschrecken **CT6**
° to scare the hell out of sb *(informal)* /ˌskeə ðə ˈhel‿aʊt‿əv/ jdn zu Tode erschrecken **2SBS**
scared /skeəd/ verängstigt **CT5**
° scarlet /ˈskɑːlət/ Scharlachrot; scharlachrot **4SBS**
scary /ˈskeəri/ furchterregend **CT8**
scene /siːn/ Szene **CT7**
° scenery *(no pl)* /ˈsiːnəri/ Landschaft **1P1**
schedule /ˈʃedjuːl/ Zeit-/Terminplan; Programm **CT7**
schedule *(AE)* /ˈskeˌdʒul/ Stundenplan **CT8**
° schizophrenia *(no pl)* /ˌskɪtsəʊˈfriːniə/ Bewusstseinsspaltung; Schizophrenie **2B5**
° schizophrenic /ˌskɪtsəʊˈfrenɪk/ Schizophrene/r; schizophren **2B3**
scholarship /ˈskɒləʃɪp/ Stipendium **CT8**
school /skuːl/ Schule; Schul- **CT5**
boarding school /ˈbɔːdɪŋ skuːl/ Internat **CT7**
school bag, schoolbag /ˈskuːl bæg/ Schultasche **CT5**
° School of the Air /ˌskuːl‿əv ði‿ˈeə/ *spezielle Schulform in den dünn besiedelten Regionen Australiens* **1B2**
science /ˈsaɪəns/ (Natur)wissenschaft **CT5**
scientific /ˌsaɪənˈtɪfɪk/ (natur)wissenschaftlich **CT8**
° scientist /ˈsaɪəntɪst/ Wissenschaftler/in **4D12, 5B/T3**
scissors *(pl)* /ˈsɪzəz/ Schere **CT5**
° scoop /skuːp/ (Schöpf)löffel; (Eis)kugel; *hier:* Schippe **5R3**
score /skɔː/ Punktestand; Spielstand; Punktzahl; Ergebnis **CT7**
to **score (a goal)** /ˌskɔːr‿ə ˈgəʊl/ (ein Tor) schießen **CT5**
Scotland /ˈskɒtlənd/ Schottland **CT7**
° scout /skaʊt/ Talentsucher/in **1R4**
° to scowl at sb /ˈskaʊl‿ət/ jdn mürrisch ansehen **3B4**
° scraggly *(informal, AE)* /ˈskræg(ə)li/ zott(e)lig **3B4**
° to scramble /ˈskræmb(ə)l/ verrühren; durcheinanderbringen **2SBS**
° to scrape by (on sth) /ˌskreɪp‿ˈbaɪ‿ɒn/ (mit etw) gerade so über die Runden kommen **3B2**
to **scream** /skriːm/ schreien; kreischen **CT6**
° scream /skriːm/ Schrei **2SBS, 4SBS**
° screen /skriːn/ Leinwand; Bildschirm **2D21, 4R2, 5D5**

screen time *(no pl)* /ˈskriːn taɪm/ Bildschirmzeit **2A6**
° to screw around *(informal)* /ˌskruː‿əˈraʊnd/ (he)rummachen; *hier:* veräppeln **4R3**
script /skrɪpt/ Drehbuch; Skript; Regiebuch **CT8**
° to scroll /skrəʊl/ scrollen **5B4**
° to scrunch /skrʌntʃ/ knirschen; zerknittern **4SBS**
° to scull /skʌl/ rudern; *hier:* runterstürzen **1R2**
° sculpture /ˈskʌlptʃə/ Skulptur; Standbild **5D2**
° to scuttle /ˈskʌt(ə)l/ eilen; hasten; wuseln **3B4**
° sea level /ˈsiː ˌlev(ə)l/ Meeresspiegel **1A3**
sea *(no pl)* /siː/ Meer; (die) See **CT6**
° seafarer /ˈsiːˌfeərə/ Seefahrer; Seemann **5D2**
° seafaring /ˈsiːˌfeərɪŋ/ seefahrend; Seefahrer- **5D2**
° seafront *(no pl)* /ˈsiːˌfrʌnt/ Strandpromenade; Strand **1P1**
° seagull /ˈsiːˌgʌl/ Möwe **2D28**
° to seal /siːl/ (ver)siegeln; verschließen **4SBS**
° search /sɜːtʃ/ Suche; Such-; *hier:* Durchsuchung **3D2, 5D5**
to **search (for sb/sth)** /ˈsɜːtʃ fə/ (nach jdm/etw) suchen **CT6**
° search result /ˈsɜːtʃ rɪˌzʌlt/ Suchergebnis **1B/T1**
to **search the internet** /ˌsɜːtʃ ði‿ˈɪntəˌnet/ im Internet suchen **CT8**
season /ˈsiːz(ə)n/ Jahreszeit; Saison **CT8**
dry season /ˈdraɪ ˌsiːz(ə)n/ Trockenzeit **1B7**
wet season /ˈwet ˌsiːz(ə)n/ Regenzeit **1B7**
° seat /siːt/ Sitz(platz) **3D12, 4R2**
° to seat /siːt/ (sich) setzen; *hier:* Platz bieten für **3R1**
second /ˈsekənd/ zweite(r, s) **CT5**
° second /ˈsekənd/ Sekunde; Augenblick **3B2**
Second Amendment (to the United States Constitution) /ˌsekənd‿əˈmendmənt (tə ðə juːˌnaɪtɪd ˌsteɪts ˌkɒnstɪˈtjuːʃ(ə)n)/ *Zweiter Zusatzartikel (zur Verfassung der Vereinigten Staaten)* **3A5**
the Second World War /ðə ˌsekənd ˌwɜːld ˈwɔː/ der Zweite Weltkrieg **5A1**
° secondary school /ˈsekənd(ə)ri skuːl/ höhere/weiterführende Schule **1B2**
secret /ˈsiːkrət/ Geheimnis; geheim; Geheim- **CT7**
° secretary /ˈsekrətri/ Sekretär/in **1B/T1**
° Secretary General /ˌsekrətri ˈdʒen(ə)rəl/ Generalsekretär/in **3SBS**
° secretly /ˈsiːkrətli/ heimlich **2B/T2**
° section /ˈsekʃ(ə)n/ Teil; Abschnitt; Abteilung **2R1, 3A/T1**
secure /sɪˈkjʊə/ sicher; fest (verschlossen) **3A7**
° security guard /sɪˈkjʊərəti gɑːd/ Sicherheitsbedienstete/r **3A10**
to **see** *(irr)* /siː/ sehen **CT5**; verstehen **CT6**
as I see it /æz‿ˈaɪ siː‿ɪt/ wie ich es sehe; meiner Meinung nach **2Intro 6**
I see. /aɪ ˈsiː/ Ich verstehe. **CT8**
See you (later). *(informal)* /ˌsiː jʊ ˈleɪtə/ Bis später.; Bis nachher. **CT5**
See you soon! *(informal)* /ˌsiː jʊ ˈsuːn/ Bis bald! **CT5**
to **seek** *(irr)* /siːk/ suchen; versuchen **CT8**
° seeker /ˈsiːkə/ Suchende/r **1A/T2**
to **seem** /siːm/ scheinen **CT6**
° segment /ˈsegmənt/ Teil; Segment; *hier:* Ausschnitt **5R3**
° segregation *(no pl)* /ˌsegrɪˈgeɪʃ(ə)n/ (Rassen)trennung **3B3**
° self-acceptance *(no pl)* /ˌself‿əkˈseptəns/ Selbstannahme **2B/T2**
self-centred /ˌselfˈsentəd/ selbstbezogen; egozentrisch **2A3**
° self-conscious /ˌselfˈkɒnʃəs/ gehemmt; verlegen **1R2**
self-defence *(no pl)* /ˌself dɪˈfens/ Selbstverteidigung **3A5**
self-esteem *(no pl)* /ˌself‿ɪˈstiːm/ Selbstwertgefühl **2A3**
° self-government *(no pl)* /ˌself ˈgʌvənmənt/ Selbstverwaltung **1P1**
° self-motivation *(no pl)* /ˌself məʊtɪˈveɪʃn/ Selbstmotivation; Eigenmotivation **Wordbank 8**
° self-obsessed /ˌselfəbˈsest/ selbstsüchtig **5B2**
° selfish /ˈselfɪʃ/ selbstsüchtig; egoistisch **1R2**
to **sell** *(irr)* /sel/ verkaufen **CT6**
° seller /ˈselə/ Verkäufer/in **3A7**
° selling *(no pl)* /ˈselɪŋ/ Verkauf(s-); Verkaufen **4Intro 2**
° semblance /ˈsembləns/ Erscheinungsbild; Anschein **4SBS**
to **send** *(irr)* /send/ (zu)schicken **CT6**
° senior /ˈsiːniə/ Senior/in; älter **3B3, 4Intro 2**
senior *(AE)* /ˈsinjər/ *Oberstufenschüler/in im letzten Jahr* **3B1**
° sensation /senˈseɪʃ(ə)n/ Gefühl; Sensation **3B2**
sense /sens/ Verstand; Sinn; Gefühl **1A5**
sensible /ˈsensəb(ə)l/ vernünftig; angemessen **CT6**
° sensible /ˈsensəb(ə)l/ *hier:* sinnvoll **5B4**
° sensitivity /ˌsensəˈtɪvəti/ Empfindsamkeit; Sensibilität; Verständnis **Wordbank 8**
sentence /ˈsentəns/ Satz **CT6**
° to sentence /ˈsentəns/ verurteilen **3R1**
separate /ˈsep(ə)rət/ getrennt; separat; einzeln **1Intro 1**
° to separate /ˈsepəreɪt/ trennen; abspalten; (sich) scheiden (lassen) **4SBS**
September /sepˈtembə/ September **CT5**
° sequence /ˈsiːkwəns/ Reihenfolge; Reihe; Ablauf **2R1, 5D11**
series (*pl* **series**) /ˈsɪəriːz/ (Fernseh)serie; Reihe; Folge **CT7**
serious /ˈsɪəriəs/ ernst **CT6**
to **take sb/sth seriously** /ˌteɪk ˌsʌmbədi/ˌsʌmθɪŋ ˈsɪəriəsli/ jdn/etw ernst nehmen **CT7**
° servant /ˈsɜːv(ə)nt/ Diener/in; Bedienstete/r **2D26**
° to serve /sɜːv/ servieren; dienen **2SBS**
° service /ˈsɜːvɪs/ Service; Dienst(leistung) **1D15, 3R1**
° set /set/ starr **2SBS**
to **be set** /ˌbiː ˈset/ liegen; spielen **CT8**
° to set *(irr)* /set/ (fest)setzen; festlegen **2D6**
° to set a fire /ˌset ə ˈfaɪə/ ein Feuer machen; einen Brand legen **5A1**
to **set up** *(irr)* /ˌset‿ˈʌp/ errichten; einrichten **4Intro 2**
° set-up /ˈsetʌp/ Aufbau; *hier:* Konstellation **4SBS**
° setback /ˈsetˌbæk/ Rückschlag **3B2**
setting /ˈsetɪŋ/ Einstellung; Umgebung; Schauplatz **2A2**
° to settle /ˈset(ə)l/ es sich bequem machen; sich niederlassen **1D3, 3A6, 4SBS**
° to settle in /ˌset(ə)l‿ˈɪn/ sich eingewöhnen **2R1, 3D10**
° settlement /ˈset(ə)lmənt/ (Be)siedlung; Ansiedlung **1P2**
settler /ˈsetlə/ Siedler/in **CT8**
seven /ˈsev(ə)n/ sieben **CT5**
several /ˈsev(ə)rəl/ einige; ein paar **CT8**
severe /sɪˈvɪə/ schwer; schlimm; heftig **CT8**
° sexual orientation *(no pl)* /ˌsekʃuəl‿ˌɔːriənˈteɪʃ(ə)n/ sexuelle Veranlagung **2D2**
° shade /ʃeɪd/ Schatten; Tönung; Farbton **5D2**
° to shake one's head /ˌʃeɪk wʌnz ˈhed/ den Kopf schütteln **2SBS, 3B2, 4SBS**

° to shake sb's hand /ˌʃeɪk ˌsʌmbədiz ˈhænd/ jds Hand schütteln **4SBS**
° shaken /ˈʃeɪkən/ erschüttert; aufgewühlt **4SBS**
shall /ʃæl/ sollen; werden **4B4**
° shape /ʃeɪp/ Form **1P1**
° to shape /ʃeɪp/ (aus)formen; prägen **1R2**
° shapeless /ˈʃeɪpləs/ unförmig; formlos **4SBS**
to **share** /ʃeə/ teilen **CT6**
sharp /ʃɑːp/ scharf; spitz; deutlich **CT8**
she /ʃiː/ sie **CT5**
she's (= she is) /ʃiːz, ˈʃi‿ɪz/ sie ist **CT5**
sheep (*pl* **sheep**) /ʃiːp/ Schaf **CT5**
° sheet /ʃiːt/ Blatt; Platte; Laken **2SBS, 3R2, 4R2**
shelf (*pl* **shelves**) /ʃelf, ʃelvz/ (Regal)brett; Bord **CT5**
shell /ʃel/ Schale; Muschel; Panzer **1B7**
animal rescue shelter /ˌænɪm(ə)l ˈreskjuː ˌʃeltə/ Tierauffangstation; Tierheim **4A5**
shift /ʃɪft/ Schicht **4A5**
° to shift /ʃɪft/ (weg)bewegen **3R6, 4SBS**
° to shift up a gear /ˌʃɪft‿ˌʌp‿ə ˈɡɪə/ einen Gang höher schalten **5R4**
ship /ʃɪp/ Schiff **CT7**
shirt /ʃɜːt/ Hemd **CT7**
° shirt /ʃɜːt/ *hier:* Trikot **1R4, 5D2**
° shite (*offensive, BE*) /ʃaɪt/ Scheiß(e) **4R1**
° to shock /ʃɒk/ schockieren; erschüttern **4SBS**
shocked /ʃɒkt/ schockiert; entsetzt **CT5**
° shocking /ˈʃɒkɪŋ/ schockierend; schrecklich **5D10**
shoe /ʃuː/ Schuh **CT5**
to **shoot** (*irr*) /ʃuːt/ schießen **CT7**
to **shoot sb** /ʃuːt/ jdn anschießen; jdn erschießen **3A2**
° shooter /ˈʃuːtə/ Schießende/r; Schütze/Schützin **3R2**
shooting /ˈʃuːtɪŋ/ Schießerei; Schießen **3A2**
° shooting range /ˈʃuːtɪŋ reɪndʒ/ Schießstand **3D7**
shop /ʃɒp/ Geschäft; Laden **CT5**
to **shop** /ʃɒp/ einkaufen **CT5**
° shop /ʃɒp/ *hier:* Werkstatt **5D7**
shop assistant /ˈʃɒp‿əˌsɪst(ə)nt/ Verkäufer/in **CT5**
° shopping mall (*AE*) /ˈʃɒpɪŋ mɔl/ Einkaufszentrum **3D4**
shopping (*no pl*) /ˈʃɒpɪŋ/ Einkaufen **CT5**
short /ʃɔːt/ kurz **CT5**
° short story /ˌʃɔːt ˈstɔːri/ Kurzgeschichte **1R1**
° to shorten /ˈʃɔːt(ə)n/ (ab)kürzen **1B/T1**
shot /ʃɒt/ Schuss **3A2**; *hier:* Einstellung **2D18**
should /ʃʊd/ sollen **CT5**
° shoulder /ˈʃəʊldə/ Schulter **2SBS**
shouldn't (= should not) /ˈʃʊdnt, ʃʊd ˈnɒt/ nicht sollen **CT5**
to **shout (at)** /ˈʃaʊt‿ət/ (an)schreien **CT5**
° to shovel /ˈʃʌv(ə)l/ (weg)schaufeln **4D4**
° show /ʃəʊ/ Show; Schau; Vorstellung; *hier:* Ausstellung **3A7**
to **show** (*irr*) /ʃəʊ/ zeigen **CT6**
° to show off (*irr*) /ˌʃəʊ‿ˈɒf/ angeben; (voller Stolz) zeigen **4A10**
to **show sb (a)round** /ˌʃəʊ ˌsʌmbədi‿əˈraʊnd/ jdn herumführen **CT8**
shower /ˈʃaʊə/ Schauer; Regen; Dusche **2A6**
to **have/take a shower** /ˌhæv/ˌteɪk‿ə ˈʃaʊə/ sich duschen **CT6**
to **shower** /ˈʃaʊə/ duschen **CT7**
° shrug /ʃrʌɡ/ Achselzucken **5R2**
to **shrug (one's shoulders)** /ˌʃrʌɡ wʌnz ˈʃəʊldəz/ die Achseln zucken **CT7**
to **shut up** (*irr*) /ˌʃʌt‿ˈʊp/ zuschließen; zum Schweigen bringen **CT7**
° to shut up (*irr*) /ˌʃʌt‿ˈʊp/ *hier:* den Mund halten **4R1**
° shutters (*pl*) /ˈʃʌtəz/ Fensterläden; Rollläden **4SBS**
shy /ʃaɪ/ schüchtern; scheu **CT5**
° siblings (*pl*) /ˈsɪblɪŋz/ Geschwister **3R1**
sick /sɪk/ krank **CT5**
side /saɪd/ Seite **CT8**
° sideline /ˈsaɪdˌlaɪn/ Begrenzungslinie; Seitenlinie **1R4**
° to sigh /saɪ/ seufzen **1R4, 2R3, 4SBS, 5B2**
sight /saɪt/ Sehenswürdigkeit **CT6**
° sight (*no pl*) /saɪt/ Sehvermögen; Sicht **4SBS**
sightseeing (*no pl*) /ˈsaɪtˌsiːɪŋ/ Besichtigungen; Sightseeing **CT6**
sign /saɪn/ Zeichen; (Straßen-/Verkehrs)schild; Spur **CT6**
to **sign** /saɪn/ unterschreiben; unterzeichnen **CT8**
° to sign off /ˌsaɪn‿ˈɒf/ zum Schluss kommen; unterschreiben **4A9**
to **sign up** /ˌsaɪn‿ˈʌp/ sich einschreiben; sich anmelden **1B2, 3B3**
° sign-off phrase /ˈsaɪnˌɒf‿freɪz/ abschließende Grußformel **5SBS**
° signal /ˈsɪɡn(ə)l/ Zeichen; Signal(-) **3B4**
° to signal /ˈsɪɡn(ə)l/ signalisieren; hinweisen (auf) **2D5**
° signature /ˈsɪɡnətʃə/ Unterschrift **5B4**
° significant /sɪɡˈnɪfɪkənt/ beachtlich; bedeutend; bedeutsam **2D10**
significantly /sɪɡˈnɪfɪkəntli/ bedeutend; deutlich **CT8**
° to silence /ˈsaɪləns/ zum Schweigen bringen **3SBS**
silence (*no pl*) /ˈsaɪləns/ Stille; Schweigen; Ruhe **3Intro 6**
silent /ˈsaɪlənt/ still; ruhig; schweigsam **CT8**
silly /ˈsɪli/ albern; dumm **CT7**
° silver /ˈsɪlvə/ Silber(-); silbern **1D9, 5D13**
similar /ˈsɪmɪlə/ ähnlich **CT7**
similarity /ˌsɪməˈlærəti/ Ähnlichkeit **CT8**
similarly /ˈsɪmələli/ ähnlich; ebenso **CT8**
° to simmer /ˈsɪmə/ sieden; köcheln **3B4**
simple /ˈsɪmp(ə)l/ einfach **CT7**
° simplistic /sɪmˈplɪstɪk/ simpel; einfach **5SBS**
° simply /ˈsɪmpli/ einfach; nur **2A4, 5SBS**
since /sɪns/ seit; da; weil **CT6**
° since /sɪns/ seitdem; seither **1P1, 5SBS**
° since then /ˌsɪns ˈðen/ seitdem **2D5, 3D12**
to **sing** (*irr*) /sɪŋ/ singen **CT5**
to **sing along** (*irr*) /ˌsɪŋ‿əˈlɒŋ/ mitsingen **CT7**
° Singapore /ˌsɪŋəˈpɔː/ Singapur **3A7**
singer /ˈsɪŋə/ Sänger/in **CT6**
° single /ˈsɪŋɡ(ə)l/ einzige(r, s); einzelne(r, s) **2R1**
single parent /ˌsɪŋɡ(ə)l ˈpeərənt/ Alleinerziehende/r **5A1**
° singsong /ˈsɪŋˌsɒŋ/ Singsang(-) **3R1**
sink /sɪŋk/ Waschbecken **2A6**
° to sip /sɪp/ nippen (an) **4SBS, 5B2**
Sir /sɜː/ (Mein) Herr; *hier:* Herr Lehrer! **CT6**
sister /ˈsɪstə/ Schwester **CT5**
to **sit** (*irr*) /sɪt/ sitzen **CT5**
to **sit down** (*irr*) /ˌsɪt‿ˈdaʊn/ sich (hin)setzen **CT5**
site /saɪt/ Stelle; Platz; Ort **CT8**
six /sɪks/ sechs **CT5**
size /saɪz/ Größe **5A5**
skateboarding (*no pl*) /ˈskeɪtˌbɔːdɪŋ/ Skateboard fahren **CT5**
° sketch /sketʃ/ Skizze **2D20**
° to sketch /sketʃ/ skizzieren **5B9**
skiing (*no pl*) /ˈskiːɪŋ/ Skifahren, **CT8**
° skilful /ˈskɪlf(ə)l/ geschickt; gekonnt; kunstvoll **2D21**
skill /skɪl/ Geschick; Fähigkeit; Fertigkeit **CT7**
° skilled /skɪld/ ausgebildet; geschickt; qualifiziert **4SBS**
to **skim** /skɪm/ streifen; überfliegen **CT7**

° skin /skɪn/ Haut **2SBS**
° to skip /skɪp/ hüpfen; auslassen; *hier:* schwänzen **3R1, 4D15**
skirt /skɜːt/ Rock **CT7**
° skull /skʌl/ Schädel **4SBS**
sky /skaɪ/ Himmel **CT8**
° skywriting *(no pl)* /ˈskaɪˌraɪtɪŋ/ Himmelsschreiben **2R3**
° slab of concrete /ˌslæb‿əv ˈkɒŋkriːt/ Betonplatte **1R2**
° to slam down /ˌslæm ˈdaʊn/ hinknallen; *hier:* sich (in einen Sitz) fallen lassen **4R1**
to **slam the door shut** /ˌslæm ðə ˈdɔː ʃʌt/ die Tür zuschlagen **CT7**
° to slap /slæp/ schlagen **3R3**
° to slash /slæʃ/ aufschlitzen; aufschneiden **5B4**
° slave /sleɪv/ Sklave/Sklavin **5SBS**
slavery *(no pl)* /ˈsleɪvəri/ Sklaverei **CT8**
to **go to sleep** /ˌɡəʊ tə ˈsliːp/ (ein)schlafen **CT7**
to **sleep** *(irr)* /sliːp/ schlafen **CT5**
° sleep *(no pl)* /sliːp/ Schlaf **1R4**
° to sleep over /ˌsliːp‿ˈəʊvə/ übernachten **2SBS**
° sleeping bag /ˈsliːpɪŋ bæɡ/ Schlafsack **5R1**
° sleepless /ˈsliːpləs/ schlaflos **1R2**
° slender /ˈslendə/ schlank; schmal **4SBS**
° to slide *(irr)* /slaɪd/ rutschen; gleiten **2SBS**
slight /slaɪt/ gering; klein; leicht **CT8**
° slightly /ˈslaɪtli/ ein wenig; etwas **2SBS**
° slim /slɪm/ schlank; dünn; mager **4SBS**
° to slip /slɪp/ ausrutschen; abrutschen; *hier:* drauflegen **3B4**
° to slip away /ˌslɪp‿əˈweɪ/ entgleiten; vergehen **1R2**
slow /sləʊ/ langsam **CT6**
° to slow down /ˌsləʊ ˈdaʊn/ verlangsamen; abflauen **2B/T2**
° to slump /slʌmp/ stürzen; zusammensacken **3B2**
° slurp /slɜːp/ Schlürfen **4SBS**
° to smack /smæk/ knallen; *hier:* einen Ruck geben **2SBS**
small /smɔːl/ klein **CT5**
° small-town /ˌsmɔːl ˈtaʊn/ kleinstädtisch; Kleinstadt- **2R1**
smart /smɑːt/ schlau; clever **2A6**
° smell /smel/ Geruch; Duft; Gestank **2D28**
to **smell** *(irr)* /smel/ riechen; duften **CT5**
smile /smaɪl/ Lächeln **CT7**
to **smile (at)** /ˈsmaɪl‿æt/ (an)lächeln **CT5**
° smoke /sməʊk/ Rauch **4SBS**
° to smoke /sməʊk/ rauchen **1SBS, 2D2, 3R5**
smoking *(no pl)* /ˈsməʊkɪŋ/ Rauchen **2Intro 2**
° smooth /smuːð/ glatt; ruhig; weich **2SBS**
° to smooth /smuːð/ ebnen; glätten **3R2, 4SBS**
° snake /sneɪk/ Schlange **Wordbank 1**
° to snap /snæp/ schnalzen; schnippen; *hier:* ausrasten **3B4**
snorkelling *(no pl)* /ˈsnɔːk(ə)lɪŋ/ Schnorcheln **1B2**
° snort /snɔːt/ Schnauben **4SBS**
snow *(no pl)* /snəʊ/ Schnee **CT8**
° snowy /ˈsnəʊi/ schneereich; verschneit **1P1**
so /səʊ/ also; deshalb **CT6**; damit **CT7**
so far /ˈsəʊ fɑː/ bisher **CT8**
° so to speak /ˌsəʊ tə ˈspiːk/ sozusagen **2R3**
so that /ˈsəʊ ðæt/ sodass; damit **CT7**
° so-and-so *(informal)* /ˈsəʊ‿ən səʊ/ Soundso **2SBS**
soap /səʊp/ Seife **CT6**
soccer /ˈsɒkə/ Fußball(-) **CT8**
° sociable /ˈsəʊʃəb(ə)l/ gesellig; freundlich; umgänglich **1R2**
social /ˈsəʊʃ(ə)l/ Gesellschaft(s)-; gesellschaftlich; sozial **CT7**
social media /ˌsəʊʃ(ə)l ˈmiːdiə/ Social Media *(Gesamtheit der digitalen Technologien/Medien, über die Nutzer/-innen sich austauschen können)* **CT5**
society /səˈsaɪəti/ Gesellschaft **1A3, 3A7**
° sociology *(no pl)* /ˌsəʊʃiˈɒlədʒi/ Soziologie **3D12**
sock /sɒk/ Socke **CT5**
° soft skills *(pl)* /ˈsɒft skɪlz/ Soft Skills *(soziale oder emotionale Kompetenz)* **4D9**
soldier /ˈsəʊldʒə/ Soldat/in **CT7**
° solemn /ˈsɒləm/ feierlich; ernst **3B2**
solution /səˈluːʃ(ə)n/ (Auf)lösung **2A4**
to **solve** /sɒlv/ lösen **CT7**
some /sʌm/ einige; etwas **CT6**
somebody /ˈsʌmbədi/ (irgend)jemand; irgendwer **CT5**
somebody can't wait (to do sth) /ˌsʌmbədi ˌkɑːnt ˌweɪt‿tə ˈduː/ jemand kann es kaum erwarten(, etw. zu tun) **CT7**
° someday /ˈsʌmˌdeɪ/ eines Tages; irgendwann einmal **3R1**
someone /ˈsʌmwʌn/ (irgend)jemand; irgendwer **CT6**
someone else /ˌsʌmwʌn‿ˈels/ jemand anders **CT6**
something /ˈsʌmθɪŋ/ etwas **CT5**
° sometime /ˈsʌmtaɪm/ irgendwann **1D14**
sometimes /ˈsʌmtaɪmz/ manchmal **CT5**
somewhere /ˈsʌmweə/ irgendwo **CT6**
son /sʌn/ Sohn **CT5**
soon /suːn/ bald; gleich **CT6**
Sorry! /ˈsɒri/ Entschuldigung!; Tut mir leid! **CT5**
I'm sorry. /ˌaɪm ˈsɒri/ Entschuldigung.; Tut mir leid. **CT5**
to **feel sorry** /ˌfiːl ˈsɒri/ bedauern; leidtun **CT6**
to **say sorry** /ˌseɪ ˈsɒri/ sich entschuldigen **CT5**
to **sort** /sɔːt/ sortieren **4B4**
° sort /sɔːt/ Sorte; Art **1R2, 4SBS**
° sort of /ˈsɔːt‿əv/ irgendwie; sozusagen **1R4, 2B3**
sound /saʊnd/ Geräusch; Klang; Laut **CT7**
to **sound** /saʊnd/ klingen **CT6**
° soup /suːp/ Suppe **1R2, 3B2**
source /sɔːs/ Quelle; Informationsquelle **2A6, 4SBS, 5Intro 4**
south /saʊθ/ Süden; südlich; Süd- **CT7**
° South Island /ˈsaʊθ‿ˌaɪlənd/ neuseeländische Südinsel **1P1**
South Korea /ˌsaʊθ kəˈrɪə/ Südkorea **CT8**
southern /ˈsʌðən/ südlich; Süd- **CT7**
° Southern Cross /ˌsʌðən ˈkrɒs/ Kreuz des Südens *(markantes Sternbild des Südhimmels)* **1A2**
space /speɪs/ Raum; Platz; Weltraum(-) **CT6**
office space *(no pl)* /ˈɒfɪs‿speɪs/ Büroräume; Bürofläche(n) **4A5**
° space shuttle /ˈspeɪs ˌʃʌt(ə)l/ (Welt)raumfähre **5B/T3**
° spacewalk /ˈspeɪsˌwɔːk/ Außerbordeinsatz; Weltraumspaziergang **5B/T3**
° spacious /ˈspeɪʃəs/ geräumig; weitläufig **5B2**
° Spain /speɪn/ Spanien **5D20**
to span /spæn/ umfassen; umspannen **1A5**
Spanish /ˈspænɪʃ/ Spanisch(-); spanisch **CT5**
° to spare /speə/ (ver)schonen; (er)sparen; übrig haben **5R1**
spare time *(no pl)* /ˌspeə ˈtaɪm/ Freizeit **4Intro 2**
to **speak** *(irr)* /spiːk/ sprechen **CT5**
to **speak out** *(irr)* /ˌspiːk‿ˈaʊt/ seine Meinung deutlich vertreten; sich aussprechen **CT8**
° to speak up *(irr)* /ˌspiːk‿ˈʌp/ seine Meinung sagen **3SBS**

speaker /ˈspiːkə/ Redner/in; Sprecher/in; Anrufer/in, **CT6**
native speaker /ˌneɪtɪv ˈspiːkə/ Muttersprachler/in **4A7**
special /ˈspeʃ(ə)l/ besondere(r, s) **CT5**
to **specialize (in)** /ˈspeʃəlaɪz‿ɪn/ sich spezialisieren (auf) **1B7**
specialized /ˈspeʃəlaɪzd/ spezialisiert **CT8**
° species (*pl* species) /ˈspiːʃiːz, ˈspiːʃiːz/ Art; Spezies **Wordbank 1**
specific /spəˈsɪfɪk/ genau; bestimmte(r, s); spezifisch **2A4**
° specifically /spəˈsɪfɪkli/ speziell; ausdrücklich **3D2**
° spectacles *(pl)* /ˈspektək(ə)lz/ Brille **2B3**
spectacular /spekˈtækjʊlə/ atemberaubend; fantastisch **CT6**
spectator /spekˈteɪtə/ Zuschauer/in **4Intro 2**
° spectre /ˈspektə/ (Schreck)gespenst **4SBS**
to **speculate (about/on)** /ˈspekjuleɪt‿əˌbaʊt/ɒn/ spekulieren; Vermutungen anstellen (über) **CT6**
speculation /ˌspekjʊˈleɪʃ(ə)n/ Spekulation; Vermutung **3B4**
speech /spiːtʃ/ Rede **1A5, 5B7**
to **give/make a speech** /ˌɡɪv/ˌmeɪk‿ə ˈspiːtʃ/ eine Rede halten **CT7**
° speech bubble /ˈspiːtʃˌbʌb(ə)l/ Sprechblase **2R1**
speed /spiːd/ Geschwindigkeit; Tempo **CT8**
° spellchecker /ˈspelˌtʃekə/ Rechtschreibprüfprogramm **4R1**
spelling /ˈspelɪŋ/ Rechtschreibung; Rechtschreib- **CT7**
to **spend** *(irr)* /spend/ verbringen *(Zeit)*; ausgeben *(Geld)* **CT6**
° spider /ˈspaɪdə/ Spinne **Wordbank 1**
° to spin *(irr)* /spɪn/ rotieren; drehen **4SBS**; *hier:* spinnen **5A1**
spirit /ˈspɪrɪt/ Geist; Stimmung; Seele; Einstellung **CT8**
° spirits *(pl)* /ˈspɪrɪts/ Gemütsverfassung; Mut; Stimmung **3B2**
° spiritual /ˈspɪrɪtʃuəl/ geistig; spirituell **1D1**
° to spit (out) *(irr)* /ˌspɪt‿ˈaʊt/ (aus)spucken; *hier:* ausstoßen **3B4**
to **split up** *(irr)* /ˌsplɪt‿ˈʌp/ (sich) (auf)teilen **CT8**
° spoiler /ˈspɔɪlə/ Spoiler(n) *(Details verraten und dadurch jemandem die Überraschung nehmen)* **2B12**
° sponge /spʌndʒ/ Schwamm **2SBS**
sports /spɔːts/ Sport(-) **CT6**
sports ground /ˈspɔːts ˌɡraʊnd/ Sportplatz **CT7**
° sports science /ˈspɔːts‿ˌsaɪəns/ Sportwissenschaft **4R2**
spot /spɒt/ Fleck; Stelle; Ort **CT8**
to **spot** /spɒt/ entdecken **CT7**
° spot /spɒt/ *hier:* (Sitz)platz **3B4**
° spotted /ˈspɒtɪd/ getupft; gepunktet **4SBS**
to **spray** /spreɪ/ (be)sprühen **5A3**
to spray-paint /ˈspreɪˌpeɪnt/ mit Farbe besprühen **5A3**
° spread /spred/ Verbreitung; Vielfalt **2A4**
to **spread** *(irr)* /spred/ (sich) ausbreiten; (sich) verbreiten; *hier:* verteilen **4A5**
spreadsheet /ˈspredˌʃiːt/ Tabellenkalkulation; Arbeitsblatt **4A7**
spring /sprɪŋ/ Frühling **CT5**
spy /spaɪ/ Spion/in; Spionage- **CT7**
° squared /skweəd/ kariert; *hier:* kantig **4SBS**
° to squash /skwɒʃ/ (hinein)zwängen **3D10**
° to squint /skwɪnt/ blinzeln; schielen **2D15**
° to squirm /skwɜːm/ sich (vor Verlegenheit) winden **3B4**
° St John fragment /sənt ˈdʒɒn ˌfræɡmənt/ *Fragment aus dem Johannesevangelium* **5D2**
° stack /stæk/ Stapel; Stoß; Haufen **3R2, 5R1**
stadium /ˈsteɪdiəm/ Stadion **CT7**
staff *(no pl)* /stɑːf/ Belegschaft; Personal **CT8**
stage /steɪdʒ/ Bühne **CT6**
° to stain /steɪn/ (ver)färben; Flecken machen auf **1R4**
° stained /steɪnd/ verfärbt; fleckig; befleckt (mit) **4SBS**
° staircase /ˈsteəˌkeɪs/ Treppenhaus; Treppenaufgang **4SBS**
stairs *(pl)* /steəz/ Treppe **2A6, 4Intro 2**
° to stalk /stɔːk/ jagen; nachstellen **2SBS**
° to stamp /stæmp/ stampfen; stapfen **1P1**; *hier:* (ab)stempeln **5R3**
to **stand** *(irr)* /stænd/ stehen **CT7**
° to stand for *(irr)* /ˈstænd fɔː/ stehen für **1SBS**
to **stand out** *(irr)* /ˌstænd‿ˈaʊt/ hervorragen; sich abheben **2B8**
to **stand up** *(irr)* /ˌstænd‿ˈʌp/ aufstehen **CT5**
° to stand up for sb/sth /ˌstænd‿ˈʌp fɔː/ sich für jdn/etw einsetzen **3SBS**
° to stand your ground /ˌstænd jə ˈɡraʊnd/ nicht von der Stelle weichen; nicht nachgeben **4SBS**
° stand-alone /ˈstænd‿əˌləʊn/ eigenständig **2R2**
° Stand-your-ground laws /ˌstænd jə ˈɡraʊnd lɔːz/ *Gesetze, die in derzeit mehr als 30 US-Bundesstaaten gelten und die Anwendung tödlicher Gewalt zur Verteidigung im Extremfall erlauben* **3D6**
° Standard English /ˌstændəd‿ˈɪŋɡlɪʃ/ englische Standardsprache **5D9**
standard of living /ˌstændəd‿əv ˈlɪvɪŋ/ Lebensstandard **3Intro 2**
° star /stɑː/ Star; Stern **1A2, 2B8**
to star in a film/play /ˌstɑːr‿ɪn‿ə ˈfɪlm/ˈpleɪ/ in einem Film/Theaterstück die Hauptrolle spielen **2B8**
° stare /steə/ Starren **5R1**
to **stare (at sb/sth)** /ˈsteər‿ət/ (jdn/etw an)starren **2A6, 5B7**
start /stɑːt/ Anfang; Beginn **CT6**
to **start** /stɑːt/ anfangen **CT5**
to **get started** /ˌɡet ˈstɑːtɪd/ beginnen **4B4**
starting point /ˈstɑːtɪŋ pɔɪnt/ Ausgangspunkt; Ansatzpunkt **CT8**
starvation *(no pl)* /stɑːˈveɪʃ(ə)n/ Hungertod; Verhungern; Unterernährung **1A3**
state /steɪt/ staatlich; Staat(s-); Land; *hier auch:* US-Bundesstaat **CT8**
to **state** /steɪt/ aussprechen; erklären; darlegen **3A10**
° stately /ˈsteɪtli/ würdevoll; majestätisch **4SBS**
statement /ˈsteɪtmənt/ Äußerung; Aussage **CT6**
station /ˈsteɪʃ(ə)n/ Bahnhof; Haltestelle; Station **CT6**
gas station (*AE* = **petrol station** *BE*) /ˈɡæs‿ˌsteɪʃ(ə)n/ Tankstelle **CT8**
underground station /ˈʌndəˌɡraʊnd ˌsteɪʃ(ə)n/ U-Bahn-Station **CT7**
° stationary /ˈsteɪʃ(ə)n(ə)ri/ ruhend; unverändert **4SBS**
statistic(s) /stəˈtɪstɪks/ Statistik **CT8**
stay /steɪ/ Aufenthalt **CT8**
to **stay** /steɪ/ bleiben; sich aufhalten; untergebracht sein **CT6**
steady /ˈstedi/ fest; stabil; gleich; stetig **CT8**
° to steady /ˈstedi/ stabilisieren; *hier:* gerade halten **2SBS**
to **steal** *(irr)* /stiːl/ stehlen **CT8**
° to steam /stiːm/ dampfen **4SBS**
° steam engine /ˈstiːm‿ˌendʒɪn/ Dampfmaschine **5D7**
° steamboat /ˈstiːmˌbəʊt/ Dampfschiff; Dampfer **5D7**
° steel *(no pl)* /stiːl/ Stahl(-) **3R1, 5D7**
step /step/ Schritt **CT7**
° step /step/ *hier:* (Treppen)stufe **3R1**
° to step /step/ treten; steigen; gehen **3SBS, 4SBS**

° stepdad *(informal)* /ˈstepˌdæd/ Stiefpapa **2D15**
stereotype /ˈsteriəˌtaɪp/ Stereotyp; Klischee; Vorurteil **CT8**
° stereotypical /ˌsteriəˈtɪpɪk(ə)l/ stereotyp *(abgedroschen)* **2B/T1**
to **stick** *(irr)* /stɪk/ kleben; stecken **5A3**
to **stick to sth** *(irr)* /ˈstɪk tʊ/ (sich) an etw halten **CT7**
° stiff /stɪf/ steif; hart **1R4**
° still /stɪl/ (Video)standfoto **2D18**
still /stɪl/ (immer) noch; noch immer **CT7**
° still /stɪl/ ruhig; reglos; still **4SBS, 5R4**
° stillness *(no pl)* /ˈstɪlnəs/ Stille **2SBS**
stinger /ˈstɪŋə/ stechendes Insekt; brennende Pflanze **1B7**
° stockbroker /ˈstɒkˌbrəʊkə/ Börsenmakler/in **3B2**
° stone /stəʊn/ Stein(-) **5D2**
° to stoop /stu:p/ sich beugen; sich bücken **3A8**
to **stop** /stɒp/ stoppen; (an)halten; aufhören; beenden **CT6**
° Stop it! *(informal)* /ˈstɒp‿ɪt/ Hör(t) auf! **5B2**
store /stɔ:/ Laden; Geschäft; Kaufhaus **CT8**
to **store** /stɔ:/ (auf)speichern; lagern; aufbewahren **4Intro 2**
storm /stɔ:m/ Gewitter; Unwetter; (Protest)sturm **CT7**
° to storm /stɔ:m/ stürmen; toben **3D12**
story /ˈstɔ:ri/ Geschichte; Erzählung **CT5**
° storytelling *(no pl)* /ˈstɔ:riˌtelɪŋ/ Geschichtenerzählen **1A3**
° stove /stəʊv/ Ofen; Herd **1R2**
° to stow /stəʊ/ verstauen; verstecken **4SBS**
straight /streɪt/ gerade(aus); direkt **CT6**
up straight /ˌʌp ˈstreɪt/ aufrecht **4B1**
° strained /streɪnd/ angestrengt; abgespannt; *hier:* gequält **5R2**
strange /streɪndʒ/ sonderbar; merkwürdig; fremd; unheimlich **CT5**
stranger /ˈstreɪndʒə/ Fremde/r **CT7**
° strategic /strəˈti:dʒɪk/ strategisch; taktisch **3SBS**
° strategically /strəˈti:dʒɪkli/ taktisch; strategisch **5A1**
straw /ˈstrɔ:/ Stroh(-); Strohhalm **1B7**
° strawberry /ˈstrɔ:b(ə)ri/ Erdbeere; Erdbeer- **4D4**
° stray bullet /ˌstreɪ ˈbʊlɪt/ verirrte Kugel; Irrläufer **3R2**
° stream /stri:m/ Bach; Flüsschen; Strahl; Strom **4SBS**
street /stri:t/ Straße **CT6**
° street art /ˈstri:t‿ɑ:t/ Street-Art *(moderne Kunstrichtung)* **5D1**
° strength /streŋθ/ Kraft; Stärke **3B3, 3SBS, 4D11, 4A/T2, 4D16**
to **stress** /stres/ betonen **5B5**
stressed /strest/ gestresst **1B7**
° stressful /ˈstresf(ə)l/ stressig; anstrengend; aufreibend **2D28**
° to stretch /stretʃ/ (sich) dehnen; (sich er)strecken **2SBS, 4SBS**
strict /strɪkt/ streng; strikt; genau **CT5**
° strike /straɪk/ Streik **5R2**; *hier: Baseball-Fachbegriff* **3B3**
° to strike *(irr)* /straɪk/ (zu)schlagen; streiken; *hier:* beeindrucken **2B6**
striking /ˈstraɪkɪŋ/ bemerkenswert; auffallend **CT8**
stripe /straɪp/ Streifen **1A2**
to strive *(irr)* /straɪv/ sich bemühen; (an)streben **1A5**
strong /strɒŋ/ stark; kräftig; fest **CT6**
structure /ˈstrʌktʃə/ Struktur; Aufbau **CT7**
to **structure** /ˈstrʌktʃə/ strukturieren **CT7**
to **struggle** /ˈstrʌg(ə)l/ sich abmühen; kämpfen; ringen **3B1**
student /ˈstju:d(ə)nt/ Student/in; Schüler/in **CT6**
to **study** /ˈstʌdi/ studieren; sich befassen mit; erforschen **CT6**
° study /ˈstʌdi/ Untersuchung; Studie **1B4**
stuff *(no pl, informal)* /stʌf/ Zeug; Sachen **CT7**
stunning /ˈstʌnɪŋ/ toll; fantastisch; umwerfend **CT8**
° stunt /stʌnt/ Stunt *(gefährliches, akrobatisches Kunststück)* **2SBS**
stupid /ˈstju:pɪd/ dumm; blöd **CT6**
style /staɪl/ Stil; Art **CT8**
stylistic device /staɪˌlɪstɪk dɪˈvaɪs/ Stilmittel **3A2, 5A5**
° subhead(ing) /ˈsʌbˌhedɪŋ/ Untertitel; Zwischenüberschrift **5B9**
subject /ˈsʌbdʒɪkt/ (Schul)fach **CT5**; *hier:* Thema **2B2**; *hier:* Betreff **4A9**
° subjective /səbˈdʒektɪv/ subjektiv **3D15**
° to subscribe (to sth) /səbˈskraɪb tʊ/ (etw) abonnieren; (für etw) Gebühren bezahlen **1B2**
° to sub(stitute) /ˈsʌb(stɪˌtju:t)/ auswechseln; einspringen; vertreten **1R4**
° subtitle /ˈsʌbˌtaɪt(ə)l/ Untertitel **2B1**
° subtle /ˈsʌt(ə)l/ fein(sinnig); subtil **4SBS**
° subtropical /ˌsʌbˈtrɒpɪk(ə)l/ subtropisch **1P1**
° suburban /səˈbɜ:bən/ Vorstadt-; vorstädtisch **5R1**
° subway (*AE* = underground *BE*) /ˈsʌbˌweɪ/ U-Bahn **3R1**
to **succeed** /səkˈsi:d/ Erfolg haben; nachfolgen **CT7**
success *(no pl)* /səkˈses/ Erfolg **CT6**
successful /səkˈsesf(ə)l/ erfolgreich **CT7**
such /sʌtʃ/ solch(er/es) **CT7**
such as /ˈsʌtʃ‿æz/ wie (zum Beispiel) **3A5**
° to suck *(informal, AE)* /sʌk/ ätzend sein **2SBS, 5B2**
° sudden /ˈsʌd(ə)n/ plötzlich; jäh **1R2**
suddenly /ˈsʌd(ə)nli/ plötzlich **CT6**
to **suffer (from)** /ˈsʌfə frɒm/ erleiden; ertragen; leiden (an/unter) **1A3**
° suffix /ˈsʌfɪks/ Suffix; Nachsilbe **2D23**
° suffragette /ˌsʌfrəˈdʒet/ Suffragette *(englische Frauenrechtlerin)* **Wordbank 2**
sugar /ˈʃʊgə/ Zucker **CT7**
° sugar cane *(no pl)* /ˈʃʊgə keɪn/ Zuckerrohr(-) **5SBS**
to **suggest** /səˈdʒest/ vorschlagen **CT6**; andeuten, (darauf) hinweisen **CT8**
suggestion /səˈdʒestʃ(ə)n/ Vorschlag **CT6**
° suicidal /ˌsu:ɪˈsaɪd(ə)l/ selbstmordgefährdet; Selbstmord- **2D8**
° suit /su:t/ Anzug **4SBS**
to **suit sb/sth** /su:t/ zu jdm/etw passen **4A5**
° suitable /ˈsu:təb(ə)l/ geeignet; passend; angemessen **4D11**
° suitcase /ˈsu:tˌkeɪs/ Koffer **5R1**
suited (to) /ˈsu:tɪd‿tʊ/ geeignet (für) **4A9**
to **sum up** /ˌsʌm‿ˈʌp/ resümieren; zusammenfassen **CT6**
to **summarize** /ˈsʌməraɪz/ zusammenfassen; resümieren **CT7**
summary /ˈsʌməri/ Zusammenfassung **CT7**
summer /ˈsʌmə/ Sommer **CT5**
° sun /sʌn/ Sonne **5D13**
Sunday /ˈsʌndeɪ/ Sonntag **CT5**
sunny /ˈsʌni/ sonnig **CT5**
sunset /ˈsʌnˌset/ Sonnenuntergang **CT8**
sunshine *(no pl)* /ˈsʌnˌʃaɪn/ Sonnenschein **CT6**
° superb /sʊˈpɜ:b/ ausgezeichnet; hervorragend; erstklassig **2B/T1**
° to superimpose /ˌsu:pərɪmˈpəʊz/ überlagern **4SBS**
supermarket /ˈsu:pəˌmɑ:kɪt/ Supermarkt **CT5**
° supernatural /ˌsu:pəˈnætʃərəl/ übernatürlich; Mystery- **4SBS**
° supervisor /ˈsu:pəˌvaɪzə/ Aufsicht; Betreuer/in **3B2, 4SBS**

° supply /sə'plaɪ/ Vorrat; Versorgung; Bereitstellung; Angebot **5D7**
support /sə'pɔ:t/ Unterstützung **CT6**
to **support** /sə'pɔ:t/ (unter)stützen **CT5**; für jdn sein **CT7**
supporter /sə'pɔ:tə/ Unterstützer/in; Anhänger/in; Verfechter/in **1A5, 3A5**
° to suppose /sə'pəʊz/ annehmen; denken **4SBS, 5R1**
° Supreme Court /sʊˌpri:m 'kɔ:t/ Oberster Gerichtshof **1D3**
sure /ʃɔ:/ sicher **CT5**
Sure! *(informal)* /ʃɔ:/ Natürlich!; Klar! **CT5**
° surface /'sɜ:fɪs/ Oberfläche **4SBS**
surprise /sə'praɪz/ Überraschung **CT6**
to **surprise** /sə'praɪz/ überraschen **CT5**
surprised /sə'praɪzd/ überrascht; erstaunt **CT5**
surprising /sə'praɪzɪŋ/ überraschend **CT6**
to **surround** /sə'raʊnd/ einkreisen; umgeben **3A5**
° surroundings *(pl)* /sə'raʊndɪŋz/ Umgebung **2D18, 4SBS**
survey /'sɜ:veɪ/ Umfrage **CT8**
to **survive** /sə'vaɪv/ überleben **CT7**
° survivor /sə'vaɪvə/ Überlebende/r **5SBS**
suspect /'sʌspekt/ Verdächtige/r **1A5**
° suspense *(no pl)* /sə'spens/ Spannung **2D18**
° suspenseful /sə'spensf(ə)l/ spannend **2D23**
suspicion /sə'spɪʃ(ə)n/ Verdacht; Misstrauen **5A3**
to **arrest sb (on suspicion of sth)** /əˌrest ˌsʌmbədi‿ɒn sə'spɪʃ(ə)n‿əv/ jdn (wegen des Verdachts auf etw) verhaften **5A3**
° suspicious /sə'spɪʃəs/ verdächtig; misstrauisch; argwöhnisch **1R4**
° to swallow /'swɒləʊ/ schlucken; verschlingen **2SBS**
to **swap** /swɒp/ (aus)tauschen **CT6**
° to swarm /swɔ:m/ (um)schwärmen **5R3**
° to swear *(irr)* /sweə/ schwören; *hier:* fluchen, derbe Schimpfwörter gebrauchen **2SBS, 4R1**
° Sweden /'swi:d(ə)n/ Schweden **3A3**
sweet /swi:t/ süß **CT7**
sweets *(pl)* /swi:ts/ Süßigkeiten **CT6**
° swift /swɪft/ schnell; rasch **4SBS**
to **swim** *(irr)* /swɪm/ schwimmen **CT5**
to **go swimming** /ˌgəʊ 'swɪmɪŋ/ schwimmen gehen **CT6**
° to swing *(irr)* /swɪŋ/ (hin- und her)schwingen; sich drehen **3R1**
° to swirl /swɜ:l/ wirbeln **4SBS**

switch /swɪtʃ/ Schalter **CT7**
to **switch** /swɪtʃ/ wechseln **CT7**
° to switch /swɪtʃ/ *hier:* tauschen **3B3**
to **switch off** /ˌswɪtʃ‿'ɒf/ ausschalten; abschalten **CT7**
to **switch on** /ˌswɪtʃ‿'ɒn/ einschalten; anschalten **CT7**
° Switzerland /'swɪtsələnd/ Schweiz **3A3**
° sword /sɔ:d/ Schwert **3SBS, 4SBS**
° sympathetic /ˌsɪmpə'θetɪk/ verständnisvoll; wohlgesonnen **3B3**

T

° T-ball *(no pl)* /'ti: bɔ:l/ *Baseballvariante für Kinder* **2B3**
table /'teɪb(ə)l/ Tisch **CT5**
to **lay the table** *(BE)* /ˌleɪ ðə 'teɪb(ə)l/ den Tisch decken **CT5**
tabloid /'tæblɔɪd/ Boulevardzeitung; Klatschzeitung **5A3**
° tail /teɪl/ Schwanz **4SBS**; *hier:* Sprechblasenspitze **2R1**
° tail light /'teɪl‿laɪt/ Rücklicht **3B2**
to **take** *(irr)* /teɪk/ (mit)nehmen; machen; (hin)bringen **CT5**; dauern **CT6**
to **take ... for a walk** /ˌteɪk fər‿ə 'wɔ:k/ ... spazieren führen; Gassi gehen mit ... **CT6**
° to take a bite /ˌteɪk‿ə 'baɪt/ abbeißen **2SBS**
° to take a (closer) look at sth /ˌteɪk‿ə ˌkləʊsə 'lʊk‿ət/ sich etw (genauer) ansehen **1SBS**
to **take a deep breath** /ˌteɪk‿ə ˌdi:p‿'breθ/ tief Luft holen **CT7**
° to take a fall /ˌteɪk‿ə 'fɔ:l/ stürzen **3R1**
to **take a risk** /ˌteɪk‿ə 'rɪsk/ ein Risiko eingehen; etw riskieren **1B7**
° to take a sip (of sth) /ˌteɪk‿ə 'sɪp‿əv/ einen kleinen Schluck (von etw) nehmen **1R2, 2SBS, 3B2**
° to take a stand /ˌteɪk‿ə 'stænd/ Stellung beziehen; sich einsetzen **5B1**
° to take a trip /ˌteɪk‿ə 'trɪp/ einen Ausflug machen **1D17**
to take a turn for the worse /ˌteɪk‿ə ˌtɜ:n fə ðə 'wɜ:s/ sich zum Schlechten wenden **2B8**
° to take a vote /ˌteɪk‿ə 'vəʊt/ eine Abstimmung durchführen **2A5, 5A6**
° to take advantage of sb/sth /ˌteɪk‿əd'vɑ:ntɪdʒ‿əv/ jdn/etw (aus)nutzen **3B4**
° to take an exam /ˌteɪk‿ən‿ɪg'zæm/ eine Prüfung ablegen **4B/T2**
to **take care** /ˌteɪk‿'keə/ aufpassen; achten auf **CT7**
to **take care of** /ˌteɪk‿'keər‿əv/ sich kümmern um **CT7**

° to take down *(irr)* /ˌteɪk 'daʊn/ abnehmen; *hier:* entfernen **2D5**
° to take hold of sth /ˌteɪk 'həʊld‿əv/ (sich) etw greifen **4SBS**
° to take (immediate) action /ˌteɪk‿ɪˌmi:diət‿'ækʃ(ə)n/ (augenblicklich) handeln **2A6**
to **take notes** /ˌteɪk 'nəʊts/ (sich) Notizen machen **CT6**
to **take off** *(irr)* /ˌteɪk‿'ɒf/ abnehmen; ausziehen; abziehen **CT7**
to **take out the rubbish** /ˌteɪk‿ˌaʊt ðə 'rʌbɪʃ/ den Müll hinausbringen **CT5**
to **take part (in)** /ˌteɪk 'pɑ:t‿ɪn/ teilnehmen (an); mitmachen (bei) **CT5**
to **take place** /ˌteɪk 'pleɪs/ stattfinden **CT6**
° to take pride in sb/sth /ˌteɪk 'praɪd‿ɪn/ stolz auf jdn/etw sein **5B/T2**
to **take sb/sth seriously** /ˌteɪk ˌsʌmbədi/ˌsʌmθɪŋ 'sɪəriəsli/ jdn/etw ernst nehmen **CT7**
to **take sth into account** /ˌteɪk ˌsʌmθɪŋ‿ˌɪntʊ‿ə'kaʊnt/ etw berücksichtigen **3A7**
to **take turns** *(BE)* /ˌteɪk 'tɜ:nz/ sich abwechseln **CT5**
talented /'tæləntɪd/ talentiert; begabt **CT7**
° talk /tɔ:k/ Gespräch; Reden; *hier:* Vortrag, Referat **1B8**; *hier:* Vortrag **3D2**
to **talk (about/to)** /'tɔ:k‿əˌbaʊt/tə/ sprechen; reden (über/mit) **CT5**
° tall /tɔ:l/ groß; hoch (gewachsen) **4SBS**
° tallow-haired /ˌtæləʊ 'heəd/ mit fettigem Haar **4SBS**
tank /tæŋk/ (Flüssigkeits)behälter; Tank; Aquarium **CT5**
° tank /tæŋk/ *hier:* Riesenauto **5B4**
° to tap /tæp/ (an)tippen; klopfen **5D5, 4SBS**
target /'tɑ:gɪt/ Ziel **CT8**
task /'tɑ:sk/ Aufgabe **CT6**
° Tasmanian devil /tæzˌmeɪniən 'dev(ə)l/ *Beuteltierart* **Wordbank 1**
to **taste** /teɪst/ schmecken **CT5**
° taste bud /'teɪst bʌd/ Geschmacksknospe **1R2**
tasty /'teɪsti/ schmackhaft; lecker **CT8**
° tater tots *(AE)* /'teɪtər tɑts/ *frittierte Kartoffelstückchen* **3B4**
° to tattoo /tə'tu:/ tätowieren **5R2**
tea /ti:/ Tee **CT6**
tea *(BE, no pl)* /ti:/ Tee; Zwischenmahlzeit **CT7**
° tea bag /'ti: bæg/ Teebeutel **4SBS**
to **teach** *(irr)* /ti:tʃ/ unterrichten; beibringen **CT7**

teacher /ˈtiːtʃə/ Lehrer/in **CT5**
teammate /ˈtiːmˌmeɪt/ Mannschaftskamerad/in; Mitspieler/in **CT7**
tear /tɪə/ Träne **CT8**
° to tear down *(irr)* /ˌteə ˈdaʊn/ abreißen; niederreißen **5SBS**
° tech *(informal)* /tek/ Technik- **2A4, 4Intro 2**
° tech-savvy /ˈtekˌsævi/ technikaffin **4Intro 2**
° technical /ˈteknɪk(ə)l/ technisch; Fach- **4D6**
° technique /tekˈniːk/ Technik; Verfahren; Methode **2D28**
technology /tekˈnɒlədʒi/ Technologie; Technik **CT5**
° TED /ted/ *jährlich stattfindende US-Innovationskonferenz* **3D2**
° telegraph /ˈtelɪˌgrɑːf/ Telegraf *(Apparat zur Übermittlung von Telegrammen)* **5D7**
phone call (= telephone call) /ˈfəʊn kɔːl, ˈtelɪˌfəʊn kɔːl/ Anruf; Telefongespräch **CT5**
to **tell** *(irr)* /tel/ erzählen; sagen **CT5** verraten **CT6**
to **tell sb to do sth** /ˌtel ˌsʌmbədi tə ˈduː/ jdm sagen, dass er/sie etw tun soll **CT8**
temperature /ˈtemprɪtʃə/ Temperatur **CT8**
° temple /ˈtemp(ə)l/ Tempel **5A1**
° temporarily /ˈtemp(ə)rəri/ zeitweilig; vorübergehend **3B4**
° temporary /ˈtemp(ə)rəri/ zeitweilig; vorübergehend **3B2**
ten /ten/ zehn **CT5**
° to tend /tend/ sich kümmern um; pflegen **3B2**
° to tend to do sth /ˌtend‿tə ˈduː/ zu etw neigen; dazu neigen, etw zu tun **4SBS, 5R1**
° tense /tens/ spannungsgeladen; angespannt **3B3**
tent /tent/ Zelt **CT6**
° term /tɜːm/ Ausdruck; Begriff **2R1, 4P5, 4R1**
terraced house *(BE)* /ˈterəst haʊs/ Reihenhaus **CT7**
terrible /ˈterəb(ə)l/ schrecklich; furchtbar **CT6**
° terrific /təˈrɪfɪk/ großartig; fantastisch; toll **3R6**
territory /ˈterət(ə)ri/ Gebiet; Revier; Territorium **CT8**
to testify /ˈtestɪfaɪ/ als Zeuge/Zeugin aussagen **2A4**
° testimony /ˈtestɪməni/ (Zeugen)aussage; Beweis **3R6**
text (= text message) /tekst, ˈtekst ˌmesɪdʒ/ Textnachricht; SMS **CT5**
to **text (sb)** /ˈtekst/ (jdm) eine Textnachricht/SMS senden **CT5**
° texture /ˈtekstʃə/ Struktur; Konsistenz **4SBS**
Thames /temz/ Themse *(Fluss in England)* **CT7**
than /ðæn/ als **CT6**
to **thank** /θæŋk/ danken **CT6**
Thank you. /ˈθæŋk ju/ Danke. **CT5**
° thanks to /ˈθæŋks tʊ/ dank; wegen **2D4**
Thanks! *(informal)* /θæŋks/ Danke! **CT5**
Thanksgiving (Day) *(AE)* /ˌθæŋksˈgɪvɪŋ deɪ/ *Erntedanktag in den USA* **CT8**
that /ðæt/ das; der/die/das **CT5**; dass; so **CT6**
that's (= that is) /ðæts, ˈðæt‿ɪz/ das ist **CT5**
That's none of your business. *(informal)* /ðæts ˌnʌn‿əv jə ˈbɪznəs/ Das geht dich/euch/Sie nichts an. **CT7**
the /ðə/ der/die/das **CT5**
the ... the /ðə ðə/ je ..., desto ... **2A6**
theatre /ˈθɪətə/ Theater **CT6**
their /ðeə/ ihr(e) **CT5**
theirs /ðeəz/ ihre(r, s); ihrs **CT6**
them /ðem/ sie; ihnen **CT5**
themselves /ðəmˈselvz/ sich; sie selbst; (sich) selbst **CT7**
then /ðen/ dann; danach; darauf **CT5**
° then /ðen/ damals **2Intro 1**
° therapy /ˈθerəpi/ Therapie; Behandlung **2Intro 2**
there /ðeə/ dort; da **CT5**; dahin; dorthin **CT6**
there is/are /ˈðeər‿ɪz/ə/ es gibt, da ist; da sind **CT5**
° there you go! *(informal)* /ˌðeə jə ˈgəʊ/ bitte schön!; sag ich's doch! **2R7**
there's (= there is) /ðeəz, ˈðeər‿ɪz/ es gibt; da ist **CT5**
° There's no point /ðeəz ˌnəʊ ˈpɔɪnt/ Es hat keinen Zweck/Sinn **4R1**
° therefore /ˈðeəfɔː/ deshalb; deswegen; daher **2D10**
° thesaurus /θɪˈsɔːrəs/ Synonymwörterbuch **4R2**
these (= *pl of* **this)** /ðiːz/ diese **CT5**
they /ðeɪ/ sie **CT5**
they're (= they are) /ðeə, ˈðeɪ‿ə/ sie sind **CT5**
° thick /θɪk/ dick **4SBS**; *hier:* rau **2SBS**
thing /θɪŋ/ Ding; Gegenstand; Sache **CT5**
to **think** *(irr)* /θɪŋk/ denken; glauben; meinen **CT5**
to **think about sb/sth** /ˈθɪŋk‿əˌbaʊt/ an jdn/etw denken; über jdn/etw nachdenken **CT5**
to **think of** *(irr)* /ˈθɪŋk‿əv/ denken an; sich ausdenken; denken an; sich ausdenken; halten von **CT6**
to **think up** *(irr)* /ˌθɪŋk‿ˈʌp/ sich ausdenken **CT8**
° think(ing) outside the box /ˌθɪŋk(ɪŋ)‿ˌaʊtˌsaɪd ðə ˈbɒks/ über den Tellerrand schauen; *hier:* unkonventionell denken **4A5**
third /θɜːd/ dritte(r, s) **CT5**; Drittel **CT8**
° third-person /ˌθɜːd ˈpɜːs(ə)n‿nəˌreɪtə/ personale/r Erzähler/in **3D15**
third-person narrator /ˌθɜːd ˈpɜːs(ə)n‿nəˌreɪtə/ personale/r Erzähler/in **3B2**
thirsty /ˈθɜːsti/ durstig **CT7**
this /ðɪs/ diese(r, s); das **CT5**
This is ... /ˈðɪs‿ɪz/ Das ist ... **CT5**
those (= *pl of* **that)** /ðəʊz/ diese **CT5**
though /ðəʊ/ trotzdem; aber **CT7**
thought /θɔːt/ Gedanke **CT7**; Meinung **CT8**
thought-provoking /ˈθɔːt prəˌvəʊkɪŋ/ nachdenklich stimmend **2B8**
thoughtful /ˈθɔːtf(ə)l/ nachdenklich; wohl überlegt; aufmerksam **2B3**
thousand /ˈθaʊz(ə)nd/ tausend **CT6**
° thread /θred/ Garn; Zwirn; Faden **5A1**
threat /θret/ (Be)drohung; Gefahr **1B7, 3A7**
to **threaten** /ˈθret(ə)n/ (be)drohen **5A3**
° threatening /ˈθret(ə)nɪŋ/ drohend; Droh-; bedrohlich **2D10**
three /θriː/ drei **CT5**
° thrill /θrɪl/ Nervenkitzel; Kick **2SBS**
thrilled /θrɪld/ außer sich vor Freude **CT7**
thrilling /ˈθrɪlɪŋ/ aufregend; packend **CT8**
° throat /θrəʊt/ Rachen; Hals; Kehle **1R2**
throne /θrəʊn/ Thron **CT7**
through /θruː/ durch **CT6**
to **get through sth** /ˌget ˈθruː/ etw überstehen **2B8**
throughout /θruːˈaʊt/ während; die ganze Zeit (über) **2A6**
to **throw** *(irr)* /θrəʊ/ werfen **CT6**
° to thrust *(irr)* /θrʌst/ recken; stoßen **2SBS**
° thumb /θʌm/ Daumen **2SBS**
° thumbs-up *(no pl, informal)* /ˌθʌmz‿ˈʌp/ Zustimmung; Okay **2SBS**
thunderstorm /ˈθʌndəˌstɔːm/ Gewitter **CT8**
Thursday /ˈθɜːzdeɪ/ Donnerstag **CT5**
° tick /tɪk/ Ticken; *hier:* Sekunde **4SBS**
° to tick /tɪk/ abhaken; ticken **3R2**
ticket /ˈtɪkɪt/ Fahrkarte; (Eintritts)karte **CT5**
tidy /ˈtaɪdi/ ordentlich; sauber **4B1**
to **tidy (up)** /ˌtaɪdi‿ˈʌp/ aufräumen **CT5**
tie /taɪ/ Krawatte **CT7**

° to tie /taɪ/ binden **4SBS**
tight /taɪt/ fest; eng; gedrängt **CT7**
° tight *(informal)* /taɪt/ knausrig **5B2**
° tile /taɪl/ Fliese; Dachziegel **4SBS**
till (= until) /tɪl, ʌn'tɪl/ bis **CT6**
time /taɪm/ Zeit; Uhrzeit **CT5**; Mal **CT6**
all the time /ˌɔ:l ðə 'taɪm/ die ganze Zeit **CT7**
for a long time /fər‿ə ˌlɒŋ 'taɪm/ lange Zeit **CT7**
on time /ɒn 'taɪm/ pünktlich **CT8**
to buy time /ˌbaɪ 'taɪm/ Zeit gewinnen/ schinden **4B4**
screen time *(no pl)* /'skri:n taɪm/ Bildschirmzeit **2A6**
at times /ət 'taɪmz/ manchmal **4Intro 2**
° timeline /'taɪmˌlaɪn/ Zeitachse **1D5**
° timeslot /'taɪmˌslɒt/ Zeitfenster **2D20**
timetable /'taɪmˌteɪb(ə)l/ Stundenplan **CT5**; Fahrplan, Zeitplan **CT8**
tiny /'taɪni/ winzig **1A4**
tired /'taɪəd/ müde **CT6**
title /'taɪt(ə)l/ Titel **CT6**
to /tʊ/ in; nach; zu; an; auf; vor **CT5**
° to-do list /tə 'du: lɪst/ Besorgungsliste; To-do-Liste **4A5**
° tobacco *(no pl)* /tə'bækəʊ/ Tabak(-) **2D2, 5SBS**
today /tə'deɪ/ heute **CT5**
together /tə'geðə/ zusammen **CT6**
° toilet /'tɔɪlət/ Toilette; Klo **1R2, 3D13**
tomato (*pl* tomatoes) /tə'mɑ:təʊ, tə'mɑ:təʊz/ Tomate **CT5**
tomorrow /tə'mɒrəʊ/ morgen **CT5**
tone /təʊn/ Klang; Ton; Stimmung **5A5**
° tone-deaf /ˌtəʊn'def/ unmusikalisch **4SBS**
tonight /tə'naɪt/ heute Abend; heute Nacht **CT5**
too /tu:/ auch; zu **CT5**
tool /tu:l/ Werkzeug **CT7**
tooth (*pl* teeth) /tu:θ, ti:θ/ Zahn **CT5**
toothbrush /'tu:θˌbrʌʃ/ Zahnbürste **CT6**
top /tɒp/ oberes Ende; Spitze; beste(r, s) **CT7**
at the top /ət ðə 'tɒp/ oben; an der Spitze **CT8**
top-left /ˌtɒp 'left/ oben links **CT8**
top-right /ˌtɒp 'raɪt/ oben rechts **CT8**
topic /'tɒpɪk/ Thema **CT7**
° to topple /'tɒp(ə)l/ umwerfen; stürzen **5SBS**
° Torres Strait Islander /ˌtɒrɪs‿ˌstreɪt‿'aɪləndə/ *Angehörige/r der einheimischen Bevölkerung der Torres-Strait-Inseln* **1A2**
° to toss /tɒs/ (zu)werfen; schleudern **4SBS**
total /'təʊt(ə)l/ Gesamt-; völlig; gesamt **CT8**
° total /'təʊt(ə)l/ *hier:* absolut, voll **4A/T2**
totally /'təʊt(ə)li/ völlig; total **CT8**
touch /tʌtʃ/ Berührung; Kontakt **CT8**
to **be in touch (with sb)** /ˌbi‿ɪn 'tʌtʃ wɪð/ (mit jdm) in Kontakt sein **CT6**
to **touch** /tʌtʃ/ berühren **4B1**
touching /'tʌtʃɪŋ/ ergreifend; (be)rührend **2B8**
tough /tʌf/ robust; zäh **CT7**
tour /tʊə/ Reise; Tour; Tournee; Führung **CT6**
to **go on a tour** /ˌgəʊ‿ɒn‿ə 'tʊə/ eine Tour machen **CT6**
° tour guide /'tʊə gaɪd/ Reiseleiter/in **4D1**
tourism *(no pl)* /'tʊərɪz(ə)m/ Tourismus **CT8**
° tournament /'tʊənəmənt/ Turnier **1D9**
toward(s) /tə'wɔ:dz/ in Richtung; gegenüber **CT6**
tower /'taʊə/ Turm **CT6**
town /taʊn/ Stadt **CT7**
track /træk/ Weg; Pfad; Gleis **CT7**
° to track /træk/ verfolgen **3R2**
° track /træk/ *hier:* Musikstück **3D2**
track and field *(no pl, AE)* /ˌtræk‿ən 'fi:ld/ Leichtathletik **CT8**
° trade /treɪd/ Handel; Branche; Handwerk **5SBS, Wordbank 2**
° trader /'treɪdə/ Händler/in **5SBS**
tradition /trə'dɪʃ(ə)n/ Tradition; Brauch **CT6**
traditional /trə'dɪʃn(ə)l/ traditionell **CT7**
° traditional /trə'dɪʃn(ə)l/ *hier:* konservativ **2D4**
° traffic *(no pl)* /'træfɪk/ Verkehr(s-) **4SBS, 5D5**
traffic lights *(pl)* /'træfɪk laɪts/ Ampel **CT6**
tragedy /'trædʒədi/ Tragödie; Trauerspiel **1B7**
tragic /'trædʒɪk/ tragisch **CT8**
trail /treɪl/ Weg; Pfad; Spur **CT8**
to **train** /treɪn/ trainieren; ausbilden **CT7**
train /treɪn/ Zug **CT6**
° train driver /'treɪn ˌdraɪvə/ Lokführer/in **5B/T3**
trainer /'treɪnə/ Trainer/in; Turnschuh **CT5**
training *(no pl)* /'treɪnɪŋ/ Training; *hier:* Ausbildung, Schulung **4A5**
° transcript /'trænskrɪpt/ Abschrift; Protokoll **3R5**
to transfer /træns'fɜ:/ (über)wechseln; übertragen **2B8**
° to transform /træns'fɔ:m/ verwandeln **5R2**
to **translate** /træns'leɪt/ übersetzen **CT8**
° translation /træns'leɪʃ(ə)n/ Übersetzung **2A/T1, 5D12**
° transportation *(no pl)* /ˌtrænspɔ:'teɪʃ(ə)n/ Transport(mittel); Verkehrsmittel **5D7**
to **travel** /'træv(ə)l/ reisen **CT7**
° travel agency /'træv(ə)l‿ˌeɪdʒ(ə)nsi/ Reisebüro **3D10**
° travel *(no pl)* /'træv(ə)l/ Reisen; Reise- **2D2, 4D5, 5D5**
° tray /treɪ/ Tablett **4SBS**
treasure /'treʒə/ Schatz **5A3**
° treasured /'treʒəd/ geschätzt; begehrt **5D2**
to **treat** /tri:t/ behandeln **CT7**
treatment /'tri:tmənt/ Behandlung **CT8**
° treaty /'tri:ti/ Vertrag; Abkommen **1P1**
tree /tri:/ Baum **CT6**
° tree house /'tri: haʊs/ Baumhaus **5R3**
° trial /'traɪəl/ Prozess; Gerichtsverfahren **3R2**
° tribe /traɪb/ Stamm; Sippe **1A4**
trick /trɪk/ Trick; Kunststück **CT7**
tricky /'trɪki/ schwierig; kompliziert; knifflig **CT7**
° to trigger (off) /ˌtrɪgər‿'ɒf/ auslösen **4SBS**
° trigonometry *(no pl)* /ˌtrɪgə'nɒmətri/ Trigonometrie **3B3**
trip /trɪp/ Ausflug; Reise **CT6**
to **go on a trip** /ˌgəʊ‿ɒn‿ə 'trɪp/ einen Ausflug/eine Reise machen **CT6**
° trophy /'trəʊfi/ Trophäe; Pokal **5D2**
tropical /'trɒpɪk(ə)l/ Tropen-; tropisch **1B2**
trouble *(no pl)* /'trʌb(ə)l/ Schwierigkeiten; Ärger **CT7**
to **get into trouble** /ˌget‿ɪntʊ 'trʌb(ə)l/ in Schwierigkeiten geraten **CT8**
° troublemaker /'trʌb(ə)lˌmeɪkə/ Unruhestifter/in **5D13**
trousers *(pl)* /'traʊzəz/ Hose **CT5**
° to trudge /trʌdʒ/ trotten; schwerfällig gehen **4SBS**
true /tru:/ wahr **CT5**
° truly /'tru:li/ wirklich; wahrhaftig; ehrlich **3R6, 4B/T2**
to **trust** /trʌst/ vertrauen **CT7**
° to trust sb with sth /'trʌst ˌsʌmbədi wɪð/ jdm etw anvertrauen **2R3**
° trustworthiness *(no pl)* /'trʌstˌwɜ:ðinəs/ Vertrauenswürdigkeit; Zuverlässigkeit **Wordbank 8**
trustworthy /'trʌstˌwɜ:ði/ vertrauenswürdig; zuverlässig **4Intro 2**
truth /tru:θ/ Wahrheit **2A4, 3A8**
to **try** /traɪ/ versuchen; (aus)probieren **CT5**
to **try on** /ˌtraɪ‿'ɒn/ anprobieren **CT6**

to **try out** /ˌtraɪ‿ˈaʊt/ ausprobieren CT8
tube /tjuːb/ Röhre; die (Londoner) U-Bahn CT7
° to tuck /tʌk/ (sich) (hinein)zwängen; *hier:* greifen (nach), klammern (an) 2SBS
Tuesday /ˈtjuːzdeɪ/ Dienstag CT5
° to tug /tʌg/ ziehen; zerren 3B4
Turkey /ˈtɜːki/ Türkei CT7
turkey /ˈtɜːki/ Truthahn/-henne; Putenfleisch CT8
° Turkish /ˈtɜːkɪʃ/ Türkisch; türkisch 4P5
to take a turn for the worse /ˌteɪk‿ə ˌtɜːn fə ðə ˈwɜːs/ sich zum Schlechten wenden 2B8
to **turn** /tɜːn/ (sich) (um)drehen; *hier:* wenden 5A1
° to turn /tɜːn/ *hier:* werden 2B3, 5R4
° to turn against sb /ˌtɜːn‿əˈgenst/ sich gegen jdn wenden 3D7
to **turn (a)round** /ˌtɜːn‿əˈraʊnd/ sich umdrehen CT6
to **turn away** /ˌtɜːn‿əˈweɪ/ sich abwenden; wegrücken CT7
to **turn into** /ˈtɜːn‿ˌɪntʊ/ (ver)wandeln CT8
to **turn off** /ˌtɜːn‿ˈɒf/ abschalten; ausmachen 2A4
to **turn on** /ˌtɜːn‿ˈɒn/ einschalten; aufdrehen; anmachen CT7
to **turn out** /ˌtɜːn‿ˈaʊt/ sich herausstellen CT8
to **turn right/left** /ˌtɜːn ˈraɪt/ˈleft/ rechts/links abbiegen CT6
to **turn up** /ˌtɜːn‿ˈʌp/ erscheinen; auftauchen CT7
° turning point /ˈtɜːnɪŋ pɔɪnt/ Wendepunkt Wordbank 7
turtle /ˈtɜːt(ə)l/ Schildkröte 1B7
° tutor /ˈtjuːtə/ Nachhilfelehrer/in; *hier:* Dozent/in 4R1
TV (= television) /ˌtiː ˈviː, ˈtelɪˌvɪʒn/ Fernsehen; Fernseher CT5
on TV /ˌɒn ˌtiː ˈviː/ im Fernsehen CT5
° to tweet /twiːt/ *eine Nachricht über Twitter verbreiten* 2D13
twelve /twelv/ zwölf CT5
twice /twaɪs/ zweimal CT7
twin /twɪn/ Zwilling; Zwillings- CT7
° to twist /twɪst/ (ver)drehen 4SBS, 5B2
two /tuː/ zwei CT5
° two-dimensional /ˌtuːdɪˈmenʃ(ə)nəl/ zweidimensional; flach *(Handlung)* 2B/T1
° two-seam fastball /ˌtuː ˌsiːm ˈfɑːstbɔːl/ *Art, einen Baseball zu werfen* 3B2
° to type /taɪp/ tippen 4R2, 5D5
type /taɪp/ Art; Typ; Sorte CT8
typical (of) /ˈtɪpɪk(ə)l‿əv/ typisch (für) CT7
° typically /ˈtɪpɪkli/ normalerweise; in der Regel 2D10
° tyre /ˈtaɪə/ Reifen 5B4

U

UK (= the United Kingdom) /ˌjuːˈkeɪ, ðə juːˌnaɪtɪd ˈkɪŋdəm/ Vereinigtes Königreich CT7
° ultimately /ˈʌltɪmətli/ letzten Endes; letztlich; schließlich 5SBS
° umbrella term /ʌmˈbrelə tɜːm/ Oberbegriff 2A1
° ump (= umpire) *(informal)* /ʌmp, ˈʌmpaɪə/ Schiedsrichter/in *(beim Tennis, Cricket und Baseball)* 3B3
° UN General Assembly /ˌjuː‿ˌen ˌdʒen(ə)rəl‿əˈsembli/ Generalversammlung der Vereinten Nationen 3D2
° unacceptable /ˌʌnəkˈseptəb(ə)l/ inakzeptabel; nicht hinnehmbar 3SBS
unbelievable /ˌʌnbɪˈliːvəb(ə)l/ unglaublich; sagenhaft CT7
° uncertain /ʌnˈsɜːt(ə)n/ unsicher 4SBS
uncle /ˈʌŋk(ə)l/ Onkel CT5
uncomfortable /ʌnˈkʌmftəb(ə)l/ unbequem; unbehaglich CT7
° unconcern *(no pl)* /ˌʌnkənˈsɜːn/ Unbesorgtheit; Unbekümmertheit 4SBS
° to uncover /ʌnˈkʌvə/ entdecken; freilegen; aufdecken 3R3
under /ˈʌndə/ unter CT5
° to underestimate /ˌʌndərˈestɪˌmeɪt/ unterschätzen 4SBS
the Underground *(BE, no pl)* /ðiˌˈʌndəˌgraʊnd/ U-Bahn CT7
underground station /ˈʌndəˌgraʊnd ˌsteɪʃ(ə)n/ U-Bahn-Station CT7
° to underline /ˌʌndəˈlaɪn/ unterstreichen 4SBS
to **understand** *(irr)* /ˌʌndəˈstænd/ verstehen CT5
understanding /ˌʌndəˈstændɪŋ/ verständnisvoll 2B3
° understanding *(no pl)* /ˌʌndəˈstændɪŋ/ Verständnis 1R2; Übereinkunft 4D14
undivided /ˌʌndɪˈvaɪdɪd/ uneingeschränkt; ungeteilt 3B3
° unduly /ˌʌnˈdjuːli/ unangemessen; übermäßig 4SBS
unemployed /ˌʌnɪmˈplɔɪd/ arbeitslos 3B1
unemployment *(no pl)* /ˌʌnɪmˈplɔɪmənt/ Arbeitslosigkeit CT8
° UNESCO /juːˈneskəʊ/ UNESCO(-) *(Organisation der Vereinten Nationen für Erziehung, Wissenschaft und Kultur)* 5Intro 1
unexpected /ˌʌnɪkˈspektɪd/ unerwartet 3B1
° unfamiliar /ˌʌnfəˈmɪljə/ ungewohnt; fremd 5R2
° unforgettable /ˌʌnfəˈgetəb(ə)l/ unvergesslich 3D11
unfortunately /ʌnˈfɔːtʃ(ə)nətli/ unglücklicherweise; leider CT5
unfriendly /ʌnˈfrendli/ unfreundlich CT6
unhappy /ʌnˈhæpi/ unglücklich CT5
uniform /ˈjuːnɪfɔːm/ Uniform CT5
° unimpressed /ˌʌnɪmˈprest/ unbeeindruckt 5B2
° union /ˈjuːnjən/ Gewerkschaft; Verband; Union 5A1
° Union Jack /ˌjuːniən ˈdʒæk/ *britische Nationalflagge* 1A2
unique /juːˈniːk/ einzigartig CT8
United Nations (UN) /juːˌnaɪtɪd ˈneɪʃ(ə)nz, ˌju‿ˈen/ Vereinte Nationen (UN) 3Intro 2
° unity /ˈjuːnəti/ Einheit; Einigkeit 3D12
° the universe /ðə ˈjuːnɪˌvɜːs/ das Universum 1A3
° university /ˌjuːnɪˈvɜːsəti/ Universität(s-) 2A4, 5A1
° unknown /ʌnˈnəʊn/ unbekannt; nicht bekannt 1A/T2
° unless /ənˈles/ außer wenn; es sei denn 5R4
unlike /ʌnˈlaɪk/ anders als CT8
° unlikely /ʌnˈlaɪkli/ unwahrscheinlich 5B4
unmatched /ʌnˈmætʃt/ unerreicht; unübertroffen 1A5
° unmentionable /ʌnˈmenʃ(ə)nəb(ə)l/ unaussprechlich 2B10
° unmoved /ˌʌnˈmuːvd/ unbewegt; ungerührt 3R6
° unnecessary /ʌnˈnesəs(ə)ri/ unnötig; überflüssig; verzichtbar 1B/T1
° unnoticed /ʌnˈnəʊtɪst/ unbemerkt 2SBS, 5R1
° to unpack /ʌnˈpæk/ auspacken; ausladen 3D10
unpredictable /ˌʌnprɪˈdɪktəb(ə)l/ unvorhersehbar; unberechenbar 4A5
° unreal /ˌʌnˈrɪəl/ unwirklich 2SBS
unrealistic /ˌʌnrɪəˈlɪstɪk/ unrealistisch; nicht realistisch CT7
° unruly hair *(no pl)* /ʌnˌruːli ˈheə/ nicht zu bändigendes Haar 4SBS
unsure /ʌnˈʃʊə/ unsicher; ungewiss 1A3
until /ʌnˈtɪl/ bis CT6
not until ... /nɒt‿ʌnˈtɪl/ erst ... 1A3
° unusual /ʌnˈjuːʒʊəl/ ungewöhnlich; untypisch 1R4, 2B3
° unwilling /ʌnˈwɪlɪŋ/ nicht gewillt; widerwillig; widerstrebend 5B2
up /ʌp/ nach oben; hoch CT6
to **be up to sth** /ˌbiˌˈʌp tʊ/ etw vorhaben CT6

° up to a point /ˌʌp tʊ‿ə ˈpɔɪnt/ bis zu einem gewissen Grad **2D4**
up and down /ˌʌp‿ən ˈdaʊn/ auf und ab **CT8**
up straight /ˌʌp ˈstreɪt/ aufrecht **4B1**
up to /ˈʌp tʊ/ bis (zu) **5A1**
up-and-coming /ˌʌp‿ən ˈkʌmɪŋ/ aufstrebend **4A5**
° to update /ʌpˈdeɪt/ aktualisieren; auf dem Laufenden halten **2R4**
° upon /əˈpɒn/ auf; an; bei; über **4SBS**
° upper /ˈʌpə/ obere(r, s) **1SBS**
upset /ʌpˈset/ aufgeregt; aufgebracht; bestürzt **CT6**
° to upset *(irr)* /ʌpˈset/ in Aufregung versetzen; beunruhigen; aufwühlen **2D7, 4SBS**
upstairs /ʌpˈsteəz/ (nach) oben **CT5**
° to urge /ɜːdʒ/ drängen; eindringlich bitten; raten **5SBS**
us /ʌs/ uns **CT5**
to **use** /juːz/ (be)nutzen; verwenden **CT5**
use /juːs/ Verwendung; (Be)nutzung; Gebrauch; Verbrauch **CT6**
to **get used to** /ˌget ˈjuːst‿tʊ/ sich gewöhnen an **CT7**
used to (do sth) /ˈjuːst‿tuː duː/ *drückt aus, was man früher (gewohnheitsmäßig) gemacht hat oder war* **CT8**
useful /ˈjuːsf(ə)l/ nützlich; praktisch; hilfreich **CT7**
° useless /ˈjuːsləs/ sinnlos; zwecklos; unbrauchbar **2D12**
° the usual suspects *(pl)* /ðə ˌjuːʒʊəl ˈsʌspekts/ die üblichen Verdächtigen **3B4**
usual /ˈjuːʒʊəl/ gewöhnlich; üblich; normal **CT6**
usually /ˈjuːʒʊəli/ gewöhnlich; normalerweise **CT5**
° utmost /ˈʌtməʊst/ größte(r, s) **4SBS**

V

° v. (= vs = versus) /viː, ˈvɜːsəs/ gegen **3D2, 5D21**
° vacation (*AE* = holiday *BE*) /veɪˈkeɪʃ(ə)n/ Urlaub; Ferien **3D10**
° vaccination /ˌvæksɪˈneɪʃ(ə)n/ (Schutz)impfung **2D8**
Valentine card /ˈvæləntaɪn kɑːd/ Valentinstagskarte **CT7**
Valentine's Day /ˈvæləntaɪnz deɪ/ Valentinstag **CT6, CT7**
Valentine's party /ˈvæləntaɪnz ˌpɑːti/ Party am Valentinstag **CT7**
valley /ˈvæli/ Tal **CT8**
valuable /ˈvæljʊb(ə)l/ wertvoll; kostbar **3A2, 5A3**
° van /væn/ Transporter; Kleinbus **3B2**
° vanguard /ˈvængɑːd/ Vorhut; Spitze **3D2**
° variation /ˌveərɪˈeɪʃ(ə)n/ Variation; Abweichung; Schwankung **1B/T1**
variety /vəˈraɪəti/ Vielfalt; Vielzahl; Art **CT8**
various /ˈveəriəs/ verschieden **CT8**
to **vary** /ˈveəri/ variieren **1A8, 2B9, 4A11, 5B5**
vegan /ˈviːgən/ Veganer/in; vegan **CT6**
vegetable /ˈvedʒtəb(ə)l/ Gemüse(-) **CT6**
vegetarian /ˌvedʒəˈteəriən/ Vegetarier/in; vegetarisch **CT5**
vehicle /ˈviːɪk(ə)l/ Fahrzeug; Vehikel **CT8**
° venture /ˈventʃə/ Unternehmung; Projekt; Unternehmen **3R1**
very /ˈveri/ sehr; außerordentlich **CT5**; *hier:* aller- **CT8**
° vet /vet/ Tierarzt/Tierärztin **5P1**
° via /ˈvaɪə/ über; per; via **1B4, 4B1**
vibrant /ˈvaɪbrənt/ lebhaft; dynamisch; lebendig **5Intro 1**
° vicar /ˈvɪkə/ Pfarrer **2D23**
° victim /ˈvɪktɪm/ Opfer **2D10**
° Victorian Gothic /vɪkˌtɔːriən ˈgɒθɪk/ Neogotik; neogotisch **5D2**
° victory /ˈvɪkt(ə)ri/ Sieg **5R3**
to **view** /vjuː/ betrachten; zusehen; ansehen **CT8**
view /vjuː/ (Aus)sicht; (Aus)blick **CT6**; Ansicht, Meinung **CT8**
° view /vjuː/ *hier:* Aufruf, Abruf **2SBS**
° viewer /ˈvjuːə/ (Fernseh)zuschauer/in; (Film)betrachter/in **2D18**
village /ˈvɪlɪdʒ/ Dorf **CT7**
° villain /ˈvɪlən/ Verbrecher/in; Schurke/Schurkin **5SBS**
violence *(no pl)* /ˈvaɪələns/ Gewalt(tätigkeit); Heftigkeit **CT8**
violent /ˈvaɪələnt/ gewalttätig; brutal; heftig **CT8**
virtual /ˈvɜːtʃʊəl/ virtuell **CT8**
° vision /ˈvɪʒ(ə)n/ Vision; *hier:* übergeordnete, langfristige Ziele **4A5**
to **visit** /ˈvɪzɪt/ besuchen; anschauen **CT5**
visit /ˈvɪzɪt/ Besuch **CT6**
visitor /ˈvɪzɪtə/ Besucher/in; Gast **CT8**
° vlog (= video blog) /vlɒg, ˈvɪdiəʊ blɒg/ Videoblog *(Blog in Form von Videos)* **2R1**
vocabulary /vəʊˈkæbjʊləri/ Vokabular; Wortschatz; Vokabeln **CT8**
° vodka /ˈvɒdkə/ Wodka **2SBS**
voice /vɔɪs/ Stimme **CT6**
° voice /vɔɪs/ *hier:* Sprach- **5D5**
voice message /ˈvɔɪs ˌmesɪdʒ/ Sprachnachricht **CT7**
° volcano /vɒlˈkeɪnəʊ/ Vulkan **1P1**
volume /ˈvɒljuːm/ Volumen; Umfang; Lautstärke **5B5**
to **volunteer** /ˌvɒlənˈtɪə/ sich freiwillig melden; *hier:* ehrenamtlich tätig sein **4A7**
volunteer /ˌvɒlənˈtɪə/ ehrenamtlicher Mitarbeiter/ehrenamtliche Mitarbeiterin; Freiwillige/r **CT8**
° volunteering *(no pl)* /ˌvɒlənˈtɪərɪŋ/ Freiwilligendienst **4A6**
to **vote** /vəʊt/ wählen **CT7**; *hier:* abstimmen **5Intro 4**
° vote /vəʊt/ Abstimmung; Wahl; Stimme **3B3**

W

° wage(s) /ˈweɪdʒɪz/ Lohn **5D7**
° waist /weɪst/ Taille; Gürtellinie **2D18**
to **wait (for)** /ˈweɪt fɔː/ warten (auf) **CT5**
somebody can't wait (to do sth) /ˌsʌmbədi ˌkɑːnt ˌweɪt‿tə ˈduː/ jemand kann es kaum erwarten(, etw. zu tun) **CT7**
waiter /ˈweɪtə/ Bedienung; Kellner **CT6**
waitress /ˈweɪtrəs/ Bedienung; Kellnerin **CT6**
to **wake up** *(irr)* /ˌweɪk‿ˈʌp/ aufwecken; aufwachen **CT6**
walk /wɔːk/ Spaziergang **CT5**
to **go for a walk** /ˌgəʊ fər‿ə ˈwɔːk/ einen Spaziergang machen **CT5**
to **take … for a walk** /ˌteɪk fər‿ə ˈwɔːk/ … spazieren führen; Gassi gehen mit … **CT6**
to **walk** /wɔːk/ (zu Fuß) gehen; laufen **CT6**
to **walk on** /ˌwɔːk‿ˈɒn/ weiterlaufen **CT6**
to **walk the dog** /ˌwɔːk ðə ˈdɒg/ den Hund ausführen **CT5**
° to walk up /ˌwɔːk‿ˈʌp/ hinaufgehen **3B2**
wall /wɔːl/ Wand **2B3**
° wall chart /ˈwɔːl tʃɑːt/ Schautafel; Wandzeitung **1Intro 1**
° to wander /ˈwɒndə/ schlendern; gemächlich gehen; *hier:* abschweifen **1R4**
to **want** /wɒnt/ wünschen; wollen **CT5**
to **want sb to do sth** /ˌwɒnt ˌsʌmbədi tə ˈduː ˌsʌmθɪŋ/ wollen, dass jd etw tut **CT5**
war /wɔː/ Krieg **CT7**
° War of Independence /ˌwɔːr‿əv‿ˌɪndɪˈpendəns/ *Amerikanischer Unabhängigkeitskrieg* **3D8**

wardrobe /'wɔːdrəʊb/ (Kleider)schrank; Garderobe **CT5**
° warehouse /'weəˌhaʊs/ Lagerhaus; Lagerhalle **Wordbank 2**
warm /wɔːm/ warm **CT6**
° warm-hearted /ˌwɔːm'hɑːtɪd/ warmherzig **2B/T1**
global warming /ˌgləʊb(ə)l 'wɔːmɪŋ/ Erwärmung der Erdatmosphäre **5B2**
to **warn** /wɔːn/ warnen **CT7**
warning /'wɔːnɪŋ/ Warnung **CT8**
was, were *(irr)* /wɒz, wɜː/ *Vergangenheitsformen von "be"* **CT6**
to **wash** /wɒʃ/ (sich) waschen **CT5**
° to wash sb over /ˌwɒʃ ˌsʌmbədi‿'əʊvə/ über jdn (hinweg)spülen **2B3**
to **wash up** /ˌwɒʃ‿'ʌp/ abspülen; anspülen **CT8**
wasn't (= was not) /'wɒz(ə)nt, wɒz nɒt/ *Vergangenheitsform von "isn't"* **CT6**
waste *(no pl)* /weɪst/ Verschwendung; Vergeudung; Abfall **CT6**
° to waste /weɪst/ verschwenden **4SBS**
° wasted /'weɪstɪd/ verschwendet; umsonst **5D4**
to **watch** /wɒtʃ/ beobachten; zuschauen; anschauen **CT5**
to **watch out (for)** /ˌwɒtʃ‿'aʊt fɔː/ aufpassen (auf) **CT8**
to **watch TV** /ˌwɒtʃ ˌtiː 'viː/ fernsehen **CT5**
° to water /'wɔːtə/ gießen; *hier:* tränen **2SBS**
water *(no pl)* /'wɔːtə/ Wasser **CT5**
° waterfall /'wɔːtəˌfɔːl/ Wasserfall **1P1**
° waterfront /'wɔːtəˌfrʌnt/ Ufer; Hafengebiet **1P1**
° wave /weɪv/ Welle **2D28**
to **wave (at/to)** /'weɪv‿ət/tə/ (zu)winken **CT8**
way /weɪ/ Weg; Art und Weise **CT5**
° way *(informal)* /weɪ/ weit; viel; voll **3B3**
all the way /ˌɔːl ðə 'weɪ/ den ganzen Weg **CT7**
by the way /ˌbaɪ ðə 'weɪ/ übrigens **CT8**
to **be on one's way** /ˌbi‿ɒn wʌnz 'weɪ/ auf dem Weg sein **CT6**
to **lose one's way** /ˌluːz wʌnz 'weɪ/ sich verirren **CT6**
° way of life /ˌweɪ‿əv 'laɪf/ Lebensart; Lebensstil **1A3**
we /wiː/ wir **CT5**
we're (= we are) /wɪə, 'wi‿ə/ wir sind **CT5**
° weakness /'wiːknəs/ Schwäche; Schwachstelle **3SBS, 4D11**
wealth *(no pl)* /welθ/ Reichtum; Vermögen; Fülle **5A1**
° wealthy /'welθi/ reich; wohlhabend; vermögend **2D21, 5SBS**
weapon /'wepən/ Waffe **3A2**
to **wear** *(irr)* /weə/ tragen; anhaben **CT5**
weather /'weðə/ Wetter **CT5**
° weaving machine /'wiːvɪŋ məˌʃiːn/ Webmaschine **5D7**
wedding /'wedɪŋ/ Hochzeit(s-) **CT7**
Wednesday /'wenzdeɪ/ Mittwoch **CT5**
week /wiːk/ Woche **CT5**
all week /ˌɔːl 'wiːk/ die ganze Woche über **CT6**
weekend /ˌwiːk'end/ Wochenende **CT6**
at the weekend /ət ðə ˌwiːk'end/ am Wochenende **CT5**
° weekly /'wiːkli/ wöchentlich **5D1**
to weep /wiːp/ weinen; schluchzen **2A4**
weird /wɪəd/ merkwürdig; seltsam; komisch **CT7**
to **welcome** /'welkəm/ willkommen heißen; begrüßen **CT8**
welcome /'welkəm/ willkommen **CT6**
well /wel/ nun (ja); tja; gut **CT6**
Well done! /ˌwel 'dʌn/ Gut gemacht!; Super! **CT7**
well-being *(no pl)* /ˌwel'biːɪŋ/ Wohl(ergehen); Wohlbefinden **2A4**
well-known /ˌwel'nəʊn/ (allgemein) bekannt; berühmt **CT7**
weren't (= were not) /'wɜːnt, wɜː 'nɒt/ *Vergangenheitsform von "aren't"* **CT6**
west /west/ Westen; westlich; West- **CT7**
° the West Coast /ðə ˌwest 'kəʊst/ die Westküste *(der USA)* **3B/T1**
wet /wet/ nass **CT6**
wet season /'wet ˌsiːz(ə)n/ Regenzeit **1B7**
what /wɒt/ was; welche(r, s) **CT5**
What a/an ...! /'wɒt‿ə/ Was für ein(e) ...! **CT7**
What about ...? *(informal)* /'wɒt‿əˌbaʊt/ Was ist mit ...?; Wie wäre es mit ...? **CT5**
What about you? /ˌwɒt‿əˌbaʊt 'juː/ Was ist mit dir?; Und du? **CT5**
° What (has) got into sb? *(informal)* /ˌwɒt həz gɒt‿'ɪntuː/ Was ist bloß in jdn gefahren? **3B/T1**
What if ...? /wɒt‿ɪf/ Was (wäre), wenn ...? **CT7**
° What the hell ...? *(informal)* /ˌwɒt ðə 'hel/ Was zum Teufel ...? **2D23, 4R1, 5R2**
what's (= what is) /'wɒts, 'wɒt‿ɪz/ was ist **CT5**
What's going on? /ˌwɒts ˌgəʊɪŋ‿'ɒn/ Was geht hier vor?; Was ist los? **CT7**
° What's the matter? /ˌwɒts ðə 'mætə/ Was ist los? **4R1**
What's the time? /ˌwɒts ðə 'taɪm/ Wie spät/Wie viel Uhr ist es? **CT5**
What's up? *(informal)* /ˌwɒts‿'ʌp/ Was ist los?; Wie geht's? **CT7**
What's wrong? /ˌwɒts 'rɒŋ/ Was ist los? **CT6**
What's your favourite ...? /ˌwɒts jə 'feɪv(ə)rət/ Was ist dein Lieblings...? **CT5**
What's your name? /ˌwɒts jə 'neɪm/ Wie heißt du? **CT5**
whatever /wɒt'evə/ was auch immer; egal was **4A5**
° whatever /wɒt'evə/ *hier:* alles **3B4**
° wheelchair /'wiːlˌtʃeə/ Rollstuhl **1D9**
when /wen/ wenn; wann; als **CT5**
° When it comes to ... /ˌwen‿ɪt 'kʌmz tʊ/ Wenn es um ... geht; In Sachen ... **4SBS, Wordbank 6, Wordbank 8**
° whenever /wen'evə/ wann (auch) immer **1R4, 3D16**
where /weə/ wo **CT5**; wohin **CT6**
Where are you from? /ˌweər‿ə jʊ 'frɒm/ Woher kommst du?; Woher kommt ihr? **CT5**
Where is ...? / Where are ...? /'weər‿ɪz, 'weər‿ɑː/ Wo ist ...? / Wo sind ...? **CT5**
where's (= where is) /weəz, 'weər‿ɪz/ wo ist **CT5**
whereas /weər'æz/ während; wo(hin)gegen **CT8**
° wherever /wer'evə/ wo(hin) auch immer; wann immer; wo (nur) **2D4**
whether /'weðə/ (egal) ob **CT7**
which /wɪtʃ/ welche(r, s); der/die/das; was **CT7**
° which one /'wɪtʃ wʌn/ welche(r, s) **4B/T2**
while /waɪl/ während; als **CT7**; obwohl, zwar **CT8**
while *(no pl)* /waɪl/ Weile **CT7**
° whilst *(BE)* /waɪlst/ während; obwohl; wo(hin)gegen **5B2**
° to whimper /'wɪmpə/ wimmern; winseln **4SBS**
° to whip /wɪp/ peitschen **2SBS**
to **whisper** /'wɪspə/ flüstern **CT6**
° whistleblower/whistle-blower /'wɪs(ə)lˌbləʊə/ Whistleblower/in *(Person, die Missstände öffentlich macht)* **2D8**
white /waɪt/ weiß **CT5**
who /huː/ wer **CT5**; der/die/das **CT6**
° Who cares? *(informal)* /huː 'keəz/ Wen kümmert's? **2SBS**
° whoever /huː'evə/ wer/wen (auch immer) **4R1**
whole /həʊl/ ganz; gesamt **CT7**
as a whole /æz‿ə 'həʊl/ als Ganzes (betrachtet) **CT8**

° **whom** /huːm/ wem; wen; der/die/das 3SBS, 5SBS
whose /huːz/ dessen; deren CT7
why /waɪ/ warum CT5
° wi-fi /ˈwaɪ faɪ/ WLAN *(Computernetzwerk mit Funktechnik)* 1R2
wide /waɪd/ breit; groß CT8
° wide /waɪd/ *hier:* weit 5D4
° wide-eyed /ˌwaɪd‿ˈaɪd/ mit großen Augen 4SBS
widely /ˈwaɪdli/ weithin 1A3
° to widen /ˈwaɪd(ə)n/ breiter werden; *hier:* weiten, aufreißen 2A2
° wife (*pl* wives) /waɪf, waɪfz/ (Ehe)frau 3R1
wild /waɪld/ wild; in freier Wildbahn lebend CT6
the wild *(no pl)* /ðə ˈwaɪld/ die Wildnis 4A5
wildlife *(no pl)* /ˈwaɪldˌlaɪf/ *die (natürliche) Tier- und Pflanzenwelt* CT8
will /wɪl/ werden CT6
will /wɪl/ Wille 1A3
willing /ˈwɪlɪŋ/ bereit; gewillt; willig 4A5
to **win** *(irr)* /wɪn/ gewinnen CT5
° to win over /ˌwɪn‿ˈəʊvə/ überzeugen; für sich gewinnen 3SBS
° to wince /wɪns/ zusammenzucken 2SBS
° to wind up *(irr)* /ˌwaɪnd‿ˈʌp/ wickeln 2SBS
window /ˈwɪndəʊ/ Fenster CT5
° windshield (*AE* = windscreen *BE*) /ˈwɪndˌʃild/ Windschutzscheibe 2SBS
windy /ˈwɪndi/ windig CT6
wine /waɪn/ Wein CT7
° winner /ˈwɪnə/ Gewinner/in; Sieger/in 1A3
winter /ˈwɪntə/ Winter CT5
° wise /waɪz/ weise; klug; vernünftig 3SBS
to **wish** /wɪʃ/ wünschen CT7
Best wishes /ˌbest ˈwɪʃɪz/ Herzliche Grüße CT6
° witch trial /ˈwɪtʃˌtraɪəl/ Hexenprozess 3R2
with /wɪð/ mit CT5
° to wither/ˈwɪðə/ verdorren, verfallen; *hier:* einknicken 5R1
within /wɪðˈɪn/ innerhalb CT8
without /wɪðˈaʊt/ ohne CT6
to **witness** /ˈwɪtnəs/ beobachten; Zeuge/Zeugin sein; miterleben 3B1
° witness /ˈwɪtnəs/ Zeuge/Zeugin 3R5
woman (*pl* women) /ˈwʊmən, ˈwɪmɪn/ Frau CT6
° wombat /ˈwɒmˌbæt/ *Beuteltierart* 1D8
won't (= will not) /wəʊnt, wɪl ˈnɒt/ nicht werden CT6

to **wonder** /ˈwʌndə/ sich fragen; sich wundern; überrascht sein CT7
wonder /ˈwʌndə/ Wunder 1A5
wonderful /ˈwʌndəf(ə)l/ wunderbar; wundervoll CT5
° wonky *(informal, BE)* /ˈwɒŋki/ wack(e)lig; schief hängend/sitzend 4SBS
° wood /wʊd/ Holz 5D7
° wooden /ˈwʊd(ə)n/ Holz-; hölzern; aus Holz 4SBS
word /wɜːd/ Wort CT5
° word class /ˈwɜːd klɑːs/ Wortart 2D23
° word formation *(no pl)* /ˈwɜːd fɔːˌmeɪʃ(ə)n/ Wortbildung 2D23
word processing *(no pl)* /ˈwɜːd ˌprəʊsesɪŋ/ Textverarbeitung 4A7
° word web /ˈwɜːd web/ Wortnetz 5D14
to **work** /wɜːk/ arbeiten CT6; funktionieren 4B1
work /wɜːk/ Arbeit CT6
° to work /wɜːk/ *hier:* wirken 2B4
° work experience *(BE)* /ˈwɜːk‿ɪkˌspɪəriəns/ Praktikum 4R3, Wordbank 8
work of art /ˌwɜːk‿əv‿ˈɑːt/ Kunstwerk 5A3
to **work out** /ˌwɜːk‿ˈaʊt/ lösen; verstehen; herausfinden; funktionieren CT7
° work-life balance *(no pl)* /ˌwɜːk ˌlaɪf ˈbæləns/ Work-Life-Balance *(Ausgewogenheit beruflicher Anforderungen und privater Bedürfnisse)* 4D5
worker /ˈwɜːkə/ Arbeiter/in CT8
° worker /ˈwɜːkə/ *hier:* Helfer/in 3SBS
° workhorse /ˈwɜːkˌhɔːs/ Arbeitstier 1R2
° working life /ˌwɜːkɪŋ ˈlaɪf/ Berufsleben; Arbeitsleben 4Intro 3
° working-class /ˌwɜːkɪŋ ˈklɑːs/ (aus der) Arbeiterklasse 5P1
° workplace /ˈwɜːkˌpleɪs/ Arbeitsplatz 4D5
° worksheet /ˈwɜːkˌʃiːt/ Arbeitsblatt 4A7
° worktop *(BE)* /ˈwɜːkˌtɒp/ Arbeitsfläche; Arbeitsplatte 5B2
world /wɜːld/ Welt CT6
° World War II *(AE)* /ˌwɜrld wɔr ˈtu/ der Zweite Weltkrieg 1D3, 4P3
° world-famous /ˌwɜːldˈfeɪməs/ weltberühmt 5Intro 1
° worldwide /ˌwɜːldˈwaɪd/ weltweit; auf der ganzen Welt 4P3
° worm /wɜːm/ Wurm 4D4
worried /ˈwʌrid/ beunruhigt; besorgt CT5
° worry /ˈwʌri/ Sorge 5D13
to **worry (about)** /ˈwʌri‿əˌbaʊt/ sich Sorgen machen (um) CT5
worse /wɜːs/ schlechter; schlimmer CT6

worst /wɜːst/ schlechteste(r, s); schlimmste(r, s) CT6
worth *(no pl)* /wɜːθ/ Wert 1A4
to **be worth sth** /ˌbiː ˈwɜːθ/ etw wert sein CT6
would /wʊd/ würde(n/st/t) CT6
would like to /wʊd ˈlaɪk tʊ/ würde(n/st/t) gern CT6
wouldn't (= would not) /ˈwʊd(ə)nt, wʊd ˈnɒt/ würde(n/st/t) nicht CT6
wounded /ˈwuːndɪd/ verletzt; verwundet 4A5
° to wrap /ræp/ (ein)wickeln; einpacken; einhüllen 5R4
to wreak havoc /ˌriːk ˈhævək/ schlimme Schäden anrichten 5A3
° wrecked *(informal)* /rekt/ zerstört; *hier:* k. o. 2SBS
° wrinkled /ˈrɪŋkld/ zerknittert; faltig; runzlig 3R2
° wrist /rɪst/ Handgelenk 3B4
to **write** *(irr)* /raɪt/ schreiben CT5
to **write down** *(irr)* /ˌraɪt‿ˈdaʊn/ aufschreiben; niederschreiben CT5
writer /ˈraɪtə/ Verfasser/in; Autor/in 2B8
wrong /rɒŋ/ falsch CT5
to **go wrong** /ˌɡəʊ ˈrɒŋ/ schiefgehen 4B3
What's wrong? /ˌwɒts ˈrɒŋ/ Was ist los? CT6
wrong /rɒŋ/ Unrecht 1A5

Y

° y'all (= you all) *(informal, AE)* /jɔl/ ihr (alle) 2R3
° to yank /jæŋk/ zerren 3B4
yard /jɑːd/ *Längenmaß (91,44 cm)* CT8
° yard /jɑːd/ Hof 4SBS
year /jɪə/ Jahr CT5; (Schul-)Jahrgang CT6
a year /ə ˈjɪə/ im Jahr CT7
° to yell /jel/ (gellend) schreien 3R5, 5R1
° to yell along /ˌjel‿əˈlɒŋ/ (gellend) mitschreien 2SBS
yellow /ˈjeləʊ/ gelb CT5
yes /jes/ ja CT5
yesterday /ˈjestədeɪ/ gestern CT6
yet /jet/ bis jetzt; schon; noch CT6; (und) doch; (und) trotzdem CT7
° Yolngu /ˈjuːlŋʊ/ *Aborigines-Stamm in Australien* 1D11
° Yolngu Matha /ˌjuːlŋʊ ˈmaːtaː/ *Aboriginessprache* 1D11
° Yorta Yorta /ˌjɔːtə ˈjɔːtə/ *australisches Ureinwohnervolk* 1A4
you /juː/ du; dich; dir; Sie; Ihnen; ihr; euch CT5
° You can't be serious. /jʊ ˌkɑːnt bi ˈsɪəriəs/ Das ist nicht dein Ernst! 5B4

° You have a point here/there. /ˌju həvˏəˏˈpɔɪnt hɪə/ðeə/ Da hast du (wohl) recht.; Da ist was dran. **Wordbank 6**

you're (= **you are**) /jɔː, ˈjuˏə/ du bist; ihr seid; Sie sind **CT5**

° You're welcome. /ˌjɔː ˈwelkəm/ Bitte schön.; Gern geschehen. **4D18**

young /jʌŋ/ jung **CT5**

your /jɔː/ dein(e); euer/eure; Ihr(e) **CT5**

yours /jɔːz/ deine(r, s); eure(r, s); Ihre(r, s) **CT6**

Yours /jɔːz/ Mit freundlichen Grüßen; Viele Grüße **CT7**

Yours faithfully *(BE)* /ˌjɔːz ˈfeɪθf(ə)li/ *Schlussformel in einem nicht an eine bestimmte Person gerichteten formellen Brief* **4A9**

° Yours sincerely /jɔːzˏsɪnˈsɪəli/ *Schlussformel in einem formellen Brief bei persönlicher Anrede* **5SBS**

yourself (*pl* **yourselves**) /jəˈself, jəˈselvz/ dich; dir; (du/Sie) selbst **CT7**

to **enjoy yourself** /ˈɪndʒɔɪ jəˌself/ sich amüsieren **CT7**

to **help yourself (to sth)** /ˈhelp jəˌself tʊ/ sich (an etw) bedienen **CT7**

° youth /juːθ/ junger Mann; Jugendliche(r) **4SBS**

° youth *(no pl)* /juːθ/ Jugend(-) **3D2, 4A/T1** ° youth club *(BE)* /ˈjuːθ klʌb/ Jugendzentrum **5B4**

° youth hostel /ˈjuːθ ˌhɒst(ə)l/ Jugendherberge **5Intro 4**

° youth worker /ˈjuːθ ˌwɜːkə/ *in der Jugendarbeit tätige Person* **4R3**

° yup *(informal)* /jʌp/ ja **2R3**

Z

° zooxanthellae *(pl)* /ˌzəʊəzænˈθeli/ *Algenart* **1B7**

W Words

Names

Girls/women
Ada /ˈeɪdə/
Alex /ˈælɪks/
Alice /ˈælɪs/
Amanda /əˈmændə/
Amber /ˈæmbə/
Amelia /əˈmiːliə/
Amira /əˈmirə/
Ann /æn/
Anna /ˈænə/
Anya /ˈænjə/
Aster /ˈæstə/
Autumn /ˈɔːtəm/
Ava /ˈeɪvə/
Bailey /ˈbeɪli/
Bella /ˈbelə/
Beth /beθ/
Bronte /ˈbrɒnti/
Caroline /ˈkærəlaɪn/
Casey /ˈkeɪsi/
Catherine /ˈkæθ(ə)rɪn/
Cathy /ˈkæθi/
Christabel /ˈkrɪstəbel/
Christine /ˈkrɪstiːn/
Corinne /kəˈrɪn/
Deborah /ˈdeb(ə)rə/
Donna /ˈdɒnə/
Ella /ˈelə/
Ellen /ˈelən/
Ellen /ˈelən/
Ellie /ˈeli/
Emilia /eˈmiːliə/
Emily /ˈeməli/
Emma /emə/
Emmeline /ˈeməliːn/
Esme /ˈezmi/
Frances /ˈfrɑːnsɪs/
Harper /ˈhɑːpə/
Holly /ˈhɒli/
Isabelle /ˈɪzəbel/
Jane /dʒeɪn/
Jasmine /ˈdʒæzmɪn/
Jen /ˈdʒen/
Jenna /ˈdʒenə/
Jennifer /ˈdʒenɪfə/
Jenny /ˈdʒeni/
Juanda /dʒuˈændə/
Julia /ˈdʒuːliə/
Juliana /ˌdʒuːliˈɑːnə/
Kim /kɪm/
Kyla /ˈkaɪlə/
Lara /ˈlɑːrə/
Laura /ˈlɔːrə/
Lily /ˈlɪli/
Lisa /ˈliːsə/
Liz /lɪz/
Lottie /ˈlɒti/
Louise /luˈiːz/
Lucy /ˈluːsi/
Malala /məˈlɑːlə/
Martha /ˈmɑːθə/
Mary /ˈmeəri/
Maya /ˈmaɪə/
Meg /meg/
Megan /ˈmeg(ə)n/
Meghan /ˈmeg(ə)n/
Meryem /ˈmeriəm/
Molly /ˈmɒli/
Monique /mɒˈniːk/
Nora /ˈnɔːrə/
Olivia /əˈlɪviə/
Orla /ˈɔːlə/
Paula /ˈpɔːlə/
Priyanka /prɪˈjæŋkə/
Rebecca /riˈbekə/
Rosalind /ˈrɒzəlɪnd/
Rose /rəʊz/
Ruby /ˈruːbi/
Sarah /ˈsɑːrə/
Shadeene /ʃəˈdiːn/
Shey /ʃeɪ/
Shobika /ʃəˈbiːkə/
Sirin /ˈsɪrɪn/
Sky /skaɪ/
Sophie /ˈsəʊfi/
Sydney /ˈsɪdni/
Talia /ˈtælɪə/
Tammy /ˈtæmi/
Taylor /ˈteɪlə/
Tory /ˈtɔːri/
Tracey /ˈtreɪsi/
Trell /trel/
Van /væn/
Yini /ˈjɪni/
Zoe /ˈzəʊi/

Boys/men
Adam /ˈædəm/
Akachi /əˈkɑːtʃi/
Alan /ˈælən/
Angelo /ˈændʒələʊ/
Anthony /ˈæntəni/
Arif /əˈriːf/
Ben /ben/
Caleb /ˈkeɪleb/
Carl /kɑːl/
Charlie /ˈtʃɑːli/
Clemens /ˈklemənz/
Dale /deɪ(ə)l/
Dan /dæn/
Danzal /ˈdænz(ə)l/
Darrel /ˈdærəl/
Delan /ˈdiːlən/
Dennis /ˈdenɪs/
Dick /dɪk/
Dustin /ˈdʌstɪn/
Dwight /dwaɪt/
Dylan /ˈdɪlən/
Edward /ˈedwəd/
Eliah /ɪˈlaɪə/
Eric /ˈerɪk/
Ethan /ˈiːθ(ə)n/
Felix /ˈfiːlɪks/
Finn /fɪn/
George /dʒɔːdʒ/
Hakan /ˈhɑːkən/
Harry /ˈhæri/
Ibrahim /ˈɪbrəhiːm/
Isaiah /aɪˈzaɪə/
Jack /dʒæk/
Jade /dʒeɪd/
Jamal /dʒəˈmɑːl/
James /dʒeɪmz/
Jesse /ˈdʒesi/
Joe /dʒəʊ/
John /dʒɒn/
Johnny /ˈdʒɒni/
Jonathan /ˈdʒɒnəθ(ə)n/
Kevin /ˈkevɪn/
Leo /ˈliːəʊ/
Li /liː/
Liam /ˈliːəm/
Luke /luːk/
Marcus /ˈmɑːkəs/
Marlon /ˈmɑːlən/
Mason /ˈmeɪs(ə)n/
Matt /mæt/
Michael /ˈmaɪk(ə)l/
Muhammad /muˈhæməd/
Nathan /ˈneɪθ(ə)n/
Nick /nɪk/
Noah /ˈnəʊə/
Patrick /ˈpætrɪk/
Paul /pɔːl/
Ralph /rælf/
Ricky /ˈrɪki/
Robert /ˈrɒbət/
Romero /rəˈmeərəʊ/
Rowan /ˈrəʊən/
Said /sɑːˈiːd/
Scott /skɒt/
Sebastian /səˈbæstʃən/
Simon /ˈsaɪmən/
Stanley /ˈstænli/
Ted /ted/
Terrance /ˈterəns/
Thomas /ˈtɒməs/
Thor /θɔː/
Tim /tɪm/
Todd /tɒd/
Tom /tɒm/
Trent /trent/
Vinnie /ˈvɪni/
Walton /ˈwɔːlt(ə)n/
William /ˈwɪljəm/
Youssef /ˈjʊsef/
Zayne /zeɪn/

Family names
Alcott /ˈɔːlkət/
Austen /ˈɒstɪn/
Baker /ˈbeɪkə/
Bancel /ˈbæns(ə)l/
Barrett /ˈbærət/
Biden /ˈbaɪd(ə)n/
Bittle /ˈbɪt(ə)l/
Bittner /ˈbɪtnə/
Briggs /brɪgz/
Brizeno /brɪzˈiːnəʊ/
Brontë /ˈbrɒnti/
Carlyle /kɑːˈlaɪ(ə)l/
Catron /ˈkætr(ə)n/
Chu /tʃuː/
Colston /ˈkəʊlst(ə)n/
Cook /kʊk/
Cresswell /ˈkreswel/
Cubbins /ˈkʌbɪnz/
Dailey /ˈdeɪli/
Dawe /dɔː/
de Wilde /də ˈwaɪld/
Delgado /delˈgɑːdəʊ/
Devine /diˈviːn/
Evans /ˈev(ə)nz/
Flores /ˈflɔːrɪz/
Flynn /flɪn/
Freeman /ˈfriːmən/
Freudenthal /ˈfrɔɪdəntɑːl/
Goggins /ˈgɒgɪnz/
Gorman /ˈgɔːmən/
Graham /ˈgreɪəm/
Grayson /ˈgreɪs(ə)n/
Hall /hɔːl/
Hargraves /ˈhɑːgreɪvz/
Haugen /ˈhɔːg(ə)n/
Hindmarsh /ˈhaɪndmɑːʃ/
Holden /ˈhəʊldən/
Holmes /ˈhəʊmz/
Johnson /ˈdʒɒns(ə)n/
Jones /dʒəʊnz/
Kale /keɪ(ə)l/

Knightley /ˈnaɪtli/
Lehr /leə/
Leung /lʌŋ/
Miller /ˈmɪlə/
Moriarty /ˌmɒriˈɑːti/
Morin /ˈmɔːrɪn/
Morrison /ˈmɒrɪs(ə)n/
Munsky /ˈmʌnski/
Naveda /nəˈveɪdə/
North /nɔːθ/
Nuttall /ˈnʌtɔːl/
Pankhurst /ˈpæŋkhɜːst/
Parker /ˈpɑːkə/
Perez /ˈperez/
Petrazelli /ˌpetrəˈzeli/
Plummer /ˈplʌmə/
Rae /reɪ/
Ramsey /ˈræmzi/
Rashford /ˈræʃfəd/
Reiss /raɪs/
Russell /ˈrʌs(ə)l/
Sandy /ˈsændi/
Sterling /ˈstɜːlɪŋ/
Stevenson /ˈstiːv(ə)ns(ə)n/
Stoker /ˈstəʊkə/
Strasser /ˈstræsə/
Stroud /straʊd/
Sutcliffe /ˈsʌtklɪf/
Stroud /straʊd/
Symmonds /ˈsɪməndz/
Taylor /ˈteɪlə/
Taylor-Joy /ˌteɪlə ˈdʒɔɪ/
Thomas /ˈtɒməs/
Tillery /ˈtɪl(ə)ri/
Trump /trʌmp/
Turing /ˈtjʊərɪŋ/
Turner /ˈtɜːnə/
Tweedy /ˈtwiːdi/
van Neerven /væn ˈneərvən/
Vance /væns/
Walsh /wɔːlʃ/
Walton /ˈwɔːlt(ə)n/
Williams /ˈwɪljəmz/
Winterbottom /ˈwɪntəˌbɒtəm/
Wood /wʊd/
Woodhouse /ˈwʊdhaʊs/
Wu /wuː/
Yousafzai /jusəfˈzaɪ/

Other names

Africaine /ˌæfrɪˈkeɪn/
All Creatures Great and Small /ˌɔːl ˌkriːtʃəz ˌgreɪt‿ən ˈsmɔːl/
Amnesty International /ˌæmnəsti‿ɪntəˈræʃ(ə)nəl/
Arsenal /ˈɑːs(ə)n(ə)l/
Athena Rising /əˌθiːnə ˈraɪzɪŋ/
Baker Boy /ˈbeɪkə bɔɪ/
Banff National Park /ˌbænf ˌnæʃ(ə)nəl ˈpɑːk/
Billy Elliot /ˌbɪli‿ˈeliət/
the Beatles /ðə ˈbiːt(ə)lz/
Blossom Street /ˈblɒs(ə)m striːt/
Boston University /ˌbɒst(ə)n ˌjuːnɪˈvɜːsəti/
BreakTheCycle /ˌbreɪkðəˈsaɪk(ə)l/
Brisbane Roar /ˌbrɪzbən ˈrɔː/
Brookwood High /ˌbrʊkwʊd ˈhaɪ/
The Canberra Bugle /ðə ˌkænb(ə)rə ˈbjuːg(ə)l/
Catani Gardens /ˌkætəni ˈgɑːd(ə)nz/
Catherine Called Birdy /ˌkæθ(ə)rɪn ˌkɔːld bɜːdi/
Chapman University /ˌtʃæpmən ˌjuːnɪˈvɜːsəti/
Chelsea /ˈtʃelsi/
Coronation Street /ˌkɒrəˈneɪʃ(ə)n striːt/
Cottonopolis /ˌkɒt(ə)nˈɒpəlɪs/
Daffodils /ˈdæfədɪlz/
Dignityville /ˈdɪgnətivɪl/
Dracula /ˈdrækjʊlə/
Earth Guardians /ˈɜːθ ˌgɑːdiənz/
Fiordland National Park /ˌfjɔːdlənd ˌnæʃ(ə)nəl ˈpɑːk/
Flickchat /ˈflɪkˌtʃæt/
Grand Canyon /ˌgrænd ˈkænjən/
Great Barrier Reef /ˌgreɪt ˈbæriə riːf/
Greenway State College /ˌgriːnweɪ ˌsteɪt kɒlɪdʒ/
Harvard University /ˌhɑːvəd ˌjuːnɪˈvɜːsəti/
HMS Buffalo /ˌeɪtʃ‿em‿ˌes ˈbʌfələʊ/
Hobbiton /ˈhɒbɪt(ə)n/
Hollywood /ˈhɒliwʊd/
Huntington Beach /ˌhʌntɪŋt(ə)n ˈbiːtʃ/
Jam Campus /ˈdʒæm ˌkæmpəs/
John Carlisle Award /ˌdʒɒn ˈkɑːlaɪ(ə)l əˌwɔːd/
John Rylands Library /ˌdʒɒn ˈraɪləndz ˌlaɪbrəri/
John St Kitchen /ˌdʒɒn sənt ˈkɪtʃən/
Kmart /ˈkeɪmɑːt/
Lake Eyre /ˌleɪk‿ˈeə/
Leeds Civic Hall /ˌliːdz‿ˌsɪvɪk ˈhɔːl/
Liverpool Cathedral /ˌlɪvəpuːl kəˈθiːdrəl/
Lockwood & Co. /ˌlɒkwʊd‿ən ˈkəʊ/
Lupo /ˈluːpəʊ/
Manchester Art Gallery /ˌmænˌtʃestər‿ˈɑːt ˌgæləri/
Mara /ˈmɑːrə/
Maritime Museum /ˌmærɪˌtaɪm‿mjuːˈziːəm/
Milford Sound /ˌmɪlfəd ˈsaʊnd/
Mount Kosciuszko /ˌmaʊnt ˌkɒziˈʌskəʊ/
Ms Frizzle /məz ˈfrɪz(ə)l/
Musgrave Park /ˌmʌzgreɪv ˈpɑːk/
NASA /ˈnæsə/
Nesyamun /ˌnesjəˈmuːn/
Nokia /ˈnɒkiə/
Old Dock /ˌəʊld‿ˈdɒk/
Old Trafford /ˌəʊld‿ˈtræfəd/
Ophir /ˈəʊfə/
Portland Row /ˌpɔːtlənd ˈrəʊ/
Princeton /ˈprɪnstən/
Queens Gardens /ˌkwiːnz ˈgɑːd(ə)nz/
Real Madrid /reɪˌɑːl məˈdrɪd/
Royal Flying Doctor Service /ˌrɔɪəl ˌflaɪɪŋ ˈdɒktə ˌsɜːvɪs/
Royal Grammar School /ˌrɔɪəl ˈgræmə skuːl/
Sackville Gardens /ˌsækvɪl ˈgɑːd(ə)nz/
Samwell University /ˌsæmw(ə)l ˌjuːnɪˈvɜːsəti/
Science and Industry Museum /ˌsaɪəns‿ən‿ˈɪndəstri mjuːˌziːəm/
Shazam /ʃəˈzæm/
Sky Tower /ˈskaɪ ˌtaʊə/
Skyrail /ˈskaɪˌreɪl/
Spiderman /ˈspaɪdəmæn/
Spinning Jenny /ˌspɪnɪŋ ˈdʒeni/
Squahamish /skwɒˈheɪmɪʃ/
St Luke's Church /sənt ˌluːks ˈtʃɜːtʃ/
Stanhope Invenit /ˌstænəp‿ɪnˈveɪnɪt/
Sydney Opera House /ˌsɪdni‿ˈɒp(ə)rə haʊs/
Taliban /ˈtælɪbæn/

Tartanya /tɑːˈtænjə/
The Hobbit /ðə ˈhɒbɪt/
The Lord of the Rings /ðə ˌlɔːd‿əv ðə ˈrɪŋz/
Titanic /taɪˈtænɪk/
Toucan Wildlife Center /ˌtuːk(ə)n ˈwaɪldˌlaɪf ˌsentə/
U-Haul /ˈjuː hɔːl/
Uluru /ˌuːləˈruː/
Wally's Wowza-Burger /ˌwɒliz ˈwaʊzə ˌbɜːɡə/
Whadjuk Noongar /ˈwʌdʒʌk ˌnʊŋɑː/
Women's Social and Political Union /ˌwɪmɪnz‿ˌsəʊʃ(ə)l‿ən pəˌlɪtɪk(ə)l ˈjuːnjən/
Whitby Abbey /ˌwɪtbi‿ˈæbi/
Wuthering Heights /ˌwʌðərɪŋ ˈhaɪts/
Youth Vanguard /ˈjuːθ ˌvænɡɑːd/

Geographical names

Adelaide /ˈædəleɪd/
Afghanistan /æfˈɡænɪstɑːn/
Alice Springs /ˌælɪs‿ˈsprɪŋz/
America /əˈmerɪkə/
Auckland /ˈɔːklənd/
Australia /ɒˈstreɪliə/
Australian Capital Territory /ɒˌstreɪliən ˌkæpɪt(ə)l ˈterət(ə)ri/
Austria /ˈɒstriə/
Ballarat /ˈbælərӕt/
Banff /bænf/
Belgium /ˈbeldʒəm/
Bendigo /ˈbendɪɡəʊ/
Bendigo Creek /ˌbendɪɡəʊ ˈkriːk/
Berlin /bɜːˈlɪn/
Blomfield Street /ˈblɒmfiːld striːt/
Borrowloola /ˌbɒrəˈluːlə/
Boston /ˈbɒst(ə)n/
Bradford /ˈbrædfəd/
Brisbane /ˈbrɪzbən/
Bristol /ˈbrɪst(ə)l/
Burlington /ˈbɜːlɪŋtən/
Cairns /keənz/kænz/
California /ˌkæləˈfɔːniə/
Cambridge /ˈkeɪmbrɪdʒ/
Canada /ˈkænədə/
Canberra /ˈkænb(ə)rə/
the Caribbean /ðə ˌkærɪˈbiən/
Castlemaine /ˈkɑːs(ə)lmeɪn/
Chester /ˈtʃestə/
China /ˈtʃaɪnə/
Clunes /kluːnz/
Colorado /ˌkɒləˈrɑːdəʊ/
Coolgardie /kuːlˈɡɑːdi/
Costa Rica /ˌkɒstə ˈriːkə/
County Durham /ˌkaʊnti ˈdʌrəm/
Darwin /ˈdɑːwɪn/
Daytona /deɪˈtəʊnə/
Fitzroy Island /fɪtsˌrɔɪ‿ˈaɪlənd/
Florida /ˈflɒrɪdə/
Georgia /ˈdʒɔːdʒə/
Glasgow /ˈɡlɑːzɡəʊ/
Guildford /ˈɡɪlfəd/
Hawaii /həˈwaɪi/
Hobart /ˈhəʊbɑːt/
India /ˈɪndiə/
Japan /dʒəˈpæn/
Kalgoorlie /kælˈɡʊəli/
Katherine /ˈkæθ(ə)rɪn/
Kenya /ˈkenjə/
Khyber Pakhtunkhwa /ˌkaɪbə pəkˈtuːŋkwə/
L.A. (= Los Angeles) /ˌel‿ˈeɪ, lɒs‿ˈændʒəliːz/
Lake District /ˈleɪk ˌdɪstrɪkt/
Lebanon /ˈlebənən/
Leeds /liːdz/
Liverpool /ˈlɪvəpuːl/
London /ˈlʌndən/
Los Angeles /lɔːs‿ˈændʒəliːz/
Maine /meɪn/
Malaysia /məˈleɪziə/
Malta /ˈmɔːltə/
Manchester /ˈmænˌtʃestə/
Massachusetts /ˌmæsəˈtʃuːsɪts/
Mattapan /ˈmætəpæn/
Melbourne /ˈmelbən/
Mexico /ˈmeksɪkəʊ/
Millennium Square /mɪˌleniəm ˈskweə/
Missouri /mɪˈzʊəri/
the Netherlands /ðə ˈneðələndz/
New South Wales /ˌnjuː saʊθ ˈweɪlz/
New Zealand /nju ˈziːlənd/
Newcastle /ˈnjuːˌkɑːs(ə)l/
Nigeria /naɪˈdʒɪəriə/
Northampton Street /nɔːˈθæmtən striːt/
Northern Territory /ˌnɔːðən ˈterət(ə)ri/
Pakistan /ˌpɑːkɪˈstɑːn/
Paris /ˈpærɪs/
Perth /pɜːθ/
Philippines /ˈfɪləpiːnz/
Port Jackson /ˌpɔːt ˈdʒæks(ə)n/
Queensland /ˈkwiːnzlənd/
Quetta /ˈkwetə/
Rio de Janeiro /ˌriːəʊ də ʒəˈnɪərəʊ/
Rotorua /ˌrəʊtəˈruə/
Roxbury /ˈrɒksbəri/
Salem /ˈseɪləm/
Seattle /siˈæt(ə)l/
Sheffield /ˈʃefiːld/
Singapore /ˌsɪŋəˈpɔː/
South Africa /ˌsaʊθ‿ˈæfrɪkə/
South Australia /ˌsaʊθ‿ɒˈstreɪliə/
Sri Lanka /srɪ ˈlæŋkə/
St Kilda /sənt ˈkɪldə/
Swat /swɑːt/
Sweden /ˈswiːd(ə)n/
Switzerland /ˈswɪtsələnd/
Sydney /ˈsɪdni/
Tasmania /tæzˈmeɪniə/
Trafford Park /ˌtræfəd ˈpɑːk/
USA (= United States of America) /ˌjuː‿es‿ˈeɪ, juːˌnaɪtɪd ˌsteɪts‿əv‿əˈmerɪkə/
Victoria /vɪkˈtɔːriə/
Vietnam /ˌviːetˈnæm/
Waitangi /waɪˈtæŋi/
Walpole /ˈwɔːlpəʊl/
Washington /ˈwɒʃɪŋtən/
Wellington /ˈwelɪŋtən/
West Africa /ˌwest‿ˈæfrɪkə/
West Yorkshire /ˌwest ˈjɔːkʃə/
Western Australia /ˌwestən‿ɒˈstreɪliə/
Whitby /ˈwɪtbi/
York /jɔːk/
Yorkshire Dales /ˌjɔːkʃə ˈdeɪ(ə)lz/

English sounds

Im Englischen spricht man Wörter oft anders aus, als man sie schreibt.
Deshalb ist die Lautschrift sehr nützlich: Sie gibt an, wie ein Wort ausgesprochen wird.
Hier ist eine Liste der Lautschriftzeichen zusammen mit Beispielwörtern:

Vokale

/ɑː/	arm
/ʌ/	but
/e/	desk
/ə/	a, an
/ɜː/	girl, bird
/æ/	apple
/ɪ/	in, it
/i/	every
/iː/	easy, eat
/ɒ/	orange
/ɔː/	all, story
/ʊ/	look
/u/	February
/uː/	food

Doppellaute

/aɪ/	eye, buy
/aʊ/	house
/eə/	there
/eɪ/	take, they
/ɪə/	here
/ɔɪ/	boy
/əʊ/	go, old
/ʊə/	you're

Konsonanten

/b/	bag, club
/d/	duck, card
/f/	fish, laugh
/g/	get, dog
/h/	hot
/j/	you
/k/	can, duck
/l/	lot, small
/m/	more, mum
/n/	now, sun
/ŋ/	song, long
/p/	present, top
/r/	red, right
/s/	sister, class (scharfes s)
/t/	time, cat
/z/	nose, dogs (weiches s)
/ʒ/	television
/dʒ/	orange
/ʃ/	sure, English
/tʃ/	child, cheese
/ð/	these, mother (weicher Laut)
/θ/	mouth, think (harter Laut)
/v/	very, have
/w/	what, word

Betonungszeichen für die folgende Silbe

/ˈ/ Hauptbetonung
/ˌ/ Nebenbetonung

The English alphabet

a /eɪ/
b /biː/
c /siː/
d /diː/
e /iː/
f /ef/
g /dʒiː/
h /eɪtʃ/
i /aɪ/
j /dʒeɪ/
k /keɪ/
l /el/
m /em/
n /en/
o /əʊ/
p /piː/
q /kjuː/
r /aː/
s /es/
t /tiː/
u /juː/
v /viː/
w /ˈdʌbljuː/
x /eks/
y /waɪ/
z /zed/

Ähnliche Wörter

Es gibt viele Wörter, die im Englischen und im Deutschen gleich sind. Sie unterscheiden sich oft nur darin, wie sie geschrieben werden. Viele dieser Wörter sprechen wir gleich aus.
Diese Wörter stehen nicht in den Wortlisten, weil sie dir ja nicht neu sind. Bei denen, die ein bisschen anders ausgesprochen werden als im Deutschen, ist die Lautschrift farbig hervorgehoben.

activist /ˈæktɪvɪst/
aggressive /əˈgresɪv/
airport /ˈeə(r),pɔː(r)t/
album /ˈælbəm/
alcohol *(no pl)* /ˈælkə,hɒl/
alibi /ˈæləbaɪ/
alliteration /ə,lɪtəˈreɪʃ(ə)n/
anti- /ˈænti/
app /æp/
architecture *(no pl)* /ˈɑːkɪ,tektʃə/
archive /ˈɑːkaɪv/
aspect /ˈæspekt/
baby /ˈbeɪbi/
babysitter /ˈbeɪbi,sɪtə/
backstage /,bækˈsteɪdʒ/
ballet /ˈbæleɪ/
band /bænd/
bank /bæŋk/
bar /bɑː/
barricade /ˈbærɪkeɪd/ ,bærɪˈkeɪd/
baseball /ˈbeɪs,bɔːl/
basis /ˈbeɪsɪs/
basketball /ˈbɑːskɪt,bɔːl/
bestseller /,bestˈselə/
block /blɒk/
blog /blɒg/
bomb /bɒm/
Brexit /ˈbreksɪt/
bronze /brɒnz/
brunch /brʌntʃ/
burger /ˈbɜːgə/
button /ˈbʌt(ə)n/
café /ˈkæfeɪ/
cafeteria /,kæfəˈtɪəriə/
camera /ˈkæm(ə)rə/
cappuccino /,kæpəˈtʃiːnəʊ/
cartoon /kɑːˈtuːn/
category /ˈkætəg(ə)ri/
chaos /ˈkeɪɒs/
check-in /ˈtʃekɪn/
checklist /ˈtʃeklɪst/
cigarette /,sɪgəˈret/
civilization /,sɪvəlaɪˈzeɪʃ(ə)n/
clever /ˈklevə/
clip /klɪp/
code /kəʊd/
colonial /kəˈləʊniəl/
comma /ˈkɒmə/
communication /kə,mjuːnɪˈkeɪʃ(ə)n/
computer /kəmˈpjuːtə/
conference /ˈkɒnf(ə)rəns/
console /ˈkɒnsəʊl/
construction /kənˈstrʌkʃ(ə)n/
contact /ˈkɒntækt/
context /ˈkɒntekst/
continent /ˈkɒntɪnənt/
cool /kuːl/
correct /kəˈrekt/
couch /kaʊtʃ/
cousin /ˈkʌz(ə)n/
cover /ˈkʌvə/
crescendo /krəˈʃendəʊ/
cricket *(no pl)* /ˈkrɪkɪt/
crocodile /ˈkrɒkədaɪl/
deadline /ˈded,laɪn/
deal /diːl/
definition /,defəˈnɪʃ(ə)n/
democratic /,deməˈkrætɪk/
demonstration /,demənˈstreɪʃ(ə)n/
depression /dɪˈpreʃ(ə)n/
design /dɪˈzaɪn/
detail /ˈdiːteɪl/
dialect /ˈdaɪəlekt/
digital /ˈdɪdʒɪt(ə)l/
disco /ˈdɪskəʊ/
discussion /dɪˈskʌʃ(ə)n/
document /ˈdɒkjʊmənt/
doughnut /ˈdəʊ,nʌt/
download /,daʊnˈləʊd/
echo /ˈekəʊ/
element /ˈelɪmənt/
email /ˈiːmeɪl/
emu /ˈiːmjuː/
experiment /ɪkˈsperɪmənt/
expert /ˈekspɜːt/
extreme /ɪkˈstriːm/
extremist /ɪkˈstriːmɪst/
fair /feə/
fan /fæn/
feed /fiːd/
feedback *(no pl)* /ˈfiːdbæk/
film /fɪlm/
filter /ˈfɪltə/
fiord/fjord /ˈfiːɔːd/fjɔːd/
fit /fɪt/
flexible /ˈfleksəb(ə)l/
follower /ˈfɒləʊə/
form /fɔːm/
format /ˈfɔːmæt/
forum /ˈfɔːrəm/
foul /faʊl/
gangster /ˈgæŋstə/
generation /,dʒenəˈreɪʃ(ə)n/
genre /ˈʒɒnrə/
global /ˈgləʊb(ə)l/
gold /gəʊld/
grass *(no pl)* /grɑːs/
hamburger /ˈhæm,bɜːgə/
hashtag /ˈhæʃ,tæg/
high school *(AE)* /ˈhaɪ skul/
highlight /ˈhaɪ,laɪt/
hip hop /ˈhɪp hɒp/
hobby /hɒbi/
horde /hɔːd/
horror /ˈhɒrə/
hotel /həʊˈtel/
HTML *(no pl)* /,eɪtʃ tiː‿em‿ˈel/
hunger *(no pl)* /ˈhʌŋgə/
ice hockey *(no pl)* /ˈaɪs ,hɒki/
idiot *(informal)* /ˈɪdiət/
infographic /,ɪnfəʊˈgræfɪk/
infrastructure /ˈɪnfrə,strʌktʃə/
initiative /ɪˈnɪʃətɪv/
inspiration /,ɪnspəˈreɪʃ(ə)n/
installation /,ɪnstəˈleɪʃ(ə)n/
institution /,ɪnstɪˈtjuːʃ(ə)n/
instrument /ˈɪnstrʊmənt/
interaction /,ɪntərˈækʃ(ə)n/
interactive /,ɪntərˈæktɪv/
international /,ɪntəˈnæʃ(ə)nəl/
internet /ˈɪntə,net/
interpretation /ɪn,tɜːprɪˈteɪʃ(ə)n/
intonation *(no pl)* /,ɪntəˈneɪʃ(ə)n/
invasion /ɪnˈveɪʒ(ə)n/
jazz /dʒæz/
jeans *(pl)* /ˈdʒiːnz/
Jedi /ˈdʒedaɪ/
journalist /ˈdʒɜːnəlɪst/
koala /kəʊˈɑːlə/
land *(no pl)* /lænd/
layout /ˈleɪaʊt/
loyal /ˈlɔɪəl/
magnet /ˈmægnɪt/
management *(no pl)* /ˈmænɪdʒmənt/
material /məˈtɪəriəl/
maximum /ˈmæksɪməm/
meeting /ˈmiːtɪŋ/
metal /ˈmet(ə)l/
mild /maɪld/
million /ˈmɪljən/
mini /ˈmɪni/
minimum /ˈmɪnɪməm/
miserable /ˈmɪz(ə)rəb(ə)l/
mix (= mixture) /mɪks, ˈmɪkstʃə/
mob /mɒb/
modern /ˈmɒdən/
motto /ˈmɒtəʊ/
multiple-choice /,mʌltɪp(ə)l ˈtʃɔɪs/
museum /mjuːˈziːəm/
musical /ˈmjuːzɪk(ə)l/
nation /ˈneɪʃ(ə)n/
national park /,næʃ(ə)nəl ˈpɑːk/
neutral /ˈnjuːtrəl/
non-stop /,nɒnˈstɒp/
offline /,ɒfˈlaɪn/
OK (= okay) *(informal)* /əʊˈkeɪ/
online /ˈɒnlaɪn, ,ɒnˈlaɪn/
organization /,ɔːgənaɪˈzeɪʃ(ə)n/
operation /,ɒpəˈreɪʃ(ə)n/
outdoor /,aʊtˈdɔː/
outfit /ˈaʊtfɪt/
partner /ˈpɑːtnə/
party /pɑːti/
pause /pɔːz/
pavilion /pəˈvɪliən/
perfection *(no pl)* /pəˈfekʃ(ə)n/
petition /pəˈtɪʃ(ə)n/
piercing /ˈpɪəsɪŋ/
pizza /ˈpiːtsə/
pizzeria /,piːtsəˈriːə/
plan /plæn/
Plan B /,plæn ˈbiː/

platform /ˈplætˌfɔːm/
plausible /ˈplɔːzəb(ə)l/
plus /plʌs/
podcast /ˈpɒdˌkɑːst/
pop /pɒp/
popcorn *(no pl)* /ˈpɒpˌkɔːn/
poster /ˈpəʊstə/
private /ˈpraɪvət/
production /prəˈdʌkʃ(ə)n/
professor /prəˈfesə/
profit /ˈprɒfɪt/
program (*AE* = programme *BE*) /ˈproʊˌɡræm/
project /ˈprɒdʒekt/
protagonist /prəʊˈtæɡənɪst/
protest /ˈprəʊtest/
PS /ˌpiː‿ˈes/
quiz (*pl* quizzes) /kwɪz, kwɪzɪz/
radio /ˈreɪdiəʊ/
rap /ræp/
relevant /ˈreləv(ə)nt/
reporter /rɪˈpɔːtə/
respect /rɪˈspekt/
rest /rest/
retro *(informal)* /ˈretrəʊ/
ring /rɪŋ/
ritual /ˈrɪtʃuəl/
rock /rɒk/
rucksack /ˈrʌkˌsæk/
rugby *(no pl)* /ˈrʌɡbi/
sauna /ˈsɔːnə/
scenario /səˈnɑːriəʊ/
science fiction *(no pl)* /ˌsaɪəns ˈfɪkʃ(ə)n/
screenshot /ˈskriːnˌʃɒt/
second-hand /ˌsekəndˈhænd/
semester /səˈmestə/
shock /ʃɒk/
shorts *(pl)* /ʃɔːts/
show /ʃəʊ/
single /ˈsɪŋɡ(ə)l/
situation /ˌsɪtʃuˈeɪʃ(ə)n/
skateboard /ˈskeɪtˌbɔːd/
ski /skiː/
skyline /ˈskaɪˌlaɪn/
slogan /ˈsləʊɡən/
smartphone /ˈsmɑːtfəʊn/
snack /snæk/
sneaker /ˈsniːkə/
snob /snɒb/
soap opera /ˈsəʊp‿ˌɒp(ə)rə/
sofa /ˈsəʊfə/
software /ˈsɒfˌweə/
song /sɒŋ/
soundtrack /ˈsaʊndˌtræk/
special effects /ˌspeʃ(ə)l‿ɪˈfekts/
standard /ˈstændəd/
statue /ˈstætʃuː/
status /ˈsteɪtəs/
strategy /ˈstrætədʒi/
stress /stres/
studio /ˈstjuːdiəʊ/
surfer /ˈsɜːfə/
surfing *(no pl)* /ˈsɜːfɪŋ/
SUV /ˌes juː ˈviː/
swimming pool /ˈswɪmɪŋ puːl/
symbol /ˈsɪmb(ə)l/
symptom /ˈsɪmptəm/
synonym /ˈsɪnənɪm/
system /ˈsɪstəm/
T-shirt /ˈtiː ʃɜːt/
tablet /ˈtæblət/
talent /ˈtælənt/
tattoo /tæˈtuː/
taxi /ˈtæksi/
team /tiːm/
teamwork *(no pl)* /ˈtiːmˌwɜːk/
techno /ˈteknəʊ/
teen /tiːn/
teenage /ˈtiːnˌeɪdʒ/
teenager /ˈtiːnˌeɪdʒə/
telephone /ˈtelɪˌfəʊn/
tennis *(no pl)* /ˈtenɪs/
terror /ˈterə/
terrorism *(no pl)* /ˈteraˌrɪz(ə)m/
terrorist /ˈterərɪst/
test /test/
text /tekst/
thriller /ˈθrɪlə/
timing /ˈtaɪmɪŋ/
tip /tɪp/
tolerant /ˈtɒlərənt/
totem /ˈtəʊtəm/
tourist /ˈtʊərɪst/
trailer /ˈtreɪlə/
training *(no pl)* /ˈtreɪnɪŋ/
triathlon /traɪˈæθlən/
tunnel /ˈtʌn(ə)l/
TV show /ˌtiː ˈviː ʃəʊ/
unfair /ʌnˈfeə/
union /ˈjuːnjən/
up to date /ˌʌp tə ˈdeɪt/
user /ˈjuːzə/
vegetation /ˌvedʒəˈteɪʃ(ə)n/
version /ˈvɜːʃ(ə)n/
video /ˈvɪdiəʊ/
video (clip) /ˈvɪdiəʊ klɪp/
video chat /ˈvɪdiəʊ tʃæt/
video game /ˈvɪdiəʊ ɡeɪm/
VIP /ˌviː‿aɪ ˈpiː/
website /ˈwebˌsaɪt/
wind /wɪnd/
workshop /ˈwɜːkˌʃɒp/

W Words

Class instructions

Add your results to ...	**Fügt** eure Ergebnisse ... **hinzu**.
Analyse the cartoon.	**Analysiere** den Cartoon.
Check G5 to find out more about ...	**Sieh** bei G5 **nach**, um mehr über ... herauszufinden.
Choose one of the tasks	**Wähle** eine der Aufgaben aus.
Collect ideas on what might happen next.	**Sammelt** Ideen, was möglicherweise als Nächstes geschieht.
Comment on his decision.	**Kommentiere** seine Entscheidung.
Compare your results with a partner's.	**Vergleiche** deine Ergebnisse mit denen eines Partners/einer Partnerin.
Complete the sentences using ...	**Vervollständige** die Sätze mit ...
Continue the story.	**Setzt** die Geschichte **fort**.
Copy the grid and **note down** ...	**Übertrage** die Tabelle und **notiere** ...
Correct the false statements.	**Korrigiere** die falschen Aussagen.
Decide if the statements are true or false.	**Entscheide**, ob die Aussagen wahr oder falsch sind.
Describe your first impression of ...	**Beschreibe** deinen ersten Eindruck von ...
Discuss the statement.	**Diskutiert** über die Aussage.
Explain ...	**Erkläre** ...
Explain the advantages and disadvantages.	**Erläutere** die Vor- und Nachteile.
Fill in the verbs in the correct tenses.	**Setze** die Verben in der korrekten Zeitform **ein**.
Find examples to support your opinion.	**Findet** Beispiele, um eure Meinung zu stützen.
Give evidence from the text.	**Führe Belege** aus dem Text **an**.
Listen and note down which aspects are mentioned.	**Hör zu** und notiere, welche Aspekte erwähnt werden.
Listen to ...	**Höre dir** ... **an**.
Look at the pie chart.	**Sieh dir** das Tortendiagramm **an**.
Make notes on ...	**Mach dir Notizen** zu ...
Match the stylistic devices **with** their definitions.	**Ordne** die Stilmittel ihren Definitionen **zu**.
Note down reasons for your opinion.	**Notiere** die Gründe für deine Meinung.
Read the newspaper article and explain ...	**Lies** den Zeitungsartikel und erläutere ...
Research the current status.	**Recherchiere** den aktuellen Stand.
Scan the blog entry and describe ...	**Überfliege** den Blogeintrag und beschreibe ...
Speculate on the reasons.	**Stelle** Vermutungen über die Gründe **an**.
Take notes on ...	**Mach dir Notizen zu** ...
Watch the interview again.	**Seht euch** das Interview noch einmal **an**.
Write a newspaper article **about** ...	**Schreibe** einen Zeitungsartikel **über** ...

Irregular verbs

infinitive	simple past	past participle	German
to arise /əˈraɪz/	arose /əˈrəʊz/	arisen /əˈrɪz(ə)n/	aufkommen; sich ergeben
to be /biː/	was/were /wɒz/wɜː/	been /biːn/	sein
to bear /beə/	bore /bɔː/	borne /bɔːn/	(er)tragen
to beat /biːt/	beat /biːt/	beaten /ˈbiːtən/	schlagen
to become /bɪˈkʌm/	became /bɪˈkeɪm/	become /bɪˈkʌm/	werden
to begin /bɪˈgɪn/	began /bɪˈgæn/	begun /bɪˈgʌn/	anfangen
to bet /bet/	bet /bet/	bet /bet/	wetten
to bite /baɪt/	bit /bɪt/	bitten /bɪt(ə)n/	beißen
to blow /bləʊ/	blew /bluː/	blown /bləʊn/	blasen
to break /breɪk/	broke /brəʊk/	broken /ˈbrəʊkən/	(zer)brechen
to bring /brɪŋ/	brought /brɔːt/	brought /brɔːt/	(mit)bringen
to broadcast /ˈbrɔːdˌkɑːst/	broadcast(ed) /ˈbrɔːdˌkɑːst(ɪd)/	broadcast(ed) /ˈbrɔːdˌkɑːst(ɪd)/	senden; übertragen
to build /bɪld/	built /bɪlt/	built /bɪlt/	bauen
to burn /bɜːn/	burnt/burned /bɜːnt/bɜːnd/	burnt/burned /bɜːnt/bɜːnd/	(ab)brennen
to burst /bɜːst/	burst /bɜːst/	burst /bɜːst/	brechen; platzen
to buy /baɪ/	bought /bɔːt/	bought /bɔːt/	kaufen
to catch /kætʃ/	caught /kɔːt/	caught /kɔːt/	(auf)fangen
to come /kʌm/	came /keɪm/	come /kʌm/	kommen
to cost /kɒst/	cost /kɒst/	cost /kɒst/	kosten
to cut /kʌt/	cut /kʌt/	cut /kʌt/	schneiden
to choose /tʃuːz/	chose /tʃəʊz/	chosen /ˈtʃəʊzən/	(aus)wählen
to deal with /ˈdiːl wɪð/	dealt with /ˈdelt wɪð/	dealt with /ˈdelt wɪð/	sich befassen mit
to do /duː/	did /dɪd/	done /dʌn/	machen; tun
to draw /drɔː/	drew /druː/	drawn /drɔːn/	zeichnen
to dream (of) /ˈdriːm‿əv/	dreamt (of)/dreamed (of) /ˈdremt‿əv/ˈdriːmd‿əv/	dreamt (of)/dreamed (of) /ˈdremt‿əv/ˈdriːmd‿əv/	träumen (von)
to drink /drɪŋk/	drank /dræŋk/	drunk /drʌŋk/	trinken
to drive /draɪv/	drove /drəʊv/	driven /ˈdrɪvn/	fahren
to eat /iːt/	ate /et/	eaten /ˈiːt(ə)n/	essen; fressen
to fall /fɔːl/	fell /fel/	fallen /ˈfɔːlən/	(um)fallen
to feed /fiːd/	fed /fed/	fed /fed/	(zu) essen geben; füttern
to feel /fiːl/	felt /felt/	felt /felt/	(sich) fühlen
to fight /faɪt/	fought /fɔːt/	fought /fɔːt/	(be)kämpfen
to find /faɪnd/	found /faʊnd/	found /faʊnd/	finden
to flee /fliː/	fled /fled/	fled /fled/	fliehen
to fly /flaɪ/	flew /fluː/	flown /fləʊn/	fliegen
to forget /fəˈget/	forgot /fəˈgɒt/	forgotten /fəˈgɒtən/	vergessen
to get /get/	got /gɒt/	got/gotten /gɒt/ˈgɒtən/	bekommen
to give /gɪv/	gave /geɪv/	given /ˈgɪvən/	geben
to go /gəʊ/	went /went/	gone /gɒn/	fahren; gehen
to grow /grəʊ/	grew /gruː/	grown /grəʊn/	wachsen

W Words

infinitive	simple past	past participle	German
to hang up /ˌhæŋ‿ˈʌp/	hung up /ˌhʌŋ‿ˈʌp/	hung up /ˌhʌŋ‿ˈʌp/	aufhängen
to have /hæv/	had /hæd/	had /hæd/	haben
to hear /hɪə/	heard /hɜːd/	heard /hɜːd/	hören
to hide /haɪd/	hid /hɪd/	hidden /ˈhɪd(ə)n/	(sich) verstecken
to hit /hɪt/	hit /hɪt/	hit /hɪt/	schlagen; stoßen (gegen); treffen
to hold /həʊld/	held /held/	held /held/	halten
to hurt /ˈhɜːt/	hurt /ˈhɜːt/	hurt /ˈhɜːt/	(jdm) wehtun; (jdn) verletzen
to keep /kiːp/	kept /kept/	kept /kept/	(bei)behalten
to know /nəʊ/	knew /njuː/	known /nəʊn/	kennen; wissen
to lay /leɪ/	laid /leɪd/	laid /leɪd/	legen
to lead /liːd/	led /led/	led /led/	führen
to lean /liːn/	leaned/leant /liːnd/lent/	leaned/leant /liːnd/lent/	sich beugen; sich lehnen
to learn /lɜːn/	learnt/learned /lɜːnt/lɜːnd/	learnt/learned /lɜːnt/lɜːnd/	erfahren; lernen
to leave /liːv/	left /left/	left /left/	verlassen
to let /let/	let /let/	let /let/	lassen
to lie /laɪ/	lay /leɪ/	lain /leɪn/	liegen; sich hinlegen
to light up /ˌlaɪt‿ˈʌp/	lit up /ˌlɪt‿ˈʌp/	lit up /ˌlɪt‿ˈʌp/	aufleuchten; erhellen
to lose /luːz/	lost /lɒst/	lost /lɒst/	verlieren
to make /meɪk/	made /meɪd/	made /meɪd/	machen
to mean /miːn/	meant /ment/	meant /ment/	bedeuten; meinen
to meet /miːt/	met /met/	met /met/	(sich) treffen
to overcome /ˌəʊvəˈkʌm/	overcame /ˌəʊvəˈkeɪm/	overcome /ˌəʊvəˈkʌm/	bewältigen; meistern
to pay /peɪ/	paid /peɪd/	paid /peɪd/	(be)zahlen
to proofread /ˈpruːfriːd/	proofread /ˈpruːfred/	proofread /ˈpruːfred/	Korrektur lesen
to put /pʊt/	put /pʊt/	put /pʊt/	legen; setzen; stellen
to read /riːd/	read /red/	read /red/	lesen
to rebuild /ˌriːˈbɪld/	rebuilt /ˌriːˈbɪlt/	rebuilt /ˌriːˈbɪlt/	wieder aufbauen
to resell /ˌriːˈsel/	resold /ˌriːˈsəʊld/	resold /ˌriːˈsəʊld/	weiterverkaufen
to rewrite /ˌriːˈraɪt/	rewrote /ˌriːˈrəʊt/	rewritten /ˌriːˈrɪtən/	neu schreiben; überarbeiten; umschreiben
to ride /raɪd/	rode /rəʊd/	ridden /ˈrɪd(ə)n/	fahren (mit); reiten
to ring (up) /ˌrɪŋ‿ˈʌp/	rang (up) /ˌræŋ‿ˈʌp/	rung (up) /ˌrʌŋ‿ˈʌp/	anrufen
to rise up /ˌraɪz‿ˈʌp/	rose up /ˌrəʊz‿ˈʌp/	risen up /ˌrɪz(ə)n‿ˈʌp/	aufsteigen; sich auflehnen
to run /rʌn/	ran /ræn/	run /rʌn/	rennen
to say /seɪ/	said /sed/	said /sed/	sagen
to see /siː/	saw /sɔː/	seen /siːn/	sehen
to seek /siːk/	sought /sɔːt/	sought /sɔːt/	suchen
to sell /sel/	sold /səʊld/	sold /səʊld/	verkaufen
to send /send/	sent /sent/	sent /sent/	(zu)schicken
to set /set/	set /set/	set /set/	(fest)setzen; festlegen
to shake /ʃeɪk/	shook /ʃʊk/	shaken /ˈʃeɪkən/	schütteln; zittern
to shoot /ʃuːt/	shot /ʃɒt/	shot /ʃɒt/	schießen

infinitive	simple past	past participle	German
to show /ʃəʊ/	showed /ʃəʊd/	shown /ʃəʊn/	zeigen
to shut up /ˌʃʌt‿ˈʌp/	shut up /ˌʃʌt‿ˈʌp/	shut up /ˌʃʌt‿ˈʌp/	zum Schweigen bringen; zuschließen
to sing /sɪŋ/	sang /sæŋ/	sung /sʌŋ/	singen
to sit /sɪt/	sat /sæt/	sat /sæt/	sitzen
to sleep /sliːp/	slept /slept/	slept /slept/	schlafen
to slide /slaɪd/	slid /slɪd/	slid /slɪd/	gleiten; rutschen
to smell /smel/	smelt/smelled /smelt/smeld/	smelt/smelled /smelt/smeld/	riechen
to speak /spiːk/	spoke /spəʊk/	spoken /ˈspəʊkən/	sprechen
to spend /spend/	spent /spent/	spent /spent/	ausgeben *(Geld)*; verbringen *(Zeit)*
to spin /spɪn/	spun /spʌn/	spun /spʌn/	drehen; spinnen; rotieren
to spit (out) /ˌspɪt‿ˈaʊt/	spat (out) /ˌspæt‿ˈaʊt/	spat (out) /ˌspæt‿ˈaʊt/	(aus)spucken; ausstoßen
to split up /ˌsplɪt‿ˈʌp/	split up /ˌsplɪt‿ˈʌp/	split up /ˌsplɪt‿ˈʌp/	(sich) (auf)teilen
to spread /spred/	spread /spred/	spread /spred/	(sich) ausbreiten; (sich) verbreiten; verteilen
to stand /stænd/	stood /stʊd/	stood /stʊd/	stehen
to steal /stiːl/	stole /stəʊl/	stolen /ˈstəʊlən/	stehlen
to stick /stɪk/	stuck /stʌk/	stuck /stʌk/	kleben; stecken
to stink /stɪŋk/	stank /stæŋk/	stunk /stʌŋk/	stinken
to strike /straɪk/	struck /strʌk/	struck /strʌk/	(zu)schlagen; streiken
to strive /straɪv/	strove /strəʊv/	striven /ˈstrɪv(ə)n/	(an)streben; sich bemühen
to swear /sweə/	swore /swɔː/	sworn /swɔːn/	schwören
to swell /swel/	swelled /sweld/	swollen /ˈswəʊlən/	anschwellen
to swim /swɪm/	swam /swæm/	swum /swʌm/	schwimmen
to take /teɪk/	took /tʊk/	taken /ˈteɪkən/	(mit)nehmen
to teach /tiːtʃ/	taught /tɔːt/	taught /tɔːt/	unterrichten
to tell /tel/	told /təʊld/	told /təʊld/	erzählen; sagen
to think /θɪŋk/	thought /θɔːt/	thought /θɔːt/	denken; glauben; meinen
to throw /θrəʊ/	threw /θruː/	thrown /θrəʊn/	werfen
to thrust /θrʌst/	thrust /θrʌst/	thrust /θrʌst/	recken; stoßen
to understand /ˌʌndəˈstænd/	understood /ˌʌndəˈstʊd/	understood /ˌʌndəˈstʊd/	verstehen
to upset /ʌpˈset/	upset /ʌpˈset/	upset /ʌpˈset/	aufwühlen; beunruhigen; in Aufregung versetzen
to wake up /ˌweɪk‿ˈʌp/	woke up /ˌwəʊk‿ˈʌp/	woken up /ˌwəʊkən‿ˈʌp/	aufwachen; aufwecken
to wear /weə/	wore /wɔː/	worn /wɔːn/	tragen *(Kleidung)*
to win /wɪn/	won /wʌn/	won /wʌn/	gewinnen
to wind up /ˌwaɪnd‿ˈʌp/	wound up /ˌwaʊnd‿ˈʌp/	wound up /ˌwaʊnd‿ˈʌp/	wickeln
to write /raɪt/	wrote /rəʊt/	written /ˈrɪtən/	schreiben

Q Quellen

Bildquellen
|Alamy Stock Photo, Abingdon/Oxfordshire: AfriPics.com 182.2; Allan, Jim 183.7; B Christopher 68.1; Blackbird, Sabena Jane 183.4; BotTastic 34.2; BRIAN HARRIS 134.3; By Ian Miles-Flashpoint Pictures 173.1; Cavan Images 93.3; Chris Howes/ Wild Places Photography 104.1; Chua, Ronnie 3.3, 91.1; Cultura Creative RF 93.1; Daemmrich, Bob 168.1; Dagnall, Ian 183.3; derek robbins 104.2; Dolgachov, Lev 66.2; Dorling Kindersley ltd 104.3; Evans, Greg Balfour 135.3; Flassig, Anett 21.2; Godong 182.1; GRANGER - Historical Picture Archive 123.3; Guillem, Antonio 163.1; Hugh PETERSWALD 18.1; i4images premium 123.2; Ian Dagnall Commercial Collection 183.1; Idir, Yanice 161.1; Imagebroker 196.1; James, David 124.1, 188.1; Jeffrey Isaac Greenberg 8+ 104.5; Joe 33.1, 238.2; Levit, Keith 21.4; M L Pearson 173.2; M-SUR 70.2; martin berry 23.3; Mather, Gary 3.5, 120.2; MBI 125.1, 126.2, 188.2; McCarthy, Andrew 141.1; Megapress 34.3; Milnes, Richard 16.3; Morrison, John 135.4; PA Images 142.1; Pain, Mark 122.3; Phanie 173.3; Pictorial Press Ltd 238.1; Prisma by Dukas Presseagentur GmbH 183.2; public domain sourced / access rights from History and Art Collection 25.2; Radharc Images 123.1; RGB Ventures 24.2; RLFE Pix 68.5; Roberts, Frances 68.7; Schonewille, Ben 173.4; Stanciu, Constantin 243.3; Sue Cunningham Photographi 104.4; Teare, Jeanette 183.5; terry bouch 135.2; Thomas, Michael 17.1; travelbild 122.1; Travelscape Images 20.2, 148.2; Vallee, Genevieve 34.1; Willis, Michael 20.1, 23.1; World Image Archive 238.4; Wyatt, Robert 23.2, 150.2; ZUMA Press, Inc. 164.2, 169.1. |Alamy Stock Photo (RMB), Abingdon/Oxfordshire: Bachman, Bill 22.1; Brain light 96.1; Classic Image 238.3; Dack, Simon / Telephoto Images 12.3; Ekstrand, Jim 211.1; imageBROKER 13.4; Life on white 26.11; MacDonald, Dennis 77.1, 172.2; MBI 207.2; MediaPunch Inc 72.1; Mueringer, Christian 26.9; North Wind Picture Archives 19.1; Panther Media GmbH 26.6; Rawpixel Ltd 38.4, 73.1, 151.1; robertharding 15.1; Standard Studio 26.1; travellinglight 26.4; Tsuguliev, Nikolay 189.1; UPI 167.2; West, Jim 76.2, 172.1. |Amnesty International, London: © Air Agency / ThePickles 165.1. |Bloomsbury Publishing Plc, London: 136.1. |Boclips.com, London: 67.1, 94.2, 164.1, 175.1, 186.1. |CartoonStock.com, Bath: Blackwell, Douglas 40.1, 153.4; Bucella, Marty 40.2, 239.1; Fishman, Loren 70.1; Martirena, Alfredo 166.1. |Colourbox.com, Odense: Nykonenko, Sergiy 103.6. |EPA Images, Frankfurt am Main: Lane, Justin 87.1. |fotolia.com, New York: contrastwerkstatt 181.2; Kneschke, Robert 66.1; totajla 11.1; underverse 179.1. |Fremantle Press, Fremantle: "Meet me at the Intersection". By Lim, Rebecca; Kwaymullina, Ambelin, Fremantle Press, ISBN 9781925591705 28.1. |Getty Images, München: Anadolu Agency 68.4; Barnes, Kelly 16.2; FPG/Hulton Archive 122.2; McIntyre, Emma 164.3; Meier, Wagner 184.1; Philbey, Martin 148.1. |Getty Images (RF), München: Bektas, Cihan 13.2; Maskot 67.3; Pekic 171.2; SDI Productions 67.2; Stephen Knowles Photography 119.1. |Guardian News & Media Limited, London: Photograph: Carly Earl/The Guardian, Copyright Guardian News & Media Ltd 2023 16.1. |Hachette Book Group, Boston: From Dare Me by Eric Devine, copyright © 2013. Reprinted by permission of Running Press Kids, an imprint of Hachette Book Group, Inc. 59.1. |iStockphoto.com, Calgary: alvarez 176.1; AndreyPopov 243.1; Balasko, Rudy 26.2; BenGoode 237.4; bennymarty 13.3; Binikins 237.5; Brainsil Titel; Coatesy, Anne 135.1; CreativeNature_nl 26.10; Goddard_ Photography 237.1; gustavofrazao 44.2; isaxar 145.2; Jonah_ Photos 13.1; JulieanneBirch 12.4; kokkai 21.3; lolostock 200.1; MarkPiovesan 237.6; Meepian, Worawee 51.1; miromiro 72.2, 170.1; mlharing 237.3; mollypix 147.1; monkeybusinessimages 203.1; Noppasin 150.1; Rigel 212.1; SAKhanPhotography 193.1; Skyimages 26.5; South_agency 206.1. |Leeds Museums and Galleries, Leeds: 182.3. |Macmillan Publishing Group, New York: Cover and excerpts from CHECK, PLEASE BOOK #1 HOCKEY by Ngozi Ukazu. Copyright © 2018 by Ngozi Ukazu. Reprinted by permission of First Second, a division of Holtzbrinck Publishing Holdings Limited Partnership. All Rights Reserved. 52.1, 52.2, 52.3, 53.1, 53.2, 54.1, 54.2, 54.3, 55.1, 55.2, 56.1, 56.2, 57.1, 57.2. |Marckwort, Ulf, Kassel: 128.1, 130.1, 191.1, 191.2, 218.1, 219.1, 220.1, 222.1, 224.1, 225.1, 226.1, 229.1, 230.1, 232.1, 233.1. |mauritius images GmbH, Mittenwald: Alamy Stock Photos / Atlaspix / Emma. Director: Autumn de Wilde 160.2; Alamy Stock Photos / Charlie Plummer in: Words on Bathroom Walls (2020) ©Roadside Attractions Film 48.4; Alamy Stock Photos / Charlie Plummer und Molly Parker in: Words on Bathroom Walls (2020) ©Roadside Attractions Film 162.1; Alamy Stock Photos / Charlie Plummer, Walton Goggins und Molly Parker in: Words on Bathroom Walls (2020) ©Roadside Attractions Film 48.3, 159.1; Alamy Stock Photos / Entertainment Pictures / Bella Ramsey in: Catherine Called Birdy. Studio: Working Title Films. Director: Lena Dunham 160.3; Alamy Stock Photos / Levine, Richard 85.1; Alamy Stock Photos / Sparks, Jon 134.2; imageBROKER/Mang, Christian 192.1; World Pictures 149.1. |Penguin Random House LLC, New York: 46.1, 157.1. |Penguin Random House UK, London: Artwork from Lockwood & Co: The Screaming Staircase by Jonathan Stroud published by Doubleday Childrens. Copyright © Jonathan Stroud 2013. Reprinted by permission of Penguin Books Limited. 113.1. |Picture-Alliance GmbH, Frankfurt a.M.: AP Images/Spencer, Mike 68.3; ASSOCIATED PRESS/Griffith, Rob 15.2; landov/Cole, Sarah 76.1. |Shutterstock.com, New York: Alexandre G. ROSA 195.2; alphaspirit.it 78.1; amenic181 101.1, 181.1; Badkin, Caron 120.1; Basnett, Garry 183.6; Bloomicon 156.5; Bona, Paolo 26.3; Colorstream 14.1; DG-Studio 25.1; Dragomirescu, Razvan 95.1; Einstock 95.2; Films, Motortion 98.2; fizkes 41.1, 45.1, 102.1, 215.1, 215.2, 215.3; Fresh_Studio 211.2; Gelpi 153.2, 153.3; Gevaert, Eric 195.1; GG Digital Arts 14.3; GoodStudio 170.2; Ground Picture 244.2; Hernandez, Jinitzail 68.2; I Shafiq 12.1; Jack_the_sparow 99.1, 243.2; Jackson, Brian A 126.1; Krakenimages.com 202.1; KVASVECTOR 146.1; Lemahieu, Melanie 121.2; leungchopan 103.2; Li, Lori 185.1; lukas_zb 103.5; Lund, Jacob 3.4, 65.1, 67.5; Master1305 242.1; milnerCreative 134.1; Monkey Business Images 67.4; Motortion Films 58.1, 112.1; mouze_art 95.3; MPH Photos 93.2, 174.1; New Africa 94.1; Odua Images 32.1, 86.1, 140.1; one photo 244.1; pathdoc 103.1, 103.3; Pavone, Sean 168.2; Pelanek, Martin 26.8; PhotocechCZ 237.2; Pretty Vectors 98.1; Rawpixel.com 239.2, 241.1; Save nature and wildlife 14.2; sirtravelalot 21.1; STILLFX 106.1; Stokkete 103.4; Tarikdiz 38.1, 38.2, 38.3, 39.1, 39.2, 39.3; TasfotoNL 121.1; Tharun 15 172.3; Todorovic, Aleksandar 145.1; vasara 37.1; WindVector 155.1; YAKOBCHUK VIACHESLAV 190.1; Zhukovsky, Leonard 147.2. |Shutterstock.com (RM), New York: JacobYakob/ LDEntertainment/Kobal 3.2, 48.1, 48.2, 160.1; Marvel/Disney/ Kobal 158.2, 158.3, 158.5, 158.7; Marvel/Disney/Moviestore 158.4. |stock.adobe.com, Dublin: ah_fotobox 177.1; Ammentorp Lund, Jacob 44.1, 214.1; ARMMY PICCA 80.1; asem arab 156.4; beau 12.2; Brian_Kinney 24.1; carballo 171.1; Chabraszewski, Jacek 156.2; cpask Titel; Diversity Studio 153.1; doomu 240.1; dvrcan 3.1; Ernst, Daniel 241.2; Francesca 158.6; Frey, Stephanie 68.6; Gorodenkoff 240.2; grafikplusfoto 156.3; Grinvalds, Kaspars 239.3; Izzotti, Andrea 167.3; Kneschke, Robert 173.6; Krakenimages.com 156.1; Lawrey 133.1; Maria_ Savenko 43.1; Martin 26.7; Nuthawut 201.1; olezzo 208.1; photology1971 161.2; Prostock-studio 152.1; Racle Fotodesign 173.5; thongsee 50.1, 158.1; vichie81 167.1; WavebreakMediaMicro 207.1.

Textquellen

S. 28–31: "Night Feet" © Ellen van Neerven. From: "Meet Me at the Intersection" edited by Rebecca Lim and Ambelin Kwaymullina, Freemantle: Freemantle Press 2018, S. 19–31.
S. 41/42: Sirin Kale: "Social media is a bad feelings machine. Why can't we just turn if off for good?", Copyright Guardian News & Media Ltd 2023, www.theguardian.com [Zugriff 21.3.2023]
S. 43: Olivia Bancel: "A Room For My Phone", LOG OFF Movement, logoffmovement.org, 14.6.2021[Zugriff 21.3.2023]
S. 46/47: "Words on Bathroom Walls" © Julia Walton. New York: Ember; Reprint edition (Penguin Random House) 2018, S. 1–4, 31–32.
S. 52–57: Cover and excerpts from CHECK, PLEASE BOOK #1 HOCKEY by Ngozi Ukazu. Copyright © 2018 by Ngozi Ukazu. Reprinted by permission of First Second, a division of Holtzbrinck Publishing Holdings Limited Partnership. All Rights Reserved, S. 4, 58, 63–66, 98–100.
S. 59–62: "Dare Me" © Eric Devine. Philadelphia: Running Press Kids (Hachette Book Group) 2013, S. 6–11.
S. 72: "Schools scared to death" © Amanda Gorman. Instagram (25.5.2022) www.instagram.com/p/Cd9QlbXPs0F [Zugriff 21.3.2023]
S. 74–77: "No Place" © Todd Strasser. London: Simon & Schuster 2014, S. 24–26, 58–60, 127–130.
S. 80–85: "Trell: Nothing But the Truth" © Dick Lehr. Somerville: Candlewick Press 2019, S. 1–4, 55–57, 73–75, 233–234, 260–264.
S. 87/88: "Malala Yousafzai: 16th birthday speech at the United Nations" Washington: Malala Fund (12.7.2013), https://malala.org [Zugriff 22.6.2023]
S. 106–111: "Forty-Five Minutes" © Anya Reiss. National Theatre Connections 2013. New York: Bloomsbury Publishing 2013, S. 493–499, 508–513, 517–518, 524–525.
S. 113–116: "Lockwood & Co. 1: The Screaming Staircase" © Jonathan Stroud. Toronto: Corgi Childrens (Penguin Random House Canada) 2013, S. 84–100.
S. 136–139: "The Summer We Turned Green" © William Sutcliffe. Sydney: Bloomsbury YA, 2021, S. 3/4, 6/7, 9/10, 42–44, 237–239, 294/295.
S. 178/179 "Die anonymisierte Bewerbung hat einen schweren Stand" wgr/© dpa Vanessa Reiber
S. 186: Jam Campus: "The Industrial Revolution Song", powered by Boclips

Wortschatzerfasser

Yücel Özyürek, Lektor und Sprachtrainer, Eresing, www.language-expert.de

Land heights and sea depths
(in metres)
Mountain peak
1344
Area below sea level
1000
500
200
100
0 (Coastline)
40
200
2000
15
2458
Sea depth
Elevation
Water features
River
Canal
Lake
Settlements (inhabitants)
Over 5,000,000
1,000,000 – 5,000,000
500,000 – 1,000,000
100,000 – 500,000
20,000 – 100,000
Under 20,000
Countries and administration
National border
London Capital
Adminstrative boundary
12°
10°
8°
6°
4°
2° West
0°
60°
58° North
56°
56°
450
Lerwick
Shetland Islands
Fair
Orkney Islands
Mainland
Kirkwall
295
Rona
Pentland Firth
Cape Wrath
Duncansby Head
Wick
Outer Hebrides
Stornoway
Lewis
799
The Minch
North Sea
Saint Kilda
531
1081
Beinn Dearg
Moray Firth
Elgin
Kinnaird Head
Peterhead
Skye
Highlands
Inverness
Kyle of Lochalsh
Loch Ness
1309
Ben Macdui
Aberdeen
Inner Hebrides
Mallaig
Scotland
Fort William
1344
Ben Nevis
Grampian Mountains
2458
Loch Linnhe
Dundee
243
Mull
Oban
Perth
Firth of Tay
Atlantic Ocean
Firth of Lorne
Jura
Firth of Forth
Edinburgh
Glasgow
Paisley
Livingston
East Kilbride
Southern Uplands
Islay
Kintyre
839
Ayr
Malin Head
Giant's Causeway
North Chann
Firth of Clyde
Great Britain
751
Coleraine
Dumfries
Newcastle
The North